Praise for the Eagles and Dragons series...

Historic Novel Society:

"...Haviaras handles it all with smooth skill. The world of third-century Rome...is colourfully vivid here, and Haviaras manages to invest even his secondary and tertiary characters with believable, three-dimensional humanity."

Amazon Readers:

"Graphic, uncompromising and honest... A novel of heroic men and the truth of the uncompromising horror of close combat total war..."

"Raw and unswerving in war and peace... New author to me but ranks along side Ben Kane and Simon Scarrow. The attention to detail and all the gory details are inspiring and the author doesn't invite you into the book he drags you by the nasal hairs into the world of Roman life sweat, tears, blood, guts and sheer heroism. Well worth a night's reading because once started it's hard to put down."

"Historical fiction at its best! ... if you like your historical fiction to be an education as well as a fun read, this is the book for you!"

"Loved this book! I'm an avid fan of Ancient Rome and this story is, perhaps, one of the best I've ever read."

"An outstanding and compelling novel!"

"I would add this author to some of the great historical writers such as Conn Iggulden, Simon Scarrow and David Gemmell. The characters were described in such a way that it was easy to picture them as if they were real and have lived in the past, the book flowed with an ease that any reader, novice to advanced can enjoy and become fully immersed..."

"One in a series of tales which would rank them alongside Bernard Cornwell, Simon Scarrow, Robert Ludlum, James Boschert and others of their ilk. The story and character development and the pacing of the exciting military actions frankly are superb and edge of your seat! The historical environment and settings have been well researched to make the story lines so very believable!! I can hardly wait for what I hope will be many sequels! If you enjoy Roman historical fiction, you do not want to miss this series!"

Goodreads:

"... a very entertaining read; Haviaras has both a fluid writing style, and a good eye for historical detail, and explores in far more detail the faith of the average Roman than do most authors."

Kobo:

"I can't remember the last time that a book stirred so many emotions! I laughed, cried and cheered my way through this book and can't wait to meet again this wonderful family of characters. Roll on to the next book!"

Join the Legions!

Sign-up for the Eagles and Dragons Publishing
Newsletter and get a FREE BOOK today.

Subscribers get first access to new releases, special
offers, and much more.

Go to:
www.eaglesanddragonspublishing.com

For Angelina, Alexandra, and Athena…

I would not walk the dark wood of this world with anyone else but you.

Για την Αγγελίνα, την Αλεξάνδρα και την Αθηνά…

Δεν θα περπατούσα στο σκοτεινό δάσος αυτού του κόσμου με οποιονδήποτε άλλο εκτός από εσάς.

ISLE

OF THE

BLESSED

EAGLES AND DRAGONS

BOOK IV

ADAM ALEXANDER HAVIARAS

PROLOGUS

A.D. 209

The rain was icy and sharp as it drove down from iron-grey clouds that clung to the jagged peaks of the hills surrounding the small valley. The rush of a waterfall cascading from hidden heights could be heard, feeding the bubbling river that ran like an artery through the village and out into the expanse of the glen.

In the heart of a gathering of village roundhouses, amid the torches that sputtered beneath the thatch overhangs of two neighbouring houses, Argentocoxus, Chieftain of the Caledonii, waited with three of his bodyguards. He stood wrapped in a long cloak of brown embroidered with silver thread, one hand reaching up to finger the thick rope of the golden torc that ringed his neck. His other hand, rested upon the silver hilt of the longsword that hung at his side.

The chieftain and his men peered into the mist and rain, down the village road, waiting for the arrival of the messenger.

"They should be here by now," one of the bodyguards said.

Argentocoxus nodded to the other group standing out in the rain. He knew the villagers were watching him from the cracked shutters of their homes, waiting to see what he would do.

The bodyguard strode out to where three Romans knelt in the middle of the road, facing into the mist. Their hands were bound behind their backs, their mouths gagged with oily rags that made the bile in their throats rise. They dared not move, for the spears held by the enemy warriors behind them would plunge into the backs of their necks before they twitched a muscle.

The chieftain's bodyguard removed the gag from the first Roman's mouth and took his hair roughly in his tattooed fist, a short blade at his throat. "You said he was coming! That he wanted to talk!"

The Roman looked up at the warrior's face, the braided, drooping moustache dripping with rainwater onto his face. "He does want to talk. He was right behind us until your men attacked," the Roman growled. "He wants to-"

"Here they are!" the warrior behind the Roman said suddenly.

The bodyguard turned to see four warriors coming toward them, their blades drawn on a single Roman in their midst. He had a sack over his head, and his wrists were bound, but he walked with his head held high.

The bodyguard turned to look at his lord, and Argentocoxus came out into the rain with the other two men at his side. The Roman had asked for this meeting. Now they would see what he wanted. Just before they arrived before him, he glanced back at the roundhouse where he had been standing, to see the open door and darkness within. The situation made him uncomfortable, but he wanted to see where it would lead.

The group arrived and the four warriors pushed the Roman to his knees before Argentocoxus.

"Remove his hood," the chieftain said.

One of the men ripped it free and there, looking up at Argentocoxus, was Marcus Claudius Picus.

"Good evening, Argentocoxus," Claudius said, his eyes darting to his three men kneeling before him. "I see you've met my men."

"You abandoned them quite easily, Claudius," the chieftain said with disdain. "Do you do that to all your men?"

"I did not trust you. I was right." Claudius made to stand, but was pushed back down.

Argentocoxus nodded and his men allowed the Roman to stand. "And I do not trust you, or any Roman for that matter."

Claudius smiled. "I am perhaps the only Roman you can truly trust." Claudius saw his men looking up at him, followed their eyes to the dark doorway of the roundhouse to his left. He looked back at Argentocoxus, and held up his bound wrists. "Do you mind?"

The chieftain eyed him warily, but nodded to one of the men who stepped forward to cut the ropes.

Claudius sighed as if bored and rubbed his wrists.

"What do you want, Claudius?" Argentocoxus asked.

"My spies tell me that the Maeatae are making plans for a large-scale assault. You wouldn't happen to know about this, would you?"

Argentocoxus' eyes went to the roundhouse quickly, but he shook his head. "My concern is for my people, and keeping to the truce I made with your emperor."

"Yes...my emperor. And the shipments of silver you continue to receive," Claudius said as he stared at the jutting hilt of the chieftain's sword. "Severus is ill, and will not live forever."

10

"So people keep saying, but he appears to live on and on, and Caracalla did not follow through on his plan," Argentocoxus said. He remembered his conversation in the woods of Caledonia after that last battle, when Caesar Caracalla had made him promises, promises that had not been kept.

"Trust me when I say that Severus will not last much longer," Claudius said. He eyed his kneeling men again. "Plans are in motion."

"What plans?"

"That is not your concern. What should concern you is what I need you to do."

"I am not your servant!" Argentocoxus said, his voice growing angry at the Roman's arrogance.

"But you are Caesar's, and I am his," Claudius said. "We have a thorn in our side...several really."

"Who?"

"The Dragon and his men."

The chieftain balled his fists, and his mouth tightened. "He is in Britannia."

"Yes," Claudius responded.

"What do you want of me and my people then?"

"I want you to slaughter the Dragon and his men."

"We tried. They are too powerful." Argentocoxus remembered all too well the thunder of horses' hooves and the roar of dragons upon the battlefield. His nights were riddled with dreams of blood and the massacred bodies of his warriors. It was a crisis his people had never faced before, and now they looked to him to make things right. *Is this my chance? A deal with this Roman?*

"If, you find an ally brave enough to face them...someone with the strength and numbers, it should be easy for you." Claudius looked to the roundhouse and back to the chieftain.

"But the truce? If we break it, war will begin again. My people have had their fill of suffering."

"They will suffer more if Rome remains here indefinitely," Claudius said. "And I for one, do not want to remain here." Even as he said it, the rainwater made him shiver beneath his cuirass. "Caesar belongs in Rome, and so do I. But the emperor's plans, and those of the Praetorian prefect, are to remain and establish a northern capital of the empire. Is that something you want? Peace here means that Rome will stay."

11

Argentocoxus was silent.

Claudius continued. "Let us make a new deal, you and I. You kill the Dragon and his men, and I will see to it that when Severus dies - and that will be soon - Caracalla will pull out of Caledonia for good."

"A death sentence for many of my people," Argentocoxus said.

"Freedom from Rome," Claudius countered. "If you do not have the courage to do so, however, or don't have an ally who is brave enough, then that is different. Perhaps we really have defeated you?"

"Enough."

The growl that came from the roundhouse froze the blood of every Caledonian there, including the chieftain.

Claudius smiled and looked toward the doorway where two glowing eyes emerged out of the darkness.

An enormous warrior stepped out into the rain. His chest was bare and tattooed upon it was a wolf, the eyes seeming to glow in the dim light as if they were alive. He had raven-black hair that fell around his shoulders and a torc that was even thicker than the one Argentocoxus wore around his neck.

Claudius noticed the Caledonian chieftain recoil a little as the man approached them, but that he tried to keep his composure.

Argentocoxus, or any of his men, could not hide the fact that they were afraid and awed by this newcomer.

"You speak too much, Roman," the new chieftain said. "You have a deal."

"But-" Argentocoxus was about to protest, but one look from the enormous warrior silenced him.

The warrior approached, his blue eyes burning with a fire that surprised even Claudius. "The Caledonii may not have the stomach for another war with Rome, but the Maeatae do."

"Ah," Claudius said. "You are the one."

"I am the Wolf. I am a son of the Morrigan, and I am sworn to destroy Rome and the Dragon."

"And I don't care," Claudius said, smiling up at the warrior. "All I care about is the death of the Dragon, and leaving this cold, filthy island."

The chieftain laughed, deep and cold as he stared at Claudius. He could use this Roman. If Rome pulled out of Caledonia, then he could rule as overlord of every tribe north of the Wall, and then, sweep south and push Rome out of the island once and for all. But

12

first, he wanted war in the land where they stood, to wipe away the shame Argentocoxus had brought on the tribes, and upon the Morrigan herself.

"I will kill this Dragon. I will make him suffer," the chieftain said, his face close to Claudius'. "But you will not tell us when. You will not dictate to us, or to me. We will bring war to your doorstep when our Gods deem it timely."

With a speed that seemed entirely unnatural, the chieftain drew his sword and slashed it through the head of the first kneeling Roman in one stroke.

"What are you doing?" Argentocoxus cried out, his voice full of as much anger and rage as he could muster.

"I am sealing this pact with Roman blood!" the other chieftain said, as he grabbed the spear from the shocked Caledonian who had been standing behind the Roman. He then bent over, picked up that bloody, gape-eyed head with one hand, and slammed it down on the spearhead. "If you betray us, if you dare to ignore the pact the way your caesar did, then it will be your head upon a spear!"

The Maeatae chieftain growled, his entire body rising and falling calmly like the blood-loving beast that covered his body.

But Marcus Claudius Picus was not bothered by the sight of his slaughtered man. "I will do my part. You worry about doing yours, Chieftain," he said, smirking. He began to walk away, but turned back to go to his remaining two men who knelt, looking up at him.

Without a word, Claudius spun, grabbed the sword from one of the men who had taken him prisoner and plunged it into the chest of one of his men, pulled it out and drove it into the neck of the other, leaving the blade protruding from the gasping man's flesh.

Claudius turned calmly to face the spear points and swords levelled at him.

The chieftain of the Maeatae smiled beside the shocked Argentocoxus and his men.

Claudius wiped his hands and began to walk away. "You may keep the heads," he called over his shoulder before disappearing into the mist and rain.

Part I

FAMILIAE

A.D. 210

I

SENEX IMPERATOR

'The Aged Emperor'

"Peace... Finally, some peace..."

Emperor Septimius Severus sat back in the great fur-covered chair that had been set up for him in the lush, green gardens of the imperial palace complex of Eburacum.

His body ached all over, but his cough had finally subsided after an entire morning of receiving various clients and hearing petitions from people wanting things from him - lands, favour, advantages over their enemies, and more.

He pulled the bear fur closely about him to ward off the cool spring air. It felt good to be alone now, after so many pulling at his attention like merchants' hands in the African animal markets. The emperor was happy to have sent everyone away, even Castor, his faithful freedman who was ever at his side, helping him, tending to him.

"I need time," he said to himself, but then laughed, and was pulled into another coughing fit. "Hmm. That is the one thing I do not have much of..."

Severus peered up at the grey clouds where they hung low, just above the red tile rooftops of the palace. He wondered if, being in Britannia, he had starved himself of the sun's light so much that it had sped the weakening of his body and soul even more.

No! he chided himself. *Fate has set its course and it would be the same were I sitting here, or in the heat and golden light of Leptis Magna.*

Since the beginning of the Caledonian campaign, Severus had missed his North African home more than ever - the sights, the smells, the colour and the light, brilliant light that penetrated the eyes such that it filled one with hope. The welcome he had received from the people of his home several years before, when he had returned, had rejuvenated him beyond measure.

Now, he fought against the waves of sadness and despair daily, as brutal an enemy as the Parthians or Caledonii had ever been.

"Time…"

How many sunrises and sunsets had he seen? How many cycles of moon and stars? He had ruled the world, believed he had been shown favour by the Gods. And yet his body wasted away with him still in it.

The emperor rubbed his eyes as they came down from the sky to rest on the ponds and tall marsh grasses before him. All was dark and deep green, the water black.

The tall grasses shivered then, despite the absence of wind, and Severus continued to stare into them, his eyes searching the spot where they seemed to part as if someone were moving through them.

"Castor?" the emperor said. "What are you doing there?"

But there was no answer.

Then, the minute amount of light that had been gracing the garden was completely choked from the sky and the emperor found himself in darkness.

The grasses rustled again.

"My son?" Severus called out, remembering with regret how Caracalla had thought to murder him before the legions in Caledonia. "Come out!"

The face that appeared was not that of his son or his freedman, or any other among the living. It was, however, the face of a man he had known.

The man approached slowly, his arms parting the reeds and grasses which hid his legs and waist. He stopped without making a sound or splash in the water.

"Clodius?" Septimius Severus sat up and forward, nearly falling over but holding on with his pale hands to the knobs of his chair. "You are dead, shade!"

Severus remembered giving the order for the murder of Clodius Albinus, his one-time friend, then rival claimant to the imperial throne. The troops had brought Severus his family seal after having cut his body up and thrown it in the Rhodanus, along with his family. Yet there the man stood, tall, his short curly hair and beard healthy and vibrant, framing his handsome face.

Albinus smiled knowingly at Severus, and extended his hand to point directly at the emperor.

You are rotting away like a corpse in the desert, Septimius.

"And you are dead!"

Yes… Murderer and thief!

18

"I stole nothing," Severus insisted. "I won the war because I was the strongest and my men the best."

Your legions cannot help you now. Not against the stars that are your fate...

Severus sat back in his chair, struggling to stay upright as the grey face seemed to stretch out to him, the eyes going from black to crimson.

Your time is near... So say the stars upon your ceiling, Septimius.

"You cannot frighten me, shade!" Severus said, his voice hoarse and angry. "I know my fate, and the hour of my death."

Albinus smiled, and teeth fell out of his mouth, even as the skin greyed and shrivelled upon his face and body, and his armour rotted and fell off to reveal his lacerated torso.

You will not see Elysium...ever. The gods will tear you apart as you tore my family apart...as you tore the Empire apart...

"No!"

Clodius Albinus' head toppled from his shoulders then, followed by the rest of his savaged form, and Severus drew back to hide beneath the furs.

"Get out!" the emperor shouted, as his hand grasped for the sword that leaned against his chair. "Be gone from me!"

"Sire!" the voice reached out, full of fear and concern. "My Emperor, I am here!"

The sword Severus had been grasping for fell onto the stone slabs with a loud clang, and he threw the furs aside to look up at Castor with rheumy eyes.

"Sire, it is me," the freedman said, his own aged eyes blinking back stinging tears when he saw the emperor in that state. "All is well, sire. It is only a passing storm cloud to block out the light. Nothing more."

Septimius Severus gripped Castor's tunic tightly and pulled him down to hiss into his ear.

"I saw him, Castor! Albinus! He is back for vengeance!"

As the emperor spoke, Castor put out his hand for one of the slaves to hand him the tonic he had prepared for Severus.

The emperor drank, rivulets running from the corners of his mouth to soak into the fabric of his purple and gold robes.

"Come, sire," Castor soothed. "I have set the braziers in your chamber alight to ward off this British chill."

19

ADAM ALEXANDER HAVIARAS

With Castor and the slave's help, Septimius Severus rose from his chair and began the long walk to his private chambers.

The darkness of the corridor was punctuated with fire from the torches, between which stood several Praetorians whom the Praetorian prefect, Papinianus, had chosen specifically for their loyalty.

Two guardsmen saluted, opened the double oak doors to the emperor's chamber, and closed them once more after Castor led him through.

Inside, Severus made his way directly to a marble altar that stood before bronze statues of Jupiter, Mars, and Baal.

Castor, well used to the emperor's routines, lit a chunk of fine Syrian frankincense, placed it in the emperor's hand and supported him as he placed it upon the altar.

Severus closed his eyes and swayed as he prayed, his mouth moving quickly, but uttering only incoherent words to the gods before him.

"Thank you, Castor," said the voice of the empress as she came up behind him from one of the secret doors to the chamber. "I shall care for the emperor now. I will call for you when we are ready to join the others in the triclinium."

"My lady," Castor said, bowing low to her, before ushering the slave out and leaving.

"Come, Husband," she said, her arm beneath Severus'. "It is time to rest."

She led him to the large bed flanked by two burning braziers with bronze lions' claws for feet.

Septimius Severus sighed once and his eyes focused on the ceiling above where he had ordered the stars painted in the pattern given him by his astrologer - the stars that reminded him his end was near, that it was written.

"I hate this feeling of weakness," he said to Julia Domna, his wife and empress.

"I know…" she said, "It is a feeling foreign to you." She held his hand in hers and squeezed.

He nodded, but his eyes widened and he shook his head, unable to forget the visage of death, of the man he had murdered, whose family he had hacked to pieces with the blades of his men.

He saw Albinus' shade more often recently. It haunted him. It undermined his strength.

Severus had told himself that all of the blood and death, of friends and enemies, had been for the good of the empire. All of it. But certainty was no longer a luxury. The only thing he knew for certain was the message in those stars painted upon his crumbling ceiling.

"I shall die soon," he said.

The empress gripped his hand tightly and nodded. "Yes," she whispered.

The imperial palace at Eburacum was a place of contrasts. At times it bustled as much inside as any market across the empire, the noise from the city's streets pouring in through every window and doorway to echo along every hall and corridor. At other times, it was silent and tense, like a prisoner awaiting sentence, or a disciplined army awaiting the call of a cornu to commence battle.

That night, the palace was silent, the darkness suspicious of the torches carried by guards as they made their rounds. Every room was carefully watched, especially the marble triclinium of the imperial family where Caesar Caracalla and his brother Geta sat opposite each other upon couches, their aunt, Julia Maesa, sitting beside the former.

"What's keeping them?" Caracalla said. "I'm hungry and have duties to attend to!" He fidgeted with a knife which he spun on the table top, a small indent forming where the blade turned round.

"Father was resting," Geta replied, popping a grape into his mouth, his eyes never meeting those of his brother or aunt. "They'll be here shortly. Mother told me when I passed her in the hall."

Julia Maesa, the empress' sister, laid her hand upon Caracalla's arm and smiled. "Your father was not feeling well today. Give him time. I think he wishes to speak with you both."

"Talk, talk, and more talk," Caracalla said, throwing his black cloak back so that it fell onto the floor behind his couch to reveal his red tunic. "We should not remain here in Britannia. The war with the Caledonii is over. We have a treaty."

"Father is not well enough to travel. You know this. Travelling will surely kill him," Geta said sadly as he wiped a drop of wine from his blue and gold embroidered tunic.

Caracalla eyed his brother over the flames jutting from several oil lamps amidst the platters of fowl, fish, fresh bread, olives, and cheese that had been laid out by the kitchen slaves for the imperial family. He was angry and resentful, like a bear that had been baited

21

too many times, not with weapons, but with laughter and derision, and the favour of their parents, which Geta seemed ever to enjoy.

Caracalla worked his jaw and ran his fingers through his dense, curly hair. It irked him that Geta walked about Eburacum as if he ruled there. While his brother had held court in Eburacum, Caracalla had bloodied his sword in Caledonia, plunged it into the flesh of their enemies. He had brokered a treaty with the barbarian chieftain, Argentocoxus, and had recovered the line of forts that made up the Roman Gask Ridge.

Much had happened since they had arrived in Britannia. As soon as he had arrived, Caracalla had been pulled into a maelstrom of blood and guts, to be spat out the other side before he had even known what happened. He was proud of his actions, of the wounds he had endured in the campaign, but the act of sitting still and tending to administration alone now irked him no end. He wanted to be in Rome.

At council meetings, his father no longer took his advice, nor did his opinion matter when it came to the running of the Praetorian Guard. Papinianus, the Praetorian prefect, no longer sought his council. In fact, he had been assured by his closest ally, Marcus Claudius Picus, that the emperor, Geta, and the Praetorian Prefect actively sought to exclude him from decisions on the future of the empire.

Caracalla slammed his fist on the table, making a carefully-stacked display of cooked fish collapse to either side, just as the double doors to the triclinium opened and the emperor and empress appeared there, flanked by Praetorians.

Geta rose from his couch and went to his father's aid, taking Castor's place at his father's left arm and helping him down the single step and around the table to the head couch.

"I'm glad to see you well, Father," Caracalla said from his couch.

Septimius Severus glanced at his son, but said nothing, reaching instead for the wine cup before him.

"I am not well," Severus replied, after taking a sip.

There was silence then, but for the splash of wine as one of the slaves went around the table to fill everyone's golden cups.

"You seem better than you were is all I meant," Caracalla said, reaching for a piece of steaming bread.

22

The emperor sipped his wine again, his eyes glancing at his sons from the top of his cup while two slaves placed braziers close behind him.

"And how are you, Sister?" Julia Domna asked Julia Maesa as she reclined across from Caracalla, beside Geta who kissed her hand as she did so.

"I am well, though I have to admit that the excitement of Eburacum is fast waning for me. I'm of a mind to go to Londinium to see what entertainments the town has."

"You'll do no such thing. The family stays here," the emperor said to his sister-in-law.

Julia Maesa nodded slowly in acquiescence, her hand reaching for her nephew's arm again.

The empress pat her husband's arm too and looked about the comfortable room, golden light reflecting off of the frescoed walls, their beauty blurred by the steam of the hot foot placed before them.

Julia Domna looked tired, her eyes betraying the weight of her worries, but beyond that, her presence soothed most, as did her calm demeanour. She reclined amid the folds of her gold and emerald tunica and stola, her shoulders covered by a matching palla. It was a simple, elegant look to match her tightly bound hair, quite the opposite of her sister who, despite the cold British climate, insisted on going bare-shouldered about the palace.

Julia Maesa's sea blue stola betrayed the actual season and place in which she found herself.

The empress smiled thinly at her, knowing that the incessantly-full wine cup her sister held aloft warmed her enough.

She did not mind, she supposed. Julia Maesa never imposed upon her own imperial powers. *She knows better...*

What the empress did mind was the way her sister always seemed to be touching Caracalla, and how, to him, it seemed perfectly natural.

We are not Ptolemies in Alexandria! she thought, uncharacteristically bitter.

Then again, a woman's relationship with her sister's son was special and complex.

Julia Maesa, however, had only daughters.

"My son," the emperor suddenly said, leaning as much as he could in Geta's direction as he ripped a chunk from a loaf of warm

23

bread. "Tell me about the newest building projects in Eburacum. We've spent much time here, and we should enrich the city for it."

"An excellent notion, Father," Geta said. He sat straighter, his eyes finally deigning to meet his brother's gaze, not without flinching at the vehemence he saw there. "The engineers have finished the improvements on the city bathhouse and the populace has begun to enjoy them. The people seem pleased. Also, the new docks along the river are improved and expanded. There are many more berths for trading traffic which will feed into the newly refurbished agora of Eburacum. Everyone is pleased."

"You've done well while we were in the North, Geta," Julia Domna said, her eyes watching Caracalla as she said so, aware that the great tension between them, one of the reasons for the Caledonian campaign, had not dwindled, but rather grown in intensity.

"There's more," Geta interrupted. "The bridge across the river, leading to the via Praetoria of the base on the other side, has been strengthened. It should now withstand the occasional rise in the river level."

"It's a shame you can't do anything about the stink of the river in this place," Caracalla put in.

Julia Domna stared at her older son for a moment and her sister removed her hand slowly. "Why don't you tell us what our second Augustus has been up to? We are no less proud."

"Really, Mother?" Caracalla scoffed. "Well, I've finally cleaned all of the blood off of my armour and weapons." He turned to Geta. "Actual fighting does get rather messy."

Geta chose to ignore him.

"The Gask Ridge remains intact and regular patrols go out to ensure that that does not change. I left Claudius Picus there to oversee things in my absence, and he assures me that all is in hand, and that the Caledonii have not broken the truce."

"If they do," Geta laughed, "will you ride out and spank them, Brother?"

"Stop this!" the emperor suddenly burst out, throwing a crust of bread that was too hard to chew down onto his plate. His sharp eyes went around the table, resting longer on his two sons to either side of him. "You both carry the title of Augustus, just as I do now, and I expect you to act accordingly. You both have your strengths and should use them to your advantage, that of this family, and the empire we rule." Septimius Severus sighed and looked up at the pine ceiling of the triclinium, the beams painted red and blue. There were no stars there, but he could see them nonetheless. He remembered the stars on the days each of his sons were born.

"Momentous," his astrologer had said. "Propitious…"

The emperor knew he had never been nostalgic before. *A waste of time!* he had thought. *The stars only ever shine their light on the way forward…*

However, as the day of his own death drew near, and the path before him grew ever shorter, his resolve to shut out the past had dissolved like mist when the sun emerged in Britannia. It was never more so than when he beheld his sons. He looked at them both, even as they spoke, unhearing of the words that escaped their mouths. He remembered their births, and the vow he had made to give Rome a new line of greatness. Before him, emperors like Antoninus and Hadrian had adopted their heirs - the 'best men for the job'. But Severus had faith in his sons and the stars they were born beneath.

Yes, Caracalla had thought of killing him, but that sort of strength was needed in a ruler. He hoped that it was only his son's love of him that kept him from carrying out the act, though his loyal troops, Lucius Metellus Anguis among them, were also responsible for stopping the embarrassing event.

All said and done, Severus knew full well that an emperor had to be prepared to kill. What mattered was the outcome of that killing, and if it left the empire, and their family, better or worse off in the Gods' scheme.

"Father!" Caracalla suddenly burst out.

The emperor snapped back out of his thoughts, and the smile upon his face faded as quickly as the thoughts of his young children.

"How dare you!" Severus said to Caracalla.

"You aren't even listening!" Caracalla said. "I told you I'm considering raising the average rate of pay for all troops. "They deserve it after this campaign, and it will bind their loyalty to you."

"Buy their loyalty to you, don't you mean, Brother," Geta said as he dropped a fish spine onto his plate and sucked his fingers. A bit of oil splashed onto the nearest oil lamp and fizzled momentarily.

"You mind your tongue," Caracalla growled. "I've learned a few new things in Caledonia."

"Enough!" Severus smacked the table, his head and face shaking visibly with pent-up rage and frustration. "Your brother is correct to

25

want to please the legions, Geta. Without them and their loyalty, we would not be where we are today." He turned to Caracalla. "But be sure that I am not yet dead, despite the rebellion of my body. We may all three be Augusti, but only I am Emperor. Do not try to undermine me."

"Gods forbid it, Father!" Caracalla said sarcastically.

Severus calmed himself and looked to his wife.

"Let us talk of other things. War is not the only way to guarantee the survival of our dynasty in the coming years…"

Julia Maesa sat up now and turned toward the emperor whom, before that, she had been ignoring as he ignored her.

"Marcus Aurelius saw fit to trust his son to the imperial throne after his death, despite the recommendations of others that Commodus was not fit"

"He wasn't!" Geta said.

"Be still," Severus silenced him. "Marcus Aurelius was a wise and warlike emperor. Yes, Commodus had his failings, but he inherited a mess. When I die, I shall leave you with an empire the likes of which has not existed before. I do so with the faith that you will both set aside your quarrelsome relationship and see fit to rule jointly and fairly so that, when the histories are written, they will have naught but good things to say."

"You should speak with Senator Dio, then," Julia Maesa put in. "He is considering writing a history of our time."

Severus paused, frustrated at the interruption, but nodded politely at his sister-in-law before continuing.

"You would both do well to make your peace, for when I pass from this world…that will be the time when the imperial throne is at its most vulnerable."

They were all silent, aware of the sad and severe truth that the emperor had just uttered. They held all the power in the world amongst them, and yet, the Gods could snuff out that flame in a heartbeat.

Caracalla stared directly at his father, and the emperor stared back at him, holding his gaze as if that would help him to ascertain his thoughts. Just as he was about to speak, say something to break the feeling of guilt that weighed upon him, one of the slaves touched him on the shoulder.

"Sire," the slave whispered. "Marcus Claudius Picus awaits you in the atrium."

26

"Tell him Caesar is busy," Julia Domna said, her voice firm.

"No!" Caracalla countered. "He may have news." He turned to the slave. "Tell him I am coming."

The slave scurried away through the open doors which were then closed by the guards outside.

"He deigns to disturb our meal?" the emperor said.

"Frankly, I don't know how you can tolerate that man," Geta said. "He's an animal from what I hear."

Caracalla stood and leaned upon his fists on the table opposite his younger brother. "Because he gets things done, little Caesar."

Geta scoffed.

Caracalla turned to leave. "I won't return this evening," he said as he pulled open the doors and went out into the torchlit corridor.

Caracalla strode quickly down the corridors, acknowledging the Praetorian troops he passed along the way.

They saluted back at him, keenly aware that he would be stepping into his father's place in the near future.

His long cloak billowed behind him as he went, always with a determined step, as if with purpose or anger, most often the two indistinguishable in him. The corridor led into the atrium where the open part of the roof allowed a mist of rain to fall into the pool of the impluvium.

There, beside the water, Marcus Claudius Picus stood with his eyes closed, the rain falling on his face to give it a sheen in the firelight radiating from the red and white walls at the outer edge of the atrium.

"What is it?" Caracalla demanded, coming right up into Claudius' face. "You had better have a good reason for this interruption." Caracalla looked him up and down. "You haven't even cleaned the mud from your armour."

Claudius slowly opened his cold blue eyes and turned to Caracalla. For a moment, he did not salute, but the young Caesar's eyes dared him not to, and so he stretched his arm out slowly.

"Augustus," Claudius said.

"Well?" Caracalla relaxed a little, but his eyes continued to bore into the man. "It must be something important for you to interrupt me at this hour."

"It is," Claudius answered, throwing back his black cloak to reveal his muddy cuirass and greaves. He had obviously been riding

27

for some time. "I received word from some of my scouts north of the wall."

"Yes?"

"They found the bodies."

"Really?" Caracalla stepped back, his shoulders caving in a little, as if a wave of relief washed over his spirit. "They're dead?"

"Not who you think, sire. The Metelli live. It was the bodies of our men…" he cleared his throat, "…your men, which they found."

Caracalla's fists balled and Claudius thought for a moment he would pommel him as he had done on occasion.

"All of them?" Caracalla asked.

"Yes. They also found the body of Centurion Kasen."

"What? So, he did go to help them." Caracalla walked around to the other side of the impluvium, his chin in his hand. He had stopped trusting Alerio some time ago, but to know that he was finally out of the way gave him some comfort, even though the Metelli were still alive.

"Alerio must have overheard us speaking and gone to warn the Metelli, or stop our men from carrying out their orders."

Caracalla looked up from the water, his eyes full of anger, and before Claudius could react, Caracalla's fist slammed into the side of his head, sending him reeling onto the black and white mosaic floor.

"You've failed again, Marcus!" Caracalla spat at him and then walked over and pulled him to his feet.

Claudius did not fight back as he would have liked to, but let himself be man-handled by Caracalla. He did, however, meet his gaze directly.

"It is only a matter of time," he said, his lip bleeding to blend with the mud upon his face.

"Make no mistake, Claudius Picus. I can put you right back where I found you on the death lists. The only reason you are alive is that I need you for certain tasks, this one the main among them. You have a great number of men and spies at your disposal, so you should be able to rid me of one troublesome man, his wife and children, no? Is that too much for you? Has Lucius Metellus Anguis proven once and for all to be the better man than you?"

Claudius' cold exterior cracked then and he stepped forward to meet his Caesar nose to nose.

"No…" he growled.

"Then prove it to your emperor," Caracalla said. "For that is what I am. And you... You are nothing unless I say you are."

"Yes, sire," Claudius found his calm again and stood down.

"Good. Now, I want you to use your vast spy network to watch the Metelli, perhaps infiltrate their surroundings. I don't care how you do it, but do it you must."

"Why can't we just kill them in their sleep?"

"While the emperor lives, such a thing would not be wise. The best course of action is to find some proof, real or not, of his guilt or suspicion of treason."

"That won't be easy," Claudius acknowledged.

"Then I can find someone else who will - "

"No, sire!" Claudius jumped in. "I shall see to it."

"Good."

"And if the emperor should...join the Gods?" Claudius asked, his voice lower now so that only Caracalla should hear him.

"Then you may dispose of them as you see fit. Just don't fail again."

"Oh, I won't," Claudius said, a smile coming to his thin lips.

As the moon emerged over the rooftops of Eburacum that night, its cold light trying to penetrate the veil of heavy rain clouds over the city, Emperor Septimius Severus lay still in his bed, staring once more up at the ceiling of his rooms.

Incense burned upon the altar, the blue smoke rising slowly to snake its way among the beams above. It reminded him of the sand serpents that wound their way across the sands of Africa when the Gods blew gently from their distant caves.

How I used to love watching them...so long ago.

He turned his head to see Castor asleep in the chair beside one of the braziers, the fold of a scroll from Rome gripped gently in his limp hand.

Severus could not remember the matter in the letter, so tedious it was. However, he comforted himself with the fact that he would leave his sons with few enemies at their gates, most of their opponents having been eliminated in the years since he had donned the purple.

He thought of their grievous behaviour toward each other, and it pained him. He worried that they would be each other's worst enemies.

29

The stars above beckoned him once more, and he gazed up. Odd that it was at such times as these that his mind now gave him the most clarity, a clarity that previously was only to be had in battle, whether on the fields of Mars or in the Senate.

There was a gentle knock upon the door, and Severus looked, expecting to see Julia Domna enter to see him comfortable before settling in for the night. It had become her habit since arriving in Britannia to bring him a cup of infused herbs to help alleviate his cough through the night, a concoction she insisted on mixing herself since the treaty with the Caledonii and their son's embarrassing display.

However, it was not the empress who entered when Castor rose sleepily and opened the door.

Papinianus, Prefect of the Praetorian Guard, appeared and whispered that he had some urgent business to speak with the emperor about.

Castor, to his credit, tried to delay it until morning, but Papinianus was persistent.

"Castor," Severus said as he sat up slowly, adjusting his gouty, aching legs beneath the thick covers. "The Praetorian prefect has every right to speak with me." He nodded to Papinianus. "What is it, my friend?"

Papinianus bowed and entered the lavish room. The glow cast from the braziers shone off of his black and brown cuirass which he kept clean and well-polished at all times.

"Sire," Papinianus sat on the chair which stood beside the bed. He waved away the cup of wine which Castor offered him and leaned close to the emperor.

"You have something important to say to me, it seems... I wonder what?" Severus looked keenly at his prefect and could discern the great discomfort upon his brow.

Severus may have been weak of body, but he was still a good judge of men.

"Do you wish for Castor to leave us?"

"No need, sire. For I know and trust Castor as well as you." Papinianus leaned in and rubbed his balding head.

The two of them had aged with time, even more so since arriving in Britannia, but whereas the emperor's body had been wasting away, his mind intact, Papinianus felt as though the worries upon his shoulders would crush him, drive him mad, though his body had not yet betrayed him.

"Sire, it is about your son."

"Geta?"

"No, sire. It is about Marcus."

"I thank you for not using that ridiculous name the men insist on calling him. For a caesar to be named after a bit of clothing..."

"Yes, sire. Well... I know you love him well - "

"He is my firstborn son." Severus' voice was slightly harder, but he allowed Papinianus to speak.

"I am afraid, sire, that he may try again to...to...harm your imperial majesty." Papinianus exhaled deeply, the sweat appearing upon his brow.

Severus' head straightened and his eyes narrowed. "You had better explain yourself, Prefect. I do not take this sort of accusation lightly."

"Nor do I, sire. Believe me. But ever since the treaty with the Caledonii, and your son's attempt to -"

"His rash thought to kill me," the emperor corrected. "He made no attempt."

"Even so, sire. It is my charge to see to your safety in this world, and so I have had a watch kept upon him at times. I believe he still harbours thoughts of harming you."

Papinianus stood and paced before the end of the bed, the emperor's eyes following him every second, boring into him.

"What proof can you offer of these harboured thoughts, Papinianus? Have you a mind-reader among your staff?"

"No sire. Some of the men I had set to watching him and his friends have gone missing. Besides, it is obvious that he bears you no love."

"As is often the case between fathers and sons."

"It is not so with Geta, though, is it?"

"Geta is different."

"I quite agree."

"What is your point? If you have no proof of further treachery on the part of my son, then all you have done this moment is endanger yourself in my eyes."

Papinianus was taken aback, and a look of betrayal lashed his old face them. "Sire, I have ever been loyal to you and your family. Your family is my family!"

"My wife's family is your family, and yes, I am aware of your loyalties. But I cannot leave this world knowing that my son does not have someone such as you minding his back at all times. You must be ruthless in this task."

"Sire, the Gods have not called you to them yet."

There was a pause and Severus pulled at his long, white and black beard. "No, they have not." He looked up at the ceiling.

Papinianus decided to push one more time.

"Sire, if it comes to light that your son, Marcus, is conspiring against you, then I must advise that you…that you execute him with all haste. As your friend and protector, I know I risk my life in telling you this, but I do so because the Gods compel me to.

He expected Septimius Severus to rise from his bed, a final image of his former self, take up the golden-hilted gladius that stood beside the bed, and dispatch him then and there to put him out of his misery.

But the emperor merely looked upon Papinianus with pity.

"My friend, you do not understand the love one has for a son… Even were it true, I could not carry out such an act, even as the divine Marcus Aurelius could not."

"Sire." Papinianus stood straight, his composure regained, his disappointment acute.

"But make no mistake, that if you come to me with such a suggestion again, I will have no qualms about ending your life."

Out of the corner of his eye, Papinianus saw Castor stiffen. They had often spoken of Caracalla and the threat he posed. They had talked of taking this opportunity to set the emperor upon the correct, though supremely difficult course he had only just suggested.

It seemed, however, that it was no use.

"There will be no need, sire, to take my life," Papinianus said. "For I remain your loyal servant, and that of your family."

"Good," Severus leaned back as if the intensity of his thinking then had exhausted him. "Remember, Prefect, that when I die, Marcus will be the Empire's greatest strength and weapon against Rome's would-be enemies. And trust me when I say that Rome will always have enemies."

II

ANGUIS DOMUS

'The Dragon's Home'

Even the Gods are capable of worry.

Most mortals do not believe it so. Most believe them harsh and uncaring, or supremely indifferent.

But some gods do worry. Some care so deeply that even on the heavenly verges of the world, they can lay awake, restless and chasing sleep when the mortals they care for, whom they have protected, are destined for trials not of Olympus' devising.

The Gods would seek to protect mortals from themselves, but there are some things that the rules of divine order strictly ordain.

From the high slopes of Olympus, in their gleaming halls, in the shade of their eternally fruitful trees beside the clarion trickle of their fountains, the Gods hear and see all.

They care, and feel. They love, and hate, the same as their mortal children, but for an eternity.

Oh yes... The Gods do worry...

It was the harsh clang of swords that drew the Gods' gaze that day.

From where Far-Shooting Apollo and Venus sat beneath the bows of an ancient, broad-limbed olive tree upon the slopes of their Olympian eyrie, their starry eyes went to the green mound far to the North, where white clouds raced across a cool blue Spring sky.

Apollo leaned against the gnarled trunk, his silver bow and quiver laid upon the emerald grass at his feet, his blue cloak snapping occasionally at Zephyrus' behest. He leaned forward to peer over the edge of the world, and Love followed his gaze from where she sat amidst long-stemmed blossoms, her stola of purest white floating just above the ground, around the feet of its heavenly wearer.

Together they stared across the lands, across time, to that one, far-distant spot.

The two opponents circled each other, their blades poised, eager.

The Gods gazed upon the sweaty brows of the fighters, the reaction of their lean muscles. They admired the way they danced around death. They could hear the rapid beat of their hearts as they thrust and parried, attacked and retreated.

"They are preparing..." Venus said to Apollo.

The Far-Shooter nodded and hung his head, his hair hiding his brilliant eyes as a cloud that passes before the sun dims the light of the world. "A storm is coming. They need to be prepared." Apollo looked up at the sky again and felt the weight of the knowledge coursing through his fiery veins.

"We can intervene..."

He shook his head and turned to her. "Not this time."

Love stood then and walked to the very edge of the precipice. She wanted to reach out and touch them, protect them. All of them.

"We must stand by and watch then?" Venus said.

Apollo turned to her, but said nothing, for even as his lips began to utter the words, the clang of swordsong reached them, then a cry of pain.

They turned back to watch once more, from beneath the shivering silver-green leaves of the tree.

"Are you all right?"

Adara Metella gazed up at the hand extended toward her, nodded, grasped it, and was pulled up.

"Lucius won't thank you for cutting me, but we need to make this as realistic as possible if I'm to be any good at it." Adara wiped the dark strands of hair from her sweaty brow, and dabbed at the blood on her arm where Briana's sword had caught her. "Again!" she panted, crouching for another attack.

"Good!" Briana said, smiling, her face rosy with the exertion of the fight. "Let's see if you've learned your lesson yet."

She attacked, and Adara parried the slash away with her own sword, spinning, and sending the fist of her left hand to strike out at the back of Briana's head as she passed.

The Briton's recovery was quick and she was instantly facing Adara again, pushing her backward on the defensive. "Attack me!" Briana yelled as she pressed her advantage. "Don't slow down! Find a way in!"

Adara stumbled then and, sensing immediately the blow to come, rolled backward twice, quickly down the slope of the hill before landing on her feet again and parrying just in time to slip in close to Briana and elbow her in the chest so that she fell backward onto the grass with Adara's blade at her throat.

Briana looked up, catching her breath, and smiled. "Good," she croaked. "And if it were a real enemy, you would not stop there, I hope, but drive your blade into the neck or abdomen without hesitation."

Adara nodded, sweat pouring from her brow as the two of them went to the table nearby where a jug of water and two cups waited for them.

There was a hooting from nearby and the two women turned to see Lucius, Einion, Phoebus and Calliope sitting near the woodpile where the two men had supposedly been chopping wood, but instead seemed to have enjoyed the entertainment just fine, with the children marvelling at the skill the two displayed.

"You're getting old, Briana!" Einion teased his sister, laughing as he took in the mud up her backside.

"You're next!" she joked before taking a long drink. She looked up the hill at the two men and children, and smiled. "Lucius seems quite impressed with your skill. I don't think I've ever seen him smile so much."

Adara turned to see her husband staring at her and returned his wave, letting him know she was fine.

"Just a scratch!" she yelled.

The truth was that in the months since Briana had begun training her everyday, she had suffered much worse injuries - bumps, bruises, cuts and gashes that would have turned her mother's hair white.

But she never felt so alive, so strong. She enjoyed her training, as well as the sisterly bond it had nurtured between herself and Briana, something she had not dreamed of having again since the tragedy in North Africa when Alene Metella was murdered.

"He worries for me," Adara said, looking from Lucius back to Briana who was tying her long, dark blond braids together again.

"Trust me, he would worry more if you did not know how to defend yourself."

"I suppose," Adara said, her gaze scanning the green landscape that surrounded them, the place that had been their home since they arrived in southern Britannia. "But I suppose here in the South, there is far less danger than in Eburacum, or north of the wall, in Caledonia."

"Aye," Briana said. "Maybe." She put her cup down "Are you ready for a bit more?"

Adara nodded. "Yes. A little more. Then I have to wash the children." She looked up at their smiling faces as they prepared to watch more practice. "Seems as though they got into the animal pens again."

They both laughed and took positions.

"Attack!" Briana said as Adara's blade whistled past her head.

From his position upon a large, downed trunk beside the woodpile, Lucius Metellus Anguis watched his wife push herself to her limits in her training. He had never imagined her to be so good at it, but he knew how hard she had worked for the skills she had acquired.

"What do you think of Mama's fighting?" he asked his daughter, Calliope, who rested in his lap with the sun on her face as she watched.

"I think she's is wonderful!" the girl said. "Like one of the warriors from the stories from Greece that you have told us. The one about the daughters of Ares."

Einion smiled and looked over at Lucius who smiled back and squeezed his daughter.

"Yes. She is magnificent," Lucius said as he watched the two women spar again.

"And you Phoebus?" Einion asked Lucius' son. "What do you think of your mother now? Maybe you won't feel so inclined to disobey when she tells you to go to bed now, eh?" the Briton laughed and ruffled Phoebus' hair.

"I knew she could do it," the boy said, not taking his eyes off of them, watching every move and sword thrust as if taking note for his own training which Lucius and Einion had taken turns at.

"Good lad," Lucius said, almost to himself.

It seemed only yesterday when he had met Adara at the banquet on the Palatine Hill in Rome all those years ago.

Has it been so long?

So much had happened to their family since then…separation, births, deaths…so much…

And now he watched his proper Athenian wife train like one of the warrior British women he'd read about, or like an Amazon of old, a daughter of Ares as Calliope had put it.

She was good too, as if some dormant fighting instinct had been awoken in her the moment a sword had been placed in her hand. At least he hoped it was that, and not the danger he had inadvertently put her - all of them - in by bringing them to those far northern shores.

The will to defend her family no doubt drove her, he suspected, as it always drove him.

He watched her and, despite the inkling of fear it gave him to see her strengthening herself, he thought her a thing of beauty more than ever, so vital and strong, her cheeks red with exertion. There was even something regal about her, as he imagined the British warrior queen Boudicca might have been.

Adara and Briana finished then, and his reverie was broken.

The two women came walking up to them.

"You're sweating more than I do, Sister!" Einion said.

"But I smell better than you," she answered, making him laugh.

Adara walked up to Lucius who put Calliope down and kissed his wife.

"I'm sweaty too," she said, trying to pull away.

"I don't care," he said, kissing her again.

"Mama, I want to learn to fight like you!" Calliope cheered, throwing her little arms about her mother's legs.

"In good time," Adara said extending her hand to her son and stroking his cheek. "In time," she repeated, her voice soothing.

"I'm not sure how much more I can teach you, Adara," Briana said. "These many months, you've learned so much."

"We'll have to teach you to fight from horseback next," Einion said in earnest.

"And with a kontos," Lucius added.

"I'll get my sword skills down first, thank you," Adara laughed. "But first, I think a nice bath to wash the dirt away."

Phoebus and Calliope began to walk the other way at the mention, but Adara grabbed them both.

"Ah, ah, ah! That means you too!" She held them fast. "You want to play with the pigs, goats, and sheep, then you need to wash. Come on!" she said, ushering the children up the slope to the stone hall. Briana and Einion followed behind them, the latter with an armful of firewood.

"I'll be along shortly," Lucius called after them.

He watched them all go up to the long, two-storey stone hall they had built in that place until the double doors closed. He then walked slowly down the slope of the plateau to the eastern rampart to peer over the edge, down to the green fields far below.

Lucius often did so in the evening, walking the perimeter of their new home, taking it all in, that place of happiness of the last several months. He turned and surveyed the work they had done since their arrival.

A new Dragon's Lair, he thought wistfully.

Lucius remembered seeing their new home for the first time as they had come along the Roman road from the North...

At first, he had thought it just another hill in a landscape that seemed to sing of green in myriad shades. But upon closer inspection of the map, and the description Publius Leander Antoninus, his father-in-law, had given him, it became apparent that the ancient mound was indeed his family's new home, including the fields surrounding it.

Lucius' soldier's eye was drawn to the four levels of strong defensive works, the ditches deep and overgrown, yet still only an echo of their former, formidable glory. He knew there must once have been walls crowning those embankments. The place grew up out of the land, a part of it, and yet distinct all at once. It had been a mighty fortress in the age before Rome had come to Britannia's shores, a home no doubt for the Durotriges, the tribe of Britons who inhabited the region.

If he had read the histories correctly, Vespasian had stormed this fortress and expelled the native population from its heights, the same as other hillforts across the South.

The eagles of Rome had come to toss the young of others from the nest, and taken it for themselves.

As Lucius walked along the top of the grassy embankments, he remembered thinking that the hillfort must once have been the fortress of kings, and he felt a hint of guilt that it had been turned into a simple Roman supply station upon which no Britons were permitted, unless they were army personnel.

It was now his family's home, a wedding gift from Adara's parents who had never even seen the place, and who had acquired it in a business deal of some sort.

"Is that our new home, Baba?" Phoebus had asked as they all stood upon the road gazing up at the titanic, grassy mound.

"Yes, I believe it is," Lucius had said to his son.

"I've heard of this place," Einion said on the horse beside Lucius' own. "It was the power centre of the Durotriges, my distant kinsmen."

"Ynis Wytrin is not far away either," Briana said to Adara and the children who were in the wagon with her, their horses tagging along behind on leads.

"I wonder what condition Rome has left it in?" Lucius mused. "I wrote to one of the magistrates in Durnovaria some time ago to ensure that it had been taken care of."

"Then let us see what they have made of it," Adara said. "Come." She flicked the reins of the wagon and it lurched forward.

Rome had done little upkeep to the hillfort, as it turned out. After all, it was not used as a defensive work, and was basically Lucius' private property, therefore his responsibility. There was no need for such defensive works in the South, especially in that area where there were more temples, villas and mines than legionary camps and signal towers.

It had been difficult to get the wagon up the narrow roadway to the north-eastern gate of the fortress, but when they did, a great expanse of grass, kissed anew with early Spring, was spread out before them like a sheet in the wind.

"It's so big!" Calliope had said, her young, bright eyes wide in disbelief, her mind already working on the array of games she and her brother could play there.

Lucius had kicked Lunaris forward up the gentle slope of the hill to see what was there, and found only the overgrown ruins of native roundhouses, a few stray, grazing sheep, and a single Roman stable block and outbuilding that served as the resupply station. There wasn't even a trooper manning it.

"I guess folks are just supposed to help themselves?" Einion said as he looked around.

"Not much to it, is there?" Briana said.

"We'll make something of it," Lucius said, turning Lunaris to face all of them.

And they had made something of it.

Living in the campaign tents he had brought for all of them, Lucius had begun planning the layout of their new home upon that ancient hillfort. For a while, they had lived like they were on campaign, sleeping in the tents, scouting the surrounding countryside, and familiarizing themselves with their new lands.

It was exciting.

They had arrived at what was really a lonely, scarred and windswept hill, and with a lot of hard work, and the funds Lucius had saved away with the imperial payroll, they had made the place a home.

The hill was large, almost eighteen acres within the ramparts. In places it was pitted with what had been lined storage holes in addition to the roundhouses on the eastern side. These were mostly grass-covered, but Einion and Briana explained that they would have been lined with baskets and used for winter food stores.

The sudden activity on the old hillfort had drawn many of the locals from the village to the South, across a clear-flowing brook. Some of the men had come up to see what was going on, and when Lucius introduced himself, they seemed at first wary, not returning for a couple of days.

They had never met the Roman owner of the land, a place that had been of great importance to their forbears. It had been over one hundred and fifty years since the Roman onslaught, but the scars and distrust still ran deep.

Some days later, a youthful man from the village came wandering up with his son to greet Lucius.

He appeared to be a potter, though he was built more like a smith, for his long brown hair rested upon immense shoulders. His hands were huge, and when he shook Lucius' hand, the latter knew he was a man of might. He was also friendly and affable as he spoke, ruffling his son's hair and nodding at the work Lucius and Einion had been doing on one of the stable blocks.

"I'm Culhwch," he said. "And this is my son, Paulus."

"Pleased to meet you, Paulus," Lucius said, kneeling down to face the boy. "I have a son too. Phoebus is his name. He's a bit younger than you, I suspect."

"You are with the legions?" Culhwch asked.

"Yes."

"On furlough then?"

Lucius looked the man up and down, and Culhwch put his hands up.

"I meant not to pry. I only ask out of curiosity, and for the safety of my family. Sure you understand that?"

Lucius nodded. "I do."

At that moment, Einion stepped up to Lucius' side. "Lucius Metellus Anguis is a friend of the Britons hereabouts. You need not worry, friend."

"A Roman with Dumnonian friends, eh?" the man smiled broadly. "Well. Then you are both welcome to Durotrigan territory."

"I've been in these lands for years myself," Einion said.

"Where? I've not seen you before."

"Ynis Wytrin was my home," Einion said.

The man fell silent and nodded, his eyes looking to the northwest. "If Ynis Wytrin welcomes you, then I shall call you friends from now on." He rubbed his beard and looked back to Lucius. "I have heard of you, I think. Some of the troops in the taberna at Lindinis mentioned a 'Dragon Praefectus' fighting in the North. 'Anguis', is it? That means 'dragon', no?"

"It does," Lucius said.

"Then this is your new lair!" he laughed, but not mockingly.

"I suppose it is," Lucius said, smiling and patting Einion on the shoulder.

"What do you intend to do with the place?" Culhwch asked. "When the winds pick up here toward October, that tent of yours will fly to the heavens."

"I'll show you," Lucius said, easing into the man's friendly manner. He led him to a roughly-hewn table where several papers were held down with rocks. One of them was a charcoal sketch of a rectangular stone hall with roof tiles.

Culhwch looked over the picture and nodded. "On the high plateau of the fortress?"

"Of the hill, yes," Lucius corrected, careful not to talk of fortifications or other defensive works that might void his building permits in the eyes of the local magistrate.

"Tiles will be quite expensive, but will last longer than thatch up here in the wind. Have you hired work crews yet?"

Lucius looked suspiciously at him then, wondering if he had only come to drum up business. "No. I haven't. We need to source the proper stone, and the tiles."

"Well, if you want help, I can give it to you. My brother has one of the best crews around. He's built several of the villas around Lindinis, some for members of the ordo there. He also has contacts at the hillfort limestone quarry south of Lindinis."

41

"Maybe you can bring him around?"

"I can."

"What of the roof tiles and timbers for the supporting beams?" Einion asked.

"The tiles are manufactured in Lindinis as well. My brother will know who to go to. As for the timbers, there is a man in our village who can find the proper timbers for you and take care of transport up here."

"And what about yourself?" Lucius asked. "Is there some service you want to provide?" He could not help sounding a little bitter now, and regretted it instantly.

"This isn't Rome, Praefectus. I offer neighbourly friendship. But, if you decide you need a new set of dishes and wine cups when your home is built, then I can offer you something." He winked, and Lucius smiled, embarrassed.

"Forgive me. My suspicions have come from dealing with too many snakes. I didn't mean to offend you."

"Not at all. Think nothing of it. But I must be going. My wife, Alma, will be waiting for Paulus and me for our supper." He turned to go. "I'll bring my brother, Cradawg, up to see you soon, as well as Silvius who can speak with you about the wood needed for that monstrous roof." He nodded toward the sketch and waved.

"I don't really know what to make of him," Lucius said to Einion as they watched Culhwch and his son walk toward the slope of the south-west gate and back toward the distant village.

"We'll see if he does what he said he'll do," Einion said suspiciously. "Can never tell with Durotrigans."

Lucius laughed.

Culhwch was as good as his word, Lucius soon found out, for he returned two days later with his brother and the woodsman.

Cradawg was a larger version of his younger brother, Culhwch, and Silvius looked like a woodland beast himself, tall, lanky, and lean, with a great beard that seemed bedecked with bits of leaf and carried a permanent scent of wood shavings.

Culhwch introduced Lucius and Einion to the two men, and it was not long before they were hunched over the rough sketches Lucius had done up, with some help from Adara's skilled hand.

"You sure you want to build up here, Praefectus?" Cradawg said after a few minutes of studying the plans. "If you built down in the field, you could have running water from the brook, and even build in some hypocausts for the winter time. It's green here now, but let me tell you, when the wind starts howling at mid-winter, you'll wish you were in a proper Roman house."

"This is the land that is ours," Lucius answered. "And..." he paused, looking around at the vast surface area of the grassy mound. "Yes. I'm sure. I want to build the domus there." He pointed at the uppermost part of the plateau where the campaign tent stood, battered by the wind.

Cradawg nodded. "Well, if it was good enough for our great grandfathers to live up here, it's good enough for you." He clapped his hands. "I can build what you want. A rectangular structure with a second level on the North side, with an inner walkway overlooking the hall. It may be a bit awkward, but I can see your reasoning."

"And I can get my lads to build a proper frame for the roof," Silvius added, looking at the plateau as if to envision the structure. "We'll have to place an order for the tiles soon. It's not too many, but the workshops in Lindinis are quite busy at the moment with a few more villas being built in the area."

"Right," Cradawg agreed.

"So how long are you thinking this could take?" Lucius asked.

"Up to a year," Cradawg said. "Things are busy, and we need to get the stone cut to size and transported from the old quarry near Lindinis."

"That's too long," Lucius said. "I'd like to have my family indoors by the end of Summer."

"Ha!" Silvius laughed. "Impossible! That's only a few months away!"

"What will it take?" Lucius asked, looking Cradawg in the eye.

The big Durotrigan rubbed his chin and appeared to be going over numbers and lists of supplies in his mind.

"Well," he said. "Since you don't want hypocausts, and the design of the building is plain enough, I suppose it could be done if we double our man-power and pay extra for speed at the quarry and tile kilns."

"The decurions of the ordo won't like that," Silvius said.

"Should I worry about them?" Lucius asked. The last thing he wanted was to make enemies in the area.

"Don't worry about it," Cradawg assured. "I know a group of hard workers who have been down on their luck recently. They'll welcome the work...and the pay."

"Which I suppose I should ask about," Lucius said. "How much are we talking?"

"I'll have to add things up, but it will be a lot for such a quick turn-around. I'll give you as fair a price as I can, Praefectus," Cradawg said. "My brother assures me you're a good man."

Lucius turned to Culhwch. "But you only just met me."

Culhwch smiled and shrugged. "What can I say? I'm a good judge of character. Besides, it's good luck to have a dragon living next door."

"All right then," Lucius said. "If I like the price, you and your men are hired. Good?"

"Good!" Cradawg extended his meaty hand and Lucius took it. "I'll stay with my brother tonight and go over the numbers with Silvius, and then I'll have a price for you tomorrow."

The next day, as Lucius was exploring the southern ramparts, he spotted Cradawg, Silvius, and Culhwch approaching with a wax tablet. He walked down to meet them.

"You're early!" Lucius said.

"No time to waste if you want this job done, Praefectus!" Cradawg said, immediately handing Lucius the tablet with estimates for the local stone, timber, tiles, labour and other items.

Lucius scanned the numbers and when he had finished, he paused, snapping the tablet shut.

The prices were half of what they would have been in Rome or even Etruria.

"Done!" Lucius smiled and handed it back to him. "And if you can do it at that rate, I'd also like two small barrack blocks on the plateau, as well as another stable. Can that be done too?"

He knew he needed to be careful, for it was like going to the agora markets while famished. He wanted everything he could imagine.

"Barracks, and a stable?" Cradawg asked. "Ha! Those will be easy compared to the house! We'll do those first so that you and your family can live within solid walls until the domus is complete."

Three days later, the work began.

That was months ago, and in the intervening period, during the building, and after, Culhwch, his brother, and their families had become permanent fixtures at the hillfort, and good friends of the Metelli.

Lucius remembered clearly what the hillfort had looked like when they arrived, and now, the work complete, he marvelled at the transformation.

From where he stood on the topmost point of the eastern rampart, he could see the wooden sheds that covered two large storage pits, and beyond those, the strong, squat stables they had built, two separate structures, each with its own paddock, and large enough to accommodate ten horses, with space for more in the paddocks outside. On the north end of the hillfort, Lucius had restored the Roman supply depot that stood there, kept it stocked with fresh hay and water from the well which was located in the middle of the ramparts on the eastern face.

He heard Lunaris neigh from within the warmth of his stable and smiled.

I should take him for a long ride tomorrow, Lucius thought as his eyes roved up to the high plateau of the hillfort where slight wisps of smoke began to fan out and over the two barrack blocks that were used for friends and guests. These structures echoed the simple, strong design of the stables on the outside, stone-faced with clean white-washed walls on the inside, blank canvases which Adara had every intention of giving colour to.

The barracks acted as a funnel onto the high plateau whose slopes were surrounded by small patches of vegetables and herbs for the Metelli's use.

The scene before Lucius was, in every way, a thing of peace to him, but no matter where one stood upon that grassy mound, it was the hall itself that drew the eye. There, on the highest point of the plateau stood their new home, not dissimilar to their villa rustica in Etruria, but in other ways very different, British even.

It was a long, rectangular building of two stories, very Roman in its outward appearance with solid, limestone blocks from the quarries to the southwest. It lay on an east-west axis with large, double doors of oak in the middle of the south side. Windows ran the length of it on the second storey, just below the earthy orange of the terracotta roof tiles that sloped down on each side from the peaked roof where three square vents allowed for smoke from the fire within to escape.

At first, Lucius had thought they would never finish it in the timelines he had set out for them. His experience with builders elsewhere had always been that they over-promised and more often

45

than not, under-delivered, except when it came to the cost of building.

Cradawg and Silvius had been men of their word on all counts. The last thing to be completed was the structure in the southeast corner of the hillfort, away from the other buildings, a place unto itself, a place of quiet.

Lucius turned and walked down the slope toward the small square structure, to stand before it as the night darkened the sky even more.

The idea for the temple had come to him in a dream not long after they had arrived at their new home. In it, Apollo had stood before him in the cold light of a silver moon, and had pointed to the spot. As the god had pointed, Lucius saw a small temple rise before his very eyes, a shrine for himself and his family, a lararium of sorts, outside of the home, but still a part of it.

He had woken and quickly sketched it out for Cradawg who nodded and adjusted his price accordingly when he saw it the next day.

"Out of curiosity, Praefectus, why there?" he pointed to the place Lucius had indicated he wanted it built.

"I'm not sure," Lucius replied. "Because that is where I saw it in my dream," he confided, quite comfortable with the Durotrigan by that time. "Why? Is that not a good place for it?"

Cradawg crossed his thick arms and shook his head. "Not at all, it is a perfect place," he said, then added. "It's where our ancestors worshiped in this very place." He said nothing after that, his eyes looking at Lucius a little differently then.

The small temple, simple as it was, stood silent sentry there, a strong symbol of Lucius' faith and a reminder of the favour Apollo had shown him. It had also served as a sort of beacon of hope to those who dwelled in the shadow of Lucius' home, as if some vague light of memory had returned to that place after years of dormancy.

One morning, not long after the temple's completion, Lucius had awoken to several offerings laid by the locals upon the steps of the temple, gifts for the Gods who dwelt in and around them all.

"You have blessed this place, Lucius Metellus Anguis," Culhwch said as he approached Lucius who was looking at the array of offerings. "I hope you are not angry with my kinsmen," he added. "They mean well, and are only grateful that the Gods have been welcomed back here."

"My gods, you mean?" Lucius said.

"All our gods," Culhwch corrected. "Your 'Apollo', as you call him," he went on, nodding to the gilded letters set into the small pediment of the temple, "he is a god of light?"

"Yes...among other things," Lucius said.

"His light shines upon us all, no? It nurtures our bodies and souls, our crops, our livestock, our children. They are right to make offerings to him, and to other gods in this place if you will allow it."

Lucius smiled and nodded. "You don't sound much like a potter right now, Culhwch."

The Durotrigan laughed. "I'm a philosophical one! And observant. I see the change in my fellow villagers since you arrived here. It seems the Gods smile on you, Dragon."

Lucius looked back at the temple and then to Culhwch.

"I'll leave the temple doors unlocked so that your people can come and pay their respects to the Gods whenever they choose."

The Briton smiled warmly and squeezed Lucius' shoulder.

Lucius noticed that the temple still smelled of fresh plaster and paint as he entered the dark interior, lit only by the flames from two braziers either side of the altar. He looked up to the ceiling where the smoke gathered before escaping into the night sky.

He watched it for a time and smiled to himself.

True, Apollo had shown him this place, in a dream Lucius believed was not merely a dream.

As he gazed upon the plain, pure walls from beneath the cowl of his cloak, Lucius knew that he had secretly harboured hopes of building a monument to Apollo ever since that day on the Palatine Hill in Rome when he was a child, the day when the eagle had come to him before the temple built by Augustus himself, the place where he had subsequently celebrated his coming of age, made numerous offerings, and where he had wed Adara in a rather unorthodox display granted by the head priest.

Now, he found himself in the small square structure that represented the fruition of that wish to build a monument to the god who had seen him through everything. In faraway Britannia he had built it, and it seemed fitting, a direct link of sorts to the great temple in the city of his birth, in Rome.

Lucius walked forward, careful not to step on any of the locals' offerings of wheat and flowers, milk and honey, and took a chunk of

47

Syrian incense, lit it, and placed it in the bowl of the altar. The offering sputtered and sparked and lit the faces of the statues on a shelf behind the altar, of Venus, Epona, and Apollo himself.

The triad of gods stared back at him and Lucius bowed his head.

"Gods... Thank you for the great metamorphosis of my life... I am awed, and grateful to you for all that has led me to this place, the joy my family is finally able to have here..."

He felt like weeping, not out of sadness, but for the feeling of relief that perhaps, maybe, just maybe, he and his family might enjoy a measure of solace, that it might continue for a long while.

The tears felt good, their burning and the tightening of his heart a reminder of the sacrifices that had led to this peaceful, personal victory.

"Thank you for this home... Bless this place, my Gods... I honour you."

Lucius gazed up at the face of Apollo, the statue of the god that was a replica of the likeness upon the pediment of the temple of Zeus at Olympia, in Greece. He had carried that statue with him over the years, from the East and Aegyptus, all the way back to Rome and then Britannia. And now, it had a home here, in the temple Lucius had built.

A part of the god dwelled in those vibrant eyes, the muscle and sinew of that powerful, outstretched arm that seemed to point Lucius in the right direction throughout his life's journey.

The two goddesses beside Apollo, no less important to Lucius, gazed on him with affection, reminding him of the other aspects of his life he would always cherish, those who saw him through pain and suffering, and who charged beside him in the fray.

His thanks to them were no less heartfelt, and though he had not seen the goddesses for some time, he knew in the fibre of his being that they were close to him, wrapping him and his family in a veil as strong and faithful as heavenly armour.

He backed away after a couple more minutes, and then, when he reached the doors, turned and went out into the night.

As he made his way up toward the high plateau of the hillfort, the outlines of the stable and barracks could be seen against the night sky, and beyond them the high roof of the hall.

The smell of food on the hearth fire reached his nostrils and he felt hungry immediately, but first he went into the stables. The wooden door creaked inward and Lucius stepped in to inhale the sweet scent of fresh straw mingled with the smell of the newly-cut beams, and manure. It had been a combination of smells that had given him comfort ever since he had become praefectus of the Sarmatian cavalry ala, the stables ever a place of peace and calm.

He walked slowly, checking on the stalls where the children's ponies, Shadow and Twilight, dozed, half-buried in the straw, their shaggy manes tangled with it.

Einion and Briana's horses looked at him as he passed, and he gave them each a rub on the muzzle before checking on Hyperion, the big mount his men had gifted to Adara in Caledonia.

Lucius could still remember how she had surprised them with her riding skills, their roars of approval of the *Dragon's wife*. Lucius smiled to himself. Hyperion was a good horse, suited to Adara's style of riding which she had learned in Athenae on the slopes of Hymettus in her youth.

Lucius stroked Hyperion's long neck before the horse lowered his great head to chew at some of the straw below the wall of the stall.

There was a pounding hoof then, not far off, and an urgent neighing as Lunaris' head peered over the edge of the door of his own stall.

"Have you grown so impatient?" Lucius said as he walked over to the beast who had become as good a friend as any of his men. Lucius leaned in and the great, dappled head and neck leaned into him, the long black mane falling over Lucius' eyes. "I know I've neglected you a bit lately," he said. "Tomorrow, we'll ride outside the hillfort."

The top of the hillfort was large enough that the horses could be exercised within its confines, enough to stay healthy and warm, but the war horses needed more, and it had become routine for Lucius and Adara to take them out on occasion, sometimes in a gallop on the road west, sometimes over the fields and up the steep hills to the east where they could see their new home from a higher vantage point.

"Do you like it here, boy?" Lucius looked into the large obsidian orbs, remembering all the two of them had been through since Numidia. "It's peaceful here, isn't it?"

The big head nudged him playfully and Lucius chuckled. "You're probably right. Adara will be waiting for me. I'll see you in the morning, Lunaris."

Lucius made his way back toward the end of the stable and the smaller door through which he had come, turned and walked along the path leading up to the hall.

Smoke continued to drift silently into the night air, above the small windows that Cradawg had built into the walls to allow light and air in. They glowed orange and yellow, and a faint sound of singing escaped their warmth.

Lucius walked up, wanting to get there before Adara had sung the children into a deep slumber. He enjoyed her voice, the song...all of it. In fact, ever since they had been on the road south to that place, leaving war and politics behind, Lucius had found a happiness he had thought lost to him. He was with his family at all times. His wife, to him, was a gift from the Gods, and his children... Well, he was finally able to be the father he wanted to be, to teach and encourage them, to give them strength and, he hoped, wisdom, such as he had. Most of all, he was there, with them, at that place and time. He could not imagine life any other way. He did not want to.

He arrived at the wide double doors in the middle of the hall, flanked by the fenced-off herb and vegetable gardens, and put his hand on the iron latch that pulled the right side open.

Warm light pooled around his feet and cast his shadow across the dark grass and earth behind him before he went in and closed the door.

The large round hearth fire stood before him in the middle of the hall, and there sat Einion and Briana, listening to Adara sing her songs to the children who leaned against her in the straw surrounding the fire, their backs to one of the great stumps that had been placed there. It was a distinctly British setting, the hearth fire a little at odds with the Roman design of the rest of the domus.

To the far left was the kitchen and food storage area, occupying the entire east end. Along the north wall were two cubicula where Einion and Briana lived, and then Lucius' tablinum where he disappeared on occasion to write his letters, though he had not done so in quite some time since his furlough had begun in earnest.

The hall was overlooked by a walkway on the second floor where three more cubicula were located, including two for the children and a larger one for Lucius and Adara. This was reached by a broad wooden staircase, which covered the privy, on the west end of the hall which Cradawg had fastened into the stonework of the wall itself.

It was simple and rough, but they had all grown to love it, more than any barrack block or villa, for it was their own. They had made it so.

Einion looked up at Lucius and nodded toward the children, indicated the bobbing heads as they struggled to stay awake, helpless against the soothing sound of their mother's voice.

Lucius poured himself a cup of wine at the small table outside the circle, and then sat down beside Adara and the children, his body relaxing as he too listened to the song.

It was a song of blue waves and a sea nymph who fell in love with the absolute beauty of the world. The words fell effortlessly from Adara's lips, the melody rolling like the wine-dark sea, for she had known it when she was a child, and had been singing it to her own children since the day of their birth.

Lucius looked up at the thick rafters overhead and then into the flames before him, waiting for that part of the song that always seemed to tear at his heart, the part where the nymph sees a fire rip through the pines lining the shoreline she had been admiring, turning all to ash. She weeps salty tears to mingle with the sea, and the Gods are so moved by her sorrow that the flames die away and green shoots explode from the blackened earth, hope springing, to bring back the forest even more beautiful than before.

The final note hung there, and Adara's voice faded away.

She looked up at Lucius and smiled, the children two tired lumps in her arms.

Her husband nodded and came over to pick his son up out of her arms, resting his head upon his solid shoulder.

Phoebus' arms clung unconsciously to Lucius' neck, and Calliope's to Adara's in like manner as the two parents made their way to the other side of the hall and up the staircase to the cubicula that belonged to the children.

Lucius' foot kicked a wooden toy horse and they paused, waiting for the children to awaken, but they continued to sleep, exhausted by a day beneath the sun and blue sky.

Lucius laid his son on his bed covered with fleeces, and Adara did the same for Calliope, kissing her gently upon the forehead before doing the same for her brother.

Outside the two rooms, Lucius and Adara stood together for a moment.

51

Phoebus and Calliope had grown, were tall for their age, mature, so much so that Lucius and Adara often had to rein their expectations in and remind themselves that they were still children. It was when they carried them in their limp sleep that that truly felt real, so vulnerable were they in their parents' arms.

So many months of joy... Adara thought, squeezing Lucius' hand as they went back downstairs.

"I don't think I've ever seen them so tired," Lucius said as he and Adara returned to the fire to sit with Einion and Briana.

"They've been busy. Phoebus is getting stronger by the day and taking on more tasks than most children his age," Einion said.

"Calliope too," Briana added. "Ula and Aina tell me that she has been a great help in the kitchen, gathering ingredients from the garden outside for them.

"She's not getting in the way, I hope, Ula," Adara said to one of the twin sisters whom they had hired to help cook and clean on the hillfort.

"Not at all, Metella," the girl said, her smile broad as she leaned over and handed bowls of stew to each of them from a large tray her sister Aina was holding. "Calliope is the loveliest child I've ever met, and she sings oh so nicely to us while we work."

"Glad to hear it," Lucius added, accepting a bowl and chunk of bread. He tasted it eagerly and his eyes widened. "This is wonderful! You've outdone yourselves."

The girls nodded proudly and turned to go back to the kitchen to clean up for the night.

"Glad you hired them then?" Briana laughed, looking at Lucius.

Lucius nodded, not saying anything as he devoured the meal.

Briana continued to laugh, and Adara shook her head, a great smile upon her face.

Lucius had always been averse to slaves, even more so since attempts on his life in previous years, including Caledonia.

But Adara had insisted that a bit of help around the domus would help free her up to do more training and spend more time with the children, rather than cooking and cleaning up after them. She had never enjoyed cooking anyway.

So, one day, Briana came back from Culwch's village down the hill and introduced Lucius and Adara to the two sisters. "They're looking for work and are skilled cooks." Briana had said bluntly, as the two newcomers stood behind her.

Ula and Aina were identical, from their pale, slightly freckled skin and sandy hair, to the birthmarks shaped like the stars of Cassiopeia in the night sky upon the left side of their necks.

"I'm sorry," Lucius had said, "but we don't need slaves."

"We're not slaves, Praefectus," Ula said, her eyes rising to meet his. "We would like to work for wages."

"We're hard workers," her sister Aina added as Lucius and Adara's eyes went from one to the other, trying to ascertain a difference they could not find.

Adara turned to Lucius, her eyes big, her back to the girls.

Briana joined them and the two girls shuffled off to the side to allow them to talk.

"Culwch recommended them when I asked," Briana said. "Last year, their mother, who did washing in the village, died, and their father was lamed by an oxen team and is unable to work."

"Gods…" Adara said, looking back at them, trying to imagine trusting them with her children.

"They've been caring for children in the village, helping some of the other women, but it is for little or no pay," Briana added.

Lucius rubbed his jaw and looked at Adara, a look that asked subtly *What do you think? I yield to your wishes, my love.*

"It would help," she said. "We could agree to a trial basis to see if it works for us, and if the children like them."

Lucius nodded and looked to Briana. "You trust them?" He had come to value her judgement in all things, her ability to read people, and their intentions, something so uncanny that he believed the Gods had a hand in it.

"They're the darlings of the village, though they don't act like it. They work hard and long, and they don't ask for much."

Lucius turned to Adara. "Well, if you're happy with them, I shall be," he said.

The girls started the next day, arriving at the first hour of daylight and leaving at the third hour of darkness, and each day, they became more and more a part of the Metellus familia.

"Good night to you all," Ula and Aina said to the four of them around the fire as they left the kitchen and made for the doors to go back down the hill to their father's home in the village.

"Thank you, girls," Adara said, smiling at them as they waved.

"They remind you of your sisters, don't they?" Lucius asked.

Adara shrugged. "Not really. I don't know. I haven't seen my sisters in so many years, I don't think I'd remember what they look like. According to my mother, the suitors of Athenae are falling over themselves to marry them."

Lucius chuckled, but Adara looked sad.

"What is it?" he asked.

"They're so far away...my family. I would like to go and see them. My parents are not getting any younger."

Lucius was thoughtful, wondered at how their lives had become so entwined with the military whims of the imperial family. True, they could have gone to Rome or Athenae after the treaty with the Caledonii had been concluded, but he had been asked to remain close to the front, to his men, to the emperor.

"I think we are all dwelling on our faraway homes," Lucius said, tossing a chip of wood across the fire at Einion.

The Briton raised his head and smiled, but sadly.

"Home is ever on my mind."

"But Ynis Wytrin is only half a day's journey," Briana said, putting her hand on her brother's arm. "If you want, we can go anytime." Briana grew excited at returning to the Isle of the Blessed, for she had missed it. But they had been so busy with their new life on the hillfort that there had been no time.

"I don't mean Ynis Wytrin," Einion said, his voice hard, his fists clenching.

"Your father's throne," Lucius said.

Einion nodded. "Everyday my uncle lives, I am shamed and our family dishonoured."

"A lot of good it will do you to go back and get killed," Briana said harshly.

"Have you heard anything out of Dumnonia?" Lucius asked, finishing his stew and placing the bowl on the log at his back.

"Nothing," Einion answered. "It's as if the land has been swallowed by time itself."

"Listen to me, brother," Briana said, turning to face him squarely. "We will take it back someday. Trust the Gods to show us the way...to tell us when. It will happen. We must be patient."

"I'm tired of being patient," he said, rising to his feet and downing the rest of his wine. "If you'll excuse me, I need some fresh air."

Lucius nodded and stood.

"When the time comes, my friend...I'll help you."

"Thank you, Lucius Metellus Anguis," Einion answered, oddly formal, before going out the double doors.

"Sorry," Briana said. "For some reason the theft of our father's throne and our family's murder has been weighing on him greater than ever lately. I think it is because we are back in the South."

"I feel like we are keeping him here against his will," Adara said. "It's not right."

"No one can keep my brother against his will, Adara," Briana said. "He is dealing with his own daemons, as we all do."

When Einion returned and went to his cubiculum, Briana excused herself and went to see him.

Lucius understood his friend's frustration at the situation, knew that it was nothing against himself, Adara, or the children. In fact, Einion and Briana were closer than family now. But the fact that he was staying there, in what was basically, Lucius' home, must have felt like he was not living his own life.

Every time thoughts of his home wormed their way into his mind, Einion had always darkened like the sky above the sea, moments before a gale.

Lucius looked down and saw Adara pick up a packet of letters.

"Did those arrive today?" he asked.

"Yes," she said, as she handed him a few with his name on it. "Here is another one from my mother. I think she's writing everyday at the rate they are coming in."

"They miss you and the children," Lucius said, taking his own letters and sighing when he flipped over the first one."

"What is it?" Adara asked as he opened it.

"It's another letter from Cassius Perrora, the procurator from Londinium. He says he is now in Lindinis and needs to meet with me to discuss the owing taxes on this land."

"Will it be very much?"

"I doubt it. But ever since he discovered we were building a home here, and planning to stay, he's been eager to meet. Now he's so close, I can't really refuse. I should go the day after next. I need to prepare a few things first. There are also accounts to settle with the tile fabricae there."

"Well, we could all go," Adara suggested. "To tell the truth, I'm sore from training with Briana, and I think we could all use a change of scenery. We can shop for the children too. They're growing at such an alarming rate. All of their clothes are either too tight or too short now. And they need sandals, and -"

Lucius laughed as Adara counted things off on her fingers, her list far too long for the number of digits she possessed.

"What?" she asked, her green eyes glistening in the light from the hearth fire.

"You," he said. "I know we're far from our homes, but…are you happy here, my love?"

He was serious. In the back of his mind, he wondered if his wife was truly happy, or if he had forced an exile on her and the children, an exile away from family, and warmth, and sunlight.

"I know what is going on in that mind of yours, Lucius." She held his face in her warm hands, her long fingers stroking his temples. "I am truly happy here, or anywhere else, so long as I am with you, and our children are safe. And at the moment, I can't imagine a safer place than this home we have built together, surrounded by wonderful and kind people. Do you understand that?"

She sat back against the log and crossed her arms in mock frustration.

Lucius got up and went to the table to get the wine jug, returning and filling both of their cups again.

"I understand," he said, holding her cup out to her and sitting right beside her, his thick arm about her neck, pulling her close. "I love you," he said, touching his cup to hers and drinking.

Together, they stared into the flames of their hearth, thankful to the Gods for the peace they were enjoying in that moment, and the place they had built together.

They were indeed happy, and the Gods smiled at that.

III

ORDO LENDINIENSAE

'The Council of Lindinis'

The moon was bright and near to full over the hillfort that night, the rain clouds coming off of the sea in the distance taking their time, holding back. They had to, for the Gods would not tolerate a downpour just yet. The peace was too blissful, there in the silver light, glistening as it was upon the dewy grass.

The darkness did its best to conceal the place, the edges of the high fortifications hidden from one side to the other. Larks called out in the darkness, their song running down the slopes to the fields below where sheep and cattle dozed in the dark, an occasional lowing only to be heard to cover the footfalls of foxes.

Love stood there, her bright eyes roaming over the place, her thoughts on the offerings that had been placed to honour her in the small shrine built by the Metelli.

She walked barefoot in the grass, the dew cold but welcome, and she put a hand to the curve of her smiling lips as she thought of the day when she had made sure to bring Lucius and Adara together, how she had ensured they met in a sea of people.

The joy such interventions gave her, when they bore fruit, was what she longed for most, perhaps because it was so rare, so very beautiful. Even a goddess needed reminding.

She wished them every joy and passion imaginable, for they never forgot her in their prayers and offerings, which came without condition. True, they were imperfect. *But then, so too are gods,* she thought.

She walked up the slope from the temple to where the stables were, for she suspected her cousin was within.

Inside, Venus came to stand beside Epona who stood at the end of the stables whispering to Lunaris, the Dragon's horse.

"Cousin…" Epona said, without taking her eyes from the stallion, her hands stroking his neck and head, healing him, giving him strength and vitality. "You have always carried your master well and done honour to him. So good you are…so good."

"You really do love them, don't you?" Venus said, her glowing hand reaching out to touch Lunaris upon the forehead so that he stilled immediately.

"I do," Epona said, her long red hair flowing behind her like the mane of a fiery mare. "If only they did not suffer so in this world..."

"There is much suffering," Venus said. "But there is also much goodness, much that is beautiful among men and women."

Epona nodded. "Their world is full of beauty and terror. The Gods have made it so, haven't we?"

"I suppose," Love said, her voice trailing away, the glow about her dimming very slightly. "Come. Let us go and see them."

Together, the two goddesses went back out into the night, the stable silent and absolutely still behind them.

Inside the hall, they rounded the hearth fire, each looking about as they went, through the strange home that the Metelli had built for themselves.

"It is very un-Roman," Venus observed.

Epona went toward the staircase and climbed, Love following her, treading silently, until they reached the children's rooms.

Venus approached Phoebus and Calliope and kissed them in turn upon the forehead, their dreams sliding away so that they stopped turning and slept soundly.

"Are they not lovely?" Venus said.

"Yes," Epona answered. "They are their father's children, no doubt."

"And their mother's," Venus added. "For she is the heart of this family, make no mistake."

"I suspect they both are, one and the same," Epona replied.

"Yes. You have it there, Cousin."

They left the children's rooms then and went to the next one.

There, they found Apollo standing in a corner of the room, wrapped in his blue cloak that contained the sky and clouds sliding across it. It cast its gentle light across the floorboards and upon the bed where Lucius and Adara lay entwined, half naked after their lovemaking of hours before.

Epona stood by the door, watching the rise and fall of their breath as they lay there, peaceful for once, content.

Venus went to Apollo's side.

"You are here too?"

"Yes. I wish them nothing but peace," he answered, seemingly troubled.

"What is it?"

"He is worn and tired."

"Surely not," Love insisted. "They have never been so happy as now. Don't you see it, feel it?"

"Life, and his toils have left scars that continue to bleed." He turned to stare at her with star-spinning eyes. "Have I failed him?"

From the doorway, Epona tilted her head and looked to Apollo and Venus whispering in the semi-darkness, then back to Lucius who held his wife close in the crook of his arm beneath the furs.

Love turned to face Apollo and placed her hands upon his broad, solid shoulders.

"Only so much is permitted. You know that. Even when it comes to Lucius, to his family. Allow them this moment, for it is times like this that mortals long for, the memories of which sustain them through hardship." She gripped him tighter then. "Do not let the sun be eclipsed by impending sorrow. Let your light shine on him, inspire him to greatness, as it always has. For if we give up, what can mortals do?"

Apollo nodded, the words ringing as true in his ears as any song sung by his Muses.

The three of them stared longer at the sleeping mortals, wishing them wellness and joy, both deserved, and when the cock crowed outside upon the grassy mound, their light faded into itself and they returned to their lofty peaks.

They woke up to the sound of thunder, deep and rumbling, followed by the sound of torrential downpour, the rain loud upon the tile rooftop of the hall.

Lucius woke up to his son's elbow in his ribs, and his daughter's humming to the rain. He opened his eyes a crack to see Phoebus staring up at the ceiling.

"Don't worry," Lucius told him raising his arms above his head. "It's just Jupiter letting us know all is right with the world."

"The thunder seems louder up here than it has in other places," the boy observed.

"It's only because we're closer to the heavens," Calliope said, ceasing her song to insert her wisdom.

59

Lucius looked sideways to see his daughter curled in the crook of Adara's arm, her face delighted and half-buried in her mother's dark curls.

"Think of it as having front seats at the theatre or the games," Lucius said.

"We've never been to either, Baba," Phoebus said.

"That's true," Calliope added, resting on her little elbow to stare across her brother's chest at their father. "Can we go?"

"Maybe. Depends on the event or play. You're too young for the gladiatorial games, and they don't have a hippodrome anywhere around here."

"Aquae Sulis has a theatre, I hear," Adara said sleepily, succumbing to the fact that she would not be able to sleep any longer. How the rain soothed her...

"Good morning, Mama!" Calliope said. "Did I wake you with my snuggles?"

"It's the best way to wake up," Adara said, kissing her daughter's forehead.

"I don't think we're going to Lindinis today," Lucius added as the rain fell more persistently upon the roof.

"No," Adara agreed. "It works for us though. I can take stock of what we have and decide what we need to get in Lindinis. And we can continue your lessons," she said to the children.

"Aww," they whined in unison.

"Come now, we don't have a tutor for you, so I shall teach you as much as I can," Adara said, sitting up and pulling Calliope onto her lap.

"I need to go over some accounts too before I meet with the procurator. He's in Lindinis for another week, so another day or two will be fine." Lucius looked at his son. "Help your mother today and do your lessons, and then maybe we can get some new rudii in Lindinis for your gladius training."

Phoebus' eyes brightened like stars bursting in the night sky, so excited he was at the prospect.

"Thank you, Baba!" he squealed, wrapping his arms around Lucius' neck.

"Work first though!" Lucius laughed.

"Yes, Baba!"

"What about me?" Calliope said, her eyes slightly downcast. "I want to train like Mama."

"And you will, over time," Adara added.

"We'll get one for you too, and your mother and Briana will work more with you." Lucius smiled, gave her a knowing look that often passed between them. That look that said *I know you are quite as capable. Do not ever worry...*

"Now go get dressed, both of you!" Adara said. "I think Ula and Aina are already here, so you can ask them for something to eat."

"Yes, Mama!" they said before rolling one over each parent and dashing out of the door back to their room.

Adara laughed and slid closer to Lucius.

"You know, there are other ways I like to wake up even more."

He kissed her and ran his hand down her leg beneath the furs. "I think we'll have to wake much sooner than our little ones to have that sort of privacy."

He touched her gently and she moaned, leaning into him again, purring like a cat lying in the sunshine.

"We're ready!" the children appeared at the doorway, and Lucius and Adara pulled apart quickly as if they were lusty youths, caught in the barn during a dinner party.

"We're coming!" Adara said, her face red as she waved them away.

The little footsteps receded and pounded down the stairs and across the hall to the kitchen.

"We'll pick this up later," Lucius said, keenly aware of the gifts Venus bestowed on both of them, that they were still interested in each other after so many years. He kissed her and stood up to dress in the grey light that filtered through the small square window in the wall.

"I'll hold you to it," she said, walking naked to the table to get her own clothes, and smiling over her shoulder.

"Gods help me."

The rain did indeed pour throughout the day, and as the children studied and grew more and more impatient within the confines of the hall where Adara went over their lessons with them at a table, Lucius sat in his tablinum gathering all he needed, including the deed to the lands that Publius Leander, Adara's father, had given him. He fretted a little over the amount that may be owing after so many years, and hoped that, like other things, it would be less costly in Britannia than closer to Rome.

They had enough, that was not the worry. For they had not squandered his considerable pay as a praefectus over the last few years. They bought only what they needed. The biggest expenses had been the ponies for the children, but that had been worth it just to see the joyous looks on their faces.

Lucius smiled to himself at the thought and took a deep breath. *I can handle the procurator.*

None of them had in fact been to Lindinis since their arrival, even though it was the closest town by far. They had been so busy getting settled and overseeing the plans, that they had not had time to go. Cradawg and Silvius had been the intermediaries as far as ordering and billing from the fabricae in town.

Lucius had to admit, he was curious about the place. He hoped there was a public bath there too, as they had all grown tired of washing in a wooden tub with water heated over the fire, either too hot or too cold by the time one got to it. If there was one thing missing in their new home, it was a bathhouse that they could all make use of.

"Baba," the voice came from the doorway and Lucius looked up to see Phoebus staring at him. "Are you all right?"

Lucius smiled. "Yes. Why?" He waved his son over and the boy came and sat on his father's lap.

Ever since that unfortunate night in Caledonia, when Lucius had lost control of his senses, his very spirit, and nearly hurt his family beyond reckoning, Phoebus was constantly asking him how he was, as if to check in on him and reassure himself that the monster that had for a time possessed his father was indeed gone from their lives.

"I'm fine," Lucius said, his hand resting on his son's arm and feeling the sinewy muscles that had begun to grow stronger in his young limbs. "I'm just thinking. I have business to take care of when we go to town tomorrow and I want to make sure I have everything."

"Oh," Phoebus said absently, looking at the large round clay dish on the table top. "Can I touch the sand?" He pointed to the dish in which Lucius had kept sand from Numidia and often ran his hands and fingers through the cool flour-like consistency.

Lucius leaned forward and pulled the dish closer to them. He took off the lid and laid it aside. Together they put their hands into the sand and raised a small handful each, watching it run between their fingers back into the dish.

Phoebus smiled. "I don't remember the desert at all."

"You wouldn't," Lucius said. "Though you and your sister were born there, at Lambaesis, we left when you were still babies."

"Would you ever go back?"

Lucius was silent for a moment. *Not there...* "I don't know. I must go where the emperor commands me."

Phoebus' smile faded then, as if the fine sand kindled a memory of sadness. He dropped his handful and pressed back into his father's muscular chest.

"That's where Aunt Alene was killed, isn't it? The place where we were born?"

Lucius felt his eyes begin to burn, and he held his son more tightly, a living talisman against the dormant grief.

"Yes." He swallowed hard to control his voice "She saved you and your sister when men came to kill us."

"I wish I knew her..."

"Me too. She was the kindest woman I knew, as much as your own mother." *If we ever get back to Etruria, the children will be able to make an offering to Alene at the shrine,* he thought.

"Baba," Phoebus continued.

"Yes, my son."

"Will men come to kill us here?"

"No," Lucius reassured him. "Listen to me." He turned Phoebus in his lap to face him. "You're safe here, understand? This is our home. We have friends close by, and there is peace in southern Britannia."

"You're sure?"

"Yes." Lucius tried to smile, to further reassure the boy who so desperately wanted to be a man. "Besides, we Metelli are not so easy to kill. Remember that."

Phoebus nodded and slid down to go back to his lessons.

"The rain is slowing," he said, his head cocked toward the ceiling."

"So it is. We should be able to travel tomorrow."

The boy began to walk away, but turned back to Lucius one more time.

"Matertera was a Metella too, wasn't she?"

"Yes."

Phoebus' head hung low and he turned again to leave.

"Phoebus!" Lucius called. "Tomorrow, we'll find the perfect rudus for you at the market. Would you like that?"

His son stared straight at him then. "Yes. I would." Then he left.

So much for playing with wooden horses... Lucius thought.

Toward early evening, the rain finally stopped completely, and as if by the summons of some god, the sun broke through the clouds which had been swept away, dismissed by a wave of Jupiter's hand.

The air over the hillfort smelled of damp grass and rich muddy earth as the children burst out of the double doors for the stables, wanting to see their ponies and brush them down.

Lucius, Einion and Briana followed on their heels, the mud squelching beneath them as they went.

Adara remained inside the hall, taking a final assessment of the clothes and shoes they needed to purchase for the children on the morrow in Lindinis.

I hope the people are friendlier there than in Eburacum, she thought.

In the stables, Lucius, Einion, Briana and the children brushed down all of their own mounts, fed and watered them.

It was a busy place suddenly, as bustling as any basilica, the children happy to be out and playing - caring for their mounts was still more a joy than a chore - and the horses were all happy to see their riders return after a night of storm and rain.

"Baba?" Calliope asked, her head peering over the edge of Twilight's stall. "Can we take a ride around the hill?"

Lucius thought for a moment and shook his head. "With all the mud from the rain, it's still quite slippery, my girl. Not safe enough for you to ride on the slopes. But if you like, you can walk them so they can have a chance to stretch their legs."

The head disappeared behind the gate, and a faintly disappointed "all right" drifted over.

Lucius smiled, almost wanted to give in, but he knew that the ponies were always jumpy after a day inside, and that though Phoebus and Calliope had become quite skilled in riding, if the ponies bolted near the top of the embankments, it could be very dangerous. The drop between each of the four layers of the ancient fortifications was in fact quite steep.

"Baba's right, Calliope," Phoebus said to his sister. "We can take a long ride another day." He looked to his father, and Lucius winked at his son, always the more reserved one, perhaps a little scared too.

Though some fear is healthy, Lucius told himself.

"I'll go with them, Lucius," Briana said, bringing her own horse out of the stall and waiting at the entrance.

"Thank you, Briana," he said.

She waved it off and led the children outside.

"You coming with us tomorrow?" Lucius asked Einion.

The Briton closed the gate of his own mount's stall and leaned on it.

"Yes. I'd like to see if there is any news from Dumnonia."

"Who would know?" Lucius asked. "I don't think many Romans get down that way."

"Soldiers like to talk, as you know," Einion said, but did not smile. "If any of them have been to Isca lately, they may have heard something."

"And if nobody knows anything?"

"Then I have to find out, one way or another what the situation is."

Lucius wanted to ask him more, to plumb the depths of his friend's grief and anger, but he also knew that when it came to vengeance, a man's business was his own. What he did know was that Einion seemed to be growing more and more distant with each passing day.

"I hope you find out something then," Lucius said. "You know," he continued. "If you ever need anything, you need only ask."

"I know, my friend." Einion lifted his head and nodded. "I know."

Lucius made to leave. "You coming? I thought I'd go down to the village and see Culhwch and Alma...check if they want to come with us tomorrow. Might get some of that farm brew they have."

Einion laughed. "You go ahead. The brew tastes like horse sweat to me."

Lucius looked surprised, but then thought about it. "You're right, but it's always offered, and it does take the edge off."

"I'm fine, Lucius. Thank you."

"Suit yourself," Lucius said, wrapping his cloak about his shoulders and adjusting the sword at his waist before heading out the stable door. "I won't be long."

When Lucius was gone, and Einion was alone, the Briton sighed loudly and leaned his head on the door of his horse's stall, his eyes burning, his fists clenched.

65

When Lucius returned a couple of hours later from the village, he was muddy and his boots soaked. But he was happy. Truly. He loved walking to the village and back, not only for the chance for him to visit with new friends, but also for the different perspective it gave them of their new home.

The fortress looked enormous from the fields to the South. The brook before him made him wonder if the well on the eastern rampart had enough flow to create a functioning bathhouse. It was an intriguing idea, but one he would have to discuss with Cradawg for the engineering possibilities behind such a structure.

Lucius continued on up the slope of the hill to join the road that led to the south-west gateway. He paused and looked away to the distant sun in the West. *Good. Not too late.* He smiled and carried on walking to climb the rampart to the right and make the circuit.

It had become Lucius' habit to walk the ramparts of their home every evening, as he had always done on the march with the men under his command. Not that he felt that constant edge he felt while on campaign, that edge that kept one alive in enemy territory. No. He had actually felt more relaxed in their new home than he had in many years.

He completed a full circuit, strolling slowly along the green embankments, his eye on the distant, reddening sun. A chorus of crows followed him, and he was entertained by the antics of swallows in the sky above.

He paused at the south-east corner to see the last of the villagers coming out of the temple where they had placed offerings. An older lady stood there and looked up at him through cataract eyes. He waved to her, and she bowed slightly, a shaky hand covering her heart before she made her way back home in the diminishing light.

After making his own offering in the temple, Lucius continued his route along the ramparts to the north-east gate, past the supply depot building on the north side, and around to stop by the usual tree on the western edge of the hillfort.

Adara was waiting there for him, wrapped in her blue cloak and watching the sun's disc as it began to bleed over the edge of the world.

"I didn't think you'd make it," she said, kissing him as he arrived.

Lucius put his arm around her and together they turned to watch the sunset.

"Wouldn't miss it," he answered. "I'm so happy here." He squeezed her.

Adara looked up at Lucius and smiled, staring at him until his eyes met hers. "I'm glad. I'm happy here too." She turned back to the sun.

Lucius held his wife close, his breathing slow. For some reason, the sight of the sun setting was a great comfort to him. It made him feel optimistic about the morrow, hopeful for what he could shape out of it, as he imagined his old friend Emrys felt when starting to sculpt a fresh piece of marble. At that moment, Lucius' thoughts and wishes would go to Far-Shooting Apollo as swiftly and surely as the god's silver-tipped arrows.

He breathed deeply, as if inhaling the sun's light, and felt strength fill his limbs again.

Once Apollo's golden disc disappeared from sight, he turned to Adara, the blue smoke from the temple visible just over her shoulder.

The wind played with their hair and cloaks as a cool breeze swept in from the distant sea, but they remained there.

"Phoebus was asking about Alene today," Lucius said suddenly.

Adara nodded sadly. "Strange. Calliope too spoke of her."

"Really?"

"I heard her humming the song Alene used to sing to them as babies - I don't know how she remembers it - and I asked her why she was singing that particular song."

"What did she say?"

"She said she liked to sing it to remember her aunt."

Lucius sighed. It had been many years since Alene's murder in Numidia, but in other ways it seemed like only yesterday, a fresh wound into which someone occasionally poured salt, or cauterized with a fresh iron brand.

Both of them wished their children had known Alene, known her well. But it was not to be. After six years, they realized the hurt they thought would diminish was never going to go away, the hole in their hearts left by her loss would never be filled. All they could do was get used to that hole being there, the emotion they felt whenever they dared to look inside again.

Phoebus and Calliope were constant reminders of Alene's sacrifice, and Lucius and Adara could imagine no greater legacy.

67

"I was thinking," Lucius continued, "that whenever we get back to Etruria, the children could make an offering to her."

"Yes." Adara shivered. "Let's go in. Ula and Aina have prepared roast meat and greens for all of us. I've invited them to stay and eat with us too."

"Of course. They're good girls, those two."

Lucius helped Adara down the steep slope and together they wound their way around the plateau upon which the hall was built, and then up past the barracks, between the family stables, and to the hall.

The smell of food met them at the door and they entered to find the fire warm and bright, and their family and friends gathered around it to share food and drink.

"Smells delicious girls," Lucius said as he sat down.

"Eat well, children," Adara said. "We leave for Lindinis early tomorrow morning."

The Gods blessed them with warmth and bright sunlight the following morning when they set out early for Lindinis. Adara, Briana, and the children rode in a covered wagon, and Lucius and Einion followed alongside on their horses.

The countryside spread out before them in a vast, rolling blanket of green fields and forest, the sun warming them more with each passing mile.

Once they exited the hillfort at the south-west gate, they wound their way around the steep slopes to the western track and took it to join the small road that headed south-west to join the main artery of the Fosse Way. That would take them directly to Lindinis.

It felt good to be out in the world, and the children's curiosity was piqued, their heads sticking out of the wagon flaps the better to see as they went.

Adara could see their excitement, shared it too, and so she stood to tie back the folds of canvas that covered the sides of the wagon.

"There!" she said, sitting down between the children, just behind Briana who was driving the wagon. "Now we can see everything."

The children still would not sit still, but balanced all over the wagon, turning this way and that, excited at the prospect of going somewhere new. They quickly grew warm and soon shed their white and brown cloaks, nibbling at the dried grapes Adara had brought for them.

"We'll buy more food in Lindinis," Adara told them. "After we go to the baths."

The children sighed, but did not protest, as even they were looking forward to washing in a proper bath.

Briana laughed at their antics as Adara shook her head in mock despair. "Gods know why they love to be so dirty."

Lucius and Einion trotted ahead of the wagon, enjoying the sunlight and open road ahead.

Lucius did not travel in his armour, but wore his black cloak, brown bracae, and red tunic. He was also armed, as always, with his dagger and sword, despite the fact that he had business to conduct, in addition to going to the market.

"Have you ever been to Lindinis?" Lucius asked Einion.

"Once, but not for long. It's a small place. Decent market. I don't know if it is as well-equipped as Adara expects, but it will do."

"I'm sure it will be fine," Lucius answered, reining Lunaris in as the stallion pranced and bounded suddenly. "I think Lunaris is happy to be out in the open now too!" Lucius said.

"Seems that way!" Einion shouted as Lunaris bolted forward, given his head by Lucius to charge along the side of the straight stretch of road. He turned to smile at his sister and Adara in the front of the wagon and charged after Lucius.

After a while, the walls of Lindinis came into view in the middle of a broad, flat, green expanse on the other side of a winding river.

Lucius and Einion stopped and waited for the wagon to catch up. When it did, Lucius turned to the others.

"I didn't expect a walled town. We'll have to leave the horses and wagon outside the walls. There should be a stabling house on the way in," he said before nudging Lunaris forward at a slower pace.

Lindinis was of a decent size, a former oppidum, the sort of native British centre where people used to live within the confines of a wall of sorts.

Lucius noted that the wall around Lindinis was relatively new and surrounded an area of roughly twenty hectares. The newer walls were thick too, at least eight feet, and were topped by a few guards whose eyes watched their party carefully as they approached and blended in with the influx of other traffic coming to the market. Lucius could hear the children's excited observance of everything as they went, from the roadside tombs and monuments, to the animal

69

pens in the fields to either side where sheep, cattle, pigs and goats milled and bleated under the watchful eyes of would-be purchasers.

To the right was a small port where barges were being unloaded, and far to the left on the other side of the river, Lucius recognized the old fortifications of a former fort with a double-ditch.

"How old is that do you think?" Einion said.

"Must be just after the invasion," Lucius mused. "Or maybe during the revolt of the Iceni." He remembered reading about it, the bloodbath of that campaign, and was grateful for the Pax Romana that now reigned in southern Britannia.

They continued on, passing homes and other shops along the road where sellers of wine, cheese, wool, and bread tried to wave them down.

"We'll be back!" Lucius called, laughing.

Finally, they came to the stables, just before the bridge that crossed the river and led directly into the main, north gate of the town.

Lucius dismounted and went beneath the broad wooden roof that covered a small smith's work area and several stalls, mostly empty.

"Who might you be?" a burly man asked, standing and coming directly to Lucius.

Lucius could tell right away the man was a retired legionary, not least because of the old gladius on a shelf behind his counter and the scars running up his thick forearms.

"Praefectus Lucius Metellus Anguis. I've just moved to the area and this is my first time in Lindinis. Do you have room for our wagon and horses while we shop in the town?"

As soon as Lucius said his name, the man's eyebrows went up quickly, and he stood just a bit taller.

"Well, Praefectus. Welcome to Lindinis," the man said, smiling. "You've come on the right day to shop. It's the market, and they've pulled out all the stops for the procurator who's here to conduct his blood-sucking business and visit with some members of our mighty ordo."

"Good timing then," Lucius said, dismissing the sarcasm in the man's voice. He had often seen such in retired veterans when talking about the mundane activities of civilian life. "Can you also shoe the horses, and give them some good feed for our journey home?"

"Aye, Praefectus. And a good deal I'll give you at that."

70

Lucius smiled and clasped the man's hand tightly. "Excellent. My gratitude…"

"Tertius Corpulo, sir. Formerly of the II Augustan."

"Really?" Lucius said, seeing the man's pride. "I myself was with the III Augustan in Numidia for a time."

"I've heard, sir. And -" the man stopped.

"You have?"

"The troops who pass through here have talked about you, Praefectus. They call you the Dragon. Gave the Caledonians a right lickin' in the North they say."

Lucius turned to look at Einion who had come up behind him, then back to Corpulo who continued.

"We was wondering when you might come to Lindinis. The men were saying they heard you were living in the area, that you ordered some building supplies from our local fabricae."

"Well, yes. We've been busy building."

"Anyway," the man hesitated now with the children, Adara and Briana standing behind Lucius. "You need anything, Praefectus, you just let me or one of the lads know, and we'll get it done for you."

"That's much appreciated, Corpulo. Thank you." Lucius started to leave, but turned back. "Can you tell me where the procurator can be found?"

"He'll be in the Curia, likely," Corpulo said. "With all the tax money," he added, a bit jaded. "Probably sitting on it like a hen upon a golden egg." He cleared his throat. "Uhm, what I mean, sir, is that -"

"Please, Corpulo. We're men of the legions, are we not? We speak frankly." Lucius leaned in a bit closer. "Between you and me, I'd rather not hand over my earnings either, but I'm here to be bled quite a bit, I've got a feeling."

"Bastards!" Corpulo grumbled, then nodded an apology to Adara behind Lucius.

Lucius nodded to the man, shook his hand, and turned to lead the way with the others following him.

"Quite a warm welcome," Adara said as they went, holding the children's hands.

"Yes," Lucius said as they crossed the bridge.

"You sure you should speak so frankly with men you've only just met?"

"He was friendly enough. Besides, there was something in the way he spoke to me. Made me feel like I could trust him."

"Adara's right, Lucius," Einion said. "You should be more careful. Remember how things were in Caledonia for you."

"I remember," Lucius answered, his voice darker, his smile gone. "I'll be careful." *I guess I just forgot how much I enjoy a bit of banter with the men.*

They stopped to stare into the clear-flowing water below the stone bridge, the children pointing at the animal pens on the eastern side, Calliope imitating the lowing of the cattle almost perfectly.

Lucius bent down and looked her in the eyes. "You sure you're not part cow?"

"Quite sure," she laughed as he poked her ribs. "But I am part dragon!" she roared and clawed playfully at him.

Lucius laughed and took her hand as they continued on their way.

They passed stalls selling local black pottery, leather goods such as satchels, saddlebags, purses, breeches and more.

Adara and the children stopped to look at every stall, but Lucius could not think of shopping until he took care of his business with the procurator.

Briana was looking at some strips of leather for her sword handle, and Einion stood beside Lucius, scanning the crowds and stalls for some of his fellow Britons.

"I'll be back," Einion said as he left the group to go to a beer seller's stall where the casks were piled high around three men in brown and black wool and leather, each with long, braided hair.

Lucius stood there watching everyone, holding his satchel beneath his arm the same way he usually carried his military helmet. He went over to Adara and Briana.

"I'm going to go ahead and see the procurator. You take your time looking at everything."

"Are you sure, Lucius? Do you want me to come with you?" Adara said.

"No, no. Just stay with the children and Briana. Keep them out of trouble." He turned to Phoebus. "We'll look for those wooden rudii after I'm finished. All right?"

"Yes, Father. I can't wait!" Phoebus replied excitedly.

"Good. Adara, be sure to buy whatever we need as far as foodstuffs, wine, cheeses and meat. You can ask the vendors to run the items back to our wagon at Corpulo's stable. I'm sure they all know each other."

"I will. But try not to take too long if you can avoid it. I'd also like to visit the baths if there are any."

"Me too," he said as he kissed her and began to walk. "Enjoy yourselves. I'll be back shortly!"

Lindinis' main roads were well-paved with stone, clean, and lined with busy shops, small dwellings, and market stalls in the centre of the town. Other roads were paved with tightly packed gravel that crunched beneath Lucius' boots as he walked.

He searched for the agora, but could not spot it, nor a basilica. In fact, to his surprise, the main roads were oddly laid out in a sort of alpha shape with the market in the middle, not the usual grid system one found in civitates or coloniae. Then again, Lindinis was just a market town and had no official status. The odd layout was, Lucius decided, due to its former existence as a native oppidum. All that was missing were the round houses.

Smoke rising into the air along the north wall told him where the baths were, and then he spotted the ring of hired guards around a two-storey building in the south-east quadrant. *The curia.*

Lucius walked along the paved road to where it intersected with another that ran directly in front of the squat, rectangular, limestone building. He approached the captain who stood talking with the two troopers either side of the oak, iron-barred, double doors of the curia.

"Salve," Lucius greeted them. "Praefectus Lucius Metellus Anguis, here to see the procurator. I believe he's expecting me."

The men stopped talking and looked Lucius up and down. A little respect crept into their observance of him, but not much.

"Wait here," the captain said, before going in through the double-doors.

Lucius nodded and waited patiently, noting the troopers staring at his sword hilt with the dragon heads jutting out from the sides. He covered it with the hem of his cloak and they stopped staring.

"This way, Praefectus!" the captain called from within the building.

Lucius climbed the stairs and found himself in a small atrium, the floor of which was covered in a vast black and white mosaic that made one feel dizzy to look at.

The captain waved him through. "In here. The procurator is waiting for you."

Lucius nodded and proceeded through a doorway that led into a broad echoing room with a high ceiling and limestone benches in three levels around the perimeter. It was like a miniature version of the Senate house in Rome, Lucius thought, but much more grey, without any marble or terracotta to speak of.

He walked past several bronze braziers, their flames licking at him as he went toward a small dais at the far end where three men in togas conversed. Two of them stood, and one sat in the middle among rolls of papyrus and stacks of wax tablets. Behind him, three scribes sat at small wooden tables jotting notes.

The two men who were standing watched Lucius approach, but the one who was sitting continued writing something as the other two waited patiently.

"Procurator Perrora?" Lucius said as he came to a stop in front of the table, nodding politely to the two men either side.

A moment more, then the procurator looked up.

"Ah, Praefectus. I'm glad you were able to finally make it here to see me. We need to conclude this business of back taxes owing on the land your father-in-law bequeathed to you a few years ago."

"That's why I'm here. I too would like everything straightened out."

"Please," the procurator motioned to the chair directly in front of his table, and Lucius sat down, placing his satchel of papers upon the table.

Cassius Perrora, the imperial procurator based in Londinium, was a short man, his patience it seemed, matched only by his stature. He was certainly no Briton, and Lucius guessed he hailed from Hispania. He had a tendency to rub his short, black, neatly trimmed beard, and to run his hand over his short head of black hair whenever in thought.

Before Lucius took out his papers, he looked at the two men to either side of the procurator.

"I don't believe I know your colleagues," Lucius said in a friendly voice.

"Ah, forgive me, Praefectus. I thought you might have known them already since you live nearby." He motioned to the man on his right. "This is Serenus Crescens Nova."

Lucius stood again and shook the man's hand firmly. "Lucius Metellus Anguis."

"I have heard of you, Praefectus," Crescens said, a friendly smile upon his face. He was tall, with short, sandy hair and pale blue eyes of the sort that old women thought carried a curse. But Lucius could see no danger in those eyes, just a friendly local citizen.

"And over here," Perrora motioned to the man on his left, "is Virgilio Carcer Hilarus."

"Praefectus," Carcer said with waving arms that jut out to shake Lucius' hand. "We welcome you to our magnificent town of Lindinis. We've been looking forward to meeting you." The second man was also very tall, thin, bald and dressed in the finest of wool togas. However his high voice struck a note in Lucius' ears so that he had to struggle not to cringe visibly.

Lucius did, however, notice the procurator raise his eyebrows when Carcer made his welcome.

"These fine gentlemen are the two executives of the elected curia of Lindinis' ordo."

"We know our dear procurator from our time in Londinium," Crescens said, smiling down at Perrora.

"Before we opted for the quieter life of country living near our investments," Carcer added.

Lucius nodded, not sure what to say to this, too distracted by the annoyed looks upon the procurator's face.

"Well, it's a pleasure to meet you, gentlemen," Lucius said.

Perrora then looked up at the two men.

"Yes, well," Crescens began, straightening. "Procurator, as always, we have enjoyed our meeting. Are you sure you won't stay longer?"

"No, no, no. I must be getting back to Londinium as soon as possible. And now that the praefectus is here, I have no outstanding business."

"But, Cassius what about-"

Crescens cut off his colleague with a hand gesture.

"Come, Virgilio. The procurator is a busy man, and we have made our case. I'm sure he will consider it strongly." The blue eyes focussed on the procurator and he stared directly back at Crescens.

"I may consider it. That is all."

Crescens nodded, then turned to Lucius and smiled. "Praefectus."

The two men walked slowly from the room toward the doors at the far end, the procurator's eyes following them the entire way as if he wanted to be sure they were out of earshot.

"Gods, I despise those two!"

Lucius turned back to Perrora, surprise upon his face. "They seemed nice enough, Procurator."

"Hmph. As friendly as vipers in a summer vineyard. Mind you watch those two upstart beggars, Praefectus. They'll whisper in your ear until you are deaf and you prefer the sound of buzzing flies in the cow yards outside to their honeyed words."

Lucius stared at the man across the table, nodding understandingly, not sure if the men were to blame, or if the procurator was just another tired, provincial official who dreamed only of the day he could leave for a posting on the shores of the Middle Sea.

"At any rate," the little man waved the thoughts away violently and sat back in his chair, his hands clasped over his belly. "Enough of those provincials. I have prepared a list of the amounts owing on your lands."

"As have I," Lucius said, taking the scrolls out of his satchel.

"Glad to see you prepared, Praefectus." Perrora smiled. "Let us compare and see if we are of like mind."

For the next half hour, Lucius and the procurator pored over the numbers, acreages owned, land uses and more, seeking to reach a balance owing that the two could agree upon.

The amount, four thousand denarii, was far more than Lucius had been hoping to have to pay, and he sat back, a little defeated by the tiny man before him. He did not like it.

"This doesn't seem correct to me," Lucius said.

"Oh, I assure you, it is," Perrora said. "And now that you are living upon the land, the taxes upon it are higher."

Lucius knew his purse was about to shrink considerably, and was just lamenting the situation, and the shopping going on in the town outside, when the procurator coughed and sat up straight.

"Oh my, I almost forgot…"

"Not more?" Lucius said, a little angrily.

"No. Less." Perrora wrote hastily on a wax tablet.

"Really?"

"Because your father-in-law continued to allow the army to use the lands for a supply depot when he took over ownership, he was given a more lenient tax. Now I remember."

"And I continue to do the same," Lucius added quickly. "In fact, I have rebuilt part of the structure and replenished supplies for the depot."

"Very good. You shall be reimbursed for that expense, and you will continue to save on the taxes... Therefore..." He continued adding. "The new amount owing is one thousand denarii."

"That is much less than before," Lucius said, feeling the relief in his stomach.

"Yes, but numbers do not lie, Praefectus. It seems Mercury is smiling upon you this day."

"Seems that way," Lucius sighed, leaning back in his chair. "I can arrange with the imperial army publicanus to transfer the funds owed from my account to the imperial treasury, if that is how it is to be done."

The procurator turned in his chair and held out his hand to accept two papyrus scrolls from one of his secretaries.

"We've already drafted two copies," he said, handing them to Lucius. "All they require are your signature and mine, and then the paperwork will be filed."

"Efficient," Lucius said as his eyes scanned the documents, reassuring himself that the amounts were as discussed and included the benefit given for partial use of the land by the army." He nodded, dipped one of the bronze styli in the ink pot and signed the papyri.

Perrora reached out to take them back and nodded when he was satisfied.

"The funds will likely come out of your accounts as soon as I reach Londinium. I don't like to delay collection," he said as he began to pack up his papers. "Gods I can't wait to get back there."

"You like Londinium?" Lucius asked. He had heard it was filthy and crowded, and he had no wish to visit there if he need not.

"Not at all! Filthy place. But I much prefer it to here."

"Don't like the countryside?" Lucius asked, descending further and further into small talk.

"I don't mind the countryside," Perrora said. "But it's the people in this town. They think they are sophisticated, elite, as if they were in Londinium or even Aquae Sulis, rather than this slight market town." He stood up, his hands clasped in front of him. "Mark me. As soon as you exit this building, those two will be on you like vultures."

"I can handle vultures, easily enough," Lucius said.

Perrora looked at him, doubtful.

"Well, Praefectus. May Fortuna smile upon you. Thank you for coming prepared."

"Thank you for your time," Lucius said, gathering up his leather satchel and turning to leave.

"Hurry up!" Lucius could hear the procurator haranguing his secretaries behind him. "Let's get going!"

Lucius was relieved when he stepped out into the fresh air, glad for the cool breeze after the brazier-heated space of the curia.

He scanned the town from the steps and spotted Adara, Briana and the children at a stall that sold leather boots. They seemed to be enjoying themselves. He was relieved.

A few groups of people stood here and there along the main roads of the town, some browsing, others talking.

Lucius scanned the crowd, and before he could be on his way to join his family, the two togas were making their way toward him, smiles blazing upon their faces, heads held high and proud, nodding to people who greeted them as they cut their way across the market area directly for Lucius.

Lucius adjusted his sword belt, tucked his satchel beneath his left arm, and descended the steps.

"Praefectus!" the gaudy, bald man, Virgilio Carcer Hilarus called out loudly and waved to Lucius, while the other, Serenus Crescens Nova, followed, smiling broadly at Lucius while still acknowledging several people as he went.

It seemed all eyes in the town were upon them and Lucius.

"Praefectus," Carcer said. "I hope you are not exhausted by your time spent with our grouchy procurator." He laughed "No lightness of bearing."

"We've concluded our business," Lucius said.

"The procurator has an important job, my friend," Crescens said to Carcer. "His responsibilities weigh heavily upon his small shoulders."

"I found him agreeable enough," Lucius said.

"As do we," Crescens added. He paused for a moment, looking around. "We did not have the chance to speak properly in there,

Praefectus - I didn't want to get in the way of imperial business after all. But we do want to welcome you to Lindinis. I've heard some of the men from our garrison talking about you and your exploits in the North for some time now. It's an honour to meet the 'Dragon' of Rome's legions."

Crescens extended his hand again to Lucius, his eyes bright and friendly, plain and sincere.

Lucius shook his hand and nodded. "Don't believe all the stories you hear. My men did much of the fighting."

"Tush, Praefectus," Carcer blurted, clapping his ring-covered hands excitedly, his voice loud enough for all to hear. "You are humble, Praefectus. Such stories! The slayer of the Boar of the Selgovae!"

Lucius held a hand up. "Actually, I did not slay him. Lord Afallach of the Votadini slew the Boar. I but captured him in battle."

"Either way, deeds worthy of legend in the annals of Rome," Carcer said, suddenly still, his toga folds held up on his left arm as if posing for a fresco.

"Baba!" A flash of brown collided with Lucius who laughed and picked up Calliope who was holding one of the biscuits Adara had purchased at one of the stalls.

Adara and Phoebus followed, with Briana hanging back, looking in the crowds for her brother.

"Gentlemen," Lucius said, beaming. "This is my family. My children, Calliope and Phoebus, and my wife, Adara Metella."

"Lovely to meet you, my dear," Crescens bowed to Adara who smiled at the two men, her hands upon her son's shoulders.

"And you…"

"These are Serenus Crescens Nova, and Virgilio Carcer Hilarus. They are the two senior members of the ordo of Lindinis."

"A pleasure to meet you, gentlemen," Adara said. "You have a lovely town here."

"We thank you, Lady Metella," Crescens said. We have tried to improve it a great deal."

"I noticed the new walls around the town," Lucius said. "Is there a need?"

Crescens paused, his face darkening a little, but his smile returned forthwith. "A minor improvement the previous ordo thought was needed when Albinus made his claim for the purple."

"Was the town for Albinus then?"

"Well, yes, but -" Carcer began, but once more, Crescens' hand was up.

"Before our time, fortunately," Crescens added. "I suppose they didn't have much choice but to support Clodius Albinus then." His smile returned. "But it is a new era for Lindinis, Praefectus. Of course, Emperor Severus has had our full support for many years, as can be seen by our diligent payments to his imperial procurator." As he said this, he turned to see Perrora coming out of the curia building, guards carrying several chests of tax money, and followed by his secretaries.

Crescens waved, but the procurator pretended not to see him.

"Well, I suppose good walls make good neighbours," Lucius joked.

"Ha! Indeed they do!" Carcer laughed.

Crescens looked at his colleague and nodded.

"Virgilio, we should let the praefectus and his family be, so that they can finish their marketing. They have journeyed all the way from the hillfort this day."

"Yes, indeed. Do enjoy the town, all of you!" Carcer smiled at the children who clung a little more tightly to their parents with nervous smiles.

"We shall," Adara said, nodding. "I think a visit to the baths before we continue with our shopping."

"Oh yes, you must," Crescens agreed. "They have been newly renovated."

"And the new slaves we've purchased are quite good at massaging aching limbs, if you are in need," Carcer added. "Oh, but the hour for women and children only has passed."

Adara sighed, though she did not mean to do so.

"We'll be back another time," Lucius said, his hand on his wife's arm. He knew she had been looking forward to a bath. *More reason to build our own at home,* he thought.

"Nonsense!" Crescens said. "Wait here a moment if you please, Praefectus." He walked across the gravel pathway directly toward the double doors of the long bathhouse, went inside, and emerged smiling a few minutes later. When he arrived, his voice was as calm and friendly as ever. "I've arranged for your family to have the entire baths to yourselves, Praefectus."

"Oh, please no. That's very kind of you but we don't want any special treatment," Lucius insisted, stepping forward. "We'll come back another day, really."

"Not at all, Praefectus!" Carcer said. "Crescens is quite right."

"There were only two men in there and they were almost finished," he said, turning to look at the bathhouse again, just as two sullen-looking Britons exited, their long hair and moustaches still wet.

"They don't look pleased," Adara added, feeling badly then.

"Please, Lady Metella," Crescens went on. "Lindinis is happy to host your family. The praefectus' reputation has preceded him, and you have provided much work for many of our citizens and fabricae."

At the mention of the fabricae, Lucius was reminded that he needed to go and pay his bills after the baths.

"Very well," Adara said. "A proper bath sounds lovely." She nodded her thanks to the two men. "Well, we should go then, so we don't prevent others. We will not be long."

"Take your time, please," Crescens said, taking her hand and bowing slightly as Carcer pretended to look around.

"Thank you. It has been a pleasure to meet you both. I suppose we shall see you next time we are in town?"

"Surely," Crescens replied, smiling at both Adara and Lucius. "In fact, I've just had another idea. "Three days from now, I'm throwing a banquet at my villa for the other ordo members and their wives. Why don't you join us? It would be nice to get to know you both more and for you to meet the others. We are a close community here, our villas dotted all around Lindinis. Will you come?"

"Crescens does have the best cooks," Carcer added.

Lucius thought about it for a moment, then answered slowly. "Very well. We thank you for the invitation," Lucius said.

"We would love to," Adara added.

"Excellent! My wife, Sabina, will be very happy to meet you, Lady Metella. I will send a wagon to pick you up at your home. Does that work?"

"I, uh, I suppose," Lucius said. "Yes. That will be fine. Though there's really no need. We can ride."

"Nonsense. That way, you won't get dirty from road travel, or have to find your way. Until then," Crescens said before they could object.

Lucius and Adara nodded as the two men turned into the crowd of market sellers and shoppers.

Adara looked at Lucius and shrugged. "Nice men, I thought."

"I suppose, yes," he answered.

"All right," Adara turned to look at the children. "Who wants a bath?"

"Do we have to?" Calliope said.

Adara smiled. "Yes, you do. You smell of horse and cattle." She sniffed loudly about her daughter's head, drawing some awkward looks from a group of ladies nearby, though Adara took no notice of them.

Calliope giggled. "But I like horses and cows!" she protested.

"But you smell so much better!" Lucius said, lifting his daughter into the air. "Come! Let's get washed."

"Briana? Are you coming?" Adara asked, waving her over.

Briana took one more look around the crowd, trying to find her brother and spotted him still talking with the beer-sellers where a large group of Britons had gathered. She began to walk over but noticed they were either laughing or speaking closely with Einion.

Good. No danger, she told herself, before turning back to Adara. "Yes, I'll...I'll come." She walked to join the Metelli and go inside the bathhouse, suddenly aware of how good a warm bath was going to feel.

Lucius and Adara thought the baths were decent for such a small-sized town. True, it lacked the rushing flow of water of a bath fed by an aqueduct, but the river which fed the baths was enough for a steady stream of fresh water. It was also clean, which made a big difference to the bathers.

The apodyteri where they all changed were small but clean and graced with fresh coats of whitewash on top, and bright red paint on the bottom half of the wall. There was no ornamentation upon the walls except for the occasional painting of a bird in flight which Calliope pointed out now and again as though she were in a summer field spotting the swallows dive in the dusk light.

The floors were not as warm as other baths, but just enough to allow them to feel comfortable, the fires of the hypocausts burning just enough to heat the floor of the caldarium.

As Lucius and Phoebus went on ahead of the women and Calliope, their eyes traced the long mosaic patterns of intertwined lines that looked like mating serpents in the steamy air.

Lucius noticed his son feeling more conscious of his naked body, especially with the women in the room behind them, and smiled to himself.

My boy's growing up... I need to do more with him, he told himself.

Since Caledonia, Lucius had done much better at being a father than previously, but he knew there was much more he could do. He realized that every time he went off to war, he might not come back, and if that happened, his son would be left adrift without the lessons that were a father's duty to pass on - right and wrong, how to treat others and honour the Gods, how and when to fight. *There's so much...*

"Would you like to come with me to the fabricae afterward to pay, and then we can go and buy you a rudus?"

Phoebus' face lit up and he turned to look at his father, his young, muscular body suddenly shuddering with excitement.

"Yes! I would like that very much, Baba!"

"Great. But first, let's take our time here. Until we build our own baths at home, this is the only option for proper bathing." Lucius wiped the sweat dripping from his face.

"You're thinking of building baths at home? But where?"

"On the eastern slopes, near the well. Would you like that?"

"Yes, I would," Phoebus said as he stepped into the cold of the frigidarium.

"Woohoo!" there was a loud splash and laughter from the frigidarium and Calliope smiled.

"Mama! I think Phoebus has jumped in!" she tried peering through the thick steam of the caldarium which they had just entered, she and Adara following the naked form of Briana into the mist where she took up a strigil and scraped her body after rubbing on the oil.

"Here, let me help you, my girl," Adara said putting the oil on her daughter's limbs and running the bronze hooked implement over her skin to scrape away the dirt.

"Ouch! That scratches, Mama!" Calliope chided.

83

"I know, but look at this…" Adara showed her the dirt and grime that was removed from her little arms.

"Oh," Calliope realized, making a face at the sight. "I see."

"We must bathe you more," Adara laughed as they joined Briana. "Small but nice here," she said.

"Yes," Briana said. "I used to think it odd to go to a bathhouse when we had cool, clear streams running across our lands, but now that I have become used to them and the warmth of the water, I can't imagine not having them," Briana said as she ran her hands through her hair.

"You have almost as many scars as my baba!" Calliope said, looking at Briana's torso.

"Not quite as many as your father," Briana answered, ruffling her hair. "Only enough to show that I've been in some battles."

"Were you scared?" Calliope asked.

"Yes. Every time. But that is normal."

Adara smiled, as she closed her eyes and let the steam envelop her. *I hope I could face danger as bravely as Briana if I had to. I must train more.*

They finished making their way through the caldarium, and then the frigidarium. A little later, they found Lucius and Phoebus relaxing on a bench in the sunshine outside the main entrance.

"Carcer wasn't kidding. The massage slave is wondrous," Lucius said.

"Truly," Adara answered, bending down to kiss her husband.

"And nothing stolen from the apodyterium either!" he laughed.

"People could steal our things?" Phoebus asked.

Lucius laughed. "Someone can always steal your things if you're not careful. But in the thermae of Rome, thievery is much more common. Some of the baths even have former gladiators as guards in the apodyteri."

"Really?" the boy asked, his eyes wide and worried.

"Really. But don't worry," Lucius said, standing to kiss his wife. "You smell good," he whispered.

"A hint of rose in the oil," she answered.

"Einion!" Briana called, waving to her brother to come over. "Where have you been?"

Einion walked up, his pace determined, his face serious. "I've been asking around among the Britons here. Trying to find out if they've heard any news from Dumnonia."

"And?" Briana gripped his arm.

"Nothing."

"Really? There must be some news?"

"It is utter and complete silence. No news at all, either coming or going. Word is the Roman garrison at Isca is going to send a patrol."

"Trouble?" Lucius asked.

"No one can say," Einion said. "Neither the local Britons or the Romans know anything."

"If they're sending a patrol, they'll find out something," Lucius reassured. "Maybe your uncle has finally ended up on Rome's bad side and gone rogue?"

Einion stood brooding, puzzling over the whole affair in his mind.

Briana knew her brother had been hoping for more information, anything, a target at which to aim his thoughts of vengeance, but news of nothing was not easy for him. He was tired of supposition and guesswork, as was she.

"You missed using the baths with us," Briana said. "You would have enjoyed them."

Einion looked at the building behind them and shrugged. "I'll use the stream beside the hillfort," he said.

Lucius looked up at the sky. "It's past midday. We should finish up and get on the road before it gets dark." He turned to Adara. "Do we have everything we need from the market?"

"We still need some new breeches for the children, some boots for Calliope, and I wanted to get a wheel of cheese from the seller on the far side of the square. Have you finished your dealings?"

"I haven't been to the fabrica yet to pay our bill for the roof tiles. That's next. After that, I want to pick up some rudii for the children. It's time they learned to use them properly."

"Can I come, Baba?" Phoebus asked, tugging at Lucius' cloak.

Lucius looked down at his son and nodded. "Yes," he confirmed, and turned back to Adara. "You go with Briana, Einion and Calliope to finish gathering everything, and I'll go to the fabrica and sword smith with Phoebus. We'll meet back at Corpulo's stable."

"Do you mind staying with them?" Lucius said to Einion and Briana.

"Of course not," Briana answered. "This town seems safe enough, but be careful, Lucius."

"We'll be fine," Lucius answered, turning with his son's hand in his, but stopping dead in his tracks.

In front of them was a group of men, their faces and skin hard and worn, their eyes staring at Lucius intently.

Lucius instinctively stepped in front of his son, his hand on the hilt of his sword beneath his cloak.

Einion was right beside him.

"Are you Lucius Metellus Anguis?" the leader of the group asked. His beard was short and grey, the colour matching his eyes.

"Yes," Lucius answered calmly, taking a step forward. "Why?"

The man rushed forward, his arm out, and Lucius' blade was out in an instant, pointed at his neck.

The man stopped in his tracks and burst out laughing.

"I told you it was him!" he yelled to the group of men behind him.

Lucius and Einion scanned the group of men who were all smiles now and began to crowd closer.

"We just wanted to shake your hand, sir, as we've heard so much about you and your actions up Caledonia way."

"Why not just talk to the praefectus instead of rush him like that?" Einion said, sheathing the long sword that was his father's.

The man looked guilty. "Well... Me and the lads here had a bet that if you were the Dragon Praefectus, you would be ready for anything. I drew the short straw in deciding who would test that."

"That was ill-advised," Lucius said seriously. He looked over the men, the calm pride in all of their faces, and knew they were speaking true, that they just wanted to meet him. He extended his hand.

"I'm pleased to meet you," Lucius said, gripping the man's hand.

The man gripped it tightly, a calloused, iron-hard grip that spoke of many campaigns across the empire.

"The young ones back in Isca won't believe me when I tell them I've met you," the man laughed, stepping aside to allow the men behind him to crowd in around Lucius.

Einion found himself shoved aside and for several minutes, Adara, the children, Einion and Briana watched as men gathered around Lucius to shake his hand and exchange a word or two about which legions they had served in and which campaigns they had endured.

Adara watched her husband and smiled. *It is not only myself that loves him. These men are awed, and Lucius doesn't even know it.*

"Mama?" Calliope asked.

"Yes?"

"Why won't those men let Baba go?"

"Because they wish to speak with him," Adara said.

"But I'm hungry."

"Shh, Calliope!" Phoebus hissed. "Baba's famous here, and the soldiers want to talk with him." The boy stepped forward to watch the proceedings until the last of the twenty or so men drifted back into the market.

Lucius turned back to his family. "Didn't expect that!" he said, his brow sweaty.

"You never do, my love," Adara said.

"I found out from one of them where the fabrica of Tellus is. It's just outside the east gate. Phoebus and I will go now and catch up with you."

With that, Lucius began to walk across the square with his son.

Einion stood and watched Lucius and Phoebus go, as Adara, Briana and Calliope went to the tanner to look at breeches and boots. If the Briton was honest with himself, he would say that he was jealous of the renown Lucius had gathered unto himself with his deeds. *What have I done to merit such words or admiration from strangers?* he thought.

"Why do you think so many people want to speak with you, Baba?" Phoebus asked as they walked along the main street toward the east gate.

"Oh, people hear stories of the war in the North. They think that I won all those battles on my own when, really, I could not have won anything without Dagon and his men." Lucius stopped and turned to his son's admiring face. "Remember that. No man can achieve greatness without strong, trusted allies. Even Alexander could not have conquered the East without his men."

"Men who loved him and would do anything for him," Phoebus added as they began to walk again.

"Yes. But Alexander earned his men's trust and love and loyalty." Lucius looked up at the gate where a few guards were standing watch, nodding to him as he passed beneath the thick, limestone arches.

"Your men love you too, Baba. I can see it."

"Yes. I am fortunate," Lucius admitted. "But I am always striving to earn their respect and love. Never forget that."

"I won't," the boy said, though to Lucius at that moment, he looked anything but a boy.

They carried on walking among the grave stelae of the cemetery on either side of the road, making for the group of buildings on their right where the various fabricae of Lindinis were located.

"The fellow said it was the third building," Lucius mumbled as they passed the first structure.

The fabricae had small fronts facing the road, but went far back to allow space for the halls where they mixed and fired the clay. Beyond those, were open yards where stacks of finished product awaited shipment to the various villas about Lindinis. The wealthy landowners were always building and adding on to their homes, so the fabricae did a steady business.

Still, Lucius' building had given them more work at once than was usual, and this was no doubt why Tellus himself came out to greet him.

"Praefectus Metellus!"

Lucius turned to see a short, dark man standing beneath a sign with the letters 'FT' upon a large clay tablet.

"I'm Tellus," he said, stepping forward to meet Lucius. "Welcome to Lindinis."

"Thank you," Lucius answered, a little surprised at how quickly word had travelled to the man that he was coming. "This is my son, Phoebus."

"Hello, laddy!" Tellus said, extending his hand to Phoebus who took the grubby, red-stained hand.

"Hello," the boy said.

"I've come to settle my bill," Lucius said.

"If only all of my customers paid as promptly, Praefectus!" Tellus laughed. "Come. Come inside. The paperwork is ready for you to look over. The exact amounts agreed upon by myself and Cradawg."

Together, the three of them went inside. The first thing Lucius noticed was that the fabrica existed both indoors and outdoors, the walls broken and roof open at intervals to allow dust and smoke to escape.

There was also a strong odour of wet earth, charcoal and sweat. Groups of men laboured at the softening of the clay, while others molded it into the forms to create the tiles.

Phoebus observed this with great interest, noting they were exactly the same as those upon the rooftops of their new home and carried the same mark. He pointed at three examples which stood proudly on a thick, rough wooden table in the front room near the counter where Lucius and Tellus looked over the accounts.

"These are the same as the ones on our home," Phoebus said.

"Why, yes they are, little man!" Tellus said jovially. "And you won't find none better in Lindinis." He winked. "We're a veteran outfit."

"So this is the final amount to be paid?" Lucius said, pointing to a number Tellus had scrawled on a large wax tablet on the counter.

"That's correct, Praefectus. That includes three thousand tegulae and imbrices, as well as the fifty anthemia."

Lucius nodded and reached for the heavy purse at his belt. He poured out the correct amount of denarii, and Tellus counted.

"Thank you," the man said. "The lads were chuffed to have all the extra work, Praefectus. If you need any more work done, just let us know and we'll cut you a discount."

"Actually," Lucius said. "I'm thinking about building a bathhouse."

"Really?"

"Yes, but I'll have to discuss the plans with Cradawg before we place an order for more tiles, and bricks for the hypocaust."

"I'm glad you're pleased with the quality," Tellus said, his chest out. "You can count on us."

"Glad to hear it," Lucius answered. "Now, if you'll excuse us, we need to get back to our family."

"Of course."

As Lucius and Phoebus were heading out the door, Tellus came around the counter again.

"Praefectus!"

Lucius turned. "Yes?"

"It's an honour to meet the 'Dragon', sir."

Lucius tilted his head and led his son out of the building.

"I told Calliope you were famous," Phoebus said, beaming as they walked back into the town.

89

It was not long before Lucius and Phoebus found Adara, Calliope, Briana and Einion in the town. They were carrying bundles of clothing and Calliope was wearing a new pair of leather boots Adara had just bought her.

"Phoebus!" Calliope called. "They had a pair that fit me!" she said, sticking out one of her legs to reveal one long, reddish-brown leather boot.

Her brother nodded and waved, running to his mother.

"They knew Baba at the fabrica too!" he said.

"I'm sure," Adara said, leaning toward Lucius. "I'm finished. I think we have all the supplies we need. There's been a steady stream of deliveries to Corpulo's stable. Everyone's so eager to help us."

"It is a bit odd, don't you think?" Lucius said. "I mean, the soldiers I understand a little - they've heard stories - but ordinary citizens?"

"Might have something to do with those ordo members I saw you talking with," Einion said. "The Britons I spoke with didn't have much good to say about the town council, I can tell you that."

"Really?" Lucius was thoughtful.

"We should be going so we arrive home before the first hour of darkness."

"Just one more stop," Lucius said, taking each of the children's hands. "It's time we got you each a rudus."

Together, they all walked across the main road to a shop along the west wall of the town.

There, a carpenter was selling all manner of tools and containers of various woods, but at the back, spreading across the wall, were a series of wooden gladii of varying sizes.

"Salve, Praefectus!" a thick, old white-haired man said. "How can I help you?"

"Greetings, citizen," Lucius said, extending his hand so that the man grabbed it right away and shook vigorously. "I would like to buy a couple of rudii for these two young ones here."

The man peered over the counter at Phoebus and Calliope. "The girl too?" he said.

"Yes," Lucius answered. "We all learn to use a sword in this family."

"Right you are then, Praefectus!" the man laughed. "Let me see what I've got here." He turned and looked at the back wall where all of the rudii were far too large and heavy for the children. "No. None of these will do." Then he flipped a leather curtain up which covered shelves below and there revealed rudii bundled like reeds. "Here we are," he said, pulling out a smaller bundle. "There should be some smaller ones in here. The local veterans all want their children to learn, so I keep a small stock for when they break 'em."

He laid out seven different rudii, mostly of the same length. "Step up then, children, and try them out."

Phoebus was eager and grabbed one immediately. He pulled one out and it immediately went to the ground.

"It's too heavy," he said, looking up at Lucius.

"It's supposed to be much heavier than a real gladius so that you can build your strength. How does the handle feel? Good? Comfortable?"

Phoebus stepped back. Adara and the others watched him from the front of the shop, as he twirled the gladius, and stabbed with it as if he were in the front ranks of a century.

Lucius could see he was working hard not to be embarrassed.

"I think that will do well for you," Lucius said. "You like it?"

"Yes, Baba! May I have it?"

"Yes."

"Good choice!" the man said. "That one is made of oak, very heavy and very solid. Mind you're careful with that, lad. Though it can't cut, it can certainly break a bone."

"What about you, my girl?" Lucius said to Calliope. "Do you see one you like?"

Calliope approached the counter reluctantly and picked up a rudus made of paler wood. It too fell to the ground quickly, surprising her with its weight, but she soon had it in the air, pointed high and looking at the tip hovering there. She had not expected to enjoy the feel of the sword in her hand. She waved it in front of herself, back and forth a couple of times, then smiled and looked up at Lucius.

"I like this one," she said.

"What is this one made out of?" Lucius asked the shopkeeper.

"Ash. Lighter than the oak, a bit more pliant, but still very strong. It'll absorb the impact more."

"We'll take them, and two full-sized rudii."

"Very good, Praefectus," the man said, taking two off of the wall and placing them on the counter.

While he added up the bill, Lucius checked the balance of each. Satisfied, he took out his pouch and paid the man.

"I'd say that was a successful day," Adara said as they walked back toward the north gate and over the bridge.

From the midst of a group of citizens in town, they were watched by the two executives of the ordo, Carcer and Crescens.

"Do you think he will help us?" Carcer whispered to his colleague, wiping the top of his bald head with a purple kerchief.

"Time will tell. We'll put it to him in a few days," Crescens said before turning away and heading back to the curia.

As they all crossed the bridge, Lucius stopped. Something had caught his eye farther along to the right, along the curving back of the river.

The others continued on their way.

"You go ahead!" he called. "I'll catch up with you!"

None of them looked back, but kept on walking, deep in the children's descriptions of the day and their purchases.

Lucius walked quickly toward the small, lone smith's shop that had caught his eye. He slowed, feeling the hairs on the back of his neck prickle, but pressed on toward the stall.

There were no other customers there, just the smith, who did not look at all like a smith. They were usually large, burly men with leathery faces and skin stained black from ash and flame. This smith was small, almost childlike, and dark of skin. He wore a sleeveless jerkin of doeskin and a hat that was almost Phrygian in appearance, beneath which twined black curls resembling the twinings of some dark forest ivy. His arms were no thicker than Lucius' wrists, but they were well-defined and quick.

"Hello there, Praefectus Lucius Metellus Anguis," he said with an odd sort of joy.

"Oh, hello. Do I know you?" Lucius said.

"I shouldn't think so. But I know you. Doesn't everyone around here?"

Lucius nodded slowly. "I guess it seems that way."

"Again, I say... Hello there!"

"Hello there!" Lucius laughed in spite of himself. The boy...man...had such an agreeable personality, Lucius almost forgot the thought that brought him there.

"You're wondering what you are looking for?" the man smiled.

"Well, a special weapon," Lucius said, leaning on the counter to look at the few pieces displayed. There weren't many items, but those that were there were exquisitely wrought. Most were the sort of longsword some Britons still carried, the blades long and straight, the hilts dedicated to whorls and interlaced animals. Not what Lucius was thinking of, but beautiful nonetheless. "You don't have much stock at the moment, I see."

"I only do commissions. I am Terdra, smith of the forest forge, and maker of heavenly weapons."

"Quite a title," Lucius chuckled.

The smile disappeared fleetingly. "I take my work with utmost seriousness, Praefectus."

"Forgive me…Terdra. I meant no insult." Lucius pushed his cloak back a little, feeling warm suddenly, though there was no fire. "May I see one of the blades? The short one with the hilt shaped like a man."

"Certainly." Terdra turned and took the odd-looking piece from its wooden pegs and handed it to Lucius hilt first.

Lucius stepped back and hefted the blade. It was extremely light. Lighter than any blade of like size he had held. He stabbed with it at the air and the point gleamed in a ray of sunlight, revealing sharp cutting edges. He spun it, and the blade appeared to sing as it cut through the air.

Lucius stopped and looked at the smith. "I've never seen anything like it!"

"Are you sure?" Terdra nodded to the sword at Lucius' waist. "Seems to me you have. No blade goes unnoticed by my eyes."

"So it seems."

"Here, test it. See that large hunk of bark at the end of the counter?"

"Yes."

"Cut it."

"But I'll ruin your client's new blade. They won't thank you for it."

"I know my work. Just cut it."

Lucius shrugged and turned to the bark, lifted the blade three feet in the air and hacked downward as if he were hammering on an enemy's collar bone.

The thick bark split cleanly through in two great pieces, and the end of the oak counter collapsed in splinters.

Lucius said nothing for a few moments, trying to gather his understanding of what he had just witnessed, the lack of any hurtful vibrations travelling through the thin blade under such an impact.

"Who are you?" he said to the smith, turning slowly and placing the blade upon the counter.

"I already told you," Terdra said, his smile warm and winking. "Now, what sort of weapon would you like?"

"A gladius for my wife."

"For a woman? Really?"

"She has become a skilled swordswoman of late and I want a blade for her to protect herself and our children."

"Tell me, was she the fine Roman lady who passed yonder toward the stables with the two Britons?"

"What? Yes, but how did you see-"

"My eyes are keen, is all," the smith answered. "I only ask to determine the size of the blade. You say you want a gladius?"

"Yes."

"And ornamentation?"

Lucius thought about it for a moment and then reached for his own blade. He drew it and held it out for the smith to see.

For the first time, the smith looked astonished. "Yes...yes...I see. Beautiful. Absolutely." His fingers hovered along the blade, light flashing in the reflection, and pointed at the dragon heads upon the hilt. "You would like dragons upon the hilt. Two of them?"

"Yes. That would work. Something to match my own."

The smith studied the pommel, handle, and all the details most people overlooked when gazing upon such works. When he felt he understood the blade, he looked up at Lucius.

"I can do it. And I promise you, it will be lighter and stronger than any blade you have seen. Even that one," he said, looking at Lucius' own sword. "The Dragon's wife is smaller and quick, and her blade should be so too."

"Yes," was all Lucius could say. Then he shook his head. "When shall I come to get it?"

"This will take some time. I return here toward the Winter Solstice."

"So long?" Lucius was a little disappointed, but he wanted the perfect blade for Adara.

Then, for a fleeting moment, he spied a face in the sheen of his own blade gazing back at him - Apollo.

Lucius took his blade and gazed at it.

"To make a blade such as this takes time, Praefectus."

"No...I mean, yes. I would like you to make it," Lucius said, confused. "Do you require some payment now?"

"None."

"But-"

"No need. I know you'll be back."

"I will," Lucius said, nodding.

"And I will wait until you arrive."

"Thank you," Lucius said, reaching out to take Terdra's hand.

The smith withheld his hand, but smiled and nodded. "Until the Solstice then."

"Yes," Lucius said before turning and walking away, his own sword gripped tightly in his left hand.

When he reached the road he turned back to see the lone stall, but the smith was nowhere to be seen.

Strange, he thought as he headed back to join the others.

"You look beautiful as ever, Adara. Would you stop worrying?"

Lucius stood behind her, already dressed in his toga, his arms crossed as he looked down at his wife where she was seated at a small table, gazing into a bronze, ivory-handled mirror she had bought in Lindinis only a few days before.

A chunk of incense burned in a dish nearby, the stealthy plumes of smoke catching in the curls of her dark hair which she had re-arranged a few times already.

"You don't understand, Lucius," she said, not looking at him, but continuing to adjust her locks yet again. "I haven't been to a banquet since Coria, and I don't want to think about that one again."

"You'll be the prettiest woman there," Lucius soothed, leaning down and wrapping his arms about her shoulders, kissing her gently to the side of her ear so that she closed her eyes and relaxed for a fleeting moment. "Besides... I'll be with you the whole time. This isn't Rome, you know? The emperor and empress won't be there. These are just local provincials, nice people...our neighbours."

"I know, I know!" she said, frustrated again by her hair which she let hang down and tied back with a single gold chain.

"You're a goddess!" Lucius said, stepping back to let her stand.

Adara wore her favourite blue stola with golden trim. It showed off her height, lengths of golden ribbon criss-crossing downward from beneath her breasts to just bellow her hips where the rest of the fabric cascaded to the floor like a straight and shimmering indigo waterfall.

"You're certain this will do?" she asked again.

"By the Gods, Adara! I can't imagine you being any lovelier," he stepped forward to kiss her on the mouth.

Once he released her, she began straightening the folds of his toga. "You look like you've been fighting in this," she said, shaking her head.

Lucius laughed. "No. Not fighting, but defending myself against Phoebus and Calliope. They were eager to try out their new rudii, so I thought I would show them a couple of things. They've really taken to it. Phoebus more, but they both have some skill."

Adara sighed. "Do you think they'll be all right?" She had been worrying about leaving the children overnight, ever since the invitation had been extended by Serenus Crescens Nova in Lindinis three days before.

"They'll be fine, my love. Briana and Einion will be here, and Ula and Aina are still going to be cooking for them. Culhwch said he would also stop in later."

"I guess they don't need us then."

"What's got into you?" Lucius asked.

"I just... I haven't really been apart from them since Coria, and that was such a horrible night."

Adara paused and closed her eyes, breathing deeply. Occasionally she would remember that horrible scene at the banquet where her former friend, Perdita, had been raped in the gardens right beneath the empress' nose, and how horribly brutalized her entire body had been afterward... *Would that the Gods rip the memory from my mind and make Claudius Picus suffer for what he did!*

She felt Lucius' hands as he gripped shoulders.

"It will be fine," he said. "We'll have a wonderful time."

She nodded.

"Lucius!" Einion's voice boomed from the lower floor of the hall.

Lucius stepped out of the cubiculum to the railing and peered over. "What?"

"There's a wagon down by the gate. Two slaves who say they're here to bring you and Adara to Crescens' villa."

"We're coming," Lucius said before going back into the room. "Ready?"

Adara checked the mirror one more time and turned, nodding. "Let's go."

Lucius turned to grab his sword and dagger beside their bed.

"You're bringing your weapons?" Adara asked.

"Yes. Why not?"

"Well...it...it might, well, scare them?"

"I said it would never leave my side."

"What if they won't allow you to keep it close?"

Lucius thought about it for a moment. It was their first time visiting the home of this prominent citizen of Lindinis, along with other members of the ordo. It really would not do to go with a sword that had seen blood beyond measure.

Slowly, very reluctantly, Lucius placed the sword back against the wall.

"Very well. But I'm keeping my dagger," he said, tucking it into the folds of his toga.

They came out into the sunlight to see the children picking carrots in the vegetable garden with Briana while Einion leaned on the fence watching the pair of slaves down by the cart.

"Watch these ordo members," Einion said to Lucius as he and Adara approached. "The Durotrigans I spoke with in Lindinis were none too fond of them."

"Don't worry, it's just dinner," Lucius said.

"I thought Romans made the biggest decisions over dinner."

Lucius pat Einion on the shoulder. "The Senate is usually where that is done, my friend."

"But these guys are just that, locally anyways."

That gave Lucius pause, but he shook his head. "We'll be fine."

"Einion, thank you for watching over the children," Adara said, stepping up and taking his hands.

He smiled. "You don't need to worry. We'll look over them like they're our own blood. You go. Enjoy time among Romans." He turned to Lucius again. "I hope you're armed at least?"

Lucius nodded and showed him the pommel of his pugio beneath his toga.

"Good." Einion nodded, satisfied, then looked in the direction of the wagon and two slaves down the hill. "You'd better get going."

Adara and Lucius leaned on the fence to kiss Phoebus and Calliope on their heads where they were in the garden.

"You be good for Briana and Einion," Adara said.

"We will, Mama," they answered, plunging their hands back into the dark soil to pull out another carrot each.

Adara knew she was going to miss them far more than they would miss her.

"Let's go," Lucius said, leading her down the path toward the stables and curving around the south side of the plateau toward the slaves.

The two men sent to fetch them were indeed slaves, as the collars about their necks revealed. However, they appeared to be well-treated. No bruises were apparent on either of them, and they each enjoyed a pair of fine leather sandals, tunics of indigo-dyed wool, and brown cloaks to cover their shoulders on the journey, and shield them from the cool evening air from the distant sea.

The smaller of the two, a young man of about twenty-three, came forward bowing and gesturing to the wagon.

"Praefectus Metellus and Lady Metella," the man said. "Our dominus sent us with the most comfortable wagon to bring you back to the villa for the banquet. There are extra blankets if you should get cold on the way, and the curtains may be drawn if you wish to have some privacy. It is not a long journey, but there is some food and wine inside should you wish it."

He extended his hand to Adara to help her up into the wagon.

She smiled, despite her nerves, and the young man blushed.

When Lucius approached, the slave cowered in awe, even backed away respectfully.

"How long is the journey?" Lucius asked, making conversation.

"Praefectus, the journey won't take more than one hour upon the road. The weather is good for travel that way."

"Excellent." Lucius mounted the wagon which was pulled by two sturdy white and brown horses.

Inside, Adara and Lucius settled into an array of soft cushions of various silks of blue, green, and yellow, all of them scented with rose water. The bottom of the wagon was softened with straw covered by a deep blue fabric, lit only by the slight amount of light that was permitted entry by the creamy canvas that covered the wagon.

The second slave, a larger, older man, turned from the front bench to see if Lucius and Adara were settled, whispered something to the other with the reins, and then the wagon lurched down the hill.

Adara and Lucius turned to look out the back and see Phoebus, Calliope, Briana, and Einion at the top of the plateau, waving them off.

Adara waved back, waiting until they were out of sight before she settled back down.

"They'll be fine, my love," Lucius said.

"I know... I know." Finally, she stopped to look at him, remembered how beautiful he was to her and she could not prevent the smile that came to her face even if she wanted to.

Adara leaned into Lucius' arms and together they sat back against the cushions to stare out at the countryside that passed them by. There were a thousand shades of green that met their eyes, dotted by yellows and purples, blues and whites. Insects flitted and buzzed in the gathering dusk, and Adara began to hum, lulling Lucius as he stroked her arm with his thumb and watched the lovely curve of her cheeks and moving lips.

"I think we're going to have a wonderful time," he said.

The slaves had been correct, the ride only took them an hour, and there was still a measure of daylight left as the wagon pulled onto the long, tree-lined road leading to the villa.

The sound of evening birdsong flooded the air as they drove among the trees, the green hills sloping away beyond the tilled fields where workers were finishing up their work for the day.

A faint sound of music reached their ears, mixed with the chatter of voices and neighing of horses. A long stone wall began from the side of the road and they followed it for several meters, passing burning braziers that had been lit to ward off the dark beneath the full trees lining the road.

"We've arrived, Praefectus," the slave driving the wagon said as he slowed the horses and turned right into a broad, square, dirt courtyard lit by more braziers and bustling with several wagon teams. The other wagons had lined up to drop their passengers off at the edge of a stone pathway that led to the main part of the villa.

"What a lovely home," Adara said as she peered out to see some of the other guests milling about and looking toward their wagon as it approached.

Lucius scanned the vast villa complex and noted that it was much larger than their Etrurian villa rustica, even though most of it was on one level. The buildings were all made of solid limestone and roofed with the best tiles Lindinis' fabricae had to offer. Stables and supply sheds were located on the north end of the dirt courtyard and opposite, on the south side, was a large two-storey home that was the main living space. The west wing consisted of guest rooms, and judging from the smoke coming out of a chimney, the entire east wing was a private bath complex.

"Very impressive," Lucius said. The villa seemed out of place in that lush, green landscape, like so many other of Rome's structures, even though the Pax Romana had held sway in the South for more than a hundred years.

It was a beautiful setting, but Lucius could not help thinking of a foreign jewel dropped deliberately in the middle of a farmer's field, something to draw attention, jealousy, something to tempt where no temptation was needed.

Guests stepped down from the waiting litters and wagons to be greeted by slaves who attended everyone, like bees to golden honey.

The wagon paused. There were some raised voices, and then it lurched past those already waiting at the front of the line where several men in togas stood watching, Serenus Crescens at the forefront.

"Praefectus Metellus!" he said for all to hear. "Lady Metella... Welcome to my home!"

Heads turned, or peered through litter curtains to see Lucius and Adara's wagon come to a stop at the end of the path that led through lush herb and flower beds directly to the main house.

The slaves jumped down quickly from their perches on the driving bench and bent their backs to putting the moveable steps in place for Lucius and Adara to come down.

All eyes were on the couple, the beautiful, dark-haired woman in the blue and gold stola, and the 'Dragon Praefectus' who had wreaked havoc on the tribes north of the Wall, only now he wore the toga angusticlavia instead of armour. It was whispered there and then that the Lady Metella was personally acquainted with the empress, almost as much as her husband was a personal favourite of the emperor.

"Welcome to you both!" Crescens broke away from the small group of men in richly coloured togas and pressed his hand into Lucius'. "We're so glad you were able to join us."

"As are we, Serenus Crescens," Lucius answered.

"Oh please, please," Crescens said. "We need not be so formal tonight. Do call me Serenus." He turned to Adara, took her hand, and bowed his forehead to it. "Lady. You are most welcome here."

"Thank you," Adara inclined her head, her left hand still hooked to Lucius' right. "You have a beautiful home, Serenus. A true piece of paradise."

"We have done well here. But such is the lot of those who dwell in Rome's peaceful lands, I dare say."

Lucius smiled and nodded, and Crescens continued.

"May I introduce you to some of our other guests?" he began to walk along the precisely fitted cobbles of the wide path flanked by manicured gardens, toward the house where the group of men had congregated. "Virgilio Carcer you already know," Crescens said, as the taller, bald man floated toward them all smiles.

"We are glad you were able to join us, that we can all get to know each other better as neighbours, and people of taste, of course," Carcer said.

The men behind Carcer muttered their agreement.

"May I introduce Cassius Bucer, Felix Inek, Renato Tulio, Nolan Phelan, and Finnian Maccus." Crescens turned to Lucius and Adara. "We are, all of us, members of the ordo of Lindinis. But we are also friends, Roman and Briton. We still await the rest of the ordo members, Medr Kendall and Arlan Blair. Though I don't suppose we can expect Trevor Reghan to join us."

"Is he ill?" Lucius asked, curious about the disgruntled or relieved looks upon the others' faces.

"No. Just not one for parties," Carcer said.

"Yes, well, let us move inside while the other guests disembark," Crescens added, leading the way and motioning for Adara and Lucius to follow.

The other ordo members remained in the courtyard and looked back to the other litters and wagons for the arrival of the remainder of the guests.

Beneath the covered peristylium that ran the length of the main part of the domus, a tall woman in a rich-looking stola of bright red approached Crescens, Lucius and Adara. Other women clung to her

101

tall form as she moved toward them. She did not smile, but took in the sight of them immediately, her eyes carefully raking them over.

Adara found it hard to smile at the woman, but managed a friendly exterior to match Lucius'. She had seen too many feline looks in the imperial court over the last couple of years, and so was naturally wary.

"Praefectus Metellus and Lady Metella," Crescens began, standing beside his taller wife. "May I present my wife, Sabina Cresca."

"Lady," Lucius took her hand and bowed a little. "Thank you for welcoming us into your home."

"You are welcome," Sabina Cresca said, staring at them down her long aquiline nose. Her forehead was smooth, and she had dark brown eyes rounded out with kohl.

"It seems Vesta has blessed your family with a beautiful home here," Adara offered, smiling.

Sabina did not return the smile. "Yes. I suppose she has blessed us. It is as good as we can do in this uncouth part of the empire."

"Now, now, my dove," Crescens soothed. "Though the Praefectus and Lady Metella do hail from Rome and Athenae, they too now live here, and that by choice. As do we."

Lucius spotted Crescens' hand grip his wife's tightly and, as if subdued, her frown turned into a smooth smile.

"Of course we are blessed in this place. For it is quiet, clean, and far from the chaos of Londinium. I wouldn't mind Aquae Sulis, but as Serenus' business dealings are hereabouts, it makes more sense to be here, despite the presence of so many Britons."

She was haughty, to say the least, but her husband's warm smile outshone her for the moment.

"I hope we can all get to know each other better this evening," Crescens said, beckoning to a well-dressed slave with a tray of hammered silver cups filled with wine. "Try this," he handed a cup to Lucius and then to Adara. "The vintage is from Sabina's family vineyard back in Italia."

Both Lucius and Adara sipped at the wine. It was good, and quenched their dry throats.

"Excellent," Lucius said, nodding to Sabina.

"Yes," she agreed. "It is one of the better ones, I agree. Our family has been selling across the Middle Sea for some generations."

"Virgilio," Crescens stepped away to speak with his fellow ordo member. "I'm going to give the Praefectus and Lady Metella a tour of the villa. Would you mind watching for the others?"

"But... I would join you if I may!" the bald man said, stepping forward, not to be dissuaded.

"No need," Crescens said. "We don't want to overwhelm our guests right away.

"Very well. But I should like to speak with the Praefectus myself this evening."

"We are all eager to hear from our new Britannic hero, I'm sure. We won't be long," Crescens said, walking away and ushering Lucius and Adara with him and his wife.

They strolled along the covered walkway and then turned right at the far end, making their way toward the bathhouse.

"Tell me, Serenus," Lucius asked. "How did you come to be in this area of Britannia?"

"Well, as I mentioned when we met, we came here from Londinium to be closer to my business interests. We deal mostly in livestock - cattle, sheep, and some pigs..."

As the two men chatted about business, Adara and Sabina walked quietly behind them.

Adara noted that Sabina's nose turned up at the talk of livestock, as though she could smell them in that moment from the scattered farms across the vast country holdings which Crescens was describing. It was odd, considering that the wealth she so obviously enjoyed was evidently accumulated through her husband's business.

"I hear your husband is on furlough after the victories in the barbaric North?" Sabina asked.

"Yes. He is."

"And you chose to remain in Britannia instead of returning to Rome, or even Athenae?"

"Yes. One never knows when duty will call him back. Besides," Adara went on. "My father gave us our lands near here for our wedding. We wanted to make something of them."

"I'm sure you did," Sabina said, following her husband and Lucius into the bathhouse.

Their voices fell to a hushed echo in the smaller space, accented by the running of fresh water.

"We built the entire villa at the same time, no stages," Crescens said. The buildings on the other side of the courtyard are for storage and horses. But this bathhouse, I can tell you, is a welcome joy on hot days or cold winter nights when the hypocausts are fully heated.

Lucius and Adara looked around as they were led through the tepidarium to the caldarium. The walls were exquisitely painted with country scenes, scenic seascapes, and forests where satyrs peered from behind the trunks of oaks. Rich red borders rose from the mosaic floors which were obviously wrought by a master mosaic maker.

"And here is my pride and joy," Crescens said as he led them into the frigidarium. "Do you recognize the story?"

Lucius and Adara looked down through the clear water to see a scene in several panels.

"Aeneas and Dido!" Adara said, forgetting the haughty woman beside her to admire the shimmering mosaic. "It's beautiful."

"Isn't it?" Crescens said, standing with his arms crossed, looking down beside Lucius and Adara, watching for their reactions. "As far as I can tell, no one has ever portrayed their story in such a way. I wanted something unique for this place and what better story than that of the two lovers, Aeneas and Dido, in the far away land of Carthage. It does warm one so on a cold British day!"

Lucius looked upon the mosaic and held Adara's hand. Before them, Aeneas and Dido rode at the hunt, fell in love, and embraced in a wood, before his tragic sailing away. In just five mosaic panels, the entire story seemed to be told, the small, square tesserae mixing the emotions and bringing them to life.

"The artist must have been a magician to make so fine a mosaic as this," Adara said.

Crescens smiled widely at her and nodded, his eyes locked on hers. "Yes, he was. Usually artists have their team of apprentices come and install the mosaic, often with pre-made patterns, but I wanted this to be something no one else had anywhere. It was very costly, but well-worth it. The mosaicist came himself to install it."

"My dear," Sabina then said. "I'm am beginning to sweat, and our other guests will be wondering where their hosts are."

"Yes, we'll walk through the main house to greet them with the Praefectus and Lady Metella," Crescens said. "This way."

They followed Crescens and his wife through a door just beyond the massage room and small apodyterium, and entered the lower level of the villa in what was a corridor with richly-decorated cubicula on either side. Ahead, slaves bustled in and out of large double doors carrying platters of delicacies and blue glass jugs of wine and water. The smells that reached Lucius and Adara's senses made them instantly hungry.

"We have had our cooks prepare something very special for all of you this evening. And each guest will have a cubiculum to themselves should they wish to retire at any point. Though," he paused and turned back to them, "I do hope you will stay up so that we may talk well into the night." This is where I receive my clients," he turned to the right and pointed into a large tablinum with walls covered in scrolls, three large tables, and several stools.

There was no room for ornamentation there, only the accoutrements of his business - stylii, papyri, ink, wax tablets, and miles of accounts, all lit by hanging bronze lamps which seemed to sway as if on the deck of a ship at sea.

"We will talk more later," Crescens said. "But first, let me introduce you to all our other guests." Crescens stepped forward through the atrium and around a small impluvium with four columns, one at each corner. Two slaves stood by the large, main double doors and opened them as their dominus approached.

As the doors opened onto the covered walkway and the garden courtyard beyond, a crowd of guests turned to see the four of them walking out.

Adara gripped Lucius' hand as they stepped forward.

It was going to be a long night.

Lucius and Adara felt as if they were on display, and they were, gods knew. However, not one of the faces before them betrayed any sort of surprise at seeing the two newcomers.

People smiled and nodded politely, waited for Crescens to wave them forward, but before he could speak, Virgilio Carcer spoke.

"Friends, friends!" He waved his arms for attention, the small woman who appeared to be his wife, moving away from her husband to stand beside Sabina. "I would like to thank our gracious hosts for the invitation to dine with them this evening. I know we are all in for a sumptuous feast!"

"I'm starving!" bellowed one of the ordo members from the back.

"We should also acknowledge the newcomers among us, Praefectus Lucius Metellus Anguis, and his enchanting wife, Adara Antonina Metella."

Crescens stepped forward then as Carcer took a breath. "Quite right!" he said. "Sip your wine and come meet our new guests before going in for a feast to sate even Bacchus."

There were some murmurs of agreement as each man and woman came forward to greet Lucius and Adara, Crescens taking care of the introductions.

"Praefectus, this is Cassius Bucer and his wife, Luciana," Crescens said.

A portly man stepped forward and extended a thick hairy arm to grip Lucius' hand. "Praefectus. It is good to meet a fellow Roman so far from home. We must talk of your choice of tiles for your buildings at some point."

"Erm," Crescens pat Bucer on the shoulder. "Cassius owns one of the fabricae in Lindinis," he said, winking at Lucius.

"Ah. Well," Lucius began. "I'm certainly open to discussion about the quality of your products."

"They're the best! That's it. Plain and simple." Bucer turned to Adara. "Lady, it is good to meet you."

"And you, Cassius Bucer," Adara returned. "Luciana," she added.

The woman's white face smiled, the hair piled high upon her head with several pins swaying a little. She wore so much jewellery that she jingled when she smiled as they moved into the atrium.

"Here we have Nolan Phelan and his wife -" Crescens stopped abruptly as Phelan rushed forward to grab Lucius' hand.

"It's a pleasure to meet you, Praefectus. I keep hearing about you."

Lucius kept calm as the man gripped his hand. He had a disconcerting look with dark eyes, and black hair that was brushed backward. For a moment, Lucius thought he glimpsed sharp teeth, but dismissed the thought.

"Don't believe everything you hear," Lucius chuckled. "Lady," he said turning to the tall woman with long hair who accompanied Phelan.

"My wife...Dana," Phelan said, nodding toward her.

"Pleased...to...meet...you," the woman said slowly.

"She has not yet mastered Latin," Phelan said, shaking his head.

Lucius smiled at the tall woman. "Nor have I mastered the language of the North," Lucius said in broken Brythonic.

106

She smiled and stared at Lucius who nodded back, just before Phelan pulled her away.

"Impressive, Praefectus!" Carcer laughed from behind Crescens.

More couples passed by to greet Lucius and Adara - Felix Inek and his wife Lavinia, Finnian Maccus and his wife Maeve, Arlan Blair and his wife, Cara. Most were pleasant and it struck Lucius how many Britons there were members of the ordo of Lindinis. A good thing as far as local politics, though he still was not sure which way the wind tended to blow in the region. Imperial politics was one thing, but when it came to local matters in remote places, Lucius' experience had taught him that the squabbles could be quite petty with a potential for violence at the slightest altercation.

As he watched everyone interact with Crescens and Carcer on the way into the villa, he guessed that, more often than not, the wind blew in whichever direction Serenus Crescens wished it to blow.

Lastly, two couples came together to meet Lucius and Adara - Medr Kendall and his concubine, Aminta, and a Roman by the name of Renato Tulio and his lover, Julio Marinos who hung off of the older man's arm as if he could not bear to be parted from him.

It was obvious from their manner of dress that every one of the ordo members was wealthy, and Lucius found himself longing partially for the honest company of his Sarmatians. *They all seem friendly enough,* he told himself as Adara laced her arm through his.

Once the other guests had all gone in, Crescens turned to Lucius and Adara.

"They are good people, if not with oddities of their own," he said, allowing himself a very slight chuckle. "But Lindinis is the better for having them on the council."

Crescens' eyes suddenly went to the gates of the villa where a tall white horse came galloping into the muddy courtyard. He frowned, his face darkening as he walked along the path. "Excuse me," he said to Lucius and Adara who watched him stalk up to the end of the cobbles where they disappeared into the mud.

The man reined in and one of the slaves took his reins before he jumped down lightly onto the path directly in front of Crescens.

"I'm surprised you came, Trevor," Crescens said, obviously disappointed.

"I'm a member of the ordo too, am I not? You invited me too, yes?"

"Yes. Of course." Crescens turned without further comment and walked slowly back to Lucius and Adara.

"What do you suppose that is about?" Adara whispered to Lucius.

"I don't know," he answered. "But I think the evening just got more interesting."

The newcomer wore plain white riding breeches which had a few spots of mud from riding, a plain brown tunic fastened with a gold belt, and a deep green cloak which he removed and handed to another slave who followed the dominus and his new guest.

"Praefectus Metellus and Lady Metella, this is Trevor Reghan. He is the last member of the ordo of Lindinis to join us. We are all here," he muttered.

"I'm pleased to meet both of you," Trevor Reghan said, bowing to Adara and taking Lucius' forearm.

Lucius liked the man immediately. He looked him in the eye, was firm in his grip, and respectful of Adara who usually could tell if someone was untrustworthy and was, at that moment, at ease. He also noticed that the man wore a thin, twisted, golden torc about his neck.

"Are you a prince of your people, Trevor Reghan?" Lucius asked, nodding to the torc.

The man smiled. "Not a prince, no, Praefectus. But my family is of noble Durotrigan blood and ruled in the lands of Lindinis when it was a humble oppidum." He turned to Crescens, not appearing to have any qualms about the man all the others yielded to without hesitation. "That is why they still give me a place on the ordo, is it not, Serenus?"

"It's tradition, yes," Crescens acknowledged. "You did not bring Lynet with you?"

"No," Trevor Reghan answered. "She is tending to the children."

"That's what slaves are for, Trevor."

Before the man could answer, Sabina came storming into the courtyard.

"Husband! Your guests await you!" she barked, her sharp eyes rolling when she saw Trevor Reghan. "Bring another couch!" she yelled at two of the slaves.

"Sabina is happy to see you as always, Trevor," Crescens said as he began to walk into the house, almost forgetting Lucius and Adara. "Forgive me... Come." He extended his hand and Adara took it

108

slowly and let him lead them inside toward the double doors and the large, glowing triclinium.

"I hear you've done some wonderful things at the hillfort..." Trevor Reghan said to Lucius as they walked in.

Lucius and Adara's senses were assaulted on all fronts as they joined the gathering. The large, rectangular triclinium was lit by hanging bronze lamps in the shape of winged victories, and in each of the four corners there was a bronze brazier with lion-clawed feet crackling and casting warm light. The walls were painted with elaborate forest scenes where nymphs frolicked by clear pools of water, watched hungrily by satyrs in the shadows. On many tree boughs were exotic birds that harkened back to the halcyon days in the lands of the Vale of Tempe where Apollo would retreat from the world.

To the left of the double doors were two musicians - one playing the lyre, another a sistrum - their music drawing the diners to their couches.

On the far side of the triclinium, between four smooth, interspersed Ionic columns of pink granite, large, floor-to-ceiling wooden shutters had been thrown open to reveal an idyllic landscape bathed in orange dusk light.

"It's lovely," Adara said.

"Thank you, lady," Crescens said. "Please," he motioned to Lucius. "You and your wife must sit here." He led Lucius and Adara to the right, to a lush couch beside the host couch. "You must honour us by taking the lectus medius for our gathering."

"Thank you," Lucius said, inclining his head and reclining on the couch reserved for high status guests. It was comfortable, they had a view of nearly every person at the gathering and, more importantly, the best view of the countryside out of the large windows.

Crescens settled himself beside his wife on the lectus imus, the host couch at the end, and Trevor Reghan, all but forgotten, made his way to the lectus summus at the far end of the gathering, to recline between Medr's concubine, Aminta, and Tulio's lover, Julio.

Lucius glanced at Trevor Reghan and noted that the man did not seem disappointed or upset at the insult, chatting amiably with Aminta and nodding to Julio who tossed his oiled black locks nervously as the Briton stared at him.

Once the slaves had gone around the gathering to refill everyone's cups, Crescens spoke up.

"Friends! I bid you all welcome to our domus. Sabina and I are thrilled that you could come."

A couple of the ordo members eyed Trevor Reghan then, but Crescens carried on, his voice deep and sincere.

"And of course a special welcome to Praefectus Lucius Metellus Anguis and his wife, Adara Metella, who have graced us with their presence. It is not so often that we have such people at our humble feast, but, I take it as a sign that the Gods do favour us."

"As they favour Lindinis!" Carcer blurted where he sat with his wife to Lucius and Adara's left.

"Here, here!" said Cassius Bucer to Sabina's right.

Crescens tipped some of his wine onto the floor in front of his couch, and the guests followed suit, Lucius and Adara pouring in concert. "To the Gods!" Crescens said loudly and everyone echoed.

Then, Crescens clapped his hands loudly two times and the doors to the kitchen opened to allow an influx of slaves carrying platters of various delicacies for the first course. There were salads of wild greens and herbs tossed in gold-green olive oil, bowls of olives from Italia and Iberia, breads and cheeses.

The bread which Lucius took from the table in front of himself and Adara was still steaming when he put it on his silver plate, the smell of it enveloping them on their plush couch.

The gathering broke into various smaller conversations then, eyes rising from time to time to observe the others around the couches or to stare out at the twilit field beyond where the slaves had set braziers in the night in case guests wished to walk out of doors between courses.

Adara was engaged in polite conversation with Jana, Carcer's wife, who was next to her, interrupted occasionally by her husband who tried to hold conversations with every person at the gathering. Jana was a pale, short creature who appeared to look up to her husband in all things, never gainsaying him, never attracting any more attention than was needed.

"Do you have children?" Adara asked her politely, eager to speak of her own for she missed them terribly.

Jana appeared to sink deeper into her couch shaking her head. "No, no. We do not. I have not been able -"

Adara felt horrible and put out her hand to touch the woman's arm, but Jana pulled it away.

"Forgive me," Adara said, retreating back over the void to her own couch. "I did not mean to pry."

"She's barren!" said Carcer matter-of-factly from Jana's other side. "The Gods do not wish us to be parents, so I must tend to business while this one runs our villa best she can."

"I'm sure she's quite able at it," Adara tried.

Carcer said nothing, but grabbed a handful of lettuce and plopped it onto his plate.

Adara noticed his eyes stray to Renato's lover and looked to Jana again. *I don't think she is the problem.*

The first course took some time, and when the slaves came in to take away the empty platters, some of the diners got up to speak with others, relieve themselves, or to walk out into the fresh night beyond the tall windows.

"Will you walk out side with me for a few moments?" Adara said to Lucius.

He turned to her, smiling broadly and touched her cheek. "Of course," he said. He turned to Crescens. "We won't be long."

"Of course, Praefectus!" Crescens said amiably. "My home is yours. Please roam at will."

"Just some fresh air," Lucius said, sitting up and giving his hand to Adara. Together they went around the couches, behind their hosts' and then Cassius Bucer's couch, and then out into the cool night.

The rest of the guests had watched them leave, Carcer and Crescens exchanging looks.

"Have you tapped the subject with him yet, Serenus?" Felix Inek asked once Lucius and Adara were far out of earshot.

"Patience, Felix," Crescens said "All in good time. He has just arrived."

"What subject is that?" Trevor Reghan asked from the far end of the room.

"Nothing you need worry about, Reghan!" snapped Carcer haughtily. "All you need know is that it is for the good of Lindinis."

"Don't you mean for all of you?" Trevor Reghan said, smiling.

"Our interests and those of Lindinis have always been one and the same," Crescens said more calmly now he had grown used to Trevor Reghan's presence at his banquet.

Trevor Reghan said no more, but drank slowly of his wine.

"What do you think of the good men of Lindinis?" Lucius asked Adara as they walked farther out, his eyes scanning the distant braziers that flickered in the darkness at the edge of the field where the trees began to climb a gradual slope.

Adara glanced back at the villa, then turned to Lucius.

"They talk a lot about themselves, don't they?"

Lucius laughed. "When you are around rich and powerful men, they talk of little else. They do love their town though, I'll give them that. Seems to me the citizenry are fortunate to have such an ordo."

Adara looked up at her husband. "Don't be fooled by the vintage wine, warm reception and honeyed words, Lucius." She dropped her voice. "I remember being warmly welcomed at the imperial court in the beginning, but there came a time when I couldn't wait to escape. We don't want to be beholden to these men in anything."

"I won't be beholden to anyone," Lucius countered, nodding in agreement. "But it is good to know people locally. What if we wish to begin a farming operation at the hillfort to expand our income? We need to keep open to new things. Someday, I will retire from the legions. Then what? From what Caecilius and mother have written, there is less and less money to be made from the Etrurian crops."

"Just be cautious," Adara said. "That's all. I too am enjoying myself. It's been a long time since you and I dined together like this, upon a soft couch." She put her hands upon his chest and kissed him.

Part of Lucius wished to stay there with her, to kiss her in the starlight and forget about the idle ramblings of these new men.

"Shall we?" he asked Adara as their lips parted and he stroked her dark hair with his fingers.

"Yes. Let's. I'll try and get to know these women more. But I must say, starting a conversation with them is harder than cracking a walnut with two fingers."

They began to walk back and the scent of cooked meats wafted out into the night. As they came back into the triclinium, their eyes adjusted to the light and they lay back down upon their couch.

"Is it pleasant without?" asked Maeve, Finnian's wife who was seated directly across from Lucius and Adara.

"Very refreshing," Adara said. "When it is not raining, I find the evenings in Britannia invigorating."

"You know," Maeve's husband began. "Used to be that on evenings such as this, our ancestors ran naked through the woods, their bodies painted with woad as they coupled beneath the moon."

"I'll thank you to keep the talk of barbarism to yourself, Finian," Crescens said.

"Such a savage land at times," Sabina echoed.

"It is only what I have heard," Finian said, his smile gone.

There was an awkward silence and then Crescens clapped again.

The second course arrived, replete with dormice stuffed with herbed grains, roasted songbirds, river eel, and oysters. There were large hunks of beef with glistening sauces upon them, roasted chickens swimming in trays of garum, honey-soaked peacock meat and more.

Lucius slowed in his eating and sipped his wine. "You put on a grand feast, Serenus," he said.

"I wouldn't dare to be so wasteful as Petronius' Trimalchio, but I have to admit that when we get together, it is nothing but the best. Sabina won't have it any other way."

Lucius took a bite of the chicken and nodded. "The garum is from Leptis Magna?"

"Yes, Praefectus!" Crescens said. "Of course, you would know that, having spent some time there."

Lucius looked at him and nodded. "But a short period of time."

"Was that when the imperial family went a few years ago?" Arlan Blair asked.

"Lucius looked across the room at him. "Yes. The same visit." Lucius remembered the enormous banquet he had attended there, but put all other thoughts of that place from his mind.

"You have spoken with the imperial family?" asked Dana, Nolan Phelan's wife.

"Yes. We have both had occasion to speak with them in the past," Lucius said, his eyes looking around the room and then at his plate.

"Very exciting," said Sabina. "And no doubt an honour given to a privileged few?"

"Not so few as you would think," Lucius added, eager to change the subject.

It was then that Crescens began to speak with him in quieter tones.

"So, Praefectus... How do you find life here in the southwest of Britannia compared with the other places you've been in the empire? Do you believe the region has potential?"

"Britannia is certainly wetter than anywhere else I've been to. I feel as if the clouds never really go away some weeks, as if they are pressing down upon my shoulders."

"It can be quite oppressive," Sabina put in. "I had never seen weeks of low cloud before Serenus brought me here."

"I can understand that," Lucius said, "but then, on those days when the sun breaks through the darkness to light the green slopes of the landscape, I think I could never again see something so beautiful as this."

"I detect a poetic streak in the praefectus," Finian Maccus said from across the room.

"Not really," Lucius said. "Just an appreciation of such things after years of blood and battle. The sands of Africa Proconsularis were beautiful to me too once, but after so much bloodletting..." he paused, and Adara leaned into him, letting him know she was there. He smiled at her. "Well, I suppose places can lose their lustre after spending any length of time there."

"That is true," Crescens said, nodding in solemn understanding. "However, I have found that the lustre of a place can be maintained if you endeavour to improve it constantly."

"Quite right, Serenus!" Renato Tulio said from the far end of the gathering where Julio held a shell up to slip an oyster down his throat.

"I quite agree," Lucius said. "I've seen how the emperor has improved various cities across the empire, especially Leptis Magna. What was once a run-down city on the edge of Rome's domains has become a jewel."

"Thanks to the imperial favour, of course," Crescens said.

"Of course," Lucius conceded.

As they spoke, Adara noticed Virgilio Carcer fidgeting incessantly to her left, as if he was in constant need to speak or interject. Finally, he could take no more.

"Of course, Lindinis is full of potential!" He edged up on his elbow the better for all to see him. "If our town were favoured even a fraction the same as Leptis Magna, then our trading activities would give a solidity to the region to cement southern Britannia's importance across the empire."

114

"You are sure you do not overstate things?" Lucius asked.

"Certainly not!" Carcer bit back, his bald head reddening.

"The problem is," Arlan Blair said, "with trying to get taxes out of the locals."

Lucius set his cup down and listened to what the Briton had to say. "Is taxation a great problem here in the South? Surely with all the great villa estates hereabouts -"

"Praefectus..." Crescens began, "...we all pay our due share of the taxes to the imperial collectors. But be under no illusions that the villa estates in the South outnumber the vast native population, scattered in so many pockets far and wide."

"Many escape taxation altogether!" barked Medr Kendall, pushing away the probing hands of Aminta beside him. "They need to be pressured into paying their share. All is peace in the South, but they live fat off the land."

"It surely doesn't appear that way from what we have seen since moving here!"

All eyes turned to Adara who had just interjected herself into the conversation. Silence followed but for a few cleared throats.

Some of the people looked to Lucius, expecting him to rein in his wife, but he nodded.

"She's correct in that observation," he said, nodding at Adara and turning to Crescens and the others. "Ever since we've arrived, I've known the Britons to be only hard-working and honest-dealing folk."

"Something I have been telling this fine gathering for some time," Trevor Reghan said from his isolated couch at the far end.

"Who asked you, Trevor?" Nolan Phelan snarled.

"No one," the moustached Durotrigan said, still smiling. "But Lady Metella and the praefectus have made a good point. And from what I have heard across the countryside, the people admire them greatly. Perhaps we would get more taxes out of people if they were better-treated by this ordo?"

"You do dream, Trevor," Carcer said with a wave of his hand. "The imperial procurator demands too much of us."

"This is true gentlemen," Crescens said, his voice smooth and calming. "But we have a duty to the empire to make a contribution. After all, we do enjoy the Pax Romana here, do we not? Praefectus Metellus has been doing battle for Rome on the edges of the empire for years now, and I wager this place in which we live is as peaceful as he has ever seen. Am I correct?" He looked to Lucius.

"Quite. Yes," Lucius agreed, sipping once more at his wine. "It is a comfort to not be on the alert at all times. And among new friends." He nodded to the others, some raising their cups.

"But the fact remains that we can do more," Carcer continued. There were murmurs of agreement around the couches. "If we had greater support and status, we could increase trade at Lindinis, and as a result, increase taxes and revenues."

"There would remain pockets of resistance that have long escaped paying their dues for the peace they enjoy," Felix Inek said.

More murmurs, more nods of heads at this.

"What pockets?" Lucius asked

Crescens cleared his throat, though his friendly demeanour had fizzled suddenly. "Well, one in particular. Ynis Wytrin."

"Ynis Wytrin?" Lucius and Adara said in concert, for they knew the name well from Einion and Briana.

"I hear it is a place of peace and sanctuary where all gods are honoured and revered," Lucius continued.

"It is!" Trevor Reghan said, his smile also having gone as he eyed his colleagues.

"Some might say that," Crescens added smoothly. "Britons only, really. But the so-called 'Isle of the Blessed' has escaped Rome since before the conquest so many years ago. It was never brought into the fold of mother Rome, and so has done as it chooses for too long. They are wealthy and should pay for the Pax Romana as much as anyone else."

"But surely a place where the Gods are so honoured contributes to the Pax Romana in other ways?" Adara said, unable to help herself.

"You sound as if you have gone native already, Lady Metella," Sabina said from her couch, looking down her nose at Adara.

Adara was not to be cowed by their hostess. "I see much good in the way the Britons lead their lives, true. But I am also Greek and Roman and know that many of the sacred sanctuaries to the Gods across the empire are exempt from taxation."

"The gods of Ynis Wytrin are not our gods!" Cassius Bucer said loudly, dabbing his face with his napkin.

"I'll thank you not to yell at my wife," Lucius said evenly. "Where I come from, and in the imperial circles, women are welcome to discourse as much as any man, so long as they make a well-thought-out argument. And my wife does indeed make a good point." Lucius eyed everyone, suddenly wanting to leave the gathering, but he stood his ground. *Who do these people think they are?*

"Of course, my colleague spoke out of turn," Crescens said to Adara. "Forgive him." He ignored the shocked look on Bucer's face. "The fact of the matter is that we have touched on a topic that has long divided our community. We would welcome Ynis Wytrin into the success of Lindinis were it to be more open to the outside world, but they refuse us constantly."

"They prefer to stay hidden in the foul-smelling marshes behind a wall of putrid mist," Carcer said with finality. He then stood and went to the latrine down the hall, followed by his slave who waited in the corridor.

"Metella," Sabina continued, staring at Adara after Carcer disappeared. "You are a woman of an ancient family, on your father's side at least. How can you defend the barbaric ways of the Britons so? Next thing, we'll see you wearing woollen breeches and fighting with a sword!" she chuckled and some of the others laughed.

Adara smiled, though Lucius felt her stiffen beside him.

"Actually, my training has been going exceedingly well, Lady Cresca," Adara said proudly. "I've been trained by a Briton who is a great warrior herself."

"A woman?" Cassius Bucer said, stunned.

"Of course. She has bested many men in her time, and I trust her implicitly."

Bucer looked at Lucius. "And you condone this...this training, Praefectus?"

"It is not for me to condone or not," Lucius said. "Besides, when I am away at war, it behooves my wife to be able to defend our children."

"That is what slaves are for," Arlan Blair added.

"Would a slave risk his life to defend his master's children at the risk of his own life?" Lucius said, shaking his head. "No. If anyone should think to attack our home, they would find those living there more than a match." Lucius looked sideways at Adara, and in her eyes she saw a pride that made him sit taller. For a moment, it seemed to the rest of the gathering that the newcomers had all but forgotten the rest of them.

117

"How rude!" Sabina muttered to her husband.

"Shh," Crescens said to her, annoyed. "More music!" he said loudly, and the slaves on the lyre and sistrum burst into a jolly tune as more steaming meats were added to the emptying platters, and wine cups were refilled, this time with a little less water.

Crescens reached out and touched Lucius' sleeve.

"Praefectus," he said, his voice low as he leaned closer. "Forgive our crass talk of business and taxation. This was not the place. Such discussions are better left for within the walls of the curia in Lindinis."

Lucius smiled, pleased that his host appeared embarrassed by the turn of events.

"I understand," Lucius said. "When soldiers get together to celebrate even the happiest of occasions, they inevitably talk of blood, fighting and battle. This appears to be the same."

"I'm glad you understand," Crescens appeared to relax.

"But some," Lucius said in a lower voice, "should be more mindful how they insult another man's wife."

Crescens stared back at Lucius, his face unreadable as he tried to figure out if Lucius spoke of Cassius Bucer, or of Sabina beside him. He nodded. "Quite."

After more food and eating, some of the attendees rose to speak with others they had not yet had occasion to converse with. They stood in small groups about the triclinium or in the hall outside.

Finnian's wife, Maeve, came around to speak with Adara about her stola and proved to be quite curious about Athenae, in faraway Greece.

"Is it as beautiful as they say?" Maeve asked. "And as hot?"

"Yes," Adara said, smiling. "And yes!" They laughed together, the younger Briton stroking her sleek, long red hair.

"It sounds like your family has adapted well to life in our part of Britannia, Praefectus," said Trevor Reghan as he walked around to speak with Lucius ahead of Crescens and Carcer.

Lucius turned and nodded.

"It is our home away from home now," he said.

"I'm glad to hear it," Trevor said solemnly. "This is an ancient land, not always appreciated by those who dwell within in." He glanced at Crescens and Carcer who stared angrily at him. "And you are correct about Ynis Wytrin. It is a sacred place, a sanctuary for both gods and men."

"Have you ever been there?" Lucius asked, suspecting that he had for all the reverence in his voice.

"Of course not. Few are ever given such a gift. Thankfully, the Gods have hidden it from the outside world."

"It sounds as elusive as Elysium," Lucius said.

"It is the same. It is the gateway to Annwn," Trevor Reghan said, his hand touching his heart instinctively.

"The Otherworld?" Lucius asked.

"Yes."

Lucius felt a chill creep up his spine at that, and a flash of a black-robed figure crept out of the shadows from the recesses of his mind. A face, as pale and grey as melted wax, with strands of greasy black hair looked up at him.

Metellusssss...

"Praefectus!" a voice called.

Lucius shook his head and he was leaning against the frescoed wall beside the brazier.

Trevor Reghan was gripping his arm tightly.

"Praefectus? Are you unwell?"

Lucius shook his head and felt the sweat beading on his forehead. He saw Adara rushing over to him.

"Lucius, my love. What is it?" she asked, helping Trevor to get Lucius to his feet.

"I don't know. I just saw... Just dizzy is all. I think I need some fresh air," he said.

"It is rather warm in here," Crescens said, coming over to the three of them. "Come, Praefectus. Let us take a walk outside. I could use some fresh air myself."

Lucius stood on his own. He felt his balance return, but the image still menaced his thoughts. *The Morrigan...*

"I'll join you," Carcer said, following Lucius and Crescens out of the tall doors into the field beyond. As he went, he shot Trevor Reghan a sharp look.

"Your husband should be wary of those two," Trevor whispered to Adara before going back to his couch to speak with Aminta who reclined upon her own, twirling a long curl which dangled down the front of her chest.

Adara returned to speak with Maeve who had been joined by Felix's wife, Lavinia. However, her eyes continued to seek Lucius out in the dark field beyond the glow of the triclinium.

119

Outside, the stars had burst from behind the clouds, and silver moonlight poured across the dark fields to lap the distant tree line like waves upon a beach.

Lucius took deep breaths of cool air and felt fine once more. He wanted to be alone for a moment, to seek Apollo's counsel, but the two men of the executive curia, Crescens and Carcer, would not leave his side. He dried his forehead with the hem of his toga as they walked.

"How are you feeling?" Crescens asked, drawing even with Lucius as Carcer strolled along behind them.

"Fine now," Lucius said. He scanned the field and spotted a brazier directly ahead. He focussed on its light and walked toward it.

"Good." Crescens was silent for a few moments before speaking again. "I do so love it here. The quiet, pastoral setting is so much more conducive to a good life than the stinking streets of Londinium."

"Cities have their uses," Lucius said. "But I have to agree with you that it is beautiful here. I can see why you love it so." Lucius could hear the words coming out of his mouth, unable to stop the idle chatter. He did not feel like opening up to this man as yet, or any of them for that matter. The conversation had been odd and at times, aggressive.

"You must forgive us our intensity," Crescens said, as if reading his thoughts. "We have talked of these things ad nauseam, and with little result or agreement among the entire ordo."

"From one member in particular," muttered Carcer from Lucius' other side.

"Let it be, Virgilio. The praefectus has no wish to hear our petty squabbles." Crescens stepped in front of Lucius and they stopped. "But you may be interested in knowing more about our plans for Lindinis. You see, we want to improve it beyond reckoning, to make it a place where any man - be he Roman, Briton or from the farthest corners of the empire - can make an honest living if he is willing to work and be a part of a great city."

"But Aquae Sulis is not far from here, correct?" said Lucius.

"That is true, but it is not the place it once was," Carcer added, shaking his head. "A Londinium in the making."

"And what of the tribal capitals of Isca, Durnovaria, and Corinium?" Lucius asked of the large civitates of the area. "Surely

Lindinis benefits from its close ties with those cities and its location at the crossroads between them all."

"The ordo members of those civitates do not deal fairly with us," Crescens said, his voice falling a little, his head just a bit lower. "We wish to do so much here at Lindinis, to make it a great centre of trade, surrounded as it is by the villas and fabricae where retired men of the legions are able to make a living after their service to Rome. We owe it to them for the peace we all enjoy."

"There are imperial settlement programs for veterans," Lucius said.

"True," Crescens said. "But I have spoken with too many families who have been forced to move farther afield in order to claim the lands granted. For instance, why would a legionary married to a Briton want to take his family to Cyrenaica when all they know and love is here on this green land?"

Lucius nodded. He had been forced to move his family around the empire, but much of it had been by choice. It was never easy. "I see your point." He shook his head. "I'm sorry I do not have much experience in this sort of thing. My duty is to fight Rome's enemies and ensure the safety of her borders. Settlement of troops is a matter for the politicians."

"I know. But as you have decided to make this region your home, I thought you ought to know what is going on," Crescens added. "If we could raise the status of Lindinis, to say, that of a civitas, then we would have more privileges and be able to do so much more for our community. We could make a case for attracting more veteran settlement, giving them an important role to play in commerce in Britannia. We would also be able to increase the tax base to please the imperial procurator."

"I suppose that would do it," Lucius said. "But with the three other civitates so close by, I don't imagine it will happen. Better for you to nurture and improve your ties with those cities, I think."

"I'm afraid you don't understand," Carcer said, frustrated. He came to stand a little too close to Lucius who stood straight and looked at the man.

"The praefectus has only just arrived, Virgilio," Crescens said, his hand squeezing Carcer's shoulder hard in the darkness.

"I'm sure there is much I don't understand about the politics of this area, about who should be taxed and who should not," Lucius said. "What I do understand is that Lindinis, no matter how wonderful a place, is a grain of sand on the larger surface of the empire. You have done well here, but there is a way in which things are done. The emperor is pleased with the way the empire is run now, and he fought many years to make it so."

"That is just it," Crescens said, his voice a little more excited. "Now that the emperor has come to Britannia, he has seen the land, the problems in the North."

"But he does not necessarily know of the great success in the South," Carcer added.

"I would not assume that. If I know the emperor and empress, they make it their business to know all that is going on, how it works, how it does not. If no changes have been made in the administration of the South, then I'm sure that is for a reason."

Lucius became distracted suddenly by something in the darkness beyond the burning brazier at the edge of the field where the forest began. His eyes probed the darkness as Crescens spoke again.

"You have struck upon something, Praefectus! The troops respect you... I have heard them speak of you time and time again -"

"And with such awe!" Carcer cut in.

"And you are closer than most to the imperial family. From what I have been told, they respect you and have shown you favour over the years."

Lucius' eyes turned on Crescens. "How much information have you dug up, may I ask?"

"You mistake me, Praefectus. When we heard you were coming to live in the area, we wanted to find out more about the man we had heard spoken of so frequently."

"Do get on with it, Serenus!" Carcer said hastily. "You see, Praefectus, as you are now a part of our community, a person who pays his taxes etcetera, we were wondering if you would speak to the emperor about granting Lindinis the status of civitas."

Crescens' face hardened in frustration at his colleague, but he bit his tongue, his eyes watching Lucius' reaction. "It would," he confirmed, "allow us to do so much more for everyone in this land."

Lucius' arms shot out quickly to grab both men's shoulders and throw them backward where they fell to the ground.

"Stay down!" Lucius yelled, then, "Ah!"

There was a flash and a humming just before the gleaming blade shot out of the dark and slashed across Lucius' arm as he spun.

"Attack!" Lucius yelled.

Confused cries echoed from the villa and several forms came running out onto the field as Lucius pulled his pugio from beneath his toga and sprang toward the darkness.

"Praefectus!" Crescens yelled.

"What's wrong with him?" Carcer screeched.

"Lucius!" Adara's voice called out as she ran toward the tangled ordo members, her eyes on her husband's running form.

Lucius could feel the blood pumping in his ears as he ran across the grass, his pugio gripped in his fingers, his senses focussed on the darkness beyond the brazier, like an animal on the hunt.

He stopped, trying to ignore the noise at the villa behind him, the calling of his name.

Whoever was out there had retreated back into the darkness. They had been close enough to throw a blade.

Then the shadows seemed to split and a man carrying a longsword sprang at Lucius from the undergrowth.

He came fast, and Lucius ducked under the killing swing and drove his short blade up and into the assailant's stomach, lifting him off the ground and driving toward the brazier again. He heard another blade singing through the air and felt it thud into the body of the man he carried like a shield before letting the wailing man drop.

Lucius kept moving, ripping the assassin's dagger from the body and throwing it into the darkness ahead.

There was a muffled grunt and then a rush of footsteps through the fern undergrowth of the forest.

Stop! he heard a voice urge within.

"Lucius!" Adara came running up, Crescens and a large group of his slaves armed with daggers and cudgels in her wake.

"Metella, come back!" Crescens was saying.

Lucius turned to see his wife, his hand up to stop her. He expected to see fear rampant in her eyes, but instead, he saw her look quickly to his wound, the body on the ground, and then to the darkness beyond assessing the danger.

She's learned a lot.

He could not help but smile for a moment before the relief washed over her features and she grabbed his arm.

"Are you all right?" she asked, a little breathless.

"It's not bad," he assured her.

"Praefectus?" Crescens said "What happened?" Even he had lost his cool composure at the experience.

"There were two of them," Lucius said. "This one threw the dagger. Another got away, though I think I injured him."

"Grawl!" Crescens barked for one of his slaves, a thick man carrying a spiked cudgel. "Get torches and search the woods with the others." He turned to another, tall man with a short sword. "Secundus, get all the guards up and surround the villa. I don't want my guests in further danger."

"Yes, Dominus," the man said before running back to the villa.

The torches carried by Grawl and the others fanned out into the woods like angry fireflies in the dark, and Lucius bent over the man he had killed, his hands glistening with blood in the firelight that was brought forward.

He flipped the body over to reveal a man with a long moustache and long, braided brown hair.

"A Briton," Crescens muttered, spitting at the ground.

"What happened?" Trevor Reghan came running up, the first of the ordo members to rush from the triclinium. He stopped before the body and looked at Lucius and Adara. "Are you injured?"

"No," Lucius said.

"Look at this!" Crescens turned on Trevor. "A Briton! Sent here to kill me!"

"You don't know that," Trevor countered.

"Oh no? If it weren't for the praefectus's quick instincts, it might be me with my guts slithering onto the grass and not him!" He kicked the body, and behind them Carcer vomited onto the grass.

"This is appalling," Carcer said as he went back to the villa with one of the slaves who had just arrived to care for him. "Get me my change of clothes!"

Lucius watched him go and then turned to Trevor and Crescens. "Do either of you recognize this man?"

They looked at him and shook their heads.

"No. I don't know the man. He might be Dobunni," Trevor guessed.

"Are you sure you don't know him?" Crescens growled, getting into Trevor's face.

"Careful, Serenus. I may not agree with you often, or even like you very much, but you should mind the accusations you throw around. If I have a problem with you, I tell you to your face." He turned to Lucius and Adara. "I can't guess why this man was sent here, but we should all get back inside."

"I agree," Lucius said. "Serenus, are you hurt?" he asked his host.

Serenus' face softened. "No. Thanks to your quick thinking. But I agree with Trevor for once. Let us get back inside."

The four of them walked back toward the light of the triclinium windows. When they walked into the room from the darkness without, everyone gasped, their eyes on Lucius.

He looked down and saw the blood sprayed all over his thin-striped toga, his own pugio still gripped in his hand.

"What has happened?" Renato squeaked as Julio went pale beside him.

"Assassins sent to kill Crescens and myself!" Carcer said, wading back into the room with a fresh toga on."

Lucius turned to Crescens. "If I may excuse myself, Serenus. I would wash the blood from my body and change."

"By all means, Praefectus," Crescens said, gripping Lucius' shoulder. "The hypocausts have been kept running. No one will disturb you."

Lucius began to leave and Adara followed.

"Lady Metella," Sabina said, rushing forward. "Stay with us. I will have the slaves attend your husband."

Adara turned to her. "No. Thank you. I will tend to my husband's wound for him."

The women in the room stifled gasps, but Adara took no notice of them as she and Lucius went out.

"I'll tell you who it was!" Nolan Phelan could be heard saying. "Ynis Wytrin sent them to kill you, Crescens!"

There was yelling then as Trevor Reghan disagreed and the others raged at him.

As Lucius and Adara followed the slave toward the bathhouse, they did not notice the bickering, focussed only on the leaching rush of energy and the explosion of nerves that now came to the fore.

Shortly after, Lucius and Adara were both alone, immersed in the warm water of the tepidarium.

Lucius was silent as Adara sponged the gash on his upper left arm before wrapping it tightly with a long piece of clean linen the slaves had given them.

The voices of the guards outside crept in through the high windows of the bathhouse, but they took no notice.

Through the faint mist, Lucius stared at the now clean blade of his pugio where it lay on the mosaic floor beside the pool's edge.

Adara looked at him when she finished binding the wound.

"You seem rather calm for someone who has just nearly been killed." Her voice was angry, and Lucius turned to her now, his hand reaching up to brush a long strand of her hair away from her face to lay across her naked shoulder.

"It's not the first time, is it?" he said. "That was the first time all evening I've felt myself again."

"I hope you are joking with me," she said evenly. "I worry when you say things like that."

He focussed on the bright greens of her eyes. "Yes. I am joking," he said, though he knew part of it was truth.

"Why do you think someone would want to kill Crescens and Carcer?" she whispered.

"I don't know. They're selfish politicians, no doubt. But to send someone to assassinate them in the middle of a convivium?" Lucius shook his head. "That doesn't make sense."

"From what Briana and Einion have said about Ynis Wytrin, it doesn't make sense that they would send assassins either."

"No. That's absurd," Lucius agreed.

"Maybe they were just bandits?" Adara wondered. "Men watching the villa, hoping to rob the guests they might have seen streaming in earlier in the day?"

"I don't know. Possible, I guess."

Lucius looked at his wife and lifted her onto his lap, the water lapping about her waist, her breasts hardening in the colder air.

"What are you doing?" she said, her eyes on him, the bloody bandage, the stubble of his face as she ran her hand along his cheek.

"You shouldn't have rushed out like that," he said. "You could have been killed."

Her hand fell. "You think I would just sit by while you are fighting for your life?"

"I'm not that easy to kill."

"Nor am I." She laid her hands upon his jaw and peered into his dark eyes. "I will stand by you through anything...no matter what. Don't you know that after all these years?"

He did, but all he could do was pull her closer, and press his mouth to hers as her arms gripped him tightly.

She guided him inside her and they gave way to the passion that overcame them in that moment, the gratitude that they were together, that they were still safe.

As the firelight danced on the painted walls of the bathhouse, they climaxed together, gripping each other fiercely as if they would never let go, unlike the submerged images of Dido and Aeneas in the frigidarium two rooms over.

Lucius and Adara both knew that they would never willingly part from one another.

A while later, Lucius and Adara returned to the triclinium. The large windows were barred shut now, and the tables had been set with jugs of sweet, golden wine and a vast array of honey cakes and pastries, fruits and cheeses.

Crescens rose from his couch as they entered, coming around to see them.

"How is your wound, Praefectus?"

"Nothing to worry about," Lucius nodded.

Lucius now wore a blue tunic and black breeches, and Adara the extra, green stola she had brought along.

"I'm glad to hear it," Crescens said. "And Lady Metella, rarely have I seen a woman rush into danger as you did."

Adara said nothing, noting the disapproving looks on some of the faces around the table. She merely held her head high, smiled, and hooked her arm through Lucius'.

"Please, sit and have some wine to take the edge off the evening's excitement," Crescens added. "Music!" he said, and the musicians began to play once more.

The conversation was not as animated as it had previously been.

Lucius suspected that Crescens had ordered the rest of them to avoid discussing what had happened, or any other unpleasant topics such as taxation, and he was grateful for it.

Instead, they spoke of the various places they had been throughout the empire.

It came as no surprise to Lucius that most of them had rarely left the shores of Britannia, and those who had, such as Sabina, longed only to return whence they had come.

At one point, after a few of the guests had drifted away to their various cubicula, the conversation turned to blaming Britons all over for the ills that beset the land, including the attack earlier that night.

"I've seen unimaginable violence across the empire," Lucius said after a long silence while listening to their talk. "And some of the most peaceful places I have been to are places where different peoples are gathered and living together."

"You make no sense to me, Praefectus!" Nolan Phelan sneered.

"Really?" Lucius answered. "One thing I've found, especially in places like Alexandria or Rome, is that different peoples can indeed live in harmony if they are happy with their lot, their society." He looked at Crescens then. "Violence does not usually start with the average person trying to get by. It starts with those who rule and chose to do nothing."

Crescens stared back at Lucius, clearly angered by the implication, but the stare was broken by Carcer.

"Sounds like a ridiculous Greek notion."

Crescens ignored Carcer. "That is why we want to better things, Praefectus. For everyone."

The guests around the couches nodded and muttered agreement.

Lucius and Adara were not convinced.

IV

SOMNIA FEBRICATA

'Fevered Dreams'

There were smiles in the shadows, the looks of gods and shades alike. Few see the signs of these presences, ever notice or heed them. They put them down to the restless imaginations and worries of mortal men and women.

But the Gods do dwell among mortals, and the dead do tread the pathways of the living with the dying of the year. The darkness can hold many things - peace and quiet, danger and menace among them.

In his cubiculum on the ground floor of the hall, Einion turned over in his sleep, like a pebble rolled back and forth with the tide. He did not wake, but his body shuddered and sweat.

And he wept...oh he wept. And the menacing form in the shadows rejoiced at his tears, the pain that was churned up like the silt at the bottom of tidal pool to cloud what was once clear, to confuse. It was all to a purpose that the man, in his weary sleep, was completely ignorant of.

Einion stood upon the distant, rainy, windswept rock of his childhood home. He had not seen it in years. It appeared the same, except there was no joy in the land, only a bleakness, a realm of deserted joys and memory.

He stared across a great void where the sea lashed the jagged fangs of rocky outcrops. A rope bridge extended over the darkness, swaying and flapping in the gale, but he knew he had to cross, even should it mean his death or immeasurable pain. One foot in front of the other, he crossed, his longsword in his right hand, his left gripping the rope of the bridge.

He clung with a white fist to that rope, the bridge writhing like a giant serpent, willing him to fall, to fly into the abyss.

Einion held fast and moved forward, every step a battle, until finally, he reached the other side.

There was no one about, save for the wind and rain and shadows.

The myriad sea birds - cormorants, puffins and others - were nowhere to be seen or heard as he walked along the wide road to the top of the fortress and the double doors of the squat great hall.

My son! Einion heard a voice call from within.

"Father!" he yelled, excited, hoping that perhaps the past had been a bad dream.

He pounded on the doors with the pommel of his sword and a great booming echoed within, the stone paving slabs cracking beneath his feet with each strike of the oak doors.

Finally, Einion burst into the hall at the south end. He stopped, unable to walk further, for at the far end of the hall, upon a dais, was his father's throne, made of stone from the land, wide and solid. It was surrounded and thrashed by waves of crimson blood which washed over it and ran in thick rivulets like veins on a thing alive.

Laid across the hard surface of the arm rests was his longsword.

Einion looked down at his hand and noticed he did not have it anymore.

He walked slowly toward the throne, blood lapping about his calves, rising to his knees. He sensed movement in the shadows, but saw none. He was about to step up to take the sword and sit, but then he appeared - his father.

Einion's father gazed down on him with a depth of disappointment the son could not recall, even when the lord of the hall was at his worst.

His father shook his head. "You have let our hall waste away, and our family line die out."

"No, Father. I have not. I've come back," Einion pleaded, feeling like a young boy despite his years.

His father made to speak, but then a shadow, a form taller than any man, wrapped its arm about his father's chest and slid a black blade across his neck.

"NO!" Einion yelled, even as he was thrown from his feet to land on the grisly floor of the hall.

He tried to rise above the crimson tide that swelled about the throne, but he could not surface, except with a mighty effort that afforded him one glance of the vacant throne where it sat accusing, and awash with his father's blood.

"AHH!!!"

Einion's voice echoed throughout the hall atop the hillfort.

Moments later, Briana came rushing into his room from the upper floor where she had spent the night beside Calliope who had been missing her parents and plagued by dreams about them.

"Einion!" Briana called, rushing to his side and sitting beside him. "Brother!" She ran her hand across his soaking brow, brushing his long hair away from his wild, confused eyes.

Einion's gaze darted about the room, every muscle in his body taught as a bowstring, but once he focussed on his sister and her calming voice, he collapsed in exhaustion.

"Einion!" Briana said more loudly, shaking him.

"Briana, what's wrong?" Phoebus said from the doorway, where he held his wooden rudus. "What's happened?" The boy's other arm was about his sister's shoulders.

"Phoebus, go and get some cold water!" Briana said.

The children ran from the doorway to the kitchen and returned moments later with a brimming clay cup which Phoebus handed to Briana.

She put it to her brother's lips and he drank unconsciously. Then, Einion's eyes fluttered open and he looked up at her.

"The Gods have sent me a terrible dream," he said, his eyes wet with tears.

Briana turned to the children. "Go and dress yourselves. Then start a fire in the hearth, and wait for Ula and Aina to arrive. Can you do that for me?"

"Yes, Briana. We can," Phoebus said, running off.

"Calliope?" Briana looked at the little girl who still stood there, unmoving, staring at Einion. She came forward, her eyes fixed on the Briton.

Briana let her approach, though she did consider insisting she leave.

Calliope extended her hand over Einion's chest and his rapidly beating heart, closed her eyes, and lowered her little palm slowly to hold it there and press down for several seconds.

Slowly, Einion's panicked breathing became normal again, his eyes focussed on the little girl. He felt joy and gratitude, so much so that tears began to form once more on his lids, burning his eyes.

Briana too wept at the sight, at the melodic humming that began low, and then rose out of Calliope's throat to comfort them as a mother comforts a frightened child.

131

When Calliope stopped humming, she opened her eyes and smiled. "There. I hope that helped," she said to Einion, taking no notice of the tears.

"Yes, little one. It did," he said.

"Good. I'll go help Phoebus now," she said, and then skipped out of the room to go to the upper floor and change.

Einion and Briana stared at one another.

"Tell me what you saw," she said, "and I'll tell you about my dream."

"Do not speak of this in front of the children," Briana told Einion when he finished and was dressed. "It would terrify them. They have had their own dreams to worry about."

"Did Calliope calm down after a while?" Einion asked.

Briana nodded. "Yes. But at the time, she was weeping much - she saw Lucius and Adara dead upon the road."

They watched Phoebus and Calliope sitting around the hearth fire with the twins, Ula and Aina, who had just arrived to get breakfast started and set about their daily work.

As she ate her porridge, Calliope sat against Aina as if she were cold.

Aina held the little girl close, protective as if she were her big sister. Her eyes found Briana's and the girl nodded to indicate that Calliope was fine.

Briana knew that once she was sitting quietly about the fire, her thoughts might return to her dreams. It was good to have others there to watch out for the children. Einion needed her at that moment. She turned to him, her hands upon his shoulders.

"We will make sense of this."

"What sense is there to make of it? For too long have I let our cursed uncle live when I should have brought vengeance to his door."

"It is not yet the time," Briana insisted "You cannot do it alone."

Einion crossed his arms as he leaned on the doorway of his cubiculum. "So many dreams - me, the children, and now you. There are too many ghosts in this place. The shades of so many Britons slaughtered by Rome."

"Rome has become our friend, Einion."

"No. Lucius and his family are our friends. To me, they are not Rome." He shook his head. "Forgive me. It's just that dream... I can't get it out of my mind." He stood straight. "You going to tell me what yours was about?"

"It wasn't really a dream so much as...well... Etain spoke to me last night." Briana smiled, but it soon faded.

"What's wrong? You should be happy. It has been so long since you two have made the connection."

"I know. I was glad of her voice," Briana said. "But she sounded different. A little weak."

Einion said nothing. Etain was like a mother to them.

"She said that we should soon expect a visitor."

"Where?"

"Here."

"She didn't say who?" Einion asked.

"No."

They were silent.

"Well, we can't stand around waiting for whoever it is. We have work to do. Lucius asked me to continue training the children with their rudii while he was away."

"They should be back tonight," Briana said.

Einion stopped. "And if they aren't?"

"Then we look for them," Briana said, her thoughts caught up in the web of Calliope's own dream.

Once they had all eaten, Einion, Briana and the children went to the stables to care for the horses and exercise them around the perimeter of the hillfort.

The children returned to their joyous selves as they rode around in morning sunlight, their ponies' hooves glistening with dew. Laughter filled the air, and the local villagers who came to make their offerings at the shrine on the hillfort smiled as they passed them.

Though all was safe, Briana and Einion never left them alone.

There was a tension in the air, as if something were about to burst.

When the ponies were exercised, brushed, watered and fed, the children ate and then began their training with Einion and Briana.

The Britons did not hold back, knowing that to do so would only give the Dragon's children a false sense of security. More than once, Phoebus went crashing down from the flat of Einion's blade, to be dressed anew in mud, and Calliope constantly held back in her swings, not wanting to hit Briana.

Briana pushed the young girl harder, encouraging her along the way, careful not to crush her peaceful nature, but to reinforce it, to lend it a sense of peace in the knowledge that she would be able to defend herself should the need arise.

"All right, children!" Einion said out loud after a couple of hours training. "You've done very well today."

Calliope threw her little rudus down on the ground and crossed her arms.

Briana bent to pick it up and gave it back to her. "It is important, love. Remember how hard your mother trains?"

Calliope nodded beside her sweating brother who was gulping water from a small clay jug.

"She trains to be able to protect you." She knelt before the child and put her hand on the side of her cheek.

Calliope was crying. "I want Mama and Baba to come home."

"They'll be back today," Briana said.

"What if they aren't?"

"They will be. They only went to a banquet. That is all. They shall be back soon. You'll see."

Calliope wiped her eyes and hugged Briana.

The Briton's heart tightened as the child's arms fastened around her neck. "They're already on the road," she said.

"Good morning!" Culhwch called as he walked up the road from the southwest gate of the hillfort with his son, Paulus.

Einion waved and Briana stood up, holding Calliope's hand.

"Good morning!" Phoebus called as he waved at the two of them. "Paulus! I've been training!"

The other boy came running up the slope to see him.

"How's it going then?" Paulus said, smiling broadly as he looked over the dented blade of the rudus.

"Well, I think." Phoebus looked to Einion for confirmation.

"Very well!" Einion said, smiling and taking Culhwch's hand as he came up.

"All is well?" Culhwch asked.

"Yes. Lucius and Adara should return today. How are things in the village. Alma is doing well?"

"Well enough. But we had a surprise last night. Alma's cousin, Sigwyll Sloane, returned after many years in the Roman cavalry auxiliaries along the Rhine frontier."

"I didn't know she had a cousin in the army," Einion said.

"She doesn't talk much of him. They were very close, but when he enlisted, she was not happy. He was a good lad, but she worried about him getting killed."

"Well, obviously he didn't," Einion said.

"No. But he has been discharged early due to an injury," Culhwch said. "A Germanic spear through his knee. He can't ride anymore, and walks with an awful limp."

"Still, he could be dead." Einion added, blunt as ever.

"Yes. He would wish it so too. He carries a weight about with him and has come home to find his father and mother dead for some years now. Alma had written to him when they passed, but it seems he never got the letters."

"Difficult."

"Yes. We've invited him to stay while we repair his home, but it's like having a storm cloud beneath our roof. He's always black of mood and everything reminds him of what he's lost." Culhwch stared at Einion for a moment. "Maybe you could talk to him?"

"What? Tell him of all that *I* have lost?" Einion shook his head, his long hair catching in the wind. "I'll tell that to him once I've regained it all."

Culhwch shrugged. "Anyway, I needed to get out with Paulus. Is it all right if we spend some time up here with you?"

"Absolutely. I'm ready for a drink myself!" Einion pat him on the back and began leading him up to the hall with Briana and Calliope as the two boys ran off to the stables.

"Oh, I almost forgot. Seems you have a visitor. I saw him coming as we approached." Culhwch turned, shielding his eyes as he looked toward the southwest gate. "There he is."

Einion and Briana looked to where he was pointing and saw the grey-cloaked figure turn up the road with another, hunched companion, both of them riding short moorland ponies. They looked at each other in surprise.

It was Weylyn.

Einion and Briana stood together with Calliope between them. They watched the old Druid approach with his servant. They had not seen him since before they had left for Caledonia to find Lucius, the one they called the 'Dragon'. It was Weylyn's dream that had sent them on that quest.

Weylyn waved and Einion pointed in the direction of the stables at the entrance to the plateau. The horses veered and the group moved to meet them at the stables.

"Who is that man?" Calliope asked Briana as they walked. Her eyes shone with curiosity, her little hand pulling Briana down the slope to the stable.

"That is Weylyn," Briana said. "He is a very wise and kind man. He knows your baba."

Culhwch tapped Einion as they walked. "He knows Lucius? He looks like a Druid to me," he said, half-joking.

"He is," Einion said. "We knew him in Ynis Wytrin."

Culhwch stopped in his tracks, and put his hand to his heart. *The Isle of the Blessed?* The Durotrigan, like many others, believed the Romans had slain all of the ancient holders of Britannia's knowledge. To him, the Druids had been relegated to the annals of the history of which they themselves had been keepers. And now, here was one standing before him, riding a spotted moorland pony, with a hunchback. He hurried to join the others, including his son who was just coming out of the stables with Phoebus as Weylyn and Morvran dismounted.

"Ahh!" Phoebus yelled as Morvran stood before him and smiled through his misshapen face.

"It's all right, Phoebus!" Briana called out. "They are friends."

The boy relaxed a little but kept his distance.

Weylyn stayed atop his pony and waited for Morvran to come around and help him down.

He looks older, Briana thought as he turned his wrinkled visage toward her and smiled. *But he is still Weylyn...*

"Briana..." Weylyn said, as he straightened his long white beard and adjusted his grey cloak. He held out his hands to her.

Briana stepped forward and took them, her hands gripping his tightly.

He felt her tremble and his eyes softened.

"You have been away long," Weylyn said.

"It is good to see you, Weylyn!" Einion said as he stepped. "You have aged."

136

"I see that tact was something you did not learn in the North," the Druid said, laughing, remembering the sometime banter he would have with the young Dumnonian. "And you have more worries than ever in your eyes, young man."

Einion said nothing, but his smile disappeared.

"We all have much to talk about," Weylyn nodded. "But who have we here?" He turned to see Phoebus and Calliope who were now standing beside each other, the former with his arm protectively about his sister.

"My father is Lucius Metellus Anguis," Phoebus said proudly, but not haughtily.

"Indeed, it must be so," Weylyn said, a broad smile spreading across his face. "I am Weylyn, and this," he turned to Morvran, "is Morvran. He is my friend, and you need not fear him. The Gods may have shaped him differently, but his heart is as pure and kind as any person across Rome's Empire."

Calliope stepped forward and without batting an eyelid, she reached up and touched Morvran's face with her little hands, her fingers running over the cracks and creases of his cheeks, the odd angle of his jaw, and the crushed shape of his nose.

"I like you, Morvran. You're funny!" she said.

Morvran blinked a couple of times, and then stuck his tongue out playfully.

Calliope giggled and Morvran howled with laughter that echoed down the slopes of the hillfort.

"How wonderful are a child's observations," Weylyn said.

"You must come inside, and have food and drink," Briana said, leading the way. "This is our friend Culhwch, and his son Paulus," she said as they approached the two others. "They live in the village below."

"It must do you good to see life flowing in and around this mighty fortress once again," Weylyn said unexpectedly to Culhwch.

The Durotrigan blinked, and for reasons he did not quite know, he bowed to the old man. "It does," Culhwch said.

They all made their way up to the hall.

"Phoebus," Briana said over her shoulder. "Please show Morvran where to stable the ponies."

"Paulus and I will help you," Culhwch said.

"Why are you here, Weylyn?" Briana asked as she led him up the hill with Calliope holding her hand.

137

"I needed to see you...and the Dragon."

"Baba's not here," Calliope said. "But he is supposed to come tonight with Mama."

"Then perhaps I may wait with you and spend the night?" the old man said.

"Of course," Briana said, hoping it would be fine with Lucius. "You risked much coming all this way."

"I had to," Weylyn said. "But she told you that, didn't she?" He smiled as he looked sideways at Briana.

She nodded.

"Still," Einion said. "It is very dangerous for you to leave the safety of Ynis Wytrin and the lake villages."

Weylyn said nothing, but focussed on walking up the slope, his staff in his left hand, tapping on the hollow hill.

An hour later, they were all sitting about the hearth fire - Briana, Einion, Calliope, Phoebus, Weylyn, Morvran, Culhwch and Paulus.

They ate silently at first, enjoying the fresh bread, cheese, and a mutton stew which Ula and Aina had prepared.

The two girls went back and forth from the kitchen to replenish bowls and the horn cups with beer before finishing tidying the rest of the hall for Lucius and Adara who were due back any time.

Fresh hay had been strewn about the hearth, and the sweet smell mingled with the scent of woodsmoke and warm food.

"This is a lovely home," Weylyn finally said, turning to Phoebus and Calliope. "Tell me... Do you enjoy living in this land?"

The children were hesitant at first, especially Phoebus who could not help staring at Morvran as he ate.

Einion elbowed the boy who sat up and looked at the old man. He was about to speak when his sister began to talk first.

"Oh yes!" Calliope said excitedly. "It is so green and peaceful. And I like the birds that dance in the sky about the top of the hillfort. It feels like the Gods can see us so much better up here."

Weylyn smiled. "Quite true, young lady. But do the Gods not also dwell in the trees...the earth...the rocks...and the wind?"

Calliope was thoughtful. "Yes. I suppose they do," she said. "Then we are certainly among gods here, for we are surrounded by all of those things!"

A joyful laughter burst from Weylyn's throat and he clapped his hands. How he enjoyed being around small children again. He turned to Phoebus.

"And what do you think, young man? Do you like Britannia?"

Einion turned to Phoebus, knowing he did not like being put on the spot like that.

"I don't like the North," Phoebus said. "It is all blood and sadness."

Weylyn nodded, his memories of blood, battle, and sacrifice rushed back to him. He thought of his son, Cathbad, the Boar of the Selgovae, fighting Rome in the northern lands. "You are right in what you say, young man."

"But I do like the South where we are now," Phoebus added. "We have good friends and a fine home which my father has built for us."

"I can see that," Weylyn said as he looked at Culhwch and Paulus. "And the home is magnificent, though not very Roman."

"The Praefectus wanted to mix the styles," Culhwch said. "Fully Roman on the outside, but only partly on the inside."

"Mostly on the inside, I would say," Weylyn added. "But for the great round hearth fire around which we now sit."

"In Rome, part of Vesta's temple is also round," Phoebus said, remembering his lessons.

"Then it is a perfect melding of the cultures here," Weylyn said.

Briana shook her head, wanting to get to the bottom of the reason for Weylyn's visit.

"Children," she said to Phoebus and Calliope. "Why don't you help Ula and Aina to clean the dishes and prepare plates for your parents when they return? I'm sure they will be famished."

Phoebus rose and went to the kitchen, but Calliope stayed.

"I want to sit and speak with Weylyn," she said.

Briana stared at her for a moment. "Now please."

Calliope stood her ground for a brief second, but her defiance soon evaporated and she went away humming.

"They are enchanting," Weylyn said.

Briana stared hard at him, and he nodded.

"We should be going too," Culhwch said as he rose with Paulus. "Thank you Ula...Aina," he said to the twins before turning to Einion and Briana. "Do you need me to stay?"

"No, my friend. You can go," Einion said. "Help Alma."

139

Culhwch nodded. "But who will help me?" He glanced at Weylyn, nodded, and then he and Paulus went out.

"A staunch friend of the Dragon's, I see," Weylyn said approvingly.

"Yes. He is," Einion added, turning to the old man.

"Etain is not well."

Weylyn spoke so suddenly that it took Briana and Einion a moment to realize what he had said, to deal with the clenched feeling in their guts.

"But she spoke to me last night!" Briana said.

"I know. She said she would try, though I feared the effort would be too much for her."

"How bad is it?" Einion asked, worried for the priestess who had come to represent both the Goddess and his own lost mother to him.

"I do not know," Weylyn sighed, and looked at the straw-strewn floor of the hall. "I have tried every herb and root I know. I believe now it may not be a physical ailment, but rather something of the spirit."

"I don't understand, Weylyn," Briana said. "She is so powerful and wise... How can this happen?"

"The mortal mind is a mystery that even confounds the Gods, child. Father Gilmore has stayed through the long nights with her and said that she often calls out in her sleep - the names of her predecessors, to Epona, to the Morrigan, and others. She has also been calling out to you, Briana."

"To me? But I have not heard her until last night!"

"You and she have a special bond, Briana. You always have had," Weylyn said. "I came to bring you back to Ynis Wytrin."

They were silent.

"Back?" Briana said. "I can try to help her, but I do not know what to do, Weylyn. My training is more martial than anything."

"I do not believe it is your training Etain needs," he said. "It is you." He turned to Einion. "And you too, Einion."

"Me?" Einion was surprised by this, for though he had always been close to Etain, it had been Father Gilmore with whom he had more often spoken.

"Gilmore said that Etain spoke of Dumnonia and a throne in her fevered sleep."

"A throne?" Einion looked at Briana. "I dreamed of such last night. A terrible vision."

140

"I do not know for certain, but I believe Etain may have sent that dream to you, Einion... To prepare you."

Einion looked up from the flames at the Druid's flashing eyes and felt Briana grip his hand.

"Then we must go as soon as possible," Briana said.

"Go where?" said a voice from doors of the hall.

They all turned to see Lucius and Adara standing there in the orange evening light with the paling blue of the sky behind them.

"Baba! Mama!" Phoebus and Calliope yelled as they ran from the kitchen. Both children collided with their parents and buried themselves in the folds of their cloaks, holding tight.

Lucius looked down at Calliope and her big eyes stared into his, questioning and relieved at the same time.

"What is it, my girl?" he asked.

Her lip began to quiver slightly, her eyes watery at the sight of her father. "I had a dream of you being attacked," she said. "But I see that it was just that - a dream." She hugged him again and Lucius realized how tall she had actually grown, able as he was to kiss the top of her head without bending over too far. "I'm so glad I was wrong, Baba!" she sobbed quietly into the black wool of his cloak.

Lucius knelt down and held her closely, aware of Briana, Einion and two others standing at the hearth fire. "My girl, all is well," he said, fighting back the odd fear he had the moment she mentioned her dream. "We weren't attacked, Calliope." He glanced at Adara. "Do not worry yourself so."

He stood up, holding his daughter's hand still, and looked to the fire. His face grew dark when he looked upon the two strangers who had been sitting in his home with his children.

"Einion? Briana? Will you tell me who our guests are?"

Adara took both children to her as Lucius stepped forward, the hilt of his pugio glinting at his belt beneath his cloak.

"Praefectus," the old man bowed politely, as did his malformed servant.

"Who are you?" Lucius demanded. He spotted something familiar in the old man's features and build, but did not say anything.

"Lucius," Briana began. "This is Weylyn, and his servant Morvran. They are our friends."

"Weylyn?" Lucius repeated the name. Then he remembered. "Weylyn... Of the Selgovae?"

"The same," the old man smiled. "You knew my son, Praefectus. And it was I who sent Einion and Briana to you in the North."

"Yes," Lucius said, his mind racing. "For which I am grateful." Lucius walked around the logs to stand before the two strangers.

Morvran tried to smile, but he was afraid before the Roman, spittle dripping accidentally from his curled lip. He wiped it and backed away.

Weylyn continued to stare at Lucius, his eyes glowing and friendly in the firelight. "Do not worry Morvran," he said to his servant. "He is Roman, but he will not harm you. The Praefectus is an honourable man."

The words hung in the air between them and made Lucius feel uncomfortable for a moment. Though he strove to be so, and though he knew what Weylyn had done for them, he struggled with the urge to lash out, for he had come home to see his children in the company of perfect strangers. *Einion and Briana let me down,* was the thought that came to him.

"Phoebus...Calliope... Go to your cubicula and get ready for sleep."

"But father!" Phoebus began. "We want to stay and talk around the fire!"

Lucius turned, his teeth gritted. "Do as I say."

The children hung their heads and began to walk, but Calliope paused and tugged on Lucius' tunic sleeve. "Baba, you need not worry. They are very nice. They are our guests."

Lucius watched them go and felt his temper doused for the time being.

"Why have you come?" he asked Weylyn.

"I am sorry for the unannounced visit, Praefectus, but I needed to get word to Einion and Briana. Our mutual friend, Etain, High Priestess of Ynis Wytrin, has been unwell, and I hoped that seeing Einion and Briana would aid her recovery."

"Ynis Wytrin?" Adara asked, the discussion at Crescens' villa still fresh and angry in her memory. "You have travelled so far?" she asked.

"It is not so far, Lady," Weylyn said, bowing to Adara "if one knows the best pathways."

"Einion?" Lucius said to his friend who was staring absentmindedly into the dancing firelight. "What's with you?"

Einion looked up, startled. "Nothing. I, uh... Weylyn has brought news of Dumnonia."

"What is it?" Lucius asked.

"I can't think right now," Einion said. "I need to think, to get outside." The Briton moved for the doors and went out into the cool evening air.

"What's happened?" Lucius looked at Briana.

"I'll tell you later," she said, also distracted by the weight of what Weylyn had told them before Lucius and Adara returned. She shook her head then looked at both Lucius and Adara. "I told Weylyn that he and Morvran could stay in one of the guest rooms of the smaller barracks for the night. They risked much to come here with news and it is far too dangerous for them to attempt the return road alone."

"Of course you may stay," Adara said quickly, putting her hand on her husband's wounded shoulder.

Lucius flinched.

"What's happened?" Briana asked.

"While at the banquet, I was speaking outside with the host when someone attacked the two ordo members I was with. They tried to kill them." He looked at Weylyn. "I stopped one assassin, but it seems another got away. "The ordo members believe the killers were sent from Ynis Wytrin."

Weylyn did not flinch. "What are you saying, Praefectus?" he asked.

"Nothing," Lucius replied. "I am asking, however, if the killers were sent by Ynis Wytrin."

"Ynis Wytrin does not deal in death, Praefectus. Of that you can be sure."

Lucius was silent.

"Absolutely," Briana echoed. "They would never do such a thing. Why would they?"

"Because the ordo of Lindinis wants to tax Ynis Wytrin," Lucius answered.

"Are you so sure it was the ordo members the assassins were trying to kill?" Weylyn asked.

Lucius was silent, staring back at the old Druid and his servant.

"You may stay the night in the outbuildings, but you leave tomorrow."

"Very well," Weylyn said.

Briana showed Weylyn and Morvran to their quarters in the new barracks block. They were grateful for two of the simple, wood-framed bunks and straw mattresses covered in wool blankets.

Einion set a small brazier burning near the door while Briana knelt before the old Druid who sat on the edge of the bed beneath Morvran who was sound asleep in moments.

"Please forgive Lucius his...temper," Briana said. "He does not appear to be himself, I fear."

"There is nothing to forgive. I took him by surprise. The Dragon came home to find his offspring with the father of his one-time enemy. And if someone did attempt to kill him, he would naturally be less than hospitable."

"Do you really think the assassins were meant for Lucius?" Briana wondered out loud.

"They did not come from Ynis Wytrin. However, from what I have been told by the people of the lake villages, the ordo of Lindinis does not look favourably upon the Isle of the Blessed. It rankles Romans when they cannot control things."

Briana smiled at the hint of the old fire that still dwelled in the Druid.

"True," Einion said. "But there have been many who have sought Lucius' death since you sent us to him, Weylyn."

"Has such happened in this place?" Weylyn asked, picturing the vast green slopes of the magnificent hillfort outside.

"No. It has been calm," Briana said.

"As before a storm..." Weylyn muttered.

"Why did you say that?" Einion pressed, leaning against one of the bunks with his muscular arms crossed. "What has Etain said to you?"

Weylyn made to speak, but stopped himself. "That is for her to tell you." He stared at the brother and sister. "Will you come back with me tomorrow?"

Einion was silent, lost again in his own thoughts, but Briana answered for both of them.

"Of course. We will come. Lucius will understand."

"I can see why my son liked the Dragon so. In some ways, they are very much alike." The old Druid was lost in a memory then, the sight of his son beside the moonlit waters of the marshes the night his

144

soul told him of Lucius before passing into Annwn. He was shining in death, strong and free of cares, save for the Dragon.

"Weylyn?" Briana said. "Are you unwell?"

"No. I am fine, child. I was just thinking of Cathbad, and of our dragon praefectus. He will need you more than ever now, and you him. I believe the Gods intend more for all of you...and his children."

Einion looked at him suddenly. "What of the children? They are good and kind. What have you seen?"

"Nothing, my boy. Be calm," Weylyn said. "I saw it from the first that they are special. Did you not see it? You do not require Etain's power to perceive it."

"Yes," Briana answered. "Please tell me no harm will come to them!"

"I cannot tell whether yes or no, for all is in motion, and the Dragon does not keep favour with all the Gods."

"Maybe we should stay here?" Einion said, against his own wish.

"No. You must come, for Etain would speak with you also," Weylyn said. "I wish I had arrived when the praefectus was not weighed so by worry, for I would have spoken with him at length."

"I can bring him here," Briana offered.

"No. Let him be rejuvenated by his children." Weylyn rubbed his eyes and turned to lie down upon the narrow bed. "I must sleep now."

"Do so, my friend," Briana said, pulling the blankets up over the old man. "Rest," she soothed.

In her cubiculum, the dam of Calliope's tears had opened once Lucius and Adara were with her, and they sat on the edge of her bed trying to calm her.

"We are well, love," Adara said and she stroked her daughter's hair. "Why so sad?"

"I saw you hurt," she mumbled. "I was worried all day."

"We're home now, my girl," Lucius said, kissing her wet face. "Do not worry so."

"And why did you speak so badly to Weylyn?" Calliope said to Lucius suddenly.

"I...I..." he could not find an explanation. "I was surprised to see them here," he finally said. "I did not expect them."

"He and Morvran are kind and gentle, Baba. And they are Einion and Briana's friends. They did not deserve to be treated like that."

Lucius stood and looked down at his daughter. *So small...but so wise. She is right. It was Weylyn who sent Einion and Briana to us. Good friends.* He nodded. "I will apologize to him in the morning."

"Please, Baba," she pleaded. "He is so kind."

Lucius smiled, ran his hand over her hair, and turned, leaving Adara to sing to her, to calm her. He went to the next cubiculum to see Phoebus sitting up, holding his rudus on the edge of his bed.

"Did you practice while we were away?" Lucius asked, sitting down next to his son.

Phoebus did not speak for a moment, but then nodded. "Yes, Baba. We did."

"Good," Lucius said. "I... I'm proud of you, Phoebus. Both of you. You are learning so quickly, growing at such a rate. I'm trying to be the father you need. Forgive me if I think you too young still for certain things. I've missed so much of your growing up that I feel you should be much younger than you are."

"I'm quite capable," Phoebus said, holding up his arm and flexing his small bicep.

Lucius chuckled. "Yes you are!" He pat the muscle his son so proudly displayed. "But being capable in this world is not just about how much firewood you can chop and lift. It is also about wisdom, and thought. About trying to improve oneself without end, to please the Gods. I still strive for these things, though I still fail."

The boy looked up at his father and put his hand on his shoulder. "But we never give up, do we?"

Lucius felt like weeping. "No," he whispered hoarsely.

"Philotimo, Baba," Phoebus said.

It was a proud moment for Lucius that his son remembered their talk on the journey to the South, that Philotimo should still be something he strove for and remembered. *He is a better person than I am,* Lucius thought. *Gods bless him.*

Adara appeared in the doorway and looked at the two of them sitting there. She had changed from her stola into a long, blue woollen tunic that reached to the floor.

"May I sing to you, Phoebus?" she asked. "Or are you too old for that now?" She smiled.

"Please, Mama. I missed your singing last night." he said.

146

Lucius kissed his son on the head and went to the door. There he stopped, and turned back. "Thank you for taking care of things while we were away, Phoebus. You did well."

"Thank you, Baba!" the boy said.

Lucius moved along the wooden walkway to their own cubiculum to change, but went slowly, enjoying the soft beauty of Adara's voice as she sang.

When Lucius and Adara came down into the hall, Einion and Briana were sitting at the fire waiting for them.

Smoke hovered in the rafters before slipping out through the high windows, and the crackle of the hearth fire sounded sweet to their ears as they came down the stairs.

However, when Lucius looked to the Dumnonians who had been with him for long now, who had risked their lives for him and his family, who had seemingly paused the cycle of their own lives in favour of his, he felt shame.

The feeling of hypocrisy made him angry.

Einion stood and strode out of the circle directly toward Lucius.

"What was that all about?" He held his arms wide and questioning, as if challenging a common thug to a tavern brawl.

"You ask *me* what that was about?" Lucius barked back. "I trusted you with our children, and I come back to find a Druid in my home! Sitting with my children!"

"He's a friend, Lucius! He had news for me!" Einion swung, unable to control the crashing of emotion within.

Lucius' arm swept up to block the half-hearted blow and his forearm slid about Einion's neck, and he jumped behind to squeeze and drag the Briton off his feet.

"Stop this, both of you!" Adara cried.

"She's right. Stop it!" Briana yelled, standing now beside Adara.

Lucius could feel Einion's body shaking with rage within his grasp. He felt dazed, the anger clouding him as if he were caught in some sort of cataract, and there, in that mist, he saw the Morrigan's face laughing silently at him. He stepped back, releasing Einion who immediately spun and caught Lucius across the cheek with his fist.

Lucius stumbled, but did not retaliate. He stood there, opposite his friend, wanting to scream to the heavens at the whirling thoughts that beset him.

But he did not. He closed his eyes…breathed.

147

Breathe Lucius... Breathe...

"Your arm," Einion said hoarsely.

Lucius looked down to see the blood seeping slowly through the wool of his tunic. He looked up at Einion and shook his head. "It's no matter. Forgive me...please," he said. "Both of you." He turned to Briana. "It has not been a good couple of days."

"There was no need to worry, Lucius," Briana said. "The children were safe at all times. We would never endanger them. You should know that."

"I know," Lucius said. "I'm sorry. Truly."

Einion rubbed his neck. "Me too. I struck first."

Adara came rushing up from where she had been in the kitchen, clutching a fresh piece of linen. She began to roll up Lucius' sleeve to remove the old bandage and replace it, speaking as she did so.

"Obviously, a lot has happened since we left," Adara said, shaking her head. "Let's sit together as friends, drink wine, and help each other, rather than fighting each other like children. I'll not have my domus turned into an poorhouse amphitheatre!"

They were silent, and then all started laughing, except Adara, who struggled to hold back her own smile.

"What?" she said. "I want a tidy home. You should have seen Serenus Crescens' villa! It was beautiful!"

The laughter was louder and finally, Adara joined in. "You're all impossible!"

"I'll get more wine," Briana howled, going to the kitchen to get four clay cups and a large jug.

They all gathered about the hearth fire, calming themselves, nursing their regret and quelling their anger. Finally, Lucius spoke.

"I'm ashamed at how I treated Weylyn," he said, his face serious, a mask of disappointment. "Is he very angry?"

"It takes much more than that to make Weylyn angry," Einion said. "He wasted all his anger and hate on the battlefields of the North a generation ago. He is a good man, for all his past faults and actions."

"I will apologize to him tomorrow," Lucius said. "The Gods do not appreciate guests being treated in such a way."

"He understands," Briana said. "So tell us what did happen at the villa. That is a bad cut." She pointed at his arm.

Lucius waved it off, but Adara spoke.

"Before the last course, everyone stood to talk. Lucius and the two head ordo members went out into the field at the edge of the forest."

"What were they like?" Einion asked.

"Politicians and greedy merchants wanting more," Lucius said.

Adara continued. "A dagger came hurling out of the forest directly for one of the ordo members and Lucius pushed him out of the way. The attacker, a Briton by the look of him, came rushing out and Lucius...killed..." Adara paused in her rushed description, her hands trembling suddenly. "Lucius killed him," she finished.

Lucius reached out to touch her arm and pull her close to him beside the fire.

"I'm sorry," she said.

"Why?" he said. "You rushed into the fray faster than anyone else there, except perhaps Trevor Reghan. Everyone else was cowering while you scanned the scene, my love. I couldn't be prouder," Lucius said, stroking the hair of her forehead back. "You've trained a lot, but true aggression and violence, someone trying to kill you, has a different effect on a person."

"I'll get better at it," she said, her eyes staring into the fire.

"Let's hope you don't have to."

"Did you say Trevor Reghan?" Einion asked.

"Yes. Why?"

"Some of the Britons in Lindinis mentioned him. They said he was the only ordo member with any sense of justice."

"His family was once the ruling clan of the oppidum."

"Was the attacker alone?" Briana asked.

"No. There was another somewhere in the wood," Lucius said. "I hit him with a thrown pugio, but he got away."

"From what you've told us," Adara began, out of her punitive reverie, "Ynis Wytrin would never do such a thing. I mean, do they even know the ordo wants to tax them?"

"I've never heard Etain, Weylyn, or Father Gilmore speak of it," Briana said. "It is a world apart."

"Well, the ordo of Lindinis has it in for the Isle of the Blessed, it seems," Lucius said. "All except Trevor Reghan."

"He's but one man," Einion said, before looking at Lucius. "Do you really think the assassins were intended for the ordo members? Or -"

"I don't know," Lucius said abruptly, trying to shake the image of the Morrigan from his mind.

"Well. Whatever it is, we need to be on the alert. The four of us are together again," Adara said.

Einion and Briana looked at each other, then back at Lucius and Adara.

"Ah," Briana said. "We need to speak to you of another matter." She righted herself and sat straighter before the fire so that she could see them clearly.

Einion stared into the flames, lost in thought.

"What is it?" Adara asked.

"Weylyn came here with urgent news for us. Etain, whom I have told you about often, is not well. She has asked to see both myself and Einion - something regarding our kingdom."

Lucius looked at the brother and sister. They were all quiet, and the sound of cracking logs in the hearth was loud and harsh.

"Has she had a vision?" Adara asked.

"We don't know. Weylyn could not say," Einion said.

Briana continued. "Weylyn thinks that by seeing me, she will feel better. She has been too weak to contact me clearly."

Lucius and Adara both thought of how bad the timing for this was, for if the assassins had been sent after Lucius - something that had happened in the past - then they would be vulnerable. However, they also knew that they had no right to keep Einion and Briana from going with the Druid. Apart from them, the triad of sages at Ynis Wytrin were their only family.

"You don't need to ask our permission to go," Lucius said. "Do what you must and see your friend well."

"We'll be fine," Adara said smiling. "I hope Etain recovers and that she has good news for you both." She turned to Lucius. "We're safe here, and Culhwch is close should we need aid."

"He's got his hands full with Alma's cousin," Einion said. "Apparently he's back from the Danuvius frontier where he was in a cavalry ala. Got a spear through his knee and has been discharged. He's come back to the village."

Lucius looked up from his wine cup. "He was serving as an auxiliary?"

"That's what Culhwch said," Einion nodded. "Anyway, I'm sure you'll meet the man at some point. I only meant to say that it has taken a toll on Culhwch. He came here to get away earlier."

150

"Depending on how long the man served, he may not have much of a pension," Lucius pointed out. "Tough times for any warrior."

Briana continued with the earlier conversation. "Weylyn's visit coincided with dreams that both Einion and I had last night. That is the reason for this urgency."

"What did you dream?" Adara asked, curious as ever about the dreams the Gods' sent mortals. She knew only too well what it was like to have dreams strike terror and worry into oneself.

Briana looked at her brother who threw back the rest of his wine and leaned against the thick trunk of the log. The fire flashed upon his face, radiating alternately through red, yellow and orange.

Einion recounted his dream of the previous night to Lucius and Adara, and all the while, the lines upon his brow and face seemed to grow deeper with the worry it caused him.

The Gods had tortured him with the dream, and Lucius could feel himself grow angry for Einion. He could understand the anger directed at Lucius earlier.

The tale made Lucius remember the rage he had felt at his own sister's death, and the want for revenge that had filled his veins from that time on. It was not a feeling he would wish upon any man, let alone his good friend.

"You must go," Lucius said when Einion finished. "If the Priestess of Ynis Wytrin can shed any light on this, you have no choice. Adara's right. We'll be fine. Stay there as long as you are needed."

"Thank you," Briana said.

Adara looked puzzled. "Thank you? There is no need to thank us. You are as brother and sister to both Lucius and myself, but you are not bound to us in anything but the Gods' plans if they have one."

Einion and Briana nodded, each chased by their own thoughts.

Lucius got up, took the pitcher of wine from the table nearby, and filled each of their cups.

"May the Gods grant you a safe journey tomorrow, my friends," he said before they all drank.

When they finished their drinking, Einion and Briana went out into the night to check on Weylyn and Morvran, leaving Lucius and Adara curled up together before the dying fire.

"I feel detached from everything for some reason," Lucius said.

"You are out of your element," she answered, her head upon his chest listening to the comforting beating of his heart.

151

"My place is with you," he said, "and the children."

"Of course it is, but that's not what I meant. What I meant was that your routines have been changed since we came to live here. Your men are not here anymore, the familiar sounds of tramping hobnails and hooves don't echo in a courtyard outside, and the rigidity of training is lessened."

"I still train," Lucius protested. "I've not grown fat either."

She smiled and rubbed the muscles of his abdomen through his tunic. "Thankfully not."

"I also know that once I get used to life in this idyll, things will change again and I'll be torn from you."

"That can always happen." There was sadness in Adara's voice. She felt as if they had had their share of upset, of tragedy and death. She prayed daily that the Gods should protect them from anymore. "What would Diodorus have said were he to hear you speaking this way?"

Lucius thought of his old tutor's white, wispy hair and beard, his joyous laugh, and his furrowed brow when he, as a young boy, found it hard to grasp the lesson. Lucius chuckled.

"He would tell me my wife is correct, that all things are fleeting, and thus we have all the reason in the world to notice what is happening and to savour it for all it offers."

"My love..." Adara said, sitting up and leaning into him, her eyes directly before his, taking in the comforting sight of his fire-lit irises. "We are here, now...together. Our children are safe. This is not war. There will always be people such as those of the ordo, but they are not us. They cannot harm us." She felt her eyes stinging as she leaned in and kissed him. "Live this life with me, my love. Live it!" she said as their mouths joined.

They kissed for some time until finally, Lucius could take it no more.

He stood, and picked Adara up as if she were a mere child's plaything. She laughed as he walked across the hall and made his way up the strong wooden staircase to their cubiculum.

He manoeuvred her, both of them laughing, through the doorframe of their room and stopped short.

There, in the middle of their bed were Phoebus and Calliope, cuddled close beneath the furs, waiting for their parents.

"In some ways, they are still so little," Adara whispered.

Lucius smiled resignedly, but happily, setting Adara on her feet.

152

She nodded, and then lay down on the bed beside Phoebus on the one side.

Lucius lay down beside Calliope and turned to face Adara, his strong arm laying across both children to touch his wife's hand.

"I love you," he said.

"And I love you," Adara answered.

Lucius watched her for some minutes as her lids grew heavy and her breathing changed.

I am happy, he thought as he too closed his eyes, only to see a sunlit isle with misty shores, a place where it seemed to him Apollo, Venus, and Epona stood watching him, waiting...

When dawn yet paled in the sky the following day, Lucius awoke with a start, the Gods' faces still hovering before him.

They had not been smiling. Quite to the contrary. Their faces had been creased with worry, a sight that reminded Lucius of black pitch seeping across the surface of the sun.

He turned to see Adara sleeping with her arms around both children, all three of them snuggled safely beneath the blankets and furs. Seeing that they were well, Lucius swung his legs over the side of the bed and put on his boots. He had slept in his clothes, and so went to the peg on the wall where he took down his thick black cloak and his sword, the gold of the dragon-headed hilt glowing even in the dim light.

Quietly, he crept outside to the gallery to look down onto the expanse of the hall.

It was empty, and the fire had completely cooled in the hearth. He made his way down the stairs to the privy, and then to the kitchen where he ate a hunk of bread, and drank a cool cup of water.

That done, he put his cloak on, hung his sword from his side, and went out of the double doors.

The air and grass were damp and dewy outside, and the few stray rays of first light illuminated droplets here and there, those upon a blade of tall grass, a gathering atop one of the fence posts surrounding the vegetable garden, or upon the clay tiles of the rooftop.

It was peaceful, Lucius' favourite time to think to himself.

He walked down toward the supply depot on the north side, and then began a circuit of the ramparts toward the north-east gate. His steps were slow and thoughtful, his eyes scanning the steep, overgrown fortifications where myriad birds trilled their dawn salutations.

Lucius knew he was going to miss Einion and Briana. If he was honest with himself, their presence had been a great comfort for a long time now. He had relied heavily upon them for the reinforcement of his own sense of security and that of his family. Once again, he chided himself for his behaviour the day before, and felt his jaw unconsciously where Einion's fist had connected.

I should write to Alerio and Dagon, he thought, realizing with regret how remiss he had been in his correspondence. It was odd that Alerio had not written in so long.

He continued his walk around the east side of the ramparts and looked down onto the roof of the small square temple. The Gods' faces still floated before his eyes, but more hidden like a shore shrouded by mist.

He turned away to look out over the valley to where the land sloped away and then struck upward, along steep cliff faces to a sort of landlocked promontory that overlooked the hillfort.

"The Dragon has come home, I see."

Lucius' hand went to his sword handle as he spun and half drew it from the scabbard, but when he saw the old Druid standing there, he stopped.

"You surprised me," Lucius said, grateful that the blade had not lashed out. He looked at the old man, wrapped in his simple grey cloak and holding his walking stick. "I did not hear you approach."

Weylyn laughed. "Moving unseen and unheard...a skill I developed during my training."

"As a Druid," Lucius finished.

Weylyn nodded. "Does that bother you?"

"It does, but not entirely," Lucius answered honestly.

"The Roman part of you?"

"Yes."

The Dragon's loyalty lies not only with Rome... Weylyn remembered the words his son's shade had spoken to him.

"But not all of you?" Weylyn pressed, trying to get the measure of the warrior before him.

Lucius shook his head. "I've fought the length and breadth of the empire for Rome, and unlike the members of the ordo of Lindinis, I've come to understand that what makes it so great is not only Rome's legions, but also her ability to welcome people into the fold, to make them a part of something greater." Lucius turned to look at the small temple and the few Britons who had already come up to the hillfort to go and leave offerings in the first hour after dawn. "It is all peoples who make up the Empire, not just Romans."

"Even Druids?" Weylyn hazarded.

Lucius stared at him. He had heard the stories about the Druids, about human sacrifices performed in sacred groves. He also knew that Rome invented such stories once staunch enemies were defeated. It was the way of victors. How much blood had Rome spilled in the name of a perceived greater good? How much had he?

"Even Druids," Lucius said. "By sending Briana and Einion to me, you have helped me and my family, and for that I owe you a debt."

"You owe me no debt, Lucius Metellus Anguis. It was I who owed you the debt for helping my son, Cathbad."

"You mean when I defeated him?"

"No. When you allowed him to die with honour. You are a warrior. You know the importance that held to him." Weylyn looked at the grass where he poked the end of his staff into the mud thoughtfully. Then he looked up. "You spoke much with...my son?"

It was an odd thing for Lucius, to look into the aged eyes of the man whose son he had captured and helped to die. A part of him wanted to apologize, but he knew he could not, for not all the stories he had heard about the Boar of the Selgovae had been false. He had only to remember Afallach of the Votadini's face when he had cut him down for all the harm the Boar had done their family.

Likewise, it pained Weylyn to look upon Lucius, the man who was in part responsible for the death of his son. But then, he remembered how Cathbad had been that night when he had come to him, shining and brilliant, like a god. His spirit had been happy, supremely content.

"Are we enemies now that our debts have been cancelled?" Weylyn asked suddenly, his bushy eyebrows up.

Lucius uncrossed his arms and faced the Druid. He extended his hand to him, palm open. "No," he said. "We are friends, I hope."

Weylyn extended his gnarled hand to take Lucius' and gripped it tightly. *The heat radiates so from him!* he thought, shocked. Then he saw a flash, a vision of vast armies spread out upon a plain, with Lucius Metellus Anguis, the Roman dragon, looking over them. And suddenly they burst into flame and he was staring at his hand in

Lucius'. He released his grip quickly. "You are come to a land of dragons, Praefectus... I have seen your struggle. You have built a home here to rival all others."

Lucius, taken aback by the sudden change in conversation turned to look over the hillfort and the buildings of their home. He nodded, proud of what they had accomplished thus far.

"It is beautiful here," Lucius said.

Weylyn smiled knowingly. "This land, it does cast a spell upon one, even more so than the northern mountains of my home. You belong here, in this land."

"I do not know," Lucius said, waving to one of the old women who came daily to the shrine. "I've travelled so far in this life, I don't know what a home is. I feel like Aeneas, adrift upon the sea, the old life burned away to ash." He shook his head. "Forgive me. My mind is often melancholy before the light."

Weylyn stared at him.

"Your children belong here too. They are...special."

Lucius stared at him, his eyes colder then. "I'll ask you to leave my children out of it. They have been through much."

"The trials of this life do not stop for any man, woman, or child, I'm afraid. That is one certainty of the paths the Gods set before us."

"I will keep them safe," Lucius whispered to himself. "I must."

"There is a place where that is possible, where safety is a certainty," Weylyn said. "This is a land of dragons, Praefectus. As I said, you belong here."

"You speak of the Isle of the Blessed."

"Yes. Will you come with us? Today? I would show you the peace that exists there."

Lucius looked at him and shook his head.

"I cannot. Not now. This is our home," he said, gesturing to the green expanse of the hillfort. "I have work to do here, letters to write. I also have business in Lindinis once new building plans are drawn up for a bathhouse."

"The world of Rome," Weylyn sighed. "I understand. I also see how much you have done for the Britons of this place. I look here and I see an ancient shrine brought back to life by you, and you alone. I see old gods and new worshipped together in the temple you have built, just as they are in the forest halls of the Isle."

"It seemed the right thing," Lucius said, proud of the offerings to different deities that continued to crowd the altar of Apollo, Venus, and Epona. "It is the least I could do for all the good the Gods have done to me."

He is still naive, even now... Weylyn thought a little sadly.

They began to walk down toward the temple, Lucius lending Weylyn his arm to lean upon as they headed down the steep slope. Once they were down, Lucius stepped forward to greet the few villagers who came out of the temple.

"Good morning to you," he said, smiling at them.

Behind him, the Druid watched with interest.

There was no fear in the people's eyes. There was peace...comfort. It was as if they knew they were protected, now that a dragon had come to dwell upon the hill. Weylyn had seen Britons of the South before, simple villagers, shudder when other Romans had approached them, like field flowers shivering in a burst of cold, cruel wind, waiting to wilt. Or others who tensed like cornered dogs, the muscles taut and snapping, teeth ready to be bared if a Roman came near to them.

"The Gods bless you, Praefectus," one old woman said as she grabbed Lucius' hands and put her forehead to them.

Weylyn saw that this made Lucius feel awkward, but he did not pull away in disgust. Rather, the Roman touched both of her shoulders and offered to walk her back to the gate.

"No need, dear," the old woman said. "I feel young and lively this day. Your Apollo's disc seems set to shine bright and warm."

Lucius looked up. "Yes, it does, doesn't it? A beautiful day ahead."

The woman made to leave, then turned and went back to Weylyn and whispered, "It *is* good to see you here. Like old times."

Weylyn touched her forehead and smiled. "In some ways, it is as it used to be."

Then she was walking back toward the southwest gate, down the road and back to the village.

When a few more of the villagers had spoken with Lucius, he turned to Weylyn and shrugged.

"I don't understand why anyone would see them as a threat," Lucius said.

"Truly? You have more experience than that, I think," Weylyn answered, giving Lucius a look not dissimilar to one Diodorus used to give him. "Is it not about power?"

157

"But I have no need of power over these people. They have as much right to live here as I do, more even."

"If all Romans thought as you, then we should truly have the world of peace which Father Gilmore dreams of."

"I know. I'm sometimes a child in my thinking. It's this place," Lucius said. "Being here, peace seems a greater possibility."

"Except two nights ago perhaps?" Weylyn said.

Lucius' face hardened. "Yes. That was…unfortunate."

Weylyn levelled his gaze at him. "No one in Ynis Wytrin would have sent those killers."

"I believe you," Lucius said. "Who then?"

"The answer escapes me, and my sight is blinded in this instance," Weylyn said. "It may be that Etain would know." This last was said to himself.

Suddenly, he felt the dragon's strong hand upon his shoulder.

"Would you bless the grounds about the temple before you leave?" Lucius asked.

For a moment, the question stunned the old Druid. No Roman, as far as he could remember, had ever asked a Druid to perform a blessing on anything, least of all their home.

"You are a puzzle, Lucius Metellus Anguis," he said.

"I've been told so," Lucius answered, "often by myself."

"Does not Apollo, in his sacred sanctuary of Delphi, compel you to *know thyself?*"

"Yes," Lucius said. "But it is a toil the end of which I do not see."

Weylyn smiled. "Then may you have a long life." He looked at the temple steps, the sprigs of rowan and holly placed as offerings, containers of milk and honey, and the grey-blue smoke of offerings snaking out of the doorway.

"I would be honoured to bless this place for you," Weylyn said.

After they had eaten breakfast and Einion and Briana's horses were readied alongside Weylyn and Morvran's, the Metelli and their friends and guests were gathered about the steps of the small temple of Apollo for the Druid's blessing

Lucius and Weylyn stood upon the steps of the temple, looking out at the faces of Britons from the village, including Culhwch and his wife and son, Alma and Paulus. Alma's cousin, Sigwyll Sloane, who stood beside her, shifting his weight constantly upon his feet and hiding behind the long strands of his black hair.

People looked up at the two men, the younger one tall and imposing, his face still smooth and dark, the older one closer to a gnarled old tree, the lines of life etched upon his his wise face.

"Friends..." Lucius said loudly, so that all could hear. "My family and I are happy you are here this morning. You have welcomed us into your lands since we arrived, and you have left plentiful offerings upon the altar of this small temple since it was completed. It is my hope that, in this peaceful place, we, as well as our gods, may continue to live in harmony."

A part of Lucius stared out at the faces as he spoke. The words he heard himself say were strange, but he felt compelled to speak them. He wondered if the conversation with the members of the ordo at Crescens' home had planted in him some form of empathy with the local Britons.

"To that end, I have invited a close friend of Einion and Briana, Weylyn of Ynis Wytrin, to also bless this place for us. Weylyn?" Lucius stepped aside.

Weylyn stood upon the stone steps and looked down. The ground felt hard there, unfamiliar in a way, and so he stepped down to stand upon the green grass that surrounded the temple.

He gripped a sprig of deep green oak leaves as once he would have gripped a blade for killing Romans, and looked at the faces before him - the young, the old, men, women. He thought of them and what he had seen this place meant to them, the gift Lucius Metellus Anguis had unknowingly given to them.

His grip upon the oak relaxed with a deep breath. He had not performed the blessing ceremony for an age, it seemed. Previously, it had always to be performed in secret, hidden away from the eyes of Rome and Romans.

Yet now, he stood beside a Roman, as odd and unmatched as rowan beside a towering palm.

Weylyn closed his eyes and raised his arms to the air. His sleeves slid back to reveal the faded tattoos upon his wrists and arms, the markings of another life.

Breathe Weylyn... he told himself. *You stand beside a dragon, and the Gods are watching you...*

And they were. He could feel their presence...in the earth, on the air, and in the light that suffused the scene, the temple.

Oh, how I've missed this. And a tear rimmed his lid as the words began...

"Gods of our land..." his voice croaked at first, but then the certainty crept into it, the power. He held the green leaves aloft. "A dragon has come to our land, and breathed new life into this ancient fortress. Come now to roam these slopes and bless the people who dwell in the mortal world. Here, in this place," he said, turning and slapping the thick columns of the temple entrance with the leaves, "may your people, Roman and Briton, lay offerings at your feet and upon your altars that they, and this land, may be protected from those who would seek to give harm. Let strength run in our veins so that we may hold onto this peace and plenty through the harshest gale."

Now the words flooded his mind, returned to him from the dark alcoves where he had safely stored them...

"Grant, O God and Goddesses of this temple, thy protection;

And in protection, strength;

And in strength, understanding;

And in understanding, knowledge;

And in knowledge, the knowledge of justice;

And in the knowledge of justice, the love of it;

And in that love, the love of all existences;

And in the love of all existences, the love of you Gods, and of the Earth, and all goodness..."

Weylyn turned to Lucius and stopped.

There, behind Lucius, at the entrance to the temple, he spied them, the Goddess Epona, and two others whom he took immediately to be Apollo and Venus, the gods honoured by the Dragon in that place.

Their starry eyes bored into him, but not with menace. They were there to ensure protection of the place, of the man before him.

Weylyn swallowed and looked back to Lucius. He gripped the oak leaves, and swung.

"Lucius Metellus Anguis..." he said as he slapped Lucius' hands, chest and face with the greenery. "May the Gods bless you and give you the strength to defend the people who are in your charge." He repeated the action another time. "May you protect this land..." He slapped his hands, chest and face a third time. "And may this land thrive along with you, and all who live here."

There was silence then as he turned from Lucius and went slowly into the temple, his grey cloak trailing behind him.

There, the Gods stared at him, divine sentries watching his every move with calm fire in their eyes.

He realized then that Lucius Metellus Anguis was under their protection, and that any who dared harm him would risk their divine wrath.

He placed the sprig of oak leaves upon the altar and bowed. "I shall continue to help them," he said, not daring to look directly at the immortals.

Weylyn backed away, his old hands shaking, and went out into the sunlight again where everyone waited for him.

The chatter started low at first, and then burst out in joyous song as birds come out of hiding after the passing of a storm. People closed in around Lucius and Weylyn with thanks and blessings of their own.

"I've never seen a ceremony like it," Adara said to Alma and Briana who stood with her and their children. "It was beautiful."

"I've not ever seen it done either," Alma said, her long arm coming up to brush away the stray strand of her golden hair.

"It isn't usually done," Briana said, "outside of the Isle. It's not been permitted in recent memory. This was special." She smiled as she watched the children gather around Weylyn and Lucius, and wondered at the unlikelihood of such a thing happening anywhere else.

"We need to go soon," Einion said in his sister's ear. "It's not safe to ride at night."

She nodded and caught Weylyn's eye, or rather, he caught her thought.

The Druid nodded and turned to Lucius. "I must go now."

Lucius, Adara and the children walked back to the stables with Einion, Briana, Weylyn, and Morvran while some of the families who had been in attendance remained at the temple to bask in the joy of what they had just witnessed. The sound of the village children playing on the grass faded away as the group entered the stables to see the horses ready to leave.

"You have everything you need?" Lucius asked Einion and Briana.

"I think so," Einion said.

"Are you ready for what you might hear?"

161

The Briton looked at him. "No. But I've been waiting for so long to hear something...anything. However terrible it might be, it will be better than the silence of years, adrift in a flimsy curragh upon a choppy sea."

Lucius gripped his arm. "If you need me...I'm here."

"I know, my friend," Einion said, slapping Lucius on the shoulder. "You take care of yourselves."

"Whatever the news," Adara said, coming up with Briana, "you have a home here with us should you need it. Always." She hugged Briana to whom Calliope was already clinging.

"We'll see you soon," Briana said, and as she did so, as she walked her horse out into the sunlight behind her brother and the others, she felt a pang of sadness.

As they mounted up, Briana and Einion realized that they had come to love the Metelli as their own family, that they would come back for them, that they would stand by them no matter the danger. And they knew the feeling was mutual.

Lucius walked over to Weylyn and looked up at the old man in whose eyes he spotted something new.

"Are you unwell?" Lucius asked.

"No," Weylyn shook his head. "I'm overwhelmed is all, Lucius Metellus Anguis. It has been an age since those words were uttered this side of the veil, it seems."

"Thank you for speaking them," Lucius said as Calliope jumped into his arms.

Weylyn looked at the little girl. "You take care of your parents, young one."

"I will," she said, matter-of-factly. "Goodbye Morvran!" she called.

"Byyeee!" Morvran howled back, his voice a sort of mountain spring laughter.

Weylyn looked back to Lucius. "You have done something wonderful here, Dragon."

"We do our best with what the Gods have given us."

"Indeed we do." He flicked the reins and the pony started off. "We will meet again soon," Weylyn said over his shoulder as he followed Morvran down toward the southwest gate.

Lucius put his arm about Adara and they held the children close as they watched the four riders descend toward the gate and then onto the road curving to the West, toward Ynis Wytrin.

"I'm scared we won't see them again," Phoebus said softly, gripping his rudus.

"Oh, don't worry," Adara said, patting his shoulders. "They'll be back soon, and all will be back to normal." She looked at Lucius and they both had they same thought.

But what is normal?

They both smiled sadly.

"Farewells are never easy," Culhwch said as he, Alma and Paulus came walking up the path with her cousin, Sigwyll.

"No, they are not," Lucius answered. "But they can be aided by the company of good friends and good wine!"

"Good idea!" Adara said. "Will you stay for a while?" she asked them.

Alma smiled, but then it faded when she remembered her sullen cousin hobbling up behind them.

Sigwyll had been as a dark cloud in their home of late, and she would have liked a respite.

Adara saw her discomfort. "Sigwyll, is it?" she asked, stepping forward. "You are also welcome to stay if you like."

Lucius remembered what Einion had told him about Alma's cousin and walked up to the man.

"You were with the cavalry auxiliaries?" he asked him.

Sigwyll tried to stand taller and stare back into Lucius' eyes. He winced at the pain in his leg.

"Yes, Praefectus. I was. Now, I'm nothing."

Alma and Culhwch sighed, but Lucius stared straight back at the man.

"Once a soldier...always a soldier." He held his hand out and the man took it. Lucius gripped it tightly, and then felt the strength in the Briton's grip returned.

"Yes...would that that were tr-"

He stopped when a loud neighing came from the stables behind them.

Lucius noticed how he gazed longingly at the building.

"Having been in the cavalry, you must have an appreciation of horses, don't you?"

Sigwyll's eyes shot back to Lucius. "I'm Durotrigan, Praefectus. We ride before we can walk in some cases."

"Come," Lucius said. "Let me introduce you to the other members of our familia and show you the stables."

"I'd...I'd like that, sir."

"Call me Lucius."

They began to walk and Lucius looked back to see Alma smiling, mouthing the words 'Thank you'.

Down on the westward road, Weylyn reined in his pony and turned to look back at the hillfort, that great sleeping beast once ruled by the Durotriges.

Usually, the future was clear to him, the nature of men, their role in the great plan, obvious. But it was not so with the Roman dragon. Lucius Metellus Anguis was something of an enigma to the old Druid.

Weylyn knew that he had an important role to play in the future of Ynis Wytrin, and that of Britannia, but the movements were lost in a mist his eyes could not penetrate. His mind grasped at the images like feathers in the wind.

He shook his head, the Gods' visages burned into his mind's eye.

"What is it?" Einion asked, riding back to Weylyn's side.

"I can't figure him out."

Einion laughed. "You only now realize this?"

They both laughed then and rode to catch up with Briana and Morvran. The distant Tor of Ynis Wytrin beckoned to them.

V

DOLORIS MISSI

'Emissaries of Grief'

Two days after Einion and Briana left for Ynis Wytrin, a storm came howling in off of the distant sea. It was in the afternoon, and the morning had been sun-kissed prior to the winds. The sky turned black and angry, and the violent tempest grew more and more spiteful in the sky.

It was the sort of storm one expected in Tartarus, not upon the green earth.

Lightning set a tall tree on the slopes of the hillfort alight, and the crack and rumble of the dark skies caused even Lunaris and the children's ponies to scream in their stalls. So much so, that Lucius ran out into the downpour to the stables to try and calm them all.

Their screams were of terror, and as he ran, he thought he spied some dark form perched atop the roof of the stable block where they were.

He threw a stone at whatever it was, but it took flight in the sheets of rain. He could swear that two fiery eyes turned toward him.

"Lucius!" Adara yelled when he came into the main hall, his body pressed against the oak door so that he could bar it shut. "Are they hurt?"

Lucius turned to see Adara and the children sitting close by the fire with Ula and Aina.

The twins had not had the chance to get back to the village before the rain, and Adara had urged them to remain in the safety of the hall with them until it was over.

"The horses are fine," Lucius said loudly, trying to be heard above the rush of wind from the high windows of the hall. "They're just scared."

"Me too," Calliope said, snuggling close to her mother.

"Don't worry, Sister," Phoebus said, gripping his wooden rudus which he kept with him at all times, practicing when he could. "It's just a very bad storm."

"It's more than that!" she insisted. "The Gods are angry."

"But we made offerings to them," Phoebus said, waving away her worry.

"Not those gods," his sister said.

Lucius did not say anything of the strange beast he had seen upon the stable rooftop, though the feeling it had given him was not altogether unfamiliar.

"This will pass like any other," Adara said. "I've told you about the great summer storms we used to get in Athenae when I was young, haven't I?"

"Yes," Calliope whimpered.

"Well, this is like that. You'll see. Tomorrow all will be clean and green, just as if nothing had happened." She looked up at Lucius who returned her gaze. "Ula, Aina," Adara said. "You should stay the night. You can stay in Briana's room if you like."

"Thank you, lady Metella," Ula said.

"I'm so relieved," Aina added. "I don't think I would want to even try going out in this."

"Has there never been a storm such as this in the years you've lived in the village?" Lucius asked.

"No," Ula said.

"Never," her sister added.

Through the night strange omens occurred across the land and around the hillfort. Trees snapped like twigs in a child's grasp, rain rushed in rivers to drown cattle and sheep, and a hillside across the valley crumbled with the weight of water and mud, exposing root and rock.

The entire night, Lucius listened for the horses' cries, and was only comforted when he could hear them, for when they paused, he worried that something worse had happened to them than the terror they experienced. He also listened to the clatter of roof tiles upon the hall, and wondered how many they were losing in the gale.

He stayed awake, watching Adara and the children sleep huddled together beneath the thick furs. A single clay lamp burned on a small table nearby where he sat in a folding campaign chair, squinting as he read one of the scrolls from his library, those precious items that had followed him across the Empire and provided him with comfort on the darkest nights. And he was awake most nights, rarely sleeping through to morning.

As the storm raged outside, and Lucius kept watch over his family, once in a while checking on the hall down below, he read from the scroll of Daphnis and Chloe which Longus himself had given to Lucius and Adara. The tale of the two youthful lovers on the island of Lesbos which the poet had recited to them at the Metellus domus in Rome, so many years ago, made him think of hot, flowery meadows above turquoise water where the sun glinted.

By lamplight, Lucius could remember his mother and sister, Adara and her family, listening to the poem's recitation in the peristylium of the Metellus domus, all of their faces rapt with interest at the tale.

Alene had been the one who invited Longus to dine with them.

Any time Lucius read poetry, she came into his thoughts.

He looked to Adara where she slept with the children as the wind howled outside, and remembered her face as Longus had recited his work, her cheeks rosy with wine and her eyes rarely leaving Lucius' the whole evening.

He spotted the two children hugging her as she slept, their sound, stable breathing pushing the furs up and down so very gently.

Where did you two come from?

He often asked himself the question, for time had flowed like quicksilver from the day he and Adara had met, and even more so now that they had Phoebus and Calliope.

So much time... He laid the scroll across his lap and stared at the lamp flame. *So much change...*

Diodorus had taught Lucius that change was constant, and not to be avoided.

Lucius did not like change in the areas of his life where he was content, the places of peace.

But his old tutor had taught him that even the most fervent wish of man, or even of an immortal, could not stop change.

"It is everywhere!" Diodorus had said, smiling during that particular lesson along the banks of the Tiber where they watched the fast-flowing water.

Lucius smiled sadly at the memory, for it was at that moment that he realized how much Diodorus himself had aged, changed in the years since their very first lesson.

He sighed.

After Einion and Briana's departure for Ynis Wytrin, life for his family had yet again taken on a new rhythm.

167

Change it seemed, was back.

His family slept before him, beneath the creaking rooftop that he had built.

We've had more time together these past few days, haven't we? Lucius thought, grateful for the time with Phoebus and Calliope, learning, teaching, playing.

At that moment, there was a loud crash of splintering wood outside, and Calliope sat bolt upright in the bed.

Here eyes were full of fear and found Lucius' straightaway.

"It's all right, my girl," he whispered, setting down the scroll and going over to her. "Just a tree breaking outside. Nothing to worry about."

"I saw fire, Baba. A great circle of fire." She gripped him tightly.

Lucius lay down beside her and put his arms about her little body, as if to shield her from the night.

"I'll always protect you," he said.

"I know, Baba. I know."

Lucius felt himself calm as he held his daughter and stared at the flickering lamp flame. Sleep finally caught up with him.

"The Gods were angry last night," Adara said as she got up from the bed, careful so as not to wake the children.

Lucius stood in the doorway of their cubiculum, already dressed in his bracae, boots, and tunic.

"It did seem that way. I think we'll have a lot of cleaning up to do today."

"Are Ula and Aina all right?"

"They're fine. I don't know that they slept very well, but they're happy the sun is peeking over the horizon."

"I'm sure everyone is happy of that," Adara said, lacing up her bracae and sliding a tunic over her head. Her hair was dishevelled and her eyes sparkled in the dim light.

"I love you," Lucius said suddenly.

She looked at him. "I love you too." She walked around and put her arms upon his chest. "Did you sleep at all, my love?"

"A little. Calliope helped me," he smiled.

"She does that, doesn't she?"

"Yes." Lucius kissed her and turned toward the door. "I'm going to check on the horses. I'll be back soon." He picked up his sword, slung it over his shoulder, and went out.

The horses were fine, if not exhausted from all the excitement of the previous night. One of the ponies, Twilight, was bleeding on the shoulder from crashing into the wall of her stable, but that was the worst injury.

The others stood scattered about the stable, manes ruffled, nerves shattered, but safe nonetheless.

It took some moments for Lucius to approach Lunaris who had raged for much of the night. It was unlike the stallion to be so unnerved, for he had carried Lucius into battle amid screaming Caledonians and other barbarians numerous times.

"Shhhh, boy," Lucius said. "It's all over now." Lucius led him back to his stall, and gave him some fresh hay.

Lunaris did not eat, but leaned in close to Lucius, his thick dappled neck and black mane pressing against him.

"I'm here..." Lucius said, wrapping his arms about Lunaris and patting him gently. He remembered the melody of one of the songs his men often sang to the horses to calm them after battle, and began to hum.

His voice flowed as best it could, like a river over rock in the grassy seas far to the East. The sound was soft and soothing, supposed to be as comforting as a warm summer breeze ruffling a horse's mane as the grass swished about his hooves.

After a couple of minutes, Lucius was able to step back from Lunaris long enough to get a brush from a nearby shelf, and set to working on the stallion. His hand brushed the smooth grey and white coat, and Lunaris, his muscles twitching, eventually bent his great neck down to eat the fresh hay.

"It's all right now, my friend," Lucius hummed, his voice still carrying some remnant of the melody.

There was a loud whinny from the stalls where Shadow and Twilight both stood waiting for the attention that was given to the elder horse in the stable.

"I'll be with you two soon," Lucius said, his voice lightening as the tension left both himself and Lunaris. "You too, Hyperion!" he called to Adara's horse.

The black gelding neighed loudly, his voice echoing through the stable, but this time it was not the sound of terror, but of impatience.

"It could have been much worse," Lucius said as he went around to the other three horses. "I swear I could see something on the rooftop."

"You did."

Lucius turned quickly at the woman's voice and immediately, his eyes locked onto those of Epona herself. He dropped to one knee.

"Goddess… I… What are you doing here?"

Epona smiled as she looked down at Lucius, her hand almost reaching out to touch the top of his head, but she refrained. She stood there in a ray of morning sunlight that came in through one of the windows, the light filled with dust motes that swirled around her.

"Am I not welcome, Metellus?" she said, her voice light.

"Always," Lucius answered, looking up at her.

As ever, her smile lifted his spirits. In Britannia and Caledonia, she had ever been with him and his men, in war and peace.

Rise, she said in Lucius' mind.

Epona walked past Lucius, just barely missing brushing his arm as she went to Lunaris.

"He is frightened of what you saw," Epona said, her hand stroking the stallion's head and muscular chest.

Lunaris calmed, as he always did at her touch.

"What was it that I saw?" Lucius asked.

"A creature of the Morrigan's… A beast meant to unsettle you and your family."

"Will it be back?" Lucius asked.

Epona was silent for a moment before answering. "No. I saw to that."

Lucius noticed a slash across the goddess' hand.

"You're hurt!" He had never thought it possible that a goddess could be wounded, but it seemed she could.

"It is inconsequential. It shall heal." She waved her hand.

"You need not have endangered yourself," Lucius said, stepping closer. He felt his heart tightening at the thought of the goddess enduring an injury. He wanted to take her hand, to kiss it, even though he knew such was not permitted between a mortal and immortal.

The goddess stared into Lucius' eyes for what felt like a long while. Then she spoke.

170

"What is important, is that your family is safe, thanks to you," she said.

"And our horses are safe thanks to you, lady," Lucius whispered. He could feel her close and, unable to stare into her brilliant eyes any longer, he closed his own.

Epona looked upon the mortal man before her, she felt the temptation to lean in and press her lips to his, but she did not. She received not only Lucius' prayers, but also those of his wife, and of his children, and so, with a great will, she stepped back from him.

"I will calm the others for you," Epona said, looking at the heads of the other horses where they peeked out at her from the stall doors. "They will be well."

Lucius opened his eyes. "And you?"

"I too will be fine. Do not worry," she said, her face serious again.

Lucius caught the gravity of the look she gave him and he knew it meant something to come, a shadow in the near future.

"It is going to begin again, isn't it?" Lucius asked.

Epona nodded.

"Why can't we live in peace?" Lucius said, his voice tired and wary.

"That is not the way of dragons, is it?"

And he knew the words to hold a truth that his ancestors had long discovered. The lives they led could be both a blessing...and a curse.

"Go back," she said. "Enjoy your family, and protect them."

"Are they in danger?"

"There is always danger...Lucius." Her eyes blinked slowly as she said his name. "But there is always goodness and strength, especially in your family. You must believe in that, even when things are at their darkest."

An image of a fast-blooming tree in a charred landscape burst into Lucius' mind then, and he was comforted by it as his eyes closed.

"Goddess?" he said, when he opened his eyes.

But she was gone, the horses calm and silent in each of their stalls.

Lucius smiled to himself, breathed deeply of the smell of fresh hay and wood, and went outside where the morning sunlight was splashing in the muddy puddles that dotted the hillfort.

The sun was full and warm upon the hillfort for the rest of that day, in brilliant contrast to the previous night. Apollo's sun beat down upon them, burning away the water and setting the world aflame with brilliant shades of emerald, and rich earthy brown.

After the morning meal, Ula and Aina went down to the village to reassure their families that they were well, and Lucius and Adara, with Phoebus and Calliope's help, began to pick up the bits of broken roof tile, shattered trees, and more that littered the ground about the hall and crops. The children especially worked at salvaging what vegetables they could from the churned garden.

When they had done what they could outside, Lucius and Phoebus set to work in the stables, mucking out the stalls and putting out fresh straw for the horses who were calmer now than they had been.

Epona's presence and touch had soothed them of their fear and panic.

When the work was done, the horses brushed down and fed, the wide doors were opened and they were all led out into the sunshine to run and stretch in the wide open space around the hill's plateau.

While the horses clipped at the grass in sunlight, their coats twitching at the stray flies darting in and out, the Metelli sat upon the grass eating some bread and goat's cheese, washed down with some cool water.

Lucius and Phoebus played with the latter's toy soldiers and horses as they ate, while Adara and Calliope lay upon their backs, gazing up at the shapes of clouds as they passed in the breeze.

A howl suddenly rent the air, and Lucius was upon his feet in a moment, his sword in hand.

"What's that noise?" Phoebus asked, his own wooden rudus gripped tightly in his hand, as Adara and Calliope came to stand by them.

Another tumultuous groaning broke in upon them, and Lucius stepped forward, his ear cocked, listening to the sound, as he twirled his sword, the sun glinting off of the blade. "Hooves," he said. "A lot of them." He turned to Adara. "Get the children inside!"

"I'll stay with you," Adara insisted, her mind going back to the other night at Crescens' villa.

"No!" Lucius said. Get them inside, and wait to see who it is. Bar the door."

Adara did not say anything for a few heartbeats, but as the sound became louder, closer, she grasped the children's arms and ran with them to the hall, her legs powering up the slope.

"Who is it, Mama?" Calliope asked as they went in.

"Probably Romans going to the depot," Adara said. "Your father is just being careful."

"Why does he need to be careful?" Phoebus asked. "He's Roman too. He's a hero of Rome!"

"Shhh!" Adara said, trying to calm her racing heart.

Outside, Lucius listened intently and realized the sound was coming up the wooded tunnel of the northeast gate. He did not know why the sudden urgency. A peel of thunder in a clear blue sky could do that, he supposed, but he had seen and heard much worse. The thunder of those hooves, and that howling, did not belong to their family peace.

He was wrong.

As the sound rushed up the road and through the gate, his heart relaxed and he felt a surge of happiness as the first draconarius came fluttering into view. He began to walk in the direction of the gate and depot station, directly for the armoured forms of Dagon, Barta, and the rest of the Sarmatian cavalry that now milled around him in the sunlight. He had forgotten that the dragon's sound - a sound that chilled the blood of all enemies upon the field - could give him such joy.

"Ave Praefectus Lucius Metellus Anguis!" Dagon yelled, and the salute was echoed by Barta, Lucius' trusted vexillarius, and the decurions Lenya, Badru, Vaclar. The mounts of three turmae stood still and raised their conti to Lucius who felt a chill run through him.

He had missed them.

Dagon swung down from his horse and strode over to Lucius, his eyes scanning the hillfort, before they embraced each other tightly, old friends reunited.

"I like what you've done with the place," Dagon said, turning around, and then focussing back on Lucius. "You've been busy." He smiled.

Lucius had known Dagon for a long time, the two of them having fought side by side for years by that point. He was one of his most trusted friends, and among the Sarmatians, that was saying a lot, for Lucius loved and trusted them all, and they him. But as

Lucius looked at Dagon, he knew right away that something was not right.

And Dagon knew he noticed. He put his hand upon Lucius shoulder, his voice low. "We will talk later." Then his smile returned "We've been given a furlough, and so I hoped we could impose upon your hospitality."

Lucius smiled. "Why do you think I've built barracks and extra stables and paddocks?" Lucius stepped around Dagon and took Barta's great thick arm. "My friend... It's good to see you. How is your eye?"

Barta squinted from the eye he had not lost in Caledonia and shrugged. "The other works well enough for two, Praefectus."

"Good!" Lucius smiled and nodded to Lenya, Badru, and Vaclar. "Good to see you, boys! Welcome!" Lucius spread his arms wide as they all gazed around the expanse of the grassy hill.

"It's bigger than I thought it would be," Dagon said. "You could hold out against legions up here."

"I don't know about that. Vespasian took this one over a hundred years ago. But it's good enough."

"Will it be an inconvenience to house all the men and horses?" Dagon asked.

"No... No. It should be fine. How many are you? Ninety-six?" Lucius asked.

"Less," Dagon replied. "We haven't received the new recruits yet from the Danuvius frontier. With the peace signed between Rome and the Caledonii, they're in no rush to bring more troops in. So, our three turmae are more like seventy men."

Lucius remembered all their faces, the men who had fallen in Caledonia, in forests and rivers of blood, and then the sacramentum ceremony from which his men had been banned. He felt his anger rising again at the betrayal, but pushed it away. This was his home, and he was able to welcome his friends, his warriors.

"The barracks on the slope of the plateau should house all of you, and the horses can go in the paddocks and stables on the north side over there," Lucius said, pointing.

"How about a bath, Praefectus?" Vaclar joked, remembering Lucius' propensity for cleanliness.

"Haven't built it yet Vaclar! If you want to bathe, you'll need to dip in the stream down the hill."

Dagon looked sidelong at Lucius. "No baths?"

"No."

"No Roman plumbing?"

"Not yet. We're going to build a bathhouse down the hill."

Dagon laughed. "I think you're becoming a Briton!"

Lucius smiled. "Maybe, my friend."

Just then there was a squeal as Phoebus and Calliope came running toward them with Adara in tow, the wind blowing her hair wildly about her head.

"Dagon! Barta!" the children yelled. They collided with the two Sarmatians.

Barta hauled Calliope into the air so that she took flight, giggling as she went up and down.

Dagon smiled at Phoebus and crossed his arms, nodding approvingly. "You've grown, Phoebus!" he said, and the boy stood proud, his rudus hanging easily by his side. "And from the look of you, I see your father has begun your training in earnest."

"Yes, he has!" Phoebus answered. "And I'm getting better and better every day!"

"I'm sure you are!" Dagon ruffled the boy's hair and turned to Adara who walked up and hugged him tightly.

"You're all most welcome here. It's good to see you." Adara stepped back and smiled at Barta and the rest of the men who all bowed to her. She had become the mortal mother of their camp, and their respect for her was as great as that which they had for Lucius.

Many of the men noted the bracae and tunica that she wore, and the gladius which she also carried.

"I see you've also been training," Dagon said to Adara.

"Yes. Briana's been training me very hard."

At the mention of her name, Dagon lit up even more, his features excited, his face red. "Where is she? I've not been able to sleep, I've missed her!"

Lucius and Adara looked at Dagon and he appeared to be a young boy whose heart has been pricked by Venus herself for the first time.

The Sarmatian stared at both of them and then nodded. "She's not here." He nodded slowly now, his smile fading as he looked up to the sky and then back at his men.

"No, my friend," Lucius said.

"All is well with her," Adara added quickly. "It's just that she and Einion received news from Ynis Wytrin that Etain was ill and needed to see them."

"Oh no! Should I go there to join her?"

Briana had told Dagon about Etain, and how much she had helped her and her brother, about the special connection she and Etain had.

"I should have been here for her," Dagon said.

"That might have been difficult," Lucius said. "But I'm happy you're here now, my friend. There is room for you...and Barta," he looked to the big Sarmatian, "in the hall with us. The rest of the men will find the barracks more than comfortable. Sigwyll has been stocking the stables too with fresh hay and oats for the horses."

"We'll not eat through your supplies, Lucius," Dagon had his hands up. "We've brought meat, cheese and bread with us, and the men are eager to use their wages in the villages nearby."

"That's just as well," Adara laughed. "We weren't expecting over seventy guests!" She hugged Dagon again. "It is good to see old friends."

Dagon looked at the Metelli and nodded, his face thoughtful. "It is indeed."

"Come!" Lucius said. "Phoebus and I will show the men the stables and barracks."

Adara watched Lucius wade into the midst of the warriors he had missed, noticed how happy he was, less thoughtful than he had been. It was a joy to see him that way, but she felt a familiar uneasiness at seeing them ride up, for it seemed that every time they came for him, they took him away or brought some ill-omened news.

"Come, my girl" she said, taking Calliope's hand. "Let's check on our supplies. I think a feast will be in order!"

"I love parties!" the girl said, dancing up the hill ahead of her mother.

Lucius, Phoebus, Dagon and Barta entered the hall a couple of hours later after seeing the troops settled and the horses cared for. It had taken even longer when Dagon and Barta had asked to walk the perimeter of the hillfort, both of them very interested in the aged fortifications and layers of defensive works.

"You're well-placed up here, Lucius," Dagon said as they had stood on the western rampart watching the sun dip away beyond the faint outline of the Tor where, Lucius told him, Briana was in Ynis Wytrin.

"She's so close," Dagon mused.

"But far," Lucius answered.

"Einion told me that Ynis Wytrin is protected by the Gods! He told me that not just anyone can make their way there, for they would be lost in the mists that surround it." Phoebus was excited as he spoke, but Lucius placed his hand upon his son's shoulder to calm him.

Dagon was quiet, staring into the distance. "A magical isle... Briana has told me much of it in the past."

"I'm sorry she's not here," Lucius said.

"I'll see her soon. I have to be content with that." Dagon turned to face Lucius. "I can't believe all the building you've done here since arriving. The barracks and stables, the hall, the temple, and now you say you're going to build a bathhouse?"

"What about the villagers, Praefectus?" Barta asked. "Can they be trusted?"

Lucius smiled at his bodyguard. He had missed him, and felt better for his family that these two and some of his men were there now. Barta had been scanning everything since they had arrived, even eyeing the villagers who had come to make offerings at the temple that Lucius had opened to them.

"The villagers are our friends, Barta. Do not worry. Their lords once lived upon this very mound, the men who watched over them. Now, it has fallen to me to protect them."

"Really? And not to Rome?" Dagon asked suddenly.

Lucius shook his head. "Of course, but... It's...the politicians of the civitas and other towns, notably Lindinis, the closest. They're not trustworthy men most of them."

"Ha! Lucius, you've been away from the politics of the court too long. What you say sounds normal."

Lucius stared directly at Dagon, his eyes hard, worried. "Dagon... Are you here to take me back to Caledonia?"

Dagon smiled and shook his head. "No. No such orders have been given to me. We are on furlough for the foreseeable future, so long as the Caledonii hold to the peace terms. You're stuck with us as long as you'll have us, I'm afraid."

"No greater news could I have from you, my friend!" Lucius sighed. He had been worried since they arrived, an ill feeling in his guts, but now that he had confirmed that the peace still held, he allowed himself to hold tighter to the hope that they would have more time in the place they had made their home. "Come! The men are settled, and encamped, the horses cared for... Now to eat around the fire!" Lucius clapped Dagon on the shoulder and led Barta away after Phoebus who had taken off like a sling stone toward the hall.

Dagon turned to look once more at the silhouette of the Tor fading into the dusky light, out of sight. *I'm here, Briana...* Then he followed after Lucius and the others. *Not all my news is good, my friend.*

Inside the hall, Dagon and Barta sat around the hearth fire and were served food upon plates by Ula and Aina. The two young girls were shy around the foreign-looking warriors, their arms covered in tattoos similar to the praefectus'. The men were kind to them, however, and the girls soon were used to them. Once the food was served and the kitchen cleaned, they went home for the night.

"You've hired help too, I see," Dagon asked.

"You know me," Lucius said. "I don't want slaves, but our new home is large and requires many hands to work it."

"You can put the men to work while they are here, Lucius," Dagon said. "After a few days of idling, they'll be happy for some work. Maybe they can help with building the bathhouse?"

Lucius nodded. "That's a good idea. The villagers have been very helpful, and hard-working, but when it comes to building, our men will indeed make a difference. It should get the job done sooner." He turned to Adara who sat with the children on either side of her. "I'll speak with Cradawg about it."

"Good idea," she said. "He might have his own crew committed already."

"Is he the brother of your Durotrigan friend, this Cul-wik?" Barta asked, having trouble trying to wrap his tongue around the Briton's name.

"Yes. And -" Lucius put his hand up. "Yes! He's trustworthy. Both of them are. You will meet them."

"Good." Barta drank more wine and then filled his cup from the pitcher that had been handed to him.

"Gods!" Dagon said. "If only we had been here a couple days sooner, we wouldn't have missed Briana." He stared into the fire, his thoughts swimming with her. In Caledonia, they had become close, very close, and he had thought of little else besides his command, her, and the news he had brought. The flames danced before him, waved at him as Lucius and Barta talked. He was tired with so much happening - the joyous thoughts rushing in his mind, the reunion with his friends who were his family too, and the tasks ahead that he had set himself, one a dream, the other a burden. He looked up and noticed Adara staring at him. She always knew when he was troubled.

"Children," she whispered to Phoebus and Calliope. "It is time you were abed. Come," she said, rising and pulling them up with her. "I'll put you to sleep. Say goodnight."

"Goodnight," the children said together to Dagon and Barta.

"May the Gods send you the sweetest of dreams, little ones," Dagon said, smiling.

Lucius made to rise to help Adara but she waved him back.

"I've got them, Lucius. Sit. You three need to talk. I won't be long."

The three men watched Adara make her way up the staircase.

Lucius looked back at his two friends. "Gods, it's good to see you!" He noticed Barta staring at Dagon, and then at the fire.

Dagon nodded. "My friend... There is something I need to tell you."

Lucius eyed Dagon now. He had begun to suspect something. Dagon was usually of a more cheerful disposition, especially around Adara and the children, but he had been quiet for much of the evening, even as more and more wine had passed his lips.

"Tell me," Lucius said, leaning forward and peering over the flames.

Dagon sighed. "Something happened a while ago. I was't able to tell you by way of a letter."

"What?"

"Alerio is dead, Lucius."

The silence was unbearable, hampered only by the cracking of the fire as the three men sat there.

Lucius felt his insides begin to burn and a great sadness welling up. Then anger. "How did it happen?" he asked.

Dagon drank and carried on. "Some time after you left Caledonia, a patrol was riding south on the main road when they spotted a cloud of carrion birds not far from the road, at the edge of some trees. They investigated and found four bodies. Alerio was one of them."

"How did you get this information?" Lucius asked, his voice even and hard.

"I know one of the cavalrymen who was on the patrol. Alerio was familiar to both of us. He told me in passing when I saw him after a briefing at Horea Classis."

"Did he recognized the other men?"

"They wore plain clothes, but he believes they might have been Praetorians. It was hard to tell for all the work the crows had done, but by the look of things, Alerio had fought all of them."

"What?" Lucius leaned forward, the fire hurting his eyes as they burned.

"They found his horse tied apart from the other three."

"How did he die?" Lucius could not help but ask questions for they helped to hold his emotions at bay.

"Blood loss, I'm sure. He had a pugio in his back, another wound in his side, and a barbed arrow deep in his thigh."

"Was..." Lucius cleared his throat. "Was he given the rites?"

"Yes. Of course. The troopers brought him back and the full ritual was carried out at Horea Classis."

"Gods..." Lucius thought of his oldest friend then. "Why was he out there in the first place?"

"That I don't know," Dagon said. "Lucius, are you all right?"

"I'll need to speak with the cavalryman who recognized him. I want to find out who did this." Lucius' fists were balled tightly, and desperate anger began to course through him.

"You can't," Dagon said softly.

Lucius' head turned quickly. "Why not?" he demanded.

"Because...the trooper's missing."

Silence again.

"Missing?" Lucius asked.

Dagon and Barta nodded.

"Lucius?" Adara's voice came out of the darkness at the far side of the hall. She came into the circle of firelight then, her eyes watery in the orange glow.

Lucius stood and went to her.

Adara wrapped her arms about him and he could feel her body shuddering. Then, she pulled back and looked up at him.

"Alerio is dead?" she asked.

Lucius nodded. It was unimaginable to hear it spoken aloud again, for Lucius had been hoping it was not true.

She had been coming out of Phoebus' room when Dagon had spoken the words, and the utterance of that news had winded her like a dagger to the stomach. For some minutes she had sat in the darkness of the upper floor breathing, her eyes burning.

Lucius held his wife tightly as her tears fell down her cheeks upon his breast. "I'll find out who did this," he said. "And I'll kill them."

"Lucius," Dagon began, standing and shaking his head. "You need to let this one go, for the sake of your family."

"What?" Lucius let go of Adara and stepped around the fire. "How can you say that?"

"For the same reason I did not write this news in a letter. His death occurred around the same time you left Caledonia, along the same road you were travelling."

"You don't mean that... But there's no reason for it!" Adara said.

Dagon breathed. "Something is going on at court, manoeuvrings that we are not privy to. You need to stay away as long as you can, and keep a low profile for now."

Lucius' mind spun out of control, and a ringing filled his ears then as he gazed at his wife and two friends.

"I need to be alone," he said. "I'm sorry. This was not the reunion I was hoping for."

"I know. I'm sorry to bring such sorrow into your home, Anguis," Dagon said. "But you need to be careful. We all do. Hopefully, here in the South, things are safer for you and your family." Suddenly, Dagon wanted more than ever to be with Briana, to ensure that she was well and safe.

Lucius stared at Dagon again, nodded, and turned to go. Words failed him, and though he saw the pain that the news brought to his friends, to his wife, he knew that he could provide no comfort in that moment. His best friend had been taken from him, and it may well have been his own fault.

Adara watched Lucius close the door to his tablinum and then turned to Dagon and Barta.

"He's lost too many friends."

"We all have," Barta said. "And we all grieve for them in our own ways, lady."

181

"Yes," Adara said, looking down at her tunic and flattening it awkwardly. "I...I should get to sleep."

"Shall I go in to see Lucius?" Dagon asked.

Adara shook her head. "No, no, Dagon. He...he needs his time. They were close friends."

"I know," Dagon said. "If it is fine, Barta and I will sit here a while longer."

"Our home is your home, Dagon. Please be at ease. I'm sorry-" Adara broke off, her hand covering her mouth as she went toward the stairs and up.

When she was gone, Dagon turned to Barta and they sat down heavily, the weight of their task lifted, but the pain only just beginning.

"We must help him," Barta said.

Dagon nodded. "We always do. We always will." Together they stared at the fire and finished the wine before going to their separate cubicula and falling into a deep sleep.

As darkness was at its fullest and most black upon the land outside, Lucius Metellus Anguis sat at the table in his tablinum, his mind turning over the news that Dagon had brought him. By the light of the oil lamp, he traced lines with the tip of his pugio in the African sand he kept in an ancient Etruscan dish. The act calmed him, but the thoughts whirling in his mind did not.

He had replenished his Samian wine cup five times, but the effects of the vintage eluded him. He was all too aware of the cloak of sadness and guilt he wore now. He had lost so many men, friends, in Caledonia, and now his very best friend, Alerio, was gone, perhaps murdered. The sketchy details frustrated Lucius no end.

He was also reminded of when Antanelis, another friend, had been murdered in Africa, and how Lucius and Alerio had investigated and brought the murderers to justice.

Here we are again... He longed for a world that was out in the open, not driving daggers into backs in the shadows, like a coward. Too many cowards had killed brave friends and skilled warriors.

Alerio's dead...

No matter how many times he said it to himself, it would not sink in. He felt as if he had let Alerio down in some way, even let the shade of his late sister, Alene, down too.

Alerio had been high in the ranks of the Praetorians, a hero due to his role in the foiling of Plautianus, the former prefect. He was also favoured by the emperor. How he came to such an end, far from base, was a mystery. How could he have been so vulnerable? The implications were horrendous, but more so, they enraged Lucius.

Alerio had hinted at his growing discomfort at court, Caracalla's lack of control, and the machinations within the Praetorian Guard itself. Had he been trying to flee others? Or was he trying to reach Lucius? It had not escaped Lucius that he was found upon the same road...that Alerio had, it seemed, left shortly after Lucius and his family.

"Gods..." he drove the point of his pugio into the tabletop. "Give me the strength to protect my family and friends. He had failed too much to protect those closest to him, and the thought of the noose growing tighter about his family was too terrible to endure.

Lucius took three deep breaths and focussed on the lamp light. He pictured Alerio's face, in happier times, before the weight of becoming a Praetorian centurion had burdened him. Ever since they were green recruits in Rome, setting out for Parthia with the emperor's legions, Alerio had always been one to laugh, to be up for an adventure. He had had Lucius' back, always, and, despite their differences, especially when it came to his love of Lucius' sister, he had always been a true brother to Lucius.

I was too caught up with my own life, my own command to be there for him. Lucius hung his head and stared at the point where his blade was planted in the tabletop.

There was a hesitant knock on the door, and Lucius looked up.

"Yes?" he pulled the dagger free.

Adara poked her head in, and even by the dim orange light, Lucius could tell she had been crying.

He stood up and went around the table to hold her.

She grabbed him and held tightly. "I can't believe he's gone."

"I know." Lucius didn't want to relay all of his suspicions and fears to her at that moment, for he knew how much Alerio had helped Adara and the children when they had arrived in Britannia. He had watched over them at all times, especially in the lion's den of the imperial court.

Adara shuddered as her tears fell, and Lucius held her close, his own tears running in smooth rivulets into her hair.

"It's like we've lost Alene all over again," Adara said.

Lucius felt his heart tighten, and he breathed deeply. "Tomorrow, we'll make offerings in the temple to him."

She nodded. "What about Phoebus and Calliope?"

"We should tell them. They should offer prayers to him also."

Adara nodded again, and looked up at Lucius. "Are we safe Lucius?"

"I won't let anything happen to you or the children, my love. And now Dagon, Barta, and the men are here... We're well protected. Trust me."

"I always have...but some things are bigger than us."

"It'll be fine."

Adara turned to go and held out her hand to Lucius. "You need to sleep."

"I can't. Not yet. You go ahead. I'll be along shortly."

Adara came back, kissed him, and then went out into the hall and upstairs.

Lucius sat in the tablinum for a while longer before going up. However, before sleeping, he went into each of the children's cubicula to check on them, to ask the Gods for their help in protecting them at all costs. It was only as he sat in the chair opposite his son's bed that sleep overtook him and Lucius nodded off to the beat of his shuddering heart.

As dawn broke upon the world the following morning, the Metelli filed out of the main hall that was their hearth and home, and made their way down from the high plateau of the hillfort toward the small temple at the southeastern sector of the hill.

As they walked, their heads covered for the ritual, the Sarmatians formed an avenue of honour for the comrade of their leader's fallen friend and ally. They too had fought alongside Alerio Cornelius Kasen in Numidia.

Lucius walked in the lead, carrying some of the sand from Numidia where he and Alerio had been stationed together at Lambaesis, and where Alerio had also met Alene and fallen in love with her.

Behind him, Adara walked slowly with the children, each of them carrying a small jug of milk, of honey, and of wine. Adara also carried a bunch of rosemarinus which would also be laid in offering. She looked down at the children and saw that their tears flowed freely, though they did not weep aloud. They had loved Alerio like an uncle.

It had been dark when Phoebus awoke to find his father sleeping in the chair beside his bed. He had seen his father's restlessness in sleep, the tears that ran from his closed lids as he slept. When he had woken him, Lucius had grabbed him and held him close. He had told him the terrible news that had arrived, and spoken of the courage they needed to muster to carry out the sacrificium for their friend.

"I will help you, Baba," Phoebus said, and Lucius had never been prouder.

It had been more difficult for Calliope to accept the death of Alerio, but she walked nonetheless beside her parents that morning, her courage melting the hearts of the battle-hardened warriors watching them pass.

As they approached the temple, Lucius saw that many of the villagers had arrived to watch, to give him courage and condolences in the misty morning light.

But Lucius saw only the temple and the light of the burning braziers within, those beacons that guided him into the cella and the images of the Gods. When he was inside the temple, Lucius stopped, and Adara and the children followed suit. He gazed at the lamps that had been lit beside the images of Apollo, Venus, Epona, Jupiter, Juno, Minerva and Mars.

The Gods gazed back at Lucius as he stepped forward to light a chunk of incense in the flame of one of the lamps and place it in a wide ceramic dish at the Gods' feet.

He raised his hands and closed his eyes.

"Gods who watch over us all, please watch over our departed friend and brother-in-arms, Alerio Cornelius Kasen. May he cross the dark river and find his way to Elysium to be among the heroes of ages past. Ever has he been loyal and brave..." Lucius faltered in his words, his voice caught in his throat, the news too fresh and raw in his heart to fully comprehend.

But it had to be done, for the sake of Alerio's shade.

"Please accept our offerings on his behalf," Lucius said as he slowly poured out the flower-fine sand in a circle about the smoking incense. Then he turned to see Phoebus come forward with the milk and pour it out.

185

Calliope came next with her small pitcher of honey which she added to the milk, something sweet for the Gods and the shade of the departed.

When the children had done their work, Adara stepped up to the altar, more slowly than them, and laid the bundle of rosemarinus in the flames before pouring the wine upon the mingled milk and honey.

"Rest and be well in Elysium...my friend-" her voice cut off from the sadness that overwhelmed her as she gripped Lucius' hand, and together they stood before the Gods with their children, praying for yet another who had been ripped from their lives.

"Gods..." Lucius said, "Oh Lady Venus... Please lead him to my sister, Alene. May they...may they be together now and know the happiness of which they were robbed." Lucius reached over and added another chunk of incense to the pile and it quickly caught, sparking and sizzling before settling into smoke.

Blue and grey haze rose into the air around the temple from the small windows set in the walls, as well as through the main doors, outside of which some of the villagers waited for the Dragon to exit.

Barta and Dagon stood there too with some of the men.

"I'll remain a moment," Lucius said to Adara.

"Don't be too long," she said. "I don't want to face everyone alone just yet."

Lucius kissed his children upon their heads. "You both did very well. You're very brave."

"I'm sad," Calliope said, clinging to her mother.

"We all are, my girl," Adara soothed. "And we will help each other through." She began to usher the children out into the growing light.

Lucius turned back to the altar where their offerings had begun to mingle and burn, and there before him, the Gods themselves stood looking at him.

Venus, Epona, and Apollo stood close to him, gleaming and bright, visible only to him, though their presence was felt by those gathered outside, something like a sense of impending Spring to lift the heart.

Lucius fell to his knees before them, his hands upon the stone floor, his face covered by his cowl.

Rise, Metellus... Apollo said in a voice that had seemed to follow Lucius the whole of his days.

Lucius stood slowly, his head still bowed as his eyes scanned their faces.

Venus approached him and ran her brilliant hand before Lucius' head and face, and over his heart. *We are sorry for the loss of your friend,* she said, her voice a song one wished never to end. *Rest assured, young Lucius, that Alerio and Alene are together.*

Lucius looked directly into the goddess' eyes for a moment at the words, and instead of the burning that should have occurred for a direct a look, a great relief and peace shot through him.

"Thank you..." he said, bowing again.

You need to be careful, Epona said suddenly.

Lucius looked to her, felt that she wanted to approach him too, but that she held back. "What is happening?"

Apollo stepped close now, his eyes, as ever, a whirling image of the heavens' brilliance. *Your enemies are plotting in the shadows, and will soon come into the open.*

"Enemies at court?" Lucius asked.

Yes, Apollo answered. *And others.*

"Others?"

The Morrigan has not forgotten her defeat, Epona said. *She has been watching you and your family.*

"My family?" Lucius felt anger rise, but the light with which Venus had blessed him overpowered it, and he felt his heart lighten at her smile.

Your family is safe, she said.

But you will be tested, Apollo added. *You will face attack on many fronts in the future.*

You need to accept help when it comes, Venus said.

And harness the strength of those who are, and wish to be, your allies. Epona took a step closer to Lucius and in her eyes she saw that strength and determination that had seen him through so many battles. It was a look that said she would not abandon him to fate.

"I'll be ready," Lucius said. "But, if I should be drawn away, please...please watch over my family for me." He scanned the faces of the Gods and saw there the love they had always shown him, a look of guardian parents, of love.

We are always there for you, Anguis, Apollo said, his voice more distant now. *You are never alone...*

Lucius blinked, and they were gone. Adara was beside him again.

"Are you all right, my love?"

He turned to her, his eyes bright and teary. "All is well," he said. His hand stroked the side of her cheek and he smiled sadly at her.

"Come... The children need us."

Together they walked out onto the porch of the temple where the children stood with Dagon and Barta.

Culhwch approached with Alma and their son, Paulus.

"We heard you had some bad news from the North," Culhwch said, staring at the two Sarmatians there.

"Sigwyll heard it from some of your men in the stables," Alma said, taking Adara's hands. "We're sorry."

"The Gods will watch over him," Lucius said to Culhwch, his eyes going to Dagon and Barta. "He will be missed."

"We are here for you," Culhwch said, his hand out. "You know that, right?"

"I know," Lucius said, taking his hand and squeezing. "And we are grateful."

"We came up with Ula and Aina this morning," Alma said. "I'll help them to prepare a meal for later. The dead should not go uncelebrated."

Adara felt her throat clench up with sadness and she squeezed Calliope tighter now. "That is very kind. Thank you."

Dagon laid his hand on Phoebus' shoulder then, reassuring the young boy that he was not alone in his grief.

"I can help you with the horses this morning if you like?" Paulus said to Phoebus.

"Thank you," Phoebus said, seeking approval to go from Lucius.

Lucius nodded and the two boys went up the hill toward the stables.

"Let's go to the hall," Lucius said to all of them. "The day has just begun, and there are many yet to come."

Lucius, Adara, and Calliope walked with the rest up to the plateau and the hall, and along the way he greeted the villagers who waited to make their daily offerings at the temple.

Later that morning, Adara, Alma, Ula, Aina, and Calliope were at work in the kitchen to prepare a feast in honour of Alerio.

Outside, the sun was bright and warm where Lucius sat with Dagon, Barta and Culhwch upon the fallen logs on the south side of the hall.

188

Lucius was distracted much of the time, his thoughts pulled back to the temple, to the Gods, for whenever they visited him or spoke to him, there was a lingering sense of their presence, the same as when one brushes against a full green herb like rosemarinus and the sweet fragrance stays with you for a spell.

Dagon spoke with Culhwch, while Lucius was lost in thought, and found that he liked the Briton and his plain honesty. It seemed that the Gods had blessed Lucius in the people who lived in the surrounding area. *That's good,* Dagon thought to himself. *I have a feeling difficult days lay ahead.*

Just as he thought it, Lucius turned to him.

"Tell me what is happening in Caledonia now."

Dagon put down his rough clay cup and put his hands upon his knees. "I don't think the peace will last."

Lucius felt his heart sink, but if he was honest, he had known that it would not. He had told the emperor as much and been ignored. His family's idyll in the South had helped him to forget that worry.

"The Caledonii are restless, and even though Argentocoxus appears to be calm, there are rumours of meetings between tribes. There is another leader, a man called 'The Wolf'. Nobody has seen him yet, but the talk is that he and Argentocoxus might be making an alliance."

"Has the emperor not investigated this? What about Caracalla?"

"Caracalla, along with Picus, are held up in Horea Classis for now, and he sees no reason to threaten the peace while the Caledonii have done nothing."

"And the emperor?"

"Lucius...the emperor is not well." Dagon glanced at Culhwch for a moment, wary of the words he was uttering in front of the Briton, but he knew Lucius trusted the man, so he continued. "He is in Eburacum with the empress and Papinianus."

"What does Papinianus say?"

"He cannot gainsay Caracalla. Severus will not hear ill spoken of his son, even from the Praetorian Prefect."

"There is nothing new there, I suppose," Lucius said. "Let's hope the emperor regains his strength. He's been ill for years and yet managed to avoid Death."

Dagon drank from his cup again.

"What about the men?" Lucius asked. "Are they well?"

Dagon smiled. "They miss their praefectus. As do the troops of the legions stationed in Caledonia and elsewhere!"

"What do you mean?"

"Everywhere we've ridden, troops ask us of your whereabouts and when you will be returning."

"Have the legions turned against us?"

"No, no, Lucius. The opposite! They ask for you, it seems. Not everyone, of course, but now and then, some group of soldiers on our way here, on or off duty, asked us about you. But they asked in such a way that made me think they look up to you."

"Strange..." Lucius rubbed his chin.

"Not really, when you think of it, Praefectus," Barta said, speaking for the first time. "What you did on the front during the war...the Boar...the bloody victories on the edges of the highlands...it is more than Caracalla has ever done."

Lucius felt a chill run up his spine as he looked around the small circle of friends. For a commander to be so favoured by the legions, even in a whisper, was a dangerous prospect.

"The troops miss the Dragon," Barta added.

"Then I'm glad I'm here for the moment," Lucius said, frowning.

190

VI

ORDINIS POSTULATIONES

'The Demands of the Ordo'

Autumn was upon the land, and the bounty and blessings of Ceres had begun to grace market stalls and tables across the land. It was time for gathering stores for the coming winter, which was some time off, but still, when the harvest was a good one, the opportunity to stock up could not be passed by.

The village below the hillfort was no different, and rather than carting all of the produce and goods to Lindinis, the local Britons decided to set up their tables and stalls along the single street of their village.

Culhwch and Alma stood at theirs with Paulus, getting ready to sell or barter small bunches of turnips and carrots, cabbages and other greens. The Gods had blessed them with an overwhelming crop and so they sought to share with their friends and neighbours once they had stored away enough for themselves. There was also a table with various wares Culhwch had made, cups, plates, bowls and platters.

Almost everyone who walked by greeted the family.

Culhwch stood in the middle of the road slapping neighbours on the back and talking with others while Alma advised some of the younger girls about matters that would have made the brawny Culhwch smile. He looked up and down the street at the faces of everyone passing by, the groaning, plentiful tables lit by the warm morning sunlight, the children running in and out of the groups of adults, playing freely and full of joy.

"I haven't seen everyone so happy in a long while," Cradawg said as he came up behind his brother.

"Me neither." Culhwch slapped his brother on the back. "When I think of the stories of the past around here, the death and suffering of our people when Rome first came to these shores, it is hard to imagine. Now, another Roman has come among us, and the Gods smile upon and grace us all."

Cradawg nodded as he looked around and waved at Silvius who stood down the road speaking with the local pelt seller. He turned back to his brother.

"The market day in Lindinis is tomorrow, you know."

"Ach, what of it?" Culhwch waved it away. "Why go all the way there when we have what we need here?"

"Because it's what's expected."

"I don't really care what the ordo of Lindinis expects!" Alma added from her small gathering of women.

Cradawg turned to her. "You should, sister-in-law. They don't take kindly to competition, and they have been trying to compete with Durnovaria itself.

"Brother, you've been doing business for too long with the Romans there. Surely they wouldn't mind people from the same village getting together to barter and sell to each other."

"But it isn't just people from your village who are here, is it? Look around. I've noticed others from the neighbouring villages too."

"It's a beautiful day and everyone is out for a nice stroll in the morning sunlight. What's wrong with that?" Culhwch stepped away to get two cups of beer from the table across from him where the brewer had just set up. He came back and handed one to Cradawg. "Drink, and be at ease. You're not working on the baths for the hillfort today, are you?"

"Not today. There's a hold-up with the shipment for the pipes from Lindinis. I need to go there tomorrow anyway."

"Well then! You can represent us all at their market day!" Culhwch laughed and drank, and Cradawg shook his head and smacked his little brother on the back of the head, making him splutter beer and laugh.

"Salve Metelli!" Culhwch burst out a moment later. The two brothers laughed as Alma came up behind both of them and gave them a wallop each before going to meet Lucius and his family.

Lucius and Adara were walking up the road holding their children's hands, greeting some of the villagers. They introduced Dagon, Barta and some of the other Sarmatians who had decided they wanted to explore the world outside of the hillfort and spend some of their hard-earned coin.

At first, the villagers seemed taken aback from the strange tattooed warriors of Sarmatia, but when they saw how Lucius

192

befriended his men, and the respect and reverence the warriors had for him in turn, all worries drifted away, and the gathering was uplifted.

Lucius was the only one armed among his men, his sword at his back, tucked beneath his black cloak. It still felt strange to him to go out in the world absent his cuirass, arm guards or greaves, but it also felt good.

As the villagers observed him, the older ones thought he might have been one of their Durotrigan princes of old, their protector with a sword.

Young Paulus came running up to see Phoebus, and the boy's eyes went to the tattooed dragons upon Lucius' forearms. He had not seen them before as the elder Metellus had always had them covered by leather arm guards when he saw him.

Alma came up after her son to greet Adara and Lucius.

"I'm so glad you came!" the tall Durotrigan said, grasping Adara's hands tightly.

Adara felt warmed by the welcome, for rarely had she felt such sincerity and kindness, certainly never in the imperial court. "Thank you, my friend," Adara said, looking back at Alma and squeezing her hands tightly. "Seems everyone is in high spirits today."

Alma's hand reached up and touched Adara's black curls gently, like a kindly sister. "Come," she said to the children. "Paulus and I have saved you each a pie. They're the best in the village," she whispered.

Adara smiled at Lucius and went with Alma and the children to their table along the road.

"Good morning!" Lucius said to Culhwch and Cradawg, approaching with Dagon and Barta.

"Good morning, Praefectus," Cradawg said.

"I don't think you've met my princeps, Dagon, and my vexillarius, Barta."

"No, I haven't." Cradawg nodded at the two Sarmatians who greeted him in return.

"They are also my great friends and allies," Lucius said. "All my men are. I hope folks don't mind if many of us have come today."

"How could we mind?" Culhwch said. "Dagon, Barta," he greeted them, then stepped aside to get cups of beer for them.

Dagon and Barta accepted the cups and drank.

"It's good," Barta said.

"Isn't it?" Culhwch laughed, then turned to the brewer at his table. "Great batch this year, Dubnus!"

The brewer nodded and placed his hand on his heart.

"Is my wife's cousin up at the hillfort?" Culhwch asked. "We thought today he might be down here and get a bit more cheerful."

"Sigwyll is already working in the stables," Lucius said. "He seems happiest in there."

"Aye. He's more one for horses than people," Culhwch agreed. "Alma's grateful to you for giving him the work. He's improved much, despite his sullenness at home."

"We've all had our share of tragedy on the battlefield," Lucius said, looking to his friends. "It wears hard upon a man's soul."

Culhwch looked upon Lucius and the group of warriors behind him. *Perhaps I have been too hard on Sigwyll?* he thought. "Come, let me show you all our village, and if you have coin to spend, the people will love you forever!" he laughed as only Culhwch could, and they spread out among the crowd to look upon tables of food and produce, pelts, pots, leather goods and more.

"Praefectus," Cradawg said as he fell into step beside Lucius.

"Don't worry about work on the villa today, Cradawg. We've been managing well enough on the hill. One day delay won't make such a difference, will it?"

"That's just it, Praefectus. It'll be more than one day. There's a hold-up with the pipe shipment from the fabricum in Lindinis. I'm going there tomorrow to see what it's all about."

"Thank you. Strange though, isn't it? I thought we had all of it worked out."

"Me too," Cradawg said. "But I'll get to the bottom of it. Don't you worry. The men are ready to work and get it all done before Saturnalia, you'll see."

"I don't doubt it," Lucius said.

Cradawg stepped aside to speak with Silvius who was providing the lumber for the baths.

"This village reminds me of those back home a little," Dagon said to Lucius.

"If we didn't live on the hillfort," Lucius said, "I wouldn't mind living here myself."

"Salve, Praefectus!" the tavern owner called from across the way.

Lucius waved back and smiled.

Dagon and Barta looked about them and saw that everyone who looked in Lucius' direction was smiling at him and waving.

"Anguis," Dagon whispered. "I think you've found your place in the world. They all adore you."

"The feeling is mutual, my friend. In all our travels across the empire, I've not met kinder folk. But I'm not interested in adoration. I just want a peaceful place to raise my family at last."

"I think you've found it, Praefectus," Barta said, smiling shyly at a maid selling potatoes.

Dagon smiled at the big Sarmatian's shyness. "Have you thought of bringing your mother and younger brother and sister here?" he asked Lucius.

"I have," Lucius said, shaking hands with another passerby. "Salve! But I'm not sure the winters would be to their liking. They love Etruria."

"Have you written to your mother lately?"

"It's been too long since," Lucius admitted. "I've been meaning to."

"Lucius!" Adara joined them. "We do need to buy supplies. The stores are lower now with all the extra people."

"I know. Let's get to it," Lucius said, kissing her on the cheek.

"The men are ready to purchase for themselves, Adara," Dagon said. "We don't want to be a drain on you."

"Ha, ha!" Culhwch laughed, turning to Lucius and Dagon. "I see that many of them are already crowding the butcher down the road. I'll go mediate and get them a good deal!" He rushed off to the butcher's table.

The next few hours were spent in friendly converse with the villagers, and a flurry of purchasing as the Sarmatian purses got lighter, and their arms more weighed down with hocks of ham, breads and other goods - a new cloak here, a new knife there. The warriors were Spartan when it came to possessions, for they were mobile and all had to be taken on horseback, but as they expected to stay at the hillfort for the term of their furlough, they allowed themselves to acquire more than was usual.

The villagers were thrilled, and new friendships were forged.

The small village, usually sleepy and idyllic, was now as festive as the Forum Romanum on a feast day, only much safer and friendlier. Carts began to roll in from other villages and the sun was

195

warm and bright in the blue sky above. Crowds of people milled
everywhere along the road, in front of the stone Roman structures of
the village, as well as upon the grass that surrounded the native
roundhouses in the fields surrounding the main trackway.

As Lucius walked and talked with his friends and the people of
the village, he wondered at how very different life there was
compared to the North. *Perhaps this is the Pax Romana I've fought
so many years to defend?*

Even Phoebus and Calliope ran free with some of the other
children of the village, racing upon the grass, playing at tag, and
playing with the locals' animals. Adara and Lucius kept their eyes
upon them, as did Barta, but there was little need to worry.

Truth be told, Lucius and Adara felt joy seeing their children run
a little wild. They too were developing bonds of friendship.

"For you, lady Metella," a young woman came up to give Adara
a bouquet of autumn flowers accented with wheat.

"Why... Thank you," Adara said to the girl. "You don't need to
give me anything, dear."

"For my grandmother," the girl said. "Since she's been going up
to the temple every day, the Gods have smiled on her. She even
seems younger!"

"Younger?"

The girl nodded. "I wanted to thank you, and -" She looked at
Lucius who turned to her smiling. "A...and you, Praefectus. I
haven't seen so many smiles in our village before."

Lucius smiled back and put his arm about Adara before the girl
trotted off, her face red about her own smile.

"I never would have thought that -"

"What, my love?" Adara asked.

But Lucius' attention had been torn away from the crowd to a
black shadow down the road. He turned to Barta behind him.

"Black cloak down the way. He just went in between those two
buildings."

"I saw him, Praefectus," Barta said, stepping forward and
motioning for two more Sarmatians to follow him.

"What is it?" Adara asked, more urgently this time. "Lucius?"

He was still staring in the direction of the man he had seen, his
eyes following Barta and the other two. He was about to go after
them when he heard loud voices behind him, one of them Culhwch's.

"We're not breaking any laws, Decurion!" Culhwch said, his voice angrier than it ever had been since Lucius had known him.

"Isn't that Serenus Crescens?" Adara asked Lucius.

Lucius waited to see Barta a moment longer and when the big Sarmatian came into view he shrugged his shoulders. Whoever the black figure was, had disappeared. Lucius indicated Phoebus and Calliope and Barta nodded. He then walked over to where Culhwch and the tall form of Crescens stood face to face.

A crowd had formed around the two men and Alma now stood beside her husband arguing with Crescens and two other ordo members Lucius remembered from the villa banquet, Cassius Bucer and the animated Renato Tulio.

"What's going on here?" Lucius pushed his way into the circle.

Crescens stopped speaking suddenly, his demeanour suddenly calmer upon seeing Lucius. He bowed.

"Praefectus Metellus. I'm surprised to see you here."

"Why?" Lucius said. "My home is nearby." He pointed to the hillfort sloping up from the field beyond the village. "My family is here to enjoy time with friends and purchase some supplies."

Crescens smiled at Culhwch and then looked back to Lucius. "Well, you see, Praefectus. That's part of the problem. They should not be holding a market here. The market is in Lindinis tomorrow."

"We're not holding a market!" Culhwch said.

"We're holding a harvest celebration in our village," Alma added. "There are no laws against that, Decurion Crescens."

"I'm sure this is just a misunderstanding," Lucius said, coming between the two parties. He spotted Cassius Bucer eyeing him, but ignored him, focussing on Crescens. "There is no law that says a village may not celebrate. In fact it is encouraged as far as I know, especially in lands where the Pax Romana has held sway for over a hundred years. I'm sure you are not against orderly gatherings such as this on a fine day. And most here are likely to go to market in Lindinis anyway on the morrow. Am I correct?" Lucius turned to look at the villagers, many of whom nodded or shouted 'yes'.

Lucius turned to Crescens and the other two. "Besides, you needn't worry now. Three turmae of my men from Caledonia have just joined me on furlough at the fort. If there were anything to dissuade trouble, it would be them, I think. Don't you agree?"

Crescens' eyes darted around the crowd where he saw the dark, tattooed Sarmatian warriors closing in on all sides, standing tall among the villagers, some drinking, others eating, and others with a woman on their arms.

Lucius wanted to smile at the strength his men gave to the villagers, but he forced himself not to. "Not to worry," he called to the crowd. "The decurions are our friends and are here to speak with me!"

The crowd began to disperse and people went back to their drinking, idle talk, and eating.

Lucius looked to make sure Barta had gathered the children and was relieved to see them with Adara again, Barta standing beside her. He extended his hand to Crescens. "How is Sabina?" Lucius asked. "You must thank her for a lovely evening."

Crescens and the others relaxed.

"Ah," Lucius nodded to Dagon who stepped up beside him. "Decurions, this is my princeps, Dagon of Sarmatian. He just arrived with a portion of our ala from Caledonia with news for me."

"Gentlemen," Dagon said, nodding to the three men.

"What news from the North, Praefectus?" Renato Tulio asked, stepping forward.

"Oh...nothing to concern you. Military matters," Lucius said. "The emperor has not recalled me, so I am able to enjoy a longer furlough here in this lovely part of Britannia."

"Ah, well..." Crescens was his old self again. He smiled and turned to walk with Lucius up the road in the direction of the river and hillfort. "I must confess that our appearance here was not to interrupt the celebrations of this lovely village."

Lucius nodded, happy that he was able to lead the decurions away. He looked over his shoulder to ensure Adara and the children were following. They were, along with Dagon and Barta and the rest of the Sarmatians who had joined the festivities.

"You wanted to see me?" Lucius asked Crescens.

"Yes, Praefectus. There is a matter we wish to discuss with you."

"We can do so over a cup of wine," Lucius said, motioning for the others to follow before leaving the village and taking the small track that led to the hillfort's southwestern gate.

The three decurions glanced at each other, Bucer and Tulio not wanting to walk all of the way, but Crescens scowled and followed Lucius. Their slaves followed with the horses.

Adara and the children, along with Barta and Dagon went more quickly ahead of them, Phoebus and Calliope running all of the way, laughing as they went, pointing to the trees upon the ancient fortifications where ravens cawed and croaked from the thinning branches of autumn.

"You seem well-liked by the people in these parts, Praefectus," Crescens said amiably.

"They are good people," Lucius said, turning to look at the other two decurions following slowly behind them, their faces red.

"And I see the construction of your baths are well underway," Crescens pointed to where he could just see construction around the south-eastern bend of the hill, the walls about waist high at that point.

"Ah, yes," Lucius said, planning to take that up with the three men when they were in the hall.

They walked alongside several villagers, mostly the elderly, who were making the trek into the fortress.

"You allow the peasants to enter your home, Praefectus?" Bucer asked, his voice dripping with disdain.

Lucius turned to him. "This fortress was once their ancestral seat of power. Now it is a Roman supply station and my home. In the interests of our Pax Romana, I'm allowing them to visit the temple I have built. They were making offerings to the Gods long before this place ever fell to Rome's legions."

"A risky business, Praefectus," Tulio said. "Allow them in at all hours and they'll never leave."

"We haven't had an issue to date," Lucius said, his legs taking him up the steep slope after his family. He found it curious that Crescens forced himself to match his pace while the other two fell quickly behind, their faces almost purple.

Crescens looked up to see several heads ranging along the fortifications and looked at Lucius. "You have manned the walls?"

Lucius stopped and stared at him. "Not at all. My men are simply stretching their legs. I can't expect them to stay in their tents or upon their horses all day everyday. They've never seen a fortress like this and are curious about its build."

"I see," Crescens said, turning to wave to the others to catch up.

They passed through the gate and the plateau spread out before them, the hall towering above, surrounded by patches of crop, horse paddocks, stables and barracks.

Lucius pointed out the temple to the decurions and waved to several of his men who saluted him.

"They salute you even on furlough?" Bucer asked.

"It is a sign of respect. They are free to come and go as they like," Lucius said.

They reached the flat area outside of the hall and Lucius led them through the double doors inside.

Phoebus was setting light to the hearth fire, while Calliope and Adara went to the kitchens to prepare food, with cups of water and wine.

"You have no couches?" Tulio's voice registered shock and dismay. "Really, Praefectus! A man of your standing dining upon the ground or upon stumps of hewn wood. It's unheard of!"

Lucius laughed. "I can see how you might find it surprising, especially after such a lavish feast at Serenus Crescens' villa. I may yet have couches made, but for now, this suits us just fine."

The three decurions watched as Adara brought in a tray of food and wine and laid them upon a table outside the hearth circle.

Lucius poured for the four of them, as well as Adara.

She looked silently at him as she bent over the bread and cheese upon which she poured olive oil. She could see Lucius was frustrated with the three men, resentful that they were there. She placed her hand upon his and he calmed.

He smiled at her and turned to the three men. "If you prefer, gentlemen, we can go to my tablinum."

"I think that would be preferable," Tulio said. "Excellent idea!"

Lucius nodded to Barta and Dagon.

The two Sarmatians watched as the decurions of Lindinis passed them on the way to the tablinum, and then went to sit at the hearth fire with Adara and the children.

"What do they want?" Dagon asked once the door of the tablinum was closed.

"I don't know," Adara said. "But I don't trust them." She did not like the idea of Lucius holed up in that room with them. *Vipers!*

Lucius lit the lamps in the tablinum and arranged three chairs in front of his table while he settled in his campaign chair on the other side.

"To the Gods," Lucius said, tipping some of his wine upon the floor.

"To the Gods," they repeated and drank together.

After a few moments, Crescens cleared his throat. "I'm glad to see you have settled in well here. Though I would have expected to see you in Lindinis more often, Praefectus. There is so much more we would like to show you. Perhaps you could bring your troops to spend some of their hard-won coin at the market tomorrow?"

"I'll certainly make them aware of the market," Lucius answered, picking up his pugio with the eagle-headed pommel from the table, turning it idly over in his hand. "For myself, and my family, we will not be able to come."

"Oh?" Bucer said, leaning forward.

"Not that we do not wish to," Lucius answered. "It's just that we received word of the murder of a friend in the North, a good friend of our familia, and it has unnerved us. I have much to think about."

"I'm sorry to hear of it, Metellus," Crescens said. "Was he one of your men?"

"He used to be…during the Parthian campaign, and in Numidia. We joined up together in Rome. He was a Praetorian centurion."

"A Praetorian centurion murdered?" Tulio asked.

Lucius nodded, trying to control the anger he felt rising again.

Crescens noted his discomfort and sought to change the conversation. If the praefectus were angry or disturbed, he would not be receptive to his request. "I myself have lost many friends in dubious ways. It is no easy thing."

"No. It isn't." Lucius stared into his cup and drank again.

Bucer and Tulio gazed uncomfortably about the tablinum, the hanging weapons, the scrolls in their pigeon holes at the back of the room, the odd Etruscan dish upon the table before them.

Crescens stared at Lucius, trying even more to take the measure of the man. He was about to speak when Lucius started first.

"I was wondering if you could tell me something."

"Yes?" Crescens said.

"You saw the bathhouse we are building beside the brook?"

Crescens nodded.

"Cradawg, my builder - I believe you are familiar with him - he told me that there has been a hold-up in obtaining the pipes required for the baths. Something about being denied supply by the Lindinis fabricum. Do you know what the reason may be?"

Crescens shifted in his seat, but his eyes did not leave Lucius'. "No. I do not. But I can look into it for you."

He's lying to me. Lucius could tell. All three of the men stared back at him.

"I thank you," Lucius smiled.

"Think nothing of it," Crescens said. "No one can say the Lindinis ordo does not get things done."

"Speaking of which," Bucer spoke up now, setting his wine cup upon the table before him. "Praefectus, you seem to have settled down quite nicely in the area. Your family is happy here?"

"Very happy," Lucius answered, his face plain. "As you could see when you arrived."

"Yes...well... As Lindinis is the closest town to you here, and the place where you will undoubtedly do most of your marketing and purchasing of supplies, it would be of benefit to you and your family, I assume, if the town were to grow and thrive?"

"That stands to reason, yes. Of course," Lucius said. "But not too big, however. You wouldn't want another Rome or Londinium marring this beautiful countryside."

"We all left Londinium to get away from the city!" Tulio said, shaking his head. "But a town can thrive and remain a manageable size."

"Yes, I suppose," Lucius said, his fingers together.

"Praefectus..." Crescens spoke and silenced the other two. "What my fellow decurions of the ordo are wondering is if you have given any more thought to our conversation of the other night, as to whether you might - whenever you next see the emperor or Praetorian prefect - if you could speak on behalf of the ordo of Lindinis in asking the emperor to grant the town the status of civitas. It would mean so much to our little corner of Britannia and be of great benefit to all of us."

"And all of the local Britons too!" Tulio threw in.

Lucius was about to start shaking his head, but stopped himself. "Gentlemen... I'm afraid you overestimate my political sway at court. To put it plainly, I have none. I'm just a soldier. I could send a letter to the Praetorian prefect and mention it, but I cannot promise it will get past his clerk."

"I do not think we overestimate you, Praefectus," Crescens began again. "We heard speak of you even before you arrived here from the North. The 'Dragon Praefectus' they call you. The man who saved Caesar Caracalla and brought down the corrupt Praetorian Prefect, Gaius Fulvius Plautianus! Almost every soldier I've had converse with has mentioned you when I've asked about the campaigns in Caledonia-"

Lucius held up his hands for them to stop. He did not like to revisit those dark days hidden in the recesses of his mind.

They continued.

"You seem to be very popular among the troops," Bucer said, his eyes set on Lucius, no sign of a smile upon his face. "Surely the Praetorian prefect would take notice of that if anything?"

Crescens turned abruptly to his colleague, his face as hard as dark marble.

Bucer said nothing more, but took up his cup and drained it.

Crescens turned back to Lucius. "Praefectus, we feel privileged to have you here in our small corner of the empire. We feel safer. The ordo is made up of ten men, and ten men only. But, we would like to extend membership to you, ex officio, as a man of the world who might better advise us on how things are done at the higher levels. We could learn much from you."

Lucius nodded at the flattery, though it made him like the men before him even less. He had grown tired of political games, but it seemed he could not escape them wherever he went, whatever he did.

"I've no wish for public life of any sort," Lucius said. "I abandoned the cursus honorum long ago when I joined the rank and file, and I was happy to do so." Lucius knew he needed to show some good faith, however. If anything, so that they could get the building supplies to Cradawg so that they could have working baths before the winter.

"That is a pity," Tulio said.

"But I wish to help...if I can," Lucius continued. "I'll send a letter to the Praetorian Prefect, Papinianus so that he might place the idea before the emperor if the occasion to do so arises. That's the best that I can do."

"That is more than enough," Crescens said, his face softening, though his eyes remained hawk-like.

Lucius poured them each a little more wine. He still needed to be seen to be a good host.

The conversation died and an awkward silence settled over them. Lucius sought to break it and see them gone.

"How is your dear wife, Crescens? Adara and I had a lovely time at your home."

"We enjoyed having you, Praefectus," Crescens nodded.

"Sabina surely knows how to entertain, Crescens," Tulio said. "You're a lucky man!"

"Are you well, though?" Lucius leaned forward on the table. "I mean, after the attack? The evening did take an ugly turn."

"Thanks to you, Praefectus, it was prevented from being worse."

"A soldier's instinct is all," Lucius waved it off. He could still feel the wound pulling where the assassin's blade had cut him. "Have you found out any more about who might have done it?"

"I think it quite clear that the swine at Ynis Wytrin are responsible. They have heard of our plans to levy taxation on them, though they have always been exempt."

"Who knows what treasures they harbour in their isle!" Bucer's fists were clenched, and he bore a hungry look in his eyes.

This was something the ordo had evidently been discussing long before Lucius had come into the conversation at Crescens' villa.

"You're sure about this?" Lucius asked the three men. He stood now, his arms crossed, staring down at them.

"Of course!" Crescens was now standing too. He left his chair and walked around behind his two colleagues as if he were addressing the council. "It seems quite obvious to us."

"Really?" Lucius said calmly. "Because, I've looked into the matter myself...asked some questions...and it seems quit clear to me that Ynis Wytrin was not responsible for the attack upon us at your villa. In fact, by all accounts, they are an extremely peaceful people who want nothing of the outside world."

"May I ask, Praefectus, with whom did you speak about this matter?" Crescens stared at him from behind Tulio and Bucer.

"It makes no difference who, suffice it to say that it is someone I trust."

Lucius and Crescens eyed each other for an uncomfortable moment across the room, the only sound Tulio's heavy breathing and the guttering of the lamps upon the table. The sounds of Sarmatian voices and horses came in through the high window of the tablinum, and it appeared to serve as a slight reminder to the three ordo members of where they were, that Lucius' loyal men were everywhere.

However, Crescens made one last attempt to bring Lucius around.

"I wonder, Praefectus, if you have heard the tales of the Durotrigan king who sat atop this very fortress before the invasion?"

"I have, yes."

Crescens smiled. "It was supposedly he who invited a group of refugee Christians to settle in Ynis Wytrin alongside Druids and other enemies of Rome."

"Your point of this bit of history?" Lucius could feel the anger rising again, but he held his tongue before the guests.

"Nothing really," Crescens smiled but looked down at the floor. "Just that others might think you fancy yourself the new king upon the fortress, seeking to protect his subjects, just like that one of the Britons long ago."

"Excuse me?" Lucius stepped around the table just as Tulio and Bucer stood.

"Oh, I mean nothing by it toward you personally," Crescens said, his hands up and his demeanour friendly as Lucius approached. "I know...*we* know...that you are a man of Rome, and absolutely loyal to the emperor. I only say this as a warning that others might perceive your protection of Ynis Wytrin and the local Britons as something more unpleasant."

"Tongues wag terribly in the provinces," Bucer added.

Tulio was silent and beginning to sweat a little.

"We are all Rome's subjects," Lucius said, "the Britons the same as you or I. I do not seek to rule anything or anyone. I only seek the truth, in all aspects of life. And I would see that my own actions give me a clear conscience."

"Of course. As do we all." Crescens crossed his arms. "We are all Rome's subjects, and for that privilege, we pay our taxes. Why then should Ynis Wytrin be any different?" Crescens relaxed, and decided to pull out of the confrontation. "We must go back to Lindinis now before it is too late in the day."

"Thank you for the wine, Praefectus," Tulio said, taking Lucius' hand.

Lucius felt at a disadvantage that the conversation had ended so abruptly. He had been ready to argue further, to make a case for Ynis Wytrin, the place that had cared for Einion and Briana for so long. He had only ever heard good of the isle, except from these men.

"I do hope you will think on joining the ordo, Praefectus," Crescens said. He stood before Lucius, almost eye to eye.

"I'll think about it." Lucius opened the door that led into the hall and they went out.

As the three ordo members walked around the hearth, they nodded to Dagon, Barta and the children who were sitting with them.

Adara rose to see them out with Lucius, but Dagon and Barta remained seated, their fire-lit faces staring at them.

Tulio shuffled more quickly after Lucius who was already at the main doors, opening them to allow the late afternoon sunshine in.

"It was good to see you," Adara said politely to Tulio as he bowed to her and went out, followed by Bucer who gave her a curt nod.

Crescens stopped and smiled at both Lucius and Adara. "Thank you for inviting us into your home. It really is a thing to see, such a blend of Roman and Briton."

"You might bring Sabina next time you visit if you like," Adara offered, though it pained her to do so. She did not like Sabina.

"Yes, thank you. Whenever she ventures from our villa or Lindinis, it is usually to Aquae Sulis to take the baths there, but perhaps she would be willing."

Lucius ignored the slight insult, only too happy to see him go by that point, his patience extremely thin. He found it in himself to smile and shake Crescens' hand.

"And, Praefectus, do not worry about your building supplies. I will ensure whatever blocks them from arriving will be dealt with immediately upon my return. There are certain benefits to being on the ordo, after all."

"I thank you for it, Crescens. And I will be contacting the Praetorian prefect soon. As I say, I make no promises, but I will contact him."

"That is all I ask," Crescens nodded and took Lucius' hand. He was his friendly self again, as if the awkwardness of their meeting had never happened.

Outside, the horses of the three men had been brought up before the hall by their servants. Tulio and Bucer were already mounted and Crescens stepped up on the back of his own servant to mount up. He waved and they rode down the slope of the plateau.

Several of the Sarmatians stood to stare at the three Romans who passed among them along the road that curved down toward the southwest gate of the hillfort.

Lucius laughed as he noted the speed with which the three men rode away, but his face darkened when the laughter of his men subsided.

206

Dagon and Barta came out with the children, the latter heading to the vegetable garden to pick some for their evening meal.

"You were in there a long time," Dagon said. "Everything all right?"

"I so dislike politicians," Lucius muttered. "They want me to be one of them now."

"They want you to join the ordo?" Adara asked.

"Yes. Ex officio."

"They just want you close so that they can use your position at court. I don't like them, Lucius. I didn't the other night, and after seeing how they treated the villagers..." Adara stopped herself. "And did you see how they looked upon our home?"

"Adara's right, Anguis," Dagon said. "You need to be careful of that lot. They mean you no good."

"I know. Nor do they mean any good to Ynis Wytrin."

"What?" Dagon knew of the isle from what Briana had told him, and though he had never been there, he respected it, if anything, for what the people there had done for the woman he loved.

"Don't worry," Lucius said. "It is an old grudge that the ordo has."

"Are you really going to write to Papinianus on their behalf?" Adara asked.

"I don't know. Perhaps. In the meantime, our building supplies should arrive now so that Cradawg can continue his work."

"That's something at least," Adara added, going to join the children who were waiving her over.

Lucius, Dagon and Barta began to walk down the hill toward the stables and a group of the men.

"Tell the men there's a market tomorrow in Lindinis if any of them want to buy supplies."

"I will," Dagon said but he wanted to know more. "What else did they say?"

"Well, they basically implied that I saw myself as a king here. They did not like how I spoke up for Ynis Wytrin or the villagers."

"I don't like it. You know how much Romans despise the idea of kingship."

"They were just trying to get a rise out of me."

"Why would they do that?" Barta asked, his deep voice coming from behind them as they walked.

Lucius turned to him. "Because they do not know who they are dealing with."

"Be careful, Anguis," Dagon said. "I have a bad feeling. I could tell they didn't like being around all your men either. They felt threatened, and men of power who feel like that don't act rationally."

"It will be fine," Lucius reassured him, and then sped up to join the men who greeted them.

Dagon stopped Barta for a moment.

"We need to be on our guard."

"Yes," Barta answered, his eyes already scanning the gate to make sure the ordo members had gone.

On the road heading west toward Lindinis, the three ordo members' horses trotted at a quick pace toward their home.

"Do you think he'll actually write to the Praetorian prefect?" Bucer asked Crescens.

"I think so. Lucius Metellus is a man who deems himself honourable. He'll do what he says."

"Idealists are so easy to manipulate!" Bucer scoffed.

"He is that," Crescens said, but turned to his colleague. "But he can be shrewd as well. You cannot survive for long in the imperial court, or in high command, without some political acumen or survival skill. He is favoured by someone, perhaps the emperor himself." Crescens turned to Tulio then. "I want you to stop the hold we placed on his building supplies. Have them delivered to the site tomorrow if possible."

"I will," Tulio nodded.

"Then the praefectus will see that we are men of our word and will, hopefully, use his position to get us what we want for Lindinis."

Bucer laughed. "Yes. For Lindinis!"

There was a loud galloping coming up from behind them and the three men turned in their saddles to see a rider all in black speeding by.

"Slow down there!" Tulio yelled after him, but the rider was already long gone, veering off on another road that led north to Aquae Sulis. "This has been such a long day. I long to be home in a civilized setting."

VII

YNIS WYTRIN

'The Isle of the Blessed'

"When is she going to get back?"

Dagon was pacing around the hearth fire early the next morning. He had dreamed of Briana that night, and it had roused his strong wish to see her without further delay. The problem was that none of them knew the way to Ynis Wytrin.

"We don't know, my friend. But she will be back," Lucius handed him a cup of sheep's milk and sat beside Barta in front of the freshly made fire. "Just be patient."

Dagon turned on him, eyes wide. "Really? Patient, Anguis? I've been patient for months now. There is much she and I have to talk about!"

"Like what?"

"How many little Sarmatians he wants to make with her."

Lucius and Dagon stopped and stared at the usually silent, stoic Barta, and they all burst out laughing, Barta included.

"I can't say the thought doesn't warm me," Dagon agreed. "But don't get too insubordinate, Barta!" He lobbed a piece of bread at him and the big Sarmatian caught it and stuffed it in his mouth.

"Yes, my lord," he mumbled through his chewing.

Lucius smiled to himself. *It is so good to have them with us again!* "Don't worry, Dagon. You know Briana is attuned to things. She probably feels you near now anyway and will be on her way soon."

"Aye. Maybe." Dagon turned his back to the other two and closed his eyes, his thoughts reaching out to her. After a minute he shrugged. "I've no idea how to reach her like that."

At that moment, Ula and Aina came in through the main doors. "Good morning, Praefectus," the twins said together.

"Good morning, girls." Lucius stood and went over to greet them.

"Thank you for giving us the day yesterday," Ula said, her eyes glancing at Dagon and Barta. "We enjoyed the fair."

"You're free people. Everyone deserves a furlough from their labours." Lucius gestured to his two friends.

The girls smiled shyly.

"Even our father was able to get himself out of our home and speak with people," Aina said. "He seemed revived."

"I'm sorry we missed meeting him," Lucius said. "We must have him up here sometime if he is up for a wagon ride."

"That's kind, Praefectus," Ula said. "We'll get to work now."

Lucius nodded and turned back to his friends, pushing his hair back.

"Good morning!" came another cry as Phoebus and Calliope came storming down the stairs from the upper floor. They were followed closely by Adara who had her hair tied back and was wearing a simple, long grey wool tunic gathered at the waist with a brown leather belt.

Dagon and Barta stood as she came down, and also caught the charging imps as they rushed upon them.

Laughter filled the hall immediately, as is often the case when children are about.

After the attack upon the Sarmatians, they rushed Lucius and he grabbed both of them in his arms.

"Seems like you've slept well!" he said.

"Oh yes, Baba!" Calliope smiled as he hoisted her in his arms. "No bad dreams last night."

"Baba?" Phoebus cut in. "Mama said we might be able to go to the market at Lindinis today. Can we, Baba? Please?"

Lucius was silent a moment. He had not really wanted to go back there after the meeting with Crescens yesterday, but he could use the opportunity to check that the building supplies were being released finally. "Do you think any of the men will want to go to Lindinis?" he asked Dagon.

"Vaclar has already gone with one turmae of men. They took a wagon so that they could get supplies to fix the horse harness - leather, moulds and some ore to smelt."

"And food," Barta added. "Always food."

Adara arrived and came to kiss Lucius upon the cheek.

He looked at her. "You feel like going?" he asked her.

"I was thinking of training today…something to chase away my sadness at the news of Alerio…but perhaps a ride would be nice. We've been blessed, it seems, with another day without rain."

"I have to admit, I am interested in seeing this little town with high ambition," Dagon said. "Besides, I only think of Briana being here."

"Very well. Let's eat and then set out."

Phoebus and Calliope wrapped their arms about Lucius and rushed to the kitchen to get food from Ula and Aina.

"Barta, you coming?" Dagon asked.

"Of course," the Sarmatian said, his one good eye staring up at Lucius. "If assassins are about, I'll not leave you or your family's side, Praefectus."

The morning meal was quick, urged on by the children's excitement and eagerness to get going. They both wondered if there would be other children in Lindinis who would be willing to play with them, having had as much fun as they did in the village the day before.

Prior to setting out, Adara had spoken with Ula and Aina about the tasks that needed completion in the hall and garden, as well as any supplies needed for the kitchen.

The girls were eager to get to work and reassured Adara that they did not feel nervous with the troops remaining at the hillfort.

Nevertheless, Dagon gave orders to the men that they were not to bother the girls or disturb their work.

Lenya and Badru assured their princeps that they planned on drilling the men who had not gone to Lindinis that day. Many had enjoyed too much beer the previous day and needed to work it out of their system.

Dagon nodded his approval and left them with their orders, a small part of him pitying the men whose furlough was about to turn to work. His two decurions were hard task-masters.

Lucius spoke with Sigwyll Sloane about work in the stables. The Durotrigan was happy for any extra work with the horses. The horsemen who had arrived at the hillfort gave him more purpose than he had had since being forced out of service.

"I'll take care of everything, Praefectus, don't you worry. Do you want me to exercise your family's horses too?"

"My thanks, Sigwyll, but we're all riding to Lindinis," Lucius said, patting him on the shoulder. "Oh, but if Culhwch comes up, tell him where we've gone. He and I were going to have a drink this afternoon."

211

"I'll tell him, though I think he might miss coming. When I left, my cousin had him working on some of the many orders they received yesterday for new pottery. He'll be elbow deep in clay already!"

Just before leaving, Lucius, Adara and the children went to the shrine to make their daily offerings to the Gods and to ask for a safe journey. When they were finished, Lucius remained a quiet moment longer to pray silently for Alerio, wherever he was. They had been busy the last couple of days, but the sadness he had felt had remained in the hidden recesses of his mind, burning and hurtful.

He pushed the black hood of his cloak back and touched the sword rising from between his shoulder blades, the pugio at his waist. On this journey, he would not go unarmed.

Grant us a safe journey this day... He bowed to the images of the Gods before him, their faces looking back at him from a haze of burning incense, and then went outside to join the others who sat waiting atop their horses.

When Lunaris spotted Lucius coming, he cantered over to him, and in a moment Lucius was in the saddle.

Soon they were heading out the southwest gate and along the track to join the main road west to Lindinis.

The Metelli and the two Sarmatians rode easily along the Roman road which stretched out into the distance before them, their horses' hooves clipping as if in jolly song.

They all wore riding bracae, thick tunics and cloaks, and the adults were all armed, causing them to receive a few curious glances from passing litters and wagons.

Most of the traffic flowed toward Lindinis for the market, but as they were not burdened with a wagon, they passed all of them easily by.

"The children's riding has improved a lot!" Dagon noted as he watched Phoebus and Calliope canter along on their ponies ahead of them.

Lucius smiled. "They have improved. Our new home gives them a lot of room to ride freely without danger. They certainly couldn't do that in Caledonia."

Barta was quiet as they rode, his eyes scanning the distant tree lines for movement the entire way.

212

"My friend," Lucius said to him. "I want you to enjoy the day too. The sun is high and bright, and there are many people on the road. I don't think anyone would dare attack us now."

"Nevertheless, Praefectus..." Barta fingered the throwing knives that were strapped across his chest. "At least the trees are far back from the road, and with the fields freshly-hewn, no one can hide in the grass."

"We'll be fine. But I am glad to have you here," Lucius said.

Barta nodded slightly and continued to ride, his eyes still scanning the world about them.

The distance closed quickly and soon they were approaching the north-south crossroads. The children were already there waiting, having galloped ahead, but they had their ponies facing north, not south toward Lindinis.

"What are they doing?" Adara asked.

All of a sudden, Calliope's horse charged north upon the road and Phoebus followed quickly after her.

"Children!" Adara called, her voice more urgent now.

"Phoebus!" Lucius yelled in his parade ground voice, shattering the birdsong silence they had been enjoying. "Calliope!"

The four adults kicked their horses and they were soon galloping hard after the children.

The fleet-footed ponies made fast progress along the road and around oncoming horses and wagons headed south, while the larger warhorses in pursuit had to slow, unable to run off on the side of the road due to the drainage ditches where it climbed up toward more thickly wooded areas and grazing lands.

"Their horses must have been spooked by something," Dagon said as they rode.

Lucius had his doubts as neither of the children called for help, which they would have done if the horses were out of control.

Adara led the way, crouched over Hyperion's neck and mane, reckless in her fear and pursuit of her children.

Finally, after some distance, they spotted the children sat atop their horses in the middle of the now deserted road.

"What in Hades is going on?" Lucius yelled, struggling to calm himself now.

The four horses arrived at a gallop and they all pulled on the reins.

213

Adara was out of her saddle and rushing to grab the ponies' bridles.

Soon, Lucius was beside her, with both Dagon and Barta nearby, watching the forest that surrounded them.

"Phoebus!" Lucius grabbed his son's tunic and shook him. "Why did you take off like that? You could have both been killed!"

"By Apollo, Baba! It wasn't me. It was Calliope!"

"What?"

"She said she heard something and then just took off, I swear to you!"

Lucius could see in his son's eyes that he was indeed telling the truth. He took a deep breath and pat him on the shoulder, before turning to join Adara and Calliope a few feet away.

"Calliope? Why did you do that?" Lucius demanded. "You could have both been seriously hurt!"

Adara turned quickly to Lucius and whispered. "She says she heard someone screaming."

"What?" Lucius stepped forward to his daughter's side where she sat upon her mount, tears running down her face. The sight immediately doused his anger, and an ill feeling came upon him. "Calliope? What happened?"

Everyone was gathered close about her now as she caught her breath and found the strength to speak.

"I'm sorry...I'm sorry," she sniffled. "But I heard screaming. A girl, crying for help..."

"Where?"

They all looked around, their ears cocked to the air, listening.

"There!" Calliope pointed to a tree-covered mound to their left where it rose out of the earth like a titan, dark and brooding.

"It looks like an abandoned hillfort," Dagon said, riding off the side of the road to look up at it.

Then they heard it. A girl's cries for help, rising out of the trees of the fort.

"You see? I'm not lying!" Calliope cried.

Lucius turned quickly to Barta. "Stay here with Adara and the children. Dagon, on me!"

Lucius and Dagon's horses bolted from the road and they charged in the direction of the cries, up a single, dark track that led up to the ancient fortress.

"Barta!" Adara said. "Let's wait in that field, off of the road."

214

"Yes, my lady," the Sarmatian answered, uneasy with having all of them separated.

The four of them cantered after Lucius and Dagon until they were beneath a single oak tree in the middle of the field before the hillfort.

"She's so scared..." Calliope muttered, her eyes unwilling to be torn from the mound.

Lucius and Dagon could hear the screams clearly now, even above the galloping of their horses' hooves on the packed dirt track that led steeply up. Then they grew frantic and terrified.

It was definitely a girl.

Lucius led the way up the shrinking tunnel of trees, both he and Dagon ducking upon their horses' backs as they charged, leaping over fallen trunks and around rocks. It was near suicide to ride so quickly, but Calliope's inexplicable panic and the sound of that girl drove Lucius on.

Someone was in trouble, and there was cruel laughter surrounding her now which both men could hear.

At last the horses burst from the path and into a wide space of open green. In the middle, a group of three young men was surrounding a fourth on the ground, cheering him, howling like beasts.

"Hold there!" Lucius yelled as he and Dagon made directly for the group.

The three standing turned and scattered, running in separate directions for the trees that crowned the ramparts of the ancient fort. Their fleeing revealed another young man who sat astride a young girl all in white.

The attacker did not turn, too busy with his clawing at her clothes.

Lucius reined in hard, Lunaris screaming and kicking above the man. He leaped down and drew his sword, kicking the man from the girl in one swift, hard motion.

Dagon scanned the trees for the others who stood watching, reticent to come to the aid of their fellow, beginning to run in and then retreating when they saw the Sarmatian's face and the deadly blade pointed at them.

"Who in Hades do you think you are?" the prostrate man cursed and spat from where he scrambled up from his back, sword drawn. "Ahh!" He charged Lucius with his sword up for a blow.

Lucius parried it easily and the back of his hand struck out to send the younger man spinning off of his feet. Lucius glanced at the young girl upon the ground, his blade still pointed at the man.

She was dressed all in white with a braided leather band about her forehead, tying back her auburn hair. No more than fifteen or so, she straightened her clothes with shaking hands, though she did not cry.

"Are you badly hurt?" Lucius asked her, leaning in.

She shook her head.

"Who do you think you are, Roman, spoiling our sport?" the group of young men had reunited now with their humiliated partner and they all four faced Lucius, Dagon, and the girl who stood behind the two men.

"I'm Praefectus Lucius Metellus Anguis, you little shit! And you're lucky we don't cut all of you down right here and now."

"What? For hunting?"

"Hunting?" Dagon said, stepping forward, his sword up.

Then the youth smiled. "Well...Praefectus... Odd way to show your appreciation after my father received you in our home!" he spat at Lucius' feet.

"I don't care who your father is, whelp!" Lucius said.

"His father is Serenus Crescens Nova of the executive curia of Lindinis!" one of the friends threatened.

"I'm sure your father wouldn't be pleased to hear you've been hunting locals for pleasure!" Lucius walked toward them. "The Pax Romana extends to all people in the empire."

"You have no idea how things work here," Crescens' son said. "My father will hear of this."

It was meant as a serious threat, to be sure, and though Lucius knew Crescens could make life unpleasant, he also knew that the youth before him was a monster. He had seen enough to confirm that. He would inform Crescens of the offence.

"I'll be in touch with your father," Lucius said evenly. "Now take your pack of wolves and get out of here."

The four young men stood rooted for a few moments, and Lucius and Dagon thought that they would actually try to fight them. They thought better of it and began to back away to gather their horses which were huddled beneath the branches of a broad tree, cropping at the grass near the edge of the overgrown ramparts.

Lucius watched them ride away down another path on the opposite side of the hillfort, and soon birdsong filled the clearing. He turned to the girl.

"We won't hurt you," he assured her. "We're Roman soldiers. My family is down in the field there, waiting for us." Lucius pointed to the path they can come up.

"We heard your cries and came," Dagon said, sheathing his sword. "How did you get here all by yourself?"

The girl looked from Lucius to Dagon as if assessing their goodness. Her pale grey eyes were no longer afraid, but bright and curious. "I came here to this ancient place of my ancestors to make offerings to the spirits of the dead. Generations ago, my family lived upon this mound." She looked down at her bloody, grass-stained gown. "I did not hear the boys from Lindinis coming."

"They're gone now," Lucius told her. "You shouldn't travel alone like that." He looked at her clothing and thought they appeared to be the robes of a priestess. "How far is your home?"

"Not far from here. A few miles."

"We will escort you there safely," Dagon said. "Is that your horse over there?" He pointed to a lone white pony tied to one of the trees.

"Yes."

"I'll get her for you." Dagon walked slowly toward the scared animal, whispering as he approached, soothing her with words the Sarmatians used after a battle.

"Your friend knows horses well. She likes him," the girl said, the hint of a smile upon her lips.

"He is from Sarmatia," Lucius told her. "He was born in the saddle."

Dagon returned and handed the girl the reins of her horse. "Are you able to ride?" he asked delicately.

"Yes," she nodded. "They were not able to harm me in that way before you arrived."

Lucius cupped his hands for her to get up but she climbed into the saddle deftly enough. Then, he and Dagon mounted up.

Dagon went first, his sword drawn, followed by the girl, then Lucius.

"What is your name?" Lucius asked.

"Olwyn Conn Coran."

"Olwyn, my name is -"

"Lucius Metellus Anguis," she finished "I have heard of you from a dear friend."

"Oh?"

"I am Dagon of Sarmatia," Dagon said turning in his saddle and bowing to her.

"You are?" the girl asked, surprise in her voice.

"Do I know you, Olwyn?" Dagon asked, very confused.

"No. But... I have also heard your name before."

The path narrowed too much for further converse and the three rode on.

A branch snapped loudly in the wood and Lucius stopped suddenly to look back as the other two went on. His eyes scanned the wood all about but he could see nothing. He did not see the tall, lean, dark shape dwelling in the wood there, watching him, observing, content to wait.

The wood on the steep slope of that ancient fort was silent but for the rustle and caw of ravens as Lucius kneed Lunaris forward after the others.

"What happened?" Adara said as she, the children and Barta rode up to meet Lucius, Dagon and the girl as soon as they came out of the trees. "We saw four riders charging toward Lindinis from the southern part of the fort." Her eyes took in the battered girl, her face swelling and bruises beginning to show. Adara looked to Lucius.

"This is Olwyn," he said. "She was attacked by those young men."

Calliope rode up to the girl. "I heard you screaming."

Olwyn said nothing, but looked back to Lucius.

"My daughter heard you from the road."

"How did you hear me?" Olwyn asked her.

Calliope shrugged, not bothered anymore now that the person she had heard screaming was safe.

"I thank you all for helping me," Olwyn said.

"Who were they?" Adara asked Lucius.

Lucius' jaw was tight and he looked at her. "Crescens' son and his friends."

"Did you hurt him?"

"He was about to-" Lucius looked at his children and then at Olwyn. "Yes. I might have. His ego mainly."

"We'll deal with it later," Adara said. Then she turned to the girl. "I am Adara Metella. This is Phoebus, and Calliope." The children nodded. "And this is Barta of Sarmatia. Where do you live, Olwyn?"

"I told her we would see her home safely." Lucius turned to the girl, his voice gentle and concerned. "You said it was just a few miles from here?"

"Yes...just to the North." The girl looked at them strangely for a moment, the Roman family and two Sarmatian warriors.

"You can trust us," Adara said.

"I'll need to lead the way," Olwyn said. "You won't be able to find it. Ynis Wytrin is beyond the Roman road."

They all looked at each other.

They were all silent as they travelled along the road, passing by the occasional villas of rich land owners to their left and right until the Roman road cut to the northwest. Then they climbed a large hill to crest it where trees atop it formed a sort of barrier.

They watched Olwyn ride slowly, calmly - more than was natural for a girl who had just been attacked. As they watched her, they realized she seemed to be allowing her horse to decide upon the way.

Dagon noted this and whispered to Barta in the rear. "You see? The pony is leading us. Not the girl!"

Barta nodded, his eye watching the way ahead.

They climbed to the crest of the hill where trees grew thickly, their branches whispering in the breeze that swept across the land from the distant sea to the West. When everyone was gathered, they looked down into a broad plain filled with mist.

"Ynis Wytrin is there?" Lucius asked, straining in his attempt to see something...anything. "All I see is a thick fog."

"The marshes protect the isle. None may enter unbidden."

"Then how will we accompany you?" Dagon said.

Olwyn looked at them and smiled. "You are not unbidden." Before they could ask her more, her horse was already taking a switchback path down the hill into the mist.

"Should we be going there, my lord?" Barta asked Dagon. "It might be an ambush."

219

Dagon shook his head. "Briana and Einion are somewhere in there," he said. "We must go."

"But what if that is not Ynis Wytrin?" Barta said, but Dagon did not answer.

"Children, stay close," Adara said. "Ride one in front and the other behind me."

"Yes, Mama." Phoebus' voice was low and full of wonder and worry as they went.

Calliope seemed at ease, however, and her gentle humming wove itself into the thickening mist.

They followed Olwyn and her horse down winding tracks used more by deer than riders, flanked by tall bushes that reached out of the mist to brush their shoulders and pull at their cloaks.

The sound of water nearby grew louder, and once they had gone farther, they came out of the bushes and found that they were flanked by deep, still and dark water on either side.

"Careful," Lucius said over his shoulder from where he rode a few paces behind Olwyn's horse. Normally, in such a situation, his senses would be prickling, highly alert and wary of danger, but that was not the case in that moment. In fact, the intense rush of the confrontation with Olwyn's attackers, and the knowledge of the problems to be caused by humiliating Crescens' son were now completely gone. There was only the mist, the water, waterfowl, and the white horse before him.

Epona...Goddess...is this your doing? he wondered, staring at the white horse before him, but no answer came on the wind in his mind, only the mist...the water...his family and friends.

They rode slowly for a long time, the path like a labyrinth of clouded reed and water. After a while they all believed night was ready to fall, for they had ridden for so long, but then the path began to open more and more until they were upon a green field filled with golden sunlight.

"Look, Mama!" Calliope said.

Olwyn's horse stopped ahead and they heard voices.

They all came out of the misty seas as if through a veil, and found Olwyn speaking with an older woman and man.

"Einion? Briana?" Lucius said.

The brother and sister looked up at Lucius and the others and smiled.

"Welcome to Ynis Wytrin," Briana said. Then she spotted the two Sarmatians coming up behind. "Dagon!" she cried, rushing around everyone to the man she had been seeking in her hopeful prayers.

Dagon leaped from his horse and caught the full force of her embrace in his strong arms. "I missed you, Briana." He looked upon the woman he had come to love as he never thought possible, and saw her eyes sparkle with a brilliance he had not noticed before. "Have you become a goddess in this place?"

She shook her head, laughing, joyous and relieved to hold him again. "Kiss me again, my Sarmatian!"

"I think she's happy to see Dagon," Calliope whispered to Phoebus.

"Shhh!" her brother hissed.

Lucius dismounted and went over to Einion. "You look well, my friend."

"Well enough. There has been much on my mind, Lucius. But I had forgotten how much easier it is to think in this place. Barta..." Einion nodded to the big Sarmatian who had left Dagon and Briana behind to come and greet him. They clasped hands.

"It is good to see you, Dumnonian," Barta said.

"We were expecting you."

"You were?" Lucius asked.

"Well...Briana was. She saw you this morning," Einion turned to his sister who was coming over, her hand clasping Dagon's.

"I saw it," she confirmed before hugging Adara and the children. "Being here has that effect. The world is so much clearer."

"How is Etain?" Adara asked.

Briana's smile faded slightly. "Not as good as I had hoped. But she is improving. I spend long hours with her." Briana looked at Olwyn who was getting down from her horse now, her legs shaky. She rushed to her side and held the young girl steady. "Olwyn tells us you saved her from some attackers, Lucius."

"Calliope heard her from very far away... Anyway, we found four men attacking her at an old hillfort north of Lindinis."

Briana looked at Olwyn's puffing, bruised face. "Are you badly hurt?"

"No. Just so very tired now," the girl said. Olwyn tipped and would have crashed to the ground if Barta had not reached out to catch her as easily as if he were catching a small sheaf of wheat.

Briana turned to the others. "We need to get her to bed and put a poultice on her face." She looked at Lucius. "Did those men -"

"No, thank the Gods," Lucius said. "We were just in time."

They all began to walk, each holding the reins of their horses as they went, Dagon taking Barta's mount as the other carried Olwyn in his arms.

"I felt you would be brought here today," Briana said to them. "But I didn't know the manner in which you would be brought."

"Why was she so far from here, and alone?" Adara asked.

Briana shrugged. "Olwyn has always been a dreamer and wanderer. She's always been at the Goddess' will and whim. She had been talking about making offerings at her family's ancient home, but to find one's way through the mists is no easy task. The Gods must guide you."

Lucius and Adara looked back, and indeed, they could not see the path from which they had emerged, only the sunlit, green way ahead. They each placed a hand on one of the children as they walked.

So this is Ynis Wytrin... Lucius thought.

The path they took threaded across green fields covered in flowers and dotted with apple trees laden with fruit for the harvest. Hills rose up above them and smoke slid into the air from a few scattered buildings in the distance. Above it all loomed the Tor, a steep-sided beacon of that otherworldly place.

The newcomers felt it as they went deeper into that sacred world. All worry and regret seemed to vanish, almost as if they could sense and feel the way you might imagine the Gods themselves did at their most joyous. They breathed more deeply and calmly as they walked.

Phoebus and Calliope sang, the former joining his sister now, the calm seeping into his spirit. Their young voices were in concert with the birds flitting through the branches of the trees and hedges, and the waterfowl skirting the edges of the sun-kissed marshes and lakes that surrounded them.

"Lucius," Adara whispered. "Do you feel it?"

He nodded and looked at her across the neck of Phoebus' pony. "Yes."

Lucius felt his heart lighten to the point where he could almost not recognize himself, so much so that were he a man of Aegyptus, he would not fear to weigh his heart against a feather in the scales of Anubis.

Adara, feeling the same longed-for sense of place and elation took in the scene around her. Everything was more brilliant and colourful than she had ever imagined. She felt more certain of herself. She felt strength well up within her, and saw clearly the people she loved most about her - Lucius, her children, their friends... And she wondered at the intense, clear and calm feeling of blessedness that filled each of them.

"Here we are," Einion said as they reached the end of the track where it opened onto a broad field with a wattle chapel, roundhouses, and several small stone structures. He waved at the two men approaching. "Father Gilmore... Weylyn..." Einion said. "The Dragon and his family have come to us."

Lucius looked up to see the old druid who had so recently blessed their home, and another man with long brown hair tied back, a beard, and wearing a floor-length shift of brown homespun belted with a rope.

"Olwyn was attacked, but they arrived to help her," Briana said to Weylyn. "We must get her to bed and care for her!"

Weylyn smiled at Lucius, Adara and the children, casting a fleeting glance at the Sarmatians, before he looked closely at Olwyn's face, his hand upon her forehead. "She is exhausted from her ordeal." He looked up at Barta. "Come. Bring her to her quarters. I shall care for her there since Etain is asleep."

"Barta," Briana said. "You and Dagon come with me. Bring her."

The two men nodded and followed after Weylyn and Briana with Olwyn in Barta's arms.

"Morvran!" Weylyn called to his servant over his shoulder. "Care for their horses, please!"

Morvran came running, all smiles for Phoebus and Calliope, and took the reins of Dagon and Barta's mounts.

"Father," Einion said to Gilmore. "This is Lucius Metellus Anguis, his wife Adara Metella, and their children Phoebus and Calliope. They are very good friends to us."

Father Gilmore smiled and outstretched his hands. "Welcome to our home. Einion and Briana have told us much about you."

223

"And you, Father Gilmore," Lucius said, hesitant all of a sudden. "Forgive me…but we were not expecting to be here. We were on our way to Lindinis…"

Father Gilmore smiled. "Few people expect to come here deliberately. But God's will works in mysterious ways."

"So it seems," Lucius answered, suddenly aware of all the priests and priestesses staring at them from the surrounding field and crops, pausing in their work to watch.

"Forgive them, Praefectus," Gilmore said. "But most of them have not seen a Roman before now, let alone the Dragon they have heard so much about."

Lucius and Adara said nothing, but assured they were close to the children.

"Do not worry. This is the safest place you will ever know on this Earth. You may be at peace here. But you must be hungry. I assume you will stay the night?" He looked at Einion.

"You should," Einion said to Lucius. "It will be dark soon and…Etain has been waiting to see you."

"Me?" Lucius said, looking at Einion and Gilmore.

Father Gilmore nodded and smiled. "Morvran will care for the horses and we will get you settled in one of the vacant rooms for the night. Come." Gilmore turned and began to walk.

"I take them…" Morvran said to Lucius, motioning to the reins of their horses. "It all right?"

At first Lucius thought to refuse, but for some reason he could not explain, he felt full confidence in the misshapen young helper of the Druid.

"Thank you, Morvran!" Calliope said, placing her hand on his arm and smiling.

He smiled back and collected all of the reins before leading the horses calmly to a stable surrounded by a paddock not far off.

Lucius and Adara held Phoebus and Calliope's hands, their satchels flung over their shoulders as they walked along the grassy path after Father Gilmore. They did not exchange words, too rapt with the sights and sounds around them - the ancient oak with outstretched and gnarled limbs with three stumps beneath it, the view of the distant marshes in the mist, the hills before them rising steeply, like islands in another world.

Father Gilmore led them to a cluster of small stone structures with thatched rooftops and opened the wooden door of the last unit.

"It's not much, but it is clean," he said as he turned to see them staring up at the hills. "Ah, yes. There is something about this place, is there not?" He came out to stand beside them, and pointed at the shorter hill where a deep crevice cut into it. "That is the Hill of the Chalice where the Well of the Chalice lies. Etain's dwelling is near there. And that..." he pointed at the Tor rising steeply to the right, its ridges lined with what appeared to be a circular pathway all around it, running up and up to the top. "That is the Tor...a place that is especially sacred to our non-Christian brothers and sisters. They believe it is the gateway to their otherworld, Annwn."

"What's 'Christian'?" Phoebus asked.

Father Gilmore smiled and knelt down to face the boy directly. "Ah, well that is a question. If you are here long enough, I will tell you, if your father permits it, of course."

Lucius smiled politely at the priest and put his hand on his son's shoulder. "This is a special place, isn't it?" he said absently as he gazed up at the Tor where it lay painted against the deepening purple of the evening sky and the few twinkling stars that had already emerged faintly in the firmament.

"It is indeed special, for all of us," Gilmore said. "Ah, Einion. There you are."

"Sorry, I was helping Morvran with one of the Sarmatian horses. He's not used to such big animals."

"I'll leave you to see your friends settled," Gilmore said. "I must go to evening prayer with...with the others." He bowed slightly to the Metelli. "It is good to finally meet you all."

Einion watched Gilmore leave along the path, nodding greetings to the priests and priestesses who were gathering their tools and implements from their work at the end of the day and lighting braziers along the path.

"If you venture out," Einion said, "be sure to stay close to the fires so that you don't fall into the marshes. They're deeper than they look."

"Where did Briana, Dagon and Barta go to?" Lucius asked.

Einion pointed toward the Hill of the Chalice. "The healing house is up there, beside where Etain lives. They took Olwyn there." He went into the room and lit the hearth fire and two lamps upon a simple wooden table in the middle of the room. "You can all sleep in here," he said, pointing at four single straw mattresses upon low wooden frames. "I know you're used to plusher surroundings, but at

225

least you can rest easy and safely here. Briana and I are two doors down, and Barta and Dagon immediately next door."

"Where do all the priests and priestesses live?" Adara asked, gazing out the open door into the night where fires glowed orange in the dark.

"There are dwellings scattered around the isle, some like this, others roundhouses."

"It must have been peaceful living here for so many years," Adara mused.

Einion nodded slowly. "Peaceful...yes. But that peace also comes with a lot of time to think on things unfinished." He smiled and went out into the night.

"I'll be back," Lucius said to Adara. "I'm going to talk to him."

Lucius made his way outside and saw Einion's silhouette against the flames of a brazier.

"What's happened?" Lucius asked. "Did Etain have news for you?"

"Not yet." Einion breathed deeply, an attempt to curb his impatience. "She's been too weak." He looked sideways at Lucius. "Briana says she's also been waiting for you."

"But how could she know? We were actually on our way to Lindinis for the market. I have business with the ordo members and the fabrica."

Einion laughed. "There are no easy explanations in this place. Trust me. When I first arrived here, I was doubtful, but after the things I have seen and heard...the things I've felt in this place...well, let's just say that my eyes were opened wide."

"And yet you still gaze toward the southwest and your home."

"Always. That is my path, or at least I hope it will be soon. That's what I hope Etain will confirm for me."

"My old tutor used to tell me that the road to vengeance is only ever a road of blood and pain."

"He was probably right," Einion conceded. He went around the other side of the brazier to warm his hands and face Lucius. "So, what was this about Calliope hearing Olwyn's cries?"

"I can't explain it. We were still very far away, Einion. We thought her horse bolted, but it seems she charged off and Phoebus went after her. We got there only just in time."

"Some thugs from Lindinis, you think?"

"I know," Lucius said. "Wealthy thugs. The leader was the son of the Serenus Crescens Nova."

"That ordo member whose villa you visited?"

"That's the one," Lucius crossed his arms and shook his head.

"Good luck with that."

"Thanks." Lucius chuckled darkly. "However we got here, it's good to see you both again. We missed you. And now we get to see this wondrous place we've heard so much about."

"You won't see much now it's dark," Einion said looking around. "I'll go and bring you some food from the stores. In the morning, we'll show you around."

"I'll help you," Lucius said, patting his friend on the back and following him toward another group of buildings among the trees of another apple orchard.

Lucius returned shortly after to find Adara sitting on a stool between Phoebus and Calliope's beds. She was singing softly and stroking their brows with her hand.

Adara looked up at him, still singing, and her face was calm and peaceful, as content as he had seen her in a long while. She finished the song and then leaned over to kiss the children. "They're exhausted."

Lucius put down the basket of food he had brought, and came to her side to look at the children. "I don't know what to make of today."

"We've suspected that Calliope had gifts, but we've never seen anything like this. None of us heard that girl's screams. Only her."

"I know. She saved Olwyn from something awful." Lucius bent to pick up the basket. "Are you hungry?"

"Famished," Adara said.

The two of them moved to the small table before the fire where four stools were gathered around it.

Lucius reached into the basket and removed a loaf of bread, a small wheel of cheese, several apples, and four squares of baked oats spiced with pepper. He then poured some water into two of the four clay cups from the pitcher that had been set there.

They ate in silence for a time, enjoying the simple fare, looking at each other in the orange glow of the hearth.

"Did you see Briana, Dagon or Barta when you were out?" Adara asked.

227

"I saw Barta when I went to check on the horses. Right now he's sitting beneath the ancient oak down the path, looking up at the night sky. He seems calm here."

"I think we all are. There's something about this place, Lucius. It really is special, like Briana described."

"I'm not sure how they feel about having a Roman here," he said, "but yes, there is definitely something about this place. It's as if...as if -"

"As if it has been touched by the Gods themselves," Adara finished.

"Yes."

They ate a bit more and when they finished, they wrapped the remaining food for the children when they awoke in the morning.

Adara stood before the fire, gazing into the flames as her thoughts began to weave about in her mind. *What would it be like to live in such a place as this?* she wondered.

Behind her, Lucius slid the wooden bolt on the door and came to her side. It was cool without in the evening air, but inside that room, warmth spread throughout, cradling them and their children who slept soundly to the side.

Lucius wrapped his arms about Adara and she turned and kissed him, her long black hair falling behind her as she leaned up.

Both of them felt life flowing inside, happiness, peace and a sense that all was right with the world, despite the start to their day. As their kisses grew more passionate, Lucius unbelted his sword and pugio and placed them quietly on the table, the golden hilt of the sword shining in the dark.

The lamps upon the table extinguished, they moved together toward one of the small beds on the opposite end of the room and began to undress each other, slowly, enjoying every moment, taking in the sight of the person they loved most fervently.

Adara's fingers caressed Lucius' muscled shoulders and his neck where his hair came down in wispy curls, her lips kissing him softly.

Lucius closed his eyes as Adara's warmth enveloped him, his own hands travelling up and down her back, over the curve of her buttocks and back up to the sides of her breasts which rose and fell as her breathing sped up.

Their eyes locked and they kissed again as Adara gently nudged her husband onto his back and she climbed on top of him.

"I love you, Lucius."

228

"And I love you, my wonderful wife," he said, gasping a little as she slid him inside of her and began to move slowly.

They took their time making love in the dying light of the hearth, and by the time calm darkness settled completely over the room, they were fast asleep beneath the blankets, content and dreaming in each other's arms.

Phoebus awoke to birdsong and a soft ray of light angling its way into the room. He stretched and looked at his sister who was still sleeping in the bed beside. Across the room he saw his parents lying together huddled beneath the blankets of a small bed. That made him smile, especially seeing his father's feet hanging over the edge.

The boy sat up and shed his blanket. It was cold in the room, but he had slept in his clothes. He looked to the hearth and saw the fire was out, so he decided to lace up his boots and go out to find some firewood, but not before putting on his cloak and taking an apple from the basket that was on the table.

Phoebus touched the hilt of his father's sword gently, and tiptoed to the door where he slowly slid the bolt and opened it. Outside he turned, closed it carefully so that the latch would not snap loudly, and then turned.

The world was covered in a faint mist, penetrated by clear, warming sunlight across the green meadow to the orchards and other dwellings he had seen when they arrived. There was no firewood along the side wall of the building where they had slept, so Phoebus walked along the path, his eyes drawn to the cloudy world of the marshes. He wondered what creatures could possibly dwell in those mists and whether they were dangerous or not, but as soon as the thought of danger entered his mind, it seemed to have been taken away, and he was humming softly to himself, happy.

The limbs of the great oak he had seen seemed to stretch into the mists, as if waving them away to make way for the sunlight, and Phoebus was drawn to it. He walked toward the ancient tree, his eyes taking in the massive limbs, and he thought how wise it appeared, if a tree could be wise. He wanted to sit beneath it and moved to do so, but stopped suddenly when he looked down and saw two children sitting on the stumps beneath its broad branches.

"Oh, hello!" Phoebus said, surprised. "I'm sorry, I didn't mean to disturb."

It was a young boy and girl, both dark and bright-eyed in the misty morning.

"Hello," said the boy to Phoebus. "You can sit with us if you like."

"Thank you," Phoebus said, taking the third stump.

"We saw you arrive yesterday," the girl said, her smile wide, slight wisps of her dark hair blowing across her face. "I'm Rachel. This is my brother, Aaron."

"My name is Phoebus."

"Was that your sister with you yesterday?" the girl asked.

"Yes," Phoebus said. "Calliope. She and my parents are still sleeping. I came out to find some wood for the fire."

The children were quiet, still smiling.

"Do you live here?" Phoebus asked.

"Yes," Aaron answered. "We always have. Father Gilmore is our guardian, but everyone in Ynis Wytrin looks after us. They are our family."

"Do you like it here?" Rachel asked.

"Yes. It's very different. You feel safe here," Phoebus looked around and could see the faint shapes of priests and priestesses moving in the mists to start their day, some feeding the animals in pens, others bringing baskets to the orchards.

Then a bell began to ring, a gentle echo in the morning.

"What's that?" Phoebus asked, looking around confused.

"The chapel bell," Rachel said. "We have to go now."

"Where?"

"To our morning prayers with Father Gilmore," Aaron said.

"Will we see you later?" Rachel asked. "Maybe we can all play together?"

Phoebus looked back at the girl and to her brother who was standing. "I would like that."

"There is firewood around the back of the building you are staying in," Aaron said as he and his sister walked away toward the distant wattle and daub chapel.

Phoebus watched them disappear inside the strange temple far on the other side of the green field. He then took a deep breath and looked up into the tangle of branches above him. It was like a labyrinth, and he found himself lost in it as he stared, until a cool breeze touched the back of his neck and he looked down to see a tall, golden-haired woman standing on the other side of the tree. She was barefoot, and wore an ornately-twisted stola of purest white.

"Greetings, young Metellus," she said. Her voice was music to Phoebus, the sweetest he had ever heard.

Phoebus took her to be a priestess of the sanctuary and greeted her back politely.

"Good morning, lady," he said.

"Did you sleep well?"

"Yes. I did. I was very tired after yesterday."

"You and your sister did well to help save that girl."

"Olwyn," he confirmed. "Well, it was really Calliope and my father. I went to keep Calliope safe."

"You did a fine job." She smiled warmly and reached out to touch his arm.

At her touch, Phoebus thought he could never be happier than he did in that moment, for it filled him with pure joy and hope. "Are you a priestess here?"

She smiled again, her brilliant blue eyes leaving him to stare out at the field and the marshes beyond. "I am not from here. I know your father well, though."

"Shall I get him for you?"

"No. I just wanted to say hello and to tell you something." There was a note of gravity in her voice, something that changed her face.

"What is it?"

The woman moved to stand before him and knelt in the damp grass, though Phoebus noted that her stola got neither dirty nor wet. "You need to be brave for your family in the time to come."

"Why?" Phoebus asked, his voice lower, a little shaken. "What is going to happen?"

"I cannot say for certain. Just know that the Gods are with you and watching over you. Do you believe me?"

"Ye...yes. Yes. I believe you."

"Good."

She reached up and put her white hand to his face.

When Phoebus opened his eyes, she was gone, and all that could be heard was the morning breeze coming off the lake marshes to rustle the leaves in the tree above him.

"Phoebus? Are you all right?"

Phoebus looked to see his mother and Calliope walking toward him. "Mama?"

231

"We were worried about you."

"I only went to get firewood," he said, noting that nothing of the sort lay on the ground about his feet. "I thought I would sit first. It is so peaceful."

"Yes. It is," Adara said, her voice soothing. "We have food and water in the room for you. Are you hungry?"

"Yes, Mama. I am, but..." He looked around. "Where is the priestess who was here?"

"We saw no one speaking with you." Adara looked around and then back at her son. "Are you feeling well?"

"Very, Mama. Don't worry." He stood and scratched his head. "Where is Baba?"

"Briana came to get him a few minutes ago." Adara sighed "Etain has asked for him."

Briana led Lucius from the stone dwelling around the edge of the base of the Hill of the Chalice. She was quiet as they went, solemn, but there was an air of relief about her.

"Is she much better?" Lucius asked as they skirted the edge of the thickly-wooded hill, and headed for the break in the trees where the healing house was beside the Well of the Chalice.

Briana stopped and turned to whisper to Lucius. Her eyes were tired and she appeared a little faint. "She is somewhat better, but still very weak. And her fever still clings to her."

"Why does she want to speak with me?" Lucius reached out to steady Briana. "You all right?"

"I'm fine. It's just... The emotion that being back here has brought about...seeing Etain so weak. I've been worried."

"You need to rest and eat something, Briana. You're exhausted from lack of both sleep and food."

"Dagon said the same thing," she said, smiling.

"He's right. Listen to him." Lucius started to walk, holding her arm, but she stopped and turned to him again.

"Lucius... Whatever she says...you...you need to take it seriously."

There was worry in Briana's eyes, and Lucius saw it clearly, even in the shielding peace of Ynis Wytrin.

"What is she going to say?" he asked.

"I don't know. All I know is that when Etain speaks, every word is sent from the Goddess with purpose. She was heard speaking of the 'Roman Dragon' in her sleep some nights ago. She never told me what that was about, but she has asked to speak with you, and that means something."

Lucius was nervous then. *Why would the high priestess of Ynis Wytrin want to speak with me? She doesn't even know me!* He continued to follow Briana until they arrived at a narrow stone staircase that went up through the trees.

The path broke and spread out on the slope of the hillside that was a garden the likes of which Lucius had never seen, not in Rome, Etruria or even faraway Alexandria. It was a paradise within the already peaceful boundaries of that sacred isle.

Lucius stopped and took a deep, calming breath. Ahead, Briana stopped to speak with one of the white-robed priestesses who helped Etain at the healing house. He looked around and saw flowerbeds of myriad herbs and flowers all in possession, no doubt, of healing properties beyond the reckoning of the average medicus. His first thought was how much Diodorus would have loved to see that place.

Autumn buds bloomed above the stalks of other plants, birds flit from branch to branch, and the soft sound of gently trickling water emerged from hidden places, as sweet as any note plucked upon Apollo's lyre. There were niches with tree stumps and soft grassy beds tucked into walls of ivy, and gnarled branches of wisteria that filled the air with their lovely scent in Spring. In some of the niches, a priestess or priest sat alone, or with one of the novices, in silent meditation or quiet converse. Towering over the green grass, beds of flowers, and woven fences, an avenue of ancient yew trees led up and away into the green dark of the Hill of the Chalice.

Lucius thought again of Diodorus. He reflected on their lessons together in the Rome of his youth, and wondered if those priests and priestesses he saw just then taught similar ways of being, and of viewing the world, to the bright-eyed apprentices with them.

"Beautiful, isn't it?" Briana said, standing beside Lucius. "Here comes Dagon."

Lucius looked and was surprised to see that one of the niches had been occupied by Dagon who had been sitting in quiet contemplation before his eyes. Neither had seen the other, so lost in thought were they. As Dagon approached, Lucius noted the look in his eyes, a look of awe and responsibility.

"Lucius," Dagon said. "Good morning." He approached and gave Lucius a hug, then turned to kiss Briana.

233

"All is well?" Lucius asked him.

He nodded, silent. Then, "I spoke with Etain just now..."

Briana was surprised. "While I was away?"

"The priestess asked me to enter shortly after you left to get Lucius. She said Etain wanted to speak with me. To meet me."

"And?" Lucius asked.

"I cannot speak of all yet, but..." Dagon paused, trying to find the right words. "Anguis..." he said. "I've never met a person like her. Ever. Listen to her, my friend."

"You both have me worried now," Lucius said.

"There is nothing to worry about, Lucius," Briana said. "You are all safe here."

"She sees things - Etain does," Dagon blurted out, shock in his voice.

He said no more, but moved off the path to go sit beside the tiny stream that ran down from uphill.

Lucius looked at the stream closely and gasped.

The water was red.

"Why is the water like that?" Lucius asked Briana.

"I'll tell you later," she said. "We must take you to her now while she has her strength." Briana turned and followed a second path that led away from the stream and went up some steep stairs to a long rectangular stone building. She pointed at the first door as she walked. "Olwyn is in here," she whispered. "She is resting and not badly injured thanks to you. Etain is in the last room." Briana continued past several doors and turned to Lucius as she placed her hand upon the latch of the final door.

Lucius could feel his heart beating rapidly, angry with himself for being so nervous. He did not understand why he felt that way, for he had only heard good things about Etain from Einion and Briana. He wondered if the fact that Dagon had seemed so shaken by her power of sight had something to do with it. But Lucius had known in his gut, when they had emerged from the misty marshes, that Etain wanted to speak with him.

Briana opened the door into a room that was dark and musty. There was a scent of cedar wood and rosemarinus, and a fire burned in a triangular brazier held upon a tripod with feet in the shape of a deer's.

Briana did not speak at first, but stood there looking at the woman upon the bed.

Lucius looked down at Etain, so still and calm, so much so that he might have thought her dead but for the subtle rise and fall of her chest.

Etain was covered in furs, except for her arms which rested on top of the coverings, palms up. Her red hair was matted with sweat, making it darker, almost bronze in the firelight. About her neck, the crescent moon pendant rose and fell.

She was younger than Lucius had expected, not a great deal older than he and Briana, but there was a sense of something ancient about her, something to be respected. Lucius wondered why he felt so strange in that room. *I've met gods and goddesses face-to-face!* he told himself.

As if she heard the cry in his head, Etain's eyes then opened and looked directly at him.

Lucius was taken aback at the sight of those brilliant green eyes set in the face of a woman who had been severely ill, for there was no sign of weakness in them or of life waning.

Without a word, she raised her left hand to Lucius, and motioned to the chair on the other side of the bed. "Briana, my dear... Leave us...please."

Briana nodded. "I'll be checking on Olwyn if you need anything."

The door closed gently and Lucius turned to the priestess.

"Come Lucius Metellus Anguis, the one they call 'Dragon'. Sit with me." Etain struggled a little to sit up in her bed, but she managed it.

Lucius went around the bed and sat down on the chair, the wicker seat creaking loudly as he did so. It was hot, and so he shed his cloak over the back and rested his elbows upon his knees. The sleeves of his tunic slid back to reveal the coiled dragons about his forearms.

"You bear the symbol of power and prophecy upon you - the dragon. How long has this symbol been a part of you?"

"For as long as I can remember, lady." Lucius looked at her and had an urge to tell her so much of what was whirling in his mind, but before he could utter another word, she grabbed his hand and held it. He was shocked to find she was not cold or clammy at all, but warm and soft, and very strong. He could not have pulled his hand away even if he had wanted to.

235

Etain closed her eyes for what seemed like minutes, her eyes twisting and turning beneath the lids as if she looked around her at many things. When she opened them, she looked upon Lucius and sighed. "You carry a great burden, Dragon. I have seen much. The Gods have whispered to me of you and your family."

"What of my family?"

She sighed again, but did not answer. "I am not ill," she told him.

"But Briana said you were near to dying before. Weylyn too when we saw him last."

Etain shook her head. "I was at first, but it was deliberate. The herbs I took made me ill, but they allowed me to go where I needed to."

"Where did you go?" Lucius asked.

"I have been wandering between worlds." She saw Lucius' look of surprise and shock and nodded. "It is no easy thing to tread where I have gone. But, like your Sibyl or Pythia, I have been both blessed and...challenged...by my ability to speak with the Gods and to have them speak to me. Epona included."

Lucius looked up and nodded.

"Yes. She values you and your men greatly. That is something to cherish, the favour of the Gods is."

"I know it."

"And you have met many."

"Y...yes. I have."

"And the Morrigan."

Lucius stiffened.

"She spoke to me of you, Lucius Metellus Anguis, and her anger will not be assuaged." Etain grasped Lucius' hand and held him fast, her eyes locking onto his. "She is a terrible enemy."

Lucius could say nothing, for he knew the truth of what Etain said, the implications of having made such an enemy of the dread goddess of war.

"You feel her and her hunters at your heels, don't you?" Etain asked.

"Not always."

"They are there...in the forests and in the skies...they watch you. You must be careful in the time to come if you wish to protect your hopes and dreams and survive your struggles."

"What is coming?" Lucius asked. "Can you tell me?"

Etain shook her head and looked down. "I cannot. But I can tell you that you are not alone. That you have friends in places you do not as yet fathom. Such is the draw of dragons, especially in this land."

"What do you mean?"

"This is a land of dragons, this isle a home and sanctuary should you need it. But you will be taken away soon, and though even your Gods will seek to prevent you, you must go so as to forge bonds that shall never break, and to repay old debts."

"Why are you speaking in riddles, lady? Please tell me." Lucius was leaning forward now, his hands grasping Etain's. He could see the struggle in her eyes, but also knew that she meant it when she said she could not tell him all.

"You do not yet know who you are...but you will pass through fire and death to do so... You will walk in realms that few ever see... You will be among them and one of them..."

Lucius let go of her hands and leaned back in the chair as if to distance himself, for what Etain uttered was all too terrifying, too confusing and cryptic to comprehend. *She must be ill still*, he told himself.

"No. I am not," Etain said, her eyes open again. "I can usually see much, but with you, only a portion is revealed to me. There is a bright and shining aspect to you that blinds me. But I suspect your hopes, your dreams...and more. Weylyn was right about you."

"I should let you rest," Lucius said, making to stand.

"I did not wish to startle you. I know you have come here by strange ways. But you are indeed welcome...always. Your entire family has a home here should you need it."

"But we've only just met. And I am a Roman."

"That is only part of what you are... But I should thank you for saving Olwyn from her attackers. She is gifted, but has often taken to wanderings outside of Ynis Wytrin."

"Without my daughter, I fear we would not have found her."

"Yes. I would like to meet your wife and children. But later. For now, I must rest from my journeys. I would see you and your family before you go."

"I was thinking we would leave today," Lucius said, though he had only just decided that.

"No. Wait another night. Rest here within the mists' embrace. Einion and Briana will return with you."

"But they will not leave while you are unwell."

"I will be well tomorrow," Etain said with absolute certainty.

"I hope that is so, lady." Lucius stood and picked up his cloak. As he reached the door she called to him once more.

"I am your friend, Lucius Metellus Anguis."

"I know," he said.

"I am glad. If you see him, please send Father Gilmore to me. I would speak with him."

Lucius nodded and opened the door to step out into the soft sunlight, closing it behind him as gently as he could. Down below in the garden, he could see Adara and the children with Dagon, Einion, and Barta. The latter was bent over one of the pools of red water, cupping his hands and splashing the socket of his missing eye with Weylyn standing beside him.

"Is everything all right?" Briana asked as she came along the path from Olwyn's room.

"Yes," he said, though he knew he did not sound convincing. "Everything is fine. She is very special."

"She is," Briana acknowledged. She looked at Lucius, expecting more, but could see that he was still processing whatever it was that Etain had told him. That was fine. That was Etain's way - to speak with individuals alone, to give them the knowledge she had if permitted, and not to tell others of it. Briana had always thought that if someone wicked had Etain's gifts, then they would be a very dangerous person indeed. As it was, Etain was the most discreet mother any of them could ask for, a true emissary of the Goddess herself. "You sure you're all right?" she asked Lucius again.

"Yes. I need to think. Etain said she wanted to see Father Gilmore. Is she friends with the Christian priest?"

"The very best of friends." Briana smiled. "I'll get him. But first, let me show you the Well." Briana walked down the path away from the healing house and through a tunnel of ivy, until they emerged on the other side in a fully enclosed garden set with stones and wild flowers growing amongst them in bursts of colour.

"There you are," Adara's voice came up a separate path that led to the same place. "Lucius, are you well? You look pale." She stepped to his side and held his arm. "Isn't this place a wonder?"

He looked around and his eyes came to rest on a wide hole in the ground. "What is that?"

Briana walked over to the hole and stared into it. "It is the Well of the Chalice."

Lucius and Adara peered over the edge of the hole into the deep well to see the red-stained walls where fern and lichen sprouted from the sides. It seemed liked another world, and Lucius did wonder if it spilled into the realm beyond the Tor which Einion and Briana had told him about in the past, the place called Annwn.

"Why is it called that?" Adara asked.

"The Christians believe that the chalice which caught the blood of the Christus at his crucifixion was brought to this land and buried beneath the earth here by a man named Joseph. Father Gilmore could tell you more of him, but he believes the water runs red with the blood of his Christus."

"What do you think?" Lucius asked. He was only slightly familiar with the beliefs of the Christians and the trouble Rome had had with some of them over the years. Diodorus had taught him about the Christians somewhat, and that their faith was their own, that they worshiped in hiding for fear of persecution from Rome. His thoughts came back to Briana.

"This well has been sacred for thousands of years. Etain and Weylyn will tell you that our ancestors here believed the blood of the Goddess ran through this water, making it a source of supreme healing. The waters are life-giving and run through Ynis Wytrin like the veins through our bodies. The water pulses with life from deep within the earth, springing from the Goddess herself."

Adara knelt beside the hole and gazed into it. "It reminds me of the Kastalian spring of Delphi," she said longingly, wanting to touch the water.

"Come," Briana said. She went through an arch in a wall of greenery and down a path of stone and sand that sparkled with crystals beneath their feet. There was a gentle trickling sound that got louder and louder as they walked. Briana turned left into a flat grassy area surrounded by upright stones covered in ivy and there, set in the middle of a squat stone wall was a lion's head. The beast's mouth was open and from out of it poured a rich red stream of water. "You may drink if you like," Briana said, pointing to three clay cups that had been set upon the ground. "The priestesses use the water in their ceremonies, and Father Gilmore uses the water for the Christian blessing ceremonies he calls baptisms."

Lucius knelt down with Adara and together they put their hands beneath the falling water.

"It's cold," Adara said, her hand squeezing Lucius'. She withdrew her wet hand then and placed it upon her forehead. "I...I feel...calm, in a strange way."

Lucius took up one of the cups and filled it with water to brimming. He smelled it at first, the coolness filling his nostrils, and then a scent of blood, or of wet iron, like so many swords in the rain. Then he set the cup down without drinking. "I'm not thirsty," he said.

"I'll try it," Adara said, her hand upon Lucius as she reached with the other to take up the cup. She put it to her lips, her eyes closed, and drank, a small sip at first, then more until a little trickled down her chin. She opened her eyes, looked around the gardens, and it seemed to her that the world was brighter in every way, more colourful and full of light, and her body was free of aches or pains. "Oh Briana..."

"Wonderful, isn't it?" Briana said.

"Where is Lucius?" Adara asked, noticing that her husband was not there. She turned to see him walking farther down the path. "Why did he leave?"

"Not all are meant to drink of the Well of the Chalice," Briana said. "It took Einion three years before he would drink. I think it is harder for men to drink of the Goddess' flow."

Adara stood and they went after Lucius who was now sitting on a bench with Dagon, Phoebus and Calliope, across from a large rectangular pool, large enough for a man to lie in. It was filled with water from the Well of the Chalice and was fed from a small waterfall that splashed down from one of the garden terraces in a rich chute.

"Are you all right, Lucius?" Adara asked.

"I'm fine. I wanted to check on the children." He held Phoebus and Calliope close on his lap, though they wiggled to get away when they saw Adara.

"Mama! Do you want to see us race flowers down the stream?" Calliope said, her eyes sparkling with excitement. "Phoebus' flower beat mine the first three times, but then I won four in a row!"

"I'll bet I can beat you again!" Phoebus said before jumping off of Lucius and running farther down into the gardens along the edge of the avenue of yew trees, with Adara in tow.

Lucius laughed and stood, his eyes fixed upon the water.

"Anguis," Dagon said. "You're awfully quiet."

"This place..." Lucius' voice sounded as if he were absent, his thoughts far away.

"Dagon," Briana said. "Come with me. I'll show you the well head."

Silently, Briana led Dagon by the hand up the path down which she had just come, and Lucius was there alone.

The quiet, the peace, closed in on him. He stared at the fluttering surface of the pool below him and saw himself in the reflection there. Then, all around him, fire leapt up, and a clang of sword and crash of spear upon shield rang out in his mind. Then a beast of such ferocity sprang up and he reached for his sword instinctively, though he had left it in the room where they had been staying.

Be calm, Metellusss... Apollo's voice whispered and Lucius looked up to see the shining god across the water from him. *You've been brought to this place to rest before a great trial.*

"What trial, Lord?"

Anyone about who would have seen Lucius at that moment might have thought him mad, unknowing of his ability to speak with the Gods themselves, but as it was, he stood alone and unobserved.

You will soon be faced with a choice...and you must choose wisely... Apollo looked into the water and at that moment a blinding sunlight reflected in the pool, setting the red water aflame in red-gold. *This place is for the blessed, Lucius, but those who come here can only stay when it is their time.*

"Can we stay here?" Lucius asked, though he did not know why the words escaped his mouth.

Apollo shook his head. *It is not your time. I will stand with you and watch over you as far as I am able, but in this land, I may not go everywhere. Be wary as ever...be wise...*

He was gone.

Lucius saw himself in the water again, and the reflection of another behind him. He turned quickly and saw Weylyn standing a few feet away.

"I'm sorry to disturb you, Praefectus. I too have had many a conversation here that I could not explain. It was your god, was it not?"

"I... Yes. Though I am blessed to speak with him often."

241

"I should say," Weylin nodded and sat down upon the bench. "I come here often in the hopes of speaking with my son, Cathbad, but I believe he is enjoying hunting in Annwn far too much to come and listen to me chatter and chide him." The old man laughed, and Lucius felt pity for him.

"What is it about this place, Weylin? Ynis Wytrin."

The Druid smiled. "It goes by many names. Ynis Wytrin... Avalon, and more. It is many things to many people with many beliefs. To the Druids, it is a place of supreme sanctity, something to be felt in the avenues of oak, ash and yew, the wooded slopes of the Hill of the Chalice and the waters running red beneath our feet. To the priestesses of the Goddess, it is here that life is created, and where it fades, as is the way of things in this world and the next. This place is the womb of the Goddess herself."

"And to the Christians?"

Weylin looked at Lucius a moment, observing the Roman before him and his reaction. He could see there was no hatred for Christians in the man beside him. "To our Christian brothers and sisters, this is the place where they were first welcomed into this land by the good king, Arviragus, to worship alongside all of us. It is a place of safety and protection for them, the one place in all of the empire where they are safe."

"Where who is safe?" Lucius asked.

"Father Gilmore," Weylin said quickly. "The world has been unkind to Christians."

Lucius sat down beside the old Druid. "I know. I have heard of the atrocities."

"And there will be more." Weylin nodded, remembering the visions Etain had described to him and Gilmore alone, and they haunted him still, for they reminded him of the cruelty of man, of Rome, and of the days when his own brothers had been hunted to near extinction with such ruthlessness. *But the dragon is different,* he told himself again, as he had several times already. He turned to Lucius, the better to face him.

"There are many who would tear this place to the ground, to burn it and sow the Goddess' bosom with salt. They would shore up the Gates of Annwn and set fire to our Otherworld. It is imperative that never happens."

242

"The Lindinis ordo has come to me again claiming that Ynis Wytrin is to blame for the attempt upon the life of the executive of the curia, Serenus Crescens."

"And what do you believe?"

"That nothing so cowardly could even be conceived of in this place of peace."

"Then you understand easily what many in the outside world refuse to see." Weylyn pat Lucius' hand the way Diodorus once did when Lucius passed some sort of test.

It made Lucius smile.

Weylyn continued. "Ynis Wytrin...Avalon... It is not just a place sacred to our ancestors, or a sanctuary for Christians in a Roman world. It is a world of faiths in microcosm, living peacefully side-by-side. It is as the world should be, but never will." Weylyn closed his eyes next and breathed as if in prayer. "It is the Isle of the Blessed...for those who walk here are blessed indeed to glimpse such potential in life, are they not?"

Lucius looked at the Druid and nodded. "I believe I understand. You have put into words what I have felt since arriving here."

"You are not very Roman," Weylyn laughed. "Words are overrated. Focus upon those feelings, for they will guide you truly."

"Is that a Druid teaching?"

"No, no. That is Etain's teaching. I learn from her everyday." Weylyn stood then and together they walked to join the others in watching the children race flowers down the red stream.

For the rest of the day, the Metelli and their friends contributed to the workings of Ynis Wytrin alongside the priests and priestesses. Adara, Phoebus and Calliope helped to pick apples in the many orchards around the isle, and Lucius, Barta and Dagon helped mend some broken fences, clear out the stables and care for their own horses who seemed to be more at ease in that place.

Everywhere Lucius went, he noticed that life seemed to make more sense and have more purpose, simple though it was. There were no strategies or worries to weigh one down, certainly the threat of death was unimaginable, except as the natural cycle of life. The latter became evident when one of the older sheep passed away that same day.

Lucius had come to one of the animal pens where he saw Phoebus and Calliope kneeling in the grass beside the two children he had seen hovering around Father Gilmore. He approached them without speaking and leaned upon the wooden rail of the pen to watch beside the Christian priest.

Father Gilmore nodded a silent greeting to Lucius and returned his gaze to Rachel and Aaron who were whispering to the fading life before them.

Phoebus and Calliope watched silently, the latter whimpering a little, her hands upon the thick grey-white fleece of the animal.

Finally, Lucius spoke. "What are they doing?"

Without removing his gaze, Father Gilmore answered. "They are easing the creature's suffering as it passes. Your children have been helping."

Lucius watched as the little dark girl, Rachel, leaned down and kissed the sheep's forehead.

The animal's eyes closed as if going to sleep, and its entire body stilled.

Calliope cried out briefly, and Phoebus put his arm around her.

The boy Aaron made the symbol of what looked like a cross to Lucius upon his chest and laid his hand on the animal.

"That is good, children," Father Gilmore said. "You gave her peace. Just as our Lord is able to do for mankind."

Calliope and Phoebus stood up with Aaron and Rachel and they all turned toward the two men waiting for them.

"That was so sad," Calliope said.

"Yes," Father Gilmore agreed. "But it is infinitely more sad to think of her passing without our Lord to watch over her."

"Was your god here?" Lucius asked.

Gilmore nodded. "He is everywhere."

Lucius could not help but notice how Gilmore's eyes went directly to Rachel and Aaron then, and he wondered what that could mean. The children were special it seemed, and Gilmore, indeed all in Ynis Wytrin, seemed to pay special attention to them. He wanted to ask about them, but decided against it. Father Gilmore was evidently quite guarded when it came to the children, and still not fully comfortable with Lucius, a Roman, walking amongst them.

"Come children," Gilmore said. "It is time for your afternoon prayers." He turned to Phoebus and Calliope. "Would you like to see our chapel?" He looked to Lucius for his approval.

"Oh, can we?" Phoebus asked.

"I don't see why not," Lucius answered.

244

The children climbed over the fence together and the four of them began making their way past the crops where some of the priests and priestesses were working, then across the green field to the small timber chapel.

"How long has your chapel been here?" Lucius asked, more out of politeness. "Weylyn mentioned that the first Christians to come to Britannia settled here."

"That is true," Gilmore said, stopping outside the chapel walls to stand in a spot of sunlight. "A wise man named Joseph came here long ago with his followers. They were fleeing…" he stopped, but continued, "…Roman persecution. King Arviragus granted them sanctuary here and they built this chapel. I am its caretaker." Gilmore walked a few paces and stood over another, smaller well in the ground beside the chapel. "This well is dedicated to Joseph."

"Is this Joseph the one I have heard of who was father to the Christus?" Lucius remembered some of what he had heard from Diodorus about the story.

"No. The Christus…" Gilmore crossed himself, "…his father is the Lord of Heaven. It was his uncle, Joseph of Arimathea who arrived on these shores with his followers. He came ashore on the slopes of Wearyall Hill there." He pointed to the northwest where the land sloped up and a long worn path led to a single windswept tree upon its crest.

"What is that tree?" Lucius said, stepping forward a pace or two to see.

"When Joseph came ashore, he planted his staff in the ground and it took root. It is a symbol of his arrival here and the welcome they received."

"It took root?"

"Yes." There was no doubt or disbelief in Gilmore's eyes when he answered. Lucius could see that his faith was strong, and he could not help but respect him for it.

Suddenly, a loud clanging rang out from the top of the chapel and Father Gilmore ran inside.

Lucius followed, covering his ears against the piercing sound. It was dark in the chapel, and he could hear Gilmore chiding the children about something.

"The bell is not a children's toy," Gilmore was saying. "It is a solemn call to prayer, a reminder."

"It is loud, whatever it is," Lucius said, coming to stand behind Phoebus and Calliope. He could see Rachel and Aaron hanging their heads.

"We only wanted to show our new friends what it sounded like," Rachel said.

"We meant no harm, Father Gilmore." Aaron looked up at the priest, his wide brown eyes sincere and apologetic.

Father Gilmore closed his eyes, breathed deeply and nodded. "I understand." He turned to Lucius and his children. "This is where we worship our Lord. This is our temple, if you will. But we do not shed the blood of animals upon the altar."

"It is small," Lucius said, thinking of the temple of Jupiter upon the Capitol of Rome, or the temple of Apollo on the Palatine hill, both held up by soaring columns of marble all leading to the cella where the images of the Gods themselves were there for all to see. In that small Christian temple, the altar was empty save for a wooden cross, and a few wooden benches arrayed before it.

"I am sorry, Praefectus, but we must to our prayers now, and then the children will have their lessons."

"Thank you for showing us your temple," Phoebus said.

"You are most welcome," Gilmore said politely.

"Bye Phoebus, bye Calliope!" Rachel and Aaron said.

"Bye," the Metelli children said before taking Lucius' hands and following him outside into the sunshine.

It was good to be out in the open after the small, dark chapel interior. Lucius breathed deeply and gazed toward the rising mound of the Tor in the distance.

"Come," Lucius said. "Let's see if we can find some food. You must be hungry after all your hard work in the orchard."

The children began to run ahead toward the building where they were staying.

As they went, Lucius watched them and was shocked to see how grown they were. It seemed they were always growing, and he chided himself for not noticing more. Phoebus and Calliope reached the building and Lucius stopped to look out at the marshes to the North. It was quiet out there, but for the song of water fowl and the final breath of Summer in the reeds.

Then Etain's words came back into his mind, and he felt uneasy. Apollo had told him of things to come, that he should be wary, that he would not be able to protect him at all times. *Oh Far-Shooting Apollo, what did you mean by that?*

Lucius sighed, allowing a deep breath to fill him with peace and quiet strength, and then followed to join his family.

The night was silent and still, with not a whisper of wind upon the water or across the fields of Ynis Wytrin. Night owls swept low among the dark, laden branches of the orchards and along the slopes of the hills.

Etain, in her bed, opened her eyes wide and sat up slowly. The dream she had been seeking had come to her, and it was time to rise, to set things in motion. It was always with a heavy heart that she set people upon the paths the Gods showed her, but it was her duty too.

She glanced down at the young priestess who was sleeping upon the floor in front of the dwindling hearth fire and smiled. *Kind girl.*

Etain walked barefoot to the door where she took her thick wool cloak from the hook and wrapped it about herself. She opened the door quietly and went outside, closing it behind her. She took a deep breath.

That feels better, she thought, having grown tired of being indoors. She had been practicing the mind exercises that kept her body from wasting away from inactivity, and thanked the Gods she could still do it, for the pain and stiffness would have been too much to bear.

The moon was near full in the dark sky above, and slivers of black cloud swept across the sky, casting shadows everywhere in the gardens and along the path.

Etain made her way down to the small waterfall and cupped her hands to fill them with water. She splashed her face and allowed the Goddess' flow to awaken and rejuvenate her. After that, she wended her way along the avenue of yew trees and down the hill toward the great oak in the middle of the dewy field. She sat herself upon one of the stumps and set her gaze upon the field and the marshes in the distance. After some time in quiet meditation, she opened her eyes and saw them, the shades of the dead making their way toward the Tor and the Gates of Annwn.

They did not look at her as they passed, but she could see them, their pain, the fear, their excitement and anticipation. Their ghostly images carried wounds and worries that had not yet been healed. Those would disappear when they passed through the veil, and when

247

they emerged on Samhain's eve to walk for one night in the mortal world, they would be whole again.

"The Gates are open to you," she whispered. "The Gods welcome you…"

When the procession thinned to a simple mist hovering upon the grass, Etain set her mind to calling her friends. Then, she waited.

She was not cold as she sat there beneath her cloak, though her feet were bare upon the earth. She felt her strength returned in full, and thanked the Goddess for it.

Soon, the shapes of Father Gilmore and Weylyn emerged from out of the darkness as they came to join her.

"You heard me," Etain said.

"Yes, my friend," Gilmore said.

"It is good to see you well again, my lady." Weylyn sat down to her right and Gilmore on her left.

"I am recovered from my travels."

"You had them all worried," Gilmore said. "Especially Einion and Briana."

"I know. I am sorry for it, but it was necessary." Etain paused and pushed back her hood so that her red hair poured out and down over her shoulders. The moonlight lit her face almost as if she were in full sunlight, and her green eyes looked to the two men. "The Dragon has finally come among us, but he cannot stay."

"I believe they will leave in the morning, to go back to the ancient fortress where they live." Weylyn stroked his beard as he spoke.

"Fitting is it not, that he should live upon the hill of the very king who patronized the Christians who first came here?" Etain looked directly at Father Gilmore, waiting for him to say something. When he did not, she continued. "I know your mind, my dear friend… You do not trust him."

"How can I? He is a Roman. They crucified the Christus and chased Aaron and Rachel's family across the Empire seeking their deaths."

"It was not only the Romans who sought his death," Weylyn added delicately.

"And did not the Romans do what your god wished for them to do?" Etain asked. "The sacrifice of the Christus was intended, was it not?"

Gilmore nodded. "Yes." He sighed. "I only fear for the children. I cannot fail them."

"Nor shall you. But you need to see Lucius not for his being Roman, but for the man he is. He is not who you think he is. Not even I know all."

"What role does he have to play then?" Weylyn asked.

"The Dragon and his family are of utmost importance to the survival of Ynis Wytrin," she turned to Gilmore, "*and* to Aaron and Rachel."

"How is this possible, Etain? He is Roman, and he has much blood upon his hands, his very soul!"

Etain was silent, searching for the patience to make her friend understand. "You are not so closed-minded as this, Gilmore. Your love and fear for the children is clouding your judgement." He appeared shamed and she placed her hand upon his, softening her voice. "Yes, he is Roman, favoured by Roman gods, but he has shown himself to be more open than most. See how he has been here, how he has listened to everyone, tried to understand everything."

"And how he has opened the temple he built upon the hillfort to the people of the surrounding villages. He even asked me to bless it for him!" Weylyn looked across at Gilmore, surprised by his vehemence in defending Lucius as much as the other two were.

"It will begin soon. Einion's time is come, and even as we speak, darkness is closing in on Ynis Wytrin. The Dragon has already sought to defend us against his fellow Romans, but I doubt they will let it go so easily. He is also hunted."

"By who?" Weylyn asked.

"Many...the Morrigan among them."

"No." Weylyn hung his head for he knew what that could mean.

"I could not dissuade her from that course," Etain said sadly. "Nor can I interfere. None can. I fear the Dragon's path is no less perilous than the Christus'."

Gilmore might have been angry at the comparison, but instead, he found his compassion and understanding. *The Christus died for love of all. Can it be so for the Dragon?* "Then we must help him how we can."

"We will, when we know how," Etain said. "But the Gods want him to walk the path unaided for now. I have seen-"

Etain's words stopped in her throat as a child's scream rent the night air.

"In God's holy name, what was that?" Gilmore was on his feet looking toward the Christian dormitory, but the sound was coming from elsewhere.

"It's Calliope!" Weylyn said, beginning to walk toward the building where the Metelli had been sleeping.

"Stay, Weylyn," Etain said, waving him back.

"But she sounds in such pain and fear!" The old man felt his heart tighten at the sound, for he had come to care very much for the Metelli children. "What afflicts her so?" he said, turning to Etain.

"The Sight, Weylyn," Etain said. "Calliope has it, and she has just seen what I have seen."

"What is that?" the old Druid asked.

"The Dragon...and fire."

When Calliope screamed in her sleep, Lucius and Adara leapt from their beds, their hearts pounding, swords in hand. When they saw that the room was empty of intruders, they rushed to their daughter's bedside to hold her thrashing body.

"What's wrong with her?" Phoebus was crying. There was panic in his eyes, an intense concern and feeling of helplessness.

"Stand back, Phoebus!" Lucius said. "I don't know!"

There was a loud knocking on the door and Phoebus rushed to open it.

Barta's form filled the doorframe and behind him Einion, Briana and Dagon gathered to see what was happening.

"Praefectus?" Barta said, sword in hand, ready.

Lucius turned to them quickly. "She's just had a bad dream, I think. Please wait outside."

Barta nodded. "I'll be right here," he said to Phoebus, pointing at the flagstone outside the door.

"Hush, my girl," Adara whispered as she gathered her daughter into her arms. "You're safe. Mama and Baba are here. Shhhh." She began to hum a tune she knew Calliope would remember, hoping the thread of the music could reach her in her dreams, something to grab onto and bring her out.

Lucius went to the table and lit the oil lamp. When he returned, Calliope's eyelids were beginning to flutter and her breathing to calm. Her body had stopped thrashing.

"Calliope?" Lucius said, his voice calm, another layer to Adara's melody. "We're here. You're safe."

250

Calliope's eyes shot open and she lunged for Lucius, her arms wrapped desperately tight about his neck.

Lucius could feel her tears on his skin, her body shuddering in silent sobs as he held her.

After some minutes, she calmed fully and Lucius pried her away from his neck.

"Calliope?" Phoebus approached cautiously, a cup of water held out to her.

She took the cup and drank, choking on the water. When she recovered, she looked up at Lucius again, one of her hands gripping his, the other Adara's.

"Did you have a bad dream?" Adara asked.

Calliope shook her head. "I saw terrible things, Mama." She turned back to Lucius. "You can't leave this place, Baba. You have to stay here...in Ynis Wytrin."

"This is not our home, my girl. We need to leave. But we have a safe home not far away." Lucius stroked her sweaty brow and touched her cheek with the back of his hand.

But Calliope shook her head and shut her eyes tightly as if still seeing the horrors of her vision. "I saw...I saw a giant ring of fire and a dragon at the centre of it... It was roaring in pain, melting away, his eyes closing slowly as he died."

"It was just a dream. You were thinking of the lamb you saw die yesterday. Remember how sad that made you?"

"No, Baba!" she said. "This was different. The lamb went to sleep. The dragon was burning to death." She began to weep again and Adara and Lucius leaned over her, Phoebus as well.

"Your whole family is here, my girl...your friends. Breathe...breathe..." Adara stroked her daughter's hair and began to hum again as she laid her down upon the bed and covered her with the blankets. She continued singing and as Calliope nodded off into exhausted sleep, Lucius tucked Phoebus back in and went outside to see the others.

"How is she?" Dagon asked.

"Exhausted. She had a vivid dream."

"It was the Sight." Briana said. "When it first comes, it is terrifying."

"What do you mean?" Lucius asked. "Calliope can see things?"

"Maybe."

"She dreamed you were in danger when you were at that Roman's villa, remember?" Einion said. "And you were attacked."

"She dreamed of a dragon burning to death," Lucius said to them. "She was saddened by the lamb that passed away yesterday. She's back asleep now."

"Do you want me to stand outside the door?" Barta asked, loyal as ever.

"No, no, my friend. Get some sleep. We will be leaving today."

Barta nodded and went back to his room.

"She just needs to rest now." Lucius looked at Briana, Dagon and Einion. "Please. We're fine."

Briana and Einion began to walk, but Dagon stayed behind. "Anguis," he said calmly, the moonlight upon his bearded face. "In Sarmatia, when we dream of our animals of strength, we always take heed and ask the Gods for guidance. It is not something to be dismissed."

"Calliope had the dream about the dragon, not me."

"Yes, but she is a dragon also." Dagon said no more, but squeezed Lucius' shoulder firmly before going to join Briana.

When Lucius was alone, he paused to breathe again of the cool night air. As he was turning, he spotted the three elders sitting beneath the oak tree in the distance, and in his mind he heard once more the words of warning imparted to him by Etain.

When the sun finally rose over the isle, it was accompanied by gusting winds that shook the trees and sent aged leaves scattering across the grassy fields and orchards of Ynis Wytrin.

Calliope awoke. She smiled to see her mother, father and brother again. It was as if she did not remember much of the night before, only that she had had a bad dream.

It was a relief to Lucius and Adara to see Calliope as her old self, despite the sliver of dread the night before had pushed beneath their skin.

"I want to climb the Tor before we go," Calliope said after eating her morning meal of bread with honey.

"We need to be going home," Lucius said. "We will climb it next time."

"Baba, please! I really want to go for a walk."

Lucius looked at Adara.

"Might be good to take the children on a walk before getting back on the horses for so long. Briana told me there is a path through the woods on the hill behind here that winds around to the Tor from the other side."

All of their things were packed, and Dagon, Barta and Briana were ready to go as well. Morvran had brought the horses to the grassy area before the guesthouse and was feeding them while Barta checked all of the straps, saddle girths and harnesses.

"Where is Einion?" Lucius asked as he approached Dagon and Briana.

"Etain asked to see him," she said. "Only him." She knelt and looked at Calliope who rushed to see her. "Did you have a long night?" She squeezed the girl, her heart going out to her, wondering at the fear she must have felt, but Calliope reassured her.

"I'm fine. I don't know what the fuss is about," Calliope said. "Do you want to go for a walk up the Tor?"

Briana looked up at Lucius and Adara. "You don't want to leave yet?"

"Phoebus and Calliope are adamant. Besides, it might do us all good to stretch a bit before going."

"Then we had better get moving!" Briana said.

"Barta, you coming?" Dagon asked.

"I'll stay and finish prepping the horses, lord."

Briana led the way and the six of them headed up the path into the woods.

From the outside, Ynis Wytrin might have seemed small to some, but as they passed through that wood and across two fields where more animals grazed and apples weighed the limbs of orchard trees, it became apparent that the isle was larger than was thought. They climbed up and up and passed through long tunnels of ivy and tangled branches. The path was speckled with sunlight. The children ran ahead with Briana who showed them different types of plants and flowers. Occasionally, butterflies flit across their paths and the beady eyes of birds in the bushes watched the party pass.

Soon enough, they found themselves at the foot of the Tor, gazing up the steep northern slope.

"It's much larger up close," Adara said.

"Einion and I spent much time up there over the years." Briana grasped Dagon's hand where he stood beside her.

253

Adara smiled at Lucius. They had both noticed how very close Dagon and Briana had become. It was more than lovers. A bond had grown between them that was rare in most, a bond Lucius and Adara knew all too well and cherished.

"What are we waiting for?" Phoebus said. "Let's go up to the top!" He and Calliope ran ahead and the adults followed.

"What are the lines around it?" Dagon asked.

"It is the processional way. The Druids and priestesses use it at Beltane and Samhain." Briana's finger traced the lines in the air before them. "This is one of the great Gates of Annwn."

Lucius felt a chill run along his spine. "It looks like a sleeping dragon," he said.

"Some believe the Tor is hollow, and that if we follow the path in the proper way, we can enter Annwn itself."

"I thought Annwn was the Land of the Dead?" Dagon asked.

"No. The living can go there...some have been lost there forever." Briana turned to the others as she began to climb. "We won't take the processional way."

"Children, stay close!" Adara called, but they continued to run, and climb up the steep grassy slopes.

When they all reached the top, Phoebus and Calliope were waiting for them.

"There's Einion!" Calliope said, pointing toward the middle of the plateau where there was an altar open to the sky and beside it, Einion, speaking closely with Etain.

"Why are they meeting up here?" Dagon asked.

"I don't know," Briana said. "I didn't expect her to leave her room."

"She told me she would be up and about today," Lucius said.

"We should not disturb them," Adara added, holding the children.

They paused to look out across the land, their sight stretching as far as it could. A land of water and green spread out before them like a blanket of the Gods. Sun and cloud reflected in the calm of the marshes, and banks of fog and mist rolled across the surface as if alive.

"Is that our home?" Phoebus asked.

Lucius stepped to look to the southeast and nodded. "Yes. That's it. Seems we have a bit of a journey ahead of us."

"Can others see the Tor from outside?" Calliope asked.

254

"That's a good question," Briana answered. "Only those meant to see it can."

"How is that possible?"

"Well, the Gods have blessed this place, and would not allow any harm to come to it."

"Because it is so peaceful?" Phoebus asked.

"That is one of the many reasons, young man."

Everybody turned to see Etain walking toward them, her red hair hovering about her head in the wind, her green eyes keen and lively as she looked upon them, smiling.

"Etain!" Briana hugged the priestess. "Thank the Gods you're well again."

"I am well. You came to me, and that helped," Etain said, her hand caressing Briana's face. She then turned to the others. "You are leaving Ynis Wytrin today."

"Yes, lady," Adara said. "Though it is no easy thing to leave." She bowed to Etain and the priestess stepped forward to take her hands.

"You are always welcome, Adara Metella. The Gods brought you here, and so you will return some day. I am sorry we did not have occasion to speak more," she turned to the children, "or that we did not have more of a chance to get to know one another. Did you both enjoy your time here? I know that Rachel and Aaron loved meeting you. They will be distraught to see you leave."

"Oh, may we come back?" Phoebus asked almost jumping at the prospect.

"I do believe you will return. The mists will always open for your family." She glanced at Lucius and then turned to Briana. "I have spoken with Einion. He will need your help, and your support. All of you," she said to the others, her eyes resting on Dagon and then again on Lucius. She nodded as she observed them, reading them as if she were reading a scroll of secrets, but smiling all the while.

But then her smile faded and she held out her hand to Lucius who moved a little slowly to take it. They walked apart from the others for a few paces. Then Etain stopped and looked down the steep side of the Tor to the Well of the Chalice and Ynis Wytrin spreading out beyond to Wearyall Hill and the lone thorn upon its crest.

"Lucius Metellus Anguis..."

ADAM ALEXANDER HAVIARAS

"Yes, lady?"

"I am sorry for the burden I placed upon your shoulders. I would have given you more to arm yourself against the coming trials, but some things the Gods hide with intent, even from me. Go carefully forward. Be wary. Be brave, as I know you are, for your friends, for your family, and…for yourself." Suddenly she grasped Lucius' hand tightly and stared into his eyes.

She had tears in her own, but it did not frighten Lucius so much as give him courage, for he knew she cared for his entire family. There was no malice there, certainly not the type he had seen in the eyes of the ordo members from Lindinis.

"Sometimes, following the path we are meant to take requires disobeying our gods for a time, just as children will disobey their parents as they find their way in the world. The journey of such an action is sometimes the only way for us to grow. Do you understand."

"I confess, lady, I do not. But I do trust in the Gods. Epona, Venus and Apollo himself guide me in all things."

For a moment, Etain observed Lucius so keenly that he felt great discomfort creep upon him.

"Forgive me," she said. "I have rarely met your like. I wish you well on your travels, Lucius Metellus Anguis, and the blessings of the Mother upon your family."

"I thank you." Lucius bowed his head, but felt her hand beneath his chin, lifting his head.

"I will see you again."

Etain then raised a hand to the others and began to descend the slope of the Tor, heading for the long avenue of ancient oaks that led away to the northeast of that ancient hill.

Lucius joined Adara, the children, and Dagon.

"What was that about?" Dagon asked.

Adara came and put her hand upon Lucius' shoulder.

"She was wishing us well and said she looked forward to seeing us again." Lucius did not know why, but he could not bring himself to tell them all that Etain had said to him just then, and the day before. He did not know if it was for fear, or something else he could not quite express in words or in thought.

"Will we come back here, Baba?" Calliope asked.

Lucius knelt down. "I'm sure we will. Etain seems to think so. But next time, Calliope, let's not charge off on our ponies to get here."

"All right, Baba."

Lucius kissed her cheek and stood to see Einion and Briana at the other end of the Tor's summit, their forms windswept and close as they talked.

"I hope he's all right," Dagon said.

As Etain took Lucius aside to speak with him, Briana excused herself and went to see her brother who had been standing still, silent, staring across the shoulders of Ynis Wytrin to the southwest.

Einion heard her footfalls approaching but did not turn.

"We spent so much time sitting up here, thinking of home, of Ynis Wytrin, of the past and the future." Briana laced her arm through Einion's and stood against him.

"The last time we were here was when Weylyn, Etain and Gilmore asked us to help Lucius, to go and find him in the North. An impossible mission..."

"And yet we accomplished that, and gained lifelong friends." Briana smiled, and Einion could tell she was.

He turned his neck to look at her and smiled. "Dagon?"

"All of them," she said, blushing. "But yes...Dagon. I love him."

"I know you do. He's a king of his people, a great warrior, generous and kind," Einion nodded, but he was distracted. "And he is trusted by the Dragon."

"Yes, Brother." Briana stood in front of him then. She was excited, her eyes aglow as he had not seen them before. "Dagon has asked me to be his wife."

Einion smiled sadly, his eyes straying over her shoulder to the southwest again, but then back at her. He hugged her. "I'm happy for you." His arms wrapped about her tightly, desperately. "Whatever your heart wishes, I support...always."

"Thank you!" Briana returned the force of the hug and then stood back to look into her brother's eyes. There was confusion...and fear...anger, and thirst, there. "What did Etain tell you?"

Einion breathed deeply, his eyes closing as the wind swept around them.

"She said, it is time for me to take back our father's throne."

VIII

AD INDAGATIO

'For a Quest'

The Metelli and their friends arrived back at the hillfort late the night before. Leaving Ynis Wytrin had not been as easy as arriving, for even Briana and Einion could not fully fathom the hidden ways through the misty marshes.

In leaving the Isle, the party also experienced the sad descent of their mood, and it affected all of them, including the children who went through bouts of plaintiveness, or yielded to sullen silence. However, a part of them yearned to return home, to see their friends there.

As they rode, Lucius went over in his mind the letters he needed to write, to his mother, and his brother Caecilius, his sister Clarinda. For years they had been distant, virtual strangers, though they were blood. For some reason, the urge to write them was more intense after leaving Ynis Wytrin than it had been before.

It was late when they arrived at the hillfort, and the Sarmatian troops who had been on duty - the decurions had maintained the regimen while Lucius was away - promptly helped with the horses. Everyone who had travelled from Ynis Wytrin immediately went to their beds, and after Lucius had satisfied himself that all was well with the troops and that nothing out-of-the-ordinary had occurred, he too counted himself among those seeking slumber.

Only Einion avoided sleep. He stood outside, cloaked by the darkness and hovering around the temple at the southeast corner of the fortress, seeking answers in the shadows.

How can I take back my father's throne? he asked again. *I can't do it alone...and yet, I would keep my friends from danger.* He knew his uncle, Caradoc, was strong, and that he had many men and some Roman administrators supporting him.

Etain had told him he would need Lucius and Dagon's help, but the thought of taking that mighty rock surrounded by the crashing seas with just three men was unthinkable. He also knew Briana would insist on going, but if he should fall, she would be the last of their house. She needed to live, especially since she had new life with Dagon.

And yet, I need Dagon's help as well!

The situation was confounding.

The following day over the morning meal, Dagon and Briana emerged from their room to see everyone save Einion gathered around the great round hearth fire. Ula and Aina greeted them warmly and brought plates of steaming bread, cheese, and honey with pitchers of water from the well on the eastern slope of the hill.

"Good morning!" Lucius said

"Good morning," Dagon answered, his smile broad.

"You look pleased, my lord," Barta said without thinking, and was followed by a burst of laughter and a wink from Briana that made the big Sarmatian blush. "That is not what I meant!" he said, rubbing his good eye.

"I know, my friend!" Dagon said as he and Briana stepped into the circle and sat upon the logs, their plates set aside for the moment.

"We have something we would like to say." Briana laced her arm through Dagon's and he gripped her hand.

"Tell us why you look so happy!" Calliope said, giggling despite herself. They seemed positively shining to her.

"Well, Calliope... Dagon, you may tell them."

"Right...well..." Dagon rubbed his beard and looked around the circle. "Where is Einion?"

"His thoughts weigh heavily upon him," Lucius said. "I think he spent the night out of doors."

Briana nodded. "It helps him to think." She shook her head. "We will tell you anyway, for he already knows of this."

Dagon nodded and carried on.

Lucius noted he looked very proud standing there. "Well? Out with it!"

"I have asked Briana to be my wife."

Adara was on her feet right away, her hands clasped together in anticipation.

"And I said 'yes'!" Briana finished.

"That's wonderful!" Adara was around the fire in a moment and hugging both of them. "Congratulations!"

"Thank you," Dagon said, kissing Briana on the cheek.

Lucius and Barta stood too, and together they went to congratulate the couple.

"The men will be pleased," Barta said to Briana, grasping her hands in his and bowing. "You wield a sword even better than my lord!" He laughed so that the whole hall shook with it.

The children danced around, both of them anticipating a great celebration.

"When will you hold the ceremony?" Lucius asked, gathering Calliope up into his arms as she danced too close to the fire.

"We haven't discussed that, but with any hope, soon," Briana beamed.

Adara hugged her again. "I'm so happy for you."

"Thank you."

Lucius looked at them both and felt a pang of sadness and regret at the thought of what Alene and Alerio had missed out on, but he pushed it aside. That had nothing to do with Dagon and Briana's happiness.

"Barta, call an assembly for this afternoon," Lucius said. "The men will need to hear this news from their lord."

"Yes, Praefectus!" Barta gathered up his plate and cup of water and handed them to Ula who came to take them. "Their voices will shake the sky."

The men were marched out onto the wide open space to the East of the plateau in their separate turmae and a makeshift dais was set up with the empty beer barrels that had accumulated since the Sarmatians' arrival there.

With Lucius and Barta standing to either side of him, Dagon mounted the barrels to address the men.

"Sarmatiana!" he roared, his sword in the air, and the men answered with a bellow as loud as any army could give.

But they knew their lord was not addressing them with ill news, for he shone with joy and life. They fell silent quickly to hear what news he had for them.

"My brothers! You are my people...my family!" More cheers erupted. "I have news that I wish to share with you."

"Tell us, my lord!" Vaclar yelled from the front of the ranks where he stood with Lenya and Badru, the other decurions.

"I am getting married!" Dagon yelled his arms open to the sky as if he wished the Gods themselves to hear him.

The Sarmatians cheered even more loudly, so much so that Adara, the children, Einion and Briana came out of the hall to the eastern edge of the plateau to look down on the assembly.

"To who, my lord?" Lenya called out.

"To Briana of Dumnonia...a princess...and a warrior!" Dagon pointed to where he saw the woman he loved standing before the small group upon the plateau with the Dragon's family, and the men roared approval as if acclaiming a general upon the field of battle.

"I think they approve!" Lucius said to Barta at the top of his voice.

Barta nodded and they both watched as Dagon jumped down from the barrel and strode through the throng of Sarmatian warriors, his kinsmen, and up the slope of the plateau to gather Briana into his arms.

The cheering went on for some time and wine and beer were brought out and passed among the troops in celebration of the announcement.

Dagon and Briana moved among them, talking with them of horses, of swords, of Sarmatia and the heirs their lord would have with his new-found queen, for queen she would be outside of Rome's empire.

Briana felt strange as she moved among them, welcomed completely by them, even though she did not know them well. *It shows how loyal they are to Dagon,* she thought. *How very much they love him and are willing to die for him. I will earn their love too,* she told herself.

Lucius, Adara and the children moved among the troops too, every one of them protective as lions around the Dragon and his family. Lucius noticed Sigwyll Sloane carousing with them also, his knowledge of horses having won him a spot among them, as well as their respect. Soon, some of the villagers from outside the hillfort came to join the festivities.

The impromptu betrothal celebration went on for hours into the evening.

"Lucius!" Culhwch called, making his way through the crowd with Alma and Paulus who promptly joined Phoebus and Calliope at the stables.

Lucius waved them over.

"What's the occasion?" Culhwch asked.

"The men are celebrating Dagon and Briana's betrothal."

"That's wonderful news!" Alma said. "When did this happen?" She turned to Adara.

"We only just found out this morning," Adara said, "after returning from Ynis Wytrin."

"Ynis Wytrin?" Culhwch said. "I thought you went to Lindinis?"

Lucius shook his head. "We were, ah…sidetracked. We never made it to Lindinis. Why? Has something happened while we were away?"

"Well…" Culhwch looked a little worried. "It's just that…well, Cradawg said the building supplies arrived finally, so that is good. But just last night, Trevor Reghan was here looking for you. I had come up to see if Ula and Aina were all right and found him speaking with some of your men."

"What did he want?" Lucius asked.

"He told me in confidence that he heard Serenus Crescens raging to a couple of the other ordo members in Lindinis about something you did to his son."

Lucius' faced darkened. "We had a run-in with his son and his friends on the road."

"What happened?" Culhwch asked.

"They were attacking one of the priestesses from Ynis Wytrin who had wandered away from the Isle to the old hillfort north of Lindinis. We got there just in time, but I had to teach the boy a lesson."

"Crescens is not a man to cross, Lucius. You know him by now."

"I know," Lucius said, patting the Durotrigan on the back. "I've dealt with others like him and worse. He needs me right now and won't risk me ignoring his request for help."

"I won't ask what that is about, but I still wouldn't trust him, or any of them for that matter, besides Trevor."

Lucius acknowledged that Culhwch had a point.

"Adara," Alma said, taking her arm. "What was Ynis Wytrin like?"

Adara noticed the awe and respect in the tall Briton's voice, her glassy eyes full of questions. "Well…" Adara said as they began to walk toward the hall, away from all the noise of the celebrations, "…it's unlike any place I've ever been to…"

"Where is Dagon?" Culhwch asked. "I would congratulate him and Briana. They will make a fine couple!"

262

"They're over there," Lucius pointed, "in the middle of that large group of Sarmatians."

Culhwch was a brawny man, but the thought of pushing his way through the warriors was not appealing, especially as they were into the drink by that point. "I think I'll get some beer first," he laughed.

Lucius watched him go and get swept up in the crowd. He then spoke to Barta whom he knew to be standing behind his right shoulder. "We need to be cautious of the ordo members."

"That is what was in my thoughts also, Praefectus. From what you have told me, and from how his son behaved, men like this Crescens cannot be trusted."

Lucius nodded. He had to admit, he was glad of Barta's strong presence. Sometimes it was the only thing that allowed him to let his guard down. He turned to his bodyguard.

"My friend, you must enjoy yourself as well. Your king is getting married. Have fun with the men. I'm going to check on the children."

"As you wish, Praefectus," Barta said. "Perhaps just one drink..." And he went slowly to join Culhwch who was pouring himself a tankard and talking with Badru and Sigwyll Sloane.

Lucius made his way up toward the stables and poked his head in to see the children brushing down the ponies. "Phoebus, Calliope?"

"Here, Baba!" Calliope said.

"Are you nearly finished?"

"Yes, Baba."

"It is getting late. I want you to make your way to the hall with Paulus to join Mama and Alma."

"Yes, sir, Praefectus," Paulus said politely.

"Come, Paulus!" Phoebus said excitedly. "Ula and Aina made some fresh bread earlier. We can have some with honey!"

The three children put the brushes away, closed the stable doors and ran up the hill.

Lucius checked everything to make sure the horses were secure, the latches closed properly, and then went outside into the gathering dusk.

Fires were being lit and his men were settling in for a long celebration with their king and queen-to-be.

As Lucius continued up the hill, he saw a lone figure sitting upon the south rampart.

It was Einion.

They had not had a chance to speak of things since Ynis Wytrin. In truth, Lucius had not been able to speak with Einion on the Isle either. He also wanted to leave him to his thoughts for a time, knowing how the Dumnonian needed time to think when a problem arose. It was time to ask Einion what Etain had said.

Lucius walked back down the hill, around the western end of the stables and passed the planted crops until he reached and climbed the southern rampart.

The sun was setting red in the West, and ravens croaked and glided along the ancient defences that fell steeply away from them.

"Mind if I join you, my friend?" Lucius asked, not sitting until Einion invited him to.

Einion turned and looked up at Lucius. "Of course not. Sit."

"What's happening? You know you can speak to me," Lucius said. "We're friends, are we not?"

"Of course we are. I just..." Einion ran his fingers through his long hair and tied it back with a leather thong he had been wrapping around his fingers as he watched the sun dip. "I've just got a lot on my mind."

"Are you not happy about Dagon and Briana?" Lucius suspected that as Briana was the only family he had left, all the others having been slain, it might feel strange to Einion that she was marrying.

"I'm very happy. If ever there was a match for Briana, it's Dagon. He's generous and kingly, and a great warrior. The Gods have smiled on them. It makes me happy, truly." He looked sideways at Lucius.

"But?"

"But the Gods have also shown *me* a path...finally."

"And you're not sure if you should take it."

"No. I'm sure. I must take it. But...I may not survive it."

"I feel the same way before every battle." Lucius had somewhat forgotten the tang of fear before an engagement. The battlefields of Caledonia seemed like a distant nightmare.

"How do you deal with it? The fear."

Lucius sighed. "I trust in the Gods, my men, and my training. I also trust in my friends, Einion." Lucius stared at the grass and then back at Einion after a few moments of silence. "What did Etain tell you?"

"She said... She said that the time to take back my father's throne was now. By Samhain."

"That's soon, isn't it?"

"Yes. A little over a month."

"You can't do that alone, you know."

"No. I can't. I don't even know if anyone loyal to our house survived my uncle's slaughter." Einion pushed himself to his feet and Lucius joined him. "I remember that night like it was yesterday, Lucius. So much blood. The screams... My mother and father cut down..."

Lucius gripped Einion by the shoulders. The red sun lit their faces. "Listen to me now. You are not alone anymore. You hear me? You have friends and allies."

Einion pulled away, not out of anger, but something else.

Lucius continued. "Etain also told us something upon the Tor. She said that we were to help you, that you would need us."

"Yes. She said that, but I cannot take you away from your family, Lucius. They also need you. I can't risk your death, or Dagon's."

"Listen, Einion. This peace here," Lucius indicated the hillfort, their home, the crops, all of it. "This is Elysium in a sense, but it can never last, as much as I would want it to. I would rather risk my life fighting for my friend than for the imperial family. That was not always the case, but it is now. I will go with you to Dumnonia, and I will fight at your side."

Lucius meant the words he was saying, for he knew how heavy a weight Einion carried upon his shoulders, had carried for so many years. He also felt a prick of dread in his gut as he made up his mind to help him. He put his arm around Einion and pulled him toward the hall. "Come. Let's pour some wine and talk about it."

It was late when Adara came down from putting the children to bed, and Dagon and Briana came inside from the gatherings around the fires without. The Sarmatians could still be heard carousing, but the start of rain was beginning to drive them to the barracks and tents which were laid out on the north side of the fortress.

"Einion!" Briana said as she and Dagon came in. "We didn't see you. I was looking for you." She came to her brother's side by the fire and sat down. Dagon sat down heavily between Lucius and Barta, but he looked across at Einion.

"Einion," Dagon said. "I hope that my wish to marry your sister has not caused you any distress."

Einion put up his hands right away to set the thought to rest. "Not at all. I am happy for you both, and as I was telling Lucius, I can't imagine a better match. I just wish you luck with her," he joked, winking at the Sarmatian, even as Briana gave him a strong elbow in the ribs.

Adara refilled everyone's wine cups and sat down beside Lucius who put his arm around her. She could feel Lucius was tense, that something was different, and then she saw Einion staring at Lucius.

"Tell them," Lucius said.

Adara looked around, as did Barta, and Dagon, but Briana looked sadly at her brother. "Tell us what?" Adara asked.

Einion looked at each of them, the only family that he had left. He thought of the two children upstairs in their beds who gave freely of their affection and trust to him, a stranger from out of the South. For years he had thought about the day he would set out to take back his family's stolen throne, and yet now, as he stood upon the precipice, ready to set out, his nerve was barely holding.

"I can't!" Einion said loudly. "I cannot ask it of you. Any of you. I'm sorry, Lucius, but my conscience will not allow it."

"What are you talking about?" Dagon asked.

The silence was uncomfortable, laced with the potential danger which had replaced the celebratory atmosphere of hours before.

"Etain spoke to Einion," Briana said. "She told him that now was the time to reclaim our father's throne in Dumnonia."

"What?" Adara squeezed Lucius' hand.

Einion looked at his sister. "Etain said it was time for *me* to reclaim father's throne."

"You can't do it alone," Briana said, leaning forward so that her eyes blazed in the firelight of the hearth.

"He won't be alone," Lucius said calmly.

Everyone stopped talking and looked at him.

"And neither will you!" Dagon said without hesitation. "I'm with you!"

"No," Briana said.

"Ah, yes, my lady," Dagon said calmly. "If Einion goes to avenge the death of your family and retake the stolen throne, then I will ride with him. You are my family now. No Sarmatian would do otherwise."

There was some arguing back and forth, but all of that faded out for Adara who turned to Lucius. "You can't do this," she whispered. Then, she stood and went through the main doors into the darkness outside. She felt faint as she stared up at the cloudy skies, droplets of cold rain falling upon her face. *Gods, do not let him leave me again.*

Adara heard the doors open and a moment later, Lucius was by her side.

"My love," he said softly. "I cannot avoid helping Einion. He travelled north to us, to help me when he didn't even know me. Even when he could have been travelling to reclaim his own kingdom. He risked his life to do that, as did Briana. And they saved my life more than once."

Adara turned to him, her eyes hard and full of fear.

"Can we so easily forget what others have done for us, for our children?"

"Of course not. How can you ask that?" She hugged him. "I'm scared Lucius. I can't lose you. We need you. Phoebus and Calliope need their father more than ever now."

"I know. And I need all of you. But I owe a debt to Einion and Briana. We all do."

"Then let us come with you."

"That is madness. No. You need to stay here. Safe within the hillfort."

"I know the troops will look out for us, but it still won't be safe."

Lucius thought for a moment. He needed to help Einion if he could, but he also knew that he could not go anywhere without ensuring that Adara and the children were safe. He turned to her, his wet hair sticking to his cheeks. "I'll ask Barta and Briana to stay with you."

Adara was shaking her head. She knew Barta would be reluctant to leave Lucius' side, and that Briana would certainly want to go with Einion. She had already said as much. "They won't agree."

"They'll have to," Lucius said, taking her hand and walking back to the hall. When they entered, the others turned to look at them.

Lucius and Adara stood before the hearth of their home, before their friends.

"Einion, Briana... You've both done a great deal, sacrificed much, to help our family. You've saved my life several times, and trusted me with yours." Lucius looked directly at Einion. "I will ride with you to get your throne back. One way or another, it will happen."

"I know this must be hard for both of you," Briana said.

"Being apart always is," Adara said.

"As are my conditions," Lucius added, and they all looked up at him. "Briana...I would ask that you stay here to help keep my family safe."

"What?" Briana was on her feet. "Of course I would do so, but I can't let Einion go alone."

"Briana," Einion said. "Etain's words. She said that it should be Lucius and Dagon. No others."

Lucius could see that Briana was torn between acceptance of Etain's words, and outright disobedience to her, a woman she admired and had always trusted implicitly.

"But I will go with you and my lord, Praefectus," Barta said then, his voice a deep, low grumbling from where he sat, his hollow eye socket shadowed by firelight.

"No, my friend," Lucius said calmly, though it was no easy thing. "I ask that you remain here to command the men and, more importantly, to guard my family with your life."

Barta looked at Lucius and then down into the flames of the fire. He was torn, and everyone could see it, but he thought of the Dragon's wife and children, how kind they were to him and how, if anything happened to them, he could not bear it.

"If it is your wish that I stay, Praefectus, then I will obey and guard them with my life."

"Thank you," Lucius said.

"If Barta is staying, then I can go with you," Briana said.

"I need you both, to stay," Lucius said, and looked to Dagon.

The Sarmatian nodded, and turned to Briana. "Anguis is right. You must stay and help Adara and Barta. I will be your proxy in the fight for your home."

"But, this isn't right!"

"Briana," Einion's voice cut through the protestation. "Lucius is right. You should stay. If I do not survive the fighting, then you will be the sole heir to the throne in Dumnonia. You need to remain behind."

Briana fell silent then. Of course she wanted to see the children and Adara safe, though she knew Adara was more than capable of protecting herself since she had started training her. She also knew that it would be difficult for Lucius to fight if he was worrying about his family, or for Dagon to fight if he was worried about her.

"Very well... I agree."

"Thank you, Briana," Adara said.

"It's not that I don't want to help you," Briana said. "It's just-"

"They know, Briana," Dagon said, holding her close. "And when we return victorious, we will be married before the Gods!"

"I'll drink to that!" Einion said, raising his glass. "To Dagon and Briana!" They all drank.

"And to reclaiming your throne!" Lucius added loudly.

They talked into the night about the route to take and the chances of success, but they had to admit that until they arrived in Dumnonia and found out more information from the locals, observed their uncle's troop movements and more, they could not plan very well.

The talk worried Adara and she excused herself to go to bed.

After more talk and more wine, Lucius excused himself and followed after his wife.

"Lucius!" Einion came running over to him before he went up the stairs to the second floor. "Thank you. I know it was not an easy decision."

Lucius smiled sadly. "It was the only decision, my friend." He turned and went upstairs, checking in on each of the children before going to his and Adara's room.

Her back was turned to the door as he came in, a single oil lamp lit on the table against the wall. There was a sniffle, but it was quickly stifled.

Lucius closed the door quietly and walked around the bed to the other side to sit down.

Adara's eyes, more grey than their usual brilliant green in the lamplit darkness, were open, staring at the window in the wall where the leather curtain fluttered in the cool breeze at the window.

Lucius placed his hand on her leg and stared with her. "I couldn't refuse to help him."

"I know," she said, her voice tremulous, which frustrated her, but she controlled her anger which was really born of the great fear she felt. *He is a man of honour! How could I expect him to do anything else?*

269

"Einion and Dagon are two of the best warriors I've ever met. The three of us will be a force to be reckoned with against his uncle's rabble."

"Briana told me the story of the massacre, Lucius." Adara sat up on the bed, the left sleeve of her tunica falling down over her shoulder.

Lucius reached up to wipe away a tear on her face with his thumb. "They won't see us coming. Men like that rule through fear and violence, threats. It is possible that when Einion kills this Caradoc, the troops will bow to the rightful king."

Adara reached up and put her hand to his cheek. "Oh, my love. How can you be so naive?"

"I'm not, Adara." Lucius removed her hand.

She crossed her arms and stood. "You do not know this enemy or the landscape."

"But Einion does."

"He's blinded by his yearning for vengeance."

"Dagon and I will look out for him. Keep him in check."

"And who will look out for you?"

"Do you forget the Gods who watch over us, Adara? How much they have helped us through all the long years and so many dangers?"

"No. I do not forget. Of course not." She held her palms up and uttered a quick wish.

"Then trust that we will succeed. That I will return." He stood up and put his arms around her. She did not pull away. "Your belief in me means more than I can say, my love. It gives me strength. There have been times when I thought I would die...many times. Times when I thought that my last breath was upon me, or that I would never live to hold you again, but then the thought of you...of our children...our family...would come into my mind like a warm, rejuvenating light and I would find the strength to fight on. I've done things I never would have thought possible, not even sure how I managed them."

Lucius turned and went to the window to stare out at the moonlit green of the hillfort and hear the voices of his men below, calling out or singing in the rain as they celebrated. He turned back to Adara.

"Some petty warlord is not going to prevent me from coming back to you, let alone thwart Einion taking back what is rightfully his. I have to help him do this."

"Lucius…I'm scared."

He hugged her tightly. "That is normal before any battle."

Adara wanted to tell him of her dreams, of the horrors she had witnessed, but she bit her tongue. Some things were better left unsaid. She did not want to weaken his resolve or faith in himself and the Gods, for in doing so, she could very well endanger him. *Sometimes, faith and resolve are the best armour.*

"Promise me one thing," she said. "Besides that you will return to us."

"Anything."

"Promise me that you will not worry about us. We'll be fine. I can protect the children, and I have Barta, Briana, and an army here with me. Just focus on the task of your quest and coming through it alive."

Lucius stared at her for a few moments, unsure if he could promise such as thing as not to worry about them, much less not think of them while he was gone.

Adara stared up at him, her eyes, her will unyielding. "Promise," she repeated.

"I promise. I will fight, and I will survive. I will come back to you."

Their hands gripped each other, the entwined dragon rings glinting in the lamplight as they kissed.

Adara pulled herself away and led Lucius to their bed where she knelt and removed her tunica, naked before him. With urgency, she then helped him to get undressed.

In the quiet of their room that night, they made love longingly, feeling every moment and shiver of pleasure, and every wave of climax before laying entwined, like the dragons upon their fingers, to fall asleep as the lamp oil burned away and they were left in moonlight.

Lucius awoke early the next morning, before the sun rose, while waves of fog yet hugged the ramparts of the hillfort. He left Adara sleeping soundly beneath the furs and, after he dressed, he kissed her cheek and went downstairs quietly. It was cold in the hall, the fire's embers long since doused.

Lucius took his thick black cloak from the peg, put it over his shoulders, and went out the double doors, his sword in his left hand.

271

He shivered as he stood outside, the scent of autumn making itself known to him.

The detritus of the celebrations was scattered on the east side of the hillfort, but he knew his men would clean it up. They were on leave and they needed a release, the prize of living at Death's dark door on a daily basis in the North.

Lucius took a few steps and turned to see the home he had built for them. *And soon we will have a bathhouse on the eastern slopes.* The thought warmed him, especially on that cold morning. But as he looked at the outbuildings, the crops they had planted which were ready for harvesting, he found himself not wanting to leave. In fact, he felt inside a part of him crying out that it was not a good idea to go on this quest with Einion and Dagon.

But I need to. I must!

As Lucius walked down from the plateau to the ramparts, he went over the various strategies for their quest that he had been formulating in his mind. But it was no use, for without detailed plans of the fortress, the landscape leading up to it, and enemy troop dispositions, it was all conjecture. They would have to rely upon Einion's memory and hopefully, support from those still loyal to him…if any were alive.

Their foray into Dumnonia would not be like meeting an army in the open field, or dealing with Caledonians whose tactics he was familiar with. This was new territory, and he could not reveal his identity in case it got back to the authorities at Isca Dumnoniorum. He walked, his boots squelching in the wet grass as he continued to walk the perimeter of the hillfort, all the while his sights on the hall upon the plateau. At the northwest corner, he stared in the direction of Ynis Wytrin and felt the chill of Etain's words upon him. *Did she speak with the Morrigan?*

The thought of that dread goddess made him angry, for she had given strength to Rome's enemies, those who had butchered Hippogriff and his men. He knew the anger did not serve him, but he also knew he could not forget what had happened. Their dead faces peered at him from across the black river of the Afterlife, pleading, weeping.

He realized it was time to move forward, to try and forget about the past. He had promised Adara he would focus upon staying alive and coming back to her, and that he would do.

When his circuit was complete, Lucius walked through the Sarmatian camp and came upon Vaclar as he was finishing relieving himself beneath one of the trees that had sprouted from the ramparts.

"Oh! Sorry, Praefectus. I did not see you coming."

"At ease, Vaclar. We're not on the parade ground." Lucius smiled and continued to walk, his decurion at his side. "Did the men enjoy themselves last night?"

"Does a Sarmatian like horses?" he laughed. "They did, yes, sir. Thank you for contributing to the festivities. It always means a lot to the men."

"It does to me as well," Lucius said with great sincerity. "Tell me... Are the men pleased with Lord Dagon's choice of bride?"

"Well...she's not Sarmatian, to be sure, but they are indeed thrilled. Lady Briana rides and swings a sword as well as the Dragon's own wife, and that is no easy task."

Lucius laughed. "I thank you for your confidence in my wife, Vaclar. Truly. Briana has taught Adara much about sword play, and I daresay the student has excelled. But I'm glad to hear that both of them are loved by the men."

"Absolutely, Praefectus." Vaclar stopped and Lucius turned to him. "Is there something the matter, sir?"

"You are always attuned to what is happening in men's minds, Vaclar. That's good. The truth is, that the Lord Dagon, myself, and Einion will be leaving soon on an important quest-"

"Then we will ride with you, sir!" Vaclar said quickly.

"No. We must go alone and in stealth. But, I will need all of you on the alert while I am away. I have reason to believe that someone might be seeking to do my family harm, that they have been for some time."

"I see." Vaclar was silent a moment. "You know, Praefectus, that any of us would lay down our lives not only for you, but for your family, for they are our family as well."

Lucius gripped his hands firmly and nodded. "That is good to hear. I'm leaving Barta in command while I'm away, along with you, Badru and Lenya as seconds. You are to protect Adara, my children, and Briana at all costs, and keep watch on the villagers down the hill, for they too are our friends and allies."

"Praefectus..." Vaclar creased his brow and stared at Lucius. "Are you expecting an outright attack upon your home here?"

"I don't know. I can't be certain."

273

"We will do all you command and more, Praefectus. Do not worry."

"Thank you." Lucius looked up the hill to the stables. "Now, I must check on our supplies. I believe we will be leaving in the next few days."

"Praefectus," Vaclar saluted and turned to walk in the opposite direction.

Lucius made his way past the storage pits that were sunk in the ground at the foot of the plateau's slope and lifted the doors. Inside, the stores of grain were about half-way full, and the stocks of beans were dwindling. They would need to replenish them before Saturnalia.

The stables were quiet, but as Lucius entered, he saw someone's shadow at the end of the row of stalls, cast by the light of a hanging clay lamp. A small voice was speaking softly and as Lucius turned to walk down the row of stalls, he saw Phoebus standing before Lunaris, brushing him and speaking into his ear.

"Phoebus?"

The boy turned quickly and then relaxed. "Good morning, Baba."

"Why are you up so early?" Lucius walked over to his son and put his arm around him. When he did so, he realized how very tall the boy had become.

"I couldn't sleep," Phoebus said, continuing to brush Lunaris down.

The big dapple grey stallion nuzzled the boy.

"He loves it when you brush him."

"Do you think so? I love to do it. I can't wait until I'm big enough to ride him." Phoebus' voice was sad then, the brush pausing upon the stallion's neck.

"What's wrong?" Lucius asked, reaching up to pat Lunaris and rub his forehead, all the while looking at his son.

"I don't want you to go."

Lucius stopped and turned to face the boy. "How do you know I'm going somewhere?"

"I heard you all talking last night, Baba. I'm not a child anymore. I know that you're going to help Einion slay his uncle and get his throne back."

Lucius did not know what to say. Usually, he told the children the minimal details of what he was doing when it came to war, but his son had grown up, it seemed, overnight, and was not to be fooled with honeyed explanations.

"You're right, Phoebus."

"Do you have to go?"

"What do you think?" Lucius pulled up two stools and they sat upon them in front of Lunaris' stall. "Caradoc slew Einion's entire family, except for Briana, and they have waited years to take their family's home back."

"But vengeance is not a path in which philotimo is possible, is that not right?"

Lucius smiled. "You remember our talks?"

"Of course, Baba. And all that you told me about Diodorus and what he taught you."

Lucius felt a pang of guilt at not having provided a tutor such as Diodorus for his own children, but he knew he was trying to pass along all the wisdom the old man had taught him over the many years, if such a thing were even possible.

"You're right. Vengeance is not a path that befits philotimo, but neither is cowardice and allowing a tyrant to punish one's people."

"One's people?"

"Well, we Romans do not believe in kings or queens, right?"

"The Tarquins were especially bad for Rome," Phoebus said.

"True. Though some were better than others. Still, it is not in us as Romans to bow to kings, though the emperor could be said to be as much." Lucius put his finger to his lips and continued. "Einion, on the other hand, is the rightful king of the land of Dumnonia, and in Britannia, before Rome's arrival, kingship was as sacred as an oath to the Gods themselves. It is a sacred duty."

"And so philotimo is central to good kingship?"

Lucius smiled. *Diodorus would be proud of my son!* He nodded. "Yes! Without question. And so, you see, it is Einion's duty to his people to protect them from tyranny."

"But why did he not go sooner?"

"I don't know for sure, except that the Gods have determined that now is the time."

"They told Etain?"

"Yes."

"Father Gilmore said many things about her."

Lucius had suspected that the Christian priest had spoken much with Phoebus, and though it did not please him greatly, he was comforted by the fact that Weylyn and Etain both praised him and trusted him.

Phoebus went on. "Father Gilmore said he had the greatest respect for, and faith in, Etain, and that all should hear and trust her words when given."

"And that is what Einion is doing. He is going now to reclaim his homeland because Etain told him now is the time."

"She speaks with the Gods?"

"Yes."

"As you do?"

Lucius paused. "I do not know if it is the same as it is for me with Etain. But yes, in a manner of speaking."

"They speak with Calliope you know... They show her things."

Lucius had been of mixed emotions when it came to his daughter and the visions the Gods appeared to be sending her. It was no easy burden to be in contact with them, as Lucius knew all too well. However, he also knew that without that contact, the divine touch upon his life, he would have died long ago, if not of wounds in battle, then of despair. For the Gods had had a hand in all the joys of his life, and he thanked them for it.

"We must be there for your sister, Phoebus, as she is there for us. To be in touch with the Gods is no easy thing. She will need you."

"She will always have me, Baba." Phoebus was quiet for a moment, reaching up to touch Lunaris' soft muzzle. "Did Etain tell you to go with Einion too?"

"Yes. She said he would need my help."

"And he saved your life."

"Yes. More than once."

"Then...I guess you have to go."

"Yes. I do. But I'll come back to you, Phoebus."

"I know."

Lucius knelt before the boy and took him by the shoulders. "Listen to me. While I'm away, I want you to continue your training with Briana and Mama, yes?"

Phoebus nodded.

"And I want you to keep your mother and sister safe. You understand?"

"I do, Baba."

Lucius could tell that Phoebus was trying not to cry, and he pulled him close.

The boy gripped onto his father tightly, inhaling the strong scent of incense and horse that seemed to constantly cling to him, to be a part of him.

"I love you, my son. Please remember that always."

Phoebus did not answer, but only squeezed harder as Lucius held him.

The day for Lucius, Einion, and Dagon's departure arrived quickly, the past two days being taken up with gathering supplies, weapons, and unassuming armour for the journey into Dumnonia.

It was still dark when everyone rose to gather in the main hall for an early meal.

The children were silent and sleepy around the freshly kindled fire, but all too aware of what was happening.

As Lucius had requested, Phoebus was already staying close to his sister, watching over her, and it made him proud.

"He seems to have grown up over night," Adara said, looking upon her son.

"They both have."

"Do you have everything you need?" Adara asked, fussing over him again.

Lucius smiled and kissed her gently. "Yes, my love. I do." Together they looked across the fire at Dagon and Briana who spoke in whispers and kissed intermittently. "It will be tough for them. I suppose you have a wedding to plan together?"

Adara laughed. "That's one thing to keep me occupied while you're gone."

"You're not convincing."

"No?" Her face grew dark. "I just... I don't have a good feeling about this, Lucius."

"Have faith, my love. Nothing will keep me from you."

As Lucius kissed his wife again, aware that it was time to be leaving, he heard the silence in the hall and felt the eyes of his children and friends upon them.

"Anguis..." Dagon said. "It is time we were going. Einion is getting the horses."

Lucius nodded and stood slowly, Adara and the children with him.

Dagon turned to Briana and kissed her again. "I'm going to get back your stolen kingdom, and then we shall be married."

Briana looked up at Dagon and thought about how much she truly did love this man, even had he no crown or warrior's build. She knew the Gods had blessed her in him, and now she thought of it, her sincerest wish at this point was not that they should kill her uncle and get back her family's throne, but that Dagon should come back to her. *At last, I understand Lucius and Adara.* And because of that understanding, Briana promised herself she would look after Adara and the children with her very life.

"All is ready, Praefectus... My lord," Barta said, standing beside Einion at the double doors now with the morning light angling in through the opening.

Everyone went outside to where the horses were waiting.

Dagon had asked that none of the men come out to wish them off, for he wanted the time alone with Briana before they left.

He went to his large black mount and turned to Briana for one last kiss.

"The Gods will keep you safe," she said to him.

"As they will you, my love." With that, Dagon mounted up and Briana went to Lucius.

"Thank you for going with him, Lucius. I know..." she stopped herself, her emotions running higher than they ever had done at seeing Dagon leave, and her brother setting out on the quest he had dreamed of for so long. "If the Gods are indeed on your side, Lucius...my friend...please keep both of them alive. For me."

Lucius took her hand and kissed it. "I will, Briana. The debt I owe is to you as well as Einion. I will never forget it." Lucius looked around and saw Adara go back into the hall. "Calliope...Phoebus...come here."

The children came and he took each of them in his arms. "Remember I love you," he said to Calliope. "I'll be fine."

Calliope nodded quickly, but it was difficult for her to look at her father, for her eyes were filling with tears she refused to shed.

Lucius picked her up easily and pressed his cheek to hers. "I'll be back soon." He put her down and she turned to cling to Briana.

"Phoebus," Lucius said, and his son came to him. "I'm so proud of you...my son. Remember that, and all that I told you."

Phoebus nodded and he wrapped his arms around Lucius' neck. "I'll look after them, Baba," he said as his lanky, muscular body hugged his father tightly.

"I know," Lucius said. He stood and turned to Barta. "Thank you for staying, my friend."

"It is my honour to protect the Dragon's family," he turned to Briana, "and my future queen."

"I know you would come with me," Lucius said. "But my heart and fighting spirit will be that much more at ease for having you here with them, at the gates of my home."

Barta nodded, and saluted Lucius and Dagon.

Lucius turned to Dagon and Einion. "Take the horses to the southwest gate. I'll be there in a few minutes."

"Wait!" Briana said, rushing to her brother. "Einion!"

Einion jumped down from his horse and hugged her. He held her face in his hands and looked into his sister's eyes. "I'm going to take back our home."

"I know. But... Einion," Briana's face was panicked, her eyes wide and fearful. "If it seems desperate...if all seems lost...just leave it. I love you, my brother, and our homeland is not worth your life. Nothing is!"

Einion looked upon his sister, his family, and shook his head. "I won't fail, Briana. You will walk in the hall of our forefathers again, I promise."

Her eyes closed and she hugged him with an iron embrace. "Then may you walk in our uncle's blood." She pulled away and went back to the children to hold their hands.

Lucius was already walking away to the temple in the southeastern sector of the hillfort.

Lucius knelt in the temple of Apollo which he had built. In the light of the bronze brazier, incense smoke surrounding him, protecting him, he prayed to Apollo, and to Venus and Epona to protect him on his journey into the southwestern reaches of Dumnonia. More so, he asked them to protect Adara, Phoebus, and Calliope while he was away.

He was filled with dread. This surprised him. He had faced massive armies in the field, forces that likely made Caradoc of Dumnonia's army look like green recruits. And yet a cloud shrouded his usual confidence.

His prayers finished, he took the sword his wife had given him from the altar and made to hang it upon the wall, a piece of him for his family to gaze upon and be comforted.

"You mustn't leave it," Adara said behind him, cloaked and silent in the shadows by the temple door as she waited for him to finish.

"But it will give you and the children comfort to know that I'll be back to take it," he answered.

"It will give us more comfort to know that you have it in your hand," Adara said, walking toward him. She reached up and touched his cheek, no tears upon her face this time, for she had cried too often at his leaving. "If you have it, I will be more certain of your safe return." She picked up the sword and slid it into the scabbard at his back so that the golden, dragon-hilted blade jutted brightly behind his shoulders. "Promise me again you'll return," she said, their arms about each other, her chin buried in the neckline of his thick black cloak.

They held each other, ever-reluctant in their goodbyes.

"I'll be fine, my love," Lucius whispered. "I owe this to Einion and Briana."

"I know. And we'll be safe with Briana, Barta and the others here. Just look after yourself. Come back to me, my dragon."

"I will." Lucius looked at the doorway and the growing light outside. "I should go. They are waiting and we have a long road."

Adara nodded. "You kissed the children?"

"Yes. Make sure they practice their riding and sword skills. The Dragon's children should be able to fight."

"The whole of his family can fight," she said, putting her hand upon the black cuirass with the winged dragon upon his chest. "Go now. And come back."

"My love…"

He kissed her, their eyes closed, and then a moment later, he was out the door, striding toward the southwest gate where Dagon and Einion waited for him.

IX

SAMHAIN TERROR

'Samhain Fear'

With the departure of those three warriors - a husband and father, a lover, and a brother - it seemed that a shroud of grief had fallen over that ancient hillfort. Life went on as ever, smoke rising from the offerings made in the temple, the sound of hammering and sawing as Cradawg continued the building work on the baths on the eastern slopes, and the sound of clanging swords and neighing horses as the Sarmatians paraded and maintained their skills in anticipation of the inevitable call to arms somewhere in the empire, if not in Caledonia once more.

One week had passed since Lucius and the others departed for Dumnonia, and Adara took it upon herself to walk the perimeter of the fortress, armed, with either Barta or Briana by her side, as if she were keeping a watch for her husband's return, though she knew full-well that it would be much longer than a week, no matter how sincere her offerings in the temple at her doorstep.

Lucius' absence felt strange to her, more so than at other times. When he was on campaign with the legions, the discomfort was something she was familiar with, and having lived in the legionary base at Lambaesis, she was familiar with the daily rhythms of that life. Now, however, Lucius was heading into the unknown, and not under the auspices and protection of the emperor, but of his own accord, despite his duty to Rome. She understood his reasons for going, of course she did. But she could not help but colour her worry with a deeper shade of red.

For days, Adara had been going through the motions of daily life, caring for the children, interacting with friends, and dealing with the occasional visits by locals from the village below. She was not present in her own life, her mind too caught up with what might be happening to her husband upon the wild road through Dumnonia. One morning, she woke from another restless slumber, rose from her bed, and splashed her face with cold water. After drying, she looked at her reflection in a bronze mirror on the table. She thought she looked tired and old, and she berated herself for her wallowing, and for her lack of faith in Lucius.

Stop it, Adara! she told herself. She then pulled on her leather breeches and boots, bound her bra band around her torso, and slipped a deep red tunica on over head. Her hair tied back in a thick black braid, and the gladius Lucius had left her in hand, she went out of the room to check on the children.

Phoebus was waking slowly, tossing and turning in his bed, his mop of dark hair waving from beneath the edge of the furs. "Good morning, Mama," he mumbled.

"Good morning, my love," she said. "Dress for sword practice today, Phoebus."

"All right," he said, almost turning over to go back to sleep but catching himself and pushing his feet over the edge of the bed. "I'm up."

Adara moved on to Calliope's room and went in.

Her daughter was sitting on the edge of her bed, dressed, and humming a tune that Lucius sometimes sang to her...one of Alene's songs.

"Good morning, Mama," Calliope said without turning. Her voice, paused in its song and was itself a well of joy and gratitude.

This amazed Adara for she suspected, yet again, that Calliope had been harassed by bad dreams in the night. She went in and sat next to her on the edge of the bed. Adara knew that they had not talked about her visions, and that that was her own failing as a mother; the news of Lucius' quest with Einion and Dagon had overshadowed everything.

"Did you not sleep well again?" Adara asked, her arm around Calliope as she kissed the top of her head.

Calliope turned to her and smiled calmly. "I dreamed of Ynis Wytrin and the Tor."

Adara felt relief. "You liked it there?"

Calliope nodded. "Yes. It was nice. Peaceful and full of life."

"You prefer it to here?"

"No, Mama. I love it here. And this place can be like Ynis Wytrin if we want it to be. We have to decide to make it like that."

Adara was often amazed by the words that her daughter uttered, but this time, Calliope's words were of such idealistic wisdom that she did not know how to answer her. It was as if the child had put into words what Adara had been feeling at the farthest reaches of her mind when she decided to come out of her wallowing.

"You're absolutely right, my girl!" Adara said, holding her daughter close and covering her with kisses.

Calliope laughed and giggled and soon, Phoebus ran in to join them.

"What are we doing today, Mama?" the boy asked.

Adara lay back upon the furs and stared at the ceiling. "Well… After we eat, we should care for the horses and go for a ride. After that, it's sword practice with Briana and Barta."

"Oh, I don't want to practice fighting," Calliope said.

"It's important, my love, but after that you will enjoy what we have to do next."

"What?" Calliope asked.

"We will begin harvesting some of the crops - Briana tells me that some of them are ready to pick - and then I was thinking we could practice your painting again. We haven't done that in a long while."

"Yeah!" the girl cheered.

"Noooo," Phoebus whined. "I don't want to paint."

"Well…" Adara remembered what Lucius had said. "You can go into your father's tablinum and pick up any of the scrolls to read. He said you could do that, so long as you're careful not to rip them. Would you like that?"

"Yes!"

"Good. So, let's get started. We have a busy day."

Adara ushered them out of Calliope's cubiculum and they all tramped downstairs to greet Ula and Aina who were just arriving.

As they had once done before, over long months of campaigning, Adara and the children settled into a daily routine of work, study, training and other tasks that required attention. It was easier than before in a way, for they were home, not at the imperial court under the constant judgment of Julia Domna's sycophantic hens who tired even the empress herself.

Adara was happy to be upon her own territory, the home they had built, and she the true head of her own household, finally. It was a task she had hoped for, though it was somewhat less without Lucius by her side so that they could make decisions together.

Prayer and offerings were also a part of their daily rituals, for in Lucius' absence, the Gods needed to be appeased. And so, in the morning and evening, Adara and the children would go to the temple to make offerings to Apollo, Venus, and Epona.

When they were there, she noted that Phoebus often stared at the statue of Venus, but she did not ask him about it. She guessed that young boys were often drawn to the Goddess of Love, and Venus had been especially good to their family.

Calliope's prayers more often took the form of humming, but Adara knew that in her head, as she sang, she also asked the Gods to watch over her father wherever he was.

Lucius...

Adara thought of him constantly, and thus the continuum of work, training and the teaching of her own children went ever on, both a distraction and a necessity.

Calliope's painting had begun to rival Adara's, and together, they began to sketch a mural they would paint upon the north wall of the great hall.

Phoebus on the other hand - when not cutting wood, seeing to the horses with Sigwyll Sloane, or sword training with Briana - could be found reading in his father's tablinum, two lamps lit and one of the many scrolls open upon the table. Each night, he would tell his mother, Barta and Briana a little of the text he was reading.

"I can't believe all that Alexander accomplished! He took his men to the ends of the earth!" he said one night as they were sitting around the fire.

Ula and Aina had just gone home, and Phoebus was staring into the fire beside his mother who held Calliope in her arms, asleep.

"Your father has told me much of Alexander, the one they called 'Megas'," Barta said, sipping his wine.

Adara nodded and smiled at her son. "Megas Alexandros has always been a great inspiration to your father, Phoebus."

"Was he really the son of Zeus?"

"What do you think?" Adara asked.

"I think so. He must have been! To be able to accomplish all that he did in so short a time. To crush the Persian Empire and march his army so far. His men were the most loyal in the world, I'll bet."

"If I remember correctly, his men did mutiny at one point, unable to go any farther," Barta added.

"And yet he brought them home."

"He did," Adara acknowledged.

"You know, Phoebus..." Barta set his cup down and leaned forward to look at the boy. The fire set his bearded face and hollow eye socket aglow. "Your father's men...my kinsmen...are even more loyal to your father than Alexander's were."

Phoebus looked doubtful.

Barta nodded. "It's true. I have seen them lay down their lives for him, and put themselves in front of danger to keep him safe. But there is a secret to having that sort of loyalty from men in your command."

"What is it?" Phoebus' hands were gripping each other quickly, excitedly.

"The secret is that Alexander, and indeed your own father, did the very same things as their own men. I have seen Anguis charge into the jaws of Death himself to save many a Sarmatian, or a regular legionary soldier. You need not be the son of a god to do that." Barta stopped talking and stood. "If you are not going out again tonight, I will sleep now," he said to Adara and Briana. "We have early morning drills."

"Thank you, Barta. Good night," Adara said.

Barta bowed to her, and then turned to Briana who sat staring into the fire. "Good night, my lady."

"Good night, Barta."

The big Sarmatian began to leave the circle of light cast by the fire and then turned back to Briana and Adara. "Lucius and Dagon will be fine. Never have I known greater warriors." And with that, he disappeared into his cubiculum to sleep the night away.

Adara looked at Phoebus, his eyes proud in the firelight as he thought of his father, but then a cloud crossed his features and he seemed worried.

"Phoebus?"

"Yes, Mama?"

"Your father is well. Do not worry so. Ask the Gods to watch over him, and Dagon, and Einion." She heard the words she uttered, but wondered if she could believe so easily herself. She knew she had to, or she would go mad with worry. "There is another reason that your father will come through whatever trials await him in this life."

"What?"

"Ponos."

285

"What's ponos?" he asked.

"Well, it is a Greek word meaning toil or struggle."

"Why is that important?"

"Well...without our ponos in this life, the struggles we face, the hard work we undertake, we cannot achieve victory."

"And Baba has toiled much?"

She smiled sadly. "Yes, my love. He most certainly has. Like Megas Alexandros, your baba's ponos has been great. You must not expect a life without it, for then it would be absent victory in whatever form that may take. Do you understand?"

"I think so... So you are saying that without ponos...without struggle in life...there can be no victory?"

"That's right."

"And so, because of their great struggles, Baba, Dagon, and Einion will be victorious?"

"Yes!" Briana said quickly, nodding as she stared into the flames.

Adara paused and looked at her before returning her attention to Phoebus. "As Briana says. Yes. Though victory is never guaranteed or assumed. Alexander toiled through to the very end...and so must your baba." She caught herself, for the thought of Lucius sharing Alexander's fate, from what she knew of it, was not a comfort. "And now that this lesson is over, it is time you were in bed." Adara propped herself up with Calliope in her arms, stood, and began to walk toward the stairs.

"Good night, Briana," Phoebus said to the Briton, giving her a hug.

"Good night, young warrior," she said, ruffling his hair.

"I'll be back," Adara said to her as she led the way upstairs.

Briana sat down again and poured some more wine.

Where are you, Dagon and Einion? She rubbed her eyes. *Lucius, please take care of them.*

After a few minutes, Adara came back with a cloak about her shoulders, poured herself some more wine and sat down beside Briana in front of the fire.

"You must be frustrated, waiting here while they go off to Dumnonia."

"I'd be lying if I said I wasn't." Briana nodded, but took Adara's hand. "But there is no other place I would rather be than here with you and the children."

"And your people," Adara smiled. "You will be their queen soon."

Briana smiled. "I don't care about that. I love Dagon."

"I know you do. But, even if Dagon has no kingdom to go back to, you are certainly the queen of his heart and of the hearts of every Sarmatian warrior now."

"Perhaps a queen of hearts is the best kind..." Briana knew it was the wine talking, but she was sullen and Adara's words cheered her.

"If you would like help in preparing any sort of wedding celebration, I would be more than happy to help."

"I haven't really thought about it," Briana admitted. "Now that you mention it, if Etain were to bind us in Ynis Wytrin, that would be very special to me."

"I suspect they wouldn't want all of the Sarmatian contingent passing into the Isle?"

Briana laughed at the thought. "Likely not."

"You could have a ceremony here at the temple, and a feast here in the hall."

"You would do that for us?"

"Briana!" Adara's voice was genuinely shocked. "You're like a sister to me. You and Dagon and Einion are part of our family, our dearest friends. How can you even doubt we would want to have it here?"

"I'm sorry...I...I'm just not thinking straight." The joy left her voice then, and Adara decided to put the subject aside for the moment.

"What is it?" Adara asked.

"I've been trying to see them in the flames, asking the Gods to show me some sign, some indication of where they are and if they are all right."

"And?"

"I see nothing, Adara. Nothing. Usually I can see something of Einion, hear his voice... But it's as if they've passed beyond a high, thick wall, and I cannot hear or see any trace of them. It's as if the Gods have cut them off from us."

Her words chilled Adara then, and now that the quiet of night had settled upon them, it unnerved her. Every night as she lay in bed alone, Adara wondered what dreams the Gods might torment her with for her weakness, her worries, or if Calliope would wake screaming again in the night, having seen some such horror in the forest of her mind.

Briana continued talking. "Etain said that it was the right time for Einion to go and reclaim our father's throne, but I can't help but doubt her."

"It is only natural to worry," Adara said. "At least that's what I tell myself. But find comfort in the fact that Etain loves you both and has been right about so much, including sending you north to Lucius."

"You're right. I know you are!" Briana said, frustrated. "I just can't help thinking that something is not right. I'm so happy now with Dagon, the possibilities of a future life together, and yet...what if it is all swept away like a pile of ashes?"

"I know what you mean," Adara admitted. "Ever since the day I met Lucius in Rome, at a banquet on the Palatine Hill, I have lived with the fear that it is all too good for me, that the Gods will, at some point, take away the joys they have given us." Adara felt like weeping then, but she held it in. She did not speak for a moment, then continued. "But I have to believe that they will not turn their backs on us."

"And your ponos?"

"Hmm. I pray that my ponos is only as painful as living with the uncertainty we are dealing with right now."

If only it were that easy, Briana thought.

The sacred festival of Samhain approached, and over the next couple of weeks, Adara had Briana, Culhwch, Alma and Paulus, as well as several of the Sarmatians, help bring in more grain stores for the storage pits. They harvested the vegetables and herbs that were ready to pick, and packed them away in barrels so as to keep better in darkness.

It was important work, taking stock of all that they had within the hillfort, trading extra produce or grain with some of the villagers from down the hill for apples, or wool, wheels of cheese and other supplies. She also had to oversee the building work on the bathhouse which Cradawg was undertaking, pressed upon by the tight deadlines that Lucius had imposed on him.

The builder was always amenable to giving Adara updates when she showed up on the eastern slopes to see how the work was coming along.

"It is moving along nicely, Metella," Cradawg said. "By Saturnalia, you'll be bathing in your own tepidarium. No more tubs of water."

"That certainly is wonderful news, Cradawg. Thank you," Adara said.

The big Durotrigan nodded and went back to work, hastening one worker who was mixing the lime cement too slowly for his liking.

The tasks were never-ending around the hillfort, but so was the waiting. Phoebus and Calliope went everywhere with Adara and Briana, learning much about the running of a household, the preparations for a winter season, and how to trade and interact with the villages of the surrounding fields.

Adara wondered at the rate at which her children took in all of the information, how they went over it verbally in the evenings with her as if trying to make sense of what they had seen, heard and helped do.

"You've both learned so much! You'll be ready to run the villa in Etruria someday," Adara said to them.

"Will we go there to see Ava soon?" Calliope asked. "It's been so long. I don't remember her well."

Adara thought about it for a moment, tried not to weep, for if they did not remember Lucius' mother well, how then should they know her own parents? *They've never even met my family! I know they would love splashing in the sea, picking oranges and lemons in the orchard, the taste of Hymetos honey warm from the sun, and the rhythmic cracking of canes in the branches of the olive trees at harvest time.*

Athenae seemed a world away.

The hearth fire jumped as Briana tossed another log into the flames and Adara's attention was pulled back to the present.

"Do you miss your own parents?" Briana asked.

"Of course I do." She clasped her hands. "I haven't seen them in years." She realized that she should be more sensitive then. Briana and Einion had lost their family entirely when their uncle had slaughtered them. She turned back to Calliope and Phoebus. "I don't know when we'll be able to go back to Etruria, or Athenae."

"I would like to go," Phoebus mused. "All I've heard are stories from you and Baba. I want to see the land of Alexander!"

Adara smiled. Her son was smitten with the texts he was reading, and she detected something of the romantic side of Lucius in Phoebus, the idealist who now seemed dormant in her husband. She turned back to Briana.

"Tell us about Samhain, Briana. Why is it important to the Britons?"

In her mind, Briana could see the bonfires being lit about the rocky fortress of her childhood home in Dumnonia, the sound of the rushing wind and the howl of the banshees upon the rooftops set above the cliffs.

"Briana?" Adara asked again.

"Oh, sorry, Adara. I was just thinking. Well, Samhain is our new year. Romans celebrate the new year with the month of Januarius, but for us Britons, it is Samhain, the time of the harvest and the death of the old year, just prior to winter." Briana thought back and she could not help but think of Einion, Dagon and Lucius and whether they might be there by Samhain. "At Samhain, the veil between this world and the Otherworld is at its thinnest, and the gateway opens."

"What do you mean?" Phoebus asked.

"That one night of the year, the spirits of the dead can roam in the land of the living. That is why we light great fires across the land. To protect ourselves from the darkness and those shades who might come near."

Phoebus gulped.

"Do not worry. We'll be safe here."

"We'll light fires around the hillfort," Adara confirmed, though if she were honest with herself, she too felt a chill run up and down her spine then.

"Then there is the Wild Hunt," Briana said.

"What's that?" Adara asked.

"That is when the lord of the Otherworld, Gwyn ap Nudd, leads the dead in a hunt across the land."

"This sounds scary, Mama," Calliope said.

"I'm sorry," Briana said. "I didn't mean to scare you, dear. The Wild Hunt would not come across this place. You have nothing to fear here."

"That's good," Calliope said, cuddling into Adara's arms.

"Did the Wild Hunt ever happen in Dumnonia?" Phoebus asked.

Briana paused. "Yes," she said, her eyes unable to look directly at the boy. "It did."

After Briana's tales of the Wild Hunt, Adara had a difficult time settling the children enough to put them to bed for the night. In the end, she managed by telling them stories of the things they would do and see when one day she took them back to Athenae for a visit.

Once Barta returned from his rounds of the camp and the doors of the hall were safely barred, Adara left Briana and Barta to go to sleep herself. The idea of Lucius being out in the wilds during Samhain terrified her. She did not need that added worry.

Ever since Lucius, Dagon and Einion had departed, Adara and Briana had been waging their own war upon the rising tide of worries that seemed to be assaulting their minds when they stopped working.

In the midst all of the activity and the tasks she had set herself, Adara felt as though she were caught in a never-ending period of waiting. She lay in her bed with the light of the lamp casting shadows upon the ceiling, and she looked to where she had left a gladius leaning against the wall, within easy reach.

Thunder began to roll outside in the night, and she closed her eyes and dozed to the first splashes of rain upon the roof tiles above her head.

Gods, please keep Lucius safe...

Despite the terrifying premise of an open gateway to the Otherworld, the atmosphere in the villages surrounding the hillfort was surprisingly jovial. The crops had been good, and the winter stores were full of wheat, beans, grains, fruit and vegetables. Those animals that needed slaughtering had undergone their own trials, and now the meat was set aside for the coming months.

Adara and Briana went over the stores again and again, ensuring that there was enough for their immediate family and appropriate orders placed for the men who were still staying with them upon the hillfort.

Barta informed them that they had received missives from Brencis in Caledonia where, it seemed, the peace was holding, if not precariously.

"Do not worry just yet," Barta told them. "There are more than enough troops stationed in the North to keep the Caledonii in check for now. Orders are that the furlough continue as planned. We just need to be ready to move out at a moment's notice."

That was not entirely comforting to either Adara, Briana or the children. At the same time, it was not surprising.

Still, they could not worry about what had not yet happened. However, there were other things to worry about as far as Adara was concerned. In the three days leading up to Samhain, there had been talk among the men of strange birds seen in the night sky above the hillfort, large ones with red eyes that seemed to be watching the hall.

"I don't want the men talking about any of this around the children," Adara said to Barta and Lenya when they told her. "It will frighten them. They're worried about Lucius as it is."

"Do not worry, my lady," Lenya said. "The mind wanders when on leave and we have too much time to think of things other than battle."

Adara wasn't convinced, especially as she spied the doubt in Barta's face, but she accepted the decurion's reassurance.

Other things had happened around the hillfort too. For one, Cradawg had told her that one of the newly made walls of the bathhouse had been knocked down, though there had been no wind that night. Three animals - a deer, a boar, and a sheep - had been found gutted on the roads leading toward the hillfort. And on another night, a mysterious horn had been heard in the night, calling out in the dark upon the slopes of the hill.

Detachments of Sarmatians were sent around the following day to scout the ramparts, but they found no tracks or anything else that would explain the occurrences.

Needless to say, by the time of Samhain's eve, there was a tenseness in the hall upon the hillfort.

The bonfires were lit early that evening and Sarmatians stationed around the perimeter by Barta as if they were on campaign. The only difference was that the villagers from down the hill were permitted to come and go, many leaving offerings of wheat and apples at the temple, and also stopping to wish Adara and the children well.

"Will you stay for an evening meal?" Adara asked Alma and Culhwch who had come with Paulus to make offerings that afternoon.

"We can't tonight, love," Alma said. "We need to get home and light the fire."

"I understand," Adara said, though she did not understand how the Britons so revered Samhain, and yet feared it at the same time. , "Please come another night soon. We've not sat and spoken in some time."

Alma hugged her. "I'd like that. So would my two boys." She smiled at Culhwch and her son.

Adara walked outside with them into the gathering dusk. The rain had stopped and a chill wind was picking up. Sharp clouds tore across the sky and in the distance, bonfires were kindled in the fields beside various villages. She watched them walk down the slope of the plateau and out the southwest gate before turning to see Briana who was coming up from the stables.

"They didn't want to stay," Adara told her, arms crossed to stay warm as the wind played with her long hair.

"Don't be upset with them, Adara. It's this night."

The two women began to walk back toward the hall where Barta was sitting upon a stump outside the doors. He stood as they approached, and opened the door.

"Thank you, Barta," Adara said. "Will you come inside now?"

"Not yet, my lady. I'll check on the men one last time."

"Don't be too long," Briana said. "Darkness is falling." She looked up and then went inside with Adara.

Inside the hall, Adara looked for the children. She could hear their voices upstairs and see them running from Phoebus to Calliope's cubiculum.

"Do the shades come indoors at Samhain?" Adara asked Briana as she filled her plate with cheese, bread and dates from the small table Ula and Aina had set out before going back to their home in the village.

"No. So long as the hearth fires are lit. It is out in the open that the danger lies."

Lucius, Dagon and Einion are out in the open, Adara thought, but she did not say anything. She felt fear then, gripping her loosely at first, but then tighter and tighter until Briana was at her side, steadying her.

"You all right? You should sit, Adara."

"I'm fine," she said, but sat anyway.

The hearth fire was bright and warm and the glow of it seemed to burn the fear away.

They ate a little, but then Adara looked at Briana.

"Do you think that...maybe... Are you expecting to see the shades of your family this night?"

Adara had been thinking of it. Would the shades have to be Britons in order to come from out of the Otherworld that night? Or

293

would all shades come forth? Briefly, Adara had wondered if she might see Alene and Alerio, or more frighteningly, Quintus Metellus pater, or Argus. The latter prospects filled her with dread, but she steeled herself, decided that she had to be strong for her children.

Briana sighed. "I've wondered if I might see them in the past, but they were not given the proper funeral rites. My despicable uncle would never have allowed it." Briana's eyes glossed over as she stared at the flames before them, and she took another bite of bread. "They are gone."

"I'm sorry," Adara said, her hand upon Briana's forearm.

Briana turned to her and forced a smile. "Just don't worry about things. Inside, with the fire lit, we're all safe."

Calliope had been uneasy when it came time to go to sleep. She had been restless throughout the day, unwilling to talk much except with her brother, but that restlessness had grown, and by the time Adara tried tucking her beneath the furs, she was outright refusing to sleep.

"I miss Baba," the girl said, her big eyes looking up at her mother, pleading for her not to leave her room.

Then Phoebus showed up in the doorway and came in. "I can't sleep either, Mama."

Adara sighed. "I miss Baba too," she told them. "But he will be fine. He always is. You need to get your sleep."

"Can we sleep with you in your bed?" Calliope asked, those big eyes luring Adara in.

"Oh, very well!" she said. "Come, let's go." Adara stood and went to the door.

"The lamp, Mama? Should we blow it out?" Phoebus asked.

"No, no. Let's leave it burning tonight." Adara had topped them all up herself so that they would burn through the night, and Briana was staying awake with Barta downstairs by the hearth fire, keeping it alive and bright. She could hear her asking Barta about Dagon as a young man, and the Sarmatian was answering his new mistress gladly, their laughter a comfort.

The children were tucked into the bed and quickly dozed, leaving Adara a small space between them in which she could warm herself.

She stood and stared at them for a few minutes. *Gods...they are ever a marvel to me...* she thought.

She removed her bracae and unwound her breast band beneath her long tunica. Barefoot, she went around the room to light two more oil lamps for a total of four. Then she reached for the gladius upon the table, pulling it from the sheath slowly to reveal the sharp edge she had put on it earlier in the day after her training.

It surprised her still to see the blade in her hand. For as long as she could remember, a paintbrush or stylus would have felt more comfortable, more normal. But that had changed. She hefted the blade and gave it a whirl before slowly sliding it back home in the sheath.

Adara walked to the bed and rolled Calliope over so that she was in the middle. Then she took the spot closest to the cubiculum door, her gladius leaning against the wall near her head. Then she turned over and kissed the children before lying on her back and staring up at the ceiling.

Be safe, Lucius...

Outside, the fires of Samhain burned bright in the night and howls rent the distant air along the crests of green hills across the countryside. The wind roared in and out of hearing, and clouds like fangs appeared to rip jagged holes in the night sky.

Adara lay on the edge of the bed, turning over in her sleep, sweating, muttering prayers as she endured visions of Lucius alone and scared in a vast wood. She called out to him, but her voice was but a breath lost on the rushing wind, unknown to her husband.

Lucius! She spied a tall shadow moving swiftly around him and ran forward to warn him, to grab hold of him, but she could go no further, for there was a wall of sorts between them, a sort of watery veil.

Then Lucius spun, a slash appearing across his chest before he spun back around to be attacked again a second, a third, and then a fourth time. *Adara!* he yelled, now upon his knees, his strength leaving him.

Lucius, come home! Adara cried, helpless and desperate as she watched him fall, the blood running from his wounds. *No!!!*

"Baba's hurt!" Calliope suddenly cried out in her sleep, her face wet with tears.

Adara's eyes shot open and she reached for the gladius beside the bed. When she heard her daughter, she moved to wake her. "Calliope! What do you see?"

Calliope shook her head, her eyes still closed. "Baba is hurt. He wants to come home. He's reaching for the door!"

Now Phoebus was awake, standing on the cold floor and looking down at his sister in the dwindling lamp light. "Mama, what's wrong?"

Adara's head spun, her mind still with those images of blood and horror, of Lucius wounded. She picked up the sword and turned to Phoebus. "Watch your sister. I'm going down to the hall."

"No, Mama. Stay here," the boy pleaded, grabbing his wooden rudus from the other side of the bed.

"I'll be fine. I just need to look," Adara said, padding toward the door of the cubiculum in her bare feet and long tunica. As she walked, her gladius probed the darkness, her ears straining to hear anything above the patter of rain upon the roof tiles.

She stared over the railing into the hall and saw that the hearth fire had almost burned down completely. She made her way down and strained to focus, her mind still reeling from what she had seen.

The hall was cold and the embers of the fire cracked and hissed, the only emanation a long thin stream of smoke that rose to the rafters to spin and make its way to the high windows.

She went to the main doors and put her ear to them.

Footsteps! Or is it crawling? Adara felt her heart pounding and made to unbar the doors. *Lucius!*

She put her gladius down, strained at the beam and set it aside. Her gladius back in her hand, she pushed open one of the doors and stepped out into the night.

"Lucius?" she said, her voice shaky. "Lucius, are you here?" She took a few more steps. "Nobody here." Relief ran through her for a moment, but as she turned something collided with the side of her head, sending her into the mud.

"Your Lucius isn't here, Metella!" a voice growled. "Bring'er here!"

Adara struggled to her knees, her hand still gripping the handle of her gladius in the mud. She was about to speak when a hand wrenched her hair, pulling her up.

Her sword arm slashed out and a man yelled. She stood and whirled as a shadow came at her and the tip of her sword stabbed and stuck in the man's neck.

"Grab the bitch!" the first voice yelled and another man rushed at her.

Adara ducked to avoid a blade lit by a crack of lightening, but a fist followed up and slammed across her face making her cry out.

The sword was about to slash down again when the attacker was knocked off his feet and thrown into the mud a few feet away.

"Adara, run!" Briana called, her dagger driving into the second man's chest in three quick thrusts.

"I'll take you both!" the growling voice said as he rushed in from the shadows, but before he could reach them his head fell from his shoulders in a mist of blood.

Barta stood above the collapsed body, his great sword poised for another blow, his eye scanning the darkness. "Alarm!!!" he yelled into the night. "Attack!!!"

Within moments, Sarmatians were pouring from the barracks with torches in their hands, rushing toward the hall and the gory scene upon its doorstep.

"Metella's been attacked. Spread out and search for any others!" Barta ordered.

The Sarmatians immediately spread out around the hillfort, the lightning glinting off of steel blades lit by rekindled firelight.

Barta and two more Sarmatians helped Adara and Briana up and back to the hall. "Why did you go outside, Metella?" Barta asked.

"I dreamed that Lucius was hurt," Adara said, her voice on the verge of tears, blood covering her hands and arms. "I thought I heard him outside."

"Whoever they were," Briana looked back at the three bodies. "They weren't going to leave you alive. The Gods love you, Adara."

But she did not hear Briana. She could only think of Lucius and her children, and of how close she had just come to dying.

"Phoebus!" Briana looked up at the railing to see the children standing there looking down, their faces horror-struck. "Get a fire going for us!"

Phoebus immediately rushed downstairs and gathered some more kindling from a pile nearby. He tossed it onto the still-warm embers and it caught right away. He looked at his mother and rushed to her. "Mama! There's blood all over you! Are you hurt?"

Adara's face was swelling where she had been hit and her head throbbed, but she focussed on her son's face. "I'm all right, my love. Just a little…just…"

"Phoebus…Calliope," Briana said to both of them as they approached. "Please go and heat some water in the kitchen. Can you do that?"

"Yes." Phoebus said.

"Mama," Calliope cried. "I had a bad dream about Baba." She wiped her eyes.

"I know, love," Adara said.

Barta stood watch the rest of the night with Briana as Adara slept wrapped in her cloak before the fire with the children.

After washing up, she had all but collapsed from exhaustion and the shock of the encounter.

When Adara and both children were sleeping, Barta spoke to Briana. "Are you hurt, my lady?"

"No. I'm fine," Briana said, placing her hand upon Barta's forearm. "Thank you for saving my life."

The Sarmatian bowed his head and then took a deep breath. "More assassins."

"Yes. But who would send them?"

"The ordo members?" Barta wondered.

"No. They need Lucius."

"I hope Dagon, Einion, and Lucius are all right." Barta shook his head. He did not know what to think at that point. He nodded to Adara's sleeping form. "She said she dreamed of Anguis, that he was hurt."

Gods, let them be safe! Briana pleaded.

"It must be nightmares brought on by the roaming shades without," he said.

"I don't know, Barta. I don't know…"

"When day comes, I'll inspect the bodies and see if there are any clues as to who they might be."

Briana nodded, but at the back of her mind, she could not shake the feeling that something sinister yet lurked outside, something more than men sent to kill. And she felt it still out there, watching.

When day arrived, the Sarmatians lined up the bodies of the three attackers. Adara's gladius was pulled from the neck of the one, and Briana's pugio retrieved from the mud beside the man she had killed.

Barta stood over them with Badru and Vaclar.

"No tattoos or symbols," Badru said.

"No," Barta answered, rubbing his chin as he kneeled beside the bodies, his hands probing in their clothing. "Nothing useful. Just black clothes and plain gladii. Nothing that couldn't be bought in any marketplace."

"What should we do with the bodies?" Vaclar asked.

"Take them down into the field below the hillfort's western ramparts and burn them." Barta stood.

"Too bad we couldn't take one alive," Badru added. "We could've tortured the bastard to find out who did this."

"The Dragon's wife and Lady Briana fought well. They would have died could they not fight."

"You did well too, sir," Vaclar said.

Barta did not answer, but turned to go back to the hall where Adara and Briana were sitting with the children.

"There are no markings or anything to distinguish the attackers," he told them. "I've ordered the bodies burned."

"We'll need to purify the house of death," Adara said, as she tried to chew some honeyed bread with her swollen jaw.

"I'll take care of it," Briana answered. "I'll send for Weylyn."

Part II

WAR

A.D. 211

X

ANGUIS CONVERTIT

'The Dragon Returns'

The weeks crawled after the events of Samhain, the cold dark days of November bleeding into the month of December when frost appeared on the grass and the sun pushed its way through the fog.

The afternoon had been a quiet one. They all were, now that the work of bringing in harvests and filling the stores was finished.

Adara sat wrapped in a blanket before the hearth fire, reading a letter that she had received from her mother in Athenae. As she sat there, warmed by the flames, an anxious feeling churned in her stomach. *Deep breath, Adara,* she told herself. She reached for the gladius that leaned against the log beside her, and picked it up. She had killed a man with it, and the feelings she had were strange still, after over a month. It was not regret she felt, nor revulsion - if she was truthful, there had been a certain satisfaction in eliminating a threat to her children.

No. What bothered her was how easily she could not have been there any more, there, in that hall, not kissing her children in the mornings or worrying about Lucius, wherever he was. It would all have stopped, living that is, for she did not know what Elysium might have held had she died. Would she have remembered anything in the Afterlife?

I'm alive, she reminded herself.

"Mama! Mama!" Phoebus said as he burst in through the double doors from outside.

"What is it? What's wrong, Phoebus?" Adara stood quickly, her sword in her hand. Ready.

"Baba and Dagon...they're back!"

Word spread quickly, and soon Adara, Phoebus, Calliope, Briana and Barta were rushing down toward the southwest gate.

Some of the guards had spotted the riders from atop the ramparts at the posts they had been assigned since the attack at Samhain.

"Yes. It's them," Briana said. "But I don't see my brother."

Mingled fear and elation gripped them all as they watched Lucius and Dagon ride up the slope of the road.

"I don't see Lunaris," Calliope said, squeezing her mother's hand tightly.

Adara could not speak, so worried was she for all the dreams she had had. *Such horrible dreams...*

"Baba!" Phoebus and Calliope yelled as they ran down the road ahead of their mother.

Adara watched her children go to their father, elated, joyful, grateful, but what Adara felt most was relief. Complete and utter relief.

When Lucius and Dagon came onto the road leading into the hillfort, their family and friends appeared. They were home.

Lucius waved slowly, careful of his stitched wounds. He felt like weeping at the sight of his family, safe and sound. *Thank you, Gods, for watching over them.*

Dagon jumped out of his saddle and ran toward Briana, sweeping her up in his arms.

"Einion? Is he..." she could not ask the question. She was too afraid, but for Dagon's smile which told her all she needed to know at long last.

"He sits upon your father's throne!" Dagon told her. "It was a victory!"

Briana buried her head in his shoulder and wept tears that had long been held at bay.

Dagon held her tightly, kissing her wet cheeks and hair, and nodding to Barta who stood by smiling with relief of his own.

"Now we shall have a wedding, my love," Dagon whispered to her as he held her tightly, not wanting to let go.

Lucius still sat in his saddle, watching them all, scanning the ramparts of their home and casting up a prayer for his safe return. He had always told Adara what happened to him on campaign, the horrors he had witnessed. In a way, it had always made things more real. But this time, he reminded himself that he could not tell her. *I can't,* he reminded himself. *Not this time.*

The children gathered around their father who was sitting atop a different horse. "Baba!" they cried, looking up at him. "Won't you come down?"

Lucius looked down at Phoebus and Calliope and his eyes watered with pain.

He's injured! Adara saw it right away.

"Barta," Dagon said. "Help Anguis out of his saddle. He's wounded."

Barta rushed to Lucius' side and helped him out of the saddle before taking the reins of the horses.

"Barta," Lucius said, wincing. "It's good to see you, my friend."

The big Sarmatian said nothing, but observed Lucius' weakened state with sadness and dismay.

The children ran up to Lucius and hugged him.

He ignored the pain that caused, and enjoyed the warmth of their arms about him, the smell of their hair, and the glow of their eyes. He saw them looking for Lunaris, but could not bring himself to tell them right away. He turned to Adara who now approached him with worry and sorrow. There was apprehension in her face, her entire body betraying it.

"I feared I wouldn't see you again," she said, putting her arms around him and holding him close.

The world around them stilled as Lucius clung to her, and he allowed himself to feel her, to finally let his guard down.

"I know," he said. "I'm home now. I've come back. I promised, didn't I?"

She let go and kissed his mouth. She saw the healing lacerations upon his face, the worn look in his eyes, and fought hard to hold back her tears.

"Thank the Gods you're safe," she said. "My love..." She looked up at him and knew that his mind was awhirl with myriad thoughts. "Lunaris?" she asked quietly.

Lucius shook his head.

"Come. Let's all go inside. There is a fire, and food, and a warm bath for each of you."

Dagon and Briana went first, followed by Barta, Adara, and Phoebus with the horses.

Lucius stood there a moment, gazing to the village in the field below, down the road, and into the distance.

What will become of us? he wondered.

Then he felt a small hand grasp his fingers.

Calliope stood beside him, her big eyes gazing up at him, tears upon her cheeks as she had realized Lunaris was not coming back.

"Come inside, Baba. Being home will help make things right again," she said.

Lucius bent over and kissed her head.

"I love you, my girl."

"I love you too, Baba."

They walked up the slope to where Adara was watching and waiting.

"Come," she said, taking his other hand. "There is much to tell..."

Life seemed to burst in upon the hall once more that night as family and friends sat around the hearth fire to celebrate the warriors' return. Troops from the barracks took it in turns to come and greet their returned lord and praefectus, and Adara sent out a couple of barrels of beer to the men to mark the occasion.

On one side of the hearth fire, Briana sat reading a letter which Einion had sent with Lucius and Dagon for her.

Lucius watched her face carefully for any sign that might indicate that Einion had revealed to her something of what had happened. Einion, however, did not know all, and Briana seemed unaware as she read.

"There was a terrible battle in the hall?" she asked, looking up at Lucius and Dagon.

"Yes," Dagon answered. "We were surrounded by your uncle's men. They were everywhere, but we managed to get inside and, with the help of the people who were still loyal to you and your brother, we won the day. Einion slew Caradoc, but not without grievous injury to himself."

"But he sounds well enough in the letter," Briana said.

"He is. The Gods gave him such strength that night! You would have been proud of him. He has certainly earned that throne."

Briana wiped the tears from her eyes as she stared at the fire and leaned on Dagon's shoulder. Part of her wished she had been there for Einion, before and after, but she could not think of anything better now than to be with Dagon and marry him as they had planned. In truth, she had never thought to love any man the way she loved him, and from the way he held her close, the feeling was mutual.

Lucius looked around the circle and was grateful to see them all, but he also knew they had questions for him that went unasked. He knew they must be thinking about him, how he could have ended up so weak, so wounded. Not even upon the bloody fields of Caledonia had he ever experienced such painful injury.

Adara looked at her husband, and stroked his cheek.

Lucius leaned into her hand, his eyes closing for a moment before he took her hand and kissed it. He cleared his throat. "So… Is anyone going to tell me why we have armed men atop the battlements as if we're in enemy territory?"

They all fell silent.

Lucius looked around the gathering, and his eyes came to rest on Barta.

The big Sarmatian looked at Adara, and she nodded slowly. "On Samhain's eve, three men infiltrated the hillfort and tried to kill Adara.

Lucius' head whipped sideways to face her. "What? Are you hurt? Who were they?"

"I'm fine, Lucius," Adara said. "I'll tell you more later," she whispered.

"Metella slew one man," Barta said, proud. "And lady Briana another."

"What about the third?" Lucius asked.

"I removed his head," Barta said.

Briana leaned toward Dagon. "Barta saved my life."

Dagon nodded at his kinsman.

"Who were they?" Lucius asked again.

"We don't know," Barta said. "They had no markings upon their bodies or their weapons, and they had no armour. They wore only black and carried nondescript weapons."

"I don't like it," Lucius said, standing slowly and pacing around the outside of the circle of logs. "I'm going to raise hell with the ordo of Lindinis!"

"You don't think it was them, do you?" Adara asked. "They wouldn't go to such lengths because you stopped Crescens' son, would they?"

"I don't know. I don't think so. That wouldn't make sense. For all they know, I'm trying to speak on their behalf to the emperor." Lucius shook his head, then looked at Dagon. "We were followed on the road southwest, weren't we?"

Dagon nodded and explained to the others. "The troops at Isca helped to waylay some men who were following us."

"Yes. But are they connected?" Lucius asked himself.

"Someone attacked you on the way?" Adara asked, standing and going to her husband. She laid her hand upon his arm and felt him shaking beneath his tunic sleeve.

"We...we would have been, if some soldiers in the local garrison hadn't helped us."

"It's true," Dagon smiled. "Anguis was popular with many troops we met along the way."

"Then it would have been no secret where you were," Briana added.

They were silent.

Lucius stood there staring at the door and the beam which leaned against the wall beside it. He wanted to bar the door right then, but it was early still, and so he resisted the urge. He turned to Briana.

"Has Etain communicated with you of late?"

Briana shook her head. "She is well, but we have not made the connection. Why?"

Lucius paced a little, beads of sweat forming on his brow. "I'm...I'm sorry. I need to sit. I'll be back..." He walked across the hall and through the door of his tablinum, leaving them all staring after him.

Adara stood alone watching him. Then she turned to Dagon. "What happened to him, Dagon?"

The Sarmatian shifted uncomfortably, his mouth tight. "Much," he said. "But it is something only Lucius can tell you, and I do not think he is ready for it."

Lucius sat down on the chair in his tablinum, his elbows upon the table and his head in his hands. His vision swam and he struggled against the thoughts that spun in his mind, the threats on many fronts that he had to keep in sight, lest he be taken unawares, or his family be harmed as they so nearly were before.

He felt his heart racing in his rib cage, and shut his eyes tightly, breathing quickly at first, but then slowing himself to deeper and deeper breaths. He heard a rustle of paper and then looked up quickly to see Phoebus sitting in a corner by the pigeon hole shelves reading a scroll by the light of a single clay lamp.

"Sorry, Baba," Phoebus said. "You seemed distraught when you walked in. I didn't want to startle you."

The sight of his son gave Lucius focus and he reached out for him to come to him.

Phoebus stood up quickly and came to his father.

Lucius took the scroll and looked at it. "Arrian?"

"Yes. He's more entertaining than Caesar, and I like reading about Alexander."

Lucius smiled. *So did I*, he thought.

"It's my second time reading it," Phoebus said proudly.

"And you're inspired to go to the ends of the earth?"

Phoebus laughed a little. "Not yet. But someday...yes." His big eyes looked up at Lucius, and then his long-fingered hands, rough from work, reached up and touched Lucius' cut face. "You look different every time you come home from war, Baba."

I am different, Lucius nodded. "It was a tough fight," Lucius said.

"But you won," Phoebus said proudly, though there was some want of reassurance in his voice.

"Yes...I won..." *Barely.*

"Calliope is sad about Lunaris, Baba."

"I am too."

"How...how did he die?"

Lucius felt his eyes burning as he thought of it, his mind trying to grasp at some description of what had happened, some reality. But he could not. Only, "he died saving my life."

Phoebus hugged him, and Lucius wrapped his arms about his son and squeezed, ignoring the pain it caused to his wounds. He was home with is family now, but for how long? How long would the Gods allow it?

"Can we put a statue of Lunaris in the temple? As a way to honour him?"

Lucius leaned back in his chair and smiled. "I think that's a fine idea." It was, and the thought of it gave Lucius some peace. "Maybe you and Calliope can come up with a sketch, like Mama showed you, and then we can commission a small statue from Culhwch and Alma?"

"We'll start tomorrow. Calliope will like that." Phoebus began to walk away.

"Your scroll, Phoebus. Don't you want to finish it?"

"You keep it, Baba. I've read it already." The boy stood thinking for a moment, then looked at his father. "Some of my favourite parts are the times when Alexander felt lost, when his men were about to leave him, and his dreams were falling away."

"Why would those be your favourite parts?" Lucius asked.

"Because, even when faced with an impossible situation, the Gods were on Alexander's side, and so were his men." Phoebus shifted on his feet. "Everything worked out."

Lucius smiled at his son. "Thank you, Phoebus."

"Good night, Baba."

When his son was gone, Lucius sat back in his chair, opened the scroll, and began to read the familiar words. Only now, his perspective, his understanding of Alexander, was wholly new.

It was late when Lucius finally went upstairs to bed. No one had attempted to interrupt him for hours. They were all asleep now. He rubbed his eyes and blew out the tablinum lamps before taking his sword from the table and going into the hall.

The fire still crackled in the hearth and the wind whistled in at the high windows of the hall. He went to the thick double-doors and saw that they were securely barred. *I should have been here!* The thought of almost losing Adara tore at him now.

Outside was silence but for the soft wind that wound its way around the hall and outbuildings upon the hillfort.

Lucius thought of all of his warriors who now slept nearby. *And yet...still...three assassins managed to get in and attack my wife!*

He was determined not to let it happen again, to protect his family no matter what. Nothing would keep him from getting to them in a time of need.

He checked the door one last time, made his way around the dark kitchen, and then to the privy beneath the stairs. Once he was satisfied that all was quiet, Lucius began to make his way upstairs to the cubiculum, but not before checking on both of the children. He stared down at Phoebus and put his hand upon his son's forehead.

The boy slept so soundly, no doubt his mind filled with dreams of Alexander and the march to the East.

Calliope's small form was huddled beneath the furs, her hair running in long strands over her beautiful and delicate features.

Lucius was tempted to brush away the strands so that he could look at her more fully, but he did not want to wake her. He leaned over and kissed his daughter upon the forehead.

She smiled in her sleep, and he felt his heart tighten.

He knew that if anything ever happened to them, he could not go on living. *Gods...you have to help me protect them...especially now...*

There had been a time when he would have thought it hubris to speak so to the Gods, to make such demands. *Not anymore,* he thought. *It is different now.*

He blew out the lamp, and went to the room where Adara lay with her back to the door. Two lamps still burned and Lucius stepped as quietly as he could to lean his sword against the wall beside the bed. On the other side, he saw that Adara had done the same thing with the gladius he had given her to use.

"I'm not sleeping, Lucius," Adara said as she turned over to face him.

When she looked at him, his face was white and haggard, his eyes so tired.

What happened to you, my Lucius?

"I didn't mean to wake you, my love," he said as he went around the bed and sat down at her feet. His hand stroked the length of her firm leg, and then he removed it, straightening to face the wall so that his wounds did not stretch.

"Let me help you," she said, getting up and kneeling before him to unlace his high boots. She wanted him to tell her everything, the way he always had before. He had always told her about the great mysteries that had befallen him the whole of his life, never once showing any sign of doubt in her belief or trust in him.

Finished with the boots, Adara stood, her hair falling over one exposed shoulder, and she began to help him remove his tunic.

Lucius winced as the fabric caught on the rough stitches.

The tunic came slowly free over his head and Adara gasped. Great, red and angry slashes raked across his chest and back in several places and the sight struck her with such fear that she needed all her will to control her emotions.

"What has happened?" she said, kissing the top of his head as he leaned against her chest.

He did not speak straight away. There was only the rise and fall of his breath, his chest and hunched shoulders as he supported himself on the bedside.

"Lucius, I've never seen you like this. Ever. What...how did this happen?"

"The battle was hard-won."

"But Dagon has nothing like these injuries. Nor does Einion, I'll wager." She turned to her table and took the ointment that she had been using on her own scars. "Should we get a medicus here to see you?"

Lucius shook his head. "No. I am healing. I'm much better than I was. A priestess known to Einion helped to care for me after the..." He winced.

"After what?" she asked as she dipped her finger in the ointment and began to apply it along the ridges of his shredded flesh.

"After the...battle..." he said slowly, his voice trailing off. "I...I never thought I would see you again. I thought I could hear your voice."

Adara stopped what she was doing and stepped back to look at him. "On Samhain's eve?"

"Yes. That is when the...battle...took place."

She fell to her knees and put her face on his lap, her arms gripping him tightly. "I was calling to you, Lucius. I saw you hurt, wounded. I thought it was a dream, but it was so real. I panicked and went downstairs to see if it was you. I believed you were outside. That's why I opened the doors and went out, and that's when the assassins attacked me!"

Lucius stared at her, confused and angry. "Why would the Gods show you such a thing if there was nothing you could do? If I was so far away?"

"I don't know, my love," she said, rising and kissing his mouth, her eyes wet with tears. "It feels as though we can no longer make sense of anything. All is in motion and I don't know how to stop it."

"We can't," Lucius whispered. He stared off into the dark as if gazing at a sea bottom through clear water, trying to spot something.

"There is more you aren't telling me."

"I've told you what happened."

She clasped his hands. "Lucius. You've never lied to me. Please don't start now. Not with me. The children and I have spent the last months worried whether you would ever come back. Nightmares most nights, and Calliope seeing things."

"I don't understand!" Lucius clenched his fists and rubbed his head. "I can't... The battle was one of the worst I've ever been in."

She could see the tension and fear in his body, and she pulled back in her enquiry. "All right, my love. I'm just grateful to the Gods that you've returned to us. This is where you belong."

"I'm sorry I wasn't here," he said, his body shuddering lightly and then heaving with sobs that pulsed up from deep within.

"We are together, Lucius. All is well. We've faced threats before, and we will face them again. But the Gods have always seen us through." She held her husband then for some time.

"I'm sorry," he said again. "You've been through so much, and here I am weeping."

"Because you've been through even more, my love. Please." Adara lay beside him. "Rest now. You need rest. And the healing will follow as it always does."

Not this time, Lucius thought, his eyes wide open as she blew out the last lamp.

They lay in silence for some time, and then Lucius heard his wife's breathing settle, indicating she was asleep. But he continued to stare into the darkness at the golden hilt of his sword, close to hand.

Over the coming days, Lucius began to mingle with the troops again, to visit with some of the villagers from down the hill, especially Culhwch who gladly took the sketch of Lunaris that Phoebus and Calliope had done and set to work on a clay image of the beloved animal to go in the temple.

"I am sorry to hear about his death," the Durotrigan said to Lucius. "He was one of the most beautiful stallions I've ever seen. And we Durotrigans know our horses!"

Lucius nodded, but said nothing, and Culhwch saw the strange look in his eyes.

"Can I get you a drink, my friend? I see that you're not feeling well."

Lucius looked up and forced a smile. "Forgive me, Culhwch. I... My wounds are draining my energy all the time."

"You're a hard man, Lucius Metellus Anguis. You must have faced an entire army by yourself to be so wounded."

"Lucius," Alma came over with the children to whom she had just fed some honey cakes. She handed Lucius a bundle. "Please bring these back for Adara and Briana to try. If they like them, I can make some for the wedding celebrations." She put her hand on Lucius' shoulder. "Do you need anything?" she asked. There was kindness in her voice, compassion and caring in her pale eyes.

Lucius smiled at both of them and took his children's hands. "I'm fine. Just taking a long time to mend," he said.

"Baba? We'll still celebrate Saturnalia, won't we?" Calliope asked, pulling at his tunic.

"Of course!" he said, more life in his voice than there had been all day. He turned to Culhwch and Alma. "You'll join us too, I hope?"

"We'd love to, my friend." Culhwch grasped Lucius' hand. "It's good to see you again. And don't worry about the effigy. I'll start work on it tomorrow and then get it to you soon." He looked to the children. "Is that good?"

"Yes, please," Calliope said. "We need to put it in the temple."

Culhwch and Alma saw them out and then closed the door.

"He's changed, Culhwch," Alma said sadly. "His spirit is struggling with something."

"Yes," he answered. "But as his friends, we are bound to help him, whatever we can do."

It was late in the afternoon by the time Lucius and the children arrived at the hillfort. The walk seemed slower to Lucius, the road up to the southwest gate steeper than ever. But he managed the climb.

The wind was cold and picking up, and Lucius held onto the children's hands as they walked, his eyes scanning the slopes of the hillfort for anything unusual.

"What are you looking for, Baba?" Phoebus asked.

"Just making sure everything is all right," Lucius answered his son.

Phoebus waved to the two Sarmatians who had been posted to sentry duty either side of the gateway.

The warriors waved back to the children and saluted Lucius.

The three of them continued up the hill, winding their way around the barracks and stables and up to the hall.

The December sky was iron grey in the distance, the clouds filtering the sun's light so that it was soft, as if seen through the smoke of a dying fire.

They opened the doors and went in.

"Weylyn!" the children cried as soon as they saw the old Druid sitting at the fire with Adara, Briana and Dagon. Morvran was there too, sipping hot wine from a clay cup beside Weylyn, laughing at the sight of the children.

313

"It is good to see you children well and safe," Weylyn said as he stood and took their hands. Then his eyes went directly to Lucius. "Dagon has told me of the successful reclamation of Einion and Briana's ancestral home, thanks to you, Lucius Metellus Anguis."

Lucius took the Druid's hand, his eyes unable to look at him. *How much have they told him?* he wondered.

"Etain knew you would need healing, and thought you could use my help. I've brought all of the herbs and remedies I know of that will help heal battle wounds." He stared into Lucius' eyes. "But I think not all your wounds are physical," he said in a low voice that only Lucius could hear.

The Roman nodded.

"Come. There is no time to waste. The sooner we apply the remedies to your wounds, the better the healing will be." Weylyn picked up his leather satchel and turned to everyone. "We will speak more later. First, I would help Lucius."

"Thank you, Weylyn," Adara said.

Lucius went across the hall and upstairs, followed by the Druid. Once they were in Lucius and Adara's cubiculum, Weylyn set his satchel down and began to remove several bottles, a mortar and pestle, and a few lead containers with some kind of resinous ingredients inside.

"How did you know I was so wounded?" Lucius asked.

Weylyn chuckled. "Have you forgotten Etain so quickly?" He coughed, the journey through the cold wind from Ynis Wytrin having taken a bit of a toll upon him. "Let's see your wounds."

"I remember her well," Lucius said as he slowly removed his tunic and bracae, leaving only his loin cloth. He tried to stand straight, but felt such stiffness in his limbs and skin that it was no easy task.

"In the days of war, I used to mend the wounds of my son and his warriors when we fought in the North," he said as he crushed some of the herbs in the mortar and then applied oil and resin to the mix, stirring and mouthing words that were known only to the Druids.

The room was filled with the tangy scent of resin, rosemary and some other herbs which Lucius could not recognize.

When Weylyn finished, he turned and gasped. He had no words for the wounds he saw upon the body of the man before him, but looked Lucius in the eyes and saw the lingering fear of a narrow escape there, a memory of glimpses through Death's door.

"No man inflicted these wounds upon you, Lucius Metellus Anguis."

Lucius struggled to breathe, to calm himself as he shook his head and looked back at the Druid. "No."

"Etain was right. But worry not. I will not speak of it if that is your wish."

"Thank you," Lucius said. "I must focus on regaining my strength. Did they tell you of the attack here?"

"Yes. Three assassins." Weylyn sighed as he observed Lucius' body up close, the gashes in his flesh. "You should be dead. Who gave you succour after the battle?"

"A woman known to Einion and Briana. Elana was her name."

Weylyn looked up. "The Gods love you, Lucius Metellus Anguis. Etain has told me of Elana. I'm not sure 'woman' is the way to describe her. It is because of her that you were able to come home."

Lucius winced as Weylyn began to spread the thick mixture on and around his wounds. It took time to administer to them all, and when Weylyn was finished, he set about making more of the mixture which he put in a covered clay dish.

"You will need to apply this everyday until it runs out. When you feel the skin less tight, you can begin light training to regain your strength, but not too soon. I know you are eager, but your muscles are torn in several places. You must give it time. Wear your armour occasionally to build strength before you lift anything heavy. Slow sword movements with no impact at first. I'll also leave some of our healing tea from Ynis Wytrin. Have three cups daily. It will help calm you."

Lucius stood there, covered in the sticky mass of Weylyn's tincture, but he already felt the healing sensation penetrating his skin and was, even then, able to stand a bit straighter. Then he looked at the Druid.

"I saw your son...Cathbad."

Weylyn stopped putting away his things and turned to Lucius. "That's not possible."

"Before going into Dumnonia, there are many things I would have thought impossible," Lucius said. "Cathbad helped me."

"Can you tell me?"

Lucius paused, his eyes tearing up. He shook his head. "I cannot."

"I understand," Weylyn said, disappointment in his voice. "When I saw my son on his way to Annwn, around the time of his death, I knew he had great respect and admiration for you. But I also know that he was dead, gone into the Otherworld." The old man shuddered and sighed sadly. "Perhaps one day…when your mind has dealt with what you have endured…when you have healed your soul…you will tell me of it?"

"I will."

Weylyn nodded. "I thank you."

"Will you remain here with us for a while?" Lucius asked. "Saturnalia is nearly here."

Weylyn smiled and shook his head. "You honour me, but I must return to Ynis Wytrin. The Solstice is a most sacred time there, and I would be with Etain and Father Gilmore for it."

"I understand," Lucius said. "But stay at least a few nights. It would mean much to us."

"Thank you," Weylyn said, making to leave the room. "One more thing, Lucius."

"Yes?"

"Live your life. Savour it. Live it without regret, no matter the pain and torment you have experienced. I have had my share of regret, and it is a sure way to dampen the soul's fire. Be strong for your family, Lucius Metellus Anguis. You are blessed to be alive."

"The Dragon is resting," Weylyn said as he came down the stairs to rejoin everyone in the hall.

"Will Lucius heal?" Adara said coming up to meet him.

"He will, but he has endured much, and I do not mean his body alone. His soul must heal."

"Did he tell you anything?" There was pleading in Adara's eyes, and the Druid felt for her.

"He did not," Weylyn said. "But you must be patient with him. He is strong. The love I can see you share will be more healing to him than anything I can prepare. Be understanding, Adara Metella, and he will rise like a phoenix from the ashes."

"I will. Thank you."

"Lucius has invited Morvran and me to stay for a few days before we return to Ynis Wytrin for the Solstice."

Briana and Dagon approached. "That is good news!" she said, looking at Dagon and then back to Weylyn.

"Is it?" Weylyn smiled. She was the daughter he had never had.

"We wondered if you would be willing to marry us, Weylyn."

The old Druid looked at the two of them and felt joy well up inside of him. He took both of their hands and nodded. "It would be an honour to do so."

"Thank you," Dagon said, as Briana hugged Weylyn.

"That settles it!" Adara said. "We have some work to do!"

The next morning, preparations were being made in earnest for the ceremony to bind Briana and Dagon together. It would take place on the steps of the temple on the hillfort, beneath an arch of ivy, cedar and winter wheat, and the sky above.

While everyone was busy, going to and from the villages to gather supplies of food and more for the festivities, Lucius knelt in the temple with his daughter by the light of a single brazier which they had lit together.

"There," he said as he placed the terracotta likeness of Lunaris upon the altar, at the foot of the statue of Epona. It was a strong, graceful portrait, a stallion with long, muscular legs, a thick neck, and long flowing mane in the Durotrigan style. Culhwch had done a good job. "He is with Epona now, riding in the grassy seas of Elysium."

Calliope sniffled and wiped her eyes. "Is there such a place as that for Lunaris, Baba? Are there horses in Elysium?"

"Of course there are, my girl." Lucius fought his own emotions as he stared at the statue, his arm around his daughter. She had always had a special bond with Lunaris, and the stallion's death, Lucius could tell, had hit her hard. "And he will see our friends there too...Alerio...and Alene too."

"Why does everyone have to die though?" Calliope stared at the faces of the Gods then, at Apollo, Venus, and Epona. The question was sincere.

Gods knew, Lucius had asked that question enough in his life. "It is the way of things, my girl."

"Did you almost die helping Einion, the way Lunaris died helping you?" She turned to her father, her big eyes full of wonder and worry all at once. It was almost as if she knew, but that she wanted him to say it.

317

Lucius hugged her close, buried his face in her long hair and breathed, trying to calm himself. When he let go, she put her hands either side of his head and closed her eyes.

A calmness came over him, a sudden clarity. "It was not in helping Einion that I almost died. We must never shy from helping those who need it...those we love and honour."

"Then what happened to you? I was so scared when I saw you." She was gripping his tunic tightly in her little fists.

"I fought a powerful warrior," he said, the sound of clanging swords deafening in his memory. Even recalling it he could feel the blade of his foe cutting into his flesh over and over again. He could feel anger like never before coursing through his body as he fought back, unwilling to yield to Death in that place of nightmare and twilight.

"Baba?" Calliope was shaking him. "What's wrong?"

Lucius shook his head and saw her staring at him. Then, startled, he spied them behind her, lighting up the shadows.

Venus, Epona, and Apollo himself stood there, staring down at the father and daughter. Their eyes were full of pity and sadness.

Calliope closed her eyes and looked up at the altar. "They are here, Baba. I know it." She did not look toward the Gods, but felt them and Lucius kissed her forehead.

"As they were with me when I fought," he said, and the bitterness in his voice made the Gods wince. Lucius held his daughter and stared at them, his eyes coming to rest on Far Shooting Apollo. "And I fought... I fought to come back to you, my family."

"I know, Baba," Calliope cried, squeezing him tighter.

At that moment, Venus stepped forward and leaned over to kiss the young girl upon her crown.

Calliope immediately stopped crying and was calm.

The next moment, they were gone, and Lucius found himself staring at the top of his daughter's head where they knelt in the small temple.

"It would take all the Furies of the Earth to keep me from you, my girl."

The following day, the sun graced the early morning horizon with a brilliance that had not been seen for weeks. The clouds were sparse in the bright blue sky.

By mid morning, the Metelli, the Sarmatians, and several villagers including Culhwch, Alma, Paulus and others, had all gathered around the temple to see Weylyn bind Briana and Dagon's hands in marriage.

The braziers were lit upon the steps of the temple and lamps burned within, upon the altar. Outside, before the steps, a sacred circle had been delineated and decorated with flowers, boughs of wood, hops, and sheaves of corn.

The guests were gathered around the edge of the circle, and Lucius and Adara stood just outside the Circle upon the temple steps with Phoebus and Calliope beside them.

Weylyn stepped forward to the edge of the circle in which Briana and Dagon stood, and he turned alternately to the four directions.

"Let there be peace in the East, so let it be.

Let there be peace in the South, so let it be.

Let there be peace in the West, so let it be.

Let there be peace in the North, so let it be.

Let there be peace through all the Worlds.

So let it be."

The old druid held a bough of oak leaves in his hands and looked about the assembly of people, warriors and citizens, friends and family.

"We gather here in peace for this sacred rite of marriage between Briana of Dumnonia and King Dagon of Sarmatia. As our circle is woven and consecrated, this moment in time and this place, are blessed. Let each soul truly be present that the spirits of those gathered may be blended in one sacred space, with one purpose and one voice."

As they watched, Lucius felt Adara grip his hand and he returned the pressure. Both felt the emotion rising in them, of the occasion, but also for the gratitude they both felt that they were yet able to stand together. They were too keenly aware of how different things might have been.

Weylyn dipped the bough of oak leaves in a broad clay dish filled with water, and walked around the circle to bless it.

"Let us call to the spirits of the four quarters of our world, that this rite be blessed by the powers of all Creation. Spirits of the North, powers of Winter, guardians of earth and stone, strength of badger, who you teach us of love and loyalty, great bear of the starry skies,

319

the Lady of the sacred womb, the rich soil of creation, I ask that you honour this circle as we honour thee. Witness and bless this rite. Hail and welcome!"

Weylyn shook the leaves and hit both Briana and Dagon's hands.

"Spirits of the East, powers of Spring, of conception, regeneration, vision of falcon and blackbird's song, swallows' freedom flight, sylphs of the wind, breath of life, my Lord of the rising sun and all new life, I ask that you honour this circle as we honour thee. Witness and bless this rite. Hail and welcome!"

He touched the tops of their heads with the wet leaves and continued.

"Spirits of the South, powers of Summer, pride of stag and fire wit of fox, dragons of the land, sprites of the dancing flame, you who teach us of courage and the power of truth, my Lord of the wild Greenwood, I ask that you honour this circle as we honour thee. Witness and bless this rite. Hail and welcome!"

As Weylyn continued, Lucius saw several people gathered there look to him. He stood still as he could, watched, saw Dagon catch his eye before turning to smile at Briana.

I am glad they are happy, Lucius thought.

"Spirits of the West, powers of Autumn, cat who stretches to hunt at dusk, wisdom of salmon and otter's play, undines of chuckling brook, daevas that dance our love and emotion, my Lady of the Seas, tides of being, I ask that you honour this circle as we honour thee. Witness and bless this rite. Hail and welcome!"

Weylyn touched their feet with the bough and walked around the circle another time.

"Hail spirits, you of beauty, power and inspiration, of the high skies that guide us to stretch and grow... You of the dark earth that holds and feeds us... You of the open seas that wash the shores of our sacred land... You who offer us freedom, nourishment and rebirth. As our ancestors knew and honoured your power, so do we now."

With that, Weylyn turned to Lucius who stepped forward with a jug of wine and handed it to him. The Druid then turned and gave it to Dagon to hold. Then Weylyn turned to Adara who handed him a round loaf of fresh-baked bread. He turned back and handed it to Briana.

"In the name of the Gods and the gods of your ancestors, we give thanks for all those who have shared with us their lives, their wisdom and their love. On this sacred day of their wedding, we give thanks especially for the blessings bequeathed to Briana and Dagon by their ancestors of blood and spirit, both those newly-departed, and those of old."

Dagon then raised the jug of wine and poured it out into the earth of the circle about their feet. When he was finished, Briana broke the bread and sprinkled it about the circle before Weylyn continued.

"Ancestors, know what is done. With thanks we bid you, Hail and welcome!"

"Hail and welcome!" everyone present repeated with one voice that rose into the windswept sky.

"Briana and Dagon, do you come to this place of your own free will?"

"We do!" they said, before walking slowly about the circle to each of the quarters as Weylyn carried on slowly.

"May you be blessed by the powers of the earth. May together you root in sweet fertile soil, that your union may grow strong. May your lives together be rich with that fertility and its perfect fruitfulness."

Back where they had begun, facing the temple, Briana and Dagon extended their hands so that Weylyn could bind them together with a long, wide cloth of deep green.

May the Gods and this community witness this hand-fasting, and know that it is lawful, true and binding, as love binds one heart to another."

Weylyn smiled and looked both Briana and Dagon in the eyes.

"Do you vow to honour each other as you honour that which you hold most sacred?"

"We do," they both said, holding each other's eyes and without hesitation.

Weylyn nodded and removed the cloth from their hands.

"And now, let your vows be sealed with a kiss."

To everyone there, it seemed as though the sky lit that very spot. They smiled and clapped and cheered as Briana and Dagon leaned together and kissed.

Amid the joy that spilled out from the circle and into the hearts of everyone there, Adara leaned upon her husband's shoulder, her eyes wet with tears.

"It's so beautiful," she whispered to him.

It is, he thought, kissing her hand and leading her forward to congratulate the couple before they were surrounded with well-wishers.

Lucius hugged Briana and turned to Dagon. "Mar would be very proud, my friend."

"I know," Dagon said, putting his hand upon Lucius' shoulder. "I'm glad you were here, Anguis."

"Me too."

"May you have years of joy," Adara said, hugging both Briana and Dagon as the children swept in to proclaim their joy as well.

"Thank you," Briana said. The Briton seemed like a new woman, brilliant and joyful, as if now the weight of her own family's ordeal had been lifted, she was able to enjoy the wonders of the world with a free conscience.

The Sarmatians congratulated their lord, foremost among them, Barta. Both Dagon and Briana were hoisted into the air and carried around the hillfort.

"I see many years of joy for them," Weylyn said to Lucius as they watched the procession.

"That is good," Lucius said.

In the Sarmatian camp, fires were lit and boar set upon spits for roasting, while loaves of bread were handed out, and barrels of beer opened for all the guests.

"Well…" Alma said to Adara as they sat upon the logs outside the hall, near the garden where Phoebus, Calliope, and Paulus played. "I didn't have a chance to make the honey cakes in time for the wedding, but I don't think they'll be missed."

"No," Adara laughed. "There's more than enough beer to keep them all distracted." It felt good to laugh, to sit with a friend and smile.

"And Lucius? Is he feeling any better?" Alma asked, looking to where Lucius stood with Barta and Culhwch just down the hill near the stables.

Adara's face dropped a little. "He still won't tell me everything. But he is feeling better. Weylyn's skills in healing are considerable."

"That is good. I'm sure you don't need me to tell you, but give it time. Men need to mull things over before they'll open up."

Adara smiled at the Briton and nodded. *But Lucius is not like most men. There is something else wrong.*

As the night wore on, bonfires were lit and the carousing continued into the night, long after Dagon and Briana disappeared from sight to enjoy each other in privacy.

"I'm feeling much better today, Adara. I promise. Weylyn's balms and teas have helped me a lot." Lucius nudged Adara where she sat beside him on the bench of the wagon. He clicked his tongue and flicked the reigns to get the horse team moving more quickly as they came onto a long, straight stretch of road turning south to see the smoke rising from Lindinis directly ahead.

Adara pulled her cloak about her and leaned against her husband. It seemed that in the days since the wedding, he had gotten better and better, that the fog that had engulfed his mind and spirit burned slowly away so that he was himself again.

It was a beautiful day, perfect for heading to the Saturnalia market in Lindinis. The sun shone full and bright above them, the wind was none too harsh, and the chill in the air was less than it had been.

"Remember to stay close when we are in the town, children," Adara said to Phoebus and Calliope who were playing in the back of the covered cart. "It's going to be crowded, and we have a lot of things to get. We're only three days to Saturnalia!"

The children yipped with joy at the thought of the celebrations, the food, and especially the sigillaria, the small gifts given during the festival.

"You know, children," Lucius said. "Catullus used to say that Saturnalia was the very best of days!"

"It is!" Phoebus said.

Lucius turned in his seat to see if the others were keeping apace with them and saw that they were.

Dagon and Briana were riding side by side, and behind them was Lenya with a turmae of off-duty Sarmatians.

The sellers of Lindinis are going to do well by my men today, Lucius laughed, knowing how much pay the men had saved and not used. The songs resonating to the sky behind the wagon told him that

323

the men were indeed in high spirits. Lucius looked forward again to see Barta leading the way.

The trusted Sarmatian had told Lucius he would not leave his side the entire time they were in Lindinis. He had not forgotten the assassins at the hillfort, nor what Lucius and Dagon had told him about being followed on the way to Dumnonia.

"Are you getting me anything for Saturnalia?" Adara suddenly asked.

"What about us, Baba?" the children echoed from behind them, kneeling and wrapping their arms about their parents.

Lucius laughed "I might have something in mind."

"So do we, Baba!" Calliope said. "But Mama said we can't tell you!"

"Well... I have something secret I need to do. You can shop with Briana and Dagon while I do that."

"We have a lot to purchase, Lucius. I'll need your help for some of it."

"I know. I won't be long," he said. Then his voice grew more serious. "I also need to find Crescens and speak with him."

"Do you have to do that today?"

"Best get it out of the way."

"But Cradawg is nearly finished the baths. We don't need any more building supplies, do we?"

"No. But the matter of Crescens' son is hanging over my head."

"Just don't lose your temper with him. You don't have to be a warrior to be a powerful man."

Lucius baulked at the suggestion, but then he realized Adara was right. Crescens could cause more trouble for him than slowing the release of building supplies from the local fabrica. "I'll be friendly."

Soon the wagon pulled up at Corpulo's horse stables outside of Lindinis' north gate, and the Sarmatians began tying their horses wherever they could. Normally, the owners of the paddocks might raise their prices upon seeing such a large contingent of visitors coming, but Corpulo thought better of it at the sight of the Dragon praefectus and the dark, tattooed warriors who accompanied him.

"Welcome back, Praefectus!" Corpulo called as he came out to greet them.

Lucius waved but carried on walking.

The guards at the city gates looked uneasy too as Lucius and his men approached, but Lucius stepped forward to explain who he was and that his men were on furlough and wanted to spend their hard-earned denarii in the town.

"As long as they stay out of trouble, Praefectus," the optio at the gate said.

"They will. You have my word," Lucius added. He began to walk back to his men, when the soldier called him back.

"Praefectus?"

Lucius turned back. "Yes?"

"The lads have been speaking about you around here."

Oh, no. What has Crescens been saying? Lucius worried.

"It's an honour to meet you, sir," the man said, his fellows gathered behind him smiling.

Lucius stared back at the man and the faces of the other soldiers. There was an awkward silence between them, even as the crowds rushed on either side like the rapids of a stream flowing about a rock in its midst.

"Sir?" the optio cleared his throat. "We've heard about all you've done in the North against the Caledonii..." the man waited for Lucius to say something, but was disappointed. "Great work, sir."

"Thank you, soldier. But it was not just me." Lucius turned to see the mass of his men coming toward them with Adara and the children, Briana and Dagon, and Barta. "My men are the best cavalry in the empire," he added.

"We know. We've heard stories!" one of the other men said, causing his optio to turn and stare at him.

"Well, we don't want to keep you from enjoying the market, sir," the optio said. The man stood back and nodded, not wanting to bother Lucius any more.

Lucius made himself look at the man and extended his hand.

The young optio took it and smiled.

"Keep up the good work, Optio," Lucius said.

The guards then nodded respectfully to all the Sarmatians as they filed past and went into the crowded centre of town where the market stalls were set up.

"You go ahead and start getting supplies," Lucius said to Adara. "I have a couple of errands I need to attend to before I join you."

"Be careful with the ordo members, Lucius," Adara warned. "I don't trust them."

"Neither do I." Lucius leaned in. "Stay close to Dagon and Briana, all right? Barta will come with me." Lucius could tell the big Sarmatian was already at his back. "And children, stay close to your mother. No wandering off."

"Yes, Baba," Phoebus and Calliope said, taking Adara'a hand.

The group set off surrounded by Sarmatians.

Lucius watched them disappear and then, when he was sure they were gone, he went back the way he had come, crossed the bridge and turned east toward the area nestled in the bend of the river. His eyes immediately spotted the little smith's stall, the man he had commissioned the sword from months before. He turned to Barta who was close behind him.

"My friend, you can stay here at the bridge. I won't be long."

"But, Praefectus, my duty -"

"Is to make sure Adara does not come this way. I am only picking up a gift for her."

Barta looked doubtful, but nodded. "I will be here, sir, watching."

"Thank you, Barta. I won't be long."

As Lucius approached, Terdra's thin frame topped by curly black hair crested the oak counter and waved.

"I've been expecting you, Praefectus," Terdra said. His eyes sparkled as he greeted Lucius, but then his expression transformed. "You are different than when last I saw you. You've been somewhere far away." The smith's eyes were sad as they looked Lucius over.

"Are you an oracle as well as a smith?" Lucius said, trying to joke, but coming across more angry.

"There was no disrespect in my statement," Terdra said, bowing formally.

"Forgive me." Lucius was frustrated with himself. He had been short with everyone since returning from Dumnonia, mostly because of the pain his body caused him. "I was in a battle and am still healing."

Terdra looked at the sword hanging from Lucius' waist. "The Dragon's blade has tasted a different sort of blood. I can tell."

Lucius stared at the little man, and his eyes must have betrayed some discomfort or fear, for Terdra stepped forward and placed his small dark hand upon Lucius' shoulder.

"You survived. And now you are here. All is well."

"Is it?" Lucius asked, looking down at him.

"I can tell when the Gods have blessed a man, Lucius Metellus Anguis, and I see as much in you."

"Really…" *You have no idea, do you?*

"How do you think I came to be here?" Terdra turned and went back around his counter.

Lucius noticed there were no wares displayed. When he said nothing, Terdra continued.

"There is much good you do not know. For instance, you might not know that I am close to the Lady of Horses, she who rides with white hounds."

"What? You?"

Terdra nodded. "Again…blessed by the Gods." He smiled at Lucius and then reached beneath the counter to bring up a long folded bundle of deep green cloth. He placed it carefully upon the wood.

"Is that it?"

Terdra nodded. "Please look. I have outdone myself in the greenwood forges. It has taken me some moons to make."

Lucius stepped forward and carefully unfolded the fabric before a brilliant gold hilt and polished blade shone from the darkness beneath. He gasped.

The blade was that of a gladius, as Lucius had asked for, but the rest was unlike anything else, except his own sword. The hilt was oval, but protruding from the sides were the heads of two golden dragons that twined about each side. The rich dark walnut wood pommel, on the other end of the antler handle, was a perfect circle with brilliant golden horses charging around the perimeter, one of them carrying a goddess with long flowing hair like river water.

Lucius hoisted it and the lightness of the object was impossible. He looked at Terdra questioningly.

"It is as strong as your blade, I'm sure. You did say you wanted one to match it."

Lucius nodded. "Aye. I did." He stepped back and stabbed with it, trying to imagine it in Adara's hand. "So light!" He twirled it and the balance was so perfect that it came easily back to rest in his grip. "It's perfect," he whispered to himself.

Terdra nodded. "Like I said. My best work."

"Thank you."

327

"It is now the twin of your own heavenly blade, Lucius Metellus Anguis. You and your lady must wield them wisely."

"I always do," Lucius answered. "But," he looked up. "How much do I owe you, master smith? I do not know if I have enough coin on me to pay for such a treasure."

"One cannot demand payment of..." Terdra's voice trailed off. "I do not require payment in coin."

"You must! I cannot accept such a gift!"

Terdra brought up a sheath of brown leather trimmed with bronze acanthus leaves, and slid the blade silently into it. He then wrapped it all up in the green cloth and put the weapon into a long leather sleeve with a shoulder strap. When he was finished he held it out to Lucius, but did not motion for him to take it yet.

"This is a precious gift." His voice was a warning. "In payment for it, I would ask that you and your lady wield the weapons always in defence of goodness, and part of that is to keep faith with the Isle of the Blessed."

"The Isle?"

Terdra nodded. "Yes. The wolves are gathering, and the Isle needs a Dragon." Terdra then handed Lucius the bundle.

The Roman took it, and for a moment, it felt extremely heavy. But the weight disappeared and Lucius slid it over his shoulder.

"Do you swear to make this payment?" Terdra asked him.

Lucius thought about Ynis Wytrin and felt a strength inside, for he had decided long before that the Isle and the people who dwelt there were good. He nodded.

"Then may the Gods continue to bless you," Terdra said before touching his forehead and bowing. "Look," he said, pointing to somewhere near the bridge behind Lucius.

Lucius turned and saw a group of men in togas approaching him hurriedly. At their head was the tall form of Serenus Crescens, his pale blue eyes focussed directly on Lucius.

Barta was following swiftly on them, one hand upon the hilt of his sword, the other fingering the throwing daggers which he wore beneath his cloak.

"I am sorry, Terdra, but I must -"

The smith was gone...the stall...any sign of him. All except the sword which still hung in the leather pouch on Lucius' back.

Amazement began to play with Lucius, but he had no time to indulge it, for the ordo members were almost upon him.

Lucius noted the others behind Crescens - Virgilio Carcer, Cassius Bucer, Felix Inek, Nolan Phelan and Finian Maccus. Coming quickly behind them all was the Briton, Trevor Reghan, the only man among them whom Lucius thought might be trustworthy. Also present, was Crescens' son.

In that moment, feelings of panic and rage filled Lucius. He had the river at his back, and this group of men approached quickly, ready for confrontation.

Crescens' face was red with anger and he was pointing at Lucius, the facade of propriety having burned away in full.

"Preafectus Metellus!" he shouted. "I have business with you!" Crescens said.

Lucius felt his heart pounding unnaturally, and in that moment he reached for the handle of his own sword and slid it free to stop just before Crescens' chest.

"Praefectus!" Barta's deep voice called out as he rushed up behind the group, passing them all to stand beside Lucius.

"How dare you draw your weapon on me!" Crescens hissed.

"Crescens, calm down!" Virgilio Carcer said, his hands pulling at his fellow ordo member.

"How dare you approach me like an angry mob!" Lucius roared.

Barta stood close beside Lucius and whispered. "Praefectus. He is no warrior. More trouble than it's worth." Barta noticed the look in Lucius' eyes and reached up slowly to still his extended arm. "Your family is in the town, sir. They wait for us."

Lucius lowered his sword and stepped forward, closer to Crescens and Carcer. "If you have business with me, then speak it."

Crescens turned and beckoned his son. "You and one of your men attacked my son and his friends."

Lucius stared at the boy who gazed back haughtily, a hint of a smirk upon his face.

"Really?" Lucius said, his eyes darting from the father to the son. "It seems to me what happened is that your son and his friends attacked and attempted to rape an innocent girl who was making offerings to the spirits of her ancestors. I thought it my duty to stop them."

"You attacked them!" Crescens said.

"They attacked us first. And we were gentle on them."

"Is that what counts for bravery among Rome's legions nowadays?" Crescens spoke aloud so that his colleagues behind could all hear him. "To bully young boys and spoil their fun?"

"You have a distorted view of the world, Serenus Crescens," Lucius said. He could feel his nerves on edge, screaming in fact, but he did not want to give the man the satisfaction of seeing it. The reaction was as much a surprise to himself. "The girl was minding her own business, spending the day beyond the borders of Ynis Wytrin. Your son had no right to accost her."

"He had every right. He is a Roman citizen! And she, she was but a British harlot!"

"You are the aggressor here, not them!" Lucius said. "Why do you threaten the emperor's peace?"

"I do no such thing!" Crescens protested.

"No?" Lucius looked beyond the ordo members.

A crowd had gathered to watch and listen, and coming in formation were the men of the contubernium manning the gate.

"Why do you defend these Britons so, Praefectus?" Virgilio Carcer asked. "My colleague's son should not have attacked a helpless girl..." he gave Crescens a stern look, "...but you appear to have a soft spot for this group of Britons who appear to live outside of Rome's reach."

"They don't even pay their taxes!" Nolan Phelan snarled.

"The people of the Isle do not bother any Roman or Briton outside of their lands. They should be left in peace, as it has been for over a century." Lucius prepared himself as the guard approached, and he saw Barta casually draw his big sword from his side, ready.

Lucius focussed on Crescens and the other ordo members. "How do you fine gentlemen expect to maintain the Pax Romana in the South if you harry the people? If you allow your sons to rape them? You threaten the empire itself when you shun disciplina!"

"How dare you," Crescens growled. "I invited you into my home."

"Where I was attacked," Lucius retorted.

"I was the one who was attacked!" Crescens said aloud. "Not you! And the assassins were sent by Ynis Wytrin!"

"I think not! Then I suppose it was also a coincidence that my family was attacked again in our home? Might you know anything about that?"

"Of course not!"

"Because if you did..." Lucius got in his face. "You would regret your part in it for the rest of your days, Serenus Crescens."

"I had no part in it. I've been working tirelessly to get your building supplies to your new home so that you might finish your construction."

"Construction which you sought to hamper."

Crescens smiled. "I did not."

"Lies come easily to you."

"This conversation is pointless!" Carcer said as the guards approached.

"What seems to be the problem here?" the optio from the gate arrived, his high crested helmet cutting through the group to the font where he stood beside Lucius and Crescens.

"Optio, this off-duty praefectus has threatened me and my colleagues. He assaulted my son as well."

The optio looked at Crescens' son and recognized him. He couldn't stand the snobby little bastard any more than the rest of the troops stationed at Lindinis. He looked at Lucius and nodded, saw the sword in Lucius hand. He said nothing, but turned back to Crescens.

"Sir... The Praefectus is a man of honour and, as far as I can see, is only here to shop prior to Saturnalia."

"What? You insubordinate dog!"

"Careful, sir," the optio said evenly. "You may run Lindinis, but we're men of the legions." He turned to Lucius and Barta. "Praefectus, I'm sorry you were inconvenienced. You should enjoy your leave like anyone else. Please, enjoy the market. My men will see no one bothers you again."

Lucius sheathed his sword and nodded his thanks to the optio. "Thank you, soldier." He also acknowledged the men of the contubernium behind the optio and they smiled back.

Crescens, Carcer and the others watched Lucius and Barta go, escorted back by the troopers. The ordo members were speechless at the insult, for in one fell stroke, the men of the garrison had shown that if it came to it, the praefectus could indeed rob them of their loyalty.

"My friends," Crescens said to his colleagues after Trevor Reghan went after Lucius and Barta. "I don't think we can count on Praefectus Metellus anymore to present our case to the emperor."

"I know someone who will," Nolan Phelan said in Crescens' ear.

331

Lucius and Barta left the troopers back at the posts and entered the town, their eyes searching the crowds for any sign of Adara, the children and the others.

Lindinis was packed to capacity that day, it being nearly impossible to go two paces without colliding with someone carrying bundles of Saturnalian cerei, myriad sigillaria, the small gifts that were given by family and friends for the occasion, baskets of food, amphorae of wine, and barrels of beer. Some people were already wearing their pileus and synthesis, the conical felt cap and loud, colourful clothing of Saturnalia.

Lucius thought briefly that no one would ever have worn their pileus and synthesis so early in Rome, but it seemed that in that faraway province, many decided to do just that, some even wearing them with the traditional plaid bracae of the Britons.

"Praefectus…" Barta tried getting Lucius' attention as they walked, but Lucius just kept going. "Praefectus, stop!"

Lucius stopped, his eyes scanning the crowd.

"Sir, what is wrong?" Barta put his hand upon Lucius' shoulder. "I've never seen a civilian get to you like that. The man and his friends are not worth it. They would not have dared to attack you."

"I'm not so sure, Barta. Any one of them could have been holding a dagger."

Barta looked confused. "None of them has the spine for it, sir. They're all soft and weak."

Lucius shook his head and pressed on into the crowd.

They entered the far end of the agora and Lucius spotted Adara and the others some distance away at a stall selling brilliant syntheses.

Lucius stepped forward, but the crowd swelled before his eyes like a great leviathan, pulling all into its slimy folds, including Adara and the children who had dived in eagerly to see the festive, richly adorned stalls of vendors from various parts of the empire beyond Lindinis.

He stared at the crowd. He did not hear Barta speaking to him. Lucius' eyes bored into the mass of people so as not to lose sight of his family.

What is wrong with me? He shut his eyes for a moment, angry and not a little confused by the fact that his fists were tightly balled and his feet remained planted, stuck in the ground like the roots of a great oak tree, when he had thought to push his way through the crowd. His fingers fidgeted with the handle of his sword as if it were a comforting talisman. He took a deep breath, and walked forward.

Lucius sought Adara's eyes and the shape of his children's bodies in the chaos, found them again, and strode toward them.

It felt like a million eyes were upon him, assessing him, judging and threatening him. For a moment, Lucius was back in that otherworldly land of dread beauty from which he had recently returned, with myriad eyes upon him, though he could see none. He knew in his bones he would, after that moment, feel more at ease in the bloodbath of battle than in a crowded agora of citizens.

Suddenly, Adara was gripping his hands and his eyes focussed upon her and the smiling faces of Phoebus and Calliope, each of them carrying bundles.

"Lucius?" Her face was all concern, her eyes holding on to him as intently as her hand.

"We need to leave...now," he said, his jaw so tight that the muscles bulged like rocks beneath his cheeks.

Adara was about to protest, but she saw the panic in his eyes.

Behind Lucius, Barta shrugged, helpless himself in the face of Lucius' sudden transformation.

"Yes, my love. We should go."

He nodded and turned, still holding her hand as he walked.

"Praefectus!" someone then called.

Lucius stopped, his hand slipped to his sword again.

Trevor Reghan stopped short, his hands up as Lucius stared wildly at him and moved on.

"What do you want with the praefectus?" Dagon stood before Trevor Reghan.

The Briton looked at the Sarmatian. "Tell him to be cautious," he whispered. "The ordo members do not take kindly to insults, and he has insulted them. Tell him it might be best if he did not come to Lindinis for a while."

"Are you threatening him?" Dagon asked, stepping closer, his voice cold and calm.

"No. I'm trying to help him."

Adara was glad that they had obtained everything they needed for Saturnalia in Lindinis before their quick departure, but her worry over Lucius' behaviour there steadily increased.

333

It cast something of a cloud over the preparations for the festival, but there was, nevertheless, jollity in the air.

The seventeenth day of December, the first day of Saturnalia, was upon them, and the food stores were close to bursting, the hall and various outbuildings on the hillfort all decorated with garlands of ivy, cedar, and holly from the surrounding forests and hillsides. Cerei were set everywhere, and wood stacked for the fires to burn brightly.

The troops, Lucius and Dagon included, thought at the back of their minds that they would be called up to Caledonia anytime, that Mars would not hide his hoary face for long. However, the call to war did not come, and so everyone allowed themselves to settle into a comfortable period for the dark days of winter.

That did not stop Lucius, however, for as his strength returned, in large part due to Weylyn's healing salves, teas, and poultices, so too did Lucius' determination to get back into fighting shape. Daily, he would train with Dagon and Barta, or the decurions Lenya, Badru and Vaclar. Despite the festival, he worked as though he were on campaign.

But Adara said nothing, for the hard, physical work appeared to keep Lucius out of the dark forests of his mind. She had not come any closer to finding out what ailed him, what had happened to him in Dumnonia, but he was becoming more and more himself. She focussed on the celebration of Saturnalia in their home.

And it was made all the better for the completed bathhouse at the base of the eastern slopes fed by the natural well in the hillside there.

Cradawg had finished putting the last finial upon the last corner of the low, stone structure when Lucius and Adara came down the path to greet him.

"All finished, Praefectus! Just in time for Saturnalia, as requested." The thickly muscled Durotrigan crossed his arms and looked at the bathhouse, even as the smoke from the hypocausts began to rise in a slim plume out of the chimney. "You can now wash in something other than a barrel!" Cradawg laughed.

"It's perfect," Lucius said. "I'm just glad you were able to get the rest of the supplies from Lindinis."

"I'm as surprised as you," Cradawg admitted. "Some of the lads at the fabrica confided in me that the ordo was none too happy with you. Luckily, the boys there know me and knew they were doing work for the 'Dragon Praefectus' of Rome, as they call you. They rushed the shipment out and into my wagons before the word came to halt everything."

"Crescens?" Lucius asked.

"Aye. Him and that wolfish one, Phelan. They've got it in for you."

"I know."

"Anyway, I hope this meets your expectations. The walls are plain, but I expect lady Metella will be able to paint something upon them." He turned to Adara. "My brother's wife tells me that you are quite an artist, lady."

"My mother taught me," Adara said, smiling. I'm sure I'll enjoy it very much."

"Well, I must get going," Cradawg said. "Alma and Culhwch will be furious if I'm late for the evening meal."

Lucius extended his arm and Cradawg took it. "Be sure to come for a drink during the festival."

"You Romans have so many festivals. It's a wonder you get any work done with all the drinking!" Cradawg howled. "I would love to. Enjoy!" he said as he walked away down the slope.

Lucius stood, his sword jutting from between his shoulders, and took Adara's hand. "We have our own bathhouse!"

"I can hardly believe it."

"Shall we take a look?"

The structure was low and long with a tiled roof running lengthwise from North to South. On the West side of the structure was a covered walkway with a door to each room of the bathhouse - the small apodyterium first on the North end, then the tepidarium, the caldarium, and lastly the frigidarium.

It was a simple hypocaust system of heating for the floors and walls, and the flow of water was enough to keep the water clean as it flowed out and down hill beneath the ground to the East.

Lucius and Adara entered the door of the apodyterium to see seven small wooden cubicles for clothing and other items.

The first thing they noticed was the tang of fresh plaster in the air.

Lucius touched the wall and his hand came away with some white upon it.

Cradawg and his men had literally just finished.

"I guess you have quite a canvas to fill now," he said.

Adara nodded.

Lucius took her hand and they walked into the tepidarium to find a warm pool of water in an alcove, reached by five steps. They knelt down and felt the water. It was still cool but was getting warmer. The fire had not been burning for long in the furnace beneath the floor.

The caldarium was not the steamy realm it should have been, but they could indeed feel it getting warmer too, bordering on hot as they continued into the frigidarium where the circular cold water pool looked icy blue.

Lucius shivered. "Maybe we should wait until the hypocausts are much hotter."

"You expected to bathe now?" Adara laughed. "We don't even have towels, clothes, or oil and strigils!"

"We wouldn't need clothes," Lucius smiled.

"Soon, but not yet," Adara teased. "We have a celebration to prepare for."

The seventeenth day of December arrived and with it, the beginning of the festival of Saturnalia, 'best of days' as it had been dubbed by the poet Catullus many years before. The morning dawned quietly, as if in preparation for the hush of winter, of frosted fields and mist-shrouded hills.

Ravens cawed in the naked branches of the trees that dotted the slopes of the hillfort, and with the wind absent, the frost and mist upon the fields below were left to gather at will.

Briana, Dagon and Barta watched as the Metelli made their way from the hall to the small temple for the sacrifice to start the festival.

Lucius had one of the young piglets they had purchased in Lindinis tucked beneath his arm, and as he walked, his cloak dragged upon the damp grass as if leaving a trail of blood. He had invited his friends to join them, but Dagon had thought it best if the family do it themselves. At least that time.

"I've seen it before," Dagon told Briana. "It is a solemn sacrifice. He needs to do it alone."

She agreed, and as they continued to watch, they saw the family pass the makeshift altar outside of the temple and go inside.

Saturnalia was one of the greatest festivals of Rome, a time of mirth rivalled by few others. Lucius had always enjoyed it, but he felt as though a cloud was hanging over the celebrations this time. His anticipation, which was usually acute, was dulled, even if he had a magnificent gift for his wife.

The truth was that Saturnalia only served to remind him of Alene.

His sister had always been the life of the celebrations, taking great care with the decorations, determining the menu with their mother, and purchasing the most thoughtful sigillaria for everyone.

He knew Adara felt the same way, but she was able to make more of an effort for the others, especially the children. She stood by Lucius' side as they entered the temple, and helped to light the lamps and cerei of bees wax which had been set all about the images of the Gods upon the altar.

Phoebus and Calliope stood back from the altar, holding hands, their heads down for the sacrificium of Saturnalia, one of the only times Romans bared their heads for sacrifices.

Once the cerei were lit and the braziers crackling to life, Lucius stepped forward, lit a chunk of frankincense, and placed it in the bowl of the altar. Smoke wafted up slowly in wide clouds at first, but then it settled into a constant rising stream to form a canopy over the Gods.

The image of Saturn with his sickle stood front and centre before Apollo, Venus, Epona and others, and about the feet of all of them, sprigs of holly and strands of ivy lay carefully placed.

Lucius gazed at the god's eyes and felt him looking upon his family, seeking the offering which Lucius held in his arms.

Adara and the children came up behind Lucius, each holding a long, thick candle which they would carry back to their home.

Lucius cleared his throat in the quiet of the temple. "Oh Saturn, Lord of the Earth and Underworld, master of the harvest fields. We honour you in these days of darkness that you might watch over us and bring us through to the light. Accept our offerings of light and life that we may be happy in this world..."

Lucius' voice faded away and he did not speak further.

Adara waited a few moments and then leaned forward to better see her husband's face.

It was a mask of emotion with eyes shut in remembrance, or perhaps worry.

The piglet began to struggle beneath his arm, but Lucius held onto it tightly. The flames flickered loudly in the braziers and the children began to fidget.

337

"Lord...grant me a torch of wisdom to hold in the darkness that I may better know myself, that I may better protect and provide for my family the length of my days. May our lights shine brightly for you, and may you remember us. Please accept our offering."

With that, Lucius held up the piglet to the image of Saturn. The beast's small eyes goggled wildly and stared at Lucius, but he forced himself to ignore it. He then stood aside so that Adara and the children could step forward and light their candles upon the altar flame. When it was done, they stood back, each child taking care to protect the flame, and Adara caring for both hers and Lucius'.

Lucius led the way outside into the cool morning to the altar below the temple steps. He pulled the left side of his cloak back to reveal the dagger tucked into his belt. Then, he placed the animal upon the altar, his left hand holding onto it while his right reached into a scrip at his waist to pull out a handful of grain. He placed his hand upon the piglet's head and let the grain fall.

The animal, distracted by the grain and eager to nibble at it, did not see Lucius' blade come to life from out of the sheath, nor the small amount of morning sun glint off of the hilt.

"Saturn... Accept the offering of the Metelli."

The blade bit deep then and after a stifled squeal, the body went limp and hot blood poured over Lucius' hands and down the sides of the altar to soak the earth below.

A cool breeze picked up then and Lucius closed his eyes and turned his face to the sky. He reached for calm within, his deep breaths and the wet of blood upon his hands giving him focus, assurance.

Adara came around the other side of the altar and handed him his burning candle which he accepted. She then placed her right hand in the blood and wiped it across his forehead.

He smiled at her and in one breath they said the words together.

"Io Saturnalia!"

Then the children came around and joined them.

"Io Saturnalia! Io Saturnalia!"

The Metelli's voices echoed over the hillfort and from the Sarmatian camp the sentiment was echoed. "Io Saturnalia! Io Saturnalia! Io Saturnalia!"

That night, the hall was lit with myriad candles for the feast, decorated with thick garlands of ivy and holly, and food and drink set out upon tables wherever space allowed. There were platters of bread and cheeses, meat and game, roasted fowl and fish from the rivers nearby. There were bowls of olives of various varieties, some of which Lucius had not seen since his time in Numidia.

As the Metelli stood by the open doors of the hall greeting the guests coming into their home, Lucius leaned over to Adara and whispered.

"How did we afford all of this?"

Adara smiled at him and laced her arm through his. "Don't worry. There are many veterans in Lindinis who were eager to sell to the family of the 'Dragon Praefectus'. I couldn't stop them giving me a deal if I wanted to!" She laughed, her voice a joyous chorus to greet the influx of warm faces.

The hall was filled mostly with Sarmatians, some of whom stood guard outside, taking the duty in rotation so that no intruder, no stranger to pose any threat, would be able to approach the Metelli or roam about the hillfort at will during the celebrations.

"Io Saturnalia!" Culhwch hailed Lucius and Adara as he, Alma and Paulus came in through the doors.

"Io Saturnalia!" the couple returned, raising their wine cups to their Durotrigan friends.

Immediately, Phoebus and Calliope ran up to greet Paulus, their three little heads pressed together in excitement as the twins described all of the food they could have.

Paulus looked up at his parents questioningly.

"Go on! Have fun!" Culhwch said, and the three ran off. He then turned back to Lucius and Adara. "What is this outfit, Lucius?" he asked, chuckling at the multi-coloured synthesis and conical pileus he wore. "Not very warrior-like, is it?"

Lucius blushed a little, but then straightened proudly. "I'll have you know that in Rome, the louder the Saturnalian garb, the better. It's tradition!"

"Well...it's...it's very..." Alma struggled to find the words but gave up, her husband finishing for her.

"Very loud!"

There was a pause before they all burst out laughing.

"I'm glad you find my Roman traditions so amusing," Lucius muttered in mock exasperation. "Come, after a little wine, my clothing will appear a wonder."

"I agree," Culhwch laughed as Lucius led him away. "But it might take a lot of wine!"

Adara and Alma watched the two men go, smiling after them.

"This is quite a celebration!" Alma said. "We've never been to a Saturnalia feast before."

"It's like many other Roman celebrations. Just more drink and more light!" Adara chuckled.

"And colourful clothing, apparently!"

"Quite!" The two women laughed again, and Adara handed Alma a cup of wine from a nearby table.

"How is he doing?" Alma asked in a low voice.

"Better everyday, I think," Adara said. But her smile faded, and Alma squeezed her hand. "I'm fine. He's fine. I still don't know how he was wounded like that except that it was in a great fight."

"Men take longer to reveal their feelings than women, if ever they do. Give him time."

"I know. And Lucius has always been open with me."

"But this time, something is different?"

"Yes." Adara shook her head and smiled again. "But this is Saturnalia, a time of joy and merriment! And so, merry I should be."

Alma retreated from her questioning. "I must say that you look like a goddess tonight, Adara. Your stola is so beautiful!"

Adara looked down at the deep blue fabric trimmed with a golden meander pattern. "Thank you. It's Lucius' favourite. Mine too in fact. I have so few occasions to wear it."

"Well, you look stunning."

Adara greeted more of the Sarmatians who came in through the door.

"I see Ula, Aina and their father with my cousin. I'll go talk to them." Alma smiled and excused herself, pushing through the press of guests.

"Barta," Adara said without turning.

The big Sarmatian emerged from the shadows behind her, near the doors. "Yes, my lady."

"Please keep an eye on Lucius tonight. I worry the crowd may upset him."

"Of course."

"And the children are to stay inside the hall."

"I'll make sure. But you should enjoy yourself, Metella."

Adara breathed deeply, comforted by the security the Sarmatian's presence ensured. "I will." She turned and smiled at him, and he bowed to her before she made her way to the hearth fire to speak with some of the guests seated there.

The night wore on, and new cerei were lit and braziers set ablaze once more as the drink flowed past everyone's lips, and the platters of food emptied.

Shouts of 'Io Saturnalia!' echoed through the hall, and Dagon laughed at how much his men had adopted the Roman expression of jubilation. The time was contagious, and he found himself relaxed, with Briana by his side, surrounded by his men.

"Will you sing us a song?" he asked Briana, who had been speaking with Alma beside her.

"Go on!" Alma said. "Something out of Dumnonia!"

Briana's cheeks were red with the warm glow of the wine, and she thought of refusing at first, but then the Sarmatians took up the chant for her to do so.

"A song from our new queen!" Vaclar cried out, his sentiment echoed around the hall.

Briana nodded and made her way to the blazing hearth fire where the children sat looking up at her, plates of food upon their laps.

Lucius turned to see and Adara was at his side, the two of them listening eagerly for Briana to begin.

"I didn't know she sang," Lucius said.

"Everybody sings," Adara answered. "They just have to want to."

A hush fell over the gathering as Briana stepped onto one of the logs to be seen by all. Her long grey and crimson tunica fell like a waterfall from the height of her shoulders, her blonde, braided hair cascading down from the golden circlet embossed with animals that Dagon had given her. She looked less like the warrior she was now, and more like a queen. It was then, after her eyes closed for a moment that the song began deep inside.

It was a single note at first, something like the wind upon the moors of her homeland, solemn and chill, like a keen. But then it rose up, higher and higher, like a tide or the sun cracking on the horizon, and a warm melody ushered forth from her mouth to blanket them all.

"I think of you
When light comes through
The dawn wind brings
My dreams on wings,
Up from the sea, over towering cliffs,
Across the moors, my heart to yours."

The words drew everyone in and they were lost in a mysterious land, longing to know where it led, what she saw when her eyes were closed. Then Briana opened her eyes to turn and gaze about the gathering.

"A goddess rides,
White palfrey strides,
To the place of silver waters deep,
Swords and spears, our hearts to leap,
Across the moors, and beneath the stars,
To my soul's very deep."

Lucius, Adara, Dagon and everyone there listened, their hearts uplifted and opened to the full emotion of the song, to what she felt for the land she had been torn from and which she had not returned to, unlike her brother who had bled to get it back, along with Dagon and, perhaps even more so, Lucius.

Briana's eyes met Lucius and Adara's as she sang the last verse, and they knew then that this was no song of old, but one that came to her even then, before the flames and surrounded by eyes and candlelight.

"We mortals thank them,
The Gods above,
For blood that was shed,
For honour and love.
For friendship fair is dear to me,
For I have dreamed of it,
Beneath the limbs,
Of the broad green trees…"

Her voice faded and she bowed to Lucius and Adara, her eyes brilliant with tear and firelight as the melody receded back into her.

The hall erupted with applause and cheers as Dagon strode forward to stand before Briana, his hands grasping hers and kissing them. He shone with pride and his men could see it, felt it too.

Lucius and Adara stood there amid the gathering, a place of stillness in the joyful, Saturnalian chaos. They smiled at their friend for the song she had sung.

In the back of his mind, the song still rang out for Lucius, for it had hit very close to the mark for him, and he shut his eyes against some of the memories that harried him. He felt Adara grip his hand again and he opened his eyes, nodding. "Beautiful," he murmured.

"I too have a gift!" Dagon was shouting, his arms upraised from his long Sarmatian robes. He stood upon the log where Briana had sung, and looked about the hall, asking for his men's quiet. When all eyes were upon him, he continued. He looked directly at Lucius and bowed, his hand upon his heart.

"I am not a man of words, more often than not," Dagon said, to the amusement of his countrymen. "Mostly of deeds, I pray. Anguis..." he began, using the sacred name the Sarmatians used for Lucius in hushed and personal conversation. "We have fought through many battles, you and I, side by side, Romans and Sarmatians, against all manner of enemies."

Dagon stopped for a moment, his eyes watery in the fire-lit hall, but he did not weep. He pressed on with what he had to say, for he knew how much Lucius had been fighting inside, though others did not.

"Long ago, Anguis, I lost the brothers of my blood to war, my mother and father. Our king, Mar..." Here the Sarmatians closed their eyes and made a symbol sacred to their god of the sword, "...he admired you above all other Romans. But...I do not."

There was an audible gasp, but then Dagon put his hands up for silence before continuing.

"I do not admire you above all other Romans, but rather above all men. To me, you are not Roman, or Sarmatian, or even Briton. You, my dearest friend, are a champion for us all!" There were loud cheers of approval at that. "And I count myself honoured to be able to fight at your side!" Dagon's eyes were wild with emotion then, and not a few there felt a chill run up their spine at the sight of the king saying such things to a Roman.

"Anguis…" he continued, the hall quieting again. "I know how hard you have fought, how you have suffered for us all. Not only are you the greatest leader I can imagine, but you are also my family and dearest friend. You all are!" Here, Dagon looked at Adara and then at the children who were now standing holding hands beside Briana, looking up at him.

Dagon was silent a moment as he gazed at Lucius again, the flames of the hearth lighting his features. He squinted briefly as he thought he spied three shining beings at the back of the hall, behind Lucius. He looked away quickly, back to Lucius, and continued.

"I think that I can speak for all my countrymen when I say that we would follow you anywhere…and we would gladly lay down our lives for you and your family."

At that point, the strangest thing occurred, and were any of Lucius' Roman colleagues to be standing in that hall at that moment, they would have baulked. For in that moment, Dagon of Sarmatia, a king of his people and lord of some of the greatest warriors in the empire, bowed to Lucius Metellus Anguis and his family.

Lucius felt chills running through the whole of his body as the room full of warriors bowed in silence to him then, the few Britons there present smiling at it all, for in the ways of their own forbears, the hall echoed with ancient familiarity.

Dagon rose, smiling at Lucius and Adara, and then he turned to Barta who stood by the door.

The Sarmatian went outside for a moment.

"And now, for you, Anguis, a gift this Saturnalia!" Dagon turned to the doors and in came Barta leading a massive pitch black stallion with white fetlocks.

The guests parted quickly to allow the great beast to enter the hall, and for Lucius to approach slowly from where he stood.

The hall was noisy and chaotic as people shouted praise, cups fell and shattered and the hearth fire crackled and flamed as more wood was added.

And through it all the stallion remained calm and alert, confident, towering and strong. He was trained to withstand the harshest conditions of battle. It was absolutely clear that this was indeed a horse bred for a king. He had been chosen, reared and trained by a people who honoured horses above all others.

Barta turned to face the animal, and even he was dwarfed by it. He glanced around with his one eye to make sure there was ample

344

space and then raised his hands in a gesture that the stallion understood.

The stallion reared so that he almost doubled in height, and even a few of the Sarmatians stood back from him.

But Lucius approached, just as the stallion came down and accepted the bridle from Barta. He was in awe, but he was also saddened. He missed Lunaris dearly, for he had been a gift from Alerio, and now they were both gone.

It was as if Dagon knew the feelings that haunted Lucius, for he was there in a moment, beside him, hand upon his shoulder.

"I know how much Lunaris meant to you, Anguis. And the sacrifice he made." It was true, for Dagon had been there when Lunaris fell in Dumnonia, and a more heroic death for a horse the Sarmatian king could not imagine. "I know that he rides now in peace and joy upon the grassy seas of the Afterlife."

Lucius looked at Dagon and nodded, then turned to look up at the titanic black head and the huge eyes staring down at him from behind the curtain of the brushed jet mane. He reached up, and the stallion sniffed at him, a warm gust of air emanating from his soft nostrils. The big neck bent down more and Lucius ran his hand along the soft warm coat. "I've never seen anything like him. What is his name?"

Dagon smiled. "Xanthus."

Lucius looked shocked then also smiled. "One of the immortal horses of Achilles."

Adara was there then, along with Phoebus and Calliope, all of them admiring the new member of their stables.

"Our ponies could gallop beneath him!" Calliope said.

"You're right!" Dagon laughed. "But I wouldn't try it."

Lucius turned to Dagon. "Where did you get him?"

"There are still some places in Sarmatia, unknown to Rome, where the ancient breeds of kingly horses are raised. Xanthus," he reached up and stroked the stallion's muzzle with a kind of reverence, "he is one of the last of a great line of sires. Some say he is descended from the Xanthus of Achilles himself."

"I can't accept him from you, Dagon. You should be the one to ride him, not me."

The people standing around them were quiet then, but Dagon shook his head and held Lucius by the shoulders.

"I told you, I...we...would follow you anywhere, Anguis. Xanthus is meant to be yours, and though he is not Lunaris, he will serve you well. Of that, I'm certain."

"Thank you, my friend," Lucius said, hugging Dagon close. He looked up at Xanthus again and shook his head. "I guess the pugio I got *you* won't do!"

Dagon and the others roared with laughter.

"Io Saturnalia!" Lucius shouted to general applause.

When Barta had taken Xanthus out of the hall and given him to the trooper to take to the family stable, the celebrations continued.

"I'll be back," Lucius whispered to Adara before cutting his way slowly through the mass of guests to his tablinum. He turned to look back at everyone and then went inside, to close the door behind him.

As he sat at his table staring at the flickering flame of the lamp, he thought of how much Dagon had honoured him just then, not only with the stallion, but with his words, the honour of friendship and praise. He thought of Briana's song, and of the many words of kindness and pride expressed to him and his family all that night by every person there. He felt safe among them all, and the feeling was welcome.

But am I worthy of so much praise? Lucius asked himself.

Of course you are... the voice said from the corner of the room where a light shone brightly from the darkness.

Lucius stood immediately and went down on his knee before Apollo.

Why do you doubt yourself after so long? After all you now know about yourself?

The questions hung in the air, expectant of answer, and yet unanswerable.

Lucius looked up slowly, shielding his eyes until the light faded and Apollo stood before him wrapped in his whirling blue cloak, starry eyes staring down with compassion. "I do not know, Lord. I...I have been weak lately."

On the contrary, you've been braver than any other in the face of it all. Knowledge is perhaps the most terrifying thing, especially knowledge of yourself.

"But why me?"

It is your destiny...Lucius. Apollo's taut, guarded body relaxed. The god wanted to raise the man from the floor with his own hands, but he could not, for he knew Lucius must raise himself up. *You were born to all of this...*

Lucius looked up, pulling himself up on the edge of the table, his muscles straining.

All of it.

"What must I do?"

Live as you always have. With purpose, strength and truth. And know that you are not alone in any of it. What you have just witnessed out there, Apollo pointed at the door, *is proof of it.*

"I need peace in my heart, Lord. I feel drained, and tired." Lucius wilted before Apollo then, and the god could see his struggle.

I cannot give you the peace you think you need, Apollo said. *But...* He stepped around the table with a long, muscular arm outstretched, and with his finger he touched Lucius' brow between the eyes. *I give you strength, as I always have, the will to carry on. To know yourself, Lucius Metellus Anguis, is to know me...*

Lucius felt life surge within himself. He felt his pain melt away, the anguish in his heart tremble and fade. A great burst of light exploded in his mind, breaking into a million points of light that descended like so many petals from a flowering tree in Spring.

He breathed deeply and sighed. "Thank you, Lord." But he found himself alone in the room, seated once more at his table before the light of the lamp.

"Open it," Lucius said as he and Adara sat beside the hearth fire. She was reluctant at first, but also curious. The bundle before her was certainly not a bangle or new stola. She looked up at Dagon, Briana and Barta and then back at the bundle.

"Open it, Mama!" Phoebus said, perhaps even more curious than she was.

It was the third day of Saturnalia, the day of the sigillaria, when Romans usually gave token gifts to each other at home, except, for Adara, this was no token gift.

She held the green cloth and slid it back, holding her breath and closing her eyes as she did so. When she opened them, she held a gladius across her lap. "Oh, Lucius..." her voice faded away as she took in the brown sheath with glittering bronze acanthus leaves, the perfectly round pommel with golden horses running around its circumference, and the golden dragons coiled about the hilt and jutting from either side as if leaping in the light of the fire.

"It's magnificent!" Dagon said.

"A blade worthy of the Dragon's family," Barta said in a low, admiring voice.

"Well?" Lucius asked. "Are you going to draw it out?"

Adara nodded silently and stood. She moved to the side of the fire where there was no one sitting and, grasping the sheath in her left hand, slowly drew the blade out.

When the light hit the blade, its reflection lit the rafters of the hall, making the others squint for a moment.

"Oh...Lucius!" Adara said, her eyes alight. She felt the balance of the blade, perfect from the pommel all the way to the razor-sharp point. "It matches the one I gave you?"

"Almost, yes."

Adara spun the blade deftly, grinning as it sang when it cut through the air and came to rest comfortably back in her hand. She sheathed it again and stepped across to kiss Lucius. "I love it."

After that, Lucius and Adara distributed the sigillaria to the others, and though there were no swords given, the gifts were cherished, and the company even more so. Dagon continued to admire the dagger Lucius had given him, and Briana the new wool cloak with embroidered interlace around the edges. For Barta a leather belt with a new set of nine throwing knives fastened across the surface, and for the children, a basket each with cerei, new writing tablets, balls, a flute for Calliope and a small knife for Phoebus.

And for Lucius, Adara had commissioned a silver bracelet in the style of a military decoration, except that the two ends were in the shape of a horse on one end, and a dragon on the other. He slid it on his wrist and kissed her, and for the first time in a long while, he felt peaceful and at ease among his family and friends.

By the time the Dies Natalis Solis Invicti arrived, the shouts of 'Io Saturnalia!' had been echoing across the hillfort for many days. The Solstice had come and gone, and the cycle of lengthening days began, days that were cool and clear and tinged with morning frost.

Lucius' mind often went back to the start of Saturnalia when Apollo had appeared to him, given him strength and a sense of calm in the midst of the storm he had been weathering. He now felt more like himself than he had in months, and as he stood in the temple, offering up to the Unconquerable Sun on that day of days, Lucius was grateful beyond words.

Adara and the children stood by his side, and Dagon, Briana, Barta and others beyond, for it was a time of year sacred to them all, not just to Romans or Greeks.

As the smoke from the offerings wended its way out the temple doors and over their heads, everyone turned their faces to the brightening, sunlit sky, the same as a field of summer sunflowers gazing toward the heavenly orb as it speeds across the heavens.

"Are we going to train later?" Dagon asked Lucius as they walked.

"Yes. I'm feeling stronger and stronger," Lucius answered. "But I don't want you to go easy on me. Our enemies certainly won't. You need to push me, Dagon."

"I will. You're ready."

Lucius stopped by the stable doors and watched Adara and the children walk up the slope to the hall.

"Our women are happy," Dagon said.

"Yes."

"And you?"

"I'm better."

"You certain of that?" The truth was, Dagon could see it in Lucius' eyes from time to time that he often recalled the images of horror and pain from Dumnonia. He may have been better physically, but he wondered if his friend's mind still lay in ruins. "Apollo has helped you again, hasn't he?"

Lucius looked up. "Yes. He has. As ever." He turned to open the stable doors and went inside. "I'll see you later for training," he said to Dagon.

"I'll be ready."

When Dagon left to go to the Sarmatian camp to check up on the men, Lucius turned to see Xanthus' head rising above all the other mounts, nearly touching the beams of the ceiling.

The huge head turned toward Lucius as he approached.

"Good morning," Lucius said, taking a brush and reaching up to run it along the horse's thick neck. "Are you ready to ride today, Xanthus?"

The big black eyes stared back at Lucius, and it was as if the animal spoke to him.

Everyday for the past several days, Lucius had spent the morning with his new mount. They needed to get to know each other, the horse as much as the rider, for the bond of trust and friendship needed to be secure before they went into battle, whenever and wherever that might happen.

Most of the time, Lucius had walked with the stallion following him, talked to him, touched him. On the third day, Lucius had put the large, customized saddle upon Xanthus' back, and mounted up, his thighs secure between the thick saddle horns that looked as big as small tree trunks.

Lucius had never sat so high upon a horse. He towered over every other rider around the camp, and with his long black cloak waving behind him, he and Xanthus together were like a titanic shadow out of a dream, covering them all.

The first time Lucius sat atop Xanthus, they had walked around the hillfort, weaving in and out of the buildings as troops came out to watch.

The stallion had, of course, been expertly trained by the Sarmatians, turning his bulk with ease at the slightest command.

That day, however, Lucius had resolved to take him down onto the fields surrounding the hillfort to give him his head and see how he fared at speed. They walked slowly down the slope to the southwest gate, and down the road to the field.

Many of the men gathered on the ramparts to watch.

When Lucius and Xanthus came onto the first field directly to the south of the fort, they stopped.

"You ready to show me what you've got, Xanthus?"

The stallion bobbed its great head and stomped the ground as if impatient to run.

"Good." Lucius looked at how far down the ground was and felt a flutter in his gut before he kneed the stallion into action. *One...two...three!*

Lucius gave the slightest squeeze with his legs and Xanthus started to walk, then a light kick with one leg brought him into a canter.

The feeling was unbelievable, for as Xanthus bobbed smoothly up and down, Lucius felt as though he were upon the crest of a tidal wave that was ready to crash down at any moment.

But the wave never broke, and Lucius found himself staring down from the top of it, seemingly above the whole world. A smile spread across his face and he found himself laughing as the stallion carried him around the eastern slopes where the bathhouse was located, and then to the northern fields.

Sarmatian riders followed along the top of the ramparts, and the sound of cheering reached Lucius' ears.

"Alexander had Bucephalus," Lucius said, "but I've got Xanthus!" He pat the stallion's neck. "Ready to run?"

Lucius kicked, a little harder this time, and the bob of the canter smoothed out, and the wind whipped into Lucius' face as they charged across the field to the western side of the hillfort.

Lucius felt a rush of emotions - elation, gratitude, childish excitement, and a little fear - as the two of them careened around the hill a second time. Ahead, Lucius spotted a fallen tree and he steered Xanthus toward it.

The stallion did not shy from it, but seemed to speed up as he approached, the jump perfectly timed and the tree expertly cleared.

Lucius cried out loud in joy and amazement despite himself, and he wondered how the enemy would feel the next time he went into battle on this horse. Then he began to slow Xanthus down as they came around to the road leading up to the southwest gate once more.

"Good boy!" Lucius said as they rode slowly up through the gate and into the hillfort.

"How was it?" Dagon asked, as he and Barta approached.

"By the Gods, Dagon!" Lucius said. "He's amazing! I've never felt anything quite like it."

Dagon could only smile at Lucius' flushed and smiling face, his cheeks red with cold and excitement. "I think it safe to say that you two have bonded."

Lucius nodded, and dismounted, the drop farther than he had expected.

Dagon and some of the others laughed as he stumbled onto his behind.

"You have to work on that dismount, though!" Dagon roared.

Lucius laughed along with him. He could not help it.

Later that day, after a heavy training session with Dagon, Barta, Vaclar, Lenya and Badru, Lucius sat in the steaming water of the tepidarium, soaking his sore muscles. His sword skills were nearly back to normal, his speed already matching that of his men. There was still some work to do, but he was satisfied that if he were called back to battle he would not get killed in his first engagement.

Don't think about battle now, Lucius, he told himself. *Rest.*

Lucius heard the door to the bathhouse open, then close, and then lock. He tried to peer through the steam to see who it was, but could not tell. His hand reached for the handle of his sword and he lifted it, careful not to make a sound on the stone floor.

He was about to challenge the person when Adara's tall, naked form came out of the mist.

Lucius smiled. "By Venus!" he said, putting the weapon back down on the floor beside the pool. "I'm dreaming."

Adara smiled as she approached. "I'm glad you still feel that way."

Lucius looked upon his wife and felt his breath taken away, for she was as beautiful and shapely as ever, from her shoulders that were partially hidden by her long black curls, down past her full breasts to her waist and hips, and to her toned muscular legs. He looked up from his admiration of her body to her eyes and raised an eyebrow.

"Where are the children?"

She smiled. "Training with Briana. We have lots of time."

"For what?"

She did not answer, but stepped into the warm pool, the water slowly covering her body which was covered in goosebumps from the cold air outside. She dipped under the water, wetting her long hair and came up into Lucius' arms.

Kneeling in the pool so that the water lapped at their necks, they held each other close enjoying the sense of calm, the quiet of the bathhouse, the feeling of their chests and hips pressed together in the warm water.

"I've missed you," Adara whispered.

Lucius said nothing at first, for he knew that he had not been easy over the past few months since Dumnonia, that he had been kissed by Fortuna to have such a caring, strong wife.

"I'm sorry, my love."

Adara pulled back a little so that she could look him in the eyes. "How can you say that? Do you think I would have it any other way? My place is by your side, no matter what the Gods have in store for us. Do you not yet know that?"

"I do. I just...I felt lost for a time." *I still do in some ways...*

"I know there are things that you cannot tell me. And I accept that." She held his face in her hands, her legs wrapped about him beneath the steaming surface of the water. "But I will never leave your side. By the lives of our children, you and our family are everything to me."

Lucius gazed back at her watery green eyes. "As you are to me. I will always come back to you," he said.

They kissed then, in the quiet privacy of the baths, as the water surrounded their bodies in their eager lovemaking.

Together, their bodies became as one, hers lithe and beautiful, and his scarred and battle-worn. They enjoyed each other for some time, as they had not done since Lucius returned from Dumnonia.

However, they knew that there were yet things unsaid, hidden fears that threatened all they held dear.

But that is the way with mortals and gods alike, is it not? Thoughts and fears coming unbidden into the forest of one's mind, a realm that each must journey through the length of their days.

As Lucius and Adara walked back to the hall from the bathhouse, they spoke of the push and pull of their lives, how the days were accented with beauty and horror and how both made up the whole of their persons, their lives.

That day, the birthday of the Unconquerable Sun, was indeed a day of beauty.

The Metelli were gathered together on the top of the northern rampart to watch the sun dive into the West at the end of that glorious day. Phoebus and Calliope huddled close to their parents, each wrapped in a thick, warm, woollen cloak against the chill breeze that came off of the distant sea beyond Ynis Wytrin.

They could see the faint outline of the Tor ten miles to the West, against a backdrop of fiery orange and pink, and they remembered their time there, the peace, the joy, the sense of wonder, all things that they would carry with them wherever they went.

Together, they sat, Phoebus with his head in his mother's lap, and Calliope sitting cross-legged in font of her father, humming a soft tune to the descending sun.

Lucius stroked his daughter's long hair and looked at Adara where her hand gently touched Phoebus' brow, his eyes closing slowly as they focussed upon the dazzling display of Apollo's light.

"Will we go back to Ynis Wytrin?" Calliope asked.

353

"Someday," Lucius said. "But not soon. We must be invited."

"I would like to play with Rachel and Aaron again."

"You will, my girl," Adara said.

Lucius took a deep breath of the fresh evening air and exhaled slowly.

"I'm glad you're feeling better, Baba," Calliope said. "I was worried."

"You will never lose me, my girl."

She did not answer, and Lucius said no more. They were relieved that her nightmares, her visions, seemed to have stopped. For how long, they did not know. But Lucius knew that the sound of his daughter's cries in the night was not something he could easily forget.

As the sun finally disappeared over the horizon, Lucius bent down and kissed his daughter's head.

"Time for sleep, children," Adara said, as she helped raise Phoebus and got to her feet.

"We're not children!"

"Even great warriors need their sleep, Phoebus," Lucius said. "Come. Calliope, perhaps you can sing us another song once you are in bed.

She yawned and smiled up at her father. "Yes, Baba. If you like."

Adara took both the children's hands and they began to walk down the slope of the rampart toward the plateau and the hall. Several Sarmatians greeted them as they went.

Lucius stared after the sun for a few more seconds and was about to turn to join his family when he heard a deep, throaty rumble, as of thousands of voices rising up in unison, chanting. He turned to the northern fields, paling in the dying light, and saw they were misty and full of movement. Then the sound came again, fuller and alive with purpose.

Metellus! Metellus! Metellus!

"No," Lucius muttered. "Not now…"

But there they were, upon the plain before his home, legions of men and cavalry squadrons, all of them looking up at him, calling out his name and raising sword and shield and spear to him.

Imperator! some warriors cried out.

Ave, Lucius Metellus Anguis! called others.

Vexilia bearing the image of gold dragons upon red backgrounds fluttered in the breeze, and the earth shook with the stomping of feet.

At the front, were rank upon rank of Sarmatian cavalry, their sixteen foot kontoi pointing at Lucius while their draconaria roared with the rushing wind.

Lucius stepped to the edge of the ramparts and gazed over the land, the tens of thousands of men who called his name in concert.

Metellus! Metellus! Metellus!

"I cannot!" he cried out, but the chill of the scene silenced him, and he felt fear and apprehension flow like liquid gold through his whole being. The very air shook with their voices, calling to him to lead them, to stand before them, to give them victory. "Gods..why are you showing me this? Why? I don't want it!"

"Baba?"

Lucius wheeled around, his brow sweaty and his eyes panicked as he saw Calliope standing before him. He turned quickly back to the northern fields and saw that they were empty, quiet, covered in winter mist as night descended and the wild deer came out to graze.

"Come, Baba. Don't you want me to sing you a song?" Calliope grasped his shaking hand. "It's all right. Come."

Lucius looked at his daughter, and the Sarmatians casually packing up things for the night, his wife and son walking ahead to the hall, the stoic black shapes of the ravens soaring in the night above the hillfort.

He nodded and followed his daughter down from the rampart and up to the plateau, but in his mind, all he could hear was the chanting of his name by thousands of men of war.

XI

ASPIS SUB PLANTA

'Asps Underfoot'

The town of Aquae Sulis slept in a haze of mist and smoke that hovered about the multi-hued, tiled rooftops of the town, nestled as it was in the crook of the river. A steady flow of traffic in and out of the town indicated that it was very much alive with Romans and Britons seeking solace, healing and help at the sacred springs.

The domes and arches of the great thermae could be seen above all else, as could the pediment of the great temple of Sulis Minerva, the goddess who kept watch over that ancient place.

Despite the Januarius chill, the streets were full of vendors, each utterly attentive in trying to catch the eyes of the wealthy men and women who passed by in perfumed litters. Aquae Sulis was a place to which the wealthy villa owners and bored classes of Londinium gravitated when the urge came upon them. There was nothing like taking the waters to soothe a complaint or illness, to meet with friends, lovers, and broker deals to decide the fates of others, all beneath the gaze of that solemn, guardian goddess.

The great gorgon head upon the temple pediment looked down on everyone who visited the sacred springs, his full beard and hair reminiscent of the sun, his eyes languid, almost pained with the power they held. The altars of the temple smoked constantly with the offerings of the people who came to seek healing and more. Most gathered before the temple steps, gazing up from the altars of the courtyard, muted prayers upon the lips of their covered heads. Others mounted the temple steps to give their offerings directly to the priests of the god who brought them inside to be lain or slaughtered upon the altar of the inner sanctum.

The god must have been pleased, but the same could not always be said of those mortals who visited the shrine.

Still, people - Britons, Romans and others - came to Aquae Sulis with hope and intent in their hearts and minds, and the fumes of the sacred spring, the baths and hypocausts shrouded it all like a pastoral Britannic mist.

In a remote corner of the elaborate bathing complex, beside the water of a tepidarium, a man sat upon a stone bench, flanked by two others who stood guard for him, their rippled arms crossed over their chests. They wore only loin cloths, but the seated man sat naked, leaning back against the red and white wall, staring at the tessellated floor that surrounded the pool before him.

His bearing told any who approached that he was a Patrician, and the look in his eyes for any who dared to approach the pool before him told others that he was not someone to be trifled with. He sat oiling his body, paying particular attention to the few angry scars he carried proudly, signs of his battles in Caledonia.

The men who flanked him, bore many more scars, one of them, the more senior of the two, had a bandaged leg and shoulder where a recent dagger wound still hampered him. The waters of the god had done nothing to soothe the pain, and it only served to make him angrier. He grunted.

"Stop your griping," the Patrician said.

"Yes, sir."

"There he is," said the second guard, motioning to a lone man who came into the room.

"Report," the Patrician said.

The man approached, his eyes darting behind him to see if he had been followed.

"So? What happened to them?" the Patrician asked.

"Sir. The men who followed them to Isca Dumnoniorum have gone missing."

"What do you mean 'missing'?"

"They were last seen being held by the garrison troops, then…nothing. They never came out." The man looked at his superior but could not hold his gaze for long.

"And our quarry?"

"Back home."

"And the men you sent there?"

The man said nothing for a moment, and the two guards moved closer to him.

"Also missing."

"What was that?"

"Missing, sir."

"You mean, dead."

"Yes, sir."

The Patrician closed his eyes and thought of Rome, of how sick he was of Britannia, Caledonia, how he longed to be back in the heat and sunshine of the Middle Sea.

"How difficult is it to kill a man?"

The newcomer looked up. "Not so much, sir."

"And yet, you seem to be failing constantly."

"We'll get him sir."

"Will you?"

With the quickness of a panther, the Patrician's fist flung out and crashed into the man's face, sending him backward into the warm pool. He then leapt upon him.

The messenger felt himself being held under water, his limbs thrashing, his fingers pulling at the fists fastened tightly about his throat. He felt his face hit another time, and then another, and blood clouded the water before his eyes and filled his mouth with its taste. Then, as he was about to lose consciousness, he was pulled out and thrown upon the mosaic floor beside the pool.

The voice that spoke next was calm, almost relieved, as if the violence had had a soothing effect.

"I'll give you one more chance to carry out your duties. If you don't bring me someone's head, I'll be having yours in its place. Do you understand?"

The man tried to nod and speak where he gasped upon the floor.

"I can't hear you."

"Yes...sir," he croaked.

"Good." The Patrician turned to the badly scarred man to his right. "Get him out of here, and see if you can't spot our three visitors out in the crowd.

"Yes, sir." The man hoisted his beaten colleague off of the floor and carried him out, pressing a towel to his bloody face as they went. "Slipped and fell on the floor," he grunted to a couple of gawkers in the next room.

The Patrician leaned back against the wall and picked up the cup of wine he had been nursing before. He closed his eyes and breathed.

He had come to Aquae Sulis to relax, to ravage the local ladies, to eat and to drink, and yet the ineptitude of his men, the bad news he received, only served to drive the thorn in his side deeper and deeper, to stoke the fires of his anger. He detested the provincials who surrounded him, men and women with thread-bare attachments to

Rome who sought to place themselves above their stations. For most of them, their only claim to fame was to have made a fortune on construction or pig farming. The men stank of sweat and shit, and the women tasted of peat and piss.

I'll get back to Rome soon, he thought, *and take what is rightfully mine. It's only a matter of time.*

"How did you say you came to know this person, Nolan?" Virgilio Carcer asked as the three ordo members approached the bath complex from the south, along the cardo.

Nolan Phelan strode forward leading Virgilio Carcer and Serenus Crescens into the main entrance of the baths. "I told you. I was here a couple of months ago with Tulio. We were talking on the edge of the large pool. The place was almost empty, so we didn't feel the need to whisper. We were talking about the situation with Praefectus Metellus and wondering if he would actually help us in getting civitas status from the emperor. Then, out of nowhere, this fellow with a nasty wound on his shoulder, a soldier-type, comes swimming up to us. He tells us he has connections close to the emperor and that his superior would be very interested in helping us, in return for some information."

"And you said 'yes' to meeting him? Just like that?" Serenus rubbed his sandy hair and shook his head. "He could have been anybody!" Having been in Londinium for some years, he was all too aware of the dangers of such easy connections. It was good to be wary of strangers in such circumstances.

"Relax. I said nothing at first," Nolan replied. "I said I'd keep it in mind, and he gave me a way to contact him here in Aquae Sulis. After our last encounter with the praefectus, it seemed obvious he was unwilling to help us anymore. So, I contacted the man we're here to meet. He got back to me quickly, said his superior was actually here on leave and that he wants to meet with us."

The three men paid the small fee and went into the apodyterium where they removed their togas and gave them to the slaves to be stored in niches until they were finished. Then, with towels wrapped about their midriffs, the three men walked into the baths.

Great torches burned in brackets around the great rectangular pool of the baths, and crowds of people moved to and fro along the walls and in the water, groups of men, of women, and both. The voices of various conversations rose to an echo in the arched roof far overhead, and misty faces floated in the water and in the alcoves that lined the walls.

"How will we know him?" Carcer asked, awkwardly clutching the towel about his waist, and longing for the private baths at his villa.

"The man I met said they would be here. Somewhere private. We just have to find them. I'll recognize him when I see him." Nolan turned to the right and led them around the great bath, into the smaller bathing rooms at the East end, and back to the other side of the large pool.

"Do you see him?" Crescens asked, feeling the sweat begin to form on his brow and shoulders.

"Not yet."

They walked slowly, peeking into rooms and alcoves, staring at faces in the water, and still no sign.

Some of the bathers looked back at them, but none spoke. Groups of off-duty legionaries kept to themselves, and those of the lower classes did not linger longer than they needed to, uncomfortable before the groups of well-to-do villa owners and their wives who, despite their nakedness, bathed in their jewels and golden ornaments for fear of having them stolen by the bath slaves.

"Let's check past the frigidarium," Nolan said, leaving the large bath and passing the entrance to the sacred spring where the sound of hot rushing water pouring into the baths drowned out their voices.

Beyond the arch, they spied the statue of Minerva standing over the sacred spring, the fire from the braziers lighting her face in the steamy mist of the waters.

Carcer made to go in, but the other two moved on and he went to catch up with them. It felt slightly odd to not visit the goddess when there, but they had other business to attend to.

They came into the room where men and women plunged into the cold waters of the large circular bath, their sighs and squeals of surprise bouncing off of the roof and walls before they extricated themselves and made for the warmth once again.

"There he is," Nolan Phelan said, as he stopped and raised his hand to the man he had met before.

He stood in the small caldarium beyond the frigidarium, and peered at the three men before raising a hand in greeting and motioning for them to follow him. When he turned, the bandaged wound on his shoulder was revealed.

"That's definitely him," Phelan said. "Come."

"Let's get this over with," Crescens muttered.

They followed the man past several small groups into an emptier room beyond where only two men stood before the entrance to a final room with a small bath. Before they were about to enter, the scarred man turned and looked at the three of them, the other two brutes staring as well.

"Do you have any weapons?" he asked.

The three ordo members looked confused.

"Remove your towels."

"I assure you," Carcer said, "We have nothing but our dignity."

The man huffed. "Towels."

Phelan, Crescens and Carcer looked to each other and then slowly removed their towels. Usually, it was not an issue, for the baths demanded such a thing, but the awkwardness of it being demanded by a stranger made the task difficult.

They stood there, naked for a few moments as the three guards before them looked them over, the two to either side chuckling a little before the man in the room beyond spoke up.

"That's enough," the voice said. "Let them in."

Crescens and the others put their towels back on and moved into the room. There, before them, stood the man they had come to meet. He was tall and fit, his muscles oiled and quick. He wore his dark hair in the Roman fashion, short-cropped and molded like a statue. His cool eyes looked them over before a broad smile and welcoming arms beckoned them to sit on the benches surrounding the pool.

"Stand outside," the man told his guards. When they were gone, he relaxed and looked at his guests. "I am Tribune Marcus Claudius Picus, first cohort of the Praetorian Guard."

Crescens sat up. *This is a man I can do business with. Perhaps he will listen? He seems nice enough.*

"Tribune," Crescens inclined his head. "I am Serenus Crescens Nova, executive of the curia of Lindinis, and these are my colleagues Virgilio Carcer Hilarus, and Nolan Phelan."

"Your man out there," Phelan cut in, "when I met him, said that you were the man to help us in our petition to the emperor, but also to deal with a certain problem we have with a man of the imperial legions."

"You speak plainly," Claudius said, nodding. "I like that." He stood and paced the floor before them, his body glistening in the light, allowing them to get the measure of the soldier before them.

Crescens noted the blood upon the floor and in the pool before them, and his bare feet retreated from it. *Is that a tooth?* He cleared his throat. As the head of the ordo, it was for him to make the case.

"Tribune Claudius, may I speak?"

Claudius smiled. "Yes, of course, gentlemen. That is why you are here. I am Caesar's eyes and ears, and anything you would say to him, you may say to me."

"You see?" Nolan Phelan hissed at Carcer who looked annoyed and almost shushed him.

"The town of Lindinis is one of the most productive centres in the south of Britannia. We have many fabricae, a thriving market, and vast numbers of livestock farms surrounding the town, many of which we ordo members own. These industries have created a thriving wool and leather market as well."

"Continue," Claudius said.

Crescens relaxed as he looked upon the man. Not quite liking the view from low down, he stood so that he was eye level with the Praetorian tribune.

"We believe that Lindinis is the anchor for the region. It is successful, industrious, and well-placed on the main road from Isca Dumnoniorum to Aquae Sulis. We have built it up over the years, with a renovated curia building, new city walls, and a bathhouse. The town can be reached by road and waterway as well."

Crescens looked back at his colleagues, waiting for them to say something, but they nodded for him to continue. He found it odd that Virgilio at least did not want to speak, for he usually insisted on being the loudest in any conversation.

"But...we would like to do so much more with Lindinis, to make it a place to rival Londinium."

"You aim so high?" Claudius asked.

"Yes. We do. Fortuna favours the bold, is that not so?"

"It is."

"We have been seeking a champion to put before the emperor our petition to be granted official civitas status."

"But are there not already three civitates in the region? I believe that Isca Dumnoniorum, Durnovaria, and Corinium Dobunnorum already hold this title, no?"

362

"They do. That is true, Tribune. But Lindinis is more prosperous, and its potential is greater. With the rights of civitas, we would be able to expand and make it a new capital in the southwest of Britannia."

"I have been told you do not have a basilica or proper forum, is that so?"

"It is."

"After all, these are things that make a civilized community."

"I agree, and we would seek to build such infrastructure in Lindinis."

Claudius was silent then, pacing with his arms crossed on the other side of the bath.

Carcer looked at him and thought that he appeared to be a man deep in thought.

"I am close to the emperor and Caesar Caracalla. They do indeed trust me." Claudius looked up at the three ordo members across the water. "But how can I be sure that I can trust you? If I were to put your petition before the emperor and Caesar Caracalla, I would not want to be shamed by inaction on your part. Trust...goes both ways, gentlemen."

"It does indeed, Tribune," Carcer nodded, believing he understood the man before him, wondering if that is why he had failed to win over Praefectus Metellus to their cause. "We have been recruiting new residents and citizens of the region to take part, to invest in Lindinis and its future, and most all of them have agreed that Lindinis is where they wish to invest, but only if the status is raised to civitas."

"And you have a plan to set in motion if this were approved?" Claudius asked.

"We do!" Carcer said, standing now and filling the room with his high voice. "Architectural plans for a basilica and forum have already been drawn up, as well as renovations to the dockyards along the river so that more sea traffic would be able to reach us to deliver goods."

"We are close enough to Lindinis, Tribune," Crescens said. "Perhaps you would like to come and see it in person? You could then give a full report to the emperor of what you have seen."

Claudius eyed the men carefully. He frowned slightly, and for a moment, Crescens worried that he had made up his mind to eject them from the room, their request all too complicated for him. But he nodded, and his smile widened until it was full across his face.

"The citizens of Lindinis are fortunate indeed to have such fine men as you to be championing them. I will put your petition for civitas status before the emperor and Caesar Caracalla!" Claudius clapped and smiled along with the three men who seemed quite overjoyed at the news. "Bring wine!"

A tray of wine was brought by the man with the wounded shoulder. He set it down upon a small table and poured for the four of them.

Crescens observed that the man was a warrior of some sort, and had to look twice at him. He looked vaguely familiar, but he could not remember where from. In the end, he put it down to the intensity of the moment and nerves.

Claudius raised his cup of wine. "To the Civitas of Lindinis!" he said.

"To the Civitas of Lindinis!" the three ordo members echoed. They drank, and each felt as if a Herculean weight had been lifted from their shoulders, especially Crescens.

Claudius called for his man to fill their cups again and then sat on the end of the bench beside the three ordo members.

Crescens noted the angry, tight and sinewy muscles of the tribune, and knew that this was a man who got things done.

Claudius' eyes were staring at the floor and the contents of his cup. Then, he spoke, his voice low and conspiratorial. "There was another matter you wished to discuss? About a man of the legions?"

Crescens set his cup down and leaned in, feeling his colleagues leaning closer behind him so that they could hear. He noticed that the tribune's man did not leave the room this time, but stood before the bench where Claudius had sat before, staring into space.

"It is a delicate matter, but one I feel it my duty to bring to your attention." Crescens cleared his throat, his mind turning over the last meeting he had had with the praefectus in Lindinis, and all the odd behaviour that he had observed since. "It concerns a certain praefectus of one of the cavalry ala on furlough in the area."

"I think I know of whom you speak," Claudius said, his face an image of understanding. Before Crescens was about to speak, he put up his hand. "Is it Praefectus Lucius Metellus Anguis?"

Crescens looked into those bright, cold eyes. "Why...yes. It is. But how did you know?"

"Part of my duty to the emperor and his family is to know exactly what is happening and where. For some time, I have suspected this praefectus. Tell me...what has he been up to here in the South?"

Crescens hesitated, and Claudius spotted it.

"Don't worry. Our conversation is completely confidential, my friend," Claudius said. "Remember, I need to know that I can also trust you as part of your petition. If you were suspected of withholding information that I should know, it would not be viewed well by the emperor. Besides, if your plans for Lindinis are to succeed, the region will need to be safe."

"Safe from what?" Carcer asked.

"All manner of threats," Claudius said, his face nearly betraying his annoyance. "Tell me... What has Metellus been doing since he arrived in the area."

I will tell him everything I know then. The Gods can roast the Metelli for all their airs. "Very well," Crescens sat up and looked directly at the tribune. "He has built a settlement upon the hillfort which he obtained from his wife's father as dowry."

"A man can build a home on his lands if he so chooses," Claudius said. "There is no law against that."

"A fortress though?" Carcer said.

"What?"

Crescens continued. "The land is an ancient hillfort that fell to Vespasian during the invasion. The praefectus has been building non-stop - walls, a hall, stables, a bath, barracks -"

"Did you say barracks?" Claudius asked.

"Yes. With his Sarmatian riders on furlough visiting him, it is as if he has fortified the place with his own personal army."

"Have his men caused trouble in the surrounding lands?"

"No, in fact. They have settled quite well in the region."

"You have received no official complaints?"

"None. The people love him, and all of the taxes that were due have been paid in full to the procurator from Londinium. The complaint, Tribune, is on behalf of myself and the ordo. You see, the praefectus seems to be trying to usurp our power, winning the people over to him."

"Especially the troops and veterans in the region!" Nolan Phelan added, knowing this would arouse suspicion.

"Troops?"

"Yes," Crescens confirmed. "Everywhere we go, we hear of soldiers clamouring for the 'Dragon Praefectus', hailing him as he goes by or anytime his name is uttered."

"It is the same in the North," Claudius added.

"Then you know the threat he poses." Crescens said it, the words that would put the Metelli under suspicion.

"You think he makes a play for the imperial throne?"

"I did not say that!" Crescens said quickly. "But it does seem odd to me that a man should be so lauded everywhere one goes."

"Tell him about the incident with your son," Carcer nudged Crescens.

"What happened there?" Claudius asked.

"The praefectus and his princeps...hardened warriors, mind you...attacked my son and his friends."

"He attacked a Roman citizen?"

"Not only that, but when I confronted him about it in Lindinis, when I saw him last, he denied it, and before I could challenge him, our own garrison stopped me and the other ordo members."

"Our own troops turned on us in favour of the praefectus!" Nolan Phelan said loudly.

"Please..." Claudius put up a hand, "keep your voice down. There are soldiers in these very baths."

Nolan Phelan shut his mouth and Crescens continued.

"The attack on my son, the praefectus said, was because the boys were having a bit of fun with a priestess from Ynis Wytrin."

Claudius waved his hand. "Boys will be boys, won't they?"

"So I said, but the praefectus dealt harshly with them when he came upon them."

"What is Ynis Wytrin?" Claudius asked.

"And there comes the fly in the ointment, Tribune. You see, Ynis Wytrin is a place that was sacred to the Druids, the Britons of the old religion, and some say, to Christians."

"Druids and Christians!" Claudius stood, pacing now, his displeasure and agitation acute and unmasked.

"Yes."

"Why has this place not been overrun?"

"It was highly sacred and, some say, it still is...protected by the Gods themselves."

"How does the praefectus come into this?"

"At a banquet at my villa, at which the praefectus and his wife were present, we, the ordo members, presented our case for taxing Ynis Wytrin."

"They don't pay taxes?"

"No. They never have, in fact." Crescens threw up his hands. "We've been trying to bring them into the fold of Rome so that they can pay their share for the peace they enjoy, but we have no contact with them at all."

"And did the praefectus think this a good idea?"

"No. He was vehemently against it. You see, he has friends there."

"He has befriended Druids and Christians?"

"Yes. Even though, on that very night of the banquet, two assassins attacked me on my own lands."

Claudius stared aghast at the ordo members, his man behind him shifting his feet.

"To his credit, the praefectus saved my life with his quick action and killed one of the assassins."

"Did the attacker have any markings?"

"No. But we know he was from Ynis Wytrin. Who else could it have been? They no doubt heard about our plans to tax them and they retaliated."

"And the praefectus has befriended them?"

"We suspect so. Yes." Crescens stood and gazed down into the pool in the floor. Claudius came to stand beside him.

"You do well to tell me all of this. But what you have told me must not leave this room. I must have your word upon it." Claudius turned to each of the ordo members who nodded consent. "Your safety depends upon it." He turned, his back to them, and smiled at the wall. "So, to go over it again... Praefectus Metellus is fortifying the ancient hillfort...he is gathering the loyalty of soldiers in the area who speak of him as if he were a god, and he has taken it upon himself to defend Druids and Christians, both of whom are enemies of the empire?"

"That is correct," Crescens said. "And he attacked my son."

"Of course. Yes," Crescens turned and put his hand upon the ordo member's shoulder and squeezed gently. "A most tragic encounter. Dishonourable for a Roman officer."

Crescens nodded. He looked forward to telling his son that he had taken care of things for him.

"This is all damning information, but the praefectus has many friends, and if you say the troops are on his side, we must tread very carefully indeed," Claudius said, facing the three men. "I will report to my superiors on this, and ensure they know that the information came from the ordo of Lindinis. That will help to ensure your petition is looked upon favourably. It is obvious that your town is loyal to the emperor. Such things do not go unrewarded."

"Thank you, Tribune," Crescens took the hand that was offered to him.

"Thank you. All of you. But there is more work to be done. I need you to keep an eye upon the praefectus and everything he does. Any rumours you hear. My man will be here in Aquae Sulis on this day every week from now on. He will be waiting in this room, and if you have any information about the praefectus, or this Ynis Wytrin, then you must bring it to him. Can you do that for me? For the emperor?"

Crescens, Carcer and Phelan stood tall and looked at the young tribune.

"We can," they said in unison.

"Excellent!" Claudius said. He stepped forward and shook each of their hands. "Then I wish you a safe journey back to Lindinis...the future civitas of Lindinis!"

The ordo members smiled and began to follow Claudius' man out of the room. At the doorway, Crescens paused and turned back to Claudius.

"It is a pleasure to see there are such men of honour at the higher echelons of the Praetorian Guard, Tribune. I thank you." Crescens bowed.

"Thank you, Serenus Crescens Nova... Thank you."

Once the ordo members were gone, Claudius' man returned.

"Do you think they recognized you from the villa that night?" Claudius asked, his face stern.

"Not a chance," the man said. "It was too dark."

"Good." Claudius stood, removed his towel and stepped into the bath where some blood yet lingered on the surface. "We've got Metellus right where we want him."

XII

ASTRORUM EXSTINCTIO

'A Flickering of Stars'

The brilliant twilight of the stars was wasted beyond the thick fog that hung over the city of Eburacum. Janus had come, and he had brought with him a deep penetrating cold that attacked the bones. Outside the walls of the legionary base and the rest of the city, the dead fields steamed as the temperature plummeted.

Beyond the crowded, torch-lit streets, the markets and gathering places of the city once more played host to the imperial family, and the halls of the royal palace echoed with the pained heaving of the emperor's lungs. Servants stood ready with hot water for bathing, teas for drinking, and bowls for vomiting should the emperor require them.

But all Septimius Severus wished for was peace, time with his thoughts and the recent arrival from Leptis Magna. Once the latest coughing fit ceased, and the warm tea relieved some of his gasping, he sat upon the edge of the bed which was covered with bear furs.

Braziers burned in every corner of the room, bronze tripods that glowed with fire and smoked with incense to purify the air in the emperor's private chamber.

Septimius Severus stood, wearing only his long sleeping tunic. He winced as his gout-besieged legs lacerated him with pain. Only his stubbornness and his will kept him upright as he shuffled along the floor to the armour that rested upon the wooden frame before him, ready for use. He knew he would not wear it again.

He reached out to touch the armour he had worn in battle, adorned with Victory and Jupiter, the ornamentation shining in the firelight like beacons, as he had once shone upon the battlefields of the empire for his men.

"Gods..." he said through his pain. "How you play with me." He chuckled briefly, but became serious as his hands roved over the brown and black leather cuirass and then to the handle of his gilded gladius. "You've served me well."

Another coughing fit came upon him then, but he brought it under control, wiping the blood from his hand upon the dark furs on his bed. He sipped more of the tea and, grasping the edge of the bed, Severus moved around to look in the other direction, to a niche in the far wall flanked by two lamps in smaller niches.

He walked toward the niche to touch the urn that stood in it. His shaking fingers caressed it, the long smooth lines of polished purple stone, the lid that was expertly fitted. "Thou shalt hold a man that the world could not hold," he whispered to the urn.

He had commissioned it some time ago, when the reading of the stars had been completed. When the day of his death was made known to him, he knew exactly where he wanted his ashes to be housed. As a child in Leptis Magna, he remembered a trader in the market selling statues made of purple stone, similar to a sort of marble. The colour had been so rich, so deep, so purple, more so than the purple of Tyre, that he had been unable to take his eyes off of it. The colour took the breath away. It was from a remote quarry in the desert to the south of Leptis Magna, a place held by the Garamantians.

Upon learning of his death, he thought first and foremost of resting in the arms of that brilliant purple stone. It had been a fortune to obtain a stone large enough and then to create it from the single piece, but he had succeeded.

He felt dizzy then, as if touching this house of the dead in miniature numbed his senses, and so he turned and stumbled back to his bed. The bandages about his calves were soaking through with blood, but he did not care to bend over to rearrange them. His eyes were drawn only to the roof of his imperial cubiculum.

There, upon the ceiling, as brilliant as ever, were the constellations of his doom and death. They were now his friends, his comfort, for in them lay certainty. The stars were not like battles or debates in the senate, easily turned with one slip. No. The stars were reflections of one's destiny, they were constant, especially if one stayed true to oneself.

"And I have done that," he said, answering himself. "I have done that."

Outside in the corridor leading to the emperor's room, Julia Domna stood with Aemilius Papinianus, Prefect of the Praetorian Guard, listening to the new coughing fit that racked the emperor. The slaves about them stood ready, but they did not send them in yet.

Julia Domna squeezed her cousin's hand, and the aged Papinianus turned to her.

"Why will he not allow us in to help?"

"It will not change the day of his death," she whispered so that the slaves could not hear her.

"But will he last so long? The stars say it will not be for some time now."

"Then I shall have my husband longer than hoped for," the empress said. She took a deep, calming breath as her husband heaved and coughed again. "I'm going in," she said.

Papinianus opened the door for her and turned to the slave with more tea, and a gilded bowl. "Follow her."

The two slaves shuffled in, followed by Castor, Severus' freedman, but before the doors closed again, Castor nodded to Papinianus and pointed subtly down the corridor where Caracalla spoke in hushed tones with three of his father's doctors.

The Praetorian Prefect stepped a little closer, the better to see, and perhaps hear, the young Caesar.

Caracalla turned in his direction for a moment, his face clearly annoyed, and motioned for the doctors to follow him farther down the hall to one of the reception rooms.

"Stay here, and go in if the empress calls," he said to the other slaves and the two guards flanking the door.

They all nodded and watched him go slowly down the corridor.

Caracalla closed the door behind him and turned to face the three doctors.

They were Greeks, all of them, dressed in their long white robes, each with a beard of varying degrees of greyness.

Caracalla gathered up the hem of his long black cloak the way he might carry the folds of a toga over his arm, and turned to them.

"My father is very near to death. His suffering worsens by the day...the hour!"

"Sire," the eldest medicus began. "The gout is too far advanced, as is the infection in his lungs."

"There is very little we can do now," said the second. "He has been suffering from this for too many years. It is not possible to cure the body of an illness so far advanced."

371

"It is really in the hands of the Gods now," the third man said. "If we could convince him to go to Epidaurus to sleep in the temple there, Asklepios might be able to cure him, but he would not survive the journey."

Caracalla looked at the faces of each of the men before him, their old, rheumy eyes gazing back with fear, but also with the arrogance that came from believing one knows better than others. His tutor, Euodus, looked at him like that all of the time, except without the fear.

Caracalla stepped closer to them and the two younger men backed away, the oldest standing his ground before Caesar.

"I don't want him cured."

"Sire?"

"You said it yourself, there is little that can be done at this point."

"We can make him comfortable and ease his pain so that his remaining days are something he can be conscious of, a time to reflect and spend with family."

Caracalla thought of those accursed stars painted upon the ceiling of his father's chamber, as well as in the enormous wagon that carried him around the Empire.

"I want you to ease his passing." Caracalla crossed his arms and stared at the three of them, the horror upon their faces barely masked.

"Sire? You cannot mean that. He is your father."

"I do mean it. And who are you to tell me my meaning?" Caracalla turned and drew his gladius, gazing at the blade in the firelight. He did not look at the doctors then, but they certainly observed him, and the blade he ran his fingers along. "The emperor, my father, is weak, and his enemies know that. The security of the empire cannot wait upon his death to take action."

"What you ask, sire, is blasphemy to us. The Gods frown upon such a thing, for we have taken a sacred oath to ease pain and suffering. We cannot interfere in such a way that it would interrupt their divine plan for your dear father."

"The emperor is strong, sire," said the oldest. "He may yet beat this bout of illness as he has done before."

"But you just said his end is near, that his illness is too far advanced! Do you lie to your emperor?"

There was silence. Then, the oldest among them spoke.

"No, sire. We do not lie to you. But we do hope to aid our beloved emperor Severus in whatever way we can."

"I would be more careful if I were you, gentlemen." Caracalla faced the three of them, sheathed his gladius, and rubbed his sparsely bearded chin. "The day is coming sooner than you think."

Caracalla turned and opened the doors to see Papinianus standing there.

The Praetorian prefect gazed beyond him for a moment to see the three doctors standing in the reception room beyond, their white forms backed by the statues along the far wall, as if they were actors upon a stage framed by the large doors. He turned to Caracalla.

"Sire, your mother wishes you to go to her."

Caracalla stopped beside Papinianus on his way and leaned in close. "Thank you, Prefect."

The doctors began to file out of the room after Caracalla, back to their stations outside the emperor's cubiculum, but Papinianus grabbed hold of the younger one. "What did Caesar say to you?" he whispered, his voice firm.

The man hesitated as he watched his fellows go up the corridor, and checked to see that Caracalla's form was inside the emperor's room.

"I cannot say."

"You must," Papinianus said, his grip firmer on the man's arm. The leather of his cuirass and pteruges creaked in the silence between them, "Tell me."

"You know his nature," the medicus whispered. "Caesar is impatient."

"Did he ask you to speed the emperor's passing?"

The man was about to speak, to tell the prefect, but he shook his head and pulled away. Evidently, his fear of Caracalla ran much deeper than his fear of Papinianus.

The Praetorian prefect watched the man shuffle down the hall to rejoin his fellow doctors who were discussing the best varieties of steeped herbs to ease the cough during winter.

Papinianus stood there for a long while before turning and going back to his quarters. He would have stayed, but he needed to make sure the palace was well-guarded by men he could trust, for even those were few and far between among the Praetorian ranks.

It had been a long day and evening by the time Julia Domna came to her private cubiculum. The servants had set several braziers burning in her chamber, the great room sectioned off by elaborately carved screens and colourful silk curtains that hung from the gilded rafters. The silks fluttered in the heat cast by the braziers and for a few blissful moments, she imagined she was back in her father's vast home in Syria.

She held up a shimmering bronze mirror to her face and gazed at her reflection. Where once a head of raven hair and wide, orb-like, curious eyes were, now there stared back the face of a greying, exhausted matron whose colourful clothing and bejewelled neck and arms could not hide the fact that she was tired beyond words. It was visible in the circles beneath her eyes which no amount of stibium or kohl could hide, in the lines about her mouth and brow and elsewhere. They were the battle scars of a mater familias.

She held up the mirror and spoke to it. "You once were my friend. Now, your allure fades with my own." She tossed the mirror into the furs upon her bed, and reclined on the couch beside one of the braziers where a cup of wine had been set out, as well as the scroll she had been reading.

She read less these days, asked fewer questions, and gathered fewer intellects into the fold for discussion. Now, when she had the time to sit and read, she was fortunate to keep her eyes open long enough to get one quarter the way down a scroll.

"But I shall try," she said to herself.

"Mistress?" A slave girl poked her head around one of the silks. "Did you call?"

"No."

The girl bowed and backed away to give the empress her space.

Julia Domna unrolled the scroll sent to her by the Christian, Quintus Septimius Florens Tertullianus in Carthage. She had been interested in what he referred to as the 'trinitas' of the Christians, and wondered if it was similar to Roman concepts of the Capitoline Triad. As ever, curiosity was her solace.

She took a sip of wine and began to read.

There was a knock upon the outer door and she closed her eyes, her leisure shattered again.

The slave girl came padding out of the silks to see the empress. "Mistress...forgive me. The Praetorian prefect is here to see you. He says it is urgent."

"Show him in and leave us," Julia Domna said. After a few moments, when she heard the hesitant footfalls in the maze of silks, she called out. "Come in, Cousin."

Papinianus appeared before her and bowed low. "My Empress," he said. His cloak fell around him where he knelt and as the empress looked upon him, she thought that she was not so badly off, for he looked much worsened by worry than she, if that were even possible.

"Please, Papinianus. Sit with me."

He rose and looked toward the door to see that the slave girl was gone. Then he turned back to the empress and took the padded chair across from her. She motioned to another cup and the pitcher of wine.

He poured some for himself and tipped some onto the floor before drinking. He then leaned back and looked at his kinswoman.

"Do you miss home?" he asked.

"Rome will always be there. I miss the great presence of Baal, ever present in the sky.

"I don't mean Rome, Julia."

"You look tired," she said.

"As do you."

She nodded. Papinianus had the weight of the world upon his shoulders, and the more ill the emperor became, the greater that burden. Plautianus would have relished that, but Papinianus had never been power hungry or violent. He was a man of learning, a respected jurist, and Julia Domna had pulled him from his sanctuary of academia to become one of the most powerful men in Rome.

He sighed.

"What is it?"

He smiled. His cousin had always known how to read him. She was the only person around whom he could be himself. They had grown up together in warmer climes.

"I have something to tell you."

"Then do so."

"It is not easy." *A supreme understatement,* he thought.

"Do so anyway. You have nothing to fear with me. I rely upon you."

He gazed at her large brown eyes for a long moment, the sound of the fire crackling near them loud in his ears.

"I have discovered something about Caracalla."

"Please," she said. "Use his name."

375

"Forgive me...about Antonius."

Her gaze grew sharper, he thought, more piercing, but he decided to press on. He was responsible for the emperor's safety after all.

"He has been asking the doctors to speed Septimius' passing."

Julia Domna held Papinianus' gaze for a long, painful moment. Then, calmly, she gazed into the golden wine cup she held as if it would reveal to her a message from the Gods, some Pythian utterance in the back of her mind to give her comfort.

But there was only silence.

"How do you know this?" she finally asked.

"I have suspected for some time, but this evening, I saw Antonius questioning the three doctors when you went into the emperor's room. I started looking into it when Castor noticed the doctors behaving oddly every time Antonius was near them. This evening, I questioned one of the doctors and he was afraid. Deathly so."

"What did he say?"

"Nothing. Only that Antonius is impatient."

"He has always been thus."

"And last year, at the Sacramentum of the Caledonii? Was attempting to kill his father mere impatience?"

Julia Domna was silent. She had always known her son had a violent streak, but she had always thought she could control it. She and Septimius had always spoken with their children about the importance of loyalty to family. *How the Gods test me,* she laughed inside, but words did not come to her. What could she say? Papinianus was her cousin, but Antonius...Caracalla...was her son.

"He will not do this. The doctors will not. I will speak with them."

"My Empress...Cousin..." Papinianus' voice trailed off and he clasped his hands together, spun his fingers as if he had a stylus in his hand to help him think through the problem before him. He could not look at her, but he could feel her gaze on him, sense the disappointment there, like a shrouded, eclipsed sun. He forced himself to look up. "Your son cannot be trusted. He seeks his father's death and, I fear, his brother's as well, should the opportunity arise."

"He is Caesar and you are sworn to protect him, Papinianus." She placed her cup upon the pedestal table beside her couch.

"I am also sworn to protect the emperor, your husband. And I am telling you Antonius is dangerous."

"He is the heir. And so is Geta."

"I know that. I also know that they hate each other. Antonius will not tolerate sharing power with his brother."

"Others have done it," she returned. "Marcus Aurelius and Lucius Verus -"

"They were exceptional men."

"And so are my sons."

"By the Gods, Julia! Will you not listen to reason? You are the most brilliant woman in the whole of the empire. Has love of your sons completely robbed you of your senses?"

"That's enough!" The scroll that had been resting in her lap flew across the room and landed softly in the folds of one of the hanging silk curtains, saved from a fiery end in one of the braziers beyond. The empress stood and faced the Praetorian prefect who also stood with her, stiff as a board, his head bowed now. "You go too far," she hissed. "My husband is one of the strongest emperors to ever rule this empire! And his sons shall carry on his work, together."

She stepped toward him and poked him in the chest, her nail clicking on the ornamentation of his cuirass.

"You know the stars as well as I. The emperor's death is at hand, and someone will have to rule the empire and keep the senate in check, someone strong. If it is not Antonius and Geta, then there will be chaos, another civil war. Is that what you want?"

"No one wants that, my lady."

"The empire is at its greatest extent, Papinianus. It is time for peace and learning, for invention and innovation. Don't you want to be a part of that?"

"With all my heart."

"And I want you there for it too. You don't have to remain Praetorian Prefect if you don't want to, but I feel better knowing it is you watching over the safety of our family and not someone else. We're family, are we not?"

"Yes, Julia. We are."

"And as a family, the Severans now have the opportunity to create a new world, but only if we stay together, if we remain loyal."

Papinianus stood tall as he looked down at his cousin. He nodded and smiled. "I suppose with you advising them, Antonius and

Geta could not help but be the greatest rulers the world has ever known."

"With *us* advising them," she corrected. She now took his hands in hers and her eyes softened. "Forgive me my anger. Septimius' illness, despite what we know the stars have said, weighs greatly on me. It pains me to see him so weak."

"Me too," he answered, clasping her hands. "He has always been a force of nature. A great man."

"With great sons." She hugged her cousin then and his arms rose slowly to return the familial gesture. "You will see," she said. "They won't disappoint us."

After a few moments, Papinianus stood back.

"I will speak no more of this. I was mistaken, Julia. Please forgive me."

"I already have. You are diligent in your duty, and I admire that." She sat down upon the edge of the couch.

Papinianus bowed. "I must go now and ensure the guards are set and awake."

"I should also check on Septimius one more time." She began to get up, but Papinianus moved to have her sit upon the couch once more.

"Please. I will do it. I'll make sure he is cared for, and if anything is amiss, I'll come get you. Rest...read... You need it, Cousin." He went over and picked up the scroll, then returned and handed it to her. He smiled. "I've not read this yet. Is the argument well-written?"

"I am about to find out," she said.

"Then I'll leave you to it. Good night, my Empress." With that, Papinianus bowed again, turned, and made his way to the doors. When he opened them, the slave was standing outside, her eyes wide as she looked at him. "Go to her. Bring her more wine."

"Yes, Prefect," the girl said before padding into the colourful and fiery cubiculum, closing the door behind her.

Papinianus' smile disappeared the moment he turned away from the doors. *She will not help me.*

He walked down the corridor toward the emperor's chamber, and there, he stopped to see the guards he had placed on duty. "Has anyone come to see the emperor?"

"No, sir. Castor has been in there the entire time."

378

"Good. Stay alert," Papinianus said as he opened the doors and went inside.

The scent of the room was a sickly mixture of frankincense, bile, and blood-soaked bandages, and it made Papinianus' gorge rise. He waved his hands to see through the billowing incense and there he saw Castor standing before the emperor.

The freedman had tears upon his cheeks as he stood there looking at the man he had served for so long, and who had manumitted him with a free heart.

"He was so formidable," Castor said, gazing down at the emperor's sleeping form. "Why have the Gods struck him so low?"

"I don't know," Papinianus said, standing beside Castor, his arms crossed. "All I do know is that the Gods have not given him much time."

"Don't say that!" Castor hissed weakly.

Papinianus pointed at the stars upon the ceiling without looking at them. He had seen them enough. "You know what is written there."

"What if the astrologers were wrong?"

"Look at him, Castor. Do you think they were wrong? He has held Death at bay for many years, but he is not immortal."

"If only we could erase those damned stars!" Castor said before storming from the room.

The door closed loudly, but the emperor did not stir. For once, he was sleeping soundly, no doubt because of the increased dose of opium the empress had instructed the doctors to give him at night.

The Praetorian prefect came around the side of the massive bed and sat on the edge, his hands upon his knees, fingers curling over the edge of his greaves.

"I don't know what to do, my friend. You always criticized Marcus Aurelius for placing so much faith in his son, and look where that led. Now, you and Julia do the same."

Papinianus inhaled like a man exhausted by life, and sighed deeply as he exhaled. He gazed at the purple, stone urn in its niche in the wall and felt sadness well up within himself. He also felt fear and desperation. He searched his mind, turning over scenario upon scenario for a way out of the situation in which the empire found itself. *So many years of war...there has to be another way...*

"Julia was right about one thing," he said to the sleeping emperor. "Someone strong will have to rule the Empire after you leave us, my friend. Someone very strong..." A thought burst suddenly in his mind and he turned to look at the emperor. "Forgive me, Septimius, but I must try to sway the stars."

Over the next several days, Papinianus' mind raced with plans, solid plans which he believed could salvage the empire. He confided in no one except Castor, for no man was more loyal to Severus, nor more knowledgeable about the family. They agreed that all could be saved, or all could fall into ruin.

They also agreed that nothing was certain yet, for they needed to speak with certain parties first, before anything else could happen.

However, the stars upon the ceiling were an ever-present threat, and the sands of time slipped quickly by.

In the meantime, Papinianus went over the list of names of the men of the Praetorian Guard, noting those whom he knew he could count upon for support, and those whose loyalty to Caracalla was unwavering, men such as Marcus Claudius Picus. He also made a note of the legionary commanders, primi pili of the legions, tribunes and other officers he believed he could count on. It was all done with utmost discretion in the privacy of his own cubiculum with the door barred, late into the night. During the day, however, he sought Caracalla and Geta's thoughts on matters of state and security, appearing to train the two young Caesars, to prepare them for their rule.

Papinianus realized how very fragile their future was, like the thinnest phial of blue glass, dangling precariously over a black marble floor. One slip, and all the world would shatter.

Then it happened. The emperor rose from his bed one afternoon, threw open the doors of his cubiculum and roared down the corridor, much to the guards' surprise and shock.

"I need a bath! I hope the hypocausts are roaring for the Emperor of Rome!" He turned back inside his cubiculum and called for Castor.

"Yes, sire?" Castor came running.

Severus smiled at him. "Where are my robe and shoes? I wish to bathe!"

"Of course, sire!" Castor hurried about, finding the items required, and dressed the emperor for the short, slow walk to the palace baths.

"And tell the cooks I'm famished! I want a feast tonight for the family, including Papinianus and my wife's sister."

"It shall be as you say, sire!" Castor said, his face smiling broadly, full of relief, his mind echoing with prayers of thanks to the Gods themselves.

That night, all the lamps and braziers in the large triclinium burned brightly, and the scent of fresh hot food wafted about the entire palace. The entire imperial family had been gathered, along with Domitius Ulpianus, Papinianus' second-in-command. They ate off of golden platters and marvelled at the emperor's rejuvenation as he sat at the head of the long table upon a well-cushioned chair eating hungrily.

The assembly, all reclined, ate and drank their fill, and music from a lyre and aulus filled their ears with soft melodies.

Julia Domna sat still beside her husband, smiling and looking much relieved at his recovery. She did not dare think the stars were wrong, but she was glad of the reprieve, however long it lasted.

She gazed at her sons, sitting across from one another. They seemed to be joking about something, or perhaps talking of their mutual love of chariot racing, no doubt wondering how their favourite teams fared in the Circus Maximus back in Rome. She thought about how they had both shown their metal here in Britannia, just as her husband had hoped they would.

Geta had proved he was an able administrator of Eburacum, and the province at large, with his trips to Londinium over the months they had been there. And Antonius had shown the he could indeed command the loyalty of the legions, and set a brave example on the battlefield.

Julia Domna's heart filled with pride as she gazed upon her sons, and she reached up to hold her husband's hand as she did so.

Severus looked at her and leaned down slowly to kiss her hand. "My Empress," he said softly.

Then there was a rapping upon the triclinium doors and one of the Praetorian tribunes entered.

Papinianus was up in a moment.

"What's the meaning of this?" the room fell silent. "Why do you enter our emperor's presence in such a state?"

The man saluted Papinianus, bowed to the emperor and empress, and stepped aside to reveal a legionary tribune behind him.

The man was filthy with mud, but also with blood, and he was so exhausted that Papinianus thought he might collapse on the spot.

"Water!" Papinianus called to a nearby slave.

The slave came with a cup for the exhausted tribune who drank thirstily.

"Forgive the intrusion, sire," the Praetorian began, bowing to the emperor, "but this tribune from the third legion brings grave tidings."

"What is it?" Severus said, his voice solid, free of coughing.

The Praetorian motioned for the tribune to step forward.

"My Emperor... There has been a revolt."

The silence in that moment was deafening, but Severus continued to stare at the man evenly.

"Where, Tribune?"

"Between the walls, and up into the highlands again, along the Gask frontier."

"Who is leading the revolt, Tribune?"

"The Maeatae, sire. They're led by someone called 'The Wolf'."

"Ha!" Caracalla laughed. "A wolf can be skinned!"

"Sire," the tribune went on. "The force is large. They've slaughtered three centuries already and are on the move. It's said they won't give up until Horea Classis lies in ruins."

"Don't believe every rumour you hear, Tribune," Papinianus said. "Give us facts."

"Quite right," Severus echoed. "The Maeatae are not so large a tribe. They must have joined forces with other clans, no?"

"Yes, sire," the tribune said. "There is a sort of confederacy of tribes led by the Maeatae." He rattled off a few inconsequential names, but then stuttered and stopped.

"There's more," Geta said.

"Who else has joined in this revolt?" Severus demanded.

The tribune was silent for a moment, but the emperor shocked him into action.

"Who is it, damn you!" Severus yelled, his voice full of anger.

The tribune bowed and spoke. "Sire...Argentocoxus and the Caledonii have joined forces with the Maeatae. It is an open revolt."

Severus stood slowly from his chair and came around the table toward the tribunes and Papinianus.

"I see," the emperor said. "I do see now..."

"Father-" Caracalla said.

"Not now, Antonius!" the emperor roared. He stood there, shaking with rage, his eyes shut tight, his fists balled.

As the empress watched her husband, she saw that his legs were bleeding again through the fresh bandages around his ankles. She was about to speak, but before she could do so, or rise to join him, to support him, he looked up, fire in his aged eyes.

"Rome shall retaliate immediately... Let no one escape sheer destruction. No one our hands, not even the babe in the womb of the mother if it be male. Let it nevertheless not escape sheer destruction! I want them all slaughtered!"

The palace seemed to shake with the order, as if the Gods gave voice to the emperor in that moment, as if the whole of Britannia were the parade ground of Severus' legions.

The emperor turned to Papinianus who was now flanked by Caracalla and Geta. "My sons...Mars pounds upon the door of our home once more, and this time, we shall honour him with rivers of blood."

Geta looked terrified, but Caracalla smiled and nodded. "We will make them pay for their treachery, Father."

Severus then turned to Papinianus. "Send out the orders immediately. Recall all the legions and auxiliaries from around the province. We march on Caledonia with fire and sword, with Death at our side!"

"Yes, sire!" Papinianus said, bowing and going out with the two tribunes and Ulpianus.

Severus turned to his family. "Before I die, I shall kill them all!" he yelled, going into a coughing fit that sent bloody spittle flying through the air and onto the chair where he had sat and laughed only moments before.

XIII

AD PUGNAM ET CRUOREM

'To Battle and Blood'

While the drums of war sounded in Caledonia, the Metelli and their closest friends and allies feasted in the warmth of the hall upon the hillfort. The days were spent in the beloved labours of home, or in training, and the nights welcomed each with quiet winter respite from the world at large.

It had been a mild winter, and it seemed the world began to blossom early, as if Proserpina had somehow escaped the halls of Hades and clawed her way through the darkness to the world above once more.

Lucius enjoyed peace of mind for the first time in a long while and, though he never lessened the guard around the embankments of the hillfort, he was able to walk with confidence and strength, to ride Xanthus across the frozen fields without the paranoia of attack settling in on him. It was not because of the presence of Barta, his loyal shadow, nor of the hundreds of Sarmatians keeping a watchful eye upon the place that was home to their leader in war, as well as their king and queen.

Peace settled upon the place like a warm, comforting blanket, and it was the perfect opportunity for Lucius to spend time with his children, for they had moved like wraiths at the edges of his tortured psyche since his return from Dumnonia. Now, thankfully, he was more sound of mind and spirit, as well as body, and his men ensured he was in top fighting shape by the month of Februarius.

He sat with Phoebus and Calliope separately, went for walks with them, and allowed them to speak their minds with him.

It showed upon his children's faces that they relished the time with their father, and he found that there was much he loved about them that he was unaware of before, but for the feelings that welled within him.

When Calliope hummed a new tune, or allowed her voice to stretch, she tilted her head and closed her little lids as if all her focus was upon some distant, heavenly connection with her own muse. She also sang differently when she was doing a chore, or painting as Adara had taught her. Calliope's songs were as variant as the chores and tasks she undertook. Lucius wondered how even a part of him could have gone into making such a beautiful creature, though it was not surprising when he looked upon his wife, as beautiful as ever. *Apollo must be delighted at my daughter,* he thought every time Calliope sang.

And then there was Phoebus, growing stronger by the day and seeking to undertake more difficult tasks. He was always pushing himself, trying to better himself, to replicate what he saw his father do, what other men he admired did.

Lucius and his son often practiced with heavy wooden rudii, the young boy determined to use the full-sized rudus the same as his father. When he got hit or went down, he never complained, but rose again, ready for more.

There had been one worrisome incident in the village down the hill, after Lucius had brought the children to visit Culhwch, Alma and Paulus.

As Lucius had sat speaking with his friends inside, the children had all gone out to play in the street. A short time later, shouting could be heard, angry words that raked at Lucius' consciousness. They had rushed out to find Phoebus standing between three older boys, the sons of a passing merchant, and Paulus whose nose was bloody.

Phoebus stood over one of the larger boys, his fists balled. The boy was wailing, clutching at his stomach as the other two stood there deciding whether or not to attack Phoebus.

Lucius could see why they did not, for in Phoebus' eyes was a look of great anger, of rage, due to the harm that had been done to his friend. The boys had instigated the argument and attacked Paulus, and Phoebus had rushed to his aid, despite the cries of his sister, who had tried to call him back.

Calliope had been shaken by the interlude, but Phoebus seemed to have been encouraged by it. It was as if he had been needing to test his strength, and his training. And he had.

Lucius stepped in quickly when the merchant approached, bellowing for a whip. The man quickly decided against facing off with Lucius, Culhwch and the rest of the village, and hauled his son up from the ground and into the wagon.

"You're Roman!" the man yelled back at Lucius. "Remember where you come from!"

Lucius only stared after the man until his wagon was gone, then he turned to his son and daughter.

Calliope struck Phoebus hard and stormed off.

"Did you need to beat him so soundly?" Lucius asked.

"You trained me to make sure that if I had to fight, the other man should not get up."

Lucius wondered if the example he had set for his son was right and true, or if it was a disservice to a boy with a wonderful and good heart, a boy who had felt at home in the peace of Ynis Wytrin.

Training took a turn after that. There was a time for attack, and there was a time for defence, and Lucius taught his son and daughter all that he could think of as they trained, walked, talked and spent more time together. He taught them of the importance of loyalty to family above all, of the responsibility of using one's strengths for good, for the betterment of the world around oneself. As he spoke to his children, Lucius could hear Diodorus in his mind, and the thought made him smile sadly at the memory of the kind old man.

There was, however, another memory that harassed Lucius in those days. It was not infrequent, despite the peaceful routines that he settled into, that Lucius thought of what he had seen from the edge of the northern rampart of the fort - that vast army spread out before him, bellowing his name as if it were a battle cry to strike fear into even the most fearsome enemies. He could still see them, rank upon rank of Rome's soldiers, the fluttering vexilla, the sound of the cornui, the rush of the feeling of ultimate power that seemed to flow from them and into him. The latter was perhaps the most terrifying aspect, and he tried to ignore the shadow of that feeling as it occasionally came back to him.

Gods...why did you show me that? he wondered in the quiet moments he had to himself.

The gathering that night was large, and the hearth fire in the hall burned high and bright, warming all of them. The children darted in and out amongst the adults, and Sarmatians, Britons, and Romans stood in friendly converse throughout. Adara stood speaking with Alma, Culhwch, Sigwyll and the decurion, Lenya, when she noticed that Lucius was missing from the gathering.

He often did that now, disappeared quietly for some time alone with is thoughts, and she would often find him breathing deeply and quietly to regain his composure. It had not happened in a couple of weeks now, but the possibility was always there.

"Excuse me," Adara said to the others as she took her cup of wine and made her way across the hall toward the tablinum.

"Everything all right?" Briana said, reaching out a hand as Adara passed.

"Yes."

Adara pulled away from the crowd and went to the open door of the tablinum. She stood leaning against the doorframe and watched Lucius standing on the other side of the large table, staring out the high window at the star-speckled night sky beyond. She heard the gentle speech of his prayer and decided not to speak yet, content to watch him and wait. She had, in fact, been waiting a long time to speak with him, and she could wait no longer. So, rather than going back to their friends, she watched and waited.

As she watched her husband stand in solitude, calming himself, she knew that the destined rhythm of their life was never meant to be one of monotony, like a single lyre string plucked over and over, or a fresco done with a single shade of blue. The sounds of the songs of their lives, the possible roads and pathways, were myriad.

It was a terrifying thought, but she recalled the writing of the late Marcus Aurelius and his thoughts on looking forward and never looking back, about being at ease with the way before us. It was small comfort, and very Roman. Stoicism had its uses, but she knew she was more romantic than that, and life was more difficult for romantics. And so, she prayed to the Gods that the way forward was the way they chose for themselves, that it was kind and beautiful.

Hope also has its uses, she thought as she took a step forward. "My love?"

When Lucius turned and looked up, he was startled for only a moment before a broad smile appeared across his worn face.

"I'm coming." He came toward her, his hands reaching for hers.

"There is no rush. I'm happy for us to be alone a little."

They held each other for a few moments, inhaling the scent of each other mingled with woodsmoke from the hearth, and the sweet aroma of wine upon each other's lips. Lucius picked his cup up from the table where he had set it and they drank together.

"To the Gods, and our home," he said, spilling some onto the floor.

"To our familia," Adara said, gently whispering into his ear. "All of us."

Lucius felt her take his free hand and pull it down to rest upon her belly. He enjoyed the sensation of her body through the silk of her stola, then looked into her eyes.

Adara smiled.

"What are you saying?"

"What do you think I'm saying, my dragon? I am carrying your child. You are going to be a father again."

"But how-" She raised her eyebrows and he shook his head. "I mean how far along are you?" Now that he really looked, he could see the rounding of her belly. "How could I not notice?" Lucius knelt and put his cheek to Adara's belly and she ran her hands through his long hair, held him close.

"It has been over a month, if I am correct," she said. She looked down at him and he up at her. "Aren't you happy?"

Lucius stood and kissed her. "The Gods bless us, my love. Of course I'm happy. I don't have the words right now. I just feel...like shouting it!"

He made to pick her up but thought better of it, and put her down quickly.

Adara laughed, her voice like the playful splash of a cool fountain. "You won't break me, you know."

He wrapped his arms around her and felt the elation sweep through him to douse the fires of worry that had been haranguing him.

"I love you."

"And I you," Adara said, her hand upon his cheek.

"Come! Let's tell our friends!"

Before she knew it, Adara was being pulled out into the hall toward the central hearth and Lucius stood upon one of the great log seats and raised his arms.

"Friends!" he called. "Friends, listen!" he said louder, in his parade ground voice.

Smiling and curious faces stared up at him.

"No more drills, Praefectus!" Badru called from the back, and the Sarmatians there roared with laughter.

"No, no!" Lucius answered. "No more drills today, my friends. Adara and I have an announcement!"

"What is it?" Dagon asked.

"She is with child!"

A great cheer burst up toward the rafters.

"Congratulations to the Metelli!" Lenya called out loudly.

Lucius jumped down, and then Dagon jumped up on the log in his place.

"I too have an important announcement!" the young Sarmatian king said. "My queen is also expecting our first child!"

An even greater cheer went up from the Sarmatians and others as the joy swept through the hall and Adara and Briana embraced each other.

"The Gods love you, Dagon!" Lucius laughed as he hugged his friend.

"They love us both, Anguis!" Dagon said just before being raised up by his men and paraded about the edges of the hall.

Adara and Briana had in fact told each other about their pregnancies, and though Dagon had known, Adara had waited to tell Lucius. He had been too lost in the shadows clouding his mind.

When all the congratulations were said and the celebrations continued, Lucius and Adara looked down to see Phoebus and Calliope standing before them, holding hands.

"Are you ready to be a big sister and big brother?" Adara asked them.

Phoebus smiled and nodded. "I'll teach him everything I've learned from Baba."

"That's good, my boy," Lucius said, ruffling his hair. "But it could be a girl!"

Phoebus looked panicked for a fleeting moment but then regained his composure, that is until Calliope stepped forward to hug her mother.

"How will we keep the baby safe, Mama, with men attacking us all the time?"

Adara looked at Lucius and felt her heart tighten as their daughter held her tightly. Lucius knelt down before Calliope.

"You are all safe, do you hear me, my girl? All is well, and Mama and the baby will be safe. Do you believe me?"

She nodded only half way before the gesture faded into worry. "I'm so happy," she said, her smile slight, though her affection and worry were eminently discernible.

"My girl," Adara said, sitting on the log behind her and looking into her daughter's big brown eyes. "Are you worried a baby will take attention away from you? Because that could never happen, you know."

"Oh, Mama. Of course not. I know that you love me. I just dream too much of fire, and it sometimes worries me."

Calliope kissed her mother on the check, touched the belly gently with her hand, and then faded off into the crowd.

That night, long after the guests had gone back to either the village or the Sarmatian camp, and the hall was locked tightly with a watch rotation set for the night, Lucius and Adara lay upon the thick furs of their bed, the brazier still burning brightly nearby to light their cubiculum.

Adara lay flat upon her back in her sleeping tunica while Lucius lay propped on one elbow beside her, his left hand tracing lines over her small belly and up and down her body. She was older now, true, but as Lucius looked upon his wife, he felt that she had never been more beautiful. Being with her, their children in the next rooms, was as a soothing balm for all that he felt.

He thought of her as he touched her and she smiled, her eyes bright in the brazier light. He thought of how proud he was of his children, of Phoebus and Calliope, and how the Gods had sought fit to bless them again with this child. His hand stopped on top of her belly, but in that moment, his face darkened, and he felt the pull of the thoughts he had been fighting daily since Dumnonia. He removed his hand and lay beside her to stare up at the beamed ceiling.

He knew he had infinite joy in his life, enriched as it was by Adara and their children, as an entire black sky is lit by a few starry beacons. He felt this with certainty in his bones.

But... He also experienced a perpetual uneasiness where he went now, a deep dissatisfaction, as if the world could never live up to his expectations of the life he wanted for his family, even more now that a third child was on the way.

Lucius explained this to Adara, and after listening quietly for a few minutes, she turned slowly on her elbow to look at him, her hand upon his pounding heart.

"Where would you have us live, Lucius? Where should we go? I love you beyond all things, as do the children..." She turned his face slowly to look at her. "Tell us where you want to go, and we will follow you."

"I don't know where," he said, his voice exhausted, as if his mind had been bent upon that single purpose for some time now. "When I was young, I couldn't wait to get out of Rome, much as I loved it. Then, for a while, I wanted nothing more than to return to her bosom. Now, the thought of living there could not be farther from my heart's desire."

"But what do you desire, my love?" There was desperation and compassion in her voice, both of them hiding the fear she too felt. Adara knew that as blessed as they were by the Gods in finding each other and making their lives one, so too had their hopes and fears become intertwined. She stroked his cheek and squeezed his hand.

"I don't know for certain... I want peace for us, for our children, our baby. But I don't know where we could go for such."

"Does such a place ever exist anywhere but in our minds, fuelled by our hopes and dreams, our fears? Not even Athenae is free of turmoil," she said sadly. "Though...I would like to see my family again."

"The only place I have felt a measure of the peace I dream of is here...or, rather...Ynis Wytrin."

The name of that blessed isle hung there between them, a comfort, a dream, memories of a place that already seemed faraway.

Adara looked at her husband and felt her heart tear for the pain she could tell he was holding inside. He wanted to hide them all from the world, behind a misty veil, but she knew, somehow, the Gods would not allow such a thing. The great in the world were not meant to hide away, but to better the world around them. And in her heart, Adara believed in Lucius' greatness.

"Lucius, my love. Why can't you tell me what happened to you in Dumnonia? Help me to understand, please, so that I can help you. You've always told me everything."

Lucius' eyes shut tightly as he struggled to stay calm. They had spoken of this before, and he did not want the poisonous thoughts to rise once more to the surface.

She cares for me, he told himself. *That is why she asks. She's scared of my silence!* He shook his head.

"This is different. I saw things...things happened that I would not dare utter for fear that they might become reality. I've never experienced such...terror, Adara."

"My love...the Gods are on your side. Ever have they been."

Apollo...why did you never tell me! "I was alone there. And it has left me fearful." There. He had said the words, given the feelings voice. He had never allowed himself to be so unguarded, not even with Adara.

"But you are not alone *here*," she stressed.

"I feel that we - you and the children - will never be safe anywhere. The world is constantly tearing itself apart, and I seem ever to be in the middle of it."

"It is peace time now. Surely that gives us hope? Besides, doesn't every man feel that way when the Fates set him upon a difficult path?"

"Yes, but where can we go beyond the reach of Rome? I can't do this anymore, Adara. My soul feels lacerated beyond recognition."

Lucius' eyes shut tightly then and tears rolled down the sides of his face as he lay there.

Adara leaned over and kissed his eyes and brow, trying desperately to smother the fire of sad emotion that was engulfing him.

"You are Lucius Metellus Anguis. It is not only the Gods who love you. I do...your children and your friends do." She sat up then, her voice steady. "Your men do, and from what I have heard and seen, the men of the legions do. With such allies, would it not be possible to *make* the world safe?"

His eyes shot open and he sat up. She had spoken in innocence, been trying to calm him, but he had to wonder if she had been inside the tangled thoughts of his mind, seen what he had seen from the high ramparts of the hillfort, felt what he had seen in the realm of Annwn.

"No," he said, standing and taking a chunk of incense from the side table and lighting it in the fire of one of the braziers. "There is always someone posing a threat. That is what I'm trying to say."

She did not understand, but knew that he needed her to. Adara stood and walked barefoot around the bottom of their bed to his side.

"Then we will defend our family together, with or without the Gods' help."

Even as she said it, and held her husband closely, a chill ran down her spine.

The night was cold and still outside the hall as everyone slept soundly in their beds, buried beneath furs and wool blankets.

For some time, Adara had lain awake, watching Lucius as his lids grew heavier and heavier until finally, he slipped into sleep. Her thoughts whirled uncontrollably, fear and doubt swarming her hopes, hopes she clung to with all her might.

Adara Metella prayed to the Gods as she lay there staring at her sleeping husband, asked them to ease his mind, to keep them all safe. Eventually, sleep carried her off and she collapsed among the furs, her breathing deep and slow, exhausted.

It was not long before she fell into the realm of dreams, however, and found herself walking through a wood of tall, dead and decaying trees, strangled by disease. She was barefoot as she walked, the ground muddy and cold beneath her feet. At first, Adara despaired of the lack of life about her, but then, out of the rotted floor of the forest came new growth, a new forest of saplings, hopeful and sinewy, with the promise of strength.

Adara walked among them, admiring the iridescent, twined leaves that lit the end of every new branch. She stopped, realizing that she knew the place, the path that led up to the Tor through the hidden ways of Ynis Wytrin. She closed her eyes, feeling the soothing calm that came over her, savouring the moment with an outstretched finger to stroke the tiny foliage at the end of the branches. In a moment, as full of magic and wonder as any child can experience, every pair of leaves took to the air as a thousand butterflies about her, and she laughed.

Adara laughed and twirled as she watched them flutter, little wings caressing her cheeks. All was perfect, until the sound of a dread horn broke the forest peace of the blessed isle.

The wings stopped fluttering in mid-air, and at the third blast of the horn, they burst into flames all around her.

Sadness overwhelmed Adara then, the sky darkened, and ash polluted the air.

The sound of marching could be heard all around.

Adara could feel the earth tremble, and heard the somewhat familiar sound of men, arms and armour approaching. They were all around her then, but where a vast circle of Caledonian spears was expected to orbit her, there stood instead an unforgiving ring of Roman iron, of scuta and gladii jutting out like the fangs of some new-born Scylla or Caribdis.

Then, Phoebus and Calliope were gripping her hands, their eyes filled with tears as they looked up at her, terror chiselled upon their faces.

Adara stepped in front of her children and gazed over the heads of the soldiers at the Tor to see it burning. Screams rent the air and the soldiers began to close in, almost near enough to run them through just before fire encircled them, and they all burst into flames.

As the burning heat raked at her body, Adara bent over her children to shield them, their screams ringing in her ears, but not as much as Lucius' own cries, somewhere…beyond the flames.

"Adara!" Lucius called to his wife as she thrashed and cried in her sleep. "Adara, wake up!"

Lucius knelt on the bed beside his wife, his heart racing in his chest as he tried to wake her, his strong hands attempting to hold her still so that she would not hurt herself or strike him.

"Lucius!" Her eyes shot open quickly, red and wet, and she was clinging to his neck, her arms gripping him tightly, her body shaking as she wept.

"Shh…shh," he soothed, stroking her hair and sweaty brow. "I'm here, my love."

He waited until she was calm again. He rarely saw her that way, so at that very moment, he was unnerved. "Was it a dream?"

She did not speak for a few moments, but then she sat up and stared directly into his eyes. "The Gods have shown me something…horror…fire everywhere, and the legions with their swords drawn on me and the children."

That was a truly terrifying vision, but it did not make sense. Lucius studied her, forcing himself to set aside his own fears and focus on her. "I don't know what the Gods showed you, Adara, but I do know that the men of the legions have a fair opinion of me. I've earned it."

"I know," she answered. "That's why I'm so confused by this." She shook her head. "But there's more… I saw Ynis Wytrin in flames."

That, Lucius could believe. If people like the ordo of Lindinis had anything to do with it, Ynis Wytrin would be burned to the ground.

"The Isle is safe, Adara. We know this. Perhaps you dreamt that because of what I said last night?"

"I don't know." She hugged him again, and he kissed her head and cheek before they lay down again to hold each other, to feel the other close and alive.

That day, Adara asked Briana to help her train again, this time harder than ever. Since Lucius' condition upon his return, as well as Saturnalia, she had grown lax in her training with so much to tend to.

In the cold, dim sunlight, Adara hefted the new blade her husband had given her and trained until it felt as much a part of her body as her own arm, until every movement and technique with the new blade came easily and instinctively. She knew her body would protest the next day, but she did not care, for the dream she had been shown harried her like furies at her back.

Phoebus and Calliope watched their mother train, but in seeing her do so with such ferocity, they felt that something was wrong, especially Calliope.

"Mama..." the girl said as Adara came to sit on the log beside them and gulp down water before tossing the skin to Briana who did the same. "Why are you so angry? Are you worried?"

"No, my girl. I'm fine. Just training."

"We haven't seen you train like that before," Phoebus pointed out.

"Your father has spoken to you about pushing yourself beyond your limits before?"

"Yes," Phoebus answered.

"That is what I am doing."

"Where is baba?" Calliope asked.

On the north rampart of the hillfort, Lucius stood with the wind howling around him, willing it to make him feel strong. The ravens cawed and dove on the breeze, and in the distance, the Tor of Ynis Wytrin caught his eye.

He remembered the lush green peace of that mist-shrouded place, the kindness in every person there, the feeling of well-being in himself that he had only ever felt when safe in the blessed isle.

It was then that he felt a need to protect it, and the people dwelling there.

What did Adara's dream mean? he asked himself, hoping too that the Gods would hear him. First thing that morning, he had gone to the temple and made offerings to Apollo, Venus, and Epona, his thoughts drifting to them as the smoke circled and flowed around him and their divine images.

The only answer that came on the wind to reach his hearing were the words: *It is time...go forward with care...*

What did that mean? He was always careful.

He looked down upon the fields below the ancient fortress and, again, as if in a mirage in the sands of Africa, the ranks of legions appeared before him once more, chanting his name in a cry that would reach the slopes of Olympus itself.

What are you showing me?

And he began to see the possibilities.

As Lucius walked back through the rows of Sarmatian tents and horse lines, he chided himself for his treasonous thoughts. *What am I thinking?*

He was about to head toward the stables to saddle Xanthus for his morning exercise, when one of the men called out to him.

"Praefectus! Horsemen approaching!"

Lucius stopped, a feeling of dread in his stomach. He turned, his hand going to the point between his shoulders where his sword jutted, reassuring himself it was there. He strode through the gathering Sarmatians who came out to challenge the horsemen charging up through the northeastern gate.

Three horsemen burst into the open area of the hillfort and reined in hard. Their mounts were covered in mud and the riders were spattered from head to foot, neither deterring from the hard look in their determined eyes.

"I'm looking for Praefectus Lucius Metellus Anguis, of the Ala III Britannorum Quingenaria Sarmatiana!" There was urgency in the man's voice, and an unmistakeable officiousness.

Barta pushed his way to the front to challenge the riders, but Lucius was there before his bodyguard could utter a word. When he spoke, all the Sarmatians turned to him, parting to allow him through.

"I am Praefectus Metellus!" Lucius declared, his voice heard clearly above the muttering. He walked forward to meet the messenger who slid quickly to the ground from atop his horse and saluted.

Dagon arrived at that moment too, to stand beside Lucius.

"What is it, soldier?" Lucius asked. "At ease."

"There is no time for ease, Praefectus," the man said, digging in his leather satchel and withdrawing a piece of parchment with the imperial seal. He handed it to Lucius who unrolled it.

Lucius read the letter and felt his head begin to spin, but he maintained control of himself, despite the fact that he wanted to roar in anger.

"What is it, Praefectus?" Dagon asked as the men closed in to hear.

Lucius looked up at the faces around him, those of loyal men and friends who had been to Hades and back with him, who had stood by him through all manner of horrors. He then turned to the messenger.

"Is it true?"

The messenger pursed his lips and nodded. "Afraid so, Praefectus. Despite the thrashing you gave'em last time... It's true."

"What?"

Lucius put his hand on Dagon's shoulder and handed him the letter from the emperor. He then stood on a nearby crate and turned around to see his men.

"The Caledonii and the Maeatae have revolted and formed a confederacy! They've broken the peace!" He felt the anger threaten to boil over then, and his vision blurred momentarily.

The Sarmatians roared in anger and anticipation.

"We ride to war in three days!" Lucius said before jumping down and marching off toward the hall on the plateau where the forms of his wife and children had been watching.

Three days...

Three days was all Lucius had to reconcile his thoughts and feelings with his chosen life. Three days to spend with his family, to lie with his wife, to study and speak with his children, to think on the life he wanted to give to his unborn child, a child who would likely be born in his absence.

Three days were not enough.

How can a man ensure that those he loves more than anything know and feel the full extent of his love for them, understand it, in a mere three days.

As he packed his satchels with supplies, maps, a few scrolls and other items he would need, Lucius wondered if he had done enough in his life, in the time given him by the Gods, to ensure that his wife and children fully understood. Certainly, he had not lifted the veil of Adara's ignorance of what he had discovered in that misty otherworld of Dumnonia. However, he found he was still not able to say it, for when one discovers a great truth about oneself, the shock can truly render one mute until true understanding dawns.

Lucius did not understand, and now, his time was to be given over to war once more, rather than seeking the understanding he so desperately needed.

Focus, Lucius! he told himself. *If you don't, you'll die!*

He sat heavily at the table of the tablinum, his head in his hands. He would have wept but for the knock at the door.

"Baba?" Phoebus' hesitant voice called out to him.

Lucius looked up and smiled at his son. "Phoebus. Come in."

The boy approached and came around the table to stand beside his father. "I've finished oiling and polishing your armour."

"Good lad," Lucius said. "Show me."

Phoebus pulled his father by the hand and led him up to the cubiculum where the armour was displayed on a wooden frame at the far end of the room.

Lucius walked up to it and looked it over.

The crested helmet shone brightly, especially the engraved dragons upon the cheek guards, and the red horse-hair crest bristled tall and proud, newly brushed. Lucius ran his hand over the hardened bull's hide cuirass and the image of the dragon with its spread wings upon the chest, cast from a single piece of metal that had been handed down in their family line for generations. As ever, it seemed to flap and roar of its own accord, unmarked, despite all of the many slashes and cuts that orbited it.

Likewise, the greaves shone with a brilliance even Lucius had not achieved in polishing his armour, matched by the shine of the leather pteruges of the skirt, and the sheath of the gladius and pugio which Lucius also wore.

Lucius smiled. "It's perfect, Phoebus. Thank you."

The boy beamed and sighed with relief as Lucius put his arm around him.

"There is one thing." Lucius took the gladius down from where it hung upon one of the arms, and turned to his son. The golden pommel with the eagle shone brightly in the angling light of day coming in from the window, and the pegasus upon the hilt seemed to rear and stomp the ground. "You will keep this while I'm gone."

Phoebus stepped back, shaking his head. "I can't, Baba. You need that."

Lucius shook his head. "I have a sword that never leaves my side." He reached up and touched the one Adara had given him. "You will keep the gladius of our family safe while I'm away, and you will use it if you have to."

"But...Baba..." His eyes glistened. "Will you not come back to us?"

Lucius knelt before his son and took him in his arms. "I will. The Gods themselves could not keep me from you." He let go and held Phoebus at arm's length. "You have trained so well, and you need to be ready to defend our family if you need to."

"But the fighting is in the North."

"Phoebus, listen to me... There is fighting everywhere in this world, not just on the battlefield. There is never joy without sorrow, love without hatred, beauty without horror. No matter how much we try to live in the light of Apollo, the darkness of Hades is always there. I need you to be strong now. I have faith in you, my son."

Phoebus wiped away a stray tear and sniffed loudly, gaining control of his sadness and fear. He nodded. "Thank you. I promise... I'll be strong for Mama and Calliope. And for you."

"I know." Lucius stood and hugged his son again. "I'm so proud of you. Please remember that."

His son did not reply, but as Lucius held him, he could feel the boy's arms tighten about his torso, his body shuddering with weeping he did his best to hide.

Where Phoebus busied himself with tasks for Lucius and Dagon to help them prepare for their departure, Calliope fell silent at the news that her father was leaving, neither speaking nor singing. She followed Adara everywhere she went, wept only in private, usually upon the temple steps or the western rampart as the sun fell away at the end of the day.

Her silence was like a dagger to Lucius' heart, though he knew she cared deeply for him. On the second day before their departure, Lucius found her sitting with Adara watching the sunset. He climbed the rampart and sat down upon the cold grass beside his daughter. His eyes found Adara's and she shook her head.

Calliope had not spoken yet.

After a moment, Adara stood and declared she was going to go check on the meal being prepared by Ula and Aina.

Lucius watched her go, the sword he had given her hanging safely at her side. She now wore it at all times, and would do so the entirety of his absence.

Calliope made to get up and follow her mother, but Lucius reached out to take her hand.

"Please, my girl. Stay with me?"

Calliope turned to look at him with her big, watery eyes and, after a moment, nodded and sat down.

Lucius looked at her and realized she was taller now, even more so than her brother. Despite that, however, she was still, to him, his little girl. *They have grown before my very eyes...* he thought, marvelling at how quickly time passed when one was a father, and how children made one keenly aware of that every so often.

"I don't want to go, Calliope. You know that, right?" It hurt Lucius to feel her so distant, so silent when her voice was everything to him. For a moment, he thought she was going to pull away and leave, but in fact, she did the opposite.

Calliope pulled herself into the crook of Lucius' arm and held him fast, as if she were willing him not to leave them.

Lucius smiled sadly to himself and stroked her long hair, kissed the top of her head. He had not been there for her the way he should have been since Dumnonia.

"So you don't hate me?" he said, more to himself, but the words made her sit up and look at him, a frown upon her gentle features.

"Of course not, Baba," she said, and the words were as music to Lucius' ears.

He held her close, relieved to hear her speak.

"I'm scared," she said honestly.

"Me too," he admitted. "But I've been through war before, and the Gods watch over me. Over you too."

She shook her head. "Not this time, Baba. I've seen it. I didn't want to tell you, but... I just can't keep it to myself any longer."

400

Now Lucius felt dread. *What has she seen?* he wondered. "Tell me, my girl."

She curled up in his lap and her breathing became quick, frantic, before she calmed and the words poured out.

"I dreamed of you fighting a great wolf," she said. "A monster. I saw a battle upon black waters…I saw watery death, and a ring of flame…" Calliope shut her eyes tight and shook her head. "I don't want to see all these things, Baba. They scare me! I don't want you to go!"

If Lucius was honest with himself, he would admit that her words terrified him.

In Ynis Wytrin it had become evident that Calliope had the Sight, that the Gods spoke to her in visions and dreams, and that it was not something easily controlled, or ignored. She had known about the young priestess being attacked, and about his fight for his life in Dumnonia. Lucius wondered what else she might see that would come to pass.

He closed his eyes as he rallied himself for his daughter, for she needed him, and her needs were greater than his own fears and doubts. He forced himself to take deep breaths and felt his daughter fall in step with him, both of them breathing in and out, calmness coming upon them.

"Calliope, listen to me," he said, turning her to face him. He placed his hands upon her cheeks. "I know you see things that others cannot. You have a gift, though that gift is scary, yes?"

She nodded.

"Our strengths can be scary, it's true. I've felt that myself. But they can help us as we pass through this life. Odysseus would not have survived without his wits, right? He toiled greatly, but he came home in the end."

"But why do you have to go to war again?"

"It is my duty, my girl. I must be there for my men, as they are there for me. I'll be safer with them than any man in the legions."

"But you won't be the same, Baba. I've seen it. I've seen you…changed."

"How?" Lucius could not help but ask.

"I don't know. Just different."

"All men change after battle. Every battle I have fought has changed me in some way. It is inevitable. But one thing will not change, and that's my love for you, your brother, and your mama. I

401

will always come for you, no matter what. I need you to remember that. I need you to see that."

Calliope stopped sniffling and wrapped her arms around him. "I love you, Baba."

Lucius' voice shook as he replied that he too loved her, more than anything, and together they watched the remainder of the sun's orb fall away.

When they returned to the hall, they found everyone gathered for a fine meal - Dagon and Briana, Barta, Culhwch, Alma and Paulus, Ula and Aina.

"I hear you're leaving," Culhwch said as Lucius joined him beside the fire.

"Yes. Day after tomorrow, we ride."

"We're sad to see you go, Lucius," Alma said.

"Me too," Lucius answered. "But with hope, we'll be back in a few months' time." He looked at Dagon and Barta, but neither of them returned the look with optimism. And Lucius knew they were right to doubt it. He turned to go to a table to get a cup of wine, and Culhwch followed to refill his cup.

"Do something for me, my friend," Lucius whispered.

Culhwch leaned in.

"Watch over Adara, Briana and the children. Too much has happened. If anything seems amiss, please help them."

The Durotrigan looked at Lucius and gripped his shoulders. "You have my word. You are friends of my people now…family. We look out for each other."

"Thank you," Lucius said, feeling a little better, despite the recurring echoes of Calliope's visions in his mind's eye.

Lucius approached the circle about the fire, of friends and family, and raised his cup as he stared across the flames at his wife and children.

"May the Gods protect us all and bring us back together again."

"To the Gods!" they said, before they all drank.

As Lucius made to sit down and eat his portion of the roasted pheasant and vegetables that Ula and Aina had prepared, there was a loud knocking at the doors.

Barta walked over with Lucius who opened the door.

There, two Sarmatians held a Briton between them. It was Trevor Reghan, the one ordo member in Lindinis whom Lucius felt he could trust. He was breathless and dirty from riding at speed.

"Let him in," Lucius said, and the Sarmatians released him.

Trevor Reghan looked inside and saw the gathering. "Praefectus...I must speak with you, but let us do it outside."

"Why?" Lucius asked.

"I have discovered something..." he looked back into the gathering darkness and then to Lucius again. "Please. There is little time, and I fear I may be watched."

Lucius turned to Barta and Dagon, and they followed Trevor Reghan outside.

Reghan stepped away from the torches so that he was hidden in the darkness.

The Sarmatians grew wary of his behaviour and surrounded them, swords drawn.

"Why are you acting like this, Trevor?" Lucius asked.

"I came to warn you."

"Warn him? Of what?" Dagon asked.

"I overheard Serenus Crescens and Nolan Phelan talking about some deal he made with a man at the imperial court."

"Who?" Lucius asked.

"They didn't say. But the deal involved getting civitas status for Lindinis."

"And the price of this?" Lucius asked.

"Information about you and your family."

Trevor Reghan disappeared into the night, reluctant to stay any longer than was needed, but the encounter gave Lucius, Dagon and Barta pause.

If Lucius was reluctant to leave before, he hated the idea now, though he knew he had no choice. Were he to be declared a deserter to the emperor and Rome, then all his family's possessions, their freedoms, could be forfeit.

They decided to tell Adara and Briana so that they could stay on the alert, though they worried what the knowledge might do.

Still, better to be prepared... Lucius told himself.

"What did Trevor Reghan want?" Adara asked after the children went to bed, and Ula and Aina were safely home in the village, having returned with Culhwch, Alma and Paulus.

Lucius and Dagon exchanged looks, and Barta, silent, stared into the flames, his jaw set like chiseled stone.

"He overheard Crescens and one of the other ordo members talking about a deal with someone at the court."

"What kind of deal?" Briana asked.

Lucius breathed deeply. He felt so much anger, he worried that it would cloud his judgement. He had not wanted to leave home like that. He had hoped to leave his family safely behind.

"What is it, Lucius?" Adara asked, squeezing his hand.

"There's just too much happening. First Alerio is murdered...then you're attacked here while Dagon and I were in Dumnonia. And now this." He looked at the two women. "Trevor Reghan said that in exchange for civitas status, Crescens has agreed to provide information about me."

"What kind of information?" Adara asked, her voice hard and cold. She had come to loathe the ordo politician.

"No doubt something about Lucius' whereabouts," Dagon said.

"But, if it's someone at court, then they would know that anyway, with the army being recalled," Adara mused.

Lucius looked at his wife and nodded. "You're right. It doesn't make sense."

"We all need to be on the alert," Barta said, speaking for the first time. "Can we leave some of the men behind here?" He looked at Dagon and Lucius. Barta remembered all too well the attack that night while Lucius and Dagon were in Dumnonia. His guard had been up since, and though he knew he must be with them on the battlefield, it was important to leave some men behind if at all possible.

"Whoever ignores the call to duty will be branded a deserter," Lucius said. He did not want to endanger any of his men, but he also wanted to ensure the safety of his family. "What if you went to Ynis Wytrin?" He turned to Adara.

She looked at him, rubbing her belly, but shook her head. "This is our home, Lucius. We built this place. I won't abandon it. I'll keep it running, keep the hearth warm and bright while you're away."

Lucius had known that would be her answer, and however much they had loved Ynis Wytrin, the hillfort was their home. He turned to Barta. "Are there three men who would stay?"

"I'll get seven," Barta answered. "They would lay down their lives for the Metelli and our new queen."

"And I'll make sure the Caledonii and this person at court regret their treachery," Lucius added, a fire and fear in his eyes that worried Adara as she looked at him.

The day to leave arrived, and Lucius awoke long before the sun's rays graced the winter landscape. His mind had been racing all night, and he had slept very little. When he woke, he turned over on his arm to watch Adara sleep.

His wife had tossed and turned all night too, but she had fallen asleep shortly before he had woken. He wanted to kiss her, to touch her again, explore her the way they had the previous night when they had believed it would be the last time for a while that they made love.

"You're so beautiful," Lucius whispered, his voice no more than a breathy exhalation. He looked at the tangle of her dark, curly tresses, the soft shape of her lips, the rise and fall of her chest. As Adara slept, her right hand rested instinctively on her slightly swollen belly.

What if it's twins again? he wondered, trying not to laugh for joy at he thought of what that would be like, how Phoebus and Calliope would react to another child, let alone two.

Then, Lucius' mood grew dark again. He would likely not be there when the time came. The enemies of Rome would not be so easily defeated, nor would they have rebelled so soon if they did not have great confidence in their strength. Threats were everywhere, and the thought of it brought Lucius back to what he had been mulling over in the dark of night - security. If Adara and the children had to flee their home for any reason, it would be left to his enemies.

With this in mind, he rose quietly from the bed and dressed in his bracae, red tunica and red cloak which he would wear for the journey. All his other clothing was packed in his single trunk for transport. His boots laced up, Lucius went out of the room and downstairs to the tablinum where he lit a lamp and stared at the pigeonhole shelves filled with scrolls.

He could not take them all with him, no. He also wanted to leave them behind for Phoebus who had shown great interest in reading them, learning as much as he could.

On the floor in front of the shelves was an iron-bound strong box with a lock. He walked over and hoisted it to carry it to the large table. It was empty, of course, but he felt compelled to use it now.

Taking the key that hung about his neck, he bent down to unlock one of the cabinet bases of the table. A door swung open to reveal over twenty leather pouches filled with gold aurea and silver denarii. He began to remove the pouches and transferred over half to the strong box on the table. Once that was done, he looked about the room for other items he wanted placed within, including the imperial pass granting him passage anywhere in the empire, the plans and deed for the hillfort given to him and Adara by her father, and the copies of the deeds to the estate in Etruria.

He did not know why he was doing this, why he was hiding away his rightful possessions like a looter hiding away his treasure to come back to. This was his home, and he was determined to keep it.

His awards, armillae and torcs, he also placed in the box, along with the corona aurea he had once received for saving a citizen's life, and a few chosen scrolls from the shelf - extra copies of Arrian and Caesar, and one of Longus who had graced their home in Rome with a reading of his novel *Daphnis and Chloe*, so long ago.

With the small fortune sealed in the box, Lucius then added the key to the thong about his neck and blew out the lamp. Once that was done, he took up the strong box and went out, across the hall, and into the early morning light, careful not to slam the double doors of the hall.

Outside, the morning was cold and frosty, though in a month, the flowers of Martius would be pushing up out of the ground. The air was suffused with a grey and white light laced with mist. He passed the naked furrows of the vegetable gardens and made his way down from the plateau, past the barracks and stables, and toward the temple at the far corner of the hillfort.

As he went, Lucius looked around constantly for any sign of watchers, other than the Sarmatians who had been placed on guard duty atop the ramparts and who stared straight out to the surrounding countryside.

The guards spotted Lucius, but turned back to their posts when they saw it was their commander. The men had kept their distance for the three days since the announcement that they were leaving, knowing the weight upon the praefectus' shoulders.

Lucius nodded to the nearest guard who saluted, and then entered the small temple. Approaching the altar, Lucius set the box down and turned to close the temple doors.

When he turned back to the altar, the faces of the Gods stared back at him, and he wondered what they were thinking, what he wanted to say to them.

Before prayers though, he had a task, and he set about removing the statues and offerings from the surface of the altar, setting them gently upon the ground to the right. When the altar was bare, he reached his fingers around the back right corner and pulled.

At first, nothing happened, but he pulled harder the second time and the entire stone altar began to swing out. Lucius pulled harder until the altar was at a ninety degree angle and stood back.

Before him, beneath the altar, was the lined pit he had instructed Cradawg to build with utmost secrecy. No one knew about it except Lucius and the Briton. Lucius lit one of the lamps he had set upon the ground and peered into the pit.

It was dry inside, the stones perfectly chiseled.

Lucius hefted the strong box and straddled the pit, lowering it as much as he could before letting it fall to the bottom with a solid thud.

At that moment, the door of the temple creaked open on its hinges, and Adara stood there wrapped in her blue cloak.

"Lucius? What are you doing?" She looked around at the displaced altar and images of the Gods upon the ground.

"Taking precautions," he said, leaving the pit and coming over to her. "I want to show you something." He led her to the pit and pointed at the box inside. "In that box, I've hidden much of our wealth, the deeds to all our lands, and some other items."

"But why?" she said as he handed her the key.

"In case..." he stopped himself. "You cannot tell anyone about this. No one at all. Keep this key safe, with you at all times. If you have to flee our home, you do so quickly with the children."

"My love," she said, her hand upon his cheek. "We'll be fine. Please only worry about staying alive for us and coming back."

Lucius shook his head. "Tell me you understand."

Adara was silent as she observed the earnest appeal in her husband's face, and nodded.

Lucius turned and pushed the altar back in place, brushing his foot over the dust lines that the motion had left. Satisfied that no one would be able to tell the altar was moveable, he and Adara began to place the Gods back on the altar until all was as it had been.

"I don't want you to leave," Adara said when they finished.

Lucius' arm found her as they faced the Gods before them, those deities who had watched over them for so long, through many trials.

"I don't want to go either. When I'm away from you now, I can't... It just doesn't feel right."

"I have that feeling also. We've spent too much time apart, my love." She took a deep, resigned breath, and stepped to the altar. "Come, let us make our offerings to the Gods together, and pray for your safe return."

As they each held a chunk of incense in the flame of the burning lamp, their minds reached out to the Gods with pleas for mercy and safe passage through the months ahead. Had Lucius and Adara turned around, they would have seen Apollo, Venus and Epona standing in the shadows behind them, unwilling to disturb the prayers they offered amid the swirling smoke of their united offering.

Will you not speak to him? Epona asked Far-Shooting Apollo beside her.

Apollo did not answer, but stared at Lucius, sadness in his starry eyes.

Epona shook her head and disappeared, heading to the stables and Lucius' mount. She would ride with her warriors to war again, to battle against the Morrigan if need be. *She will pay for Dumnonia.*

As Apollo watched Lucius, Venus stepped forward to lay her hands upon Lucius and Adara's shoulders at once, her golden head hovering between them, joining them as she had so long ago with the breath of deep-born love. They leaned closer together, their prayers fervent, their tears and wishes burning. *Your love binds you in this world and the next, Venus whispered to them. It is a light in the darkness. Hold onto it, believe in it, and it will not abandon you.*

At that moment, husband and wife turned to face each other and kissed, their tears mingled upon their cheeks, and their arms held each other tightly, as if their lives depended upon the memory of that private embrace.

When they turned, Lucius paused, seeing the face of Apollo for a fleeting moment at the temple's door, and then the light dimmed in that sacred space as the two deities departed, leaving Lucius and Adara alone.

Bowing to the altar, they turned and left the temple, heading into the morning light and back to the hall that was their home, their own.

Outside, the Sarmatians were gathering supplies and saddling their horses for the journey north to war. The hillfort rang out with the familiar sounds of campaign, only this time, directly upon Lucius' doorstep. Harness jingled and horses neighed and stomped. The air was filled with the scent of fresh hay and manure, of newly oiled leather and polished armour. Lance tips glinted and the harsh, guttural voices of the decurions broke the morning air.

"They'll be ready soon," Lucius said as they walked together, up the hill to meet Briana, Dagon, and Barta who stood outside the hall with seven armed men in plain tunics and cloaks.

The men bowed to Lucius and Adara as they approached.

"Praefectus," Barta said, stepping forward and saluting. "These men wish to stay behind and protect the Dragon's family and our queen."

Lucius stopped before the men and recognized each of them, grateful for the relief their presence gave in that moment, especially Lenya, the decurion. "You all know what you risk not returning with us to the front? Are you sure you want to do this? I will not oblige you."

Lenya stepped forward, his fair hair tied back to reveal his stern, bearded face, the tattoo of the chimera upon his body snaking its way up his neck.

"Praefectus, we know. It is our decision. For us, it is a high cause, granted us by the Gods themselves, to protect our queen and the Dragon's family. It is an honour we could not have hoped for, and we will remain steadfast in our duty, until death."

Lucius did not know what to say. These men would be reported deserters, and that by himself as their commanding officer. Lucius would have to claim not to know of their desertion. The thought pained him, but they all knew it was the only way.

"I cannot thank you enough, my friends," Lucius said, taking Lenya's hand and squeezing it, then doing likewise with the other men. "It has been an honour to fight alongside all of you."

They bowed.

"We will move into the barracks and keep the horses hidden in the stables," Lenya said. "Two of us will remain on guard at the hall doors day and night, or remain close to your family and our queen wherever they go. You have my word, Praefectus."

"Thank you," Lucius said, nodding and walking slowly on toward the hall, Adara thanking the men as she passed too.

"I'll be ready shortly," Lucius said to Dagon and Briana, leaving the two of them to their farewells, patting Barta on the shoulder as they went inside.

About the hearth at the centre of the hall, the fire crackled warmly, welcoming, as if the very place made an attempt to keep Lucius there.

Phoebus and Calliope ate their breakfast about the fire, Ula and Aina sitting with them, evidently trying to comfort the children.

Adara nodded to Ula and Aina and the girls rose to go back to the kitchen to make the final food preparations for Lucius as she had instructed.

Lucius sat down on the ground between his children. "You will help your mama while I'm away?" he asked, unsure of what else he could say. There was just too much.

"Of course we will, Baba," Calliope said.

It sounded good to hear their daughter's voice again, and Adara leaned over and kissed her on the head.

Lucius turned to Phoebus and noticed that he was fully dressed in bracae, boots, tunica and cloak. He also wore the ancestral gladius that Lucius had entrusted to him, and Lucius' heart clenched at how grown his son suddenly seemed.

I hope he never needs to draw that blade.

"I want to tell you both something," Lucius began.

The children stopped eating and set their plates aside, turning to their father.

"I...I'm very proud of both of you and...well...I love you very much. I want you to remember that, now and always." Lucius felt Calliope squeeze his hand, and it gave him strength.

"We love you too, Baba," she said.

"I know." He turned to Phoebus. "I know."

The boy nodded.

"We will be together again, children," Adara reassured them all. She noticed her son's face, the pain there, of memory and monsters, and motioned to Lucius.

"Phoebus," Lucius said, putting his hand upon his son's cheek. "I know that last time I went to war, I was not myself after. I know I hurt you." Lucius' eyes began to water at the memory of it and he breathed deeply to calm himself, and stared into his son's eyes. "That will never happen again. I swear to you now."

"I believe you, Baba," the boy said, before hugging Lucius. "I believe you."

The four Metelli sat there together for a while longer, making every attempt to perceive the world as normal, to speak of their home, all they had built since arriving at the hillfort, and all that they planned to do.

Adara and Calliope spoke of the frescoes that would be adorning the walls of the hall and bathhouse when Lucius returned, and the new vegetable crops they would plant.

Phoebus talked of the training he would undertake with Lenya, who was one of the most skilled swordsmen among the Sarmatians.

Most of all, both Phoebus and Calliope discussed how they would help Adara as her pregnancy advanced, and how much fun it would be to have a younger brother or sister - or indeed, more twins! - to care for.

The family smiled, and it felt good. They felt blessed indeed by the Gods. But when the sounds of ordered men and horses reached their ears, Lucius knew it was time to prepare to leave.

The children accompanied Lucius and Adara upstairs to watch her arm him for war, a solemn ceremony of leather and iron, of whispered prayers and wishes to the Gods.

Soon, Lucius stood before them in his full armour - the pteruges surrounding his arms and waist, the ornate greaves over his boots and the black cuirass with the ancient dragon upon it.

"Anguis," Phoebus said, and his father smiled and nodded.

"Yes," Lucius said. "It is a part of each of you as well."

He felt different with the armour on, the crested helmet high atop his head, the pugio tucked at his waist, and the golden-hilted sword jutting from between his shoulder blades. Dressed for war, he felt in direct opposition to the man of family he was at heart.

Lucius Metellus also knew he was a warrior, from a long line of warriors.

We are, all of us, children of Apollo... his mother had said when he left for war in Parthia, so many years ago. And now that he knew, he would put that to the ultimate test in the months ahead.

"Lucius?" Adara broke his revery. "Are you ready, my love?"

He looked at her. "Yes. I am." He knew he had to be, for if one was not ready when war came, it meant only death. "It's time."

Adara took his hand, and together, followed by the children, they went out of the room to find Dagon, Briana, Barta and others standing in the hall below, waiting.

They descended the stairs and Dagon, Barta and the others saluted their praefectus. All wore their armour now, Dagon his leather cuirass and scale armour, and Barta in full scale armour with the crossed daggers over his chest.

"The men are ready, Praefectus," Dagon said.

Beside him, Briana gripped his hand tightly. They had shed their own tears, and had now come to terms with the impending separation.

"I'll bring him back safely," Lucius told her, winking.

"Take care of yourselves, Lucius Metellus Anguis," she said.

"You too." He turned to the children one more time and knelt down.

Calliope threw herself into his arms and he held her fast in an attempt to brand the memory of her size and smell in his mind.

"I love you," he whispered.

"I love you too, Baba."

Phoebus approached his father more slowly than his sister, but as he came close, Lucius pulled him in and hugged him tightly.

"I love you, my boy. Be strong."

"I will, Baba."

Lucius stood and Barta and the others filed outside. He turned to Adara and gazed into her green eyes one more time.

"I'll be back." He kissed her and they lingered there, wanting to delay the inevitable one more time. As their lips parted, he spoke. "I love you, my soul."

"Psyche mou..." she said in Greek. "I love you with all of mine. Come back to me."

He kissed her again, and then turned to go out into the sunshine.

"Metellus! Metellus! Metellus!" the rows of Sarmatians roared from atop their horses, lined up the entire way from the hall to the northwest gate.

Lucius felt a chill run up his spine.

"Praefectus," Lenya saluted and handed him Xanthus' reins. "Slay some Caledonians for me," he said.

"I will," Lucius answered, accepting the reins and climbing up onto the enormous black stallion so that he was taller than everyone around him.

412

"Are we ready to ride, Princeps?" Lucius asked Dagon who was mounted beside him.

"One last thing, Praefectus," Dagon said, turning to Barta upon his own horse.

Barta reached down to accept the long staff from Lenya and then raised it to the sky.

The spear-tipped dragon vexillum unfurled, a brilliant splash of red in the winter light, and the men roared, their own draconaria raised down the line.

Lucius felt the pride of leading his men fill him up, and it was only when he looked down at his family again that he felt that pride at odds with the sadness at leaving.

But the look in their eyes, of pride, of their own strength, gave him courage.

"To Caledonia!" Lucius yelled and the men echoed the call to war.

With a last glance at his family, Lucius wheeled Xanthus and together with Dagon and Barta, rode down the avenue of Sarmatian warriors, each row falling in behind their leaders in perfect step, following the dragon, a glinting array of scaled armour and shining lance tips, followed by the pack-horses. They were watched by the many partners from the village who had grown close to several of the Sarmatian men who had lived among them for many months.

The crowd of villagers, led by Adara, the children, and Briana, moved to the northern rampart to watch the Dragon and his men ride out to join the Fosse Way for the journey north.

As they watched, Adara and Briana flanked the children, holding each other close, fighting their tears and fears with hope and courage and prayers to the Gods.

Lucius and Dagon rode in stony silence, all too aware of the people and place they were leaving behind. Once they had ridden eagerly to war, in the Spring of their lives, as young green recruits. But now, with loves and lives outside of the ranks of Rome's armies, they could not help but look back at what they stood to lose.

Lucius reined in his mount as the men carried on past him, and turned to stare at the lush green slopes of his fortress home to see his family watching him from the ramparts, a final look at his own private Ithaca.

413

Pain shot through his chest then, as if that part of his heart where happiness dwelled were being dug out by savage hands.

However, the glinting lights behind his wife and children told him their gods were with them.

Apollo...Venus... Let me come back to them. Keep them safe...

And I shall watch over you, Lucius Metellus Anguis.

Lucius turned to see Epona sitting atop her brilliant white stallion, smiling at him from the fire of her brilliant hair and flowing white robes.

It is time to ride, she said, her three white hounds charging ahead from her side to lead the way, and the three white birds soaring in the sky above them.

"We are with you, my lady," Lucius said as he kicked Xanthus and charged ahead, side-by-side with the goddess.

XIV

AVE ANGUIS!

'Hail the Dragon!'

Lucius Metellus Anguis and his Sarmatians travelled quickly once they joined the Fosse Way, the Roman road that cut northeast from Aquae Sulis to Lindum. The Roman road network that veined southern Britannia made travel easy and quick, and with every man mounted, and pack-horses used instead of wagons, they made good time.

Something seethed inside of every man, something to drive him on. It was as if furies lashed their backs and horses' rumps, encouraging them to the slaughter ahead. As they rode, they thought not of comfort as they bivouacked beside the lonely stretches of road that crossed the vast dales and moors, nor of food as they went through the rations of hard biscuits, dried meat and sour wine. Comfort and warmth were forgotten on the many miles of travel as if the journey were a dark catharsis to prepare them for war, and while Lucius and Dagon's thoughts often drifted back to their wives and the children, most of the men grew excited for battle, their anticipation palpable.

When they arrived in Lindum, the rough-looking force was greeted with consternation, many of the citizens in the vicus apprehensive of the foreign-looking troops tattooed with animals and riding horses of a size most had never seen.

However, the troops in the small garrison there, when they spotted the dragon vexillum of Lucius Metellus Anguis, surrounded by the draco standards of the Sarmatians, rushed out to see them, cheering for Lucius and his men.

The sounds of those cheering troops was a shock at first.

"It's like riding into Isca all over again," Dagon said, referring to their journey into Dumnonia when every trooper they met hailed Lucius.

They reined in before the fortress' walls where the centurion on duty approached and hailed Lucius.

"Ave, Praefectus!" the man said. He was an older member of the centurionate, an echo of his former self, close to retirement, and though he had a limp when he walked, he stood proud. "It's an honour to meet you, sir."

"Salve," Lucius raised his face mask and saluted in return. "We're riding north and need to stay one night and resupply. Can you accommodate my men and horses?"

"Sir, there is always room for the Dragon Praefectus and his men. You can have the run of the place. Most of the troops have been sent north to fight over the last couple of days. It's bare bones here, sir. Stay as long as you wish."

"We only need to stay one night, Centurion. I thank you."

The man saluted and turned to his men behind him. "Open the gates!"

The old doors of the fortress creaked open and Lucius and his men entered.

"Does everyone know who you are?" Dagon asked Lucius as they reined in beside the principia.

Lucius said nothing, dropped to the ground from Xanthus' high back.

"We're staying only one night!" he called out so all the men could hear him. "I want guards on the horses."

"I'll give the order," Dagon said.

Lucius turned, gave him a wink, and went inside.

They set out again early the next morning, along the broad curving road from Lindum to Danum, their file flanked by misty woodland and intermittent pasture lands.

It had to be said that it was nice to sleep on a bed, hard as it was, for one night, rather than upon the ground, but Lucius tried to push the memory of comfort from his mind. He expected little comfort or sleep in the months ahead, and no peace of mind. What worried him was that he did nor relish the fight now. He used to, or at least it did not bother him. However, his heart was not in it. He fought hard to stave the fears that beset him, the uncertainties. He knew he had to, at all costs, mask the weakness and worry that was constantly laying siege to his psyche.

If he was weak, his men would die. It was that simple.

Xanthus seemed to feel Lucius' anxiety and shifted uneasily beneath his rider.

Dagon and Barta looked at the horse and Lucius riding ahead of him. They were both keenly aware of the relationship between a man and his horse, and Lucius had not yet fully worked out his with Xanthus.

Lucius bent over and pat the beast's massive neck. "Sorry, boy. My thoughts are heavy. I won't let you down." He took a deep breath and thought of the peace of Ynis Wytrin, and at the same time, the stallion's gait evened out.

The truth was that Lucius and Xanthus had not yet bonded the way he had with Lunaris. That sort of thing took time. Trust had to be developed, nurtured, allowed to grow. Yes they had trained together, and much, but they had not been in battle yet, survived a battle together. Both man and horse would feel a degree of uncertainty until that happened.

Many days after they had left the hillfort in the south, the Herculean walls of Eburacum came into view. Lucius reined in the force on the side of the road to allow the mercantile and citizen traffic that flowed to and from the city to pass by.

Most gawked at the force of cavalry as they passed by, not wanting to linger long.

Some of the Sarmatians laughed at the frightened reactions they received, and their mood lightened as they thought of heading into the markets to buy supplies that were more palatable.

A guard was set up and Lucius, Dagon and Barta stood to the side.

Lucius set about cleaning up his mud-splattered armour and face, before brushing down Xanthus.

"The emperor is in residence, and I may be asked to attend him," he said, looking worried.

"Shall I come with you?" Dagon asked, cleaning his own armour. The Sarmatian looked across at the walls of Eburacum, their heights covered with a mist of smoke and steam in the cool spring air. "Something tells me I should."

Lucius squinted as he looked upon the large settlement. Something unnerved him about it. "Maybe you should. Barta," he turned. "You're in command while we're away. I'll find out if there is room in the fortress for us. If not, we'll camp out in the fields."

Once they had finished making themselves presentable for an imperial audience, Lucius and Dagon mounted up.

"Riders approaching!" Badru, the decurion said suddenly.

Lucius turned to see a group of riders flying a Praetorian banner. He did not recognize any of the men, but did note that none of them looked upon him or his force with the respect that most other troopers did. There was even an air of hostility about them.

"Praefectus, Lucius Metellus Anguis?" the leader said to Lucius as they met upon the road.

Lucius looked at the man. "That's correct. I received orders while in the South to proceed north with all haste. Is the emperor in residence?"

"The emperor and empress are in residence, yes."

"Good. I would like to meet with the emperor if he is able to -"

"The emperor is not available at this time, Praefectus," the man interrupted.

Lucius eyed him, but decided not to push things. There was a sudden tenseness that he did not like.

"I understand. Please advise the emperor or the Praetorian prefect that I am here should they wish to speak. My men and I will resupply before continuing north."

"Your orders are to proceed north at once without delay." The man produced a short rolled scroll with Caracalla's seal.

"Surely Caesar understands the need to resupply for the journey?" Lucius said evenly.

"Orders are orders, Praefectus," the man said, already turning his mount back toward the city. "You are not to stop in Eburacum, but carry on your way. Unless you have not the stomach for the fight."

At that, the Sarmatians bristled with anger and moved toward the Praetorians, but at a raised arm from Lucius they stopped immediately.

Lucius eyed the man and nodded. "We will do as commanded by Caesar. Please inform him we'll meet him at the front."

Without another word, the Praetorians kicked their horses and rode back to the city.

"What now?" Dagon asked.

"We ride for Trimontium."

"Why won't they let us resupply here?" Dagon asked.

"I don't know. Something's wrong." Lucius rubbed his face. "We can get everything we need at Coria before crossing the wall."

With that, they set off north again, leaving Eburacum behind them.

Their reception in Coria was the exact opposite of what had happened in Eburacum. As Lucius and his small force approached the town along the wall of Hadrianus, shouts and acclamations could be heard on the air as the soldiers on duty came out to greet them.

The name of 'Lucius Metellus Anguis' could be heard on the air, as well as shouts referring to the 'Dragon Praefectus' or simply 'the Dragons'.

It was uncomfortable, and Lucius felt as though he were being given an impromptu triumph, despite the fact that they had not yet fought.

Every accommodation was made for the force of cavalry and their leader.

"We'll spend one night," Lucius said to Dagon, Barta and the decurions. "The sun is falling. We'll reach Trimontium tomorrow evening."

"Several of the horses need their harnesses repaired," Badru said. "And we could use more grain rations."

"I wouldn't mind a visit to the baths myself," Dagon offered in a low voice.

"I don't know if there will be time for that," Lucius said. "Let's pay the urban praetor a visit and see how accommodating he is willing to be." Lucius turned to the decurion. "Badru, you're in charge while Dagon, Barta and myself go into town."

"Yes, Praefectus!" the Sarmatian saluted and went back to the waiting men.

With that, Lucius, Dagon and Barta rode toward the western gate of Coria where they left their horses, and were permitted entry by guards.

The streets were packed with pedestrian traffic headed for the forum - armies of slaves, women and children, and men in and out of uniform.

Lucius was uneasy as he walked through the parting crowd, mainly because he remembered what had happened to Adara the last time she had been in Coria at the empress' banquet. His wife had come close to being a victim of Marcus Claudius Picus, but her friend Perdita had not been so lucky. He decided he wanted to spend as little time there as possible.

Coria was a frontier town, there was no mistake. Everywhere one looked, there were veterans and armed civilians, off-duty

419

troopers carousing and gaming, and guards upon the town walls at regular intervals.

Lucius, Dagon and Barta were making their way toward the main administrative buildings when a loud series of screams cracked the air and the crowd ahead began to rush in every direction in a panic.

With little thought, Lucius drew the sword from his back and rushed forward against the oncoming pedestrians.

Children and women were screaming and there was an unmistakable sound of clashing steel. Then, a great barbaric battle cry above it all.

Lucius arrived to see the bodies of a soldier, a Roman woman and two children lying hacked upon the cobbled street. Above them, a bearded barbarian with blue tattoos over his body roared and challenged all about him. When Lucius stepped into view, his eyes taking in the massacre, the barbarian smiled at him.

"Anguis, wait!" Dagon yelled, rushing forward with Barta.

But Lucius was already facing the man, his guts twisted and angry at the sight of the slaughtered children at his feet and the cries of the people all around him.

The barbarian lunged, spittle flying from his gaping maw as his bloody blade swept quickly toward Lucius' head.

Lucius parried the swing, swept beneath the man's raised arms and slashed his side so that the barbarian cried out in even greater anger. As he turned to attack once more, Lucius' blade was already embedded in the man's throat, a grisly gurgling sound emanating from his mouth. He struggled momentarily before Lucius kicked him down and pinned him with his blade to the road to finish the job.

The crowd was silent then, except for the crying of children who had been witness to the atrocity, and the high-pitched wailing of the father and husband who wept bitterly over the bodies of his wife and children.

Lucius stared at the man for a moment, horror-struck by the scene, his bloody blade hanging limply by his side.

"Anguis!" Dagon's voice broke in upon his thoughts. "You all right?"

Barta went over to the body of the attacker and kicked it. "He's dead."

"It's all finished!" Dagon called out to the gawping crowd. "Go back to your homes!"

420

"What is the meaning of this?"

Lucius turned to see the urban praetor and a few men coming out of the headquarters building and almost trip over the body of the attacker.

"What happened here?" he demanded. The urban praetor was a tall, older man, dressed in a clean toga and wrapped in a cloak. He turned to see Lucius, Dagon and Barta. "Who are you?"

"I'm Lucius Metellus Anguis, Praefectus of the III Ala Britannorum Sarmartiana."

There were whispers among the crowd, and even the guards accompanying the praetor.

"Praefectus?" The man shook his head. "Of course. Yes, Praefectus Metellus. I've heard of you. But how did this happen?"

"I was on my way to see you, Praetor, when I came upon this barbarian cutting away at the people you're supposed to be protecting."

The praetor stood tall, a vague look of insult upon his face. "This is horrible. But how did he get in here?" The praetor looked around him at his men, but none offered an answer.

"He was obviously cloaked and armed and walked right into the centre of town," Dagon said. "He might have been coming for you."

The man gulped and wiped his brow.

"What is he?" Barta asked, his deep voice crushing all other sounds about them.

Someone from the crowd yelled. "Looks like a Maeatae warrior!"

Lucius gazed in the direction of the Briton who had spoken up and then went to the body. The man's body was as taut as a bowstring and highly muscled. No doubt about it. He was a warrior."

"But why would they slaughter innocents in the street?" the praetor asked.

Lucius looked at the man, incredulous at the stupidity of the question. "We're at war again, Praetor. This will not be the last attack." He wiped his blade upon the barbarian's trousers and turned to the praetor again. "You need to set more guards out, and check everyone who goes in and out of the town. The great wall is not far off, and beyond that, the Maeatae and Caledonii could appear anywhere at any time."

"Of course. I'll see to it, Praefectus." He shook his head as if remembering his manners. "How can I help you?"

"We need some grain supplies and a place to repair our harness."

"Of course. You'll have everything you need, Praefectus. We can also billet your men inside the walls for the night."

"No need. We'll fortify ourselves outside and leave before dawn. Before anything else, you need to help that man!" Lucius pointed to the wailing man beside the bodies of his family.

"There would have been more deaths if not for the Dragon Praefectus!" someone else in the crowd yelled, their comment finding more and more backers.

Lucius ignored the chanting and cries of thanks. At that point, he only wanted to get away from the scene of blood and death. There would be plenty more in the days to come.

"Send your men into town to gather the supplies you require, Praefectus," the praetor said. "I'll see they get everything."

Lucius nodded and turned to Dagon and Barta. "Let's get the hell out of here!"

As the three of them marched back the way they had come, citizens reached out to touch Lucius as he passed. To him, the grabbing hands were more an annoyance that made him want to run from that place, but to everyone else, it meant much more.

Talk of the 'Dragon Praefectus' was upon everyone's lips that night in Coria, and not just the troops. Later that evening, torches appeared outside the Sarmatian camp.

"Praefectus," said one of the troopers as he saluted Lucius who spoke with Dagon and Barta about their route the next day.

"Yes?" Lucius said, looking up from the well-used map he had been so familiar with on the first campaign.

"The praetor's men are here. He invites you to join him at the administration building so that he can give you what information he has on the situation."

Dagon looked across at Lucius. "Trap?"

"I don't think so. Not here. He might have something useful to say."

"I can watch things here, but bring Barta with you."

Lucius looked up at his massive bodyguard. "Shall we?"

"Only if I can remain with you at all times, Praefectus."

Shortly afterward, Lucius and Barta were following the praetor's men across the cold field toward the city gates. The sky was free of cloud for once and above, the stars began to appear, growing brighter and brighter as the darkness deepened.

Lucius' eyes scanned the roadside. If there had been an attack in the town during the day, the likelihood of an assault during the night was much higher.

They did not leave their horses outside the gate this time, but rode through and down the main thoroughfare to the administrative buildings. Guards took their horses' reins there and Lucius and Barta were ushered inside.

"He stays with me," Lucius said, as one of the guards began to protest Barta's entrance into the building from the courtyard.

The man looked up at Barta's one-eyed, bearded face and nodded slowly.

The praetor was alone in his tablinum, poring over wax tablets with lists and dispatches from the wall - calls for more supplies of grain from the huge stores in Coria, requests for word of recalled units and their progress to the front. He looked up from his work and smiled when Lucius and Barta stood before him.

"Ah, Praefectus Metellus. Thank you for coming. I know you probably prefer to be resting for your journey tomorrow, but I wanted to make sure we had a chance to talk before you move on. Please, sit." He motioned to the two backed chairs before the table and then proceeded to pour three cups of wine.

Lucius was pleased to see he did not question Barta's presence.

"To the Gods," the praetor said, spilling a little upon the floor.

Lucius and Barta did likewise and drank after the praetor.

Lucius observed the praetor more closely now. He was older than himself, greying, but fit for his age. Lucius thought that he must once have been a good fighter, but had opted for a life of administration when campaigning had become too much for him. From the look of his tablinum, he was organized and astute, but perhaps overwhelmed judging from the number of dispatches and unfinished replies scattered about the table before him. He was obviously up late trying to finish work.

"I thought this was all finished...the war, that is," he said, looking over all the work before him.

"I'm sorry, Praetor, but I don't know your name," Lucius said politely. There was nothing more unnerving than speaking to a title and not a person.

"Forgive me, Praefectus. Quite right. I know yours, of course. Who doesn't? I'm Cornelius Cinna. I haven't been in this position long, but it certainly has been a dire introduction."

"We have the Caledonii and the Maeatae to thank for that."

"Yes. Traitorous barbarians." His eyes glanced quickly at Barta, but he looked away.

"You can trust Barta, Praetor. He is my friend and bodyguard and has been with me for many years."

"It is good."

"What is?"

"That you have him near."

"Really? Many find his presence unnecessary."

"On the contrary, Praefectus. Around here, he is absolutely necessary. There are things going on which I don't quite understand...between you and me." There was fear and worry in the man's eyes.

"This conversation will remain private, Praetor. Do not worry. I appreciate any information you can give me going into this campaign. All I know is that the Caledonii and Maeatae have formed an alliance and rebelled. I've been ordered to join the legions and quell the rebellion."

"This is much more than simple rebellion, Praefectus," the praetor almost whispered. "The attack today. It was not the first such attack, though it was the bloodiest. These assassins appear like wraiths everywhere, but how do they get across the Wall? It's supposed to be fully manned right now. Praetorians keep knocking upon my door too-" He stopped himself then, and Lucius could see he felt he overstepped.

"I've had my own run-ins with Praetorians, Cornelius. Speak freely. I am on good terms with the Praetorian Prefect."

The man actually sighed. "Funny that you should mention Papinianus! He passed through here just yesterday with a small guard. The Praetorian prefect himself! Why, when the emperor and empress are in Eburacum?"

"That is odd," Lucius acknowledged. "He doesn't usually fight at the front. Was Caesar Caracalla with him?"

"No. But Caesar passed this way not long before with some other Praetorians."

"Where were they headed?" Lucius asked. He could guess who the other Praetorians were. The thought made him think briefly of Alerio and his face darkened.

The praetor noticed this and nodded. "If I may... Caesar is, well, not an easy man." He cleared his throat. "But he was on his way to Horea Classis. Is that where you are headed?"

"Not that I know of. We're headed for Trimontium tomorrow."

"I think you are earlier than expected." The praetor held up a small piece of parchment. "This arrived today shortly after the incident. It has Caesar's seal upon it and requests for word to be sent when you arrive in Coria on your way north."

"That's odd."

"You must travel quickly, Praefectus. The letter - which I doubt is in Caesar's words - says to expect you days from now."

"I have the privilege of commanding the best cavalry in the empire," Lucius said. "We can travel the length of Britannia at speed in only a few days."

"I can see that." He put down the paper. "I can also see the high regard in which all the troops hold you, and how the people look up to you." He looked down at his hands on the table, then back at Lucius. "I want to help you."

Lucius thought about it for a moment, wondering how much he could trust this man. He looked to Barta and the big Sarmatian nodded slightly. Even with one eye, Barta was a good judge of character.

"Would you mind answering the letter in four days rather than now, to let them know I've arrived in Coria?"

"Of course. With all of the Maeatae attacks in the town, I've been quite tied up."

Lucius inclined his head. They had an understanding. "I appreciate your help."

"There is one more thing, Praefectus."

"Yes?"

"The Wolf."

"Yes?" Lucius felt a strange sensation then, and for some reason, the Morrigan's face came to mind.

"The leader of the Maeatae. They call him 'The Wolf'."

"What of him?"

"Rumour is that he was once a man of the legions, or even in the Praetorians. They say his brutality and skill far surpass those of

Argentocoxus, or that of the Boar of the Selgovae, whom you defeated previously."

"Sounds like they say a lot of things." Lucius tried to sound unphased.

"They also say that he is a dark god of some sort. His hatred of Rome knows no bounds and all who face him have been sent back in bloody pieces."

"Then I suppose we'll meet him in battle in the near future," Lucius said.

The praetor was silent, his eyes fixed on the flame of the lamp upon the table. "Praefectus," he said, still staring at the flames. "Do you think the Gods have abandoned Rome in this fight?"

The man's question was not what was terrifying, or what sent a chill down Lucius and Barta's spines. What unnerved them was the sincerity, the belief in the man's voice.

"Praetor?" Lucius said, waiting until the man looked at him directly. "Not while we're in the fight."

The man said nothing, but gazed from Lucius to Barta and back.

"It seems we're about to go on a wolf hunt."

On the way back to the camp from the town, Lucius could not help but think of his daughter's dreams.

Calliope had dreamed of Lucius fighting a great wolf, and now it seemed that it was only a matter of time before that came to pass.

With their provisions replenished from the grain stores of Coria, and their tack and harness repaired, Lucius and his men set off for the Wall before the first hour of daylight.

He had briefed Dagon on what the praetor had said the previous night, and thought more about it as they rode toward the Wall. Lucius was suspicious of Caracalla and the letter asking the praetor to notify him of Lucius' arrival in Coria. Something was not right, but he comforted himself with the fact that he was ahead of rumour and expectation.

Dagon shared his concerns, and wondered what exactly they were headed into. Was it a war to quell a rebellion, or was it something else?

Only the Gods knew, it seemed, and of them, Lucius had seen very little on the road north.

Toward the second hour, the force of Sarmatians arrived at the fort of Cilurnum. With the dragon vexillum flying high above Lucius as they approached, a cornu sounded from the ramparts and several men of the garrison appeared.

"Open the gates!" the centurion on duty yelled, and the great wooden gates creaked open to reveal the interior of the fort and the road running directly through it to the other side.

Lucius led the way, flanked by Dagon, with Barta flying the banner behind them. The horsemen followed, two by two, with the pack-horses riding in their midst, lowering their kontos lances as they passed beneath the first gate.

The garrison looked upon the strange cavalry force as they passed, and where they might have taunted other foreign cavalry ala in the same situation, they looked upon the Sarmatians with a respect that was owed to the role they had played in the previous campaigns with the Caledonii. Now, each man breathed a silent sigh of relief knowing these warriors were now in the fight, especially as they were led by the Dragon himself.

"Ave, Lucius Metellus Anguis!" the centurion roared within the fort, saluting Lucius.

"Ave, men of Rome!" Lucius returned.

The centurion approached. "Glad you're here now, Praefectus, to teach these traitorous bastards a lesson they won't forget!"

The garrison cheered, and Lucius could feel the anticipation in his men behind him, in the grunts of approval they uttered, in the stomping of their horses' hooves upon the road.

"We'll do our best, Centurion!" Lucius returned "May we pass through? We're headed for Trimontium."

The centurion nodded and turned to his men on the walls above. "What do you say, lads? Shall we let the Dragon and his men pass?"

"Metellus! Metellus! Metellus!" the legionaries roared, at which the far gate was unbarred by several men and the heavy, studded doors facing the war zone opened to reveal the vast rolling plains, stripped of trees, and the road leading north.

"My thanks, Centurion!" Lucius said loudly above the tumult.

Dagon leaned close to Lucius. "If there was any doubt about your whereabouts before, there certainly isn't now."

Lucius nodded gravely, waving casually back at the men upon the wall.

The centurion saluted. "Gods go with you, sir," he muttered.

It had been a long time since Lucius had been to Trimontium. Much had happened since then. Clouds were gathering in the West as they rode along the undulating road, and in the distance, native scouts could be seen for fleeting moments.

They were being watched.

"Don't engage them," Lucius ordered. "Let them think we don't see them."

They rode on, unfriendly eyes following them along the way, and it was only when three white birds dove in the windswept sky above them that Lucius relaxed a little.

Epona, stay with us.

Before long, the three peaks of Trimontium came into view.

Lucius raised his hand to stop for a moment as he looked ahead to the high hills, and the fortress in the mountain's shadow. A torrent of memories came back to him - his first meetings with Coilus of the Votadini, and his son Afallach. The Praetorian assassin who had come for the Boar of the Selgovae in the depths of the fortress, Lucius' own wailing voice from the top of the mountain overlooking the plain.

So much happened here...

Most of all, he remembered his conversations with his defeated enemy, the Boar, the bond they shared, and how much Lucius felt he owed to the Selgovan warrior, now long dead, having been slain by Afallach upon the very road he now followed into the fortress.

From a distance, the fortress of Trimontium appeared busy - smoke hurled itself into the sky from the fires and forges within, and the silhouettes of soldiers upon the walls moved back and forth on alert watch.

If Coria had been targeted occasionally by enemy warriors in disguise, then Trimontium was ripe for attack, sitting as it was in the middle of the damp, deep green plain below the hills.

The turf and timber walls loomed larger as they approached, and Lucius noticed that the three ditches had been dug out anew with fresh stakes protruding from their steep slopes. He also noticed that the vicus and east and west annexes of the fortress appeared to be uninhabited. No smoke rose from those quarters.

"Only the garrison," Dagon said, noting the same thing.

"Seems that way," Lucius replied. "No one is staying here long this time. Trimontium is just a stopping point on the way to the front and Horea Classis."

"The vultures are probably hawking their wares up there then," Dagon shifted in his saddle and pushed back his cloak to free his weapons as they approached. "You see him above the gate?" he asked, noting the lone Praetorian trooper standing among the legionaries atop the gate house.

"I do."

A cornu sounded and orders were shouted. The gates swung open like titans roused from a long slumber. It was oddly quiet as they approached the first ditch, the garrison's eyes studying the new arrivals closely in the cold grey light, but as Lucius, Dagon and Barta led the way beneath the gate and onto the Via Decumana the call rose up from a lone voice among the men.

"The Dragon has returned to the fight!" the man called. "The Gods are with us!"

"Metellus! Metellus! Metellus!" hundreds of men chanted all at once.

Lucius felt a shiver run down his spine as the sound crashed over their heads like a great wave in the sea.

He saluted men as he reined in before the praetorium where several Praetorians stood guard. *Is Caracalla here?* he wondered. "Dagon, see that the horses are stabled and the men given space in the barracks. Hopefully they're in good repair still. The men need a decent night's sleep."

"I'll see to it, Praefectus," Dagon said, saluting and leading the way to the stables in the northern quarter of the fortress.

"Praefectus Metellus?" one of the Praetorians said, approaching and saluting.

Lucius saluted back out of respect, but his suspicions were growing. "Yes. Is Caesar here?" he asked.

Troopers chanting his name and smiling were milling about them from either end of the Decumana.

"Ave, Praefectus!" some called.

"Good to have the Dragon among us!" said others.

The Praetorian looked around before responding to Lucius, a slight smile on his face.

"No, sir. He is not. But your presence is required immediately."

"By whom, may I ask?"

The man said nothing this time, but turned and went into the praetorium that had been Lucius' home at the outset of the previous campaign. He led Lucius through the courtyard toward the tablinum where two more guards stood to either side of the doorway. The men stood still as Lucius passed and entered the room.

The tablinum was dark after the light of the open road, lit only by two crackling braziers. Behind the table, a man in ornate armour sat hunched over dispatches, a cup of steaming hot wine within reach.

"Sir," the trooper leading Lucius said. "Praefectus Metellus is here."

The man set down his stylus and looked up.

It was Papinianus, prefect of the Praetorian Guard.

Lucius had to try very hard indeed not to gasp when he saw Papinianus, for he looked very different from when he had seen him last.

The Praetorian prefect, one of the most powerful men in the empire, looked ten years older than his actual age, with a warren of worry lines about his eyes and forehead, and the little bit of hair he did possess having gone completely white around the edge of his bald head. His eyes were darker, sunken, as if he were constantly rubbing them or found sleep as elusive as peace of mind.

Lucius thought that the burden of guaranteeing the emperor's safety at all times was finally too much for his shoulders, and he felt a great pity then for Papinianus.

"Prefect!" Lucius saluted sharply.

"Praefectus Metellus," Papinianus stood and came around the table to greet Lucius, his hand extended. He actually smiled as though he were relieved to see Lucius. "It is good to see you." He turned to the guards behind them. "You may leave us."

The guards saluted and went out, closing the door behind them, leaving the two of them completely alone.

"Sir, I didn't expect you to be here," Lucius said. "Is the emperor to follow?"

Papinianus released Lucius' hand, which he had still been gripping firmly, and went back around the table to pour a cup of hot wine for the younger man. He handed it to Lucius and motioned for him to sit in the backless chair opposite.

Lucius realized that he had always liked Papinianus, a far cry from his opinion of his bloody predecessor, Gaius Fulvius Plautianus. He was not power-hungry, and he was respectful to those who ranked lower than himself. Learning had always been foremost among his pursuits, rather than the abuse of the great power he did possess. Though, to look upon him then, one would think that he had indeed become powerless.

"The emperor is unable to travel at all at this point. His end is near."

Lucius felt the air go out of his lungs as if he had been punched, and there was a ringing in his ears as he stared across the table.

Papinianus' eyes glossed as he said the words, the veil of power drawn aside for a brief moment before he sighed loudly.

Lucius shook his head and set his cup upon the table for fear of dropping it. "Is he so ill?"

"You know as well as I do, Metellus, that our beloved emperor has been unwell for some time."

"But he always seemed to recover, to find strength when needed. Surely this time..."

Papinianus shook his head. "It seems that this time, the stars do not lie. It will be soon."

Lucius wanted to ask what would happen if the emperor did die, but he knew the answer already, and he could see that Papinianus knew the answer too, and that he did not like it.

"I was told that Caesar Caracalla has gone north to Horea Classis."

Papinianus nodded slowly. "Yes. He is leading the campaign to quell this rebellion now, while Geta administers the empire from Eburacum. The two of them are to succeed their father."

Lucius was surprised to hear the prefect speak so plainly to him. Surely, he was not a close confidant of Papinianus, but, the man was clearly in earnest. He eyed Lucius uncomfortably then, as if some internal debate were raging inside his head. He suddenly rubbed his eyes and took another sip of the hot wine.

"Are you unwell, sir?" Lucius asked.

"The burdens of this position are great, Metellus, as I'm sure you suspect. And planning for a possible succession is...well..." his voice drifted off.

"Is there anything I can do to help, sir?"

Papinianus smiled. "You can quell this rebellion."

"That is why my men and I are here." *And why I was forced to leave my family behind.*

Papinianus almost read his thoughts. "I'm sure it was extremely difficult to leave your family and new home in the South, Metellus. Being away from home is...not easy."

431

"No. It is not." Lucius' voice sounded more bitter than he had intended.

"If you can stomp out this resistance among the tribes, then all manner of things become possible, Metellus."

"I'm not sure I follow you, sir. Surely Caesar will be the one who quells the rebellion."

Another sigh, and a frown upon the prefect's face. "We both know you were right previously. We should not have trusted Argentocoxus. He should have died before."

Lucius nodded, but said nothing.

"Now, we are back upon the bloody field with new orders."

"What are the orders, exactly?"

With a sadness in his tired voice, Papinianus recited the emperor's words verbatim. "Let no one escape sheer destruction. No one our hands, not even the babe in the womb of the mother if it be male. Let it not escape sheer destruction! I want them all slaughtered!" He leaned back and looked up at Lucius. "Those were the words of our emperor."

Lucius felt a darkness descend upon the room. It was obvious neither of them liked the orders, but both were all too aware that to gainsay them would be treason.

"Genocide?"

"Yes," he said quickly, his disappointment palpable. "You are right to feel shocked by this."

"I've been told of a new enemy," Lucius said. "They call him 'The Wolf'. He is leading the Maeatae contingent."

"Yes. I've had reports of him too. He's already massacred several detachments of the legions. You defeated Argentocoxus before, but this man - this animal! - he is the one you must defeat."

"But surely Caesar Caracalla -"

"*You* must be the one, Metellus." Papinianus' eyes blazed with more life than Lucius had previously seen, and there was an anger there that was not native to the person before him. The prefect breathed deeply and then spoke again. "It is true, that Caesar requires a victory, especially if he is to succeed his father. That is how it has always been. Military victories secure the loyalty of the legions. As does coin."

"I have always understood it to be thus," Lucius said, his mind trying to work out the convoluted way in which the prefect spoke.

Papinianus shuffled a few papers and tablets upon the table, ordering them as if he were preparing to leave. As he did so, he spoke again. "I heard the men hail you as you rode into the fortress. And I have word that the same happened in Coria."

Lucius looked surprised.

"Do not worry, Metellus. I have my own eyes and ears throughout the empire, and they are friendly toward you. How else do you think I knew you would arrive in Trimontium today?"

"You did not stop here on the way to Horea Classis?"

"I'm not going to Horea Classis. My place is with the emperor. I only came here to speak with you."

The crackle of the braziers seemed louder in Lucius' ears then as he stared across the table and his eyes met Papinianus'.

"The men of the legions love you, Metellus. They always have. Equally important, the people seem to have an affinity for you as well. Many more would have died in Coria had you not rushed in."

"It was my duty, sir. That is all."

Papinianus laughed, but not maliciously. "It was more than that. You possess qualities that many men lack, including Caesar Caracalla." He stopped himself there.

Lucius saw the tension in Papinianus' face, the working of his jaw, the clenching of his fists around the wax tablets he picked up. The praetorian prefect obviously did not find himself in accord with Caracalla. Lucius pitied him for it.

"Sir," Lucius began. "The praetor at Coria said that Caesar asked that he be notified when I arrived there. Did the letter come from you?"

"No. It did not." They stared at each other.

"Is there anything I need to know going into this fight?"

"Only that you should win. At all costs. Then, much is possible, Metellus."

The words left Lucius' head spinning, his blood cold. He wondered what was going on. *What is Papinianus reluctant to say?*

"We will see each other again soon." Papinianus stood, drained his cup and extended his hand to Lucius who took it. "In the meantime, keep me apprised of your movements and needs, and I will ensure they are met. More men, supplies, horses, anything. When you have slain the 'Wolf', send word immediately."

"I will." Lucius walked with him to the door where they stopped. "Do you know where the rest or my men are stationed, sir? Are they still based at the fort of Bertha?"

"No. They are not. Caesar ordered them moved to Fendoch."

"Fendoch?"

"You know it?"

"Yes." Lucius felt the anger rising in his gut, a familiar rage that he had hoped not to feel again. "I lost many men there."

"Then let us pray you do not lose more." Papinianus put his hand upon Lucius' shoulder. "May the Gods guide you to victory, Metellus."

"Thank you, sir."

"I almost forgot!" Papinianus said, as he opened the door. "I've sent for reinforcements to help you. The Votadini will be arriving tomorrow. They will be joining you in the fight."

Lucius smiled. "That is good news, sir. Thank you."

Papinianus' expression turned to one of grim determination. "Ride to victory, Dragon." And with that he strode across the courtyard, followed by his guards.

Lucius watched the Praetorian prefect ride away to the South with his small guard of men from the top of the gate. So much had been said, and yet not said in their conversation that it left Lucius uneasy and confused.

He was in a contemplative mood, but he could not indulge it for all the activity around him, the troops hailing his name as he walked, the centurions and optios wanting a quick word or pressing him with questions about the tactics for the coming campaign. It seemed that Lucius' previous successes against the Caledonii had made him something of an expert in their eyes. The name of 'Metellus' continued to be chanted or whispered in every corner of the fortress.

Dagon eventually found Lucius in the stables brushing down Xanthus in his stall. It was the first quiet moment either of them had had since arriving.

"All is well?" Dagon asked as he looked around to make sure they were alone.

Barta approached from out of the shadows to stand with them.

"Papinianus was in the praetorium waiting for me."

"The Praetorian prefect?" Dagon was stunned. "What did he want?"

Lucius stopped brushing and leaned his forehead against Xanthus' massive rib cage. The sound of the massive heart beating inside the beast seemed to match his own - a mixture of anticipation and anxiety.

"Much that I can't discern exactly." Lucius straightened and looked at his two friends, the confused looks on their faces. "He told me I had to win this war at all cost."

"He came all this way just to say that?" Dagon asked.

"There was more..." Lucius shook his head and looked around. "We shouldn't speak here. Finish your rounds and then we'll talk in the praetorium."

Lucius took a fresh armful of hay and put it down for Xanthus before walking away.

"Stay with him," Dagon said to Barta. "Something's not right."

Thunder tore across the dark skies around Trimontium that night, a greater storm than any man there could remember experiencing in Britannia or Caledonia. Reports from the guards upon the walls came to Lucius and the commanding centurion of shadowy figures ranging in the fields around the fort, seen only by the flashes of lightning. There were also reports of dark winged creatures seen in the night sky that caused more than a few troopers to panic at their posts. The centurion grumbled that he would be hard-pressed to discipline the men the next day.

Many of the Sarmatians left the comfort of their barracks to calm the horses whose panicked cries could be heard along the fortress' streets.

"The Gods are angry, it seems," Dagon said as he, Lucius and Barta sat in the tablinum of the praetorium, thunder rolling continuously in the skies above.

Lucius was silent. He had just relayed to them all that Papinianus had said and they too had questions left unanswered.

"I think Caracalla is giving Papinianus trouble. Did he say anything else about it?" Dagon asked.

"No. He stopped himself from saying too much," Lucius said. "Papinianus is a good man, extremely loyal to the emperor."

"But not to Caracalla," Barta added.

Lucius looked at him. "It doesn't seem that way, no."

"And he stressed that *you* win the campaign?" Dagon asked again.

"Yes." Lucius thought about Papinianus again; the Praetorian prefect was in one of the most powerful positions in the empire, often feared. But Papinianus did not wield his power the way Plautianus had. In fact, Papinianus was the antithesis of the previous man.

"Lucius, the Praetorians are not to be trifled with," Dagon said, rubbing his beard and sipping his wine. "You yourself have told me how they murdered Caligula, and how, when you were young, they auctioned off the imperial throne to the highest bidder after the death of Commodus. They can make or break the empire. Can you trust Papinianus?"

"I think he was the one trying to figure out if he could trust me."

"For what?" Barta asked.

"That's what I'm not quite sure of. He is having trouble with Caracalla, that much seems to be clear. And he is worried about the succession."

"The emperor is that ill?" Dagon asked, leaning forward to rest his elbows on his knees.

"Yes. Apparently, the end is near."

"A great loss. Though Rome conquered my people, Severus has always seemed a just and capable ruler, at least compared with others."

"Yes," Lucius agreed. "But I think what worries Papinianus is the change that will come afterward. With Caracalla and Geta ruling together, who knows what will happen?"

All three were silent for a few moments, and as they each mulled over the future possibilities, Lucius remembered his conversation with Adara.

She had told him that he should make the future he wanted to better the world.

He knew she was right, and the word *philotimo* drifted into his mind again as it had so many times before. The idea of every action and decision being for the love of honour, for the betterment of the world around oneself, the world at large.

It was a humbling and sometimes terrifying thought, one that he did not voice in that moment.

"One thing is sure, Lucius," Dagon finally said. "We need to go carefully into this fight. It seems that Caracalla has deliberately stationed us at Fendoch, and that this 'Wolf' is a foe to be reckoned with."

"I too have heard many of the troopers in the garrison here speak of this 'Wolf' with fear," Barta said.

"And the men of the legions do not scare easily," Lucius added.

"At least the Votadini will be with us too," Dagon said. "Our men work well with them."

"That is a consolation, yes," Lucius said. "I just hope that Afallach is up to it." Lucius thought of the young Votadini prince who had become lord of his people after the violent death of his father, Coilus, in battle with the Caledonii in the previous campaign. It had been a bloody fight and Afallach had fallen with a badly injured leg. "I guess we'll see tomorrow when they arrive."

The Sarmatians were not to remain long in Trimontium. As daylight dawned on the fortress, the morning light glinting on the broad puddles dotting the muddy streets, the men immediately began packing provisions, sharpening weapons, and repairing armour and harness for the imminent fighting. They waited only for the Votadini.

By the sixth hour of daylight, a horn sounded from the top of the eastern gate. The Votadini had been spotted.

As had happened years before, Lucius, Dagon, Barta and several of their men rode out to meet them, except this time, when the red banner with the white horse upon it came into view, it was not greeted with apprehension, but rather with a chorus of cheers.

Lucius smiled to himself as he watched the Votadini horsemen approach, the bosses of their oval shields and spear points glinting in the midday light. He was pleased to see Afallach riding at the front, his red cloak and long hair blowing in the wind, trailing behind him as if he were charging into battle.

Lucius, Dagon and Barta reined in before Afallach, the dragon vexillum fluttering above their heads.

"The Stallion and the Dragon meet again!" Lucius said as their two banners flapped together in the breeze. "Hail, Lord Afallach of the Votadini!"

The Sarmatians roared their approval at that.

Afallach smiled and saluted. "And hail to Lucius Metellus Anguis and his dragons!" Afallach returned, his men cheering.

Lucius nudged Xanthus forward so that he was beside Afallach, and took his arm. "It is good to see you, my friend."

Afallach smiled sadly. He looked tired and pained, but the smile was genuine. "And you, Praefectus. Though a part of me wishes we

437

were dining together at Dunpendyrlaw, upon silver plates, rather than quelling another rebellion."

"We'll crush them this time," Lucius said, seeing that the memory of his father's violent death still lay heavy upon Afallach.

"I look forward to it."

"Come," Lucius said. "You can rest the night, and then, tomorrow, we ride to war."

They rode together through the gates and stopped before the doors of the praetorium.

Lucius swung down from Xanthus' back and turned to Afallach whose smaller horse was still quite large compared to others.

The lord of the Votadini tossed his spear and shield down to one of his men who appeared at his side, and then busied himself with unstrapping his left leg from a contraption attached to his saddle horns.

Lucius watched closely, remembering the terrible injury Afallach had endured in battle, wondered if he would be able to fight in such a state.

Afallach, supporting himself on the saddle horns, swung his right leg over and dropped to the ground beside Lucius, landing only on his good leg.

"The old injury," Afallach said. "It's an annoyance, nothing more. My man here," he nodded to the younger man who handed him back his spear and shield, "devised a way of keeping my leg close to the saddle girth."

"Ingenious," Lucius said, putting his hand upon Afallach's shoulder. "Come. There is wine and meat. Let us eat and you can tell me all that has happened since I last saw you."

"Wine...sounds good!" Afallach laughed and followed Lucius, limping stiffly upon his once-broken leg and using his spear to steady himself.

The Votadini horses were stabled, and the men prepared to set out the following morning. As the Sarmatians and Votadini remembered the bonds of friendship they had developed over the course of the previous campaign, Lucius, Dagon, Barta, Afallach and the decurions met in the tablinum.

The old map of the frontier was spread out before them as Lucius explained what he knew. When he pointed his finger at

Fendoch, where they were to be based, there were glances about the table as dark memories flooded back.

"That place is cursed, Praefectus," said Badru, the decurion, unable to hold the anger he felt.

"Why would Caesar base us there?" Vaclar added. "It's so exposed."

"The tribes are sticking to their highlands and it's going to be our job to flush them out. The orders are to kill everyone, men, women, and...children."

The men about the table were silent. The Votadini decurions stared at their lord who was silent upon the stool he occupied.

"It will be a tough fight. To go so far beyond the protection of the Gask Ridge. The bogs alone will be our enemy, let alone the Wolf's forces."

"These are our orders. Caesar commands from Horea Classis," Lucius said, forcing himself to keep the disdain from his voice.

"While Conn Venico of the Venicones pours honeyed nectar in his ear," Afallach added.

"No doubt." Lucius looked at Dagon, and together they watched Afallach focus on the map, his finger tracing a line inland from Fendoch, through the known glens, to an area in the mountains that had not yet been mapped.

"Fendoch has one advantage," Afallach said.

Everyone looked surprised.

"Whatever could that be?" Dagon said.

"It allows us to strike at the heart of the rebellion, to charge with fire and sword into the Wolf's own den."

"Tell me," Lucius said, leaning upon his fists. He could feel his heart quicken. "How do you know?"

"Because. I've been there."

An hour later, when Lucius, Dagon, Barta and Afallach sat alone over a last drink before turning in, Lucius turned to the Votadini lord.

Afallach, for all his resentment of Rome, had, it seemed, successfully filled his father's boots. The men respected him greatly, and despite his injury, he could ride and fight as well as any of them.

"Will you be able to wield the lance in battle?" Dagon asked, knowing full-well how much strength of leg was needed when manoeuvring a mount in battle.

"I've got used to it."

"What if you're knocked down?" Barta asked.

"I make sure that I'm not," he answered confidently.

"I'm glad to hear it," Lucius said. "But tell me... How did you come to know the location of the Wolf's den?"

Afallach set his cup down and smiled.

"I got my sister back."

Lucius looked at him, stunned. "I thought she was lost to the Selgovae, sold into slavery to...what was the tribe? The Ulstermen?"

"She was!" he said, leaning forward. "But Lucretia was always strong-willed. A fighter. I had always hoped I would find her, but wasn't sure the Gods would ever grant it. Anyway, there is a wine merchant who has been coming to Dunpendyrlaw since I was a child. He loved my father greatly. On one of his visits last year, he told me that he had seen Lucretia being unloaded in chains on the west coast. She recognized him, and he got close enough for her to whisper to him that she was being sold to Argentocoxus as a gift to the Wolf of the Maeatae."

"And that was enough information?" Dagon asked.

"Yes," Afallach said. "The merchant came to me and told me that he had seen Lucretia. He told me what she had said. I sent spies out to find the exact location of the Wolf's dwelling."

"But... I've heard this Wolf is exceptionally brutal," Lucius said. "Did he not harm her?"

Afallach sat taller and shook his head. "Argentocoxus, it seems, enjoyed parading a royal hostage in his hall beside his wife, and so he kept Lucretia there for some time, time that gave me a chance to gather my best men and ride out. She never made it to the Wolf."

"How did that happen?"

"We hit the riders who were delivering Lucretia to the Wolf on the road, just before they reached his den. Killed them all and returned home to Dunpendyrlaw."

The group was stunned.

"The Gods must love you to have brought you through this safely," Dagon said.

Lucius smiled, truly happy for his friend.

Afallach had, previously, been highly impatient and quick to action, but in this instance, he had stayed calm, thought strategically, and won the day...and his sister.

"Where is Lucretia now?" Lucius asked.

"She rules in Dunpendyrlaw while I'm away."

"Her captivity must have changed her, no?" Lucius asked.

Afallach was saddened at this, but nodded. "Yes. In some ways. She is harder and less joyful than she once was. But her strength and the fire in her heart burns fiercely still. I only wish my father had seen the day of her return, the cheers of his people at seeing their princess return to the hall of our fathers."

"It must have been quite a sight." Lucius raised a cup. "To your victory!"

They all raised cups and drank to Afallach.

"But tell us," Lucius continued. "Did you see the Wolf's den?"

"Once we slew the men carrying Lucretia, we did not linger long. The Wolf's men are everywhere. But we could see smoke down the mountainside hovering over a distant lake. The road led in that direction."

"How do you know it was his base?" Dagon asked, doubtful.

"The mist was thick upon the valley floor and lake, but I could spy what seemed like a large settlement within the veil. There are no settlements that large in those highlands. If there are, it is the home of a powerful warlord. And the Wolf is that."

"How many men does he have?" Lucius asked.

"Many thousands follow him."

"I heard he was perhaps once a man of the legions himself. Is this true?"

Afallach nodded. "It's possible. He seems to be able to anticipate Roman tactics from what I've heard. He knows how Romans work."

"Then we'll have to be unpredictable in our actions," Dagon said.

"There is one more thing," Afallach said, his features darkening. "They also say the Wolf is a child of the Morrigan herself. Her eyes are everywhere around him. She protects him."

The air in the room seemed to grow cold at the mention of that dread goddess.

Lucius was quiet as he stared blankly at the map, not wanting to let the others on to the fear he suddenly felt as he saw her face hovering before him, laughing at him.

"Lucius?" Dagon said, putting his hand upon his friend's shoulder.

Lucius looked up at Afallach. "Tell me. Where do you think the Wolf's den is?"

441

Afallach leaned forward and pointed at a spot in the middle of the mountains. "Here."

When grey dawn light lit upon the rain-soaked fields surrounding the fortress of Trimontium the following day, the three Sarmatian turmae, along with many more of the Votadini allies, thundered out of the fortress gates.

They rode hard to join their comrades who were already on the front lines, and before long they had crossed the rushing waters of the Bodotria, making their way for the defensive line of the Gask Ridge which they had fought so hard to win back for Rome many months before.

Lucius drove the men hard, his dark form constantly at the head of the massive column, towering over all the other riders as he sat upon Xanthus' back.

Even as the offerings still smouldered upon the altar in the centre of the praetorium's courtyard, the horsemen led by the Dragon were already of a mood for blood, for the place they had been assigned to held little memory for them other than just that - blood.

XV

FLUVII SANGUINORUM

'Rivers of Blood'

It was the screams that brought him out of his battle frenzy, the cries of the Caledonian women and children the enemy were now using as shields in the village before them. Their voices pierced ear drum and soul, so full of fear and pain, anguish and horror.

The attack had begun quickly, expertly, with a hail of arrows and spears from what had appeared to be empty hillsides sloping down to the river in the broad glen. The enemy sprouted from the rocks and gorse, from the grass itself. Several horses and cavalrymen went down in the deathly rain, and even more legionaries with razor-sharp barbs ripping out their throats, or tearing their legs from beneath them.

As the Roman forces turned to either side in the sudden confusion, shouted orders to form up amid the curses and cries of anguish, the enemy column turned to run, to try and disappear into the land as suddenly as they had been born from it.

But Lucius and the others rallied their men, the Sarmatians, the Votadini, and the men of the legions.

It was then that the world slowed, and enemy blood was shed upon the cold muddy earth and grass of the glen.

Lucius' lungs heaved as he pushed up his cavalry mask to gulp at the cold air. He caught sight of the cleaved and broken bodies of the five men he had just dispatched, the bodies crushed by Xanthus' massive hooves.

The screams reached his ears again and he shook his head as if to shed the haze that surrounded him. Red legionary cloaks were rushing among the squat stone dwellings of the village that the fighting had moved into. Gladii stabbed and cut and thrust at any Caledonian that moved.

Lucius watched in horror as a legionary struck a babe in its mother's arms, even as he was run through by an old grey-beard wielding an axe.

"Ahh!" Lucius yelled as he kicked Xanthus' sides and the great black beast exploded onto the scene.

"On the Praefectus!" Dagon yelled from somewhere behind as the Sarmatian turmae followed the dragon vexillum, the draconaria howling in the frozen wind as if a storm were coming to wipe out the village.

"Dunpendyrlaw!" came the Votadini war cry from the other side of the river as they charged into another part of the village.

The spearheads of the cavalry formed, with Lucius and Afallach at their heads, the legionaries of sixth legion turning from their blood work to allow them through to the other side to where the warriors had fled and formed up. One of them held a woman before them with a knife to her throat - one of his own people - supposing this would slow the Romans advancing on them.

A moment later, the man fell with a short javelin through the face, the woman he held screaming as she ran headlong into the oncoming legionaries.

"Ahhh!" Afallach roared as his javelin hit home. He cut left and right and wielded javelins in every direction, taking down four, five, six of the enemy before drawing his sword and slashing, all while strapped tightly to his saddle, bending his body and weaving away and under any blow that sought his death. "No!" he yelled at the legionaries who were now rushing the woman he had saved, but she fell dead beneath their frenzied and furious blades, trampled as the troops crashed into the Caledonian remnants beyond her broken body.

All was chaos, and blood. Those who pleaded with the Romans were hacked down as quickly as those who fought to the last and, in the end, every warrior and villager lay dead upon the very threshold of their village.

"Stop this now!" Lucius yelled as his enormous mount reached the legionaries, having finally made his way through the confines of the village behind them. "Halt!"

It was as if he had slapped every man there, even the centurions. He struggled to catch his breath then, to speak to the confused and blood-spattered faces that stared up at him.

"What are you doing slaying the villagers?" he asked the centurion who approached him from the tangle of Caledonian bodies.

"Orders, sir!" the centurion said. "Every Caledonian man, woman and child to be slain. Is that not correct?"

Lucius spat blood and turned his horse to see the rest of the cavalry approaching. Some of his men had enemy heads strapped to their saddle horns already, others the scalps, but he was relieved to see that they were from men, warriors, not women and children. He closed his eyes.

Gods give me strength in this fight...

He looked at the centurion. "You are correct," Lucius said. "But my orders are to win at all costs, and in winning this particular fight, it was not necessary to slay women and children. Do you understand?" he yelled.

"Yes, Praefectus!" Lucius' men replied, all of them staring down at the legionaries.

Lucius addressed the legionaries. "If you seek glory...if you wish to fight at my side...if you wish to achieve victories you can be proud of... You will follow my orders and strategies! Do you understand?"

"Yes, Praefectus!" the legionaries answered, ignoring the disgruntled looks of their centurions and the young tribune present who stepped forward.

"Praefectus," Gaius Fulvius Regulus said. "You overstep, sir."

Lucius looked down at the man. He too had been a young tribune, very young, and he could remember following orders at all costs. But sometimes the costs were too high, and he was all too aware of the price to be paid. He softened his voice, though it held no less confidence.

"There will be killing enough in the days to come, Tribune."

The man nodded, his chest heaving from the rush of battle, his eyes wide. "Yes, sir."

"Now, have your men go around and dispatch any enemy warriors who may yet be breathing."

The tribune nodded and went to speak with his centurions.

The ringing in Lucius' ears eased up and he could now hear the sound of the gurgling river that ran through the middle of the glen and the village. Its melody seemed unchanged by the sheets of blood that skirted across its surface. In the distance, falling from the top of the cliff overlooking the glen, was a waterfall that fed the river.

The spray from it misted down over the scene and the blood upon his and the men's armour turned to pale rivulets. The sound of the falls was a rushing whisper upon the wind and Lucius' eyes followed it to the top where he spied a group of Caledonii staring down at them, safely out of the way of Roman steel.

Dagon and Afallach reined in beside him and looked up to see a man in a chariot surrounded by several others.

"Argentocoxus," Lucius said.

"The coward," Dagon added. "Watching his men die from a safe distance."

There was the slither of a blade then and Lucius turned to see Afallach pointing it up at the Caledonian chieftain. "I'll have his head this time," the lord of the Votadini said.

Lucius spat and turned his mount as the distant enemies disappeared from their clifftop perch. He looked at the village behind them, the river, the glen stretching away to the East with the sun only now just breaking through the clouds.

It would have been a peaceful place, a place of beauty, but all he could see now was a place of blood and death, a place where the shades of women and children would be forever weeping in the long dark nights of winter.

He kneed Xanthus around the back of the houses where they crept like ivy up the slanted hillside, and dismounted. He dropped to the ground and almost fell, his legs wobbling beneath him, and with the cries of those women and children ringing once more in his ears, he turned and vomited against the stone wall of one of the dwellings. His eyes burned as he did so, his thoughts reaching out for goodness, for images of his own family.

I should have prevented this! he told himself, though he knew that the Caledonii had put their own people in harm's way. *If I am to lead, I must lead... Ahh!*

A white bird perched upon his shoulder then and cheeped softly for a moment. Lucius turned to see Epona standing beside Xanthus, her lithe hands running up and down his forehead as he bowed to her.

"My lady," he said.

"This slaughter is not your fault," she said sternly, her bright eyes reaching out from the orbit of her red hair.

"I could have prevented this," Lucius insisted.

The goddess had no words, only a look of sadness and pity. She knew all too well what was going through his mind, what he had been through mere months before in Dumnonia. It crept into his every thought and fear, challenged him at every turn. She stepped closer to Lucius and placed her hand upon his face.

Lucius closed his eyes, felt the warmth fill him in that cold place, grateful for the temporary recession of pain and torment. When he opened his eyes, Epona's face was close, but she made no move to come closer, nor would he ever dare.

"You must focus upon the task at hand," she said. "Fighting and staying alive."

"I know," Lucius said.

"Staying alive," she repeated, her eyes so intense he had to look away. Something about the way she spoke frightened him. "There is much more fighting to come."

He nodded.

Then Xanthus was standing over them both, nudging Lucius' head.

Epona smiled. "He has finally bonded with you. If any good has come of this horror, it is that. He will be your rock now."

Lucius reached up and stroked Xanthus' thick black neck and cheeks, and for a moment, he spied Epona's reflection in the large eyes.

Then, she was gone.

"You did well today, boy," Lucius said as he led Xanthus from the back of the building out into the open where the men were being formed up by their decurions and centurions.

"There you are," Dagon said. "You all right?"

"I just needed a minute," Lucius answered, looking around the scene of slaughter, at men eating dried bread or oatcakes with bloody hands. "Any survivors among the villagers?"

Dagon was quiet before speaking. He had seen the mangled bodies, the hacked limbs and blank faces of the villagers. "No. No one left alive."

"May the Gods save us from ourselves," Lucius muttered.

"It won't happen again," Dagon said. "I've heard the muttering among the men, the discontent with the original orders. They would follow the Dragon." He smiled.

"Well...that is something," Lucius said. "Let's get out of here." He looked around and gave the order. "Back to base!"

The turmae formed up in orderly rows, as did the centuries of the cohort. The dead and wounded were already upon the backs of horses and on a couple of carts taken from the wreck of the village, solemn among the ranks of marching troops.

As they turned and headed back to base, the smoke from the flaming thatch rooftops of the village spiralled into the sky above.

At the head of the column, Lucius, Dagon, Barta and Afallach kicked their mounts into a canter and led the way out of the glen, back to base at Fendoch.

The village where they had fought was not far from their base. In fact, every battle Lucius and his men had fought since returning to Caledonia did not require travelling a great distance, for the war was now taking place upon their front doorstep, in the myriad glens beneath snow-capped hills, and fens bordered by forest.

This was mostly due to Fendoch's exposed location, jutting out farther as it was from the rest of the Gask Ridge frontier forts, like a man extending his neck for the executioner's axe.

Since arriving, Lucius had instituted the strictest routines at the fort among the Sarmatians, Votadini, and the cohort of men from III Parthica Legion. He was grateful that the tribune and centurions from the latter agreed with him and yielded to his command, respecting the role he had played in the previous campaigns. It made the job much easier.

What was more difficult at Fendoch was maintaining a steady supply line. Whereas supplies could reach Bertha by the river that led from the Tava, the streams, burns, and rapids that led to Fendoch were not navigable, even for the smallest of barges. And even if they were, the Caledonii would have sprung from the earth to massacre them and interrupt the supply lines. The only way to maintain supply was to transport it with a heavily-armed escort of three turmae.

The camp was another matter entirely. When Brencis and the Sarmatians, along with the men from III Parthica were ordered to leave Bertha, the Dragon's Lair, and encamp at Fendoch, there were no permanent structures on the site.

The Sarmatians, under Brencis' command, had dug in deep with three rows of ditches and a high palisade of sharpened stakes made from entire pine trees that could have pierced an elephant's underbelly. These larger stakes were fronted by smaller ones, the sharpened tips of which stood solid, ready to run through any attacking force day or night.

However, with the constant rains, the stakes often became loose in the soggy ground, and so constant maintenance of the defences was required.

448

They had to be ready for anything.

That day, as Lucius and the men returned from yet another bloody battle, enemy heads and scalps hanging from the Sarmatian saddle horns, he observed the state of the defences again, ensuring that the ditches were still steep-sided enough, and the nettles and gorse filling them still menacing, covering the stakes planted at the bottom of each ditch.

As they approached, a horn sounded, followed by orders to open the tall, wooden gate where men stared down at them grimly, seeing the number of wounded upon the horses and carts.

"Hail, Metellus!" the guards saluted from the gate's roof, and the call was taken up around the entire fort.

Lucius saluted back as his name was chanted, but he did not smile. His thoughts were dark and panicked as he entered the confines of the fortress.

From atop Xanthus' back, Lucius looked out over the orderly rows of newly-built, timber barrack blocks, store houses, two granaries, the small principia and praetorium, and the valitudinarium, the field hospital which would now be overrun with wounded. The men had been grateful to stop sleeping beneath the thin leather of their campaign tents once the barracks had been built, for the highland air was chill and fell, and penetrated the bones of even the heartiest warrior.

Lucius' eyes sought out the principia at the centre of the fort. The mud squelched beneath the horses' hooves as the rest of the men made their slow progress toward the open stables where only sheets of leather covered the animals. Still, the fresh straw and wood shavings the Sarmatians provided for their horses lessened the effects of the cold earth and wind howling out of the mouth of the next glen.

Lucius reigned in before the timber principia, along with Dagon and Barta.

They were met by Brencis who saluted Lucius and Dagon, and spoke, his voice low. "How many did we lose?" he asked, noting the wounded being taken to the medical tents.

Lucius turned to him. "Too many. Dagon, do we have a count?"

"Not yet. Badru is looking into it. But the legionary cohort bore the brunt of it."

"I'll speak with Tribune Fulvius about the losses and see what he needs from Horea Classis to bring them back to full strength."

449

"We'll get no help from Horea Classis, Praefectus," Brencis said bitterly.

Lucius looked upon the younger Sarmatian noble, Dagon's cousin. Brencis used to be good-natured with a ready wit and a laugh that echoed around the room at meetings, but he had since lost his humour. From the time Caracalla had ordered them to the front at Fendoch, from the moment the Caledonii and Maeatae had rebelled once again, breaking the peace, he and the Sarmatian turmae he commanded had been hard-pressed, under constant attack, even as they were building up the defences of Fendoch.

When Lucius and Dagon appeared earlier than expected before the deadly defences of the fort, Brencis had almost wept with relief in the privacy of his own tent, where he had been living before the barracks were erected.

Dagon had spotted it immediately, and felt a pang of guilt for all that his cousin had been through while he was on furlough in the South and celebrating his marriage to Briana.

"I look forward to congratulating our new queen in person," Brencis had said when he embraced Dagon. "I wish I had been there."

Dagon knew the bitterness his cousin might have felt would not last, but he did ask Lucius that he and the men who had remained behind be given lighter duties for the time being to make up for the difficulties they had endured, and the furlough they had never taken.

Of course, Lucius agreed. He too felt somewhat guilty when he saw the state of things at Fendoch. He had arrived feeling well, all things considered, for as they had travelled north along the Gask Frontier from the Bodotria, every garrison, whether auxiliary or hardened legionary, had been inspired by his and the men's presence upon the field.

The Dragon and his men were hailed every step of the way, the fighting spirit of every man along that dread frontier raised by the appearance of the dragon vexillum, the roar of the draconaria, and the thunder of hooves pounding the muddy ground as the Sarmatian and Votadini cavalry rode to war once more.

Meanwhile, men on the front wondered what Caesar Caracalla was doing in Horea Classis with his Praetorian advisors and the leader of the Venicones, Conn Venico, whose men were distinctly missing from the fighting.

Lucius had been happy not to have to deal with the Venicones, his trust in them utterly destroyed after Conn Venico's man tried to kill him in his own quarters during the previous campaign. He put his hand on Brencis' shoulder.

"If we don't get help from Caracalla, we'll win this war ourselves. More the glory for us."

Brencis nodded, and a glimmer of his old smile appeared.

As the men cared for the horses, tended to their injured comrades, and built pyres for the dead upon the field outside the fortress, others hung the heads and scalps of their slain enemies upon the palisade as reminders to the enemy that only death awaited them.

Lucius, Dagon and Barta entered the principia and went directly to the table where a map of the region was laid out.

With a stylus and ink, Lucius made a mark of the location of the village they had just destroyed, one more added to the many actions they had already fought since arriving several weeks ago.

The orders that had been awaiting them were to reconnoitre the glens, flush out the enemy, and to wipe out every village they encountered.

Lucius leaned on the table, his fists hard upon the surface. They were all tired, and the sudden change in their lives from the peace of the South weighed heavily upon the three of them.

He poured water for them from a pitcher and each drank.

"How long can we keep doing this?" Afallach said as he entered.

Lucius looked up and shook his head. "I don't know. As long as it takes to find the Wolf."

Afallach limped over to the table, using a spear shaft to walk, and bent over the map.

"Are you still certain of the location of the Wolf's den?" Lucius asked.

Afallach shook his head. "It's in this region here," he pointed to an area far into the highlands. "But we'll never get there if we keep having to fight Argentocoxus and his Caledonii every step of the way."

Lucius agreed. "And the Maeatae are like ghosts."

"Sorry I'm late," Brencis said as he entered, followed by the tribune, Gaius Fulvius Regulus, and his first centurion, Rufus, Rutilius Corax. "A messenger just arrived from the fort at Strageath."

Lucius stood straight. "What's happened?"

451

"The Maeatae swept in, slew the small garrison, and then torched the signal station. All in a matter of minutes."

"Did the men at Strageath pursue them?"

"No. They were already gone. But a farmer reported seeing a huge warrior with a wolf tattooed upon his back and body."

They all looked at each other.

"The Wolf," Lucius said.

"Likely," Brencis said.

Afallach continued to stare at the map, searching his memory for clues that would lead them to the Wolf's den.

Lucius was quiet, then remembered the day's fight. He turned to Tribune Fulvius and Centurion Rutilius. "I'm sorry for the heavy losses today. Your men fought bravely."

"They're trained to," the young tribune answered calmly but with resignation. This was his first campaign.

Lucius could tell he was shaken, could still see him on the field of battle, his lungs pounding so hard he thought the man would drop from exhaustion.

"Are the biers nearly ready to receive the dead?"

"Almost, Praefectus," Rutilius answered, rubbing his thick red beard. "But I suggest we hold the rites in the morning. We're going to lose more men to injuries throughout the night."

The mood was heavy about the table, but they all knew the truth of what the centurion had just said.

"Very well," Lucius said. "If you all agree, we can hold the rites in the morning. Dismissed for now." He turned to Dagon and Barta. "You both stay."

The centurion went out first, followed by Brencis and Afallach, talking about the rites in the morning, but as the young tribune was about to leave, he turned back to Lucius.

"Praefectus, a question if I may?"

"Of course, Tribune."

"On the Parthian campaign, years ago…"

"My first campaign. Yes?"

"When you were in the Parthica legions… Was it different then? The enemy, I mean."

Lucius looked at the tribune. Even in the few weeks he had known him, he seemed to have aged, lost his fine veneer, though his confidence had been growing steadily.

"Everything was very different. The enemy, but also the politics. Times are changing," Lucius said.

The tribune sighed and nodded. "I'm beginning to see that." He looked up at Lucius and the two Sarmatians. "At least now that the Dragon is among us, the men's spirits have risen. You can count on my cohort, Praefectus."

"I appreciate that, Tribune."

Fulvius saluted, turned and went out into the night.

"You know, strictly-speaking, he's not your inferior in rank, is he?" Dagon asked.

"No. And I wouldn't pull rank on him anyway. I've been in his position. It's not easy. He's lucky to have Rutilius to help him. Good man."

"Yes."

The three of them sat down upon the rough wooden stools and Lucius poured them some of the wine he still had from a small amphora.

"I wonder how Briana and Adara are doing?" Dagon said aloud, staring into his cup.

Lucius smiled sadly. "I'm sure they're sitting around the hearth right now, wondering the same about us."

"War is not the same as it once was," Dagon said. "I used to revel in it - not the killing - but the cavalry charge itself, the heft of my kontos in my hands, the wind in my face and the howl of the draco above my head. It's as close as I'll ever come to feeling like a god."

Lucius looked at him abruptly, about to speak, but stopped himself. As they all changed, as the world around them changed, their individual perceptions of war had changed. Dagon was now married with a child on the way; that changed a man, even a king and warrior.

When Lucius did not speak, Dagon spoke again. "Do you want me to come on the rounds with you?"

"No. You sleep. I'll do it myself."

"I'll stay with you, Praefectus," Barta said. It was not a question.

Lucius nodded, grateful for Barta's constant presence.

When Dagon left the room for his own quarters in the praetorium, Lucius stood, put on his red cloak and helmet, and adjusted his sword on his back. He and Barta went out into the night. Torches burned everywhere and an eerie orange light gathered in the mist that pressed in upon the fort from the vast glen without its sharp walls.

Men were stationed on guard duty everywhere they went - Sarmatians, Votadini, and legionaries from III Parthica. Every unit shared the burden on the frontier, and not a man was dozing or distracted at his post, for if they did, it meant death.

The Caledonii and Maeatae had not attempted an attack since the fort had been completed, but they were out there. Lucius felt sure. He could feel their eyes upon the fort, hundreds of them. It was only a matter of time.

"Praefectus!" men saluted Lucius as he passed, and he too greeted each of them, reminding himself of their names, those he had known for years now, and the new ones from III Parthica. They were all respectful, all well-disciplined, and that was a comfort, for the lack of such on the Caledonian frontier would mean only disaster.

They reached the turf platform of the defences and made a slow, full circuit.

Lucius ensured he spoke with each man there, that he gave encouragement where needed, strong comfort a few other times to men who had lost friends that very day. Every time he left a group of men, they stood a little taller, their eyes brighter as they stared keenly into the darkness of that wild world beyond.

At the northwest corner of the defences, Lucius stopped and stared out into the dark.

Barta stood beside him, silent as ever.

As the moon appeared in a crack between the clouds rolling across the sky, the silhouette of the large oak tree upon the field came into view.

Lucius stared at it and the memories flooded back, of finding his disfigured and massacred men hanging from it, above the bodies of their slain horses. He felt a great sadness well up inside which gave way to anger, an anger that he had made use of in the fighting the last few weeks, and which he would use in the days and weeks to come.

"We should cut that tree down, shouldn't we?" he asked Barta.

Barta had been looking in the same direction, remembering the same images of horror and blood, the burning pyres of his countrymen. "No. Not yet, Praefectus. Let it be a reminder of the sort of men Argentocoxus and his allies are. It will harden the men's resolve. I've heard them talk about it."

"You have?" Lucius turned to him.

454

He nodded. "Once we have defeated them, then...let it burn."

Alone in his quarters, after having cleaned his armour himself, Lucius knelt before the flame of the lamp and the incense he had just lit. For a few minutes, he stared at the swirling smoke, breathing in the heady scent of the myrrh.

It still felt strange to kneel before a single flame rather than the effigies of his gods which were now housed in the temple he had built. He knew Adara and the children would maintain the offerings there in his absence, but he was bound to do so wherever he was, be it in a temple, or before a single flame, kneeling upon the muddy ground of his temporary timber home.

"Oh Gods... Epona...Venus...my lord, Apollo. Hear me... I feel the world closing in around me, suffocating me like a noose about the neck of a condemned man. I pray to you for the strength and skill to survive this fight, whenever and wherever it may be." Lucius closed his eyes and felt himself sway upon his knees. "Are you not with me?"

You are never alone, Metellussss... the words chilled Lucius. There was no comfort there.

When the laughter came, he opened his eyes and turned.

The Morrigan rushed at him, a shadow with fiery eyes and claws as strong as adamant gripping his throat, lifting him off the ground.

Lucius felt his body begin to freeze, slowly immobilizing him before he was thrown across the room to slam into the wall.

The Morrigan rushed again, and Lucius drew his sword.

You dare!!! She screamed in his mind, a deafening banshee cry as she raised both her hands, the words of power and death encrusting her lips.

A brilliant flash of light exploded between them in that moment, and both Lucius and the Morrigan tumbled backward, blinded. When they rose again, Far-Shooting Apollo stood between them, his body radiating sunlight and wrath.

At his sides, Venus and Epona each appeared then, and the three gods faced down the dark goddess that had nearly snuffed out Lucius' life.

Leave here! Apollo roared at her.

You cannot harm him! Venus said.

Epona helped Lucius to his feet and stood beside him, her arm through his.

The Morrigan laughed at the three gods standing before her, at Lucius standing there with Epona. *My son will pull out your entrails, Dragon. Your mortality will soon be at an end!*

He is no mere mortal, Epona hissed at her.

The Morrigan chuckled. *We shall see... When the fangs of wolves tear into his flesh...and he burns in his own dragon fire...we shall see...* she laughed again and then in a dark light that imploded upon itself, she was gone.

Lucius leaned against the wall and made to go onto one knee before the Gods who had just saved him. "Thank...you," he said, rubbing his neck.

Epona raised him up so that he was standing again, and held onto him.

Apollo turned, his dark face and starry eyes full of anger and worry. *You are not alone,* he said to Lucius.

"Is...is the Wolf the Morrigan's son?" Lucius asked.

Venus and Apollo looked to Epona. The goddess nodded. *He is.*

Lucius looked at the ground and felt extremely tired then. "Am I..." He thought he would ask the question that had been hounding him since Dumnonia, that had haunted his dreams and cast all that he thought he had known into doubt, about the world around him, about himself. But he decided against it, for in the utterance, he would not be the same. "Am I able to defeat this enemy?" he asked, staring into Apollo and Venus' eyes as he had never dared to before.

Yes, Apollo said, stepping forward to place his mighty hand upon Lucius' armoured chest. *You are able...*

There was a pounding on the door, and Barta shouting to Lucius. "Praefectus!"

The Gods looked at each other, then at Lucius, and disappeared just as the door burst open.

As it did, Lucius felt Epona's lips upon the crown of his head.

"Praefectus!" Barta said, his voice full of worry as he strode into the room.

Lucius knelt as before, in front of the burning lamp, the ashes of the incense only just smouldering as he swayed upon his knees in the exact place he had been.

Lucius looked up and Barta saw in his eyes a cloud of confusion.

"Anguis," Barta said, kneeling beside Lucius and lifting him up as if he were a thick pine trunk from the forests beyond. Barta carried

Lucius to his cot and set him down. Then, he brought the cup of water that Lucius had been drinking from and put it to his lips.

Lucius drank and the fog clouding his eyes seemed to clear, the memories still fresh and terrifying in his mind.

"Barta... Thank you, my friend."

"Are you unwell, Anguis?"

"Lucius shook his head. I'm fine. They were here," he said, too exhausted to explain.

"They? The...Gods, you mean?" Barta sat back, casting his eyes about the room.

Lucius nodded. "And the Morrigan...she was here." Lucius pointed at his neck, but Barta could not see anything.

"Rest now, Anguis. Dream of home and of your family..." He drew his short sword and laid it across his knees. "I will stay and watch over you."

In his tortured sleep, Lucius saw many things - the whirling and merging faces of the Gods, explosions of light and dark, forest trees reaching to the skies like black teeth, and dark waters as thick as honey, ready to swallow him. Then he saw him, the Wolf, huge and muscled, standing upon the surface of a lake, a sword in each of his hands.

He looked up slowly, smiling with fang-like teeth and pointed a blade at Lucius, and as he did so, the tattooed eyes upon his chest burned with yellow hatred, and his black hair bristled.

Baba! cried a voice in the darkness behind Lucius. *Baba, beware of wolves!*

Calliope! Lucius yelled, recognizing his daughter's voice. *Calliope, run home!*

Baba, no! You are surrounded!!!

Run, Calliope! Lucius yelled. *Run!!!*

The Wolf charged, and from the water all about him, dark warriors burst out of the surface to rush at Lucius, howling and baying for his blood.

Lucius drew his sword and charged, swallowed by a chorus of screams and the rush of black water...

No!!!

In the battle-filled weeks that followed, the Sarmatians and the Votadini hacked away at the small Caledonian and Maeataean forces that they had tracked deeper into the glens of the highlands in every direction to the West of Fendoch. It was the same with other auxiliary and legionary forces who attempted to push out from the Gask Ridge to hunt down an elusive enemy that refused to meet them in an open field of battle.

The Maeatae and the Caledonii chose rather to maintain their campaign of harassment, like a selfish lover who picks and prods, licks and withdraws, but never fully allows the other to engage. They seemed to be controlling everything that happened, and it frustrated the legionary legates to no end.

What was more frustrating was that every time a Roman force went out, they came back with their ranks much thinner than when they had left, if they came back at all.

The casualties were high, and all the while, men spoke in whispers of the Wolf's depravity and the horror of his actions.

Lucius had had enough, and he cursed his whirling mind, full of worry and doubt which he buried deep. He knew he was losing control of himself, and the feeling scared him. If not for Barta, who was constantly at his side, he would have been walking with his sword constantly drawn, slashing at shadows.

However, the anger Lucius felt at the enemy's cunning and cowardice also gave him focus, helped him to forget the haranguing thoughts that assaulted him every day. He sent scouts out, men who wore native clothing and had picked up some of the local Caledonian dialects, to track movements and speak with remote farmers who were not concerned with war on Rome, but rather simply surviving to see the end of the conflict raging all about them. Sometimes these men returned, sometimes not, but the information on enemy movements which they were able to ascertain was invaluable. They were getting nearer to their quarry, and everyday, turmae of Sarmatian and Votadini cavalry stood ready to ride out at a moment's notice.

After the grain shipment was intercepted yet another time, and only two of the men returned to base, Lucius reached his breaking point.

"Damn them!" he slammed his fist on the table. "I'll send them to Hades, every last one of them!"

The men about the table in the principia were quiet, each dealing with his own frustrations. They stared at the map, waiting for Lucius to speak, but the latter shook his head.

"I need air," Lucius said grabbing his cloak and going outside.

They all saluted as he left, and Dagon glanced at Barta that he should follow, for even in daylight, in the morning, danger lurked around the fortress.

Lucius strode down the via Principalis to the western wall of the fortress. He stopped there, hands gripping the rough wood of the palisade wall, to stare out at the glen, at the iron grey clouds that, once again, threatened rain.

The wind rushed around him, and the men on duty stared, wondering what he was thinking.

The desolation of that cold, inhospitable place spread out before him, the bogs and burns, the icy rippling river coming out of the mouth of the next glen, leading to yet another and another... Caledonia was itself a deadly labyrinth in which men were lost and slain, their blood feeding the veins of the rushing rivers, washed away by the rain.

How many of our men's ghosts roam those hills? Lucius wondered. Then he saw it, a fluttering some distance beyond the Roman palisade. Hovering patiently, about fifty feet or so above the ground, was a kestrel. Lucius focussed on the bird seeking its prey, felt himself calm in watching it.

The kestrel's wings flapped rapidly as it appeared to scan the ground, to wait, its wings channeling its impatience and yet its head and eyes calm and watchful. It was beautiful to watch.

Lucius could not spot what the kestrel observed, but knew it must be there.

Then, the bird dove with deadly speed to sink its talons into what appeared to be a mouse or some other rodent.

The engagement seemed small and insignificant, but Lucius took note of it, the surprise with which the kestrel had lain its attack. It had not swept in with lightning speed from the side like other birds, swooping down on the fleeing creature. It had waited patiently in the sky above, unseen, unheard, waiting for the right moment to strike, and then it had come down out of the heavens to deal death quickly, and decisively.

Then Lucius spotted another movement upon the broad glen, a man charging toward the fort on a small pony. He waved one hand as the animal strode deftly over the burns and around the tussocks of grass.

Immediately, Lucius heard the sound of drawn bowstrings on either side as the guards atop the wall snapped to and pointed their deadly barbs at the approaching rider.

"Hold," Lucius put his hand. "He's one of ours."

"Praefectus!" the man called, his voice mostly carried away on the wind.

Lucius waved to the man who rode faster, recognizing one of the scouts he had sent out. "Open the gates!" Lucius called down, the order repeated by the Sarmatians on guard duty. Lucius and Barta went down the stairs to meet the man who jumped off of his mount and fell to the ground, lungs heaving. "Get him some water!" Lucius ordered.

A bronze ladle of water was brought and the man gulped at it, choking in the process before he regained his composure and saluted Lucius.

"Praefectus, it's Argentocoxus!"

Lucius' fists clenched and he stepped closer to the man. "What about him, soldier? Tell me!" Lucius felt a flutter in his gut then, something akin to excitement, the flapping of that kestrel's wings.

"He and a large force of Caledonii have been spotted two glens over heading this way." He pointed toward the mouth of the next glen. "They just burned out more of the Gask signal stations."

"How quickly are they moving?" Lucius asked, taking the man by the shoulders.

The Sarmatians and Votadini surrounding them closed in, the better to hear.

"They're moving slowly enough, sir. They've gorged themselves. Argentocoxus rides in his chariot at the front like a peacock. But sir, I stayed ahead of them and scanned the terrain. If we ride now, we can engage them!"

Lucius' eyes widened. His mind turned quickly. "How did you see all of this without them spotting you? Argentocoxus' scouts always spread out ahead."

"I stuck to the forested ridges atop the hills. There are small paths looking down on the glens if you know where to go."

Lucius clapped the man on the shoulders. "You will show us." He turned to the gathered men all around him. "Two turmae and the men of III Parthica, are to hold the fortress. The rest of the cavalry rides out immediately!" Lucius called out as he strode back to the principia.

Men were already rushing to their mounts as Lucius threw open the door to see Dagon, Afallach and the others.

"We've got him!"

Lucius charged at the head, with the scout on a regular mount now, leading them into the next glen and then up to follow a steep path that led to the forested ridge of the glen after that. It was a hard ride, speed being essential but deadly on the precarious path. But the cavalry was skilled, the best in the empire, and they kept apace.

They climbed higher and higher until they looked down on the glen. Fog was settling in, but the terrain was still visible. During the breakneck ride, Lucius mulled a plan over, but was unsure if it would work until he saw the terrain. Now that they were there, it seemed it would work. From where they stood, hidden in the trees atop the ridge, the walls of the glen sloped away steeply, but smoothly, the grassy carpet broken only by the occasional boulder or gorse, leading to the muddy road that ran through the middle of the glen. To the right, far below, was a river that came out of another copse of trees to run parallel to the road where it curved away. On the other side of the glen, along the road's edge, was a forest of thick pine, usually a domain for deer, but there Lucius saw something else.

He thought quickly, gazing in the direction of the approaching enemy and then at the terrain laid out before him.

Dagon, Barta, Brencis, Afallach, and all the cavalry awaited his orders, their mounts champing at their bits.

Lucius nodded, and Dagon and Afallach approached.

"Dagon, take half of the Sarmatians and hide yourselves in the trees beside the river down to the right, and out of sight. Afallach, you and the Votadini need to get yourselves quickly and quietly into that forest on the other side of the glen, far beyond the road so that they won't spot you."

"How do we know when to strike?" Dagon asked, gazing warily down the slope to the road far below.

Lucius turned to Brencis. "You feel like flying today?"

Brencis smiled and nodded, his hand gripping his kontos easily.

"Good," Lucius said. "Brencis you and I, with the rest of the Sarmatians, will lead the charge from up here."

"Lucius," Dagon said, leaning in, his voice low. "That's madness. Our horses are the best, but they're not eagles."

461

"They will be today," Lucius answered. "Once Argentocoxus' army comes into the glen, I will charge down and hit them in the centre. Dagon, when you hear us, you come out and hit them in the front. Afallach, you then come out of the trees while Brencis flies down on the left and blocks off their escape if they should try to go back the way they came."

The men were silent for a moment, but there was not time to ponder it.

"We can do this!" Lucius said. "It all hangs on surprise. Muffle the draconaria for now, but when you change, let them howl!"

Their resolve hardened, Dagon, Afallach, and Brencis quickly gathered their men and went to take up position. Lucius turned to the scout and motioned for him to come closer.

"Yes, Praefectus?"

"Hide yourself down below with your bow and take out any advance scouts. Then, I want you to focus on one thing during the engagement."

"What's that, sir?"

"Get close to Argentocoxus, and kill him."

The man nodded grimly. "My pleasure, sir."

The Caledonii took longer than expected to arrive, and the wait for the Roman force hidden among the trees, beside the river, and looking down on the glen, seemed interminable. Fog began to form as the temperature dropped and the rainclouds thickened on the hillside.

Lucius worried that they would not be able to see enough to navigate the perilous charge down the hill, but they could still make out the ground ahead. Besides, the fog masked any trace of their hiding and muffled the occasional shifting of horse harness.

He felt Xanthus beneath him, calm and warm, great whiffs of breath emanating from his nostrils. Lucius leaned over and spoke to him. "We can do this, boy. I'm with you. We'll protect each other." He rubbed the stallion's neck and tried to calm his own racing heart. The task he had set his men was mad, he knew, but if it worked, Argentocoxus would be lying dead in the mud once and for all.

"Praefectus," the rider beside him whispered and pointed into the glen.

A lone rider on a small, native pony trotted along the road into the glen. As he neared the end of the glen, approaching the banks of the river, he pitched backward off of his saddle with a thump. His horse bolted, but two more arrows took the animal down before it could get far.

Lucius watched as another scout came into the glen, more slowly this one, cautious in the fog. As he approached the end, he stopped and saw his clansman upon the ground. He turned quickly to yell, but an arrow through his neck stoppered his mouth. Gasping, he kicked his horse but more arrows took down the animal, leaving the rider gasping upon the ground.

"Shoot him," Lucius whispered, hoping his man would not leave the scout gasping out in the open.

An arrow struck home, pinning the man's face to the earth and all was silent.

A few minutes later, the front of Argentocoxus' marching column appeared at the mouth of the glen.

First came a squad of about twelve warriors on highland ponies, each carrying an axe and a short spear. Their torsos were bare, painted with the blue whorls, crescents and Z-rods they favoured.

As Lucius watched, he wondered if these men in front acted as a sort of talisman, but he soon remembered that most of the Caledonii bore such markings when going into battle. Then came a group of about twenty warriors, taller than most, also bare-chested above their multi-coloured leggings. Each of these men carried a long-handled axe and a round shield. These were Argentocoxus' bodyguard, for after them, the chieftain rode in his war chariot, pulled by agile mountain ponies. He was flanked and followed by twenty more of his hulking guards.

Lucius stared down at the chieftain as he passed. The Caledonian was a survivor, that was sure, but Lucius hoped that this time the man would pay for his cowardice and treachery. Lucius gazed at the trees on the other side of the glen and wondered if Afallach could see Argentocoxus from where he was, what thoughts of vengeance were running though his mind.

That was the man who had killed Coilus of the Votadini, Afallach's father, and the latter would not readily forget it.

Lucius only hoped that Afallach would hold his men until he saw the signal.

Argentocoxus' bodyguard was followed by the bulk of his force, warriors in the tunics and plaid trousers favoured by the Caledonii. There were many of them, perhaps three hundred marching in threes, armed with round shields, short javelins, swords of varying lengths, and compact bows.

They were something of a rabble, Lucius thought, but they marched confidently into the glen, seemingly unaware that they were about to fall beneath the hooves of the cavalry waiting to pounce on them.

Lucius' men looked down the line at him, waiting, each savouring that moment of sweet terror and anticipation before the signal was given and they were ordered to charge headlong down that steep hillside. Their disciplined mounts stood still as the men gripped their long kontoi, loosed their longswords in their scabbards, and picked a path down the treacherous descent.

Finally, the last of Argentocoxus' army came into the glen, almost filling it like a great, armoured serpent, slithering along the banks of a Hyperborean stream.

Lucius felt the tension mount as he drew the gleaming sword from his back and raised it above his head.

Gods...give us victory this day...

Barta raised the dragon vexillum and down the line the draconaria of each turmae were raised.

Lucius' arm cut down and the earth suddenly began to shake.

Marching along, Argentocoxus was standing proudly beside his crouching charioteer on the basket weave platform of his prized chariot. He had just been thinking of how the Gods had favoured him with this alliance with the Maeatae, how easy it had been to pick away at the Romans. *This time,* he thought, *we can win and keep them out forever.*

He felt it, that victory and freedom from Rome were at hand. He was in the late autumn of his life now, and eager to leave a legacy for his family and people, but he had never felt so young as he did then. The feeling surrounded him like a comforting blanket of mist that shielded him through the days of his life.

However, when he heard his men begin to cry out, to shift and look quickly to the right and left, Argentocoxus felt his misty shield blown away in a sudden gale.

Then, the hills shook, and a great avalanche seemed to be rushing down from their forested heights.

A great howl and roar rent the air in every direction as the chieftain turned in his chariot to shout at his men.

"Romans!"

As the Sarmatians broke from the trees at the top of the glen, Lucius felt his stomach lurch as Xanthus plunged down the steep slope. He felt as though he had been launched from a high precipice into a void of fog, rain and sharp edges. In his peripheral vision, Lucius saw the line of his men begin to break as one, two, then three horses went down, unable to keep their footing on the steep and slippery hillside.

Far away to the right and to the left, the forces commanded by Brencis and Dagon emerged to crash into the Caledonii lines which were already attempting to form up to meet them in a chaotic mess.

The draconaria howled as the mad descent progressed, and many of the riders' mounts baulked at the pace and fast-approaching wall of enemy shields and spears.

Xanthus' powerful bulk, however, carried Lucius as if he pulled the sun's chariot across the heavens, never slowing or speeding, but maintaining the pace that Lucius had set for him.

Lucius' legs gripped tightly, and more than once he had to lower his left hand to grip the saddle horn, fearing that he would be thrown to his death before he even drew Caledonian blood. Then he saw it, a great boulder looming high before him. There was no room to manoeuvre around it, and Lucius prepared to jump from his saddle, hoping he would not be crushed by the cavalry to either side of him.

Xanthus slowed, and then jumped.

Lucius looked down on the tops of his men as they soared over the boulder and landed not fifty feet from the Caledonian line. It was all he could do not to yell to release his fear.

"Sarmatiana!" Lucius cried.

The call was met by another battle cry.

"Dunpendyrlaw!" the Votadini yelled as they burst from the forest to smash into the other side of the Caledonii.

Lucius slashed down as he slammed into a group of Caledonians at full speed, sending their bodies and weapons in every direction.

It was the same down the line as the Sarmatians who had survived the descent careened with the enemy shield wall.

In that moment, chaos reigned.

It was hard to know how many men one killed, how many slashes or cuts one endured, or that glanced off of armour and shield.

The screams of horses and of men were woven together over the battlefield, even as the Votadini and Sarmatians passed each other in the middle of the slaughter and then wheeled about separately on the other side.

As Lucius, Barta, and the riders turned about in the forest under a hail of Caledonian arrows and javelins, the battle raged furiously at the ends of the Caledonian column where Dagon and Brencis' turmae were pushing the Caledonii warriors inward upon their fellows, giving them less and less room.

Waves of Caledonii attempted to run uphill the way Lucius had come but they soon found themselves impaled on the points of Sarmatian kontoi as if they were a carrion feast for the crows that were now hovering in the sky above.

The enemy also attempted to flee into the woods, but their escape was cut off in most cases with only a few making it through the charging and turning cavalry.

Then, Lucius spotted Argentocoxus.

The chieftain's chariot sped along the Caledonian line as if he were trying to draw his warriors out of the Roman noose. His bodyguards slashed at horses and riders and a wall of sorts began to form between them and the roiling mass of fighting men and mounts where the road turned to a bloody, churning mass.

Lucius was about to ride for the chieftain when he spotted the white horse of the Votadini rushing toward him, Afallach crying out as he hacked his way toward his father's murderer.

The Votadini lord, still in his saddle, reaped his way toward Argentocoxus whose bodyguards fell beneath the speed and ferocity of his attack. "Dunpendyrlaw!" Afallach cried again.

Lucius watched, but then felt a massive blow to his head that almost sent him from his saddle. He looked down and saw that he was surrounded suddenly by several jabbing Caledonian spears. Blood flowed from somewhere under his helmet, down the neck of his tunic beneath his armour, but he was not yet dizzy. He slashed and took one man in the face, and removed the arm of a second.

Still, the enemy warriors closed in, and as they did so, Xanthus reared and kicked out, sending their bodies flying fore and aft, knocking them to the ground as he spun.

Barta found his way to Lucius' side again and together they hacked and slashed, the dragon vexillum still flying high above the enemy heads.

"Sarmatiana!" Dagon's voice rang out over the dwindling fury of the battle as his men slammed into the force facing off against Lucius.

Lucius turned as the attacks abated and looked for the Votadini.

The white horse banner flew around Argentocoxus, and the chieftain's bodyguard fell before it.

Lucius spotted arrows flying around the chariot too and saw his scout on the hillside, firing at the chieftain. One of the arrows found the charioteer's neck and Argentocoxus lunged for the reins as the chariot turned abruptly.

The scout was running then, and leapt into the cab beside the chieftain, his dagger jabbing quickly in and out, trying find a window.

But Argentocoxus was strong and he wrested the dagger from the scout, butted him in the head and threw him from the chariot to be trampled by the Votadini hooves directly behind.

"Now you die!" Afallach roared, swinging his spear and taking the chieftain across the chest to send him flying onto the bloody earth.

The cavalry passed him quickly and wheeled, but before they could reach Argentocoxus, he was already springing onto a Sarmatian mount that had lost its rider, and speeding in the direction they had come, leaving his men to die to the last.

"After him!" Lucius ordered as two Votadini turmae and one Sarmatian pursued the fleeing chieftain.

"Coward!" Afallach yelled as he rode after his father's slayer, swinging his spatha in the air.

"They're surrendering!" Dagon said to Lucius as he rode up beside him. "Praefectus!"

Lucius, feeling light-headed now, looked at Dagon and then beyond to see where a mass of Caledonii warriors were surrounded by a great orbit of Sarmatian and Votadini lances and swords. He rode over to the group and looked down on them, wiping the blood from his eyes as he did so.

"Do you surrender to Rome?" Lucius asked them.

One of the Caledonii, the final surviving bodyguard, stepped forward and spat, his axe pointed at Lucius.

He wanted single combat.

Lucius knew he was in no state to fight long, hand-to-hand, but he also knew that his men valued single-combat, that he would appear less than a leader if he should deny the challenge.

He dismounted and gave the reins to Barta.

"No, Praefectus," Barta whispered. "Let me fight him."

Lucius shook his head, his eyes on the Caledonian as he approached.

"When I kill you, Dragon, you let my countrymen go." The man was tall with a long blonde moustache and spiked hair, and blue designs covering his body. His axe dripped with the blood of Lucius' men.

Breathe, Lucius. Breathe.

"When I kill you," Lucius said to the man. "Your men will die."

The man rushed in immediately and the Sarmatian horses nearby reared in surprise.

The rush attack was skilled and deadly, and Lucius found it hard to pinpoint a pattern in the man's moves. He was wild, unpredictable.

The parries clanged over the field and up the walls of the surrounding hills which were eerily quiet now after the cries of battle shortly before.

The Caledonii cheered for their man, but the Sarmatians and Votadini stared in stony silence as they watched the Dragon sidestep and parry, preserving his energy, before moving in with amazing speed beneath a deadly slash to stab his blade into the warrior's side, then his leg, and then the shoulder.

The Caledonian cried with rage as the blood flowed from his wounds and charged at Lucius as he moved backward.

Lucius tripped over the body of a horse that was behind him.

"Anguis!" Dagon yelled out.

The Caledonian was in the air, his axe speeding toward Lucius' face on the other side of the horse's body, but as he came down, Lucius rolled quickly to the side and swung with all his might into the man's flying body to strike him on the neck.

The Caledonian crashed into the ground, his body convulsing as the blood pulsed from his jugular.

Lucius scrambled to his feet and drove the blade into the man's spine. Bile rose in his throat, but he forced it down, not wanting to vomit in front of the men. When he turned, visible now above the horse's body, it was then that the Sarmatians and Votadini roared with victory in their hearts. They waited for the order.

Lucius looked at the Caledonii before him, each of them with hatred in their eyes, and no doubt in their hearts. He nodded to his men.

"Kill them!"

As kontos, spear and sword were driven into the bodies of the surrounded Caledonii, and as their screams of pain and defiance rose into the sky above, Lucius watched, somehow removed and uncaring of the death being meted out before him. He told himself that he was following the orders he had been given - to kill them all, to let none escape - but he knew that was not true. He despised those orders. He was simply tired of war, of battle and blood. There were no women and children upon the gory ground all about him. He saw only warriors who had tried to kill his men, who had killed Romans. He also saw men who prevented him from reaching his family again.

The anger was exhausting.

When the killing was done and the Sarmatians and Votadini were going over the field to take up their own dead and wounded, as well as gather what riderless horses there were, Lucius leaned against Xanthus' great neck and held onto him as his head began to spin.

"Praefectus," Barta said behind him. "You're pale."

Lucius turned to Barta and saw the cuts across his face and thick arms that resembled sappy axe wounds in a tree trunk.

"You're wounded, Barta," Lucius said.

"I'm fine. Just glad I survived the charge downhill."

Lucius smiled grimly. "Me too."

"That was mad, Lucius," Dagon whispered as he too approached, bleeding from several wounds. "Here. Take off your helmet." He held a length of linen in his hand. "We need to bind your head."

Lucius undid the straps of his helmet and slowly pulled it off. As he did so, his hair fell down, matted with blood.

Dagon looked him over carefully. "Your skull is not cracked. It's just cut where your helmet is dented. But we need to wrap it now to stanch the bleeding."

Lucius did not argue. He bent his head while gripping onto Xanthus' calm bulk, and let Dagon wrap the linen about his head three times. He then put his helmet back on, carefully, so as not to show his wound to the men.

"Any sign of Afallach?" Lucius asked, as the three of them gazed back to the far end of the valley. "When he brings

Argentocoxus' body back, we'll drive him into Fendoch in that damned chariot of his."

"We should send a force to search for them," Dagon said. "It's going to be dark soon."

"Yes. We need to get back to base." Lucius looked around them to see the men's progress in gathering the bodies and wounded. "Leave the Caledonian dead for the crows!" he called over to a trooper who was moving enemy bodies.

The man saluted Lucius and then bent over to cut the head from the enemy body - another trophy for the fortress walls.

"Yes. Dagon, you go with two turmae and see if you can find him."

"Yes, Praefectus." Dagon saluted and was about to go when Barta spoke.

"No need. He's here."

At the end of the valley where the road wound its way in, they saw the white horse vexillum of the Votadini appear with Afallach riding beneath it.

Men began to gather and approach the riders, cheering as they did so.

Lucius, Dagon and Barta walked toward them, their horses following.

From the look upon Afallach's face, Lucius could tell the news was not good.

Afallach reined in before Lucius. His face was pained not from wounds, for he seemed to have escaped the battle unscathed apart from a few cuts on his hands.

He saluted Lucius and spoke. "He escaped, Praefectus."

Lucius was disappointed, but he knew Afallach was even more so. "We'll get him, my friend."

"We had him. I inflicted several wounds on him. Nearly took his arm off as we rode abreast of each other. My sword was nearly in his back as he ran away, but..."

"What?" Lucius looked at the men who had returned with Afallach. Their faces were white, their eyes wide. "What happened?"

The lord of the Votadini took a deep breath and spoke low so that none of the others could hear. "The sky darkened suddenly, almost to night, and then barbed arrows tore into us. We lost a few men. Then ahead of us, standing upon a huge rock was..."

470

"Who, Afallach. Tell me!" Lucius' voice was impatient, and he felt his heart beating faster in his breast.

"It was the Wolf and...her."

Lucius knew, even though Afallach did not say it. "The Morrigan?"

Afallach nodded, and Dagon and Barta looked at each other.

"Together they laughed at us, as arrows rained down." Afallach hung his head. "We couldn't get at them. It was as if an invisible wall appeared before us, beyond which the skies were even darker, as if it were a different land of unearthly sound."

"You need to rest, my friend," Lucius said, and turned to some of the Votadini. "Help your lord. We need to get back to base."

"I'm fine, Praefectus," Afallach said. "But that place...I wanted to say. I recognize it somehow."

"What do you mean?" Dagon asked.

"That is the way to the Wolf's den."

Lucius heard a ringing in his ears at this, a laughter.

"We need to get back to base," he said absently as his eyes stared in the direction Argentocoxus had fled. Then he looked one more time at Afallach. "We'll get Argentocoxus," he reassured the lord of the Votadini. "And he'll pay for all he's done."

Afallach nodded, but his face showed little sign of hope. *Forgive me, Father...*

"Back to base!" Lucius ordered so that the men around him could hear. "And bring that chariot!"

That night, back at base, the Sarmatians and Votadini tended to their wounds and the wounded, and cleaned the blood and offal from their horses and armour. Many tales were recounted of the Praefectus' mad plan, and many a man spoke in hushed whispers of how the Dragon had swooped down out of the sky to destroy the enemy. It did not matter that the chieftain of the Caledonii had escaped alive. He had been badly wounded and his chariot had been captured, a prize that groups of men came to gawp at where it stood in the small courtyard of the principia.

After caring for his own wounds, and writing a report which he would send to Horea Classis the following morning, Lucius completed his rounds of the fort, checking on the men who had fought and were wounded, and those who had remained behind to hold the base. As he walked the battlements, men saluted him with something approaching awe in their eyes.

Lucius thought how odd it was that men built stuff up in their minds, not only to raise a person, but to give themselves courage in the face of great odds. He had heard the whispers of the magnificent battle, of the charge he had led out of the very skies.

If only they knew how afraid I was, he thought.

He stopped again at the western edge of the fort and stared out at the moonlit glen and the oak tree standing there.

In the dark hush of that night, a lone bird called out, harsh at first, like a woodcutter's axe among the trees of a silent wood, driven and impatient. The bird, once answered, subsided into something softer, an eerie echo like water in the olive wood of an Etrurian idyll.

Lucius closed his eyes and breathed deeply of the night air, imagining the warmth and clear sky of the place of his youth. When he opened his eyes again, he shuddered.

Standing beneath the oak tree beyond the fortress walls was the Morrigan herself and, beside her, the Wolf, her son.

Together they stared at Lucius, smiling and arrogant, inviting him to die. The Wolf stepped forward and pointed his sword at Lucius.

None of the guards upon the walls could see them.

Lucius felt alone then, cold, but then a warmth settled in beside him and he felt strength fill his veins, defiance.

You are not alone, Epona said, her hand gripping his.

Lucius closed his eyes momentarily and the pain in his head and body faded away. *Thank you,* he said, and together they stared back at the dark goddess and her son until they disappeared into the darkness of night.

When Lucius finally lay down upon his cot that night, his mind reached out to his wife, son, and daughter. Before long, he gave way to exhaustion, words of love and tenderness upon his lips as he slipped into sleep.

To the East of the front lines, where the northern seas lapped at the sandy shores of the one-time kingdom of the Venicones, the legionary base and command centre of Horea Classis sat squat in stony silence along the banks of the Tava estuary. Beneath a clear spring sky of sea-swept air, smoke from the fires within the base and the surrounding camps and vici swirled up into the sky above the settlement like a hazy nimbus before disappearing, like the units of troops themselves who had been sent to the front and were not seen again.

The seaside beyond the walls of Horea Classis was choked with ships carrying supplies of grain, arms, oil and more to supply the army. So numerous and tightly packed were the transports that they resembled their own cargoes of amphora, tightly packed in a great hold beneath the sky.

From these, a steady stream of laden wagons, slaves, and beasts of burden flowed to distribute the cargoes in various sectors outside of the base, there to be separated and distributed to the front.

Tens of thousands of men - legionaries and auxiliaries - were already spread across the Gask Ridge frontier, and many thousands more were arriving by land and sea to join the fight to exterminate the Caledonii and Maeatae rebels.

At the centre of it all, in the hall of the principia of Horea Classis, Caesar Caracalla sat at a large table reading over incoming reports and going over supply chains with the help of Domitius Ulpianus, Marcus Claudius Picus and others. In a corner of the lavish room, Conn Venico, chieftain of the Venicones, sat in silent attendance upon Caesar as if he too were one of the statues scattered around the periphery of confidants.

"Yes, Caesar," Ulpianus said. "The coastal prefect, Nearchus Chioticus, sends word that the shipment of ballistae and onagers has arrived. It will be unloaded as soon as the ship can approach the quayside."

"Good," Caracalla muttered absently as he scrolled through the endless lists. It was hot in the room, due to the braziers burning brightly in each corner, and so Caracalla threw back the long cloak he had been wearing.

A slave came to pick it up and another refilled his cup of wine.

"Any word from Eburacum? Does my father still breathe?"

Ulpianus cleared his throat. "The Praetorian prefect sends word that the emperor is well and likely to recover."

Caracalla snorted. "He's lying. My father is near death."

"Perhaps," Ulpianus said. "It is in the Gods' hands now."

Caracalla nodded. They had the same conversation every few days when Papinianus' regular letters would arrive.

"There is something else," Claudius Picus said, approaching Caesar's side.

473

Caracalla looked up. "What is it?"

"The men…"

"Which men?" Caracalla asked.

"All of them…" Claudius said, pausing purposefully. "They are talking about Praefectus Metellus' battles on the front, regularly too."

Caracalla stopped writing and leaned back in his chair. "Ah yes. The Dragon is back and haranguing the enemy. No doubt his men are pinning heads to the walls of Fendoch."

"Savages, sire," Claudius said.

"But good fighters," Caracalla returned. "We will use them for now."

"As I was saying, sire, the men… They speak often about Praefectus Metellus. He is highly regarded for his bravery and skill in battle, though he has not yet engaged the Wolf."

Caracalla looked up at Claudius then, his frown intense and simmering. "Then let us hope he meets this foe sooner rather than later."

"Yes, sire. But we may wish to… How shall I put this? Monitor the praefectus' behaviour. He is very popular."

"What are you saying, Claudius?"

"Only that we should be cautious. He could win this war for you, sire, but his popularity among the troops continues to grow stronger with each battle. Even men who have not met or seen him speak of him."

"Men love a victorious general," Caracalla said.

"Yes. But men are fickle."

"Has Praefectus Metellus sent in any report recently?" Caracalla asked Ulpianus.

"No, sire. He has not. Not recently."

Caracalla stood and walked around the table, stretching his arms and neck. He took up a sword from the wooden dummy behind his desk and swung it around a few times.

"Gods! Would that we were back in Rome."

"Yes, sire," Ulpianus said as he bent over his own table to make a few notes in the margin of a manual he was writing on the duties of governors and other officials, something he could leave behind for whomever commanded in Horea Classis when Caesar took him back to Rome with him.

Claudius went over to Conn Venico and looked down at him. "And what about you, Chieftain?" he smirked. "Have you heard anything from your spies about Argentocoxus and the Wolf's movements?"

Conn Venico looked up at the man he had come to know as a viper, and shook his head. "I have no reports, sire," he said to Caracalla.

"Perhaps if I rub your head, I will glean something from it?" Claudius teased, actually placing his hand upon the chieftain's bald head.

Conn Venico grabbed his wrist and took the hand off of his head. "How dare you?"

Claudius laughed, but Caracalla silenced him.

"Enough! Claudius, you insult our guest." Caracalla put up his hand suddenly for silence. "Wait! What is that sound?"

A loud cheering crept in through the door from the courtyard of the principia where several Praetorians stood guard.

"The legions are cheering," Caracalla said. "What for?" He took up his cloak and strode out of the room into the daylight of the courtyard. Outside, in the street, a large crowd of men had gathered to shout and cheer at something in their midst.

Out on the via Principalis, surrounded by cheering legionaries and even some Praetorians, was a turmae of Sarmatian cavalry. Each one of them wore long, battle-worn scale armour and carried a long sword or the battle club used by the Sarmatians. Hovering above them was a draco standard, its long wind sock wavering gently in the cool breeze that swept up the street, Beside that, the dragon vexillum fluttered and jingled, the golden dragon with outspread wings upon a red background visible to all around. It was this to which the cheers were directed.

"Where is Praefectus Metellus?" someone among the legions yelled. "Where is the Dragon of Rome?"

"Metellus! Metellus! Metellus!" the chant was taken up.

The Sarmatians paid no heed to the chants, but dismounted, and a few among them began to pull something that had been travelling in their midst. The decurion leading them tucked his helmet beneath his arm and walked forward until he was before the open principia gates. He saluted. "Permission to approach Caesar and report?" he said.

In the courtyard facing the gate and street outside, Caracalla stood surrounded by several Praetorians with Claudius, Ulpianus, and Conn Venico beside him. He nodded to the guards flanking the gate and the Sarmatians marched through.

"What do they have there?" Caracalla asked.

Conn Venico stepped forward, his eyes wide. "It is Argentocoxus' war chariot, Caesar."

Caracalla broke from the group and walked toward the decurion who stopped and saluted him formally. Claudius Picus remained close my his side. "Decurion Brencis," Caracalla said. "You bring news?"

"I do, Caesar," Brencis said, bowing his head.

All around them, as the Sarmatians pulled the war chariot into the courtyard and then stood at attention behind Brencis, men began to gather closer so as to hear what was said.

"Give me your report then, Decurion," Caracalla said, glancing at the small and speedy chariot of his enemy and truce-breaker.

"Sire, Praefectus Metellus sends his greetings to you," Brencis began, his voice loud so that all could hear. "He also offers the war chariot of Argentocoxus, Chieftain of the Caledonii."

"Do I take it that Argentocoxus is dead?" Caracalla asked.

Conn Venico cocked his head to listen, to hear if it was true.

Brencis paused, then spoke. "No, sire. He lives, we think."

"You think?"

Brencis pressed on. "A great battle was fought against a large contingent of Argentocoxus' forces in a valley beyond the fort of Fendoch. Praefectus Metellus' forces and the Votadini allies charged the enemy and slew them all. Argentocoxus' charioteer was slain and his chariot taken, but he fled from the battle on a stolen horse."

"Why did you say you think he lives?" Caracalla asked.

"Because he was badly wounded in the battle."

Caracalla was silent and went to look at the war chariot sitting in the midst of the courtyard. In the last campaign, he had prevented Praefectus Metellus from killing Argentocoxus. He had even brokered the deal with the Caledonian chieftain, certain that it would have permitted him to return to Rome.

In breaking the truce, Argentocoxus had made Caracalla look a fool, and he now hated him for it, wished his bloody and hacked corpse were lying in the bed of that chariot so that he might spit upon it. The fact that he likely survived now only served to fuel his anger.

Claudius Picus was at his shoulder then. "Sire... Praefectus Metellus has failed to bring you the head of Argentocoxus, and he sends this chariot only to make Caesar look bad. Hear how the men chant his name in the street still."

Caracalla looked up. He could still hear faint shouts of 'Metellus!' in the street where troopers were approaching the Sarmatians standing there to get news from the front. Already, tales of the mountain charge were spreading.

Brencis chanced a glance at Caracalla and Claudius, who was whispering in his ear. "Sire, there is more to report."

Caracalla turned abruptly and strode to Brencis, his face now close to the Sarmatian's. "Then tell it to me, Decurion."

"The Wolf of the Maeatae, sire."

"What of him?" Caracalla almost shouted the question. It had been the Wolf he heard constantly spoken of in whispers, the Wolf who had convinced Argentocoxus to break the truce.

Brencis spoke loudly again. "Praefectus Metellus commanded me to report that he will soon engage the Wolf and his forces, that he knows the location of his base."

"He seems confident, our praefectus. Is this true?" Claudius asked.

Brencis stared directly at the Patrician in his Praetorian uniform. "The Praefectus always speaks truth."

Claudius spat.

Brencis would have slammed his fist into the man's face were it not for Caesar's presence. Instead, he turned to Caracalla again.

"Sire, Praefectus Metellus asks that reinforcements be sent for the march inland to the Wolf's den."

"And when would Praefectus Metellus like these reinforcements?" Caracalla asked, not without sarcasm.

"We will move out quickly, sire. Three days at most."

"There is fighting all along the Gask frontier, Decurion. Praefectus Metellus' battles are not the only ones being fought. We are suffering heavy casualties everywhere. If the praefectus has a plan of action, he must carry it out as he sees fit. If he is successful, he will have our thanks. If not..." Caracalla's voice faded away as if he were lost in some sudden, pleasurable thought.

Claudius spoke up. "If not, he will come to Horea Classis to explain himself."

Brencis did not look at Claudius, but remained still before Caracalla.

477

After a few moments, Caracalla turned to Brencis. "You are dismissed, Decurion. Thank the praefectus for this symbol of his failure," he said aloud, pointing at the chariot.

Brencis, his jaw taut, his face expressionless, saluted stiffly and properly to Caracalla, then turned and ordered his men to mount up.

Back on the street, while Caracalla and his entourage went back into the meeting room of the principia, Brencis and the Sarmatians mounted up again, hoisting the dragon vexillum and draco standard, and rode out of Horea Classis to another tide of rising cheers.

Back in the room amid the piles of reports and dispatches, Caracalla paced back and forth, like an angry, caged lion. The cheers of the men out in the streets still echoed in his ears, salt upon his wounded pride.

The guerrilla war being waged by the Caledonii prevented any large scale battle in which he could be seen commanding the legions. As supreme commander of the armies in this campaign, Caracalla could not engage the enemy in the myriad small skirmishes that were taking place in the wild, ambushes in which he might very well be slain and never get back to Rome to sit upon the imperial throne. The only way to command was by giving commands from within the high walls of Horea Classis.

The problem was that the troops, with whom he had always been on good relations, never saw him, nor heard of his deeds.

Frustratingly, once again, Lucius Metellus Anguis, managed to steal the glory that Caracalla believed was his own. The praefectus and his men managed to engage the ghostly enemy somewhere in the damp world of those misty highlands, to make himself victorious in the eyes of the legions, even though he had all but failed.

Caracalla pounded his fist on the table, making Conn Venico jump a little. Papers and wax tablets skittered over the edge onto the floor, and a slave emerged from the shadows to pick them up.

"You've failed me, Marcus," Caracalla said, not looking at Claudius Picus. "I'm very disappointed. He was supposed to be dead long ago."

"Sire...he will be."

Caracalla's fist swept around and landed squarely on Claudius' jaw, sending him tumbling backward and nearly landing on the slave who had just cleaned up.

At that moment, Ulpianus came back into the room from outside and stopped in surprise to see the Patrician on the floor. He did not dare smile, though he wanted to.

"Perhaps I should leave you, Caesar?" Conn Venico said.

"No. Stay," Caracalla said. "See what fools I am surrounded by." He drew his gladius from his side, and the audible slithering of the blade from its sheath sent a chill down Conn Venico's spine.

Claudius felt the blade at his neck and looked up at Caracalla. Through clenched teeth and a cracked lip, he spoke. "Sire, we will have him soon, I promise you. I have a plan, and the report that we have just received confirms that it is in motion.

Caracalla pressed the razor-sharp, triangular tip of his sword against Claudius' neck, and for a moment, the man upon the floor thought that Caesar would indeed end his life.

"Sire, if this goes well, you will find yourself in Rome by the end of the year."

The pressure upon the blade eased, and Claudius got to his feet as Caracalla went back to his table to continue his work.

Conn Venico cleared his throat. "If I may," he said to Claudius, "how do you propose to catch the Dragon? They say he is protected by the Gods themselves."

Claudius looked at the chieftain, his eyes cold and narrow. "You need not concern yourself with these things. Your own incompetence has caused enough trouble. You were supposed to help maintain the peace in Caledonia. If you had, Caesar would be back in Rome by now."

At that moment, Ulpianus moved away from the chieftain's side to hand Caracalla more dispatches that had just arrived.

Claudius and Conn Venico continued to eye each other.

Claudius wiped his mouth. "Why don't you go back to that mud hut of yours, Conn Venico?"

"I wait upon Caesar. Not you." Conn Venico straightened, his expression one of defiance and disdain for the man before him. *Who does he think he is? I'll see him dead!*

"Leave us, Conn Venico," Caracalla's deep, angry voice said from across the room. "You are no longer needed today."

For a moment, the chieftain was speechless. The humiliation Claudius was permitted to heap upon him was intolerable.

Claudius was not finished, however. As he approached the chieftain, a maddening smirk upon his face, he said, "And if you speak a word of what you heard here, I'll have your head on the end of a spear. Do you understand?"

Conn Venico looked past Claudius to Caracalla, hoping for some word of rebuke for the Praetorian, but he was only to be disappointed by Caracalla's apparent disinterest for the crude treatment of an ally and chieftain. He bowed to Caracalla, and turned to leave.

Claudius laughed, but then only did Caracalla raise his head. "I don't understand your mirth, Claudius. I meant what I said. If you don't do as you've promised, you'll receive worse than Conn Venico."

"I would expect nothing less, sire," Claudius said.

Darkness blanketed the plain surrounding Horea Classis that night. The clouds were thick and low, choking out any trace of moonlight that might have illuminated the forts upon the field leading up to the main base.

Fires sparked in orderly rows along the walls of the fortifications, or burned in torches and braziers flanking the guarded gates of Rome's armies. Men on guard duty upon the walls, or roaming the streets in alert contubernia ensured that the enemy could not approach Caesar within his high walls.

Little heed, however, was paid to the hunched, cloaked man who carried a basket of oysters through the streets. The man walked slowly and awkwardly with his burden, stopped only occasionally to be robbed of an oyster or two by the guards before being dismissed.

He was no threat, after all.

"Move along, grandfather!" one legionary said, giving the man a good-natured kick in the backside.

The man moved on silently along the muddy pathways of the gathering of Rome's eagles, past groups of exhausted whores from the vicus, or the bastard children and wives of the legionaries based there. Civilians ignored and avoided him, and the troops only paid him cursory attention as he went, finally arriving at the gates of the main fortress.

There, a full century was on guard duty, and as he approached the brightly-lit area of the gate leading onto the via Principalis, the Praetorian centurion on duty poked his vinerod into the old man's chest.

"Where do you think you're going?"

The old man, his face far below the great bulk of the soldier, said something faint.

"What? I can't hear you! State your business or I'll have you flogged!"

Some of the troopers behind the centurion laughed. A flogging would be entertaining and distracting during the dark hours of the watch.

The centurion bent down the better to hear and the man spoke again.

"Bloodletting."

The colour drained from the centurion's face immediately when he heard the word spoken to him. He remembered all too well the order that had come from Marcus Claudius Picus, that if a man came to the gates, no matter who he was or what he looked like, if he spoke that single word, he was to be brought to him immediately.

"Come with me," the centurion said.

"You're letting him in, sir?" the optio on duty asked.

"Shut your mouth, and do your duty!" the centurion snapped, pointing his vinerod at the man. "I'll be back."

The men stiffened as they watched the centurion lead the hunched old man through the gates and down the street into the heart of the fortress.

They walked slowly, none asking questions of the centurion as they passed groups of officers or slaves skirting around in the dark like rats upon a ship at night.

After several turns, they came to a wooden door. The centurion knocked twice with the end of his vinerod.

The door opened and the face of Marcus Claudius Picus appeared.

"Bloodletting," the centurion said.

"Leave us," Claudius commanded.

The centurion nodded, turned, and disappeared back down the dark street.

A few lamps were lit in Claudius' quarters, quarters not located in the Praetorium, but in a more remote, private part of the base. The room was simple, the walls of plain plaster, hung with a few weapons. In the middle was a table set with pitchers of water and wine, and clay cups.

Claudius closed the door.

The old man straightened then and shed his cloak. His back unbent, he became taller before Claudius' eyes, and a thickly muscled body emerged from beneath the dark cloak.

"Speak," the man said to Claudius.

Claudius walked over to the table and poured some wine. He looked at the man who only shook his head. After drinking, Claudius turned to face him, his hand upon the hilt of his sword.

"Tell your master the Dragon is coming to him in the next three days."

The man smiled, his dirt encrusted face stretching to reveal sharp, white teeth. "My master will be pleased."

"He cannot fail," Claudius said, pouring more wine.

Before he knew it, the man's hand was clenched about his throat, the other crushing Claudius' hand where it rested upon his sword's pommel.

"You do not give orders to the Wolf of the Maeatae, Roman," he hissed in Claudius' ear. "You only obey. When the Dragon is dead, his flesh devoured by the Morrigan, you will ensure that Caesar and his legions return to Rome. If you do not, the Wolf will tear your flesh and crunch your bones."

Claudius pulled away and put up his hands.

"Tell your master all is in hand." He straightened, straining for some form of courage in that small room. "Just tell the Wolf the time has come. Tell him to do his worst!"

Without another word, the man put the cloak back on, opened the door, and disappeared into the night.

"You're dead, Metellus," Claudius smiled as he downed another cup of wine.

XVI

SUFFOCATIO

'The Drowning'

It had been three days since Lucius' request for reinforcements from Caesar Caracalla. As every man prepared to ride out at his command, Lucius stared out at the broad mouth of the glen. In the courtyard of the praetorium at the centre of the fort, Lucius' offerings to the Gods still smouldered and smoked upon the altar he had erected there - rosemarinus for Apollo, frankincense for Venus, and a thick sheaf of wheat for Epona, whom Lucius prayed would be riding with him into battle.

Dagon, Barta, Afallach, Tribune Fulvius, Centurion Rutilius, and the Sarmatian and Votadini decurions stood nearby.

Word had come that the Maeatae and Caledonii had been warned of the imminent attack and were preparing to move their highland base to another location. Everyone knew this could well be Rome's last chance to stomp out the rebellion and bring the enemy chieftains to justice. Every man knew this could be the battle that ended the war. They all waited as Lucius Metellus Anguis stared out at the land and sky, though none knew what he thought or to whom he had spoken in his silent prayers.

Lucius knew they were all watching him, waiting for the answer they deserved to know, but his doubts crept in on him again, like a poison working its way into the system to slow the movement of every limb, every thought.

From the distant peaks of the rising mountains to the West, it appeared that the clouds had been splashed across the sky in a permanent mixture of grey, pink, orange, and fiery red. It was as if Eris had thrown her heavenly palette in anger to deliberately deface the canvas of the world.

Lucius took a deep breath and turned to the gathered men looking up at him from below the ramparts, as well as those standing beside him, waiting patiently for his command. He nodded and put his crested helmet upon his head.

"We ride now!" he said loudly.

Cheers erupted from the men as the decurions, centurions and optios passed along the order that they were to march on the stronghold of the Maeatae and Caledonii, hidden somewhere in the teeth of those distant mountains.

Lucius turned to Dagon. "I want Akil to remain here with his turmae to guard the base."

"Yes, Praefectus," Dagon answered and saluted before going to find Akil.

"Tribune?" Lucius turned to the younger man from the Parthica legion. "Can you leave behind at least one contubernium to help guard the fort here?"

"Absolutely, Praefectus!" the man answered, nodding to his centurion who went to relay the order.

The base exploded to life as men checked their weapons and horse harness one last time, mounted up and ordered themselves into their turmae outside the walls. The men of the Parthica legion joined them, hoisting their gear - satchels, pick axes, pila, pans, and stakes - and forming up for the march beside the massive force of cavalry auxiliaries.

As Lucius went to mount Xanthus, sitting where all could see him, he inhaled deeply of the scene. With the incessant rains of that inhospitable land, all was soaked through, leather, man and beast. The scent of damp and mold had been a constant in Lucius' nostrils since they had arrived in Caledonia. The sky was dark once more, low, crushing, and gave them the feeling of living in the confines of a dark tomb.

Gods, Lucius asked, remembering his prayers of that morning. *May we soon leave this land forever. Watch over me that I may return home to my family. Grant us victory!*

"We'll win this together," Lucius whispered to Xanthus once he was settled snugly between the four saddle horns of the huge saddle, his red cloak draped over the stallion's rump.

Xanthus' thick neck turned and the orbs of his black eyes looked to Lucius who stroked him before turning to look at the men crowding the via Principalis.

"Warriors of Sarmatia and of the Votadini..." Lucius began, his voice loud and clear, his heart racing, causing a shiver in the words as he spoke. "Men of Rome's legions... My friends! Today we ride into the heart of Caledonia, to battle!"

At this, every man cheered and raised his weapon to the sky as he gazed up at Lucius.

"For too long, the coward, Argentocoxus, and the Wolf of the Maeatae have gorged themselves on the blood of our countrymen, our brothers-in-war... They have broken oaths and a sacred truce!"

Shouts of anger met this, the rage filling men's voices and hearts as Lucius addressed them.

"They would rip from us the lives of our loved ones, our families, they would tear asunder the bodies of our children if we let them...but we will not allow it!"

All along the street and atop the ramparts, a sea of red cloaks billowed in the highland breeze as if it were Lucius' words rousing every corner of the fortress. Horses' manes bristled like the hair of giant angry boar, and men clenched their weapons more tightly, more determinedly as they thought of all they had to lose, all the blood they had seen in that land.

"Today...men...we will ride into the very heart of the Wolf's den and drive the barbed spear of war into his beating heart! We will rip his limbs...and nail them to the walls of our fortress in the wild! And then...then...will the enemy know that the Dragon and his men cannot be beaten!"

In that moment, Lucius felt a wave of strength rush through him as every man there, every soldier and cavalryman, the tribune of Parthica legion and his officers, his decurions, every man around him, saluted him and chanted his name.

"Metellus! Metellus! Metellus!" from the men of the legions.

"Anguis! Anguis! Anguis!" from the Sarmatians and Votadini.

Lucius spread his arms wide and gazed up at the sky where a brilliant ray of sunlight pierced the thick ceiling of cloud. He closed his eyes to feel the heat of Apollo's light upon his face and breathed deeply of it.

"The Gods are with us!" he yelled to the men.

At that moment, Barta raised the dragon vexillum high above their heads, and it was joined by the horse of the Votadini and the centaur of the Parthica legion.

Lucius drew his sword from his back and lowered the face mask of his war helmet.

"Ride with me to battle and blood!" he yelled and kicked Xanthus' sides, sending the great stallion cantering down the centre of the street.

485

Amid the cheers of all present, Dagon, Barta, Afallach and the rest of the horsemen fell in behind Lucius. Then the men of the legions followed, led by their tribune and centurions, their hobnailed march loud and determined as their voices rang out with marching songs above the din of their clanging kit.

Once they were all across the ditches of the fort, the gates were barred and the skeletal force of men remaining behind climbed to the ramparts to watch their fellows march to battle, some to death, most, they felt, to victory.

With the Dragon leading them, the long force of men and horses followed the flow of the river into the maw of the next glen and disappeared from view.

In the dark sky above, peals of thunder rolled in the distance.

They marched westward along rivers and over burns, along the green and brown pathways of the glens, heading farther from base, from the world of Rome. When night came, they dug in with the skilled help of the men of the legions.

The stars were hidden from their eyes at night, their comforting beacons effaced by the blackness that assaulted them.

Men's minds went to the stories they had been told of the disappearance of the Ninth legion in that land of Hades, and when expressions of fear or concern were voiced, they were answered with 'the men of the Ninth were not led by the Dragon!'.

The next day, they struck camp, filled in their ditches, and set out again.

As Lucius and his men marched, there was a growing concern that there had been no sign of the enemy, no scouts atop the peaks of the hills that towered over them, no flanking attacks mid-march, no tracks. They appeared to be in a no-man's land of river and rock.

Afallach assured Lucius that they were headed in the right direction, that according to the map, the place he had seen on his quest to free his sister, Lucretia, was not far off.

But, just as Lucius began to doubt his friend and ally, when he was about to order a change of course, they came to a sign at the mouth of the next glen.

There, barring the way, high upon the sharpened trunks of three mountain pines, were the impaled, naked bodies of two Roman soldiers and a Sarmatian warrior in the middle.

Lucius called a halt before the grisly posts and raised his face mask to look up. "Keep alert," he said as he rode forward slowly with Dagon, Barta, Afallach, and Tribune Fulvius.

"Who did this?" Fulvius asked.

"The Wolf," Afallach answered.

Lucius recognized the Sarmatian as one of the men who had gone missing on patrol a week prior. He did not recognize the legionaries, but knew they were indeed Romans, for about the bottom of the stakes were the broken remains of lorica segmentata and helmets. He felt his gorge rise as he took in the sight of their lacerated bodies, and the holes in their bellies from which their guts dangled in the breeze for the Morrigan's carrion fowl.

"Get them down!" he ordered, looking around them. There were no trees but for the stakes upon which they had died. "Have the men gather rocks for a cairn."

The men set about it immediately, and when the bodies were brought down, they were lain side by side upon the sloping hillside and covered with rocks from the land in which they had died.

"Gods...may these men find their way to Elysium...may they find peace now, far from here..." Lucius lit a small chunk of incense he had in his saddle bag and set it upon the cairn.

When they were finished, they marched on into the next glen, each man's eyes taking in the resting place of their fallen comrades as he passed, fanning the flames of his anger and rage and will to defeat the enemy lurking upon the road ahead.

As they marched, Lucius and his men found an increasing number of Roman remains. The road became so littered with scattered arms and armour, severed limbs and broken bodies, that they began to suspect that a great battle had taken place.

But there had been no battle, and just as the Sarmatians adorned the walls of their fortress with the limbs and heads of their slain enemies, the Caledonii and Maeatae decorated their land with the gruesome trophies of their own fallen foes.

And so, the trail of blood and guts led them on, deeper into the highlands until the road began to lead upward, seemingly disappearing into the tree-clad cliffs bordering the dark sky above.

Afallach rode to the front and stared out, his keen eyes scanning the surroundings.

"What is it?" Lucius asked as he and Dagon joined him.

Afallach turned to them. "This is it," he said. "We're here."

487

Lucius had to be sure before he led the entire force up and over the hillside, and so he sent Barna, one of his decurions, and three other Sarmatians to scout ahead and peer over the hillside.

The men watched the scouts climb the steep hillside like mountain goats, weaving around boulders and rock faces until they disappeared into the trees.

"We're exposed here, Praefectus," Dagon said and he gazed around the broad bowl of the glen. "I don't like it. If the enemy were here, he would have attacked us by now."

"Might be a trap," Barta said, and Lucius believed he was right. He had suspected as much for some time now, but the remains of his countrymen scattered beneath their horses' hooves had driven him on, farther into enemy territory.

"It could be," Lucius said. "But we're here now, and we need to end this."

"There they are!" Dagon said, pointing at the four men running down the steep hillside directly for them.

When they arrived, Barna stepped forward and saluted Lucius. "This is the place, Praefectus. Just as Lord Afallach described. On the far side of the next glen is a lake with a settlement in its midst. It's surrounded by scattered trees and roundhouses."

"Is there an army there?" Lucius asked.

Barna shook his head. "No, sir. Just small groups of enemy patrols moving around the perimeter of the lake."

"Is there any activity in the settlement?" Afallach asked, searching his mind for what he knew of the layout he had but caught a fleeting glimpse of when he had rescued his sister.

"It was difficult to see, but there were several people moving along the lakeside and upon what appear to be roads." Barna shrugged. "Torches were burning everywhere though. It's definitely a large settlement."

The men were silent as Lucius thought about it.

We're so close... Lucius thought, and as he did so, the Morrigan's laughing face flashed in his mind.

My son will destroy you, Dragon!

Lucius closed his eyes, trying to block out the thought of that dark apparition.

"Anguis," Dagon whispered. "Are you all right?"

Lucius did not answer right away, for he saw him again - the Wolf - standing upon black water, waiting for him, his daughter's screams echoing in the distance.

"Anguis?" Dagon had his hand upon Lucius' arm, gripping him tightly, aware of the men's eyes upon them.

Lucius looked up at the men standing beside him. "We go in, quietly at first. I want to see it." He turned to Barna. "Is there space for a cavalry charge?"

Barna smiled and nodded. "Apart from the trees and roundhouses, it's wide open around the lake. Just scattered crops."

Lucius felt the thrill of the prospect enter him. "Give the order," he said. "We go up to scan the glen, spread out, and move in quickly. Prepare the men."

With the excess baggage and legionary packs staying behind and under guard, the bulk of the force of men and horses made their way up the steep paths to the forested heights of the glen. When they arrived, they spread out among the trees. Lucius and his fellow officers moved forward to get a better look as darkness began its slow settling in the sky above.

Crouching close to the ground, Lucius, Dagon and the others crept forward between the great pine shafts with their swords drawn until they came to the edge of the tree line. When they peered over the edge, they gasped, for they looked down onto another world. If there was said to be one major settlement, a base for the Caledonii and Maeatae rebels, that had to be it.

Far away from the great, gradual slope of the mountain, set in the middle of the western end of that hidden valley, was a lake, the water of which was as black as Cerberus. The lake was surrounded by stands of lumbering alder, willow and birch, some of which jutted from the dark depths, creeping out of the blackness like sentinel ghosts, their bodies lapped by water.

But it was the settlement itself they had never seen the likes of. Apart from the scattered roundhouses dotting the land around the shoreline of the lake, the bulk of the settlement was made up of an entire labyrinthine village suspended above the water on thick pylons. He had seen such cranoghs before in other parts of Caledonia, but they had only been made up of three or five huts at most. The cranogh before them now was vast and confused, with what appeared to be hundreds of roundhouses of varying sizes,

489

bunched in groups at the end of various termini of broad wooden walkways. All was haphazard with no apparent pattern, but for the split of the main walkway into two main roads that splintered off to the North and West.

The broad roads and their domestic tributaries ran in great curves toward the centre at the back of the settlement to converge on a massive round hall with a great peaked thatch roof that reached into the dark sky. Around the hall was a wide gallery that was higher than the rest of the village and commanded a view of the surroundings. The main hall was approached from two sides, both entrances flanked by two guardhouses, and at each they could see several armed men. Off of the back of the hall, was a wide square quay surrounded by fishing boats, and where fish dried on wooden frames, their silvery bodies dulled in the flat light.

There were people present, moving in and out of the various huts and along the wooden avenues like ants around the great mound of the hall. They appeared to be going about their daily tasks, with no signs of panic or hurried packing at the rumoured approach of the Romans.

"They don't know we're coming," Tribune Fulvius whispered behind Lucius.

Lucius held up a hand for quiet as his eyes went back to the great hall. Above it, ravens circled in the sky, some perched upon the rooftop peak that appeared to be carved like a great wolf's head.

There was movement then, around the hall, and as Lucius crawled forward a little more, he spotted them.

There, standing together beneath a skull-covered arch in front of the main hall, were Argentocoxus and the Wolf of the Maeatae.

The enemy leaders were deep in discussion about something, surrounded by their guards who were armed and alert. The Wolf stood taller and thicker than every warrior there, like a solid oak tree among birch saplings. His black hair was pulled back tightly to allow him to fight, to hunt, to kill more freely, and the growl of his voice could be heard among the murmur of the settlement. A great battle axe hung at his back, and Lucius thought no one but Hercules could have hefted it.

"If we can reach that hall, we'll have them," Lucius whispered to the others.

At that moment, as if he had heard him, the Wolf looked in their direction, and Lucius felt that he gazed directly at him, smiling,

490

laughing. He saw the Wolf standing in the middle of that black lake, challenging him.

Lucius felt his hands begin to shake and Dagon, who was beside him, gripped his arm.

"Anguis," he whispered. "What is wrong? Have the Gods shown you something?" Too many times, Dagon had seen the effects that contact with the Gods had had upon his close friend. He feared not that it would affect his ability to command, but that being so close to Them would burn his body and soul from the inside out. "Should we not attack?"

Lucius gazed down into the valley, at the vast, stilted settlement in the water, and shook his head.

"We attack now. It's our only chance," he whispered. *Apollo, Venus and Epona...see me through this alive.* He closed then opened his eyes and forced his mind upon the strategy. The men gathered close.

"We have to move fast, for once we come out of the trees here, we'll be visible to all. Sarmatian and Votadini cavalry will charge down the road that leads onto the main walkway of the cranogh. Where it splits, I'll lead the Sarmatians to the left, and Afallach and the Votadini will take the right. The main walkways are broad enough for three horses abreast, but expect there to be enemy warriors coming out of every one of those huts along the way. We'll be hit from every side, and so we'll have to hack our way as quickly as possible to converge on the hall." Lucius turned to Brencis. "You take four turmae and sweep around the edge of the lake to clear the settlements and watch our backs."

"What about women and children, Praefectus?" Brencis asked.

Lucius breathed. The orders had been to kill them all, but he hated the orders, and these were his men. "Spare them, let them run if that is what they do. If they fight...disarm them if you can. If not..."

Brencis nodded.

"Fulvius," Lucius turned to the young tribune. "You and your men follow as quickly as you can behind us with the same dispersement of troops. Hold the beachhead where the road leads onto the walkway and then split your force. Search every hut for warriors along the way, but order your men to spare women and children."

"Yes, Praefectus."

Lucius nodded. "On my signal, sound the cornui for the charge. May Epona guide us."

The officers went back to the men and the orders were given. Soon, hundreds of horsemen stood silent among the trees gazing down at the settlement, the men of the legions at their backs. Torches were lit along the walkways of the settlement then, casting an eerie orange glow everywhere.

The cornicens of the Parthica legion stepped forward with their great curved horns and looked to Lucius for the signal.

Lucius, sitting atop Xanthus' calm bulk, lowered his face mask and looked from side to side, nodding to Dagon and Barta.

The dragon vexillum was hoisted, as was the horse of the Votadini, and the centaur of the Parthica legion.

Lucius drew his sword and pointed it downhill.

"Charge!"

The legion's cornui sounded out from the mountaintop like tremors in the earth, and all at once the cavalry exploded from the forest, the sound of the draconaria ranging over the valley as the horses sped toward the lake.

Screams burst from the various houses around the water's edge, and people were suddenly running in every direction, either for the hills or for the maze of the cranogh.

Once the cavalry was on the flat of the plain, careening down the main road for the settlement, they picked up their speed.

Brencis and his four turmae veered to the wings of the broad cavalry charge to sweep the shoreline, and it was then that arrows began to fly.

As the Sarmatians and Votadini drove forward in formation, the hail of arrows came down on them like ice in winter, chips of iron assaulting their arms, faces and legs to be deflected by the scale armour of both horse and man.

A couple of horses went down beneath their riders, but the rest drove on, each man's eyes on the dragon vexillum ahead, on the red crest and billowing cloak of the Dragon leading them from the front of the charge, as inspiring to them as Alexander ever was.

In the foremost arrowhead formation, Lucius fell into his battle trance, his mind and body one with his mount's, his men behind him, Dagon, Barta and the others. The only other thing upon his mind were the three white birds soaring in the sky high above him, and the three white hounds following Epona's white stallion into the fray directly beside him, her fiery hair and white robes flowing in the breeze like a shield against the death-seeking iron barb's that sought them.

The draco standards howled in the dark air as the cavalry charged down the main road, between the first roundhouses flanking it, and from there emerged numerous enemy warriors swinging spear, blade and axe. Even as they ran up, the cataphracts of Rome ploughed through them, slashing at their faces and limbs, impaling them on the long tips of their kontoi so that the screams of their onlooking families and countrymen began to keen over the black lake ahead.

The Sarmatian and Votadini lances did their bloody work, the warriors spending them before they reached the confined space of the cranogh pathways which, Lucius could now see, were crowded with bare-chested and screaming Caledonii and Maeatae warriors.

As they approached the great, skull-covered arch leading onto the wooden walkways of the cranogh, Lucius raised his voice.

"Sarmatiana and Epona!"

And Afallach added to the voice of his own people. "Dunpendyrlaw!"

The men roared behind him, and the horses strode faster as the settlement loomed and enemy warriors amassed themselves behind the arch to block the way.

Lucius sought a space between the shafts of jutting spears and as Epona's stallion leapt over them all, chilling the enemy's courage, the Sarmatian spearhead exploded into the mass of armed bodies to send them flying in every direction.

Lucius' sword sang as he slashed to the left and right, every blow making contact with an enemy blade or skull, shoulder or collar bone. The pace slowed, as he led the Sarmatians to the left path and the Votadini veered to the right, their force driving away where the road split.

Both walkways were crowded with the enemy, and men began to fall on both sides, either onto the walkways to be trampled, or splashing into the dark depths far below to disappear beneath the surface.

Lucius felt his arms burning, and his cuts bleeding, but he kept swinging and was comforted by the call of the legions who had now arrived at the water's edge.

"Pila iacite!" came Tribune Fulvius' voice above the din and in that moment, Caledonian and Maeatae screams rent the air as the men of Parthica legion launched their pila into the enemy just ahead of the cavalry, clearing the way for Lucius and Afallach before beginning the clean butcher work with gladius and scutum.

Lucius turned briefly in the respite to see Afallach leading the Votadini in a great arc to the right, but they were slowed more as a dozen or more warriors rushed from every roundhouse flanking the broad, bloody walkway.

"Look out, Praefectus!" Barta suddenly yelled, and as Lucius looked forward he leaned his body steeply to the side to avoid the spear shaft flying for his chest.

The Maeatae who had launched it from atop one of the thatched roofs fell with one of Barta's knives in his chest.

The Sarmatian charge slowed then, almost to a standstill, and as Lucius searched for Epona ahead, he saw the thick wall of spears and stolen Roman shields facing them. Beyond it were the guardhouses where the monstrous bodyguards stood waiting and roaring, opening their mouths as if to swallow the flow of men and horses coming at them.

Beyond them, stood the Wolf, his axe pointed directly at Lucius.

The shield wall rushed up to them quickly, and Lucius hoped his men behind him would find their way through after him.

He kicked Xanthus' flanks and the stallion sped forward, himself screaming as he leapt over the tops of the enemy spears and shields.

Time slowed for Lucius as they soared through the air, possessing the viewpoint of gods for a brief second before dropping out of the sky to land among the enemy.

All was chaos and madness, sword, spear, axe and dagger slashing and stabbing in every direction.

Xanthus began to spin and rear as they were surrounded, and it was then that Lucius felt the saddle girth loosen, cut by a spear as they had soared over the enemy. He straightened and charged forward, but even as they picked up speed, two of the Maeatae bodyguards rushed forward with a log wielded horizontally and slammed into Xanthus, sending him over the edge of the walkway to splash into the black water.

The girth broke upon the impact then, and Lucius was thrown from his saddle onto the walkway at the other bodyguards' feet.

"Anguis!" Dagon's voice called from the other side of the shield wall where they were locked in bloody combat.

No time to think, Lucius rolled and his god-made blade swept around him in a protective arc, taking two of the bodyguards through their bare ankles.

"Kill the Dragon!" the Wolf howled from not twenty feet away, laughing as he watched his men surround Lucius.

Behind his mask, Lucius gasped for air, his eyes stinging from sweat, his body trying to ignore the myriad stabs and slashes that sought to find a way through the chinks in his armour.

Suddenly he was lifted off of his feet by one of the bodyguards who had wielded the log and, too close for a swing of his sword, he reached for his pugio, drove it into the man's eye and twisted. He fell to the blood-slick planks and spun into the next oncoming bodyguard, his cloak tangling the man's axe swing, his own blade crashing into the bared spine of the man's back.

Lucius looked up quickly to meet the Wolf, but he was gone.

"Xanthus!" he yelled, but could not see the stallion anywhere in the depths below. He felt a flow of anger and despair then, but rallied himself as his men broke through the shield wall, Dagon and Barta almost with him.

The cries from the other side of the settlement told him that Afallach was still fighting his way to the hall.

Lucius, help!

The words rang out in his mind and he knew then that Epona was calling for him.

Lucius took the steps up to the hall two at a time, dispatching the warriors who waited there for him and kicked open the great double doors before rushing in.

"Praefectus, wait for us!" Barta yelled from the mass of fighting, but Lucius was already gone.

As Lucius burst into the hall, he saw two men come out of the shadows from the corner of his eyes, ducked, and slashed at their midriffs with one swing, sending them both screaming to the ground.

Two more warriors came at him, and he was sent hurling backward into the wattle and daub wall as the haft of a battle axe slammed into his armoured chest. He dropped and rolled, his blade driving upward into the man's throat while his other hand drove the pugio into the chest of the other.

The attacks ceased, and Lucius looked up.

There, in the middle of the hall, the Wolf held out the glinting blade of his battle axe to rest beneath the neck of Epona herself.

Lucius stepped forward, but even as he did so he felt his blood run cold, for out of the shadows stepped the Morrigan.

Epona's eyes did not plead, but Lucius could tell that there was fear there, even then, for him.

Lucius held up his dripping blade and pointed it at the Wolf. "Let her go."

The Wolf laughed. "You fight well, Dragon. Are you ready to die?"

"You are the one who will die today," Lucius said, but as he spoke, the Morrigan laughed and approached him.

"You are wrong, Dragon."

Her voice chilled Lucius, and sapped his strength. Her very presence darkened the room about them.

Suddenly, at Lucius' side, Epona's three white hounds appeared, growling, their red eyes intent upon the Wolf, but even as their courage flamed, it wavered under the gaze of the Morrigan.

The dread goddess laughed again. "You may have defeated the Lord of Annwn, Dragon. But you cannot defeat my son. He will devour your flesh, and your family, your friends, will all burn in fires of despair."

No, Lucius! Don't! Epona cried in Lucius' mind, but he did not heed her.

Lucius rushed the Morrigan and the hounds leapt for the Wolf.

The huge warrior swung his axe at the oncoming beasts, and as he did so, Epona appeared in a burst of light between Lucius and the Morrigan.

Lucius cut off his attack and leapt for the Wolf then, even as the two goddesses grappled with unimaginable power that lit up the entirety of the hall.

The Wolf and Lucius circled each other for a moment, and before Lucius could adjust his mind to the task, the Wolf was rushing in to grab Lucius and throw him over the flames of the hearth to roll like a child's toy in the dirt beyond.

There was a pounding at both sets of doors of the hall then and even as the Sarmatian and Votadini warriors burst through, they dropped to their knees before the bright light of battle emanating from Epona and the Morrigan.

Lucius felt his head snap back as the Wolf's great fist connected with the cheek piece of his helmet, sending it flying into the wall as the leather strap broke. He shook his head, unable to gain his feet, his hands still clinging to his sword and pugio as he was thrown against the wall again.

The Wolf rushed, howling, the tattooed eyes upon his chest coming to life as he charged, the great spike upon the tip of the battle axe driving for Lucius' heart.

But Lucius side-stepped as quickly as he could and drove his elbow into the Wolf's neck, giving his attacker pause enough to allow Lucius to slash his blade across the Wolf's tattooed eyes.

Lucius followed it up by driving his pugio into the Wolf's right shoulder blade, but was knocked backward and through the back doors of the hall to tumble down the wooden stairs and onto the fish-drying platform of the quay.

As Lucius opened his eyes, a black carrion crow dove for his face. He slashed up to hack the bird in half, and in that instant he heard the Morrigan scream inside the hall.

The Wolf appeared in the doorway at the top, as more of his warriors came around the walkway to rush into the hall to meet the arriving Sarmatians and Votadini who were battling, unbeknownst to them, alongside the two goddesses.

Lucius got to his feet, his lungs heaving painfully, and pointed his sword up at the Wolf.

"Come now! Let's finish this!"

The Wolf smiled, but his smile turned to anger as Lucius slashed at another carrion crow descending upon him, causing the Morrigan to cry out again.

The Wolf leaped from the top of the stairs, his axe just missing Lucius' neck as he retreated and parried in amongst the fish racks.

The blows and swings came quick and full of fury, scything through everything as the Wolf advanced, his eyes like fire, his titanic bulk bristling with rage and a thirst for the kill.

Lucius parried, and ducked, spun and lunged, inflicting myriad small wounds upon the son of a goddess rushing upon him. Behind them, the battle had spilled onto the platform, the cries of the two goddesses rising to a crescendo above the din of battle, the sounds of dying men, and screams of horses.

All of it rang in Lucius' mind at once, a chaotic symphony of death and dying. He felt he was at the eye of a great storm, staring Death in the face at that very moment.

The Wolf kicked out and Lucius spun, but not enough to avoid the blow. He was knocked into a tangle of fish racks, his left hand reaching up to stop the descending blow, his right hand gripping his sword still, unwilling to release it.

The Wolf's axe buried itself in the planks of the quay beside Lucius' face, and Lucius reached for the handle of his pugio, still jutting from the Wolf's shoulder, and fastened upon it.

Lucius pressed the blade deeper into the Wolf's body and twisted it, but the Wolf seemed to gain strength from his pain and rage. He lifted Lucius up to headbutt him.

Lucius kneed him, his sword arm flapping to the right as his head reeled.

"No!" Lucius cried as his blade slipped from his bloody hand into the dark water directly below him.

The Wolf laughed and fastened his hands about Lucius' neck.

My Lord Apollo, Lucius cried out in his mind. *Give me strength!*

Lucius' hand reached up and grabbed hold of the eagle-headed pugio there. He pulled with all his might and the Wolf cried out in anger, his grip loosening even as they both fell into the black abyss of the water below.

Darkness encircled them as the weight of their struggle, and Lucius' armour, pulled them down, farther and farther.

As they sank, the Wolf pushed Lucius toward the bottom, his raging eyes visible to Lucius who held onto his enemy's neck.

Lungs came to bursting point, and in that moment, Lucius felt that the end was near.

Then it came, a singular note in those dark depths, a clear ringing, a light from below.

Lucius craned his neck to see his sword jutting up from the bottom of the lake, illuminating their surroundings. His hand reached up for the pugio still embedded in the Wolf, withdrew it, and drove it into the Wolf's ribs.

The Wolf's grip fell away and Lucius stabbed again, turning them both over once, then again as they struggled until Lucius was on top, pushing his enemy downward.

The brilliant blade of his sword exploded through the Wolf's face, and they came to a sudden stop on the bottom.

Lucius felt his vision going, the strength in his body at an end, and for a moment, he thought of giving himself up to death, letting the dark water fill his lungs, to be done with all of the pain and torment and confusion.

Then, he felt heat and light, and through the cracks of his closing eyes, he saw her, Lady Venus. She glowed in the depths, her hair swirling like streams of seaweed in the current. She leaned forward and placed her hand upon his chest, filling him with strength and a will to live.

Do not let go now, Anguis! she said.

With a last breath of godly air in his lungs, Lucius pushed off of the bottom with all his might toward the moonlit surface of the lake above.

He felt his strength wane however, as he rose to the top, unsure if the goddess' touch were enough. The weight of his armour, and of his worries, threatened to drag him down again, but he pumped with his burning legs, his mind bent on living, on life and love, and the world above that black and watery Hades.

Finally, he broke the surface of the blood-churned water, and the stars appeared in the sky above.

Lucius gasped at the fresh night air, but he could not call to his men, his voice too weak to rise above the ongoing sounds of battle above.

Bodies floated all around him, choked him, and threatened to push him under until he heard a splashing and heavy breathing coming nearer and nearer, and a moment later, Xanthus' great bulk was beside him.

Lucius gripped the stallion's mane and felt himself dragged away, cutting through the water, away from the great fire of the burning cranogh.

There was a crying in the air, the weeping of a single child, her heart on the verge of breaking absolutely. The sound travelled in and out of the world of the living, twining its way among the thick wisps of morning mist, even as the chariot of the sun sped into the sky from its distant halls.

Baba? the voice said. *Wake up, please... Wake up!*

The voice was familiar, a beacon of light and heat and love.

Lucius' mind awoke, still trapped in black depths, surrounded by wolves, but the voice of his daughter called out to him again.

Leave him alone! Baba! You must wake up!

"Calli...ope?" Lucius' cracked lips formed the words of his daughter's name where he lay face down, unable to move. His body ached all over, and it was cold...so cold.

Baba, she is coming to help you...the goddess. You must stay awake! Calliope's voice pleaded once more in the recesses of his mind. *Stay awake...*

His eyes opened, but all he saw was darkness and mist.

Lucius reached out a hand to search the dark before him and felt a warm, solid, heaving bulk.

"Xanthus?" Lucius said, straining to raise his face and look up.

The stallion groaned and awakened, the heaving of his great belly revealing the wound that had only been stopped short of fatality by the severed saddle girth.

"Praefectus!!!" came the call from the misty world beyond.

"Anguis!!!" came the voice of another.

But Lucius could not speak, could not recall immediately where he was or how he got there. He was not even certain he lived, for his body felt cold, heavy, and wet, as if he had been dumped from on high into the very depths of Tartarus.

Then, the mist to his side swirled, and Xanthus raised his head.

Lucius searched for his sword, but it was not there. He struggled to turn over, to meet the Morrigan face to face as her carrion birds swarmed the world about him.

But the world brightened instead, and out of the mist, walking toward Lucius was Epona.

She was barefoot, her robes torn, her face and body bloodied and rent with fiery tears in her flesh from her struggle with the goddess of battle and death. She paused when she saw Lucius, then rushed to his side.

Anguis, she said, kneeling beside Lucius and taking his hand in hers. *It is over. You have a victory.*

Her voice shook, and as Lucius looked upon her, he realized that they had both come close to death that night. "And you?" he asked. "The Morrigan?"

She is defeated for now. When you slew her son, she retreated.

Lucius closed his eyes. *The Wolf.* Images of blood and a watery struggle flashed in his mind, and he felt strong hands clamped around his throat.

Victory, she repeated, and then leaned over Lucius to place her lips gently upon his.

Just as saplings and trodden blooms returned to their glory upon Epona's divine touch, so too did Lucius then feel heat and strength re-enter his body. Through the strands of the goddess' fiery hair, he saw the sun break through the canopy of cloud.

Epona stood and looked down upon him with love and kindness in her eyes. *I must go...* she told him. *I must heal, and so must you...* She reached out again, but this time to Xanthus, whose great eyes could not be torn from the sight of her, and as she laid her hands upon his belly and forehead, the stallion was soothed of pain and fear, the same as his rider.

"Anguis!!!" Dagon's voice tore through the mist until, not far off, a large group of warriors emerged along the shore. "There he is!"

Barta and Dagon were the first to fall to their knees beside Lucius, both breathing raggedly. Their panicked hands hovered over him, afraid to touch him, to feel his skin cold as death.

But Lucius slowly opened his eyes, and both Sarmatians sighed loudly, their eyes full of relief.

"Is it finished?" Lucius asked, his eyes open wider now, his mind searching for Epona, though she was now gone.

"You have a victory, Lucius," Dagon said.

Lucius looked up at his friend's bloody, cut and bruised face and smiled painfully. "*We* have a victory."

"Praefectus..." Barta said. "I thought we had lost you. I'm sorry I wasn't at your side. When we saw you go over the edge and into the water with the Wolf...I feared..."

Lucius put his hand upon Barta's armoured shoulder and squeezed with what strength he had. "Do not fear, Barta. I am well-" He looked up as more and more men came to see him - Sarmatians, Votadini, and men of the legions - including Tribune Fulvius whose young face was covered in blood and soot.

"Help me up," Lucius said to Dagon and Barta.

The two men lifted him slowly and held onto him until he found his balance. As he stood, Xanthus rose too, towering above everyone there. Lucius walked up to him and stroked his long neck. "Thank you for saving me, my friend," he whispered, then turned to Dagon. "He pulled me from the lake."

Dagon looked upon the stallion with pride, for he and Lucius had bonded as closely as any horse and rider ever could have. It was the way of their people to do so, and the Dragon and his mount had exemplified that.

Lucius' face darkened as he and the rest of the warriors about him looked down the shoreline to see the smoking remains of the cranogh. Carrion birds and gulls circled high in the sky above the litter of bodies of men and horses. The losses had been heavy, he knew, but he was reluctant to ask.

"How bad?" Lucius said.

Dagon wiped his face, and some of the crusted blood fell away. "We're still counting, but it's bad. I'd say we lost two turmae of men at least, and the same number of horses. Most fell into the water during the charge, and many of the horses snapped legs when they got caught between broken planks." Dagon paused, fighting back the tears that threatened to fall. "We've been putting down horses as we find them."

"I don't want our fallen men left here," Lucius said. "Use the Caledonian boats and find them." He turned to the tribune nearby. "Fulvius...what of your losses?"

"My centurion is still tallying things and searching for missing men, but I'd say we lost about seven contubernia in total. The Maeatae and Caledonii came from every direction."

"Can your men begin building pyres for our fallen comrades?" Lucius asked him.

"I've already ordered it, Praefectus."

Lucius nodded to the man. "Thank you." He was silent then as he watched the men working around the lake. "How many of the enemy survived?"

"All of the Caledonii and Maeatae warriors have been slain!" Afallach said as he rode up to Lucius.

Lucius smiled, happy to see the lord of the Votadini still alive.

"We spared the women and children as you commanded," Afallach said, anticipating the next question. "They are under guard beside the road."

"Good. Ensure that they are given food from their own stores, if there is any left, and release them into their highlands." There were some grumblings at this, but Lucius put his hand up to silence the men around him. "We've fought hard, and those who fought against us have fallen. I'll not murder or enslave women and children just for being present here. This was their home."

Lucius turned back to Afallach. "What about Argentocoxus? Do you have him?"

Afallach once more looked dismayed and full of anger, gripping the spear that rested upon his legs. "He escaped...fled across the lake in the night in one of the boats. We're combing the shoreline, but..."

Lucius sighed, angry that the Caledonian chieftain had, once again, escaped punishment for his treachery. However, he knew that it pained Afallach even more to have missed slaying his father's murderer.

More and more men gathered around the group of officers then, their voices rising in talk of the battle, of how hungry they were, who among them had been lost, and who had fought most bravely.

"And what of the Wolf?" Lucius asked loudly of his men. "Has anyone seen him?"

There were confused looks all around until Afallach answered. "I think our Dragon Praefectus should turn around and see what has become of the Wolf of the Maeatae," he said, pointing with his spear to a spot on the pebbled shore where a massive body, tattooed with a wolf, lay face down with Lucius' golden hilted sword and pugio jutting from it.

The men about them began to mutter loudly and cheer.

"The Dragon has slain the Wolf!" someone yelled.

"The Wolf is dead!" others cried.

Lucius walked over to the Wolf's body which lay there, like a great, slain leviathan upon the beach. Gazing down at his fallen enemy, he knew that the Morrigan would not forget, that she would ever seek his life, just as he would have anyone who would have done such a thing to his own children.

And then there was the sword, gleaming in the cold, misty morning air of that lake of death. At the back of his mind, he had feared it lost forever.

The men grew strangely silent about him, for they all remembered the tales of the Wolf's brutality, his slaying of many a friend during the war.

Lucius pulled his pugio free from the Wolf's ribs, wiped in on his sodden cloak and sheathed it. He then put his boot upon the body, grasped the sword's handle with both hands and pulled hard.

Slowly, the gleaming blade came free, and Lucius raised it into the air. *Thank you, Apollo...*

The men erupted in cheers then, their faces battle-worn, filthy, and relieved, proud of the leader before them.

"Metellus! Metellus! Metellus!" they chanted.

"The Wolf is dead!"

"Barta, flip him over," Lucius said, looking down at the body.

Barta bent, wedged his hands beneath the body, and heaved.

The tattooed eyes upon the Wolf's chest stared back at Lucius, and the dead mortal eyes gazed blankly into the sky as if disappointed in his divine mother.

It was then that Lucius felt anger, and the power that came with surviving such a battle. This enemy deserved the death he had received and in thinking that, Lucius breathed deeply and swung his sword downward into the Wolf's neck.

All around him, men roared their approval, and chanted the name of Lucius Metellus Anguis to the sky above the battlefield.

They remained at the cranogh for two days, taking stock of losses, preparing the pyres for the rites of their fallen friends and comrades, and taking care of the wounded. It would be a long march back to Fendoch, but the thought of their enemy's final defeat, and their role in it, gave every man a strength of step and spirit.

Offerings were made to the Gods upon the beach where wooden altars had been erected to Apollo, Venus and Epona, Mars, and the warlike gods of the Sarmatians, of the sacred sword and sky. When the rites and prayers were set, the pyres were lit, the brave remains of men and horses consumed slowly by the flames, making the transit from flesh and bone to ashes and dust.

Many a man wept to see such a sight, the cost of hard-won victory, but now they were able to imagine a return to base, to warmer climes, and to family.

Lucius, Dagon, Afallach and Tribune Fulvius, as commanders, made the rounds of the men, thanking them for their bravery, encouraging them in the rush and inevitable emptiness that came with victory, so that no man felt truly alone.

When all was done, when the trophies of death hung heavy upon the saddle horns of the Sarmatian warriors, the cranogh was set ablaze to dissolve and fall away into the murky depths of the lake.

Lucius and his men turned their backs upon it, and marched for Fendoch.

When the fort came into view, there were cheers from the ramparts at the sight of the dragon vexillum, the horse of the Votadini, and the centaur of the Parthica legion. The gates were thrown open for the first time since the army had set out.

Those inside the fortress were keen to hear of the battle, but their enthusiasm was tempered by the losses that were recounted to them. Every man among them knew someone, or many, among the dead, and each survivor offered his own private prayers for their safe passage to Elysium, should the Gods decide that is where they should wander.

As Lucius approached the fortress at the head of the army, he thought of his family, and how he would see them again. He could not help feeling that no amount of prayers or offerings could make up for the life he had managed to hang onto.

However, as the battle haze dissipated from his mind, he felt panic begin to settle on the fringes of his mind, and he wondered about himself and his own role, for there, he still felt confusion.

He forced himself to focus as the broad oak tree upon the plain of the glen came into view, and he remembered all of the death it represented. He looked down at the wagon that pulled the Wolf's monstrous body, and gazed up at the kontos that held his head. That night, there would be one final blaze.

Beneath a black sky pocked with stars, the surviving Sarmatians, Votadini, and men of Parthica legion stood upon the grassy glen before the great oak tree.

The Sarmatians present all remembered the death that tree represented, the images of their dismembered countrymen hanging from those gnarled limbs. Now, before them, the headless body of the Wolf of the Maeatae was nailed to that broad trunk, the limbs of the oak doused in pitch.

Lucius stood at the front of the ranks of his men and allies with Dagon, Barta, Afallach and Tribune Fulvius, gazing up at the tree.

Orange light from the burning braziers cast shadows from the branches of the tree, whose limbs appeared to wring like hands upon the grass. A wind picked up, as if attempting to blow out the flames, but Lucius stepped forward to grasp the shaft of a torch from the brazier. The cold wind bit at his face, and pulled at his cloak, but he pressed on, the torch held aloft, the flames alive.

He looked up at the body upon the broad trunk.

For the deaths of my men...my friends...

He reached out then, touched the flaming brand to the black pitch and the tree came alive with writhing flames, spreading, climbing, consuming.

Lucius stepped back and watched as the body of the Wolf sizzled and burned and blackened. He thought of all the men who had died upon that tree, and upon the stilts and shoreline of the cranogh, and his heart raced with satisfaction, and with fear.

The action could not be taken back, the deaths undone, but there was some glory to be had in the sound of the Morrigan's keening on the rushing wind of the glen as her hateful son burned, the flames rising into the night sky to illuminate the darkness.

XVII

MATER CAMPESTRUM

'Mother of the Camp'

Low, dark clouds had settled over the city of Eburacum for several days now, weeks perhaps. The warmer weather had done nothing to push out the darkness, and the mud and cobbled streets of the settlement were dank and damp beneath boot and wagon wheel. There was still a buzz in the air with the imperial court still in residence as the armies battled in the North against Rome's foes. The central agora of Eburacum remained alive in the grey light, the vendors and merchants of livestock, imported oils, wines, garum and more, ever-eager to cater to the imperial slaves who frequented their stalls.

However, a pall hung thick over the palace precinct of Eburacum, for there, the emperor and empress remained locked within. Rumours of Severus' health were rampant, and even more so were the rumours of what would happen should he die. These were answered with optimism by some, that the emperor had been ill for years and yet always recovered, so favoured by the Gods was he. Those of a less positive bent of mind believed that if he passed from this world into the next, another civil war would ensue, and the Pax Romana they all enjoyed would burn to ashes.

The corridors of the palace complex were quiet, but for the flickering of the braziers that burned both day and night to light and warm those cold corridors of stone, plaster and brick. Praetorian guards stood sentry everywhere, keeping careful watch, by order of Papinianus.

Meanwhile, in the imperial chamber, the emperor lay abed, fighting upon the battlefield of his soul as he faded in and out of sweaty dreams, sometimes delirious, sometimes lucid, and with a will to take care of the business of empire.

The whole of her husband's illness, Julia Domna, Empress of Rome and Mother of the Camp of Rome's legions, sat at his bedside, speaking to Severus, updating him on the reports she received from across the empire, going over correspondence, family news from

Syria or Africa, and updates from the front in Caledonia which Papinianus brought on a regular basis.

The rebellion of the Maeatae and Caledonii had filled Severus with an anger and rage that, she thought, would raise his breaking body from his bed, but even as he had prepared to lead the army, his illness had struck him low once more, and it was all she and her kinsman, Papinianus, could do to dissuade him to remain abed and entrust the campaign to Caracalla, and administration of the empire to her and Geta.

Severus had not fully agreed, but he was in no state to countermand their wishes. He was frustrated with his weakness. He had hoped to fight, to wage one last war to show his might to the world, but such hopes were but dreams.

The stars upon the ceiling of his chamber, and the great stone urn staring at him from its niche in the wall, were reminders of the approaching time.

As the fire crackled and she sipped lightly of warm, honeyed wine, Julia Domna looked upon her husband as he slept peacefully for a time, at least, without the fevered mumblings he was usually beset by.

She was afraid.

It was a sentiment she had not felt for some time, not since the dark days of Plautianus' choking hold upon the empire and her husband. She laughed silently at that, for those days now seemed halcyon compared to the current predicament. Too much was unknown, and it was difficult to know who one's enemies were. Though friends abounded in the shadows, they were too afraid to step forward, to stand beside her with what loomed ahead. She stood in the sunlight by herself, beside her husband's bed while all but a few like Papinianus and her sons stood beside her, burning beneath the Gods' gaze and the light of those stars above.

She looked up at the ceiling and felt anger in her heart. *Why?* she demanded of the painted constellations, but there was no answer, as there had been no answer in the blood of her offerings to Baal. The days of her colourful youth in Syria were long past.

Julia Domna had also fallen into the habit of remembrance, of longing for the past, that she knew was unhealthy, unhelpful, weak. In the deep of night, she had often risen from her own bed to come to her husband's side, dismissing Castor, and sitting there with tears in her eyes, tears she would allow none but the Gods to witness.

As she looked upon the white hair and bearded face of her husband - a man who had conquered the world - she had been unable to stop herself remembering him young, and dark, and muscled again. Before her eyes, she saw Severus as such again, his olive skin and oiled beard, the battle-scarred body that had held her and given her two sons, that had begun a dynasty Rome would never forget.

She wrote the history of this man, her husband, upon her heart in that room, but ever those stars loomed above her head and his, and then the colour would fade from his face, his skin, and the scars of disease would appear and blossom in horrible reds, pinks and browns, while the bulky, taut muscles of his body would shrivel and collapse as quickly as her momentary hopes and dreams.

The vibrant man the Gods had sent her, whom she had wanted from the moment she had laid eyes upon him in the bright sunlight, was now old and wasting, and he would remain so until the writing on those dreaded stars came to pass.

When Julia Domna closed her eyes, she thought of the Syrian sun she missed so much, the blueness of the thrashing sea, the feel of the sand beneath her bare feet. It felt good to think of such things, but in her mind, she heard her sons' angry voices pulling her back, and her worries began anew. With her eyes closed, she frowned, her once smooth face creased beneath her greying hair.

"What...are you thinking about, Julia?" Severus said to her one day when he emerged from a long, sweaty sleep. His rheumy eyes stared up at her for a moment before seeking the stars upon the ceiling.

The empress leaned forward to place her hand upon his brow, to bring his eyes back to her.

"Why do you weep?" he asked.

"For you, Septimius...and for our sons."

"Our sons..." he said, nodding very slowly as if there were nothing to worry about. "Good boys."

"They loathe each other. This war has not helped them to grow closer, but farther apart."

Septimius Severus stared at the ceiling above and wondered how much time was left, though he suspected very little. He could hear the Gods calling him from afar, he could see the sand seas of Africa Proconsularis, the honey-coloured streets of Leptis Magna... "I dreamed of the desert," he said to his wife. "Swaying palms and dunes that touched the horizon, they were so tall...beautiful."

Julia Domna looked at her husband and nodded, unsure what to say.

His hand reached out for hers and she took it. He squeezed with a surprising amount of strength. "The desert," he repeated. "There is beauty in the unknown...that which we cannot see. There is uncertainty..." he breathed slowly, not wanting to fall into a coughing fit. "But...I know...that our sons, though they do not love each other...they will find accord between them, they will do what is needed to preserve this empire I have fought for."

The empress leaned forward and kissed her husband's hand, a tear falling from her cheek onto it.

"No tears," he whispered, and with his thumb, he wiped her cheek.

Julia Domna sat back up, her silk stola ruffling beneath the thick wool cloak she had taken to wearing about the palace. "No tears," she repeated, sniffing once and wiping her eyes. "You are right, Husband. Our sons will find harmony between them. And Euodus has been schooling them to that end, speaking with Geta daily and writing to Antoninus."

"Good," Severus said, his voice weaker, his eyes closing and opening. "They must also have harmony at home," he added. "Antoninus must reconcile with his wife...with Plautilla, and her brother, Plautius, when back in Rome. And you must find Geta a wife. A man must have family. In this way, the Gods have blessed us, have they not?"

Julia Domna looked down at her husband and smiled sadly. "Yes, they have," she said, thinking *But our sons are not the men you are. They are not capable of wise rule.*

Just then, there was a knock on the door, and Castor entered followed by Geta.

"It is morning, my lady," Castor whispered to the empress. "I can take over if you wish."

"Thank you, Castor. The emperor and I were just discussing our sons." She stood, turned toward Geta, and smiled. At twenty-two, he was the mirror-image of his father when he was young. Since coming to Britannia, Geta had come into his own, it was true. The administration was running well, and supplies flowed smoothly due to his astute management. The troops loved him, and for a time, he seemed to grow less selfish than the young man who had been taken away from Rome to the frontier. It was only when Geta was near his brother that things changed.

"Mother," Geta said, bowing and kissing her hand. He removed his cloak, laid it across the back of the chair, and straightened his indigo tunic with embroidered stars in gold about the hem. "How is he?"

"Come closer...my son," the emperor said, his hand reaching for Geta.

"Father." Geta approached slowly, and knelt beside the bed.

Severus managed a smile, and pat his son's cheek.

Geta, it seemed to Castor, who was tending the bandages of his emperor on the other side of the bed, wanted to pull away in disgust at the smell that lingered, but the freedman said nothing, and went about his business.

"My son," the emperor continued. "Remember...you and your brother must rule harmoniously if you are to keep power."

"I know, Father. You have told me this already."

"Enrich the soldiers...and scorn all other men."

Castor looked up as he finished his work, and saw the young man nodding at his father's advice. Glancing around the room, he saw the slaves adding fuel to the braziers and lighting more incense.

"Thank you, Castor. My friend..." Severus broke off to address his freedman.

"Sire..." Castor bowed, his eyes filling with tears that fell not only because of the imminent death of his former master and friend, but at what might become of them if the boy before him were permitted to rule alongside his older, more hateful, brother.

"That will be all for now, Castor," the empress said. "Geta and I will stay with the emperor for a while longer."

"Yes, my lady. I will return with broth and bread soon."

"Very good."

Castor bowed and went to the double doors of the chamber, opened them and went out.

"There must be harmony," the emperor said as the doors closed.

In the corridor, Castor stopped for a moment between the two silent Praetorians guarding the room. He breathed deeply, and turned left down the corridor, his steps going quickly as he passed the sentries on duty, standing guard between the torches in their brackets along the red and white painted walls. He came to a peristyle and made the circuit until he reached the other side where two more Praetorians stood guard.

The guards recognized him and nodded for him to enter.

Inside the tablinum, he found Papinianus sitting behind his broad table covered in piles of scrolls and missives upon wax tablets.

Sitting across from him was Euodus, long-time tutor for both Caracalla and Geta.

"Ah, Castor," Papinianus beckoned him to enter and sit with them.

A slave offered the freedman a cup of wine, and Castor accepted it, drinking a little and then setting it down.

"Here we are then," Euodus said, patting Castor's arm. "Three old men, uncertain about the future."

"Life is uncertain," Papinianus said.

"Quite," the tutor added. "Though I have hope that my work with our young Caesars over the years will bear fruit. As harmony is essential in playing music that is pleasing to the Gods, so to is it essential in wise rule. The emperor believes it so."

Castor and Papinianus looked at each other, then Castor spoke.

"But the question remains, do Antoninus and Geta believe it to be so?"

"I believe the lesson has sunk in, yes," Euodus said confidently. "When the day comes - and it will, sadly, - they will be ready to rule with the harmony their father wishes."

"Then there is hope for the future," Papinianus said.

Euodus nodded.

"How is the emperor today, Castor?" the Praetorian prefect asked.

"He is awake, and speaking," Castor said. "He speaks to Geta of harmony."

Euodus smiled. "You see? Geta understands. But I am pleased to hear the emperor is speaking."

"He still looks to the stars above, and awaits the day of his death," Castor said sadly.

"That reminds me," Euodus added. "I must seek out his astrologer and ask if the stars reflect harmony."

Castor and Papinianus were silent for a few moments and then the latter spoke. "Then, by all means you must do so, Euodus. The guards informed me just before you arrived that the astrologer

ISLE OF THE BLESSED

returned early this morning after spending the night making his observations."

"It was an unusually clear night," Euodus said. He nodded and got up. "I shall seek him out. Gentlemen."

When Euodus was gone and the door closed, Castor looked to Papinianus, his face incredulous. "I think he's gone senile!"

"I fear that may be true. He believes his lessons have had such a positive effect upon the boys. Perhaps they have with Geta, but with Antoninus…"

"Geta?" Castor shook his head. "When I was changing the emperor's bandages just now, Geta looked as though he would vomit. He was disgusted just being around his father. Harmony…pah! They don't know the meaning of the word."

"Euodus has done his best, but you are right, I'm afraid. The message has not got through, nor will it." Papinianus lowered his voice. "That is why new leadership is required…to preserve the harmony that does exist in the empire."

Castor nodded, his eyes glancing at the silent slave in the corner, far enough not to hear. "But you have no answer there. No certainty."

"I have the favour of the troops as a certainty," Papinianus said. "I only require agreement."

"He's too good and honest. Would he be up to the task?" Castor's voice was full of doubt, and fear. "And what of our beloved Augusta? Where does she fall in all of this?"

"We must care for her at all costs. She has saved this empire as much as Severus himself. We cannot go back to the dark days of Plautianus."

"Never!" Castor said.

A loud knock came at the double doors and they opened.

Daylight filled the room, illuminating the black and white mosaic floor and the pigeon holes filled with scrolls behind Papinianus.

"Yes? What is it?" the Praetorian prefect asked.

"A messenger from the front, Prefect," the guard said. "He's with the Sarmatian cavalry ala of Praefectus Lucius Metellus Anguis."

Castor and Papinianus looked quickly at each other.

"Send him in," Papinianus told the guard.

The guard saluted, and went out. A moment later, the jingle of scale armour approached and in came a bearded warrior, his armour

513

dirty from the road, his long sword swinging by his side. He saluted Papinianus.

"You're a long way from the front, Decurion…"

"Brencis, sir."

"You have news?"

"Yes, sir. Praefectus Metellus sent me with all haste to hand this message to you and you alone." Brencis stepped forward and handed a small leather tube to Papinianus.

Papinianus took it, undid the laces and shook it out. He unrolled the letter and read the short message. When he finished, he looked up at Brencis with wide eyes. "Is it true?"

Brencis nodded, and smiled proudly. "Yes, sir. It is. The praefectus struck at the heart of the enemy. The Wolf of the Maeatae is dead."

In her chambers that afternoon, the empress sat alone again with her thoughts, feeling more optimism since her conversation with her younger son than she had in a long time. Julia Domna sat at her table by the fire of a brazier. A fresh sheet of papyrus was laid out before her. She wished in that moment that her eldest, Caracalla, was not so distant, that he was right there and able to sit down with her, the emperor, and his brother to shape a brighter future.

With the firelight glinting off of the gold and jewels bedecking her fingers, she dipped her bronze stylus into the ink pot. Her hand stood poised just above the paper, but she found it difficult to begin. Just as the ink was about to drip, she began writing…

Dear Antoninus,

My son, I hope that this letter finds you well and happy at Horea Classis, and that you have not endured injury in the fighting. I trust not, as we would have received word of it. We have received news of many victories accompanied by heavy losses to raiding, but this is war, and that is to be expected.

The legions are fortunate to have you leading them.

But this is not a formal missive. There are no orders from the emperor here. This is a letter from a mother who deeply loves her son and wants only the very best for him. I prevail upon the Gods to this end daily, and hope, as ever, that they hear my fervent wishes.

Your father remains alive, but the Gods could take him any day, and as the day written upon the stars approaches, I find myself thinking more and more of you and your brother and how it is crucial that you both mend the rift between you so that you can rule the empire your father has built up, in harmony, for the benefit of all.

Though I do not want to think of such things just yet, your father's time is very short, and we need to plan for the future. We cannot afford another civil war, though you do not have the opponents your father had.

It is crucial that you continue to nurture your relationship with the legions and their commanders, even those you despise, for their loyalty in the days ahead will prove essential. Your father taught you that.

Men such as Lucius Metellus Anguis you need not worry about, for he has always been loyal to your father, to me, to us, and has always proven himself to be a true Roman. With his support and that of others, including members of the senate, the transition should be smooth.

But there are always wolves in the shadows, rats in the sewers, who will creep out of hiding when the time is right. Papinianus and I have these men in our sights, and our spies will take care of them when the time comes.

In the meantime, you must win this war. Finish it, so that you and Geta can return to Rome together... when the time comes.

Here, Julia Domna let fall a tear onto the stiff papyrus sheet to mingle with the ink. It still seemed strange to her to be writing such things, but she needed to have the same talk with Caracalla that she had just had with Geta. She wiped her eyes with a silk cloth, and carried on.

My beloved son, you and your brother are my world, and I would gladly give up my life to see you both safe upon your father's hard-won throne. By Baal, and the Sun and Stars, I swear it!

When war passes - as it must - I beg you to find it in your heart to love your brother, to accept him and stand beside him. Geta has grown much, and learned a great deal in the administration of this campaign and the empire itself. And with your learned skill among the men and upon the battlefield, you will complement each other perfectly. You will be as Castor and Pollux upon the imperial throne.

515

You will be better than Romulus and Remus. I know it in my heart, you will.

I must return to your father's side now, for he wakes often in confusion, and only faithful Castor and I can soothe him.

Until we meet again, I commend you to the Gods and give you all my love.

Your loving mother,
J.D.

Julia Domna finished and sat back in her chair, staring at the sheet of parchment. How strange it was to pour so much emotion, so much hope, onto the surface of so mundane an object as a sheet of papyrus.

She removed her signet ring with the image of a radiant sun and rolled the parchment. She then took a stick of wax, melted the end in the flames of the bronze lamp beside her, and let it drip onto the sheet. With her insignia pressed into the wax, she took the roll, blew upon the seal, and then slid it into a leather case.

The empress stood from her table then and went to the door to open it.

"I want this sent directly to Caesar in Horea Classis," she said to the Praetorian standing outside her door.

The man took the leather case and bowed. "Yes, my Empress."

After he departed down the corridor, his place taken by another guard, the empress went in the opposite direction, back to her husband's chamber, to see how he fared. She would have preferred to remain in her chambers where the ceiling was plain, empty, but she knew it was easier for her husband to gaze at the stars with her.

There will be time enough for me to gaze at the stars alone, she thought.

The spring air was cold, but the sun was shining along the banks of the Tava estuary where the walls and fortifications of Horea Classis and the surrounding forts rose up from the plain. Out in the water, dolphins skirted the surface of the sun-speckled sea, playing about the hulls of the bobbing ships that had arrived with supplies for the legions and now awaited orders, or made space along the quayside for those still arriving.

In every camp and along the streets of Horea Classis itself, the troops who had stayed behind went about their duties, their eyes watchful for any sign of the enemy, but also of Caesar, who three days before, had ridden out at the head of his Praetorians, and the first cohort of II Augusta legion, to fight an action near the old legionary fortress of Inchtuthil where scouts had spotted some of the enemy massing.

There was a tenseness in the air. Every man left behind could feel it.

It was as if the sun and its spring warmth were a diversion to mask the movement of something greater behind the scenes of a play, the calm before chaos.

Beside burning braziers, at mess, and on guard duty beside closed gates, men spoke of their friends and brothers who were out in the wilds fighting the Caledonii and Maeatae on the edges of those distant highlands, that were clearly visible on a day such as that.

The highlands loomed distant like brown teeth, and some imagined that their friends had been eaten up by them. The stories of surprise attacks and of massacres, of the human sacrifice of Roman prisoners of war in barbaric rituals, were rampant among the men of Rome's legions.

Men began to wonder what they were doing in Caledonia at all, for that land held nothing but anger, pain and regret for most. And yet, the rumour was that the emperor and his administration sought to built a great city there, a 'northern Rome', to lord it over the tribes of Caledonia and bring them into the empire's fold.

The despair, however, was kept at bay by the tales from the distant front, of the Dragon praefectus and his cavalry who had crushed a large Caledonian army in a surprise charge that was now the stuff of legend, and nearly captured the enemy chieftain, Argentocoxus. With men like Lucius Metellus Anguis leading the offensive, giving pain and torment back to the enemy, men took heart.

Now, they waited for Caesar, who had, up until that point, commanded from within the walls of Horea Classis on that second campaign in Caledonia.

Caracalla had received intelligence from scouts that a large force of Caledonii and Maeatae fleeing north had gathered at Inchtuthil, and so he had decided to take action. The legionary commanders who remained at Horea Classis had jostled to join him, and in the end, it was the Capricorn vexillum of II Augusta that flew high beside the thunder bolts of the Praetorian guard, and the legionary aquila and the imagina of the emperor.

Toward the tenth hour of daylight, Caesar's forces were spotted from the ramparts of Horea Classis, and the clear ringing of brass cornu could be heard across the plain.

Men rushed to the edges of the fortifications to see the force of Praetorians and men of II Augusta marching toward them, snaking their way along the banks of the Tava to the west, the banners caught high in the chill breeze.

The cornu sounded out again, and it was answered by those of the returning force.

As they approached, the men could see Caesar Caracalla at their head, surrounded by his Praetorian tribunes. The troops cheered as they approached, and a buzz went through the camps, guesses as to what had happened. It became clear as Caesar approached, smiling broadly, exchanging banter with the men, that they had won a victory, and the men cheered him even more for it.

"See how they adore you, Caesar?" Claudius Picus said from the horse beside Caracalla as they rode between the camps, making their way to the main gate of Horea Classis and the via Principalis.

Caracalla smiled and nodded slightly, saluting his men as they rode by. The adulation made him feel strong, happy, and he knew that this was where he belonged - at the head of his legions. He could now understand the power his father had felt over the years of war and campaign across the whole of the empire. *No one will ever take this from me,* he thought. *The legions are loyal to me now.*

The sound of cheering men was loud in Caracalla's ears, so much so that he could barely hear Claudius Picus beside him. The man had fought bravely at Caesar's side, and so Caracalla decided he would reward him with one of the Caledonian girls they had taken, who now rolled along at the back of the marching column in a cage upon a wagon.

Behind the Praetorian ranks, the men of II Augusta marched stern-faced and guarded, as did their own tribunes and legate commander. When this force came into view, men wondered why they did not share in the celebration of Caesar's victory over the enemy.

The men had been ordered by their tribunes to keep quiet and not speak of it, but some men, when their brothers in arms approached to walk beside their marching column, could not help but speak.

"Oh yes, we won!" one man said. "We slaughtered children, old men, and grandmothers, and took their women."

"Orders is orders," said another. "We did what we were told."

Soon, spreading quietly like blood or bile in a clear-running river, the whispers of what had really happened came to be known. The men had believed that Caesar had met a great force of the enemy and engaged him in a great battle, but it had not been a great slaughter. Those had been the original orders of the emperor in distant Eburacum, true, but the lustre of victory was greatly lessened by the act itself.

Caracalla continued to smile and nod and salute his men as he turned into the gaping gates of Horea Classis, staying just ahead of the rising tide of grumbles behind him. He and the Praetorian tribunes, Claudius at their head, turned into the courtyard of the principia as the rest of the Praetorian troops continued on to the barracks.

"Have the women washed and kept under guard in the Praetorium," Claudius ordered one of the centurions as they dismounted.

"Yes, sir!" the man said, turning on his heel and going out.

"You can take your pick, Marcus," Caracalla said to Claudius Picus. "You fought well."

Caracalla did not notice the sudden silence that had replaced the cheers without the walls then as the men of II Augusta returned to their own camp and the word spread. To his mind, they had followed the emperor's orders and successfully eliminated a large number of the enemy and, besides, the sound of the troops cheering for him still rang in his own ears, the same way that the sea sounds in the hollow of a shell.

"I thank you, Caesar," Claudius said. "We must celebrate your victory this night."

"Excellent idea!" Caracalla said as the Praetorian commanders gathered around him. "There will be food, wine, and captive women for us all to enjoy!"

The men about him cheered.

"And a few captive boys for others among you!" Claudius added, and they laughed.

At that moment, slaves brought out bronze basins of scented water and set them upon tripods in the courtyard for Caracalla and the others to clean their hands. Fresh towels were handed to them, and afterward the men dispersed to their offices about the courtyard to disarm and receive the lists of dead and injured from each of their cohorts. Once the tallies were received and reports finalized, they would join Caesar for a celebration.

"Ah, Ulpianus!" Caracalla said as the jurist approached from where he had been waiting along the wall outside the door.

Ulpianus saluted. "Hail, Caesar!" he said. "I hear you have a great victory."

Caracalla shrugged his shoulders. "We made short work of them, though there were many."

"The troops and the carrion birds will sing your praises to Olympus!"

Caracalla guffawed and made to leave, but Ulpianus stepped forward urgently.

"Sire, this letter from the empress just arrived from Eburacum."

Caracalla grabbed the letter and broke the seal. His heart fluttered and he felt an excitement building in his gut as he walked apart from the others to the centre of the courtyard. He stopped beside the altar of Jupiter, where a fire burned, and read.

"Harmony?" he muttered, his teeth gritted, his brow tight. "Accept him? Stand beside him?" Caracalla let out an enraged cry and balled the papyrus in his fist before tossing it on the fire.

"What is it, sire?" Claudius Picus approached slowly, his own hopes up. "Is the emperor...has it happened?"

Caracalla wheeled on him, his eyes wild and full of rage. "The emperor yet lives, you idiot!" he growled.

Claudius Picus nodded. "Then that gives you more time for further victories that will win you the loyalty of the troops, sire. Did you hear them? Listen again."

The air was silent, but for the neighing of their horses in the courtyard and the cracking of the empress' letter in the flames behind them.

Caracalla craned his neck, hoping to hear more of the adulation that had greeted him upon his arrival, but all that greeted him was silence and the boring sounds of camp life.

But then, there it was, louder than ever it had been, the roar of the men of the legions!

Caracalla smiled.

"Word of your victory must have spread among all of the camps now," Claudius said, feeling his own relief. "Listen how they cry 'Victory!'"

Caracalla turned to the altar where the offerings to Jupiter yet burned, and raised his hands to the sky above.

Just as he was about to utter the words of thanks, compelled as he was in that rare moment, one of the Praetorians on duty came rushing into the courtyard from the via Principalis.

"Caesar, come quickly!" the man said.

"What is it, soldier?" Claudius Picus turned on the man who stopped immediately and saluted.

Caracalla lowered his arms, and turned to face the man. "Yes?"

The man stepped forward and bowed. "Sire, forgive the interruption, but you must come with all haste to the south gate."

"Caesar will come," Claudius Picus said to the man, pointing that he should go. The man saluted and Claudius turned to Caracalla. "The men of the legions cheer for you and want to see you, Caesar. You should show yourself to them, armed and freshly returned from battle and victory."

"Excellent idea, Marcus," Caracalla said, smiling once more, his mother's letter all but forgotten. "You come too."

Claudius bowed to him and together, with Ulpianus and the other tribunes who had emerged from their offices, they all made their way down the via Principalis which was filling with men on and off duty, their centurions calling them back to their posts.

The sound was deafening, the cheers of 'Victory!' and 'Imperator!' constant and rising to the sky, building like the pressure in Vulcan's forge.

"This is incredible!" one of the tribunes behind Caracalla and Claudius said.

They arrived at the gates however, and saw that the men upon the ramparts were not looking down on them, on Caesar, but outward to something on the field outside the gates.

Caracalla emerged from the open gates onto the broad, muddy road to see the area choked with cheering men, their swords and spears in the air, their voices soaring to the sky. Caesar felt numbness and hate then, for the men of the legions were not calling to him.

521

They did not even notice him at first. Their attention and adulation was directed instead at one man - Lucius Metellus Anguis.

"Metellus! Metellus! Metellus!" the men chanted, like an adoring mob in the heart of Rome itself.

Lucius stood in front of Xanthus, flanked by his decurions who formed a sort of arched fan from either side of him as if there to present something.

When the Sarmatians had first joined the first campaign in Caledonia, the legions had looked upon them with distrust and doubt, but the elite cavalry force had become Rome's hammer in that land, bringing victory after victory, as was evidenced by the trophies hanging from their saddle horns, and the limbs upon their fortress walls wherever they were based.

The dragon vexillum fluttered serenely, confidently in the breeze above, flanked by the humming draco standards.

The Sarmatians stood stock-still, their hands clasped over their battered scale armour, stained with enemy blood, their long swords and clubs sheathed or hanging at their sides.

Caracalla stared directly ahead at Lucius who met his eyes, his face devoid of expression beneath the bristling red crest of his war helmet. Caesar put up his hand for silence and gradually, the chanting died down.

Lucius stepped forward, his hand grasping the one trophy that drew the gaze of every man there. High in the air, on the end of a kontos lance, Lucius held aloft the head of the Wolf of the Maeatae.

Blood ran down the shaft of the spear and gathered about Lucius' hand as he approached Caracalla and held it out.

Caracalla looked up at the extremely large head, its purple tongue jutting from the gapping mouth, the black hair fluttering like a barbaric war standard, the eyes, oddly enough, still colourful, as if the Wolf yet lived and bled. Caracalla looked at all of this, and then met Lucius' eyes again.

"Praefectus Metellus," he said loudly. "What have you brought me?"

Lucius came closer to Caracalla. "Sire, I bring you the head of the Wolf of the Maeatae. He is dead."

From among the men of the legions, someone shouted. "The Dragon of Rome has slain the Wolf!"

"The war is over!" shouted another.

Caracalla looked annoyed, but tried to hide it.

Lucius extended his arms to hand the kontos to Caracalla, his head bowed. He did not take a knee to offer his Caesar the gift.

For a moment, Caracalla only stared at the bloody lance, at Lucius' fists caked with blood as they gripped it.

Claudius ordered the Praetorians to move closer, but Caracalla put up his hand to stop them. He reached out and took the trophy in his hands. Then, he put the end of the lance down on the ground, holding it in his left hand, his right hand upon his hip.

"Is there no more?" Caracalla asked.

Lucius frowned, his eyes upon Caesar. "Sire?"

"Rome had more than one enemy in this war. You have brought me the head of the Wolf. But where is the head of Argentocoxus?" he said loudly so that all could hear.

There were rumblings among the men, and as word of what Caracalla said spread, angry voices rose. But they were not in agreement with Caesar. They were a chorus of rising anger at the disrespect shown to the hero of that war. The Wolf had massacred Rome for months, and none had come near to defeating him. Stories had already spread among the troops of the fight between the Dragon and the Wolf, of how Lucius had defeated him alone. And now Caesar dismissed the victory?

"Shame, Caesar!" someone yelled from the crowd.

Caracalla turned to Claudius. "I want whoever said that to be put in chains."

"Yes, sire," Claudius said. He turned and spoke to a couple of the guards behind him and they spread out to find the culprits, which legions and centuries they were in.

Lucius kept his face calm, though he wished to reach out and shake the man before him.

"Argentocoxus fled the battle, sire," Lucius finally said when the shouting voices calmed a little. "We're searching for him."

"I should think so!" Caracalla shouted. "One head, does not end a war, Praefectus! I should have thought a man of your experience would have known better."

If you had let me kill Argentocoxus the first time, we would not have found ourselves in this situation! How dare you shun this victory? Lucius felt like saying all of it and more, but he caught Claudius Picus' hateful gaze, his smirk, over Caracalla's shoulder and knew that anything he said would be of no consequence.

"The Wolf of the Maeatae, sire, has been leading this second rebellion from the beginning. He has been using Argentocoxus. Without the Wolf, the chieftain of the Caledonii will not last. We will find him!"

"Then do it!" Caracalla said, "And do not return to Horea Classis until Argentocoxus' head stands upon a lance!"

Lucius saluted calmly to Caracalla.

"Get out of here now, Praefectus, and go finish the job if you are able!"

Without another word, Lucius turned and went back to his men to mount Xanthus. From atop his mount, he could see all the faces looking up at him, a sea of men who longed for peace, who wanted to go home to their families and sweethearts, who had lost brothers, friends and so much more.

Once the rest of the Sarmatians were mounted, Lucius spun his horse to face the men of the legions, and he saluted them, his back to Caesar.

They raised their voices in his name, and their gladii beat upon their scuta as Lucius and his men rode away, back to the front, to the fighting.

As Lucius put distance between himself and Horea Classis, between himself and Caracalla, he felt a mixture of dread and anger in his gut, for the future, for the sort of leader Caracalla had turned out to be, and the sort of men Caesar surrounded himself with, mainly, Marcus Claudius Picus.

The latter was more of a danger than any other. Lucius felt certain of it.

"What are you thinking, Anguis?" Dagon asked when they were a couple of miles out.

"That Caracalla is not half the man his father is, or his mother."

XVIII

HOSTES ANTE PORTASI

'Enemies at the Gates'

"How is she today?"

Adara turned from Calliope's bedside to see Briana standing in the doorway, her hands holding her swollen belly. Adara sighed and turned back to her daughter's soundly sleeping face.

"She is getting better and better everyday, stronger too." She leaned over and kissed Calliope's brow and the girl sighed in her sleep.

For weeks, Calliope Metella had been out of sorts, her nights sleepless or riddled with nightmares, her days spent worrying about wolves and fire.

Briana had remembered the first time she had experienced a small iota of the Sight that Calliope seemed to possess, and that it had exhausted and terrified her. She knew the signs, knew that the girl was experiencing something powerful.

But Calliope was also young and afraid, and could not put into coherent thought the things she saw, though it was obvious she worried for her father, fighting far away in Caledonia.

Adara felt helpless, for though she felt the Gods near, watchful over them, she did not receive such visions, and found it difficult to understand how she could help her daughter, how she could ease her mind.

Thankfully, Briana did, and had received some instruction from Etain in Ynis Wytrin when Calliope's gift had become evident.

"It's not what I had wanted for her," Adara said as she pulled Calliope's blanket up. "I didn't want her burdened with such a thing. She's a child." *She's my child.*

Adara winced as she felt a kick in her own swollen belly, the young Metellus therein awake for the day now.

"She is strong, Adara," Briana said, coming to her side and placing her hand upon Adara's shoulder. "Come, you should eat. We all should." Briana felt her own belly again. "Phoebus can look after her. You've eaten already?" she asked the boy who sat on the other side of the bed watching his sister sleep.

"Yes," he smiled. "I'm fine, Mama. You go and eat. I'll watch her so that someone is here when she wakes."

Adara smiled and rose slowly from her stool to go around and kiss her son's head. "My big boy. How grown up you are."

The two women went out of the room and down to the hall below where Ula and Aina had set out food for them, and Phoebus had already built up the fire in the hearth.

When they were gone, Phoebus turned to his sister, his eyes focussed on her face. He set aside the gladius he had been carrying around with him, practicing with, since his father had given it to him, and held her hand gently.

"Sister...don't worry about Baba. He is safe now."

How do you know?

Phoebus stopped and wondered at his sister's words inside his head, though her face was calm and sleeping before him.

He could not speak for a moment, but once he calmed himself, he knew there was no danger. She could hear him as she slept.

"The lady Venus appeared to me. She told me that Baba slew the Wolf. He is safe."

Calliope's sleeping face smiled, but then a frown formed upon her lovely young features, like spilled ink upon a fresh sheet of papyrus, and she began to sob.

So many enemies... she said in Phoebus' head. *And fire...*

Phoebus began to panic, but forced himself to stay calm. Instead, he bent his thoughts to Venus.

Goddess, please help my sister...

Calliope's weeping grew louder and Phoebus shut his eyes, willing her to be calm, telling her that all was well, and then, she was calm.

He opened his eyes to look, and instead of the dim light of the room, Calliope's face was lit by a brilliant light, almost of starlight, for standing on the other side of the bed, leaning over her, was Venus.

She smiled tenderly at Phoebus, and placed her hand upon Calliope's brow.

Phoebus stared at Love, his heart full of emotion he could not explain or comprehend. He knew only that he had never felt such joy, such happiness. He could not understand why, in that remote

526

fortress-home, he could hear the gentle lapping of waves upon the sea.

Thank you, Goddess, he heard Calliope say.

All will be well, Love answered. *You are both strong.*

Calliope smiled and her eyes opened to behold the goddess.

Venus' smile to her was purest love, like light after a year of darkness.

Calliope nodded and turned to look at her brother, smiling joyfully.

Venus stood and walked around to Phoebus, bending over him so that her golden, luminescent hair poured over his head which she kissed gently.

Phoebus felt himself full of calm, his mind only of clear thought and joy as he gripped his sister's hand.

Take care of each other, young dragons, Venus said.

We will, the twins answered.

Venus was gone, and the sound of Spring birdsong came in at the window.

Down in the hall, Adara and Briana sat eating with Ula and Aina around the fire. It had become their daily ritual to do so. The women's pregnancies had progressed together and healthily, both of them sharing in the trials and tribulations, the joy and anticipation of being heavy with child.

It was not often they spoke of their worries for their husbands, for there was nothing to be done except pray daily to the Gods for their protection and safe return.

Adara had been more worried about Calliope. However, that had not stopped her from seeing to the proper running of the hillfort, the planting of the year's crops, maintenance of the bathhouse etcetera.

Both women continued to train, as much as was possible to do safely, but riding was becoming more and more difficult.

Adara was grateful for the help and support she received from Alma and Culhwch, Sigwyll, and of course the Sarmatian, Lenya, and the men who had remained behind.

The Sarmatians had been vigilant in their duty, and their watchful eyes were aware of what went on day and night about the hillfort.

Adara wondered that they slept at all, for there were not many of them.

Lenya ensured that the ramparts of the fort were in good repair after the winter had passed, that all of the horses were taken care of and exercised daily, and that fresh supplies for the animals were not lacking.

Adara could tell that, at times, the Sarmatians were restless, that they longed to be fighting alongside Lucius and Dagon, but they were also content with life at the hillfort.

Spring had blossomed early that year, and as snowdrops and crocuses poked out of the ground, the sight of spring lambs in the fields below became a thing of beauty and peace. Birdsong was a constant too, and sunlight. It seemed the whole world was awake after a long slumber.

The people of the village were of great support, especially Alma, Culhwch, and even Paulus who had taken to helping his uncle, Sigwyll, in the stables.

Alma had taken it upon herself to watch over the two pregnant women as well, bringing with her occasionally the local midwife to check on them.

"We will need to go into Lindinis for supplies tomorrow," Adara said to Briana and the girls as they ate that morning.

"I don't know if I have the strength," she sighed. "My little Sarmatian prince is quite demanding," she laughed.

"They'll be more demanding if we don't keep food coming," Adara joined in the laughter.

"We can bring supplies from the village," Ula offered. "There may be enough extra for purchase."

"No don't worry," Adara said. "They don't have extra at this time of year, and we need to top up the stocks here."

At that moment, there was a knock upon the double doors of the hall. The doors opened and Lenya came in. "Lady Metella... My Queen," he said, bowing to both Adara and Briana."

"Good morning, Lenya," Briana said. "All is well?"

"A quiet night, my Queen, yes. And a beautiful day."

"Please eat something, Lenya," Adara said, pointing to the platter of cheese and bread.

The Sarmatian shook his head. "No thank you, Lady Metella. I have already eaten."

Adara smiled. It was still strange to her to see the Sarmatians out of their armour on a regular basis, dressed only in their knee-length breeches, tunics and cloaks. It had been decided that they should go

528

un-armoured at the hillfort in case someone chanced to recognize them as soldiers and realize they had not obeyed the summons back to the front.

The villagers could be trusted, but beyond that, anyone could have a wagging tongue.

"Lenya," Adara said. "The children and I need to go into Lindinis. Would two of you be able to escort us?"

"No, my lady. Four of us shall escort you." He smiled and bowed.

Adara laughed, used by now to his wry sense of humour. "I thank you. If you could prepare the wagon and horses, I would be most grateful."

"It shall be done," he said, bowing again to both ladies and turning to go out.

Briana noticed both Ula and Aina blushing as they watched him go, and she nudged Ula with her foot. "He's a handsome young man," she said.

The girls shifted awkwardly and giggled.

Briana laughed and turned back to Adara.

"Are you sure you don't want to come?" Adara asked. "It might be the last trip there for a while."

"I'm sure. I'm feeling quite tired today. I might make use of the baths."

"I'll come!"

They turned to see Alma's tall, lithe form coming into the hall.

Adara clapped and pushed herself to her feet. "Excellent!"

Alma came over and hugged her and Briana. "How are you ladies today?"

"Heavy and tired," Briana said.

"And yet, I'm sure you could swing a sword just as well as ever you could," Alma said, almost proud. "But are you sure you should travel to Lindinis, Adara? Perhaps Briana is right to stay behind?"

"Just one trip. We need supplies."

"Lenya told me that he and three of the men will be going with you. I should be a chaperone for you," she winked.

"I'll be happy for the company. Will Paulus come too?"

"If Phoebus and Calliope are going, there will he be too. He talks of them all the time!"

Adara was happy to hear it. For too long, Phoebus and Calliope had had no friends of their own, but there, in that place, their home, they all had something of a community. It felt wonderful.

"How is Calliope feeling?" Alma asked, but before Adara could answer, the twins appeared at the top of the stairs.

"I'm fine!" Calliope's voice rang over the hall, clear and joyful.

Adara went over to them and hugged her daughter. "My love...are you...feeling better today?"

"So much, Mama. And did you hear the birds singing outside today?" Calliope beamed.

"Yes, I did," Adara answered.

"Are we going to Lindinis, Mama?" Phoebus asked.

"Yes. And Alma is going to join us."

"Will Paulus come too?"

Adara looked to Alma and the two of them laughed.

"I don't think we could stop him!" Alma said.

The wagon rolled slowly down the path to the southwest gate. Phoebus and Paulus sat on the front bench with Lenya, his sword slung around his shoulder, and Adara, Alma and Calliope reclined among some cushions in the back of the wagon, the mother and daughter singing some of the songs they used to sing when Calliope was very little. As they left the safety of the hillfort, Adara began to feel strange and a little exposed, though four hardened Sarmatian warriors rode with them.

She looked up the path to the haze above the temple where she had just made her daily offerings to the gods of their family for Lucius' safety, and for a safe journey that day.

What was I thinking going out? She began to doubt her decision to go to Lindinis, even though the journey would not take long. The birdsong, fresh spring air, and sunlight had made her a little reckless. It was not so long ago that an assassin had come in the night to try and kill her and Briana at the hall. She began to feel a panic that she was unused to.

"Adara? What's wrong?" Alma asked, reaching out to touch her belly.

"Oh, it's nothing. Just... Lenya?" she said.

The Sarmatian turned quickly to look at her, immediately aware of the change in her voice. "Yes, my lady? Are you feeling unwell?"

"No. I feel fine. I'm just..." she looked at the boys, seeming to enjoy themselves, being out, at Calliope who was happier than she had been in some while. "Is all well for travelling?" she asked him, her eyes staring hard at him, then beyond to the road.

He nodded, turned to exchange a few words in their Sarmatian dialect with his brothers, and then turned back to her. "It should be a fine day for travelling. The roads are busy with farmers heading to the market."

At that moment, one of the riders moved his horse directly behind the wagon and he bowed his head to them.

Calliope waved, and he waved back.

"Don't worry, Lady Metella," Lenya said. "Try to enjoy the outing. We won't leave your sides."

"He's right," Alma soothed, saddened by the worry spreading across Adara'a face. "It's market day in Lindinis and the road will be busy from dawn till dusk. Try to enjoy it." She looked at her belly. "You may not have the chance to go beyond the walls of your home at all soon."

Adara acquiesced to her friend's wisdom. "You're right." She turned to look at Calliope whose big eyes were staring up at her, and placed her hand upon her cheek.

"Don't worry, Mama. Today is a good day."

It was not long before the walls and terra cotta rooftops of Lindinis came into view. It appeared to spread out before them like a paint palette in the middle of the green fields, wrapped in the bend of the glittering river where waterfowl skirted the edges of the shoreline.

In the front of the wagon, Phoebus was pointing out the remains of the fort of II Augustan legion to their left, along the river, a remnant of the Boudiccan revolt. "My father told me all about it," he said proudly to Paulus. "Why did your father not come today?" he asked.

Paulus shrugged. "Father doesn't like Lindinis. He says it stinks."

Alma chuckled. "No doubt the smell is made worse for him by the members of the ordo."

Adara looked down at her clothes, the long, belted tunica, her boots, and the sword she carried beneath her cloak. "Will we see the ordo's wives, do you think?"

Alma sighed. "No doubt they'll be clucking around the front of the curia and tax office while their slaves do the shopping."

The wagon came to a halt at the stables, and the voice of Tertius Corpulo could be heard approaching.

Lenya got down and reminded the man who the wagon and horses belonged to.

"I will take extra care of your wagon and horses for you!" he said. "While the praefectus fights for us in the North..." he stopped, looking at the four Sarmatians. "Are you men not part of his force?"

Lenya stepped up to the man, his hand upon his shoulder. "We work for the praefectus on his lands."

"Really?" Corpulo looked doubtful.

"We were gladiators in another life," Lenya said. "The praefectus freed us. Do you have more questions, stable master?"

"No, no!" Corpulo shook his head. "None at all." He turned to Adara, Alma and the children. "You needn't worry about your horses or wagon while you shop, Lady Metella."

"Thank you," Adara said, placing a coin in his hand.

The man nodded as they began to walk away toward the main gate of the town. "Congratulations as well, my lady! May the Gods bless you!"

The crowds were thick on market day, the spring sunlight having encouraged the population from the surrounding region out of doors. The gates of the town were wide open and there was a steady flow of people to and from Lindinis, children weaving in and out of adults' legs, laughing as they made their way to a stand in the centre of the market where a puppet show was underway.

"Can we go, Mama?" Calliope asked.

Adara looked at the crowd, the faces of the people, and shook her head. "I don't think so, my girl. You should stay with us."

Paulus looked at his own mother and she shook her head.

"Not today, Paulus."

The children's disappointment was fleeting as they approached the stalls to see the wooden toys, an instrument maker who plucked at a lyre while his daughter played an aulos, and of course, a weapons seller that drew the boys to it like moths to a midnight flame.

Adara and Alma allowed the children to lead them to whichever stalls they wanted for a time before they undertook the more serious matter of purchasing food, oil, wine, olives, flour and a few other items.

Adara was efficient in her ordering, and fair bargaining with each of the sellers, some of whom recognized her from previous visits, and wished her well with her imminent birth.

The entire time, Lenya and the three others hovered around the women and children like a nimbus of protection.

At one point, Adara heard Lenya speaking to the others.

"The garrison is completely different than the last time we were here with the praefectus." He spotted Adara looking at him. "Nothing amiss, just a different set of guards here, my lady." He turned his head to look in different directions, the chimera tattoo running up his neck straining as he did so. "Are you nearly finished?"

"Almost," Adara said. "I want to go to the cloth seller. That will give the other vendors time to deliver my orders to the stables."

Lenya nodded and relayed the message to the others.

"The bigger I get, the less my clothes fit me," Adara said to Alma as they walked, arm in arm behind the children."

The cloth sellers were gathered in the centre of the market where their fabrics were on display, fluttering in the spring breeze and sunlight like the sails of ships at a trading port.

With the arrival of Spring, and thoughts of distant Summer, Adara was drawn to the lighter fabrics of blue, yellow, and pink, rather than the earthy wools she had become accustomed to wearing in that colder climate.

"You'll be able to wear those silks out of doors only a few days in the summer," Alma joked.

"Don't I know it!" Adara said, reluctantly moving on to the warmer fabrics. She was about to enquire about the price of one of them when a voice called her by name.

"Lady Metella," the voice said, as if the name was one of displeasure.

Adara turned to see Sabina Cresca approaching from beneath an awning. She wore a long midnight blue stola with a matching cloak that set off the gold about her neck. Beside her were the much shorter Jana, wife of Virgilio Carcer, and the smiling Lavinia Maia, wife of the ordo member Felix Inek.

All three women had their hair done up in elaborate patterns which they had been told, no doubt, were the latest fashions in Rome. As they approached Adara and Alma, Sabina leading the way as if at the point of an arrowhead formation, the eyes of several marketers watched them. The three ladies were well-known.

"How lovely to see you again, Metella," Lavinia Maia said, her voice catching as Sabina gave her a look that said 'Silence!'.

"And you, Lavinia Maia," Adara answered, glad she was able to remember the name from the banquet which seemed ages ago. Her focus, however, was on Sabina Cresca, for she felt immediately that the woman meant no good.

Sabina stopped and looked Adara up and down, laughing to herself as she saw her long black hair with a few simple braids, like a Briton. "I see you are expecting another child," she said, her eyes glancing at Phoebus, Calliope and Paulus with something approaching disgust or disdain.

Adara unconsciously placed her hand upon her belly. "Yes," she answered. "And where are your children?"

"At home where they should be," Sabina answered.

"Your son as well?" Adara could not help herself. She remembered the screams of the priestess of Ynis Wytrin when Sabina's son and his friends had attacked her.

Sabina was about to say something, but caught herself. Instead, she approached Adara a little more, her own bodyguards following, not unnoticed by Lenya and the others who closed in around Adara and Alma.

"To be frank, Metella," I'm surprised you have the gall to show yourself in Lindinis. Your husband has proved to be a disgrace."

"Very disappointing, he is!" added Jana.

Adara looked from one to the other of the women, and felt anger rising in her. "For someone who hopes to slither up the ladder of society, Lady Cresca, you are incredibly ill-informed. My husband's achievements on the battlefield, and his service to Rome, have only served to ensure the safety of the empire, and quaint towns such as Lindinis."

Sabina smirked. "While he lords it in a fortress with armed warriors," she said. "I wonder what Caesar would think about that?"

"My husband fights at the front with Caesar."

"For Caesar you mean."

"It's no wonder you don't have any real friends, Sabina!" Alma said, unable to keep silent any longer.

Sabina pretended not to hear the tall Briton, but wrinkled her nose as if an ass had relieved itself in their midst.

Adara laid her hand upon Alma's arm. "You know, Sabina Cresca, it strikes me that the only reason you invited us to your home was not to welcome us to the community, but to try and use my husband for your own selfish ends."

"How astute, she is," Sabina said to the ladies beside her.

Lavinia looked down at the ground, silent, evidently uncomfortable with how the conversation was going, but unwilling to gainsay her peer.

"Your husband might have proved useful, once, but that time has passed. He, and you, are of no consequence really. Serenus and the ordo have a new friend, very close to Caesar, who has taken up Lindinis' cause and promised to approve the request to make this an official civitas."

"I would be mindful of 'friends' who promise what they cannot give," Adara said.

Here, Sabina looked disdainfully at Alma for the first time. "And you speak of friends!"

Adara looked at Alma and smiled. "I am certain of my friends." She looked at Lavinia and Jana. "Are you?"

"You must feel very alone in your fortress farm with your husband so far away. I wonder how you sleep at night knowing you are so exposed." Sabina's eyes changed then, from the eyes of an arrogant upstart to something more akin to a wolf.

Adara felt Calliope grip her hand then, brushing her cloak back to reveal the golden hilt of the sword that hung from her shoulder, beside her pregnant belly.

Sabina glanced at the sword and took a fraction of a step back.

"Oh, Sabina Cresca..." Adara said. "We are not alone." she glanced at Lenya and the others who stood calmly by, their hands upon the hilts of their longswords. "And anyone who were to threaten my family would deeply regret it. Of that, you can be sure." Adara's voice was measured and low, surprising even herself, but the feel of a threat to her children, and her friends, gave her a strength she had not expected. She stepped forward. "There are those who have attempted to harm us before, and they did not survive to cause further harm."

The silence that hung between the two women was deafening, and was only broken by Calliope then.

"Mama, may we go now?"

535

Adara nodded, still staring at Sabina Cresca's hateful face. "Yes, my dear. It is time to leave. We have everything we need." With that, Adara turned her back on Sabina Cresca and the other women, and pulled Alma and the children back to the cloth seller.

Lenya and the others closed in to form a wall between the women, their own bodyguards, and Adara.

"Come ladies," Sabina said. "It is uncouth to be seen too long in the company of barbarians."

The bodyguards eyed the Sarmatians, but the sight of the warriors before them gave them pause, and they quickly turned and followed their mistress and her friends to disappear into the crowded market.

As Adara looked at the fabrics, the fabric seller and his wife approached her, smiling.

"Lady Metella, that was a wondrous thing to behold," said the woman. "It's about time someone knocked her from off her high horse."

Adara looked at a roll of light, green wool. "I'll take this please."

"Very well, my lady," said the man. "And here," he reached up and took a roll of the blue fabric she had been looking at earlier. "Please accept this gift. Please the Gods, it will suit you better than any other here."

"I couldn't," Adara said.

"Please," the seller added, his hands up. "For your courage."

"Thank you," Adara added, giving him the coins for the wool.

As they were making their way back to the stables, having purchased some roasted meats upon small skewers for the trip back, Alma walked beside Adara and leaned in.

"Thank you," she said.

"What for?" Adara asked.

"For being a good friend."

Adara looked at her and smiled, squeezed her hand. "She's a horrible woman."

"It did sound like she was threatening you though, didn't it?"

"Yes," Adara said, stopping suddenly, her heart racing a little, feeling breathless.

"Adara?" Alma stopped and held her by both arms.

"I'm fine...I'm fine. Just tired. Let's get home."

A short time later, the wagon was rolling away from Lindinis for the hillfort.

Later that night, after the children were finally asleep in their beds, and the double doors of the hall barred and guarded by the Sarmatians for the night, Adara and Briana sat beside the hearth fire eating some bread, dates and cheese, washed down with some watered wine.

Adara felt better being at home. The day had not gone as she had planned. For some time, Calliope had spoken of the mean woman they had met in Lindinis, and had clearly been shaken by the encounter, and the menace in the woman's demeanour. Adara too had been shaken by it, and wondered who could possibly be Serenus Crescens Nova's new contact at the imperial court that would make his wife confident enough to threaten the Metelli in the middle of the marketplace.

"I'm sorry I wasn't with you," Briana said to her as they sat beside each other, watching the flames sway before them. "I would have knocked that smirk off of her face."

"I came close to doing the same thing," Adara said, the thought of it giving her some momentary comfort. "But I'm not sure that it would have helped matters. It seems that wherever we've gone in the empire, we find vipers underfoot... Except in Ynis Wytrin."

They were both quiet again as they thought of the Isle of the Blessed. The place had that effect upon those who had been there, for once it was seen, it was always remembered.

"Funny you should mention it," Briana said, shifting to adjust her position. "I've been thinking of Etain lately. I think she's been reaching out to me, but I've been so tired that when I did try to calm myself and listen, I fell asleep." She laughed, but it soon faded and she was serious again. "I miss Dagon." She shook her head. "I feel ridiculous pining after a man like that, but I feel more whole when he's around."

Adara smiled and laid her hand upon Briana's arm. "That's because he is *your* man. It has always been that way for me and Lucius. We both feel whole when we're with each other, and the children too."

"It's a new feeling for me," Briana said. "But I like it. The only time I felt something like it is with Einion."

"I've heard that said about twins. I know that Phoebus and Calliope are different when they are apart than when they are together. There is a comfort I see in them, an easiness in their behaviour, when they're together." Adara took a bite of the bread and sipped some wine. "Have you heard from Einion at all?"

"Oh! I forgot to tell you. A messenger did come!"

"Really? What did he say?"

"You know Einion," she laughed. "He's not one for long descriptions. But he did say that they cleansed our ancestral home, and that they have begun the task of rebuilding."

"Did he ask you to go to him?" Adara felt a little dread at the prospect, for it would mean that Briana would be gone for a long while, and with all that she imagined after Lucius' return from Dumnonia, she wondered if she would ever see her friend again.

"No. He says I should remain where I am." She looked at Adara. "He did ask how Lucius was."

"He did?"

"He said we should watch out for him, that his ordeal in helping him regain the throne was..." Briana stared at the flames, the feelings of sadness and guilt that washed over her like the sudden, cold splash of a spring upon the moors. "That it was terrifying."

Briana looked at Adara again and saw her tears running silently in the light, like two rivers of fire down her face. "I'm sorry. I didn't want to upset you."

Adara shook her head. "I just wish Lucius would have told me what happened. He seems to have sworn Dagon and Einion to secrecy. I've never known him to be so afraid."

"Is it fear? Or is it something else?"

"I don't know. But he changed after that quest."

"Every quest changes a man, though, doesn't it? Look at the stories I've heard you tell the children of the Greek, Odysseus."

For a moment, Adara feared that Lucius had met his own Circe, or another Calypso, but she dismissed it. To her, Lucius was a better man than Odysseus, his own ponos, his life's toils, having been no less to her mind than the hero of legend.

"I just pray to the Gods that they watch over Lucius now. Calliope's visions give me some comfort, but they also fill me with dread."

"The Sight does that," Briana said. "But if Calliope says that Lucius is safe now, you should believe her. That must mean the war will be finished soon."

Adara smiled at that, her eyes dry again as she stared at the flames and finished her wine.

"Besides, you have to worry about that new Metellus growing inside you."

The next day dawned clear and rosy, and it was early when Adara rose from her bed to use the privy beneath the stairs. She then opened the doors of the hall to allow the fresh air to sweep in over the ashes of the cool fire.

The two Sarmatians on guard outside, bowed to her as the doors opened. "Good morning, my lady."

"Good morning," she greeted them. "Have Ula and Aina not arrived?" she asked.

"Not yet. But the decurion said he will go soon to the southwest gate to see if they are approaching from the village."

"Very well," Adara said. "I'm going to go to the temple."

"One of us will go with you."

Adara waved it off. "The gates, have been closed all night. I'll be fine. Besides, I'll call if I need anything."

The men looked doubtful, but yielded to the wishes of the Dragon's wife.

Adara put on her cloak, took her sword, and made her way down toward the temple in the southeast corner of the hillfort.

"Good morning, Sigwyll!" she greeted Alma's cousin who was just coming out of the stables with one of the horses.

"Good morning, Lady Metella!" the man said, waving.

Adara smiled to herself. Alma had told her that the change in her cousin had been tremendous, that he was a new man since Lucius had invited him to work for them as a stable master.

She continued her walk down the road toward the temple where it was tucked away on its own, enjoying this quiet moment in her days when she could be alone with her thoughts and prayers, when she felt the Gods could hear her best.

Before going in, she saw Lenya making his way toward the southwest gate to look for Ula and Aina.

He waved to her and she waved back before unlocking the temple and going in.

539

Dim morning light filled the cella of the temple, and the statues of Apollo, Venus, and Epona appeared against the back wall, standing above the candles, oil lamps and offerings from the previous days. The air was pleasant, scented with incense, dried herbs, and the tang of oil.

Adara took the tinder box from a side table to the right, and lit the lamps and candles before pausing before the altar and gazing at those divine visages. She laid her sword upon the front edge of the altar and turned her palms upward, her eyes closed.

"Oh Gods...Apollo, Venus and Epona...hear my prayers and accept my offerings. I feel a shadow closing in on our family, and it fills me with dread. I do not know if it is because I am heavy with child that I imagine horrible things, or because of my daughter's visions. Whatever it is, please...I beg you...watch over my family. Keep my children safe...please...keep Lucius safe, wherever he is. Bring him back to me."

Adara opened her eyes and went to another table where she took one of the tied bundles of rosemary and a pitcher of oil. She returned to the altar and in the carved bowl on its surface, she placed the rosemary and poured the oil over it. Then, after setting the pitcher back upon the table, she lit a chunk of incense and set it upon the altar, blowing gently upon it until it caught and smoke began to weave up into the air about the Gods' faces in gentle wisps.

"I ask you, Gods of our family, to watch over us and keep us safe from those who seek to do us harm. Please." Her eyes were shut tight as he reached out to the immortals before her. She was about to finish when, at the back of her mind, like a faint sound out of doors at twilight, Venus' voice whispered in her mind.

Lucius is safe. You will be together again...

Adara felt gratitude fill her heart, and tears burn the rims of her closed lids.

"Thank you," she said, her voice fervent as ever it was. Then, she opened her eyes, bowed to the Gods, and took up her sword from the altar. She backed away, one hand gripping her sword, the other caressing her swollen belly. She stepped out into the growing daylight and breathed deeply of the fresh Spring air.

"Ahhhhhh!"

A sudden scream rent the air, sending birds from the nearby trees into the sky above Adara's head.

Her heart began to pound, as she saw one of the Sarmatians running down the road to the southwest gate where Lenya was leaning against the bar to open them.

"Ahhhhhh!" the scream came again, and Adara began to run as best she could in the direction of the gate. It seemed to take forever to make her way along the ramparts, but when she arrived she looked down onto the road outside the gate to see Ula and Aina grasping each other and screaming.

Beside them, on the road, was the body of a young man. He lay upon his back in a pool of blood that stained the dirt about him. His throat was slashed roughly, gaping almost as much as his mouth which was set in a rictus of pain or surprise.

Adara made her way down from the rampart and onto the road to the girls' side. "Shh, shh," she comforted them, feeling her gorge rise at the deathly sight so nearby. "Don't look. Don't look," she said as Lenya and the other Sarmatian bent over the body to examine it.

"His throat was slit right here," Lenya said. "Some hours ago. He was gagged and bound." He pointed to the burns about his cheeks and wrists where ropes - now removed - had rubbed his skin raw as he struggled.

Lenya turned and gazed about the road leading up the the gate. "No wagon tracks or visible foot prints in the dirt." He turned to Adara and the shuddering girls. "Who is he?"

Adara hugged the girls and whispered. "Do you know him?"

"He...he's..." Ula struggled to get the words out. "It's Gwri," she wept. "A young man from our village."

"Why would someone do this to him?" Lenya asked, nodding as Adara put her hand up for the questions to stop.

"My lady," Lenya said. "It's not safe here. We need to get you inside and close the gates." His eyes continued to rake the area, the body a secondary thought now.

Adara nodded. "Come girls, come inside the hall, away from here."

They nodded, still shuddering, looking a last time at the body of the boy they had known for years, and weeping again as they went.

Adara went with them, but stopped, dizzy all of a sudden as she turned to the side and vomited.

"My lady," Lenya was at her side. "Come. This is too much for you. We'll take care of the body and I'll go down to the village to find his family."

Adara nodded. "Go to Alma and Culhwch's home. They'll know. They'll help."

"Yes, my lady," Lenya said as they passed beneath the gate which the other Sarmatian closed immediately.

The death of Gwri came as a shock to everyone in the village, and it was with no small amount of guilt that Adara wondered at the reasons someone might have for killing him upon their very threshold.

Who had the boy angered that they would do such a thing? Or was it a warning to them? Who would dare to approach the hillfort in the night and lay murder at the Metellus door?

The Sarmatians were on high alert after that, and none of them, Adara, Briana, or the children were permitted to go anywhere within or without the hillfort without an armed guard.

The boy's family came with a wagon up the road from the village to collect the body and take it back for cleansing and burial in the small cemetery beside the village.

Adara went with Briana and Lenya to see them, to offer what she could in the way of sympathy, condolence, food or anything else, but she was only greeted with silence and stern gazes of betrayal.

"Don't take it personally," Briana said. "They're in shock. They've lost a son."

"The whole village will hate us now."

"No. They won't."

"We'll need to keep the northeast and southwest gates closed permanently now," Lenya said. "I'll have the men patrol constantly on horseback around the perimeter."

Adara nodded. "Thank you, Lenya."

"My lady... My queen," he bowed to both of them and went to speak with the others.

"Are the children all right?" Adara asked.

"They're fine. Sigwyll is with them in the stables," Briana said. "Come, let's walk."

The two of them made their way up the slope to the top of the rampart and began their circuit.

The sunshine felt good upon their arms and faces, but the events of that morning cast a gloom over them that could not be shaken. They walked in silence from the southern rampart around to the eastern slopes to gaze downhill to the bathhouse. That building had been searched by the Sarmatians and it was still locked safely.

"What is that?" Adara said, stopping to look to the East, at the one hill that rose higher than the hillfort.

Across the valley, upon the promontory of rock that jutted out to overlook the hillfort from a distance, a man stood there, watching.

"Who's that?" Briana asked.

"I don't know."

"Is something wrong, my lady?" the Sarmatian who had been following them asked, coming up the slope to their side.

Adara turned to him. "We saw a man on the far hill. He seemed to be watching us."

The Sarmatian rushed to their sides and looked up, but the man was gone. "Are you certain, my lady, my queen?"

"Yes," Briana said. "There was definitely someone there."

"I'll go and check," he said, bowing before running down the slope to his waiting horse and hopping into the saddle. He kicked, and the animal charged for the northeast gate.

Adara and Briana watched the Sarmatian's horse charge up the crest of the hill to the northeast, curving upward to where they had seen the man. They could see the Sarmatian clearly enough as he turned his horse around, sword glinting in his hand, to search for any sign of the intruder. After a while, he returned, the northeast gate securely closed behind him.

"There was no sign of him, my lady," he said to Adara. "Are you quite sure you saw someone?"

"Yes."

"I'll inform the decurion and we'll keep a watch out. Don't worry, my lady...my queen. You're all safe."

"Thank you," Adara said. "But I worry also about our friends in the village."

"I understand," he said, "but my orders are to keep you safe. Not the villagers."

Adara thought about chiding him, but knew that he was only following his orders. There were not enough of them to mind the hillfort, and the village. Besides, Alma had told her that most of the men in the village - and many of the women - were capable fighters.

"Come," Briana said. "We need to rest. Let's go inside."

That night, as Adara lay awake in her cubiculum, the children snuggled beneath the furs to either side of her, both sleeping soundly, Briana remained awake in the hall below.

The Briton sat before the flames of the hearth fire, staring into them. She was not eating, nor was she dwelling on the life of the boy that had been slain outside the hillfort's gate, though that had saddened her a great deal.

Briana gazed into the flames, her breath slow and deep, her eyes searching for something and then relaxing, closing.

Etain? she reached out in her mind.

After a moment, as the flames continued to crackle, there came a response.

I am here, Briana.

I miss you.

And I you, Etain's voice said. *I have been trying to contact you.*

I thought so. Is all well?

No. We cannot leave the Isle, for there is a threat upon the road.

Who? What? Briana asked.

I cannot tell. But we are safe in Ynis Wytrin. It is you, we fear for.

Us?

I have seen death and fire, Briana. There is danger.

A boy was murdered here last night.

Etain's voice was silent at that. It was a minute before she spoke again.

Only one?

Yes. Why, Etain? Briana felt fear clenching at her breast, and her hands went to surround her belly.

There will be more. You must be vigilant...for you, for your friends. Keep the children close. Keep them safe.

And Dagon and Lucius? Are they safe?

For now. But be mindful, Briana, my love. For you dwell among dragons, and they have enemies at their gates.

The fire flickered violently, and then fell in upon itself so that all that was left was smouldering ash.

"Etain?" Briana called. "Etain?"

But there was no answer.

Part III

FIRE

A.D. 211

XIX

IMPERATORIS MORS

'Death of an Emperor'

When the mighty of the world stand upon the shores of the black river, their gaze fixed on the possibility of the afterlife that awaits them, it is as though the Gods themselves sit in debate. As the mortal's life, a single spark in the palm of their divine hands, flickers and fades, the Gods determine the appointed time, place, and manner of dying. Perhaps they base this upon the life that individual has led? Maybe those gods the individual propitiated argue on the mortal's behalf, and those whom the mortal ignored or forgot voice their reasons for wishing pain and torment?

There is no way to know the will of the Gods. Each man is a product of his daemon, his ponos.

Septimius Severus, Emperor of the Roman Empire, Parthicus, Britannicus, thought of these things as he approached the broad banks of Death's river. He could walk, yes, and stand tall as he did so, though the urge to turn and run was incomprehensibly strong. He stopped, hearing the voices of Olympus, and gazed up at the myriad stars spread across the clear, dark firmament.

Beautiful...

The stars he had become familiar with over many months were there, and they shone out brighter than all the rest. They called to him as if he were returning to a street he had once visited in happier times. After a lifetime of mortal experience, of war, and learning, and of love and hate, he came back to that street. It was time to knock upon the great door of destiny, to request admittance to the Hereafter.

Ave, Destiny, he said, raising his hand.

But something stopped him. He saw his teary-eyed empress, his love, standing over him, grasping his raised hand.

"Septimius?" her voice echoed about her features.

"Come," he said, feeling strength for one last fleeting moment. "Give it here, if we have anything to do."

He knocked, and the door swung open to reveal the river beyond...

The emperor's chamber echoed with soft weeping. Many there gazed up at the painted stars upon the smoke-stained ceiling to either curse them, or to thank them for having given them the privilege of knowing such a man.

Surrounded by her son, Geta, her sister Julia Maesa, Papinianus, tearful Castor, Euodus, the emperor's astrologer, and several servants, Julia Domna fell silently upon the furs of her husband's death bed and wept through her silent prayers to Baal that His light might shine upon her husband's way.

Geta stood there in a red tunic trimmed with gold, and a deep purple, almost black, cloak of wool, looking down at his father's body with tears in his eyes. Only a week ago, the emperor had bestowed the titles of 'Augustus' and 'Britannicus' on his youngest son, so that now, he stood the full equal of his older brother.

Geta bent down and kissed his father's forehead once, his tears spilling onto the aged brow. "I will do as you ask, Father. Antoninus and I will not fail you."

Julia Domna looked up at her son and reached across the body to grasp his hand.

Julia Maesa came up behind her sister and placed her hands upon her shoulders. "I am sorry, Sister, for he was a man of greatness." When Julia Domna made no reply, but continued to stare at her husband's still face, Julia Maesa turned and left the hot, stinking confines of the room.

When Geta left the bedside to sit in a chair nearby, Castor, Severus' loyal freedman began tidying the bedclothes about his former master and friend. He wept openly for the loss, drying the emperor's face of sweat one last time, wiping the spittle from his beard. "Be at peace, my emperor."

The empress looked up at Castor and nodded to him. They had often disagreed, the two of them, but they were united in their grief.

An hour passed, an hour in which more incense was lit, an hour in which Julia Domna sat and stared at the body of her husband and wondered what was next. Though she had her family about her, she was more alone than she had ever been. *Baal, Lord of Light, guide me through the days to come...*

"Julia..." Papinianus' soft, caring voice broke into her thoughts. "You should get some sleep."

She turned and he handed her a silver cup filled with unwatered wine. She took it and drank, feeling its sweetness run down her throat to quench her shuddering gullet. She looked up at the ceiling, at the stars, and nodded. "Artimodoros was right about the stars. He was right."

Papinianus looked up too. "Yes. He was." He looked back down at his cousin. "And now, other stars are at play, Julia. We must see to the arrangements for the funeral."

"A funeral for Rome's greatest emperor," she said, her eyes gazing into the distance, before she came back and focussed on Papinianus. "Yes. I know what we shall do."

"As the heirs, Geta and Antoninus should have the final say."

"They will listen to me. They will agree," Julia Domna said. "The world will speak of this funeral for ages to come."

"I'll write to Antoninus at once and tell him to come with all haste."

"Thank you," she said. "Tell him that if the war allows, he should come with the commanders who knew my husband well...Nearchus Chioticus for one..." She strained to remember the names of anyone at that moment, her mind awhirl with fresh grief, and all that needed to be done.

"Do not worry. I know who to recall. But you must sleep now, Julia. I'll see that the slaves clean him, and that the priests prepare and anoint him." Papinianus stopped, his voice cracking. *Can this really be happening? Has it come to pass?* He bowed to her and took her hand, helping her up.

The empress set her cup down on the table beside the bed, looked another time at her husband, and went to the doors. They opened and she went out.

The guards in the hall went quiet immediately and bowed to her. "The emperor is dead," she said, though she knew that word had already spread. She looked at her servant who had been waiting for her. "I will retire now, for the days ahead shall be long, and there is much to do."

"Yes, Domina," the servant said, bowing low and falling in beside her mistress.

Inside the room, Papinianus stood above the body of the emperor, gazing down at him. "Farewell, my friend. It's been an honour." He placed his hand upon the emperor's still chest. "May the boatman carry you through smooth waters with the sun on your back." He paused, aware of Geta sitting at the back of the room, sipping wine as he stared at his father's still body. "May you also forgive me, for what has to be done," he whispered, before turning and going to Geta. "I'm sorry, Geta. Truly. Your father was a good friend and a great man."

"Yes." Geta nodded, not looking at Papinianus.

Papinianus bowed slightly to the young man, and turned to leave him alone. As he reached the doors, Geta spoke.

"Papinianus."

"Yes?"

"You will address me as 'Augustus'."

Papinianus stared back at Geta for a moment, too shocked to speak, but he rallied himself, and his resolve, and bowed deeply. "Forgive me, *Augustus*."

Geta smiled and turned back to his father's body as Papinianus went out and closed the doors.

In the corridor, Papinianus turned to the six Praetorians on duty. "I want to know the names of all who come." He turned to the centurion on duty and whispered. "Notify the rest of the men who are here. There may be trouble in the days ahead. I want everyone alert."

"Yes, Praefectus," the man answered, saluting.

"I'll be in my tablinum, writing to Caesar Antoninus."

At that moment, Castor came out of the room and joined Papinianus.

"Castor, see to it that the slaves clean him up right away so that the embalmers may get to work. The body won't last long."

"How can you speak like that, Papinianus? He's only just passed away!"

Papinianus stopped and turned to him. He sighed deeply and put his hand on the freedman's shoulder. "I know how much you cared for him. How kind he was to you. You were perhaps his greatest and truest friend."

Castor nodded, wiping another tear from his eye.

"But you know now what is at stake."

Castor looked him in the eyes and nodded with certainty. "Yes. I know."

"It will not be easy, but for the good of the empire, we must."

"Yes."

"I need you to see to the care of our departed emperor's body. In the meantime, I have an urgent letter to write."

Papinianus turned down the corridor and disappeared around the corner to go to his chamber. Before entering, he turned to one of the two guards who stood there. "Get me our two fastest riders."

"Yes, sir!" the men said.

"Is it true, sir? Is the emperor dead?" one of them asked.

"Yes. It's true." Papinianus went into the tablinum and closed the doors.

At his broad table, he took a fresh sheet of papyrus and sat down. His heart was beating quickly, and his hand shook as he took up the stylus and dipped it in the inkpot beside the burning lamp.

I'm Praetorian Prefect! he reminded himself. *It's my duty to see to the good of this empire!*

Determined now, his grief pushed farther back in the recesses of his mind, he began writing.

To Praefectus Lucius Metellus Anguis
Ala III Britannorum

Praefectus,
The emperor is dead.
Ride with all haste to Eburacum. Bring your men.

Aemilius Papinianus
Prefect of the Praetorian Guard

Papinianus reviewed the words quickly, fully aware of the events this would set in motion. He sprinkled some sand upon the paper, shook it off, and then rolled it tightly before affixing his seal and placing it in a small leather case.

The doors to the Praetorian prefect's tablinum swung open, and there stood the guards with two riders, ready to go. Papinianus recognized both men, trusted them completely. He went to the first and handed him the leather tube.

"Flavius, I want you to ride as quickly as you can to the fort of Fendoch, on the Caledonian front, and put this directly into the hands of Praefectus Lucius Metellus Anguis. Do not stop along the way but to change horses. Do you understand?"

"Yes, sir!" The man saluted and disappeared down the corridor, his cloak billowing behind him.

Papinianus turned to the other rider. "Plautus, I'll have a most important dispatch for you. Wait here for it."

"Yes, sir!" the man said.

Papinianus went back inside and sat down to write a second dispatch, only this time, he was not so urgent about it, a fact that made his heart beat all the faster for what that meant.

To Augustus Caesar Antoninus,

Antoninus, I write to you as your mother's cousin, and as one who has served your father loyally for years.

It pains me to relay the news to you that Septimius Severus, our emperor and your father, has died...

After the insult and humiliating dismissal by Caracalla at Horea Classis, Lucius had fallen into a deeper state of anger and rage than he had known for some time. It was not that he had been insulted personally by Caesar - the voices of the legions raised in his honour had been a shield against that - rather that after the deaths of so many of his warriors, and of the Votadini allies, Caracalla had sent them away, even as he held the enemy's head in his hands.

So many lives...and for what? So Caracalla could send us away like children after all the blood we've shed?

Lucius had been asking himself what the alternative would have been. To see the war carry on so that more lives were lost? To slaughter the population of Caledonia so that they did not need to return? Those were the original orders, and Lucius hated them.

Since the death of the Wolf, the enemy's assaults had all but completely stopped. All along the frontier and into the grievous glens of those cursed highlands, they had been hunting for Argentocoxus in vain.

Has Rome lost its way, or have I?

Lucius wished that Diodorus were still alive to counsel him, for his old tutor had always had a way of helping him to see beyond the obvious, to find the truest answers hidden in the rough of life.

But Diodorus did not know what I know now...what I heard from the lips of the Gods themselves...

In the loneliness of his cubiculum at the heart of the fort, and as he stared at the charred remains of the oak upon the plain where he had burned the Wolf's corpse to spite the Morrigan herself, Lucius felt the confusion, the burden and anger of his own existence.

Since Dumnonia, he felt an irrepressible rage pulsing in the depths of his soul. It pushed into his senses, and then spread throughout his body so that he hurt everywhere. It felt as though his teeth and bones ground together and were heavy, like the rocks of the earth. His blood pulsed all over, like the veins of a volcano. His vision blurred at times, and his mind was drawn into further battles with all that he saw in the world around him and had seen and heard when he had fallen into the trap in Dumnonia. The words he had heard Venus whisper to Apollo as Lucius bled to death upon the grass of that faraway place...

Lucius shut his eyes tightly as it came back to him, as it always did in the hauntings of the mind's night. The only solace he felt was when he was with, or thought of, his family and his men, his friends.

What are we doing out here at the edge of the world? he wondered. *Surely, the Gods want more of Rome than blood upon the field?*

When his mind drifted, Lucius saw it again, that vision of legions laid out before the ramparts of his home, the dragon vexillum flying high in the breeze at the head of the insignia of so many others, the rising tide of his name chanted on the wind, the power felt as thousands of men raised sword and spear in his honour.

It was all terrifying, and every day that he and his men lingered at Fendoch, he felt it was another day wasted, time lost in which he could have held his wife and children, or contributed to some greater purpose for his life and that of the people who relied upon him.

Philotimo is far from my grasp, Diodorus...

For you...Lucius...it is never far...

Lucius looked up suddenly from where he knelt before the lamp-lit altar in his quarters and there, standing before him, was Apollo. Lucius bowed his head quickly, but the god reached out to place his brilliant hand upon Lucius' shoulder.

You should know that you no longer need to bow before me.

"I don't know what to say anymore. I don't know what I'm supposed to do, my Lord. I'm tired of killing."

Apollo reached down and pulled Lucius to his feet so that they faced each other. His eyes whirled with the stars for a moment, but then they became still, the pupils like pebbles in the middle of clear, light-filled pools.

Killing is the way of men.

Lucius shook his head. "That can't be all."

Not for you. But sometimes we must all walk a bloody road to peace...to the destiny determined for you.

There was a loud racket in the courtyard at that moment, and Lucius heard the commotion.

Apollo looked to the doorway of that room, waved a hand, and the sound disappeared briefly.

Listen to me.

Lucius looked back at the god before him and froze, unsure what to say or do. There were so many questions, but somehow, he knew it was not the time. Apollo's eyes were urgent, insistent.

Events have been set in motion that not even I can affect. The burning of her son has deepened the Morrigan's hate against you. We are with you, Lucius, but you will be tested. The Lord of the Silver Bow grasped Lucius' shoulders tightly. *You must be strong in the days to come - stronger than you have ever been in your life. Do you understand?*

Lucius was silent, his body hurting not from the god's touch, but from the fear he felt welling up.

You are right to feel fear, but know that I believe you will come through these trials.

Lucius nodded.

Then, will you understand.

The sound from the courtyard burst in upon them again and there was a loud knock upon the door.

Apollo placed his glowing hand upon Lucius' chest and all traces of physical pain fled from his body.

Lucius' closed his eyes and breathed more deeply than he had in a long while. When he opened them, Apollo was gone.

There was another knock at the door.

"Praefectus! A messenger from Eburacum!" Dagon said loudly.

Lucius looked around his cubiculum and grasped his chest. The strength and calm he felt surprised him, and gratitude replaced the anger that had been poisoning him. He took up his sword where it leaned against the altar, and walked over to the door to open it.

In the light of the braziers outside in the courtyard, he could see dozens of Sarmatian and Votadini warriors standing there, surrounding a single messenger.

"At ease!" Lucius said, seeing the worry in the messenger's eyes. "Forgive my men. Attempts have been made upon my life."

The man nodded.

"You come from Eburacum?"

"Yes, Praefectus Metellus. From the Praetorian Prefect himself. He asked me to ride to you in all haste to give you this." The man held out a small leather case.

Lucius stared at it for a moment as if it were a thing of fire, or burning quicksilver, an object to set things in motion that he was not sure he wanted.

"Sir? You must read it immediately. It is urgent!" the messenger said.

Lucius took it and walked over to stand beside the burning tripod nearby so that he could see the writing. He had to read Papinianus' message three times before he understood what had happened. His hand shook as he read, and his heart beat quickly. He looked at the Praetorian messenger and the man nodded.

"Praefectus?" Dagon said, as Barta, Afallach, Brencis, Fulvius and others pressed in around them. "What news?"

Lucius stood to look at the fire-lit faces around him, each eager, worried, curious, for they knew that something great had happened.

"The emperor is dead!" Lucius said loudly.

At first, the men's faces registered shock or confusion, but then the murmur of their voices became louder and louder as they discussed the implications, his deeds.

Dagon, Barta and Afallach were silent, as was the messenger. They all stared at Lucius as he stepped into the middle of the courtyard beside the altar.

The men quieted down.

"Men... Warriors!" Silence again. "Break camp with all haste!" Lucius yelled. "The emperor is dead, and we ride for Eburacum in the morning!"

Caracalla dreamed he was lying on the desert sand, flat on his back, gazing up at the stars. *Where are they?* he thought, his eyes searching the million tiny fires for those that he recognized from their painted signals in his father's chamber. *Ah, yes...there they are.*

He looked longingly at them. How long till they came to pass, those cursed stars? Pray as he might for his father's demise, try as me might to speed him from the world, those stubborn stars insisted on having their say, on being correct. Like Euodus, his teacher, their arrogance knew no bounds. *How dare they tell me what I may and may not do in this world!*

He picked up a handful of soft sand, raised his fist and let the wind take it, swirl it up into the sky like a serpent leaping from his fist. That was how he felt - powerful one moment, impotent the next as that power was swept from his hands, carried away on the wind.

He thought of Hercules, and of Alexander the Great; they had made no compromises, had taken what they wanted and achieved glory. And yet, here lay Marcus Aurelius Severus Antoninus Augustus Britannicus upon his back in a quiet room in...

Those cursed stars! I'll show them! I'll show them all...

Caracalla's eyes shot open and all he saw was the pale white ceiling of his cubiculum. There were no stars there, no painted destiny. Just a plain ceiling.

He felt something stir and thought to reach for the dagger beneath his pillow, but the naked leg that lay across his own reminded him of the woman. He turned to look at the mess of tangled red hair beside him. The woman slept soundly upon her stomach, her back rising and falling slowly, pressing her pale, naked breasts into the bed.

He had been curious about the red-haired women of the Caledonii, whether what the men said about their fiery demeanours had been true. This one had been lustful, but more like an animal. She was no northern goddess as he had hoped, and once his curiosity and lust had been sated, he saw only a highland heifer.

He swung his legs over the bed and cracked his neck, frowning at the dim dawn light that came in at the upper window. He rose, went to the corner where the piss pot was, and relieved himself.

The air was cold, and made his skin prickle and tingle. When he turned, the woman was sitting up, her hair falling over her shoulders to cover her breasts. Her green eyes gazed at his naked body.

"Come back to bed, Caesar," she said, smiling. "I'm still wet with morning dew."

Caracalla stared back at her, and her lustful smile faded immediately.

"How dare you address me, slave! Get out!"

"But, my lord. Did I not please you?"

"Get out!" he screamed.

The woman hurriedly gathered her things and ran naked to the door where she stopped to put on her tunica.

"Get dressed outside. I want you out of my sight!"

She fumbled with the lock and went out, only to be laughed at by the guards in the falling rain.

Once the woman had left, Caracalla's usual slave, who had been waiting outside since before the first hour of daylight, opened the door and went in. He neither spoke to the naked woman who had come out, nor even looked at her.

Inside Caesar's cubiculum, the scent of sweat, sex and wine filled the slaves nostrils, but he went in, head bowed, to begin lighting the lamps.

Caracalla was already dressed in brown bracae and a black tunic with purple stripes around the cuffs and hem. He stood, staring at the sky through the high window, silent and unmoving.

Once the lamps were all it, and a bronze, lion-footed brazier crackled in the centre, the slave stood silent against the wall, head down, staring at the floor.

"Bring me food," Caracalla said.

Without answering, the slave bowed and went out.

Caracalla turned then to sit at the broad table, to stare at the map of the empire which he had laid out. He gazed upon that map everyday, imagining the plans he wanted to put into action once it was all his.

And Geta's, he heard his mother's voice in his mind, and his hands turned to balled fists.

"Harmony!" he said to the map, shaking his head and pounding his fist on the tabletop.

He thought of the dream he had had, and felt anger. The stars had conspired against him for all of his life to that point, his own constellations of imperium ever over-shadowed by the success of others.

It was not just the stars he cursed. No. Mortals had stood in his way - his brother, his wife, Papinianus, Euodus, Castor and more. *Men like Lucius Metellus Anguis...*

Caracalla still seethed when he thought of Lucius, of how the troops had chanted his name. Those who gainsaid Caesar had been dealt with. They would never march again. Some small consolation that Claudius had found them and brought them to Caracalla for punishment.

556

He thought of the rotting head of the Wolf that hung outside the main gate of the fortress, and how Metellus had handed it to him. *So arrogant, setting himself above Caesar!*

Thunder rolled then in the distance, another storm pouring out of the highlands to the West.

He thought of how warm it would be in Rome at that time of year, how bright and full of prospect. And yet, he was there, wet and waiting, and full of rage. The feeling of impotence made him want to scream, to kill, but even the fighting had stopped since the Wolf had died.

Caracalla slammed his fist on the table and rose to put on his gladius and pugio and his long black cloak. When he opened the door onto the courtyard, the slave was approaching, carrying a tray of food and drink.

As he approached, his head bowed, Caracalla drove his fist into the man's face sending him onto his back in a puddle on the courtyard floor, the dishes and food flying through the air to crash all about him.

"Good morning, Caesar!" Claudius' voice said from behind as he and two more guards followed Caracalla.

Caracalla did not speak, but continued to stride out of the courtyard, along the via Principalis to the principia where the Praetorian tribunes were already busy with troop dispositions for the day.

Every man there present stopped immediately and saluted Caracalla as he passed them by and only when he had entered the main tablinum of the principia did they continue on with their business.

Inside, Ulpianus was already at work on the ledgers. He stood and bowed to Caracalla when he and Claudius entered.

"Any word of enemy movements?" Caracalla asked Claudius once he was seated at his table among the piles of dispatches, maps and accounts.

"No, sire. Nothing," Claudius answered. After a moment, he spoke again. "Did the woman not please you last night?"

Caracalla looked up at shrugged. "Only so much as a slaughtered beast pleases the mouth, but once eaten is not thought of." He looked back down at the letters upon the table. "You can have her, Claudius."

Claudius bowed and sat. "I thank you, Caesar. I'm afraid the one I had last night did not survive the ordeal."

Caracalla did not speak.

Ulpianus looked up at Claudius, and then back down at his work.

"Are there any special orders for the legionary commanders, sire?" Claudius said.

"The usual. They're to patrol, search for the enemy. That is all we can do right now."

"Yes," Claudius said, catching Caracalla's eye. "Searching."

"I want the Wolf's head taken off of the walls now. Dispose of it!" Caracalla said. "I'm tired of looking at it, and it only serves to remind the troops of Metellus."

"Gladly, sire," Claudius said. "You know, you should have punished him on the spot."

Caracalla looked up at Claudius. "And what do you think would have happened? Hmm? The men were chanting his name. He slew the Wolf."

"He's dangerous, sire." Claudius glanced around the room at the slaves working in the background, and at Ulpianus who appeared to be too involved in his work to listen. He leaned forward over the table to speak. "Metellus may be the slayer of the Wolf, but how great would be the man who slew the Dragon?"

Caracalla looked up, and in a second his fists reached for Claudius' tunic and pressed his face to the tabletop with a loud thud, a pugio at his throat. "How dare you!" he growled, his face pressed against Claudius'. "You were supposed to get rid of him. How many times have you failed me, Claudius? Tell me! Perhaps it is you I should kill. The legions don't even know who you are. They wouldn't care, they wouldn't mutiny if I killed you. You're like a nameless whore, you are!"

Claudius felt the blade press harder into his throat and break the skin, but he stayed calm, his eyes on Caesar. "Like any difficult quarry, sire, many attempts must be made. He is surrounded by his men at all times. But trust me. I will bring you his head. His family too."

Caracalla's eyes bored into him, but the pressure of the blade upon his neck, and the crushing force of Caesar's forearm upon his neck eased. Caracalla sat down again.

Claudius rose slowly from the tabletop, allowing the blood to flow from his cut without touching it.

"If the day ever comes to pass when you make good on your promise to kill his family, I want Metellus' wife brought to me." Caracalla remembered the first time he had seen Adara in Rome. The thought still aroused him. *A much sweeter prize than the red-haired heifer,* he thought.

Claudius spotted the inkling of a smile on Caracalla's lips. "It shall be as Caesar wishes." *But not before I have her first.*

There was a loud pounding upon the door then, and Claudius went to see what it was about.

He opened the door and there, standing in the rain, flanked by two guards, was a Praetorian messenger. "You have something for Caesar?"

"Yes, sir," the man said.

Claudius held out his hand, but the man shook his head. "I'm to hand it directly to Caesar Antoninus."

Claudius eyed the man whom he knew to be one of Papinianus' lackeys, and after a moment stood aside to let the man enter.

The man strode in, leaving wet boot marks and mud upon the paving slabs, and saluted Caracalla sharply.

"What is it? What does Papinianus want?" Caracalla looked up at the man and stood with his hand upon the pommel of his sword. Something told him he should be standing.

"Urgent news from Eburacum, sire." The messenger handed him the leather dispatch tube and bowed.

Caracalla reached out slowly to take it. He turned it over in his hand and undid the leather thong before letting the rolled dispatch fall out to reveal Papinianus' seal. He stared at it a moment longer, the eyes of all of the men in the room on him, then broke the seal, unrolled the papyrus, and read the short letter.

After a minute, he looked up at the messenger. "The emperor is dead?"

"Yes, sire. I'm sorry, sire." The man truly did seem saddened by the news he had just brought Caesar, and bowed his head.

In that moment, Caracalla felt many things as the ringing sounded in his ears, things that, perhaps, a son who had just lost a father should not feel, relief and excitement among them. But a part of him also regretted not being there when his father had passed, as surely others were, including Geta. He remembered the dream he had

had that very night and wondered if the Gods had sent him the dream to say that the stars had finally aligned with their message of death, that he was now emperor.

The ringing in his ears stopped and Caracalla looked up at the messenger. "Stay here. You will accompany me back to Eburacum."

"Yes, sire." The man saluted and went out into the courtyard. When he was gone, Caracalla turned to Ulpianus and Claudius.

"So?" Claudius asked.

"We ride for Eburacum."

"You are emperor now, sire," Ulpianus said, bowing his head.

Caracalla nodded.

Claudius bowed too, his own mind turning with the plans he wanted to carry out.

"Ulpianus," Caracalla said. "Notify the Praetorian tribunes and centurions that we will be marching in two days."

"What of the legions and their commanders? The fleet?"

"The legates are commanded to attend as well with a small part of their force - officers etcetera. The rest remain to guard the frontier...for now."

Ulpianus saluted and left.

Claudius looked at him but did not speak. He noticed that Caracalla gave the orders with a dull, flat voice, that he went through the motions of what was in the letter, but that he thought of other things. When Caesar looked up at him, he spoke. "Why wait to leave? You could go now and the legions could follow."

"I'm not coming back to this place. I want to make sure of that, Claudius." Caracalla walked around the table, his hand upon the pommel of his gladius. "The Caledonii have stopped their raids for now, and the Maeatae are weakened without their leader. We can end this."

"How, sire?"

Caracalla looked at him across the flames of one of the braziers beside his table. All around the room, the faces of the busts of greater men gazed back at him - Hercules, Alexander, Caesar, Hadrian, Antoninus, and even his father, Severus. Their eyes watched him in the dim light, their lips seeming to move with advice for or against the actions he mulled over in his mind. He wanted to cover them all in black shrouds at that moment so that they could not accuse him, for this time was now his. He was emperor, and no one would take that from him.

"Are you still in contact with your man, or has he run since his master was slain?"

"I can reach him easily enough, sire."

"Good."

"Do you want me to bring him in?" Claudius asked.

"More than that. I want him to bring Argentocoxus to me. He's to tell the chieftain I want to talk."

"Argentocoxus will be wary. He'll want specifics."

"Tell him he is safe and that he is to come to Horea Classis immediately. Tell him that I want to talk peace."

Claudius stared across the fire and slowly, a smile began to spread across his face. "I'll have him here by tomorrow morning."

Later that day, the legions were assembled before the walls of Horea Classis to be notified of the death of Emperor Septimius Severus. It was a bright spring day by that time, the mud and puddles of the early morning downpour dotting the roads and pathways about the legionaries' feet as they stood at attention, awaiting Caesar. The legates and tribunes of the legions stood together at the front, conferring, wondering what this could be about. Some of the tribunes wondered if the war was over, but the experienced veterans thought that something darker was at play, and so they waited quietly.

After a while, a cornu sounded from the top of the southern gatehouse and Caracalla appeared before them all. He was dressed in his full armour, flanked by his Praetorian tribunes, including Claudius.

The legions saluted, but they were silent.

The wind picked up, pulling at the sea of red cloaks, whistling among the lorica plates of thousands of troops.

Caracalla looked down on them all, no trace of a smile upon his face. He began to speak.

"Men of Rome's legions!" he waited a moment until it seemed they were intent upon the words he uttered. "I have received word today from Eburacum!" He held up the piece of papyrus that was Papinianus' letter to him. "My father, the emperor, is dead!"

At this there were exclamations of sadness and outrage, and it got louder as the news spread from the front ranks of the legions all the way to the back. Some men wept openly, while others hung their heads where they stood, no longer hearing the voice of the young

Caesar standing above them, but uttering silent prayers to the emperor who had handed them victory over the enemies of Rome.

Caracalla raised his hands for quiet, but he could not calm the waves of emotion that ran through the ranks. The gathering of legates and tribunes at the front stared up at Caracalla silently however, aware of the delicacy of the situation then. Some of them had survived the previous violent succession and civil war. They had no appetite for another bloody period such as that.

"Men of my legions!" Caracalla said loudly, deliberately. "We are marching for Eburacum for the emperor's funeral. Some of you will accompany us, most of you will remain here to guard the frontier. But you are all in my thoughts! I will not forget my loyal legions!"

There were some cheers at this, but not many, not enough to drown out the sound of the wind along the banks of the Tava.

"I promise you!" Caracalla said loudly. "You will not remain here for long. You will soon see your families again, and return to them with coin enough for celebration of your victories in Caledonia! I will take care of you, and this war will soon be at an end!"

With that, Caracalla paused to gaze out over the sea of red, but there he saw not only sadness at the death of his father - obviously loved by all of them - but also confusion instead of the joy he hoped would meet his announcement of the imminent end of the war. He turned without another word and disappeared with his Praetorians from the top of the tower, leaving the legates and tribunes standing about in confusion as the centurions of each legion ordered the men back to their various camps and duties.

Caracalla was up early the next morning and had already broken his fast when a group of cloaked men arrived at the western gate of Horea Classis escorted and guarded by a group of Praetorians that had met them on the road to the West when it was still dark. Caracalla was in the principia with Ulpianus who was packing up letters and dispatches while Caracalla paced back and forth across the wide room. He wore his full armour, and a purple cloak was draped over his shoulders. He was nervous, but sought to control it, his hands upon the pommels of his pugio and golden gladius, his mind focussing on the journey ahead, and the weeks to come.

There was a knock on the door, and Claudius stuck his head in. "Sire…"

Caracalla stopped and looked up.

"Argentocoxus is here."

Ulpianus looked to Caracalla and joined him. "You must still be careful, sire."

Caracalla nodded and Claudius opened the door wide to reveal the dimly-lit courtyard where braziers crackled around the edges, and the offerings he had made that morning smoked upon the altar at the centre.

Argentocoxus stood there, flanked by two of his massive bodyguards, and attended by two of his eldest surviving sons. They were unarmed, outwardly anyway. The chieftain of the Caledonii still stood tall, his fur-covered shoulders rising and falling with his breathing. He was still a strong man, but he was tired. He had lost many of his people, his family. His remaining hair and beard were greyer than before, but set in that aged, weathered face were a set of wily, willful eyes. He had survived for so long for a reason.

Caracalla noted his own guards all around the perimeter of the courtyard, and relaxed a little. He approached the Caledonian chieftain, their eyes locked.

"Caesar," Argentocoxus said without bowing. "You asked to speak with me?"

Caracalla stopped before him. "I did."

"You wanted to talk peace?"

"I do."

"We have done this before," the chieftain said. "It did not last."

"That was your fault, oath-breaker."

At this, the bodyguards and Argentocoxus' sons bridled and stepped forward, but the slither of gladii all around them stopped them in their tracks.

Caracalla smiled.

"We both know, that oaths made under duress are short-lived," Argentocoxus said. "When we spoke in the woods after that battle, my life was in your hands. This time, I was assured that this was a peaceful converse."

"It is. But your life is still in my hands."

Argentocoxus smiled, his teeth barely visible behind the hairs of his beard. "The emperor is dead."

Caracalla tried not to betray his emotion then, but could not keep the surprise from his eyes at seeing that the chieftain already knew, that he no doubt suspected his plan.

"He is."

"And you are emperor now."

Caracalla nodded. "Yes. And I could order more legions here from Gaul and Germania. More men to hunt down your people and every member of your family, and crush them into the bloody mud and rock of your highlands. I could do this."

Argentocoxus was silent for a moment, his face a mask as he stared back at Caracalla. He remembered standing upon the field outside of Horea Classis a few years ago, the humiliation of surrendering his weapons and bowing to the sickly emperor Severus. The Wolf of the Maeatae had given him hope for redemption in the eyes of his people, but the Wolf was dead now, killed by Rome, though he was a son of the goddess. Argentocoxus also remembered the pale dead faces of his sons who had fought in battle, the broken bodies of the women and children of his people, a result of the savagery of the man before him. *How much more punishment can my people endure?* he thought as he gazed upon Caesar. *He would send more legions, and my people would cease to exist.*

"What do you propose?" Argentocoxus asked.

Caracalla smiled only then. "A truce. A lasting peace in Caledonia. I am emperor now, and I must return to Rome to secure my position. I have no wish to settle this land, but I will not see the borders of the empire disrespected. You will cease all hostilities to Rome and her allies in Caledonia now and forever. You will farm your own lands, and rule your people in peace, but you will never raise a sword against a Roman soldier or citizen again. If you do, I will return and burn this land to the ground."

The chieftain nodded, looked back at his sons, and then back to Caracalla. "And for all of this, for peace at your back while you secure your ivory and gold throne, Caesar, what do I get?"

"You live. You get peace and an end to the slaughter of your people. There is also an entire ship at anchor in the Tava right now that is full of gold and silver enough to ring the necks of you, your children, and all their successors with heavy torcs of kingship. You will be the richest of Rome's clients."

"Subject to Rome," you mean.

"Of course. But you will never see us if you keep to the truce."

Argentocoxus was silent for a few moments. He looked at Caracalla, at the men behind him, the Praetorians, including the man who had made contact. These were men he did not trust, whom he wanted far away from his people, his lands. *They will leave forever,* he thought, *and when they are all dead, my successors can take back the lands they have lost. They can fight another day.*

He nodded. "We have fought long enough, Caesar," he said. "I agree to your terms." He extended his hand and Caracalla grasped it.

"What is going on here?"

Conn Venico and his attendants entered the courtyard to see the chieftain of the Caledonii and Caracalla shaking hands, and he stopped dead in his tracks, only remembering to bow to Caracalla after a few seconds of shock.

"Ah! Conn Venico!" Caracalla said, turning toward him. "You're just in time."

Argentocoxus stared at the chieftain of the Venicones who had been tied to Rome for so long, and he smiled.

"What is he doing here, sire?" Conn Venico asked.

"I have news for you, Conn Venico," Caracalla said. "The war is over. You will have peace at your doorstep from now on."

Conn Venico looked from Argentocoxus to Caracalla, and back again. He did not trust the Caledonian, but he trusted Rome even less. He turned to Caracalla and bowed slowly. "That is excellent news, sire. The Gods have smiled on us all."

The swift ride south to Eburacum had passed like a fleeting, unwanted dream. Lucius had been quiet the entire way, his mind racing over the possible outcomes of Severus' death, and none of them seemed good. He felt nervous, and his men felt it too.

Dagon and Barta kept a close eye upon him the entire way, wondered what he was thinking, where his mind was at.

Lucius did not hear the chants of his name as they passed through the war zone near Trimontium, nor the cheers of the garrison along the Wall when they passed through. In Coria, his name resounded to the sky, 'Hail, Dragon!', or 'Hail, Slayer of the Maeatae!'.

The only time their pace was broken, the only time in which Lucius came out of his thoughtful silence was to bid farewell to Afallach and the Votadini. After crossing the Bodotria, they reached the eastern road that led to the fortress of Dunpendyrlaw. The entire force stopped to rest the horses, and the Sarmatians bid farewell to their friends among the Votadini yet once more.

"We seem to be doing this all time, bidding farewell," Afallach said to Lucius as they walked along the grassy slopes of a nearby hill overlooking a wooded valley. "Are you sure you won't come to Dunpendyrlaw, Lucius?"

"Thank you, my friend, but I must get to Eburacum as soon as possible. The Praetorian prefect needs me urgently."

"Did he say why?" Afallach looked at Lucius from behind the long strands of his dark hair that swayed in the breeze. He looked Lucius in the eye.

"No," Lucius said, but he suspected, and that suspicion filled him with dread.

"Be careful, Lucius," Afallach said. "We need the Dragon. This entire island does."

Lucius looked at the man before him and smiled. Afallach had once been an angry young man, and now, looking upon him, Lucius saw only a king of his people.

"I want to thank you for all your help. You and your men are among the best I have ever fought alongside."

"It's been an honour, again. I only wish that..."

Lucius knew what he would have said, the thought that tortured Afallach now, as always. He could see the pain and frustration in his friend's face, the anguish it caused him to have missed slaying his father's killer yet again. "We'll get him, Afallach. When the war resumes - as it must - we'll bring Argentocoxus to justice."

"I pray the Gods give me that chance."

"So do I." Lucius was silent and stared out at the men and horses beyond the two of them. Dagon, Barta and Brencis were walking toward them.

"You know you can always count on us." Afallach's voice was intense then, and he reached out to grab hold of Lucius' arm. "Remember that. If you need us to come to you, anywhere. Anytime. We will help." He stared deeply at Lucius, as if trying to say something.

Lucius nodded as he looked back. "I know. And the Gods bless you for it, my friend. Until that time, be careful. If Caracalla is on the throne, the world will be a very different place. Be wary, and take care of that sister of yours."

"I will. I would that she could meet you, and that I could see your family again." Afallach smiled. "Who knows? Perhaps when this is all over, you and your family and men will dine with us in the halls of Dunpendyrlaw? A feast to remember!" Afallach looked younger then, like a young man dreaming impossible dreams with absolute certainty.

"That sounds good to me!" Brencis said as he approached with Dagon and Barta. "Farewell my friend," he said to the lord of the Votadini.

"Take care of each other," Afallach said to him. "Take care of our dragon," he said to Barta next, as he grasped his forearm.

"Until I die," Barta answered, his voice deep and thoughtful.

That gave Afallach pause, but he nodded. "Until death. Yes." He turned to Dagon and they embraced, one lord to another. "As I told Lucius, if you have need of us, send word, and we will come."

"My friend, may the Gods bless you and your men. Take care," Dagon said.

The Votadini were mounted up now and Afallach's horse was brought to him. He pulled himself up in the saddle and secured his legs. The wind picked up his red cloak as if blowing him in the direction of home.

Afallach's vexillarius came to his side, and Lucius looked up at the red banner with the white horse upon it. He would miss the sight of it.

With the Votadini assembled in marching order, their spearpoints glinting in the daylight, and their shields hanging from their sides, they waited for their lord's order.

Afallach smiled. "To Dunpendyrlaw!" he yelled. "Home!" The men cheered and their horses moved out. "May Epona guide you safely home, my friends!" Afallach called over his shoulder to Lucius, Dagon and the others.

Lucius waved at the young lord and watched the Votadini disappear into the East.

"When this is over," Brencis said. "Perhaps we can visit them at Dunpendyrlaw?"

Lucius turned to him. "I don't think this will be over anytime soon, Brencis." He began to walk. "Let's ride!"

After that, their pace was quick, and they covered the distance as if furies were at their backs.

In his mind, Lucius sought out his family, his wife, daughter and son. He tried to let them know that he wanted to come home, that he was thinking of them. He always was, no matter what events took place in the maelstrom around him. So long as he thought of them, he had a hold on the thread that led out of the labyrinth.

He was happy to have left Fendoch, that place of death, behind them, but he wondered if Eburacum would be any different. With the death of an emperor, there was always much uncertainty, and he guessed that that was why Papinianus wanted him and his men there.

After a couple of days of hard riding, the solid walls and high towers of Eburacum finally came into view.

They were met by a Praetorian patrol who had been on the lookout for them, and Lucius was relieved when they pronounced that Papinianus had sent them.

"Praefectus Metellus," the optio said, saluting sharply. "The prefect will be glad of your arrival. He told me to inform you that you and your men should encamp as close as possible to the walls, outside the annexe and northwest gate of the via Principalis. He will send for you and your decurions soon."

"Has Caesar Antoninus arrived yet from Caledonia?" Lucius asked.

The man was silent for a moment, and shook his head. "Not yet, Praefectus. Caesar Geta is in the city, but Caesar Antoninus and the legions are yet to arrive. The prefect expects them soon. For the funeral, that is."

"Of course." Lucius nodded to the man. "Thank you, Optio. We'll set up camp and be ready when Papinianus calls for us."

The man saluted again, turned and marched his contubernium back to the city.

"It's better this way," Lucius said to Dagon. "I'd rather be in our own camp than billeted within the city walls."

"Are you worried, Anguis?" Dagon asked.

Lucius looked at him. "I'm always worried these days." He looked around the fields ahead of them, near the city gate, and pointed. "Let's set up camp over there, on the other side of the road, opposite the annexe."

"Should we entrench?"

Lucius thought about it for a moment, and shook his head. "No. Not fully. That would not be...appropriate. I want a single ditch with stakes though. Not a full war-time camp, but enough to dissuade the curious."

Within a few hours, the Sarmatian camp was fully set up outside the walls of Eburacum where the heads of the garrison could be seen watching them. Citizens, merchants and camp followers also came out of the annexe and the city itself to see the Sarmatians, and to try and catch a glimpse of the Dragon Praefectus they had heard so much about, the man who had slain the Wolf of the Maeatae.

Inside his campaign tent, his armour cleaned and oiled, Lucius waited by the light of his lamp, gazing at the hilt of his sword. It was getting late, and Papinianus had still not sent for him. He had wanted to write to Adara, but his mind was too busy, too uncertain, and he did not want to start the letter only to be interrupted by a summons. He wondered what was going on inside the fortress and city. Julia Domna came into his mind and he wondered how she was. Her sons were heirs to the imperial throne, but she had also lost her husband. Lucius wondered how she would be when he saw her. Ever had she been his ally, but since arriving in Britannia, things had felt different, more uncertain, when it came to the empress. She was, perhaps, no longer the woman who had helped him to escape Leptis Magna all those years ago.

"Praefectus?" Dagon's voice came from outside the tent.

"Enter, Dagon."

Dagon entered, also wearing his full armour, polished to a sheen. "Papinianus has sent word. He'll see us first thing in the morning."

At the first hour of daylight, Lucius, Dagon, and Barta made the short walk to the looming gate of the via Principalis where the Praetorians on duty had been expecting them. They were escorted down the street to the principia of the fortress where they turned into the courtyard and were led directly across to the offices of the Praetorian prefect.

The guards on either side of the door nodded to their approaching comrades and turned to open the door.

Lucius turned to Barta and Dagon, indicating that they should follow him.

Inside, the room was still dimly lit, the slave still in the process of filling and lighting the lamps and braziers. Still, Papinianus, fully dressed in his armour, was already seated behind his table, going over the preparations for the funeral.

"You made it," he said, looking up at Lucius, his eyes also studying Dagon and Barta.

"Prefect," Lucius said, and the three of them saluted. "You remember my princeps and my vexillarius."

569

"Yes, indeed. Welcome to Eburacum, gentlemen. Please sit." Papinianus turned to the slave. "Water and wine for the men."

"Yes, Prefect." The slave busied himself finishing lighting the lamps, and then brought cups of watered wine to the three men.

"So, here we are, Metellus," Papinianus said, looking across the table at Lucius.

Lucius found he had a strange look in his eyes, something nervous, too nervous for a man in his high-ranking position.

"Leave us," Papinianus said and the slave disappeared.

"I am saddened by the emperor's death, sir," Lucius said. "He was a great leader."

Papinianus could see that Lucius meant it, for in many others who had delivered their condolences to him, Geta, or the empress, he had seen in their eyes that they only mouthed the words. The real sincerity came from Severus' troops. They knew the metal of the man who had ruled the empire.

"It is a loss we had been expecting for some time, but which feels completely unexpected now that it is here, if that makes any sense."

"It does," Lucius said. He sipped his wine and then looked at Papinianus. "The guardsmen who met us on the road yesterday said that Caesar has not yet arrived in Eburacum."

"We expect him sometime today. He is bringing some of the legions with him - the men should have a chance to mourn their emperor, but the frontier needs to be guarded too."

"I left the men from Parthica legion at Fendoch. It has been quiet, but Argentocoxus is still at large and could attack any time without warning. I don't trust him. I never did."

"And you were right not to, Metellus. Everyone knows it. Your instincts were right." Papinianus shook his head. "Septimius has left us with quite a mess, now he's departed for the Afterlife."

Lucius glanced at Dagon and Barta, and then back to the Praetorian prefect.

Papinianus looked at Dagon and Barta and nodded. "It is good you are here, all of you. You must stay close to your Praefectus, for he must have you ready at a moment's notice."

"Ala III Britannorum is always ready, Prefect," Dagon confirmed.

"Good. For now, I wonder if I might speak with your praefectus alone?"

ISLE OF THE BLESSED

"Of course," Dagon said, rising, followed by Barta. The two of them saluted and then went out.

When the door was closed, Papinianus looked at Lucius.

"What mess did the emperor leave you with, sir?" Lucius asked, though he suspected the answer.

"The empire hangs by a thread, Metellus. Strong leadership is needed to keep it strong, and I don't mean the senate. There are only so many Dio's in the world. With dear Septimius upon the throne, things were stable, even when he was an invalid. His very presence was enough. But he is gone now, and in his will, he made his sons Geta and Antoninus his heirs. They both already carry the title of Augustus - one of Septimius' final acts. Can you see them ruling peaceably, together?"

"They hate each other, don't they?" Lucius asked.

"That is an understatement. And yet, my cousin - excuse me, the empress - believes that she can sow a great harmony between them."

They looked at each other, and Lucius wondered what was going through Papinianus' head. At the back of his mind, he suspected, but he would not voice the words. He could not.

Papinianus continued. "If I need you, if Rome needs you, will you be ready to act at a moment's notice?"

"I am always ready to fight for Rome," Lucius said. *Even though my path seems to have diverged from Rome's.*

"That is good, Metellus. I'm relieved to hear you say that."

"Sir, can you tell me what is going on?"

"Not yet. But soon. I'm still looking into things and will know more when the legionary legates arrive with Caracalla. For now, make yourself seen in the city, meet with my Praetorians, and the regular troops. Speak with them. They will want to know of your battles."

"That seems an odd thing to do, Prefect. I would rather wait in my camp and prepare for the funeral."

"That will be tomorrow, should Caracalla arrive today. Go into the city for now, visit the baths, the market - purchase something nice for your family. It is the normal things in life that we miss when the world goes awry." Papinianus stared at the table for a moment and then snapped out of his reverie, his features darkening. "Come," he stood up. "It is time for you to see him."

"Who?" Lucius asked.

Papinianus looked at him, his eyes glossy in the lamplight. "Why, the emperor, of course."

Papinianus and two guards went with Lucius, Dagon and Barta across the courtyard, turned left onto the via Principalis, and then went into the complex of the praetorium, the imperial residence within the fortress.

They were led down guarded corridors, past the peristylium, and to a set of open double doors where some guards stood at attention. The scent of burning myrrh and frankincense was extremely heavy on the air.

Lucius, Dagon and Barta had to cover their mouths for a moment until they adjusted to the smell, for it was not just incense, but also death and decay.

Papinianus turned to them. "If you wish, you may see him."

"I will," Lucius said. "Barta and Dagon will remain here." Lucius looked at them, and knew that they were relieved he said that, though they showed no outward signs of it.

"Come," Papinianus said, leading the way in.

The large cubiculum had been completely emptied of furniture, and in each corner of the room scented smoke billowed from a large bronze brazier with clawed feet. In the middle of the large chamber lay the body of Septimius Severus, Emperor of Rome.

Lucius walked forward and stopped.

"I'll leave you alone," Papinianus said, turning and going out into the corridor to speak with the guards.

Lucius watched him go, then turned back to the body.

Severus was laid out on a broad couch, upon a bed of laurels and bows of cedar. He was dressed in a toga of rich Tyrian purple that was trimmed with rich gold brocade of the meander, and there were doeskin slippers upon his swollen feet. Upon his white head, there rested a corona of golden laurels. His aged hands were clasped upon his stomach, and just visible at the edge of his grey lips could be spotted the glint of a brilliant aureus placed in his mouth, his payment for the Boatman.

Lucius approached, ignorant now of the scent, for all he could see was the body of the man who had raised him from the ranks to the position of tribune and then praefectus, the body of the man who had believed in him, who had taken a chance on him, the body of a man who had been more fatherly to Lucius than Quintus Caecilius Metellus had ever been. Lucius remembered Severus leading them

572

into battle in Parthia like Alexander himself, but now he found it hard to reconcile that man with the corpse lying before him, swollen, bandaged legs beneath a grey, emaciated and wrinkled body.

No matter how much purple a body was draped in, the Gods' work could not be hidden from sight. Even the greatest of emperors turned to dust and ash.

Lucius bowed his head. "You always believed in me, sire. You gave me the chance to prove myself. For that, I thank you..." He did not know why, but the tears that formed in Lucius' eyes then surprised him.

"He loved you like a son, you know."

Lucius wiped his eyes quickly and turned to see Empress Julia Domna standing behind him. He bowed to her, falling to one knee, his greave grating on the stone floor.

"Empress," Lucius said, staring at the floor. "I'm sorry for your loss." He felt her hand touch his head, linger on his hair, and then she moved silently past him to look upon her husband's body.

The empress was dressed in many layers of black silk, and fine black wool that once would have matched exactly the sheen of her tightly woven hair. She wore a black fur cloak over her shoulders, even though it was Spring. She had never felt warmth in Britannia.

"Stand with me, Metellus," she said, her voice laced with exhaustion.

Lucius rose from the floor to stand beside her, looking down at the emperor's body.

"I can't believe the day came to pass," she whispered, looking up at the ceiling and then back down.

Lucius looked up too and saw the stars painted there, then he looked at her. Her large brown eyes did not weep, but they were dark, lined with black kohl to cover the dark circles. The eyes suddenly looked at him.

"How is your family?"

Lucius was taken aback by the question, especially as they stood over the body of the dead emperor, her husband.

"They...they are well. We have found a home here, in Britannia."

"I imagine your wife must miss the Middle Sea, the sunlight and heat."

Lucius smiled. "We all do, my lady."

"I think things will be a little less bright beneath the sun for me now." She looked back to her husband's body.

"I will be forever grateful to him," Lucius said, bowing his head.

Julia Domna placed her had upon Lucius' on the edge of the couch, her long, bejewelled fingers falling over his rough, warrior's hands.

Lucius would have taken his hand away, but she held him there, he thought, for comfort.

"He was a magnificent ruler, my husband."

"Yes he was, my lady. And I suspect that much of that success was owed to your own devotion and faith in him."

At this, she smiled and looked at Lucius again. It seemed that perhaps that was something that few people had ever told her.

"I did my best with what the Gods gave me, in order to help him achieve greatness and found a new dynasty. And I will do the same for my sons who are his heirs." Her eyes narrowed a little.

"They could not ask for better support, my lady," Lucius said. At the back of his mind, he knew that he had to be very careful in that moment about what he said or did.

"They could also use your support, Metellus. The legions love you, by all accounts. You could be the greatest legate commander Rome has ever had under the new, joint emperors."

Lucius could not help but look surprised at this. He hoped the disgust that he actually felt was not revealed on his features. *More wars? More death? I would not want to be a legate for Caracalla or Geta!*

"With you helping them...us...we can carry on the work my dear husband fought so hard for." She looked down at the body again, lifted her hand from Lucius', and reached out to touch the swollen legs draped in purple cloth.

"Of course, my lady," Lucius managed to say. "I serve Rome. I will always serve Rome."

"That is good." She said, turning to face him and look up into his eyes. With the hand that had been resting upon her husband's body, she touched Lucius' cheek. "I rely on you for this," she said.

"Hail Caesar!" came a chorus of voices from the corridor outside then, followed by the swift marching of hobnails upon the stone floors.

The empress removed her hand slowly from Lucius' face and they both turned to face the doors where, a moment later, Caracalla appeared with several other Praetorians behind him.

"Sire, we must speak," Papinianus could be heard saying behind him.

"Not now, Prefect. I must see my father!" As Caracalla turned to face into the room, he stopped suddenly, his eyes taking in the death couch and his mother standing there with Lucius Metellus. "What is this?"

Lucius saluted quickly and bowed his head, not taking a knee upon the floor as he had done for the empress. "Sire. I grieve for you and your family."

Caracalla marched into the room, his face and armour still splashed with mud from the road. He was about to ignore Lucius and walk past him, but stopped and spoke very closely to his face. "How did you get here so quickly? I did not send word to you at your wilderness fort, Metellus."

"I...we...my men and I were ordered by the prefect to ride swiftly and clear the road of any threats so that you would have safe passage, my lord."

"Did he now?"

Lucius turned to see Marcus Claudius Picus standing at the back of the room with Papinianus opposite him. He stared at Papinianus.

"Of course, I did," Papinianus said, standing tall and staring at the upstart beside him. He looked at Caracalla then and bowed. "Sire, the Sarmatian cavalry is the best and fastest, and as Argentocoxus is still at large, I wanted the way to be secure. Metellus was the best man for the job."

"How thoughtful of you, Papinianus." Caracalla's voice, full of sarcasm, was harsh as a newly-sharpened gladius blade. He turned to address all of them, including the empress. "But we don't need to worry about Argentocoxus any more."

"What do you mean, sire?" Papinianus asked.

"I've made a truce with him that will last. The war is over. I've permitted him to continue to rule his people in exchange for the promise of no threats to Rome, her citizens or allies, in perpetuity. We spoke quite frankly about it at Horea Classis."

"You had him before you, sire?" Lucius asked, unable to help himself.

"Do you question me, Metellus?"

"No, sire. But, Argentocoxus is not to be trusted. He betrayed Rome before, he will do it again."

"He betrayed my father." Caracalla looked quickly at the body, and then back to Lucius. "He knows it will be death to betray me. Besides, I made it worth his while."

"You paid him in gold and silver, didn't you?" Papinianus said, his voice shocked, and angry. "Your father wanted to build a new polis of the north there...sire."

"Yes, I paid the barbarian off with a ship load of gold and silver. And plans change, Papinianus. Much *will* change. Caledonia is not worth Rome's resources. The land can offer us very little. Argentocoxus will remain north of the Wall, and not bother us." Caracalla went to stand beside his mother before the body again, but stopped in Lucius' face one more time. "And remember, Metellus, those are *my* men, not yours."

"Of course, sire." Lucius bit his lip hard to keep from saying any more, bowed as he backed away, allowing Caracalla to approach his mother who took his hand and kissed his cheek.

"After the funeral for Father, we will get out of this accursed land and get back to Rome," Caracalla said.

"That's the first brilliant idea I've ever heard you utter, Brother!"

Everyone turned to see Geta approaching.

"Geta," Caracalla growled.

Julia Domna placed her hand upon Caracalla's arm and reached out with the other to take Geta's hand. "My sons," she said. "We must honour your father now, and then there is much to do."

"Yes, Mother," they said together, all of them turning to face the body.

"We know, Mother," Caracalla added. "Harmony..."

Lucius backed away from the empress and the two Caesars and walked toward the doors, but not before Claudius Picus stood in his way.

The Praetorian looked Lucius straight in the eyes, his smile supremely confident and challenging.

"I must confess, Metellus, that I'm surprised to find you here, alone with the empress, seemingly so close to the heart of things."

"Metellus is here at my invitation, Claudius," Papinianus said, standing at Lucius' side. "He has served the emperor for longer than you have. Severus honoured him, and as such, Metellus deserved to be able to pay his respects to the emperor's shade on his own. You on the other hand…"

"You flatter me, Prefect."

"No. I do not."

Claudius actually laughed in Papinianus' face then, the sound like shattering glass in that solemn room.

Caracalla glanced back, his scowl deep and rigid, but he did not say anything. He turned back to the body.

Claudius turned back to Lucius, still smiling. "How is your family, Metellus? You wife? Your children? I hear Adara is expecting yet another?"

Lucius' hands were gripping the edges of Claudius' cuirass faster than anyone could have imagined. "You do not speak of my family," he growled. "Ever!"

"Not here, Metellus," Papinianus said in his ear. "Let him go."

Lucius released Claudius, who still smirked at him.

"Get out of here!" Caracalla bellowed. "Or I'll have you flogged!"

Papinianus pulled Lucius out into the corridor where Dagon and Barta were waiting for him, their eyes wide with worry.

Lucius looked back to see Claudius waving at him from inside the room, that hateful smile upon his face, and a wink thrown in for good measure.

"Go," Papinianus said as he walked with Lucius, his men, and his own guards down the corridor. "Go back to your camp. I will send for you if…" He stopped speaking as Ulpianus walked past him without saluting.

"Papinianus," Ulpianus said as he smiled and walked right by on his way to join Caracalla and the others.

Papinianus watched him disappear into the room. When he turned, Lucius and his two men were already far down the corridor, storming off as ordered.

At that moment, Castor came rushing up to him. "You saw Caesar?"

"Yes," Papinianus said. "It's already starting."

As they left the busy streets of the fortress, Lucius, Dagon and Barta exited the gate at the northwest of the city to find the fields beyond the annexe and their own camp brimming with the men of the legions who had accompanied Caracalla from Caledonia and were setting up their camps.

The air was filled with the songs men sang upon the march, or as they dug and shifted the earth for their camps.

Many spotted Lucius as the three of them walked, and they shouted his name.

"Hail, Metellus!" men cried.

Lucius tried to smile and salute back, but his mind was spinning with anger and fear. "How did Claudius know Adara was expecting a child?" he asked Dagon and Barta.

"I don't know," Dagon said. "But I don't like it. The bastard has spies everywhere."

They arrived at the outskirts of the Sarmatian camp to see several centurions milling around one of the gates, men from the Valeria Victrix, the Parthica, and the Augustan legions.

"What's going on here?" Barta wondered.

"I don't know," Lucius said, approaching a primus pilus he recognized from the sixth legion. "Centurion!" Lucius saluted.

The grizzled veteran turned and saluted, his horizontal crest swaying in the breeze as he saluted sharply back. "Praefectus! The Gods themselves must have blown you and your men here to have arrived so quickly."

"What news?" Lucius asked the man.

"There is a lot of confusion, Praefectus. The legates are within, waiting to see you."

"All three of them?" Lucius asked.

"And some tribunes," the centurion nodded. "You're quite popular. You fight too well!" He laughed, but his eyes betrayed that he knew something was amiss.

Lucius nodded, and went past him and the other centurions into the camp. His men saluted as he went in, and Lucius noticed that Brencis had ordered some men to mount up and stand at attention with the arrival of so many troops.

"Praefectus," the decurion Barna said as he arrived. "Brencis is in your command tent with them," he said as they walked.

"Is there danger?" Lucius asked, his voice low.

"No, sir. I think they just want to talk."

They arrived at the tent entrance where Sarmatian guards stood at attention. "I want the guards doubled," he said to Barna.

The decurion saluted and went to see it done.

Lucius turned to Dagon and Barta and took a deep breath. They could hear the hum of voices within the tent. Lucius nodded, and the three of them went in.

"Gentlemen," Lucius said as he entered.

Before him, gathered around his campaign table with cups of water, were the legates of the three legions, each accompanied by their broad-striped tribunes.

"Praefectus Metellus," said the legate of the II Augustan legion, Antonius Valerius Lyco.

"Commander," Lucius said, taking the man's extended hand.

"Sorry for the intrusion, Metellus, but we wanted to meet with you as soon as possible."

"I'm sorry for the delay. The Praetorian prefect wanted to see me.

"So your princeps said," Valerius added.

"I also paid my respects to the emperor."

"So, it's true then. The emperor is dead," asked Demetrius Valens Boscu, the legate commander of II Parthica.

Lucius nodded. "The Gods have taken him. Severus is dead."

The men in the tent began grumbling and shaking their heads.

"I also saw Caesar," Lucius added.

"With his snake, Claudius, no doubt?" asked Marcus Aemilius Fronto, legate of the XX Valeria Victrix.

"Yes," Lucius said, balling his fists and leaning on the table. Lucius looked up at them all. "Caesar said that he has made a truce with Argentocoxus. Is it true? He let him live?"

"Yes," Valerius said, rubbing his temples. "It's true. Tens of thousands of Roman troops dead over the last few years, only to pay the barbarian off with a boatload of treasure. You were right the first time, Metellus. The Caledonian should not have been trusted."

"The treaty is disgusting!" Aemilius said, his face red with anger.

Lucius looked at the men there before him and wondered that they were so open with him. Were they not worried about retaining their commands, worried about their lives?

Lucius cleared his throat. "Caesar said that once the funeral is finished, he wants to pull out of Britannia."

"That is the plan," Valens confirmed. Valens was the youngest of the legates, but he had seen plenty of war already. "The three legions that garrison Britannia will stay, but the rest will pull out and be posted elsewhere. As to where, your guess is as good as mine."

"This is a precarious time, Metellus," Valerius said. "I remember when Commodus died. It did not go smoothly."

"Papinianus would not auction the throne," Lucius said. "And no one wants another civil war."

"With those two brothers," Aemilius began, "there may well be one."

Everyone of them was silent then, uncomfortable, the tribunes behind the legates distinctly so. Normally those men of patrician rank would have felt the need to insert themselves into a conversation with their legates. Their advice was normally sought and respected, but at that moment, the space in that crowded tent was tense.

Lucius could feel it. Too much had been said, but these men were clearly unhappy - angry and betrayed - with the treaty, and worried about the future. He could understand that. He was still reeling from the news that Argentocoxus was permitted to live and carry on ruling his people. *After all he has done, the men he's killed. My men!* Lucius could not help but think of the betrayal to Afallach and the Votadini, Rome's only true allies north of the Wall. He noticed the legates staring at him and wondered what they expected. There was a time when men such as these, and their broad-striped tribunes, looked down on him with utter disdain as an upstart equestrian. But now...now they appeared to be looking to him for a lead.

"Gentlemen, I'm not sure what else to say," Lucius said, standing up and crossing his arms.

Valerius stepped forward. "Metellus, when last I saw him, my old friend Flavius Marcellus spoke very highly of you."

Lucius smiled at the thought of his old legate commander in Numidia. The man had believed in him, but because of the fear of the men around him, and the events that had hampered Lucius and his family, he had sent Lucius back to Rome. *How times have changed,* Lucius thought. *At Lambaesis, men were afraid to be near me...now they chant my name in the camps and streets of Britannia. All I want is to go home.*

Lucius shook his head as if trying to clear it, and took a deep breath. "At the moment, we need to focus on the emperor's funeral, for that is why we are here."

Valerius put up his hands for his colleagues who were about to speak up more vehemently. "Metellus is right. We must honour our fallen emperor. Then will come the debate about the matters of war and empire."

"If we speak with one voice, perhaps Caesar will see that finishing the war and Argentocoxus will be a better, long-term solution. Stability will follow. Else, we will be back in Caledonia a year from now to feed the crows." Lucius knew that what he had just said sounded foolish and naive, but he did not know what else to say to these men.

"I'm afraid, Metellus, that Caesar's mind is fixed on Rome and nothing else," Valerius said. "We will speak more of this, I'm sure." He stepped forward and extended his hand to Lucius who took it. "The men in all of our legions admire you and your deeds, Metellus. If we get the order to return to the fight...in Caledonia...they would all be behind you. As would we."

"Then let us hope the Gods help us to finish what we started," Lucius said.

The legates and tribunes bid Lucius farewell until the funeral, and all filed out of the tent to return to their respective camps.

When they were alone, Lucius turned to Dagon, Barta and Brencis. "That was unexpected."

"And dangerous, Anguis," Dagon said. "What are they thinking coming here and speaking so openly with you about Caracalla."

"I don't know."

"I think you do." Dagon's voice was worried, and the expressions on Brencis and Barta's faces revealed that they too were uncomfortable with what had just happened. "Do you not see it? They look to you to lead, Anguis."

"The emperor is just dead, Dagon. And he has two heirs who are already stepping in."

"Yes. He does. And they are." Dagon began to turn to leave, but stopped. "This is bigger than Caledonia and Argentocoxus."

Brencis saluted, having no words for once, and followed Dagon out of the tent.

Lucius turned to Barta and the big Sarmatian nodded.

"We heard what was said in the praetorium when we waited for you in the corridor. When Caesar arrived..." Barta shook his head. You need to be careful, Praefectus. We all do."

"You're right, my friend."

Whatever worries men nurtured in their minds as to the future of the empire, and themselves, they were silenced over the next day, for fear, and out of respect for the emperor. The day of the funeral of Septimius Severus had arrived, and Eburacum was shrouded in black.

Papinianus and Castor had seen to it that preparations had been underway since the day the emperor passed from the world. They, and Julia Domna, had known his wishes.

Almost two miles to the southwest of Eburacum, in a flat broad field away from the river, the site of the funeral, the burning place, the ustrinum, had been prepared under the auspices of the priests, with the men of the legions building the actual pyre itself.

Rumour in the city was rampant as citizens who had been to the site brought word of a massive construction that rose by the hour, higher into the silver sky. In the markets of Eburacum, the citizenry also spoke of the legions encamped outside of the northern walls, including the 'Dragon Praefectus' who had just ridden to victory against the savages of Caledonia.

Papinianus had also, in conference with Caracalla and Geta, sent orders to the legionary legates to arrange for their men to be ready to march in the funeral cortege from the praetorium and through the southwest gate to the distant site of the proceedings.

It was widely whispered among the Praetorian troops that the prefect and Caesar were at odds and could not agree on anything, and that only the empress' interference had prevented a falling-out prior to the funeral.

The entire time, Lucius, despite Papinianus' advice that he be seen out in the city, at the baths and markets, remained inside his command tent in the Sarmatian camp. He stayed out of the city, away from Caracalla and especially Claudius.

It would not do to shed blood on such an occasion as that.

The only time Lucius ventured out of the camp was to meet with the men of the legions who were encamped nearby. He enjoyed the camaraderie between them, the shared experience of blood and death, battle and loss in Caledonia having formed a bond between them all. And with the death of their emperor, they were also united in their grief, sharing stories around cook fires, or around clusters of men outside the gates of the various forts, about their own experiences over the years with Septimius Severus, that generous leader who was loved and admired by the men of the legions.

When the dispositions came from Papinianus about the orders of march for the procession, every man returned to his tent to prepare for the following day.

The night, however, proved to be one of chaos. As often happens in that land of rain and cloud, the skies darkened and black clouds rolled in from the moors and dales to the West. Then the rain started, followed by lightning that cracked like a Titan's whip over their heads the whole of the night.

In the Sarmatian camp, the horses whinnied and screamed at the noise, and even though they were used to the chaos of battle, the sound of the Gods' wrath or weeping was too much for them to handle.

Many of the Sarmatians went from their tents to spend the night with their mounts, soothing them and reassuring them that all was well.

At one point, Lucius too went out to check on Xanthus in the horse rows, and it was only upon seeing Lucius that the stallion became calm. His eyes had been wide with fright and panic, and constantly gazing toward the sky.

With his hand upon the stallion's neck as the rain poured out of the sky, Lucius looked up, squinting at the sky laced with spiderwebs of lightning, to see several dark shapes circling there. For a moment, he thought he was imagining the fast-whirling clouds were alive, but then he thought he spied wings, and heard the sounds of screeching on the wind.

With the braziers and torches guttering to minuscule points of light throughout the camp, the entire Sarmatian force remained alert through the torrential night, as did men in the camps of the legions surrounding them, their own dim lights visible through the watery haze of the downpour.

The next morning, word spread everywhere of omens throughout the camps, and Eburacum itself.

Three men had been struck by lightning and killed in the camp of II Parthica Legion, and to the northeast of the legionary fortress, the river had swelled so much that it broke its banks and swept away all of the pack animals from the XX Valeria Victrix that had been set out to graze, their bodies washing away in the river.

Within the walls of Eburacum and throughout the civilian annexe, perhaps the most frightening thing of all was the sighting of ghostly legionaries marching calmly through the streets, over and over again. Men and women there began to wonder if those slain in Caledonia had returned to march in the procession of their dead emperor and escort him to the Afterlife.

For all this, when the sun's chariot crept over the horizon, a wave of relief spread throughout every camp and home of Eburacum.

The funeral was to begin late in the morning, and so at the first hour of light, after brushing down and feeding Xanthus, making sure he was calm, Lucius went back to his tent to close his eyes for a short time before rising again to dress in his full armour. He was just finishing brushing the tall, red horsehair crest upon his helmet and checking the sword at his back when Dagon and Barta came in.

"Did you rest?" Dagon asked him.

"A little. Did you?"

"Not really." Dagon shrugged. "There will be time afterward." He looked around the tent and then back at Lucius. "What are the orders from Papinianus?"

"They want us mounted for the procession. We're the only cavalry force in the funeral. We're to report to the Principia gate at the fifth hour."

"All of us?"

"We can leave two turmae here."

"I'll give the order." Dagon sat down beside Lucius at the table, and Barta followed. "The Gods were angry last night."

"It seemed that way," Lucius said. "Did you hear about II Parthica?"

Dagon nodded, then looked Lucius in the eye. "Something doesn't feel right, Anguis. Something is coming. I sense it. I also felt that…"

"What?"

"In the chaos of last night, I felt like Briana was reaching out to me…telling me to be careful."

"She's worried you won't make it back in time for the birth of your child." Lucius shook his head. "She and Adara must both be very near their birthing time." Lucius thought of his wife, heavy with child, and how he had not had time to write to her in a while. He hoped she heard his prayers, or that the Gods winged his thoughts and feelings to her across the miles.

584

Outside then, they heard the call of cornui on the morning air.

Lucius looked up at the roof of the tent. "Gather the men. It's time to say farewell to our emperor."

The three of them rose and Lucius put on his black cloak instead of his red one this time, but fastened it with the blue and red enamelled brooch he had always worn.

Together, the three men emerged from the tent to see many Sarmatians waiting for the orders which Dagon gave, and apart from the two turmae that were to remain behind, the rest of the warriors mounted up.

Xanthus, already harnessed, was brought up for Lucius who pulled himself up into the saddle. The golden hilt of Lucius' sword jutted up behind him and glinted in the morning light, and his horsehair crest swayed with the movement of his head as he looked around at the men. As ever, he was proud to lead them, be it in battle, or in a funeral cortege.

To his right and left, Dagon and Brencis were mounted, the scales of their armour polished as well, and glinting like serpents after a rain, or the Nile crocodiles newly emerged from the river of life. When Barta raised the dragon vexillum behind them, Lucius looked up at it fluttering in the breeze.

The draco standards of every turmae were hoisted down the line, their tails filling with wind and the slight hum of their voices beginning low and deep.

"Move out!" Lucius said, kneeing Xanthus so that the enormous stallion led the way through the guarded gate where the troops remaining behind saluted Lucius and his princeps on the way out.

On the road outside, the legions were marching toward the gate of the via Principalis in orderly blocks of centuries, their own aquila, vexillia, and other battle standards held high and proud. Every legionary's lorica shone brilliantly in that rising light, and beneath the solemn song of the cornui, blown by the bear-pelted cornicens, there could be heard the rhythmic tramp of the hobnails of thousands of men.

Many of those men, including the legates and tribunes at the head of the armies turned to see Lucius and the Sarmatians riding up to await their turn to join the flow into the fortress, and as they did so, they saluted Lucius upon his titanic black horse as he watched them.

Lucius saluted them in return, and when the last of the legionary units passed, he led his cavalry onto the road and toward the gate.

In the courtyard of the praetorium of Eburacum, the priests and augurs had just finished with the sacrifices and the taking of the auspices. There was a tenseness in the air, especially after the violent night, but as the blood of the offerings pooled upon the altar, and the smoke curled into the sky, the auspices were declared favourable.

That done, the couch bearing the body of Severus was carried out by eight Praetorians, followed by the imperial family who emerged from the praetorium.

The courtyard was surrounded by legates and tribunes and men of the Praetorian guard, as well as senators such as Cassius Dio and many others. All of their eyes were on the body of the man they had called 'Emperor' for over a decade, and who was now gone.

Behind the deathly couch, Empress Julia Domna walked slowly. She was dressed entirely in black, but for a ribbon of Tyrian purple, to match her husband's robes, that wound its way about her torso. Covering her entire face, masking it from hundreds of eyes, was a thin black veil, beneath which she did her best not to weep, for she had anticipated that day for a long while.

To either side of the empress were her sons, those whom her husband had declared joint rulers upon his death. The two augusti were dressed in full parade armour, their new cuirasses oiled and gleaming, Geta's with images of Victory and Jupiter, and Caracalla's with a raging Hercules. Upon both of their heads were crowns of golden laurels, and at their sides hung ornate gladii, newly forged for them in the fires of Eburacum by the emperor's order before his death, a final gift with which to rule.

Mother and sons followed the couch slowly around the courtyard, and they in turn were followed by Julia Maesa, draped in black like her widowed sister, and the ladies of the court who flanked her. Behind them came Castor, the emperor's weeping freedman and friend, Domitius Ulpianus, and Euodus, Caracalla and Geta's teacher who strained to see his pupils over the heads of the black-clad women.

Papinianus then emerged from the praetorium with a large contingent of Praetorians, those men loyal to him. He was dressed in his full parade armour with a high crest of red horsehair upon his black helmet which matched his polished armour with Helios in his sun chariot upon the muscled chest. He had been rushing about all morning to ensure that the proper orders were given and that everyone knew their role for the funeral. Castor had helped, but Caracalla had hampered his plans by insisting on changing the order of march for the funeral.

When Claudius Picus had shown up at Papinianus' tablinum to convey Caracalla's orders, he had come with such arrogance into his presence that Papinianus considered locking him up for insubordination. But he quickly considered what this might mean, how it could hamper his own urgent plans. He had nodded and told Claudius to return to Caracalla to inform him that the changes would be made.

As the mourners made their voices heard about the courtyard of the praetorium, Papinianus scanned the crowd of legates, tribunes and centurions for Lucius Metellus Anguis, but he could not spot him anywhere, and wondered if the horses were delayed in the choked streets where the legions waited. Just as he was considering how bad it looked that Lucius was not there, he saw him.

Lucius entered the courtyard just as the funeral couch came to a stop before the gates facing the intersection of the via Principalis and the via Praetoria. He stopped suddenly, surprised by the sudden sight before him and quickly moved to one side where the legates Valerius and Valens stood at attention.

Caracalla and Geta looked in his direction, slightly annoyed, and Lucius bowed to them, the empress, and the funeral couch of his emperor.

To Lucius' surprise, all around the courtyard, men followed his lead and bowed to the imperial family.

Papinianus felt a wave of relief run through him at this. He nodded to Lucius who had also seen him. The procession could now begin. He was about to give the order to the guard to begin when he heard Claudius Picus' voice.

"Praetorians! It is time to bid farewell to your emperor! First cohort, on me!"

Papinianus was outraged at this, but the look in Caracalla's eyes at that moment was challenging and defiant. It was how *he* wanted things. Papinianus nodded and watched as Claudius marched through the gates of the praetorium with the first cohort of Praetorians. These were followed by the aquilae, vexillia, imagines and other standards

587

of the legions which had been held aloft around the fringes of the large courtyard.

Behind the first wave of Praetorians, led by Claudius, the standards of the legions followed like a forest dressed in victory, and behind them came the funeral couch bearing the emperor's body. This was followed and surrounded by the masked mourners who, all dressed in black, tore at their clothes, scratched at their faces, and wailed so loudly that it was heard in the civilian town even before they left the via Principalis.

Behind the mourners came the imperial family, Julia Domna flanked by her two sons, Geta and Caracalla. The empress walked silently, like a shadow, facing directly ahead as if she could not rip her gaze from the body of her husband where it lay hoisted on the shoulders of his Praetorians.

Caracalla and Geta both seemed more interested in the gaze of the troops lining the way, acknowledging them as they went, nodding to the men as they passed in their polished and resplendent armour.

They ignored Lucius when they passed him and walked down the via Praetoria straight ahead.

Behind Caracalla and Geta there followed Julia Maesa and her daughter, Julia Mamaea, as well as the other ladies of the court who never left the empress' side. Papinianus and Ulpianus, Julia Domna's cousins, fell in with them before another group of Praetorians followed.

The latter were led by Claudius Picus, and as he passed Lucius he turned directly to face him.

"You and your men are the horse's ass of the procession." And then he laughed.

The legates standing with Lucius stiffened as if waiting for Lucius to reach out and grab the man.

Lucius made no reply, but carried on watching the next group which included Castor, Euodus, and various senators, including Senator Dio who gave a polite nod to Lucius as he passed. They were joined by the army of imperial secretaries, freedmen, and other bureaucrats who had been helping to run the empire from Eburacum.

Once the main parties were out of the courtyard, making their mournful progress down the via Praetoria, the legates joined the men of their legions - the II Augusta, VI Victrix, IX Hispana, XX Valeria Victrix and representatives from the II and III Parthica legions. Century by century, each led by their legate, tribunes and other officers, the men of the legions marched in perfect unison along the via Principalis and then turned down the via Praetoria. The sound of their hobnails rose to the sky, and once each cornicens blew on his great curved horn, the true chorus of the funeral began, for Severus made his empire with the help of his legions, and by the Gods they would see him out of it.

Lucius felt a chill run up his spine as he walked past the marching legionaries, many of whom looked to him, some even saluting, as they passed. When he reached the Sarmatians, still waiting at the northwestern gate of Eburacum, enough space had cleared for them to follow.

"Ala III Britannorum!" Lucius yelled. "Forward!"

Beneath the dragon vexillum held by Barta, Lucius, Dagon, and Brencis led the men forward, each decurion keeping his men in perfect formation as they rode three-abreast, down the cobbled street.

When they turned right down the via Praetoria, past the tribunes' houses and barrack blocks of the fortress, a gust of wind swept up the street to fill the draco standards of each turmae with air.

The dragons howled in the street then, adding a new dimension to the procession that would rouse every citizen and soldier who watched along the processional way.

Beyond the heads of the marching legionaries, from where he sat on Xanthus, Lucius could see the funeral bier crossing the bridge over the river before heading into the civilian quarter where the streets were stuffed with people who had come to watch. They hung out of windows, perched on rooftops and crowded the steps of the temples of Serapis, Minerva, and other structures.

When Lucius passed beneath the fortress gates, the great stone towers rising up to either side of him and his men, he breathed deeply of the river air, the waters rushing beneath them as they crossed the bridge. He could see civilians pointing in his direction, at the dragon vexillum, at his men, and at him. For some reason, he lowered his mask, more comfortable beneath it, hidden from all of the eyes riveted upon him. It was a funeral, and so he rode in iron-faced silence, the only sound made by him and his men coming from the click of their horses' hooves and the dragons that fluttered wildly above their heads.

It took some time to pass through the civilian quarter of Eburacum, many approaching the procession to throw flowers upon the emperor's bier, others coming forward to offer a word of condolence to the empress who was enclosed by her sons.

The procession carried on, however, the Praetorians keeping things moving on down the street, the tramp of the legions behind adding a severity to the occasion.

As he rode, Lucius thought about how odd it was that he should be there. He remembered marching among the troops in the emperor's triumph all those years ago. That had been a joyous time, a time when it seemed anything was possible. Beneath his mask, he smiled to himself, remembering that that had been the day when he had met Adara at the imperial banquet on the Palatine Hill. *So long ago...*

The triumph and banquet of those halcyon days were forever etched on the record of his happy memories.

Now, he found himself far from Adara and his children, closed in by walls and thousands of confused and grief-stricken faces. He now marched in the funeral of his emperor. There was no cheering, no shower of bright flower petals from the tops of buildings. All was silence among the people as they passed through the civilian quarter. Here and there a child cried or complained, or someone might have coughed. Only the sounds of war echoed along the streets - the grating of hobnails, the clap of horses' hooves, the dirge of cornui, and the howl of the dragons above his head.

Far down the swaying line, the sound of the mourners crept back like smoke skipping over the heads of the procession, faintly to be heard at the back where Lucius and his men brought up the rear.

Eventually, they broke through the outer wall and gate of the settlement onto green fields. The funeral site was located almost two miles from the fortress, but the slow, mournful pace was maintained as they went, free of the crowds of civilians and buildings.

To the right side of the road was the large necropolis of Eburacum where a sea of monuments, large and small, spread out on the green grass. Lucius gazed at the city of the dead and felt a wave of sadness wash over him.

The time for mortals is so fleeting, he thought, turning away from it to look to the left on the other side of the road. There he spotted another, smaller necropolis. It was farther from the road and surrounded by scattered oak and yew trees. The monuments there were less grand, but there was something more dire about that smaller place of burial than there was about the large one on the other side of the road.

A choking feeling came over Lucius then, that dreaded panic he now sometimes felt, as he looked at that place.

Xanthus felt it too and bridled as he walked, tossing his head.

Lucius pushed up his face mask quickly and sucked in the cool air. He tore his gaze and thoughts from the small cemetery and stared straight ahead.

"Anguis," Dagon whispered beside him. "Are you ill?"

Lucius shook his head. "No. I'm fine."

"I think I see something in the distance," Brencis added. "That hill wasn't there before, was it?"

They looked ahead, beyond the legions marching before them, and in the distance, perhaps a mile away, there appeared to be a hill where there had been none, rising out of the ground as if placed there by the Gods in the night.

Eventually, the cortege began leaving the road, and as Lucius and his men approached, they could not help but be filled with awe.

"Papinianus has outdone himself," Dagon said as they came to a halt on the road while the legions took up positions around the burning site.

Lucius said nothing but looked up at the site before them.

A hill had indeed been created. It was of hard-packed earth, no doubt erected by the men of one of the legions. It rose up like the steep-sided embankment of a signal tower, only larger. Stairs were set into to sides of the mound, and the top was broad and flat. But it was not the hill itself that surprised Lucius so much as the pyre which rose like a wooden temple on top of it.

It was the biggest funeral pyre anyone had ever seen.

Upon the solid roof of the hill were set four massive platforms, each one slightly smaller than the one beneath, rising up to the top. Each level was stuffed with logs and boughs of cedar and pine. From the scent on the air, Lucius suspected that a large amount of pitch had been poured among the kindling as well, so as to ensure that the pyre would catch and the flames burn hot enough to consume the emperor's remains.

It was, however, not a simple pyre of wood and fuel. All around, each platform was decorated with draped and flowing sheets of purple and black that fluttered in the wind upon the field. It was a temple to be burned with the emperor upon it. It rose out of the earth

591

to reach for the sky and, perhaps in some way, lift Septimius Severus closer to the sun than any other.

Lucius and his men were ushered forward to a position on the far side of the pyre, and as they rode, he could see the emperor's couch sitting upon the grass before a large, covered dais where the empress, Caracalla, Geta and the imperial entourage were seated.

As they passed the body of Severus, Lucius and his men turned in their saddles and saluted. The sounds of drums and cornui began to slow as they came into position in the shadow of the funeral pyre.

The drums and horns stopped completely, and an eerie silence fell over the field, though thousands were present.

At an altar before the funeral couch, the priest of Baal, wearing black robes and his headdress of gilded ram's horns, raised his arms to the sky above and asked the Gods to take the shade of Severus to them, to the land of eternal light where the sun ever shines.

Many could not hear the priest, for his words were lost on the wind, though his actions spoke enough. As the victimarius held a large black ram upon the altar, the priest of Baal sliced the animal's throat slowly and deeply until the blood poured out to cover his hands which he raised to the sky above. The man bowed, and with his hands seemed to offer Severus' corpse to the Gods.

That done, Senator Dio stepped forward from where he stood to the right of the dais, and approached the body. Staying back from the bleeding altar and the blazing tripods that had been lit on either side of the funeral couch, he cleared his throat to give the eulogy.

Lucius doubted whether he would hear anything, but Dio was a trained orator, and his voice swept around the field in defiance of the wind itself. Standing there in his immaculately white toga with the thick, dark senatorial stripe, he was indeed fit to bid farewell to an emperor.

"My fellow Romans...friends..." He paused, bowed to the empress and her sons upon the dais, and then looked around at the gathered troops. "Today we bid farewell to our beloved emperor, Lucius Septimius Severus Parthicus Maximus Britannicus... Our August father of the empire. For years he has brought stability and prosperity to the empire. He has defeated the Parthian empire, Rome's long-time enemies, and brought to heel the raucous Caledonii. He came to a throne in turmoil, an empire under threat by those who would have sought to destroy Rome for their own selfish ends."

Dio looked around slowly, as if trying to catch the eye of every person there, and then he looked down upon the body. "There are no words of gods or men that could do justice to such as he." Dio outstretched his arms as if in apology. "I am no poet. I am a humble servant of Rome and her people." Here, he indicated the body of Severus. "As was Severus. For he has left the state better than when he found it. He has given us...hope...for the future of Rome. And it is up to each one of us to honour his work, to carry it on with honour and strength!"

Lucius felt a tightness in his chest at Dio's words, their power overwhelming him.

But though Dio's words were spoken to all, he had turned to Caracalla and Geta when he spoke the last sentence.

"May the Gods grant us the strength and grace we all need in the days...no...the many glorious years to come, so that future generations of Romans will look back on this time and say that with Severus, a new golden age of Rome was born!"

Here, Dio walked closer to the body of Severus that was dressed in full military regalia to bid farewell to the world of men like the warrior he had always been.

"Romans!" Dio cried, his voice high and steady. "Today we bid farewell to Septimius Severus, Emperor of Rome...Dominus et Deus!...and we commend him to the Gods themselves that they might receive him in Elysium and the very halls of Olympus!"

Lucius watched and listened, and upon his face, he felt the tears run down his cheeks.

Dio then backed away and bowed to the empress as she stood from her seat with her sons, and descended from the dais to approach her husband's body one last time.

All eyes were upon the black-veiled figure of Julia Domna as she moved slowly across the grass, through the scented smoke of the braziers, to her husband's side.

No words were spoken as she looked down at him, her hand resting gently upon his armoured chest. Slowly, shaking beneath her thick gown and robes of mourning, she leaned down to kiss her husband's cheek one last time, her lips meeting his pale skin through the thin film of her black veil.

Julia Domna stood then and backed away a few steps as her sons approached the couch, side-by-side.

The troops all watched as the two Caesars looked down on the body of their father.

Geta could not help but weep silently, the tears running down his cheeks as he stood there.

Caracalla's face, however, was dry, a blank facade devoid of emotion. After a few moments, he turned to look at Claudius and the Praetorians who stood nearby.

Before Claudius could move, Papinianus stepped forward with the men who had borne the couch forth from the city. He marched directly toward the couch, pausing by the empress' side to bow, and then directed the men to hoist the couch.

Claudius Picus remained rooted where he was, fuming, but silent as he watched.

The Praetorians, under Papinianus' direction, slowly and very carefully, carried the couch with the emperor upon it up the successive levels of the pyre.

As Lucius watched, he saw Papinianus glance in his direction.

It was no easy thing for those men to carry the heavy couch up the steep stairs to the top of the monumental pyre, and several times, he thought that the body might actually slide away. But it did not, and eventually, the Praetorians reached the top-most level of the pyre where they set the couch down.

All around the mound, men craned their necks to look up at the body of Severus, windswept and surrounded by fluttering purple and black.

Then, in the sky above, a sight that none had expected.

Julia Domna turned her head to the sky and there, high above her husband, even as the sun shone, there glimmered the stars to mark that day. It was only then that she wept beneath her veil, and her son Geta was at her side, holding her hand.

As if to add to the solemnity of the occasion, the cry of an eagle could be heard on the wind. High in the sky above, it could be seen circling and crying out in its shrill voice.

Papinianus nodded to his troops and they proceeded to light the braziers that were located all around the pyre, and beside which were buckets of torches.

The Praetorian prefect took up two of the torches and handed them to Caracalla and Geta who accepted them.

Then, the two brothers approached the pyre together, and mounted the steps on either side until they met at the top beside their father's body. As the drums and cornui sounded once more, slow, steady and rhythmic, the two caesars held their lit torches above their heads and circled the body so that the men of the legions could see them. Then, together, they lit the couch on fire.

As they descended the levels of the pyre, they set light to the pitch and timber within each platform until they reached the bottom and stood near the bloody altar.

It was then that Papinianus invited the legates of each legion to step forward with firebrands of their own, and in this act, he included Lucius to whom he pointed.

Seeing this, Lucius dismounted from Xanthus' high back and handed his reins to Barta who had dismounted as well.

Lucius walked across the grass and accepted a torch from the Praetorian prefect.

Lucius joined the legates before the burning funeral pyre, and was surprised to see that they would not add their torches until he had done so first. He looked at each of them and then at Papinianus who nodded.

"It is for you to do, Metellus. Bid farewell to him. Lead the way." Papinianus' face was in deadly earnest. He leaned in closer to speak again. "Come and see me after all of this. It is urgent."

Lucius nodded, then glanced around at all the eyes of the troops upon him, but also at Caracalla and Geta who frowned at the proceedings. He turned, and approached the pyre, followed by the legates.

"Farewell, my Imperator," Lucius said, and he then threw his torch high onto the third platform where it stuck in the pitch-soaked logs and caught at once.

The legates followed suit, and then it was the turn of the legions.

All around the smoking pyre, men from each legion then took up the torches which were set around the pyre and added to the flames that crawled up the hill to consume their emperor's remains.

At that moment, Caracalla and Geta approached the pyre and began to jog around it, an echo of the rites of old, going as far back as the funeral games held beneath the walls of Troy.

The troops, including Lucius, joined in, and soon the violent fires of the pyre were surrounded by a maelstrom of legionaries running around the burning body of Severus as the cornui sang and the drums of war pounded.

Papinianus and the legates stood together, watching, along with the imperial family and their entourage upon the dais.

For hours, they watched as the pyre dissolved and fell in upon itself in a pile of ember and ash. The black smoke rose into the sky and was visible from across the land, signalling to the world that an emperor was dead.

As the sun began to fall out of the sky, and the fires died completely, the emperor's ashes were collected and placed in the urn of purple stone he had chosen himself for his journey back to Rome.

XX

SALVA NOS!

'Save us!'

After the funeral of Septimius Severus, there was no public banquet, no celebration at which to speak of his great deeds. The imperial family retreated in on itself in the praetorium of Eburacum's fortress, the troops returned to their camps, and all civilians went back to their homes and the tabernae of Eburacum to speak of all they had seen that day, the rumours they had heard spoken in the crowded streets and agora.

Some wondered about the succession, or how the two young caesars would manage to rule jointly and peaceably. Others spoke of what they had heard of the lighting of the pyre, of how the Praetorian prefect himself had handed a torch to the Dragon of Rome to be the first to light the pyre after the sons of Severus.

Rumour was rampant among the people, and among the troops, so much so that its echoes could be heard in the corridors of the praetorium itself. The tension was as thick as the fog that swept in from the moors to engulf Eburacum. Britannia had seen emperors declared before; the memory of Severus' fallen rival, Clodius Albinus, was still a sort of fresh wound.

This time, however, the heirs were present in Britannia.

It was common knowledge that Caracalla and Geta lacked the age, wisdom and experience of their father and those before him. They had proved only too wild in the past, incapable of getting along or working together. People wondered, how then would they rule an empire?

The bigger question, however, the one that terrified people who had much to lose in a civil war, was that if the Gods did not want the sons of Severus to rule, who would?

In his tablinum at the heart of the principia, Aemilius Papinianus' mind debated this very question. He paced his room, wearing his battle armour and weapons, cloaked as if unsure to go out or remain within. Pacing helped him to think. He could not sit still, for when he did so, he began to sweat. He had always prided himself on his ability to think rationally of a situation, to analyze the actions of himself and others to come to a logical course of action, but this time it was different.

Caracalla, Geta, Julia Domna, and Julia Maesa had not been seen since the funeral. They had locked themselves away as if in a private, mournful banquet for the departed Severus.

When Papinianus had gone to see them, to check on them, to offer to get them anything, he was turned away by Claudius Picus who stood smugly with the guards outside the doors of the imperial triclinium. Papinianus had threatened the man and his guards - after all he was their superior, the Praetorian prefect! - but they stood still and resolute, certain of their defiance. The troopers had been men Papinianus had known well over the years, but it was clear that Claudius Picus' hold on them was stronger, for he had Caesar's support.

"Go back to the principia, Prefect. There you may wait for word from Caesar," Claudius said, that hateful, thin smirk stretching across his Patrician face.

"You mean, Caesars. We have two rulers."

Claudius said nothing, but pointed down the corridor to the exit.

Papinianus felt somewhat reassured that the men who were stationed in the principia were loyal to him. They stood guard at the gates leading onto the via principalis, and around the torch-lit courtyard day and night.

An eerie feeling had settled over the city and fortress, the fog clouding the streets as much as if they were out upon the grass of a pre-dawn battlefield. Only this time, the enemy, it seemed more and more clear, was not a distant threat, but rather next door in the praetorium itself.

It was clear that Papinianus had lost favour, and that his hold on the Praetorian guard was not as it had once been. When he had been appointed prefect by Severus, he had told himself he would run the guard fairly and firmly, that he would never fall to the disgraced level of a wicked, self-serving man such as Plautianus. But the more he realized that his position, and perhaps his life, were in danger, the more he was determined to take swift action.

A solid knock on the door roused him from his pacing, and he stopped in the middle of the tablinum, his hand upon his sword.

"Yes?"

One of his trusted guards opened and saluted. "Prefect, Castor and Euodus are here to see you."

"Send them in, Rufio," Papinianus said to the centurion.

The man hesitated. "Erm, sir, Senator Dio is also here."

"Dio?" Papinianus began to feel mixed panic and hope. Senatorial support could help things. "Send them all in."

The centurion saluted and opened the door wide.

Castor came in first, wearing a black tunic and cloak of mourning, followed by Euodus in his floor-length tunic, and then Cassius Dio in his toga, obviously doing nothing to disguise his visit to the Praetorian prefect.

"Gentlemen, welcome," Papinianus said, pointing to the chairs set out before the table. He looked to the slave who had been sitting quietly in the corner and the man immediately set about pouring wine and handing a cup to each of the visitors. "What news?"

Dio spoke first. "Let me say that I am here first as your friend, Aemilius. We've known each other for some years."

Papinianus nodded, but wondered at Dio's tone.

Dio continued. "I'm also here on behalf of the empress, your cousin. She has been wondering what is in your mind. As I have."

Papinianus eyed the senator for a moment, and searched for some reassurance in Castor or Euodus' faces. He found none, and looked back at Dio. "Why, the succession, of course."

"The succession is clear, is it not? Caracalla and Geta," Dio said, almost automatically. He cleared his throat. "My friend...you need to be careful. There are rumours everywhere. And the empress is aware of all of them."

"What rumours?" Papinianus asked, though he knew he offended Dio by even pretending.

"I think you know. The rumours that you have a different successor in mind. The well-known fact that you and Caracalla and Geta are at odds." He turned to Castor and Euodus too. "That all three of you are at odds with them."

"Senator, do not lump Geta with his brother," Euodus complained. "He is a good young man, and but for the unfortunate circumstance of his older brother, these...rumours...would be non-existent."

"If I could only see my cousin, I may be able to help her see reason," Papinianus said, remembering long ago days in the East

599

with Julia Domna, the time before she had been empress of the Roman Empire.

Dio shook his head. "Reason has nothing to do with it, Aemilius. These are her sons. Her flesh and blood, and all that she has left of Septimius. No gods or signs in the stars above will pull her from their sides. You must see that."

Papinianus sat forward, his hands clasped tightly upon the table before him. "What I see is the possible unravelling of everything Severus built, unless we do something about it."

Cassius Dio set his cup down on the table and looked at the three men in earnest. He knew them all, had respected them all. He still did. But in that moment, he knew they could not be swayed. He also thought of the man he had heard spoken of in the rumours, the one with the most to lose. "Aemilius. The man you are thinking of... He is not an emperor. A hero, yes, absolutely. But not an emperor. I know him. He won't want this, and by even considering this course of action, you're putting him in grave danger."

"The emperor loved him dearly," Castor said, adding his voice for the first time. "His shade would not hate us for it if it saved the empire."

Dio looked at the freedman, unbelieving of what he was hearing.

Papinianus spoke more certainly now, his voice deep and unwavering. "Everyone has their role to play in this. True and honest servants of the empire know this. He'll come around."

"I see why you would think such a thing, but you forget Caracalla - never mind Geta for the moment. We know him, and the men loyal to him. Claudius Picus has been at work on him for a long time now. You know this. Am I right?" Dio looked at Papinianus and the prefect nodded gravely. "Then you know how dangerous this situation is."

"Believe me, Cassius. I do. But I can also see a dire future if we don't do something. I love my cousin Julia dearly, but over the years, I have come to love the empire and what it stands for, the good it could achieve, even more. That is why I must do this."

"We," Euodus corrected, reaching out and gripping Castor's arm.

"We," Papinianus smiled. "All true Romans." He reached out to Dio then, his palms facing up. "The legions support this, Cassius. All of them. They support our choice. He's a born leader. Can we count on the senate to support him?"

Cassius Dio looked across the broad expanse of the Praetorian prefect's table at Papinianus. "If I've learned anything over the years, Aemilius, it's that history is not with you. Such actions have only led to rivers of blood."

"Believe me, Cassius. If we do nothing, we will all drown. Will you speak for us?"

Cassius Dio looked at each man there. He was silent, contemplating the possible outcomes, the future. He shook his head. "I cannot. But that does not mean I do not wish you well."

"Coward!" Euodus barked.

Dio turned calmly to the philosopher. "No. A realist and strategist. I cannot support you openly, but," he turned to Papinianus, "should you succeed, you will need allies, as will the new emperor." Even as he said it, he doubted it all. "You have my word that I will not report anything to the empress. I will tell her that you are only worried for your relationship with her sons, and that you will serve the empire to the best of your abilities."

"That is no lie," Papinianus said. "Thank you."

"Do not thank me, Aemilius."

"What will you do, then?" Castor asked Dio.

"Tomorrow, myself and the other senators here will return to Rome as escort to Julia Maesa and her daughter."

"Is there any word as to when Caracalla and Geta will return with the empress?" Papinianus asked. "I've been told nothing."

"I don't know," Dio said. "There is much to do to pull out of Britannia. There will be many waves, and the empire has been run from here for the last few years. However, I suspect they will not linger long. You don't have much time."

"We have what time the Gods give us," Papinianus said.

There was no more to be said.

Cassius Dio looked at the three men and bowed his head slightly to all of them as he stood. "I must leave you now, but, whatever happens, I do hope to see you all again in Rome."

"You will," Papinianus said, rising from his chair to come around the table and grip Dio's hand. "In Rome. A new Rome."

With Castor and Euodus remaining seated, Papinianus walked Dio to the door.

Dio turned one last time to him. "Just remember...he's a good man, the one you would see upon the imperial throne. And that seat, as great as it is, is a perilous one. For all that he has done for the empire, does he truly deserve that?"

Papinianus did not say anything, but opened the door where the centurion was waiting.

"Farewell," Dio said, and then turned as the door closed. He walked slowly to the centre of the principia courtyard and stopped by the altar to look up at the sky.

The stars were shrouded, invisible. All was darkness and fog, a blank canvas for the heavens.

All is uncertain, Dio thought. Part of him wanted to go to the Sarmatian camp, but the more reasonable part of him knew that that would be a mistake. There were spies everywhere, and nothing went unseen. *The Gods will decide...* He went out into the street where his slaves were waiting for him. "Back to the domus. I have packing to do."

In the Praetorian prefect's office, Papinianus, Euodus and Castor discussed how they planned to save Rome.

"You spoke to all the legates?" Euodus said.

"Yes," Papinianus said. "They are with us. As is most of the Praetorian guard."

"You're certain?" Castor said. "Claudius Picus has much support."

"I'm certain. They know right."

"There's just one more thing to do then," Euodus said.

Papinianus nodded and began writing on a small piece of papyrus. When he finished, he rolled it and sealed it. "Castor, you'll take this to him. Tell him it is urgent."

"I'll do it," the freedman said with conviction. "Now."

Papinianus stood, handed the note to him, and went to the door where the centurion was waiting.

"Rufio," Papinianus said, his voice low. "Take Castor to Praefectus Metellus in the Sarmatian camp at once. It's time."

The centurion nodded gravely. They had spoken about this, about where the meeting would take place. "Yes, Prefect," the man said. "I'll see it done."

In the Sarmatian camp, Lucius sat at the table of his command tent staring at a blank sheet of papyrus which he had weighted down in order to write a letter to Adara, but he had been unable to start. He had also been unable to sleep, as if a constant reverberation within his mind would not let him.

He wondered if the Gods were trying to tell him something, and wished he could walk out beneath the fullness of the bright moon to speak with them as he once had done in the peace of the desert. Here, however, in the middle of his men, surrounded by legions, and with the imperial family so close, with a feeling of death hanging in the air, the Gods did not come to him at all. Though, in recent months, he had been able to speak with them more often, as if he kept one foot at all times in that realm usually forbidden to mortals, they now stayed away. It was as if he was on the brink of a decision that he was destined to make on his own.

Apollo...guide me in the time to come...I beg you. Venus...watch over my family.

As if in reply, Dagon called Lucius from outside the tent. "Praefectus?"

Lucius looked up and stood from the stool. "Come in, Dagon."

The guards outside pulled back the tent flaps to reveal Dagon standing in front of a what appeared to be a Praetorian centurion, and behind him, Castor.

Lucius felt his heart begin to race for some reason, but he took a deep breath, unwilling to reveal his nervousness.

The three men entered, followed by Barta who kept a close watch on the Praetorian who came to a stop before Lucius and saluted.

"Praefectus Metellus," the centurion said.

"You're Papinianus' man," Lucius answered.

"Yes, sir."

Lucius wondered at the deference paid to him by the trooper. The Praetorians never really cared about officers of the legions or alae.

Castor stepped forward and bowed very slightly to Lucius.

"What brings you here, Castor?" Lucius asked. He had always seen the man with the emperor, moving about the palace, waiting in the wings to attend upon Severus or even engage the emperor in discussion and debate at times. He had never spoken with the man privately.

"Praefectus Metellus," Castor said, coming forward. "I come to you on an urgent matter. The Praetorian prefect, Aemilius

Papinianus, asks that you come to meet him in one hour. Here." He handed Lucius the note that Papinianus had written.

Lucius looked at it and went to Dagon's side to show him the seal of the Praetorian prefect.

"Why did Papinianus not come here, to my camp?" Lucius asked.

"That would not have been ideal," Castor replied. "For him to be seen visiting one camp in particular...it would have raised suspicions."

Lucius eyed the man, then broke the seal and began to read.

Metellus,

We must meet urgently to discuss a matter of the utmost importance and urgency. Meet me tonight at the granary office, just off the via Decumana of the fortress. Come armed and bring your bodyguard.

It is imperative you come, for the good of the empire rests upon it.

Papinianus.

Lucius finished reading and looked up at the Praetorian centurion and Castor. "When does Papinianus want me to meet him?"

"In one hour," the centurion said.

Lucius frowned. He did not like this. He turned to Dagon and handed him the letter.

Castor began to baulk, but Lucius put up his hand.

"Do not worry. I trust these men with my life. They are my friends."

Dagon shook his head and looked up at Lucius.

"Gentlemen, can you wait outside for a moment while I have a quick word with my princeps?"

The centurion and Castor looked at each other, then nodded acquiescence.

When they were outside, Lucius turned to Dagon and Barta, the latter now reading the short missive.

"This is no regular meeting," Lucius said, though the obviousness of his statement almost made him laugh, but not for hilarity, but fear.

"I don't like this, Anguis," Dagon said. "Something is going on behind the curtains of this world. Can you even trust Papinianus? Or this freedman outside?"

"I think Papinianus would not have told me to come armed and to bring Barta if he meant to do me harm."

"It's not him I'm worried about." Dagon gripped Lucius' arm as if to emphasize the point. "Caracalla and Claudius Picus are in that fortress."

"I know."

"And you don't know how much of the Praetorian guard is loyal to Papinianus or Caracalla. Alerio is no longer here to watch your back."

Lucius was silent, staring at the words upon the papyrus - *for the good of the empire...*

"I'll hear him out."

"Then let me and some men come with you, Anguis."

"No. That will draw more attention. Barta will be with me and we'll both be armed."

Dagon was clearly frustrated, the muscles of his jaw beneath his beard working as he stared at Lucius. "Fine. But if you aren't back two hours after you leave here, I'm coming with a turmae of men to find you."

Lucius smiled. "Agreed." He turned and went outside where Castor and the centurion were waiting between the torches and guards flanking the entrance. "Tell him I'll be there."

Castor nodded, a wave of relief giving the colour back to his face as he turned to leave.

"Sir," the centurion saluted and followed Castor.

Lucius stood there for a moment watching them disappear down the road of the camp and back to the walls of Eburacum.

One hour later, Lucius and Barta, both cloaked in black, their weapons hidden beneath, made their way along the walls of Eburacum until they reached the northeastern Decumana gate.

They had been challenged once on their way by the guards of the legion encamped closest to that part of the city walls, but in truth, so many off-duty soldiers were about that no one thought it odd to see two more walking in the misty night. When Lucius revealed his cuirass beneath his cloak and the dragon emblazoned upon the chest, the guards recognized him immediately.

"I have business in the city," Lucius said, not wanting to give more information than that.

The guards nodded. "Yes, sir, Praefectus Metellus."

Lucius and Barta carried on until they reached the gate and there, the Praetorians on duty spotted them immediately.

Centurion Rufio was there and waved Lucius in his direction. "Praefectus. The men on duty here are loyal. When you leave, you must only go back the way you came."

"Where is Papinianus?" Lucius asked the men.

"This way, sir."

Lucius and Barta followed the centurion a short distance down the via Decumana, the way lit by torches that cast an orange glow over the street, at odds with the fog that had swept in. As they went, both men had their hands upon their pugionis, ready for anything or anyone, but soon enough they turned left down a smaller street and came to a door where two Praetorians stood guard in the shadows.

The guards saluted Rufio, and one opened the door to the granary offices.

As they went in, Barta's eyes scanned the darkness, the rooflines of the building, and the looming towers of the granaries across the street. No one else was around.

When they went inside, Rufio closed the door and stood beside it.

The main room was empty, and smelled of timber and burlap. There was no table.

Lucius turned to the centurion, his hand upon the handle of his sword. "What is this, Centurion?"

The man's face was calm, and he nodded to the other side of the room where, from behind a curtain on the other side of the administrative counter, Papinianus emerged.

"I'm sorry to alarm you, Metellus, but it is not safe for us to meet in the open, or in the principia or praetorium."

"A lot of things seem unsafe lately, Prefect."

Papinianus nodded, and stood still. He looked tired, his eyes slightly sunken.

"What did you want to speak with me about?"

As Lucius began, Barta moved to the side wall where he had a good view of the centurion and the curtained area behind the counter.

"The time has come for action, Metellus," Papinianus began. "Our beloved emperor is dead now, and we must take immediate

606

measures. I know you share my doubts about Caracalla and Geta, but like any good soldier, you do not voice them aloud."

"I ah...I've never said -"

"Let us be frank," Papinianus said. "Geta is inept, and Caracalla is a monster. They are not fit to rule the empire any more than a green recruit in the legions.

"Severus' will though. They are his heirs."

"Only if the Praetorians allow it."

Lucius felt the skin on the back of his neck prickle. When Praetorians spoke like that, history said they were on dangerous ground. But he let Papinianus go on.

"I know what you are thinking. You remember Caligula and Claudius, or even Pertinax, and how the Praetorians' plans did no good for the empire in those days. They were selfish and arrogant, no better than Plautianus was."

Lucius' eyes registered the name of Plautianus, and Papinianus saw this.

"I know what he did to you and your family, Metellus. And I know that you were the one to rid us of him. Let me assure you that I am not Plautianus, or a creature like him."

Lucius collected himself. "I know this, Prefect. But Plautianus is long dead. What do you want?"

Papinianus was quiet, obviously deliberating with himself in that moment, searching for the words he had been thinking of for a long while, words suited to this very moment of treachery, but which he viewed as a moment of redemption and assurance for the future of Rome.

"Rome needs a strong leader. A new leader." Papinianus began to walk, finding it easier to think as he did so. "You have always been a man of honour, Metellus. Severus knew it. And the legions know it. For some time now, I've seen how the men revere you, almost like a hero of old."

"I am no hero, Papinianus." Lucius found himself gripping the Praetorian prefect's arm.

"True heroes do not claim to be as much. Rome needs an honourable man upon the imperial throne, Metellus, and neither Caracalla or Geta are that man. I love my cousin, the empress, but she is misguided in her faith in her sons, as was our late emperor."

Lucius released his grip on Papinianus who stepped back stiffly, the tone of his voice now more formal.

607

"I have spoken with the legates of every legion here, and we are in absolute agreement."

"About what?" Lucius felt dizzy. A ringing sounded in his ears and he struggled to focus on Papinianus' face. He breathed deeply and focussed on the man before him.

"We want you to be our emperor, Metellus."

Lucius could not believe the words that had just been spoken to him, the audacity of them, the extreme danger that being in that room at that exact moment meant to him, to his men, and to his family.

"Why?" Lucius asked. It was s simple question on the surface, but the import of it was far-reaching, like the tremors of a mountain quake.

"Because we need you. The empire needs you. If Caracalla and Geta rule, all of Severus' work will turn to dust. You are a good man, a just man. But you're also a leader whose men are loyal to him. The legates and I have spoken with soldiers from every legion, and they all praise you, look up to you. You have set an example to which all others would aspire, Metellus. And *that* makes you an ideal ruler. With you leading us...uniting us across the empire...we have a chance to be better than ourselves." Papinianus stepped forward and placed his hands upon Lucius' shoulder. "With you as emperor, Lucius Metellus Anguis, we can make this world a better place."

Lucius looked back at the man before him and there he saw conviction and belief, the sort that every man did not know he wished directed at himself until it actually was. A world ruled by Caracalla and Geta, and men like Claudius Picus, was terrifying, but a world ruled by himself was...unthinkable. Or, at least it had been until that very moment.

Papinianus could see the doubt upon Lucius' face, the turmoil. "I know you worry for your family, but with you as emperor, they would be safer than ever. The legions support you, the Praetorian guard supports you...and the senate will support you."

"The senate?" Lucius looked doubtful. "They would support an Equestrian upon the throne?"

"Men of lesser rank have risen to such heights. But the world has changed, Metellus. Deeds speak louder than blood. Never was a man more clearly supported than you are at this moment in time." Papinianus turned, paced back and forth a couple of times as Lucius stared at the floor. He could feel the presage of time, the urgency of the moment, and the need for a decision. Their lives depended on it.

He stopped pacing and faced Lucius. "How many times in the past have the Metelli come to Rome's aid?" Papinianus swayed on his feet. He was sweating now. He had been gone too long. He began to worry about what was being said in the confines of the praetorium, in the halls he had been shut out of. The time was ripe. He needed to know.

"What say you? Save us, Lucius Metellus Anguis! Save Rome! For if you do not, a world of pain awaits us all!" Papinianus outspread his hands to Lucius and bowed his head. "Will you be our emperor?"

Lucius stared at the man before him, prostrating himself in all but body. He looked past the prefect to the centurion at the door and the man seemed to nod, and with that nod, to plea that Lucius say 'yes'. Lucius turned to Barta and the big Sarmatian stood there, eyes wide, his face speaking of danger and fear. Lucius shook his head.

"I need to think about this."

"There is no time!" Papinianus said loudly.

Lucius looked at him. "If I were the sort of man who grabbed at this opportunity like a beggar grabs at a denarius on the street, I would not be the sort of man you wanted upon the throne, would I?"

"No. But -"

"Give me a day to consider, Papinianus. I know the faith you place in me is great. Trust me when I say that I will consider this carefully...by the Gods, I will."

Papinianus was resigned, accepted that he must wait. He had hoped that the following day, he could put his plan into action, but it would have to wait a little longer.

"We will all look forward to your response."

Lucius nodded. "Thank you. I promise you, by tomorrow night, you shall have it."

XXI

FATALITAS

'Fate'

"Emperor?" Dagon stared across the table at Lucius. He had been ready to set out with some men to find Lucius and Barta just as the two of them returned to the camp. The moment he had seen Lucius' face, he knew that something of great import had happened, but he had not expected what Lucius had just told him.

As Lucius, Dagon, Barta, Brencis and some of the other decurions sat around the table, it felt as though the focus of the Gods' eternal gaze had now shifted to that very place and time. Each man there felt it, feared it, and pondered the possibility of it.

Other than Lucius, each of them had dreamed of an emperor who would treat them as Lucius, their own leader, had treated them - with respect, honour, and understanding. He had always shared in their toils, their pain, and led from the front in every battle, as much as Alexander had ever done.

And the Gods blessed him. They each knew it, and they wondered if he had been groomed by the immortals for the very purpose set before him at that precise moment.

"Say yes, Anguis!" Brencis said, his face alight with excitement. "Think about it! Think about all that you could achieve!"

Some of the men around the room nodded, but Lucius shook his head as he stood there.

"My friends… We've fought for many years. We've lost many friends in battle-"

"The way Sarmatians dream of dying!" said Deva, the ala's imaginifer.

"Yes, but how many of our friends dreamed of having their bodies desecrated alongside their horses and then hung from the limbs of a broad tree?"

That silenced them.

Lucius regretted the words immediately. No one needed reminding of that. "Forgive me, my friends," he said. "I know

Caracalla and the men who serve him. He will not simply set aside the imperial throne. I don't even expect Geta to do so."

"Papinianus said that the majority of the Praetorian guard is with you, as are the legions encamped here?" Brencis' eyes flashed in the lamplight above the table. It was clear he was eager for Lucius to take action, and he was not alone. He turned to Dagon who had been silent. "What do you think, my lord? We will follow you," Brencis said.

"And I will always follow Anguis," Dagon's voice was serious, the voice of a king who must decide on behalf of more than himself. He had his men to think of, but also Briana, his queen, and their child. "Anguis is right to think. We are not talking about command of a small region or province, we're talking about the entirety of Rome's empire."

"Other men will help to run such a beast, won't they?" Brencis said.

"Yes, but an emperor must make everyone believe so that there is unity across all lands and peoples within the empire's borders," Dagon said. "Otherwise, there will be civil war. Are you not tired of blood, my brothers?"

Some of the men nodded, but other Sarmatians were uncertain. They were warriors, had always been warriors. It was all they knew.

"Then answer me this, cousin," Brencis said. "If Caracalla and Geta are emperor, will there be no more bloodshed? No more war?"

Lucius looked up at Dagon, and then to Brencis. "There will always be blood and war, Brencis. And I suspect that with Severus' sons ruling, it will not be lessened."

Boas, a burly decurion with snakes tattooed around his arms and legs stepped forward. He had been silent till then, only nodding or shaking his head. Now, he cleared his throat and waited for the nod to speak to come from Lucius.

"Boas?"

"Praefectus...Anguis..." he bowed, "We have followed you through all perils. Our dragons have flown into battle and bled, but they have always carried on flying. With you, and our king, we have, I believe, amazed the Gods themselves. You have conquered the Gods of war. Of course, more battles will be fought, but we will win them. Some will die, others will live." Boas looked around the circle at his countrymen and commanders. "I'm not afraid of death. Were I to die tomorrow, I would do so willingly, for I have truly lived beneath your banner. No warrior or man can ask for more."

The men cheered the older warrior, for he spoke truth, and each man there felt a prickle of pride run through his limbs and echo in his heart.

But Boas was not finished. "That said, to conquer and nurture a peace in which we can all live and thrive...that...that would be infinitely more difficult than battle. Perhaps that is your...our...next challenge. The Gods love you, Praefectus, as do we all... And if you have a chance to truly change this world, to better it by leading it, then is it not your own duty to do so?"

Lucius stared at the bearded, wise warrior for a moment, and found himself nodding, not in agreement, but in sincere thought and consideration for what was being said.

"Many a time, I heard Hippogriff speak of 'philotimo', a word I have heard you utter in conversation. By taking up this challenge - by accepting the imperial throne - would you not be allying yourself with the very principle of that Greek word Hippogriff loved so much? If you do not do it for the power - which every one of us believes you deserve - then do it for the love of honour and the wish to better the world around you." Boas stepped back.

Lucius could not speak, nor could the others in the tent. They all stared at Boas as he faded back into the shadows, away from the table, having said his piece. The shades of Hippogriff and all of their slaughtered brothers were there with them at that moment, urging Lucius and Dagon to agree with Boas' words.

After a few moments, Lucius cleared his throat. "Boas...your words have hit home, and well do I remember my conversations with Hippogriff and others about 'philotimo'." *Including my own son.* "I do not wish to risk your lives needlessly. You've been loyal, and commanding you has been my greatest honour. And...I feel that I owe it to you to give you this world, to give you all a life without blood, for you have shed enough."

Brencis slammed his fist on the table. "For you and your family, Anguis, we will shed more! And if the heads of Caracalla and Geta must decorate the walls of our fortress, then so be it!"

Lucius reached out to calm Brencis with a hand upon his shoulder. If they had been anywhere else but in the heart of their well-guarded camp, they would be dead already for the words he had

612

uttered. "I know you would, Brencis. And I would bleed for all of you. But I won't lead you to slaughter. I must be sure about this."

"There isn't much time, Anguis," Brencis said. "Did not Papinianus want to do this tonight?"

"Yes. And I delayed him until tomorrow."

Brencis stood tall then, ignoring that fact that he was not king. He looked at Dagon, then back at Lucius. "We have said what we must. You know we are all behind you in this." He looked at his fellow decurions and they all nodded, the certainty etched upon their faces like the finely chiselled features of any godly statue wrought from marble. "Whatever you decide this night, we'll be ready." He bowed to Lucius, as did all of the others.

"I thank you all," Lucius said. "I will seek the Gods' guidance this night, and tomorrow, we'll see what the day brings. Dismissed."

The men filed out, including Brencis who was caught up in conversation with some of the others. Only Dagon and Barta remained.

Lucius sat down and stared at the surface of the campaign table. He was shaking his head. "I find myself standing on a precipice, my friends. I don't know what to do. Part of me suspected what Papinianus wanted with me a while ago, but I didn't want to believe it."

"Boas was right," Dagon said, sitting down with Barta opposite Lucius.

"Yes. He was," Lucius said. "And by the Gods, it terrifies me."

"No man is fearless, no matter how much he convinces himself he is," Dagon said. "Lord Mar taught me that. He also taught me that acknowledgment of that fear is your greatest weapon, for it will never conquer you by surprise."

Lucius smiled. The old Sarmatian king, Dagon's uncle, had been one of the wisest men he had known. "I wish he were here to advise us. I wish Diodorus was here too. So many."

"Don't you see, Lucius?" Dagon leaned upon the table, the leather from his arm guards creaking as he did so. "They are all here...Mar, Diodorus, Hippogriff...all of them. We are not alone. They are in the flames of this lamp, and they are upon the wind outside. They walk among us, watching, listening, and speaking to us from that wall of fog that has surrounded us. It isn't just the Morrigan or our enemies who linger in the shadows, but also our friends and fallen allies, our ancestors..." Dagon looked up at Lucius. "And with you, Anguis, the Gods themselves are near."

Lucius stared blankly at the table, then shut his eyes as if trying to focus his thoughts. He heard the words Dagon spoke. He believed them, but doubt assaulted his psyche on all fronts, resisted the urges of hope, of right itself.

Dagon saw his friend struggle, and offered a few last words. "Anguis..." He waited for Lucius to look at him and Barta. "I will not say that I'm not afraid of what may happen either way. I am. Even more so now that I worry about Briana and our child..." he smiled to himself as he thought of her. "But long ago, we all swore to follow you, and it was the wisest decision we have ever made as a people. We will follow you now if you decide to do this, if it is what the Gods have set before you. The possibilities of what could go wrong are...well...not good. It's true. But the more I think of what you could achieve...the good that could come of it...I am awed. From Sarmatia to Ynis Wytrin itself, you could help. I would prefer a world ruled by you, than one ruled by Caracalla, Geta, or any ordo member from Lindinis."

"And we would die for such a world," Barta said, the only words he had spoken since the men left.

Lucius looked at both men, his staunchest friends and supporters. With them...with all of the Sarmatians...he could achieve the impossible. They had already done so many times.

"The Gods have indeed blessed me with friends like you," Lucius said. "Thank you." He stood and walked around the table, staring at the patched walls of the tent. He had travelled across the empire with that tent, that table and chairs. He had fought upon many fields. *Perhaps there is one more battle to be fought?* "I need to be alone. To think some more, to see if the Gods have any advice for me."

"Of course." Dagon rose from his chair and Barta followed. "We'll be nearby should you need anything, Anguis."

Lucius stood before them. "Thank you, both." Instinctively, he reached up to touch the jutting pommel of his sword. "In the morning, I'll let you know my decision."

Dagon and Barta saluted Lucius, turned, and went out of the tent into the fog-laden night air. The camp was not asleep yet, and those many men who were not on guard duty, stood in groups, speaking in excited whispers about what they had heard, what the morrow might bring.

Dagon did not worry about them endangering Lucius by speaking, for they were always discreet and utterly loyal. It was the men outside the walls of their fort he was uncertain of. "Brencis," he said to his cousin who was standing nearby. "Triple the guard tonight." He turned to Barta. "There will be no sleep tonight, Barta."

"Then we will wait, my lord, and see what the morrow brings."

Despite all the support he knew he had from his friends, from his men, from the legions, and from the Praetorians, Lucius had never felt so alone as he did in his tent that night. The decision he had to make loomed before him like a monumental stone set in the ground by giants or titans. And he, a mere man, stood tiny before its swaying mass, waiting to see which way it would tumble. Would it fall upon him, and douse his light, or would it fall forward to bridge a great gulf to a world of infinite possibilities?

You are no mere man, Metellus...

He heard the voice in his mind then, reminding him of the thought that had truly terrified him in recent months. With that, as he gazed at the small altar where incense and flame burned in honour of Apollo, Venus and Epona, he was back in Dumnonia overhearing the whispered words from the lips of the Gods themselves as he bled to death.

Lucius fell to his knees before the altar and shut his eyes tightly. He was home then, upon the grassy mound of the hillfort, standing upon the northern rampart and looking out to see it again, his men and legions of Rome's warriors waiting for him, saluting him, and chanting his name to the heavens.

The noise in his mind was deafening and thrilling, for it filled the forges of his toils with a great fire and heat that could not be doused.

But then, the chanting stopped, and all that he could hear was the sound of birdsong, and the calm whisper of the wind in the trees. The valley before the hillfort was empty, but for the puffs of white sheep, and the swaying of green crops. In his reverie, he turned to see his fortress home and his family, his friends. They milled about the the hillfort, laughing, playing, seemingly secure. He saw Adara, Phoebus and Calliope, and a young child, a girl. They seemed happy, turned to him and waved, called to him.

Even as he waved back, dark clouds formed above their heads, and the poison of dread and fear crept into his heart. Laughter turned to cries for help, and his vision was blurred by sheets of bloody rain.

Lucius shut his eyes against the scene within his vision then, reaching out for the calm of his tent. "Gods help me... I need your guidance more than ever... I cannot do this alone."

He felt a hand upon his head then, and the whirling of his thoughts came to a standstill. The flames upon the altar slowed to almost absolute stillness. Lucius looked up from where he sat upon his knees and there he saw Apollo reaching down to pull him up.

You are not alone...Anguis... Apollo said.

Lucius looked back at the god and saw a sadness in his eyes, something he had not seen before.

"Tell me what to do, Lord."

Apollo shook his head slowly. *I cannot. You are not alone, but you must decide which road to take on your own. That is the way of things...the way of Fate. It is thus for all of us, for men and gods alike.*

"But I don't want to be burdened with this decision," Lucius said, his voice like a young boy's, a boy who is leaving home for the first time.

You already are burdened with it. Apollo said.

"I know that with such power, the possibilities are endless. I would seek to have good prevail, but is that my purpose?"

Apollo looked kindly on Lucius, but said nothing.

"A part of me also only wishes to go home to my family, to be done with war and blood. Have I not fought enough upon the banks of red rivers choked with death?"

Not all battles are fought wading through war and blood, Anguis. There are always battles to be fought, and sometimes the most intimate ones are born of the greatest terrors.

"I would live with my family in peace, and love... Perhaps in the Isle of the Blessed, where there would be no pain, no worry?" Lucius wanted to beg now. He shook with fear, a fear so acute that it was like the leaf of a spear point directed at his gut, writhing on the end of a long shaft of ash, but he could not see who held the spear. "My Lord, I beg you to help me. Help my family. I only want to keep them safe, to do what is right for them."

But Apollo shook his head, though it was obvious it pained him to do so. The god himself held back tears, his immortal hands tied from action by the decrees of the world and universe.

There are many battles, and a longer road leading to the blessed isle you seek, my...Anguis. We will watch you upon it, but we cannot tell you which winding path to take. That decision is yours.

Lucius felt like weeping then, but he did not. He hung his head, suddenly exhausted. He felt Apollo's hand upon his chest then, and a feeling of warmth, of light, filled him, gave him calm strength.

Sleep now, Anguis... Apollo's voice, like the music of his lyre, sounded in his mind. *Sleep and rest...for with the rising of the sun, you will know your path.*

In his rest, Lucius dreamed silent dreams. He saw his family, his friends. They spoke to him, but he could not hear them, not clearly. He could see Calliope step forward from the group, calling to him, urging him to do something. Was she warning him? Was she crying of fire? He could not tell, nor could he understand the expression upon her face.

Lucius wanted to reach out to her, to Phoebus, and to Adara who stood there, holding her swollen belly, ready to give birth to their child. He wanted to run to them, to embrace them and tell them he loved them...but he could not, for every step he took brought him no nearer to them. He turned on the spot to look behind him and there spotted that same roaring army of men, men loyal to him, and all he could hear was his name chanted over and over, like a drum of war calling him to battle, to destiny, to fate.

As the drum pounded, he felt his head spin, and he fell to the grassy ground, his eyes focussed on the sun and moon in the sky above, their mingled light blanketing him as his eyes closed and he saw only himself in a deep blackness.

Lucius sat up suddenly in his cot.

Rays of early morning sunlight penetrated the canopy of his campaign tent to lay a patchwork about the ground, his cot, the altar and his face. It dizzied him at first, made him rub his eyes, but the more he awakened, the more he felt strong and calm.

A certainty burned inside of him that had not been there before, a confidence that he had not felt for a long time.

Is it hubris? he asked himself.

617

He shook his head. How could it be hubris if one considered a path set before you by the Gods, something that was a part of your fate, your destiny?

Adara and the children entered his mind then, and he felt a deep sense of loss without them, an urge to protect them anyway he could.

Apollo had visited him, of that Lucius was certain. But the Far-Shooter had also told him of many battles to come, of a long road...

I need to protect my family from those who have been seeking to hurt us.

It was then that he knew what he needed to do, what would protect them, what would help him to shape a world in which they could live in peace. He had always admired Alexander's dream of a pan-Hellenic world, a unified world, but such things seemed only to be the stuff of day dreams and idealists.

Lucius had been an idealist once, but the rough world had hacked away at that part of himself over the years.

Now, however, with the choice the Gods held out to him, the help offered, perhaps he could sow new ideals for a new world.

That will be my legacy to my children...

He stood and went over to the table where he took a sheet of papyrus, a stylus, and bronze ink pot. He sat there and stared for a moment at the paper before writing...

Adara, my Love.

I do not have much time to write all that I have to tell you. Things are changing quickly.

The emperor has died here in Eburacum, and all is chaos.

But there is hope, my love, for us, and for our children. I have been made an offer, and I am going to take it. I cannot say what at this point, but I feel that it is the right thing to do, for all of us.

Things will happen swiftly now, and fast action is needed.

I hope that you have not yet given birth to our child, that I have not missed it. If all goes well, I will see you soon.

In the meantime, if you are able to travel, you must go to Ynis Wytrin with Briana, Phoebus and Calliope as soon as possible. The men will accompany you. When you arrive, stay there. Wait for me. I will come to you as promised.

Soon, Adara, we will be together again.

You and the children have all my love.

Your loving husband, Lucius

618

Lucius re-read the missive once, his heart pounding as he did so, but no less certain of his decision. *They will be safe there,* he thought. He blew on the ink and folded the papyrus. Then, in the still-burning lamp upon the table, he heated the wax and sealed the letter.

Rushing to the tent flap, he flung it open to reveal men standing everywhere. "Princeps!" he called for Dagon.

"Yes, Praefectus?" Dagon came out of a nearby tent, already fully armed. His face was tired and drawn, as if he had been up all night, worrying, fearful.

"Get me Vartan!" Lucius said loudly.

Dagon saluted and turned to see the young Sarmatian warrior coming from his nearby guard posting.

"Yes, Praefectus!" Vartan saluted.

"Come inside," Lucius said. "And you, Dagon, Barta…"

The three men followed Lucius inside his tent and he turned to them.

"I've decided to follow the path the Gods have set before me," he told them. "Dagon, we need the men to be ready for anything. Do so discreetly." Lucius turned to Vartan. "You are one of the fastest riders we have, Vartan. I need you to do something for me and my family, as well as for your queen."

Dagon looked at Lucius, confused.

"I need you to ride like the wind upon the plains to my wife and children at the fortress in the South. You will give this letter to my wife immediately, and then help them, along with Lenya, Akil, and Shura, to get themselves to Ynis Wytrin."

"Ynis Wytrin?" Dagon asked.

"Yes. That is where they will be safest." Lucius held out the paper and the Sarmatian took it.

"I won't fail you, Praefectus," Vartan said.

"I know," Lucius slapped his armoured shoulder. "Now, go as soon as you may by the most direct route. Do not stop at all. With luck, you'll be there in a few days."

"Praefectus!" Vartan saluted, tucked the letter in a leather scrip belted around his waist beside his sword, and turned to leave.

When he was gone, Dagon spoke up. "Lucius, what is going on?"

"I can't stand by while Caracalla and Geta destroy the empire, Dagon. I'm going to take up Papinianus' offer. As emperor, I will be able to make this world a better place."

Dagon stared at his friend then. He could see the life pulsing in Lucius' eyes, that they were brighter and more animated than they had been in a long while. But he was still afraid. "Anguis...are you sure about this? There is no turning back from such an action."

Lucius did not speak for a moment, and Dagon could see that he struggled yet more, as if he were making one last effort to come to terms with his decision. "With you both, my friends, and our men, we can do this. Do I feel uncertain? Of course I do. But since when have we been certain about anything except the love of our families, and our loyalty to each other? I'm not doing this because I want to wear the purple."

"Then why are you, Anguis?" Dagon stood before Lucius, the sunlight shining upon his scale armour as it came in more intensely through the roof of the tent, dappling it like the surface of the sea.

"Because it's my duty, Dagon. My duty to you all, and to our family and friends. If I have a chance to make this world of ours safer...better...then am I not bound to take the opportunity the Gods have presented me with?"

Dagon thought about it and bowed his head forward. "We are with you, Anguis. You need no laurel crown or purple cloak to be our imperator. You always have been."

Lucius hugged his friend fiercely then. "Thank you." He was about to start giving the orders that needed giving when there was a struggle outside the tent.

"I must see him now!" a voice cried outside.

Barta drew his blade and rushed to the tent flaps. "What's going on?" When he opened the tent flaps wide they could see the black-cloaked figure of Castor being held by two of the Sarmatian guards.

"I must see him now!" Castor insisted.

"It's all right, men. Release him."

The Sarmatians released Castor who stumbled forward. He flushed red, but said nothing as he regained his balance and stepped forward to meet Lucius at the threshold of the tent.

"Praefectus Metellus. Papinianus sent me." He spoke so low that it was difficult to hear him, but Lucius extended his hand and invited the man in. In truth, he felt badly for the freedman, for he had been at

Severus' right hand for many years, and now he no doubt felt adrift in chaos.

"Be at ease, Castor," Lucius said.

Castor looked annoyed, even angry as his brow creased and he grimaced as if he had been punched in the gut. "At ease?" he shook his head violently. "I'm afraid you do not understand the situation, Praefectus. There is no way to be at ease. The situation is perilous."

"I understand. Of course," Lucius said. "Now. Be calm, and tell me."

Castor took a deep breath and regained something of his usual composure, however slight. "We've been up all night... I've been slinking in shadows the entire time, speaking with some of the guards, the staff and slaves-"

"About what? I hope you did not name me?" Lucius began to panic, for if things were revealed too soon, then they would lose the element of surprise that was crucial to success.

"I did not name you. I was merely assessing loyalty, and promising gain where needed, financial or otherwise. But before things go further Papinianus needs to know... Will you lead us, Lucius Metellus Anguis? Will you accept the throne Papinianus and the legions are offering you?"

Lucius looked at Dagon and Barta one last time, then back at Castor.

"Tell the Praetorian prefect that I agree. Yes."

Castor looked supremely relieved for a moment, and once he comprehended Lucius' answer fully, he fell to one knee.

"Please, get up, Castor. I'm not emperor yet." *That sounds so strange to me,* he thought. *Emperor?* "Go back and tell him I will have my men ready when the time comes."

"There is more, Praefectus..." Castor's face looked worried again, and Lucius felt a prickle of doubt. "I just found out."

"What?"

"Geta. He fled with a small retinue in the night. He's gone back to Rome. Caracalla does not yet know."

Lucius stared at him, trying to ascertain how bad that was, whether the entire endeavour was already doomed. "What will Papinianus say of this?"

"He does not worry so much about Geta. The boy is young and inexperienced. The troops like him, but they do not love him. They will not follow him."

In a fight or battle, Lucius was accustomed to quick assessment, to finding and eliminating the opponent who was of greater risk before taking on the others. From fights in the street, to the broad span of a battlefield filled with thousands, it was a concept he was used to.

"We need to worry about Caracalla, Claudius Picus and their followers first. Once they're out of the way, we can follow Geta."

Castor nodded. "I must go now, Praefectus. Papinianus needs your answer in order to set things in motion." He stopped talking and stared at Lucius for a moment. "I heard Severus speak of you often, Praefectus. Never did I hear him speak so warmly of a man who was not his son."

Lucius extended his hand and Castor took it slowly, his grip light and a little feeble. "And it is my goal to preserve our emperor's work."

The freedman nodded and smiled. "Until later." He bowed, backed away, and went out of the tent to disappear into the brightness of day.

"Praefectus," Barta said when Castor was gone. "Are you sure that Geta is not a threat?"

"I was thinking the same thing," Dagon added. "He is Severus' heir also."

"He is a threat. But Caracalla and Picus are by far the greater danger. We need to deal with them first. Once that is done, we can ride with speed to catch Geta on the road south, or in Gaul if he has already crossed the channel."

"What now then?" Dagon asked.

"I want all the men armed and the horses saddled. Wherever this fight takes place, we'll be ready."

Dagon and Barta saluted and went out.

Lucius turned back to the small altar at the back of the tent where he had prayed the night before, and lit another chunk of incense.

Gods...grant me wisdom and strength in the time to come...

When Castor came out of the Sarmatian camp, his black cloak pulled low over his face so as not to be recognized, he looked from side to side along the road, like a deer moving slowly through a misty forest, searching for predators.

For so many years, he had gone where he wanted and done as he wished under Severus' protection, but now, the act of moving in shadows, the burden of secrecy, and the urgency of their plans filled him with fear. And it was not only that fear that drove him to do what he was doing, but also his hatred of Caracalla and Geta.

All about him, groups of legionaries marched about the camps in which the legates also awaited word from Papinianus about what would happen. For a moment, Castor thought about going to tell them, but he stopped himself.

No, I must tell Papinianus first. He must have Metellus' answer, and he must know about Geta.

He made his way toward the road that led past the fortress annexe and to the via Principalis. Behind him a contubernium of legionaries was marching in order, led by their optio with his tall horsehair and feather-crested helmet and carrying his staff with the brass ball on the end.

Castor glanced back a couple of times at them, but moved on. There were so many troops around Eburacum, on duty, off duty, that they were everywhere, like ants at a picnic. He carried on, passing beneath the open gates of the fortress, his hood back by then so that Papinianus' guards recognized him and allowed him to enter.

The tramp of the contubernium's hobnails echoed on the cobbles behind him as he pressed on. The men of the legions had been coming and going from the fortress as usual, using the baths, getting repairs done in the forges, or simply passing through in order to get to the civilian settlement on the other side of the river where the agora, better baths, and brothels were located.

Castor turned into the courtyard of the principia and headed straight for Papinianus' offices, passing the nervous-looking Praetorian tribunes who were loyal to the prefect.

The contubernium passed by in the street, the optio glancing into the courtyard of the principia as they passed, to see Castor rush into the Praetorian prefect's office. They carried on marching but instead of turning right down the via Praetoria to go to the civilian settlement, they turned left into the courtyard of the praetorium and there, the optio was met by Claudius Picus.

"What news?" Papinianus asked immediately as Castor came into his tablinum.

Euodus was there too.

Castor poured himself a cup of wine and drank it before speaking.

Papinianus noticed the freedman's hands shaking as he did so. "Speak, Castor."

"Geta fled in the night. He's headed for Rome. Trying to get there before Caracalla."

"I know. Euodus just told me."

Castor glanced at the teacher of Severus' sons. "Did you know he would do this?" His voice was accusing.

"No," Euodus said, his voice bitter. "After all I have devoted to that boy." He wagged his head as if he were still the disapproving tutor. "It's very disappointing."

"And smart," Papinianus added before turning back to Castor. "And Metellus? What did he say, Castor?"

Castor set down the cup and stood a bit taller. "He says 'yes'."

Papinianus sat heavily in his chair. The feeling of relief was enormous and welcome. "Thank the Gods... Did he say anything else?"

"He seems determined now. He says his men will be ready, and he'll wait to hear from you."

Papinianus looked to Centurion Rufio in the corner of the room and the man nodded and smiled back. "Rufio. Go gather the men - quietly. Bring them here in one hour. Our timing in this must be precise and swift."

Rufio saluted and went out.

The relief in the room was palpable, and when Rufio left, Papinianus, Castor and Euodus closed in on the table to speak.

"The question now is, how do we take Caracalla and Picus by surprise?" Euodus said.

"I have a plan for that..." Papinianus said, and he set about explaining it, and the roles each of them were to play.

Claudius Picus smiled to himself as he made his way through the corridors of the praetorium. In fact, he almost laughed.

Castor had been so predictable, and dressing his Praetorians in legionary uniforms so that they looked like any other contubernium had been a stroke of genius, for they were able to move among the camps without raising suspicions.

Now, if only the centurion holds his nerve... He smiled again, as if in anticipation of a meal to savour, something he had been smelling eagerly in the corridors of power for a long while now. He entered the peristylium and made his way around the columns until he arrived at the guarded door of Caracalla's large cubiculum.

"Caesar?" Claudius said.

"Enter." Caracalla's voice was deep, laced with coupled worry and anger.

Claudius entered and bowed easily to him.

Caracalla sat alone at a table on the far side.

"The empress is not with you?" Claudius asked.

"She and her ladies are packing for the journey back to Rome," Caracalla said. He then looked up, his brow lined with tight furrows. "So? What news? I know your little birds have been flocking around Eburacum. What have they discovered, Claudius?"

"I was right about Castor. He's been slinking everywhere. He was last seen coming from the Sarmatian camp."

Caracalla stood up quickly. "So. The rumours are true?" He pounded his fist on the table, and the ink pot tumbled, spilling its contents onto a pile of clean papyrus sheets. Caracalla let it lie and stared at Claudius. "Do we know what was said?"

"No. There was no way to get a man inside the camp. It's too well-guarded and his men are too loyal. Not much is known by the troops. My men were gaming and drinking with them all night, but no news came to light."

"Papinianus is planning something," Caracalla said. "I know it!"

"And we'll make him pay, sire. I've set a trap he'll fall into easily enough."

"You sure you can trust the man?"

"I can trust the vast fortune I've promised him."

"Good." Caracalla sat down again. Things were coming together. "What of my brother? Does Geta suspect anything?"

"That is the other thing I wanted to speak to you about, sire."

"What?" Worry raked Caracalla's face again and he leaned forward on his elbows.

"Geta fled in the night. He's headed for Rome."

XXII

MORTIFICATIO

'The Culling'

Claudius braced himself for the impact of Caracalla's fist on his face, and a second later he was sprawled on the floor with Caesar's hands around his throat. He struggled enough for show, but he knew how long he could withstand the choking before he blacked out or worse.

A little more... Give Caesar a sense of power for now... The time for revenge is almost here...

Claudius began to kick his legs a bit more violently now, and his hands grasped at Caracalla's hands where they were around his neck. His eyes bulged as they stared up at the enraged face scowling blankly down at him. One day he would rearrange that face, but not yet. *Not yet...*

"Cae...Caesar!" Claudius gasped. "I...I..." His vision was starting to blur as Caracalla's grip grew tighter. "Plan...I have a p...plan."

Caracalla's features focussed on Claudius now as if he only just realized where he was.

The pressure on Claudius' neck released and he turned over gasping and coughing on his hands and knees.

Caracalla stood and paced the room like a caged lion. "We need to take care of this. We need to do it now. Geta will get back to Rome and win over the senate and people before I even arrive. I need to finish things here in Britannia, but there are so many enemies. So many against me... Ahhhhhhh!"

Caracalla screamed with rage as his thoughts whirled and his anger ran like cold, icy rapids in the highlands of Caledonia.

Two Praetorians burst into the tablinum with their swords drawn, but Claudius immediately stepped in front of them, still rubbing his throat.

"Stand... Stand down!" he croaked. "Caesar is upset."

The two men gazed past Claudius at Caracalla and saw that he stood with his back to them, staring out of a high window in the wall.

They nodded and went out, closing the door behind them. Such outbursts from Caesar were not uncommon.

"Sire," Claudius said, moving slowly toward the table where Caracalla now stood on the other side. "The time has come..." he gulped, his throat sore and dry. "You need to make your move now, before Papinianus and Castor do."

Caracalla turned and it was all Claudius Picus could do not to smile at the supreme hatred he saw in Caesar's eyes, almost a madness.

Excellent, Claudius thought.

"You should have known of Geta's plans," Caracalla growled.

"Forgive me, sire. He kept it secret, but I believe I know how."

"How?"

"The empress, your mother." Claudius could see another change upon Caracalla's face. *Now to take care of the imperial bitch too!* "I said nothing because I was not absolutely sure. There were only whispers..." Claudius spread his hands wide. "It is a sensitive matter, and I could not be certain, but I believe that the empress is the one who urged Geta to leave for Rome in the night. Her, along with Euodus."

Caracalla's fists clenched and unclenched. The mere mention of his and Geta's tutor was enough to enrage him, but the thought that his mother would do such a thing came as an unpleasant surprise. "She always preferred my brother, as did Euodus," he growled. He looked up at Claudius. "What is your so-called plan?"

"I'll tell you, sire."

"Do. But know this. If it fails, I will have you torn limb from limb and hang the pieces from the walls of Eburacum. Do you understand?"

"I do, sire. I also know that if we do not succeed, that could well happen to us all."

Once Claudius Picus left to speak with their men, Caracalla burst from his tablinum and stormed down the corridors of the praetorium until he reached the empress' rooms.

"Sire!" Julia Domna's body servant moved to block his way. "My lady asked not to be disturbed, for she is not feeling well and-"

Caracalla's hand lashed out to strike the woman's face sending her onto the floor to the right.

She cried out in pain as she slammed into a column.

Another slave dropped a silver tray of glass perfume bottles with a fearful yelp and a crash upon the flagstones. Immediately the air was filled with the sickly, pungent smell of a dozen mixed oils.

Caracalla swept forward, past a large table of scrolls which he swept to the ground, sending one flying into a nearby brazier where it smouldered and then caught fire, disappearing in a matter of moments among the ash and flame.

Ahead, in a small peristyle garden, Julia Domna stood up from a bench where she had been sitting, reading in the sunlight. "What is the meaning of this?"

Caracalla did not slow as he approached her and his fist was up, ready to strike.

She did not move as his fist came at her, she did not need to, for his hand stopped just short of her face, as she knew it would.

Caracalla stood there, frozen before her, his chest rising and falling quickly, his nostrils flaring like those of a crazed stallion.

"You've betrayed me!" he yelled.

"How so?" she asked, her voice calm, her large brown eyes looking up at her son. "What have you heard?"

"You sent Geta back to Rome!"

Julia Domna was quiet for a moment, waited as his breathing slowed, and then placed her hands upon his arms.

Caracalla quickly shrugged them off and stood back.

"Of course I did," she admitted.

"Why? You seek to betray me? To undermine me?"

"Of course not. I seek to save you, my son."

Caracalla shook his head.

She continued, seeing an opening in his rage. "You have enemies, both of you. Every emperor does, especially at the beginning of his reign. And yours and Geta's are preparing something."

"You have no idea, Mother. Of course they are!"

"There is a difference between fact and rumour."

"Sometimes. Not this time!"

"Antoninus...listen to me... Geta needed to get away so as not to arouse suspicion. If you are to rule together, in harmony, then swift action is needed by both of you. I told Geta that he needed to get to Rome first so as to secure support for you both there."

"Of course," Caracalla said, exasperated. "You can see no fault in little Geta! He passes wind and you praise him! Are you so blind, Mother?"

"Do not insult me," Julia Domna answered, her voice low and even. "Your aunt left for Rome days ago with several senators, before Geta. She'll make sure your brother behaves accordingly, which he will."

Caracalla was silent now, though his mother could see the fiery rage in his eyes, marring his features.

"Geta has work to do in Rome, but you have work to do here so that you do not leave things unfinished. You cannot proceed with enemies at your back."

Caracalla smiled then, and took another step backward from his mother, stepped out of the sunlight in which she stood, and into the shadows beneath the overhang of the tiled roof above.

"On that, at least, we agree." He nodded. "Fear not, Mother, for I am about to take care of everything. After tonight, there will be no enemies at my back." Caracalla turned and walked from the garden, back the way he had come, ignoring the slave sweeping up the broken glass in a haze of oil scent, and the lady-in-waiting being tended by a slave upon a nearby couch.

As he walked down the corridor, more slowly this time, and speaking with the guards along the way - he would need them soon - Caracalla smiled to himself. Claudius' plan might just work, and if it did, then there would be a glorious night of blood ahead.

After her son had gone, Julia Domna sat heavily upon the bench in the garden, the scroll she had been reading having fallen to the ground, forgotten among the broad green leaves of fern that surrounded her.

She had known it was a risk sending Geta ahead, but she had also known that he was in danger from his brother. The animosity between them had not dwindled, despite the feigned show of accord between them. She was sure that the viper, Claudius Picus, had informed her son of Geta's departure and her role in it, hoping that it would alienate her from Antoninus. *It almost worked,* she thought. For some time, she had thought about having Claudius killed or poisoned, but he was a dangerous opponent, more cunning than Plautianus had ever been. He had bored his way into her son's confidence, so deep that it would take surgical skill to remove him.

629

Papinianus was a great disappointment to her. They had always had a loving relationship since they were young. He had always looked out for her, and she him. That is why she had urged her husband to appoint him Praetorian prefect, someone to balance out Ulpianus. Never would she have thought that her cousin would work against them.

But he has, and he has used the one man I thought more trustworthy than any other.

She thought of Lucius Metellus Anguis, but the feeling she had was only one of sadness. He had saved her family at one point, saved her husband and son. She had rewarded him and his family for it too, helped them. *And now...* She shook her head. The rumours just did not sound like him. *But men change, and he has not been treated well these last years.*

She could still hear his name chanted by the men of the legions, the citizens of Eburacum. She could see the looks of awe as hardened men of war looked up at him upon that giant stallion as if he were a god in their midst. If he were harmed, the army would not look kindly on it.

My family must come first, she thought. Then, she had an idea. One last thing she could do for Metellus while still securing her sons' succession. Julia Domna rose from her bench and went to her writing table in the room beyond.

Upon a small square of papyrus, she wrote a short message. Once she had finished, she folded and sealed it.

"Cousin?" she called the man who had always been by her side and had been waiting in the shadows. He had come from Syria to help her when Severus had taken the throne, and he had watched over her since.

He also knew Lucius, having watched over him and his family outside of Rome, before the fall of Plautianus.

"Yes, my lady?" he appeared at her side.

"Take this to Praefectus Metellus at the Sarmatian camp. Do not let anyone overhear your conversation. Tell him it is one last gift to him, for all that he has done for my husband and our family."

The man took the small letter and looked at it for a moment.

"It is urgent." She stood and spoke lowly into his ear. "Go by backward ways. Claudius' men should not see you deliver this."

"I understand." He bowed low to the empress and then went into a room at the back of the peristylium.

Julia Domna watched him leave and then stepped back into the sunlight of the garden. She bent over to pick up the scroll among the foliage. With a deep breath, she sat again upon the bench, and continued with her reading.

The day had worn on, and inside the Sarmatian camp, Lucius, Dagon, Barta and all of the men were growing impatient and uneasy.

Lucius had been waiting for word from Papinianus, but none had come. Not yet. He understood that there were a lot of men to coordinate, but time was of the essence now, and the Gods were watching.

Patience, Lucius, he told himself. *You cannot rush into battle unaware.*

"Praefectus?" one of the guards said beyond the tent flap which opened a moment earlier.

Dagon and Barta stood with Lucius as the guard came in.

"There is a messenger at the eastern gate. He has an urgent message for you, but he will not enter the fort."

"I'm coming," Lucius said, eager for some news, any news. He went out, and Barta and Dagon went with him.

The men saluted Lucius as he walked along the rows of saddled horses and armed warriors to the eastern gate of the Sarmatian camp. He could see they were all impatient, and anxious.

Lucius arrived at the eastern gate and there, just outside, was single man surrounded by five Sarmatians.

The man stood calmly against the wall, his face hidden by the hood of a plain brown cloak.

The guards parted to let Lucius through, and as he approached, the man raised his head and smiled.

"It is good to see you again, Praefectus."

Lucius stopped in his tracks. "You?"

The man bowed his head.

"What are you doing here?" Lucius asked, his hand was upon his dagger beneath his cloak.

"My mistress sent me with a message for you. Here it is." He held out the small folded papyrus.

Lucius took it and read.

Praefectus,

For all that you have done for my husband and for Rome, I offer you this last bit of advice. Do not proceed, for it can only end in misery for us all. See to your family, for I believe they are in danger. Go, and live in peace, for you cannot hope to do so by the advice of doomed men. May the Gods watch over you.

J.D.

Lucius looked up at the empress' cousin. "This is from the empress?" he asked.

The man bowed his head.

"How can I be sure?"

"I serve only her. You know this."

Lucius nodded. He knew the empress had been kind to him and his family in the past, but she had also deceived him at times, allowed Adara to be treated with contempt in her presence. She had allowed him to be locked up for standing up to men such as Claudius Picus back in Horea Classis. The sweet scent of the empress' perfume that he remembered was now rank in his memory. He had been used by her, and though he did not hate her for it, he would not allow her to manipulate him for her sons anymore.

Lucius looked at the empress' cousin. "Thank you for bringing this."

"A debt owed," the man said. "I must return to her now." He made to leave, but stopped when Lucius' pugio blade appeared before his chest.

"Forgive me, but I cannot let you do that." He turned to his men. "Guards." The Sarmatians closed in quickly and held the man. "Don't harm him," Lucius added. "He's a good man. Lock him up quietly until this is all done."

For the first time, the Syrian's face looked uneasy. "Praefectus. Think of what you are doing. Is this really wise?"

"I am sorry," Lucius said. "You need not fear for your life." He nodded to the men and they ushered the empress' messenger inside to a holding cell hidden away in a far corner of the fort.

Lucius handed Dagon the letter from the empress. "She's trying to scare me."

Dagon nodded as he read it, but he was worried. "What if she's right? What if there is a danger to Adara and the children? To Briana?"

Lucius looked at him. "We know there is a danger to them. They'll be safe in Ynis Wytrin once Vartan reaches them with my letter. Right now, there's a danger to us all if we don't succeed."

Dagon nodded. "You're right."

"If Papinianus doesn't contact me by the first hour of darkness, then we'll move without him."

It was late afternoon, and all was quiet within the walls of Eburacum. Sacrifices smouldered upon the altars of the principia and the praetorium, before the temples across the river, and in the private homes of citizens in the fortress annexe. It was still daylight, but a fog had rolled in as the sun dipped into the West, and orange light angled its way across the fields surrounding the city.

Torches and braziers were lit prematurely among the camps and along the streets as farmers came in from the fields or the last of the merchants' wagons arrived for the market on the following day. Patrols changed, and guards rotated.

In the camps of the legions, it seemed like a collective breath was being held among the legates, tribunes and other officers. The waiting had been interminable, but when the time came, they would be ready. They had to be.

In the corridors of the praetorium, all was quiet, but for the muffled sound of sweeping as one of the slaves cleaned the paving slabs before Caesar's cubiculum. The guards ignored the slave as he swept around their planted feet, hurrying past to go along the way toward the distant garden.

A gut-wrenching howl came suddenly from Caesar's rooms and the slave dropped his broom with a wooden clatter upon the floor.

Caracalla burst from his cubiculum crying out loudly.

"Caesar has been betrayed! I've been wronged by Castor! Traitor!" He repeated this as he paced up and down the corridor, pulling at his hair and rubbing his face in frustration and panic.

"Sire! Sire! What has happened?" one of the Praetorian centurions came rushing up to join the concerned guards who stayed near Caracalla.

"Castor the freedman! He's conspired against me."

The centurion immediately echoed the words up and down the corridor. "Caesar has been wronged by Castor! Castor the freedman! We must find him. Defend Caesar!"

The Praetorians took up the cry throughout every building and along every street of the fortress of Eburacum, shattering the evening silence and alerting all within hearing that a plot against Caesar was imminent, that Castor was to blame.

"Find Castor the freedman! He has wronged Caesar!"

Like a frightened mouse running along the streets of a cat-infested city, Castor moved quickly along the walls, staying to the shadows, his cloak pulled over his head. He had been writing a letter in his cubiculum in the praetorium when he had heard the shouts, and immediately stole from his room, down a smaller corridor, and out a back door that led onto the small alleyway between the praetorium and the principia.

It seemed like the entire fortress echoed with is name. His heart pounded as he ran, the blood pumping in his ears as tears of fear and frustration burned the lids of his eyes. He needed to get to Papinianus quickly so that they could alert Praefectus Metellus and the legionary legates. It had almost been time for their plan to begin, but Caracalla's outcry had surprised them. Things needed to happen now.

He pounded down the street on the northwest side of the principia, rounded the corner onto the via Principalis and arrived breathless at the gates of the principia.

"I need to see the Praetorian prefect now!" he yelled. He stared in panic as two large groups of Praetorians could be seen rushing in his direction from both directions down the via Principalis. "Quickly!" he said, pushing past the guards and running to Papinianus who was coming out of his tablinum, fully armed, on the other side of the courtyard. "Thank the Gods!" Castor said when he saw Papinianus.

"What is it? What's happened?"

"They're coming! Claudius and his men! They're yelling that I've wronged Caesar!"

"Guards!" Papinianus called to his men who had been waiting in the rooms surrounding the principia's courtyard. "To arms!"

Fifty fully-armed Praetorians came rushing out of the surrounding rooms and into the courtyard to form up around Papinianus.

"It is time!" he said, as the sound of rushing hobnails in the street outside came closer and closer. "Castor," he turned to the freedman. "Lock yourself in my offices."

Castor nodded and ran to the back of the principia, slamming the door behind him.

"Rufio!" Papinianus called for his centurion.

The centurion appeared at the gates, alone, the two guards having rushed into the courtyard to join the others at Papinianus' side.

"How many of them are there?" Papinianus asked Rufio.

The centurion turned quickly and peered down the street in both directions. "Too many," he said.

"Go! Get to Metellus and the legates!" Papinianus ordered. "Tell them to march on the city at once!"

The centurion stood there, his hands upon the pommels of his gladius and pugio.

"Rufio do it! Run!" Papinianus yelled.

But the centurion stood there, saluting as Claudius Picus arrived with two cohorts of Praetorians filling the street outside.

The slither of gladius blades sliding free of their sheaths could be heard, cold and hard in the street outside.

"Traitor!" Papinianus yelled at Rufio, his gladius levelled at the gates where Claudius and his men poured into the courtyard to surround them.

Deadly blades were everywhere, and death waited in the wings. An eerie silence settled over the courtyard, and all that could be heard were men's rapid breathing and the slow, steady footsteps of Claudius Picus as he approached the Praetorian prefect.

"Hello, Papinianus," Claudius said, his smile broad.

"It's dark," Dagon said to Lucius as they sat atop their mounts in the middle of the via Principalis of the Sarmatian camp.

Lucius nodded and looked up and down the street at his mounted men. "It's time!" he said. "On me!" he said, nudging Xanthus forward as the eastern gate swung open. Just as he, Dagon and Barta came out into the open, a Praetorian centurion rode up before them. "Rufio?" Lucius recognized Papinianus' man.

"Praefectus! Thank the Gods I've caught you in time. The prefect asked me to bring you to him in secret as quickly as possible. Something has happened. He's waiting for you with the legates,

Castor, Euodus, and some of the men outside the eastern walls. Plans have changed."

Lucius felt his heart racing. *Can it be falling apart so quickly?* "What's changed?" Lucius asked.

"It's Caracalla and Claudius Picus," Rufio said. "Papinianus will tell you everything. But we must go quickly, sir!"

At the mention of Claudius, Lucius felt the anger inside him begin to burn. He had wanted to bring that man to justice for a long time. He turned to Dagon. "One turmae. With me now."

"I'm coming with you," Dagon said. He then turned in his saddle. "Akil! Bring your men. On the praefectus now. The rest of you remain on alert and ready!"

"Come Praefectus," Rufio said. "This way!"

Lucius and his men rode across the grass after the Praetorian centurion, rounded the octagonal tower of the northeast corner of the fortress and made their way toward the river.

The sound of the river became louder as they rode, the ground squelching beneath their horses' hooves. Lucius, Barta and Dagon scanned the darkness ahead, the stand of trees near the river's edge, and the length of the via Principalis that stretched from the southeastern gate of the fortress to the distant wharf to their right.

It was quiet, and they could not see any sign of torches.

"I don't like this, Praefectus," Barta said.

Then, out of the shadows, a hail of arrows whistled through the air.

Lucius felt his head jarred as an arrow glanced off of his helmet. "Attack!"

"It's a trap!" Dagon said loudly.

"Back to camp!" Lucius ordered as two Sarmatians went down. Whoever the attackers were, they were shooting in darkness, but they appeared to be closing in. "Rufio! Where are you? Back to camp!" Lucius called for Papinianus' man. Xanthus wheeled, and out of the corner of his eye, Lucius only saw Rufio charging at him out of the darkness with his sword levelled at him.

Lucius drew his blade and it swept from the sheath down just in time to parry the Praetorian's blade, and with a lightning-quick stroke of his sword, he cut both of Rufio's hands off at the wrists.

Rufio screamed.

Lucius moved in quickly, reached down from Xanthus' back, and grabbed him by the neck. "Where's Papinianus? Tell me!"

Rufio looked up at Lucius from his bleeding stumps and spat at him. "He's already dead! And the legates!" He shook his head and began to laugh. "You chose the wrong side, Metellus! You and your men will be slaughtered!"

Lucius pulled back his blade and drove it into Rufio's face, killing him instantly.

The body slumped in the saddle as Lucius pulled his blade out, and Rufio's spooked horse charged away. Lucius watched it go and there he saw a wave of soldiers coming out of the dark, running on foot.

More arrows flew, finding targets now, and more of the Sarmatians went down.

"We need to move!" Dagon called as the sound of clanging swords broke the evening silence.

"On me!" Lucius yelled, kicking Xanthus toward the river.

The survivors of the turmae followed Lucius, trampling the Praetorians rushing at them, arrows slamming into the muddy ground behind them.

They charged, away from the walls, and swept left, to the north along the river, and when a century of men appeared in the darkness ahead, Lucius lowered his mask and charged with his sword levelled.

They slammed into the Praetorians at speed, even as the attackers' pila took out three more Sarmatian riders, but they did not stop to finish them. Kontoi impaled the enemy on the way, and swords, long battle clubs and axes swept and cracked bone and armour as they made a furrow of blood and screams, and came out the other side. Lucius turned to see Dagon and Barta still with him, the other men, including Akil tightly formed behind them.

The lights of the legionary camps burned in the darkness ahead and as they got nearer, Lucius could see that Brencis and a turmae of men were outside the camp. Lucius reined Xanthus in before them.

"Treachery!" Lucius said, and even as the words left his lips, he knew that Claudius Picus had got to Rufio, that all of Papinianus' plans had turned to ash.

"Who attacked you?" Brencis asked.

"Praetorians!" Akil said, reining in hard before him.

Lucius' head spun. They did not know now who was loyal, whom they could trust.

"Praefectus, what are your orders?" Dagon asked, kneeing his mount closer to Lucius. "They'll be here any moment."

Lucius looked to the walls of Eburacum and there he could see a gathering of torches and Praetorian uniforms upon the ramparts. He felt panic rising, but forced himself to focus. His men needed strong decisions then, but he kept thinking of one thing - that he must reach his family.

Lucius shook his head. "Sound the cornu!" he yelled. "Cavalry form up!"

The Sarmatian turmae began to pour out of the fort, but even as they did so, the cornui of the legions could be heard upon the fields surrounding them.

"The legions! Look!" Brencis yelled, pointing at the approaching cohorts.

Lucius turned to Dagon, Barta and Brencis. "Papinianus and the legates are dead!"

"What?" Dagon said, his face betraying his own panic then as the legions approached. "Are the legions with us or not?"

"I don't know!" But even as Lucius said it, the cohorts began closing in around them. "We need to get away now!" Lucius yelled. He knew then that the legions were not with them, for whatever reason he could not say. There was no time. He turned to Dagon and the others.

"We ride south! Split into two groups and meet at home! Brencis!"

"Yes, Praefectus!"

"Take half the men and make for Deva. Then head south. We'll ride for Lindum and take the Fosse Way."

Brencis' horse whirled on the spot and a crazed look entered his eyes as the legions closed in. He looked at Dagon, his cousin and king, and nodded.

"May the god of thunder and the sacred sword see us through this!" Brencis said, saluting and then turning to the turmae behind him. "On me! Charge!"

"Brencis!" Dagon called, but his cousin and the men were already slamming into the first century of an oncoming legion. "There are too many!"

"Dagon, we've been betrayed! We need to break free and get home. Now!" Lucius looked at his friend, then lowered his visor.

Barta was handed the dragon vexillum and hoisted it above Lucius.

The sound of fighting erupted in the distance and cries of pain and battle rent the air as Brencis' charge slammed into the first of the legions' cohorts.

Lucius raised his sword and called to his men. "Sarmatiana!" he yelled, kicking Xanthus' flanks and charging into the oncoming troops to the West.

The Sarmatian cavalry followed the dragon banner like a beacon in the night, and with the earth shaking beneath their hooves, terror filled the troops before them, so much so that they broke apart before the thunderous charge.

"Metellus, wait!" Lucius heard some men yelling at him as he passed, but the Sarmatians carried on, slashing their way free, hacking, crushing at speed until after what seemed an hour of blood they finally broke free and rode into the night.

I'm coming Adara...I'm coming!

Barta and the banner were directly behind him and once they were in the open, upon the road, Xanthus and Barta's mount began to swallow the miles ahead.

In the dark of night, he did not see that Dagon and the others had fallen behind. He could not hear their hoofbeats falling farther and father away. All he heard was the pounding of his own maddened heart and the Gods' warning beneath the cold, starry sky above the road.

The sounds of battle could not be heard in the civilian settlement of Eburacum on the other side of the river, especially outside the southern wall, in the small necropolis near the gate and beside the road south.

That small city of the dead was normally quiet, rarely visited, but on that night, as the Sarmatians were slaughtered with sown betrayal, the necropolis was alive with torchlight. From the outside, with fires burning within, the stands of oak and yew that surrounded it looked like great hands reaching out of the earth, their fingers like the bars of a massive cage. In ages past, it had been a ceremonial site of the druids, but for some time now, it served as a cemetery for slaves, the grass dotted with sad memorials of rotting wood or cracked plaster; these were the slaves none cared for, the abused and nameless ones. Favoured slaves were given monuments by their masters in the larger necropoli around the city.

Within the dark embrace of the trees, among the rows of grave markers, four long, deep trenches had been dug, and on every side of the dark pits, kneeling before the dark, were rows of men with their ankles tied together and their wrists bound behind their backs. Each man had a sack over his head, and was unaware of the movements around him, the faces of his fellows awaiting the torment to come.

Strategically placed among the prisoners, bronze tripods had been set up and lit to cast fiery light over the entire cemetery, and around the edges, in the dark line of the trees, stood Claudius Picus' Praetorians.

The men stood waiting for word from the broad table at the back of the glade. Their eyes watched as Marcus Claudius Picus and Caracalla drank from gilded cups that had been set out, the wine poured continuously from two full amphorae of Falernian wine.

Caracalla and Claudius' conversational voices were as out of place in that dreaded glade as was laughter at the side of a man's deathbed. As the wine flowed, and the two pored over the proscription lists that Claudius had written up, the kneeling men awaited their fate.

Some of the prisoners tried to peer through the sacks over their heads to look for some form of escape. Other trembled and pissed themselves, and some cursed the side they had chosen as if they had bet too much on the wrong chariot team at the Circus Maximus.

"These lists are very thorough, Claudius," Caracalla said, his voice almost joyful with drunkenness. "You've done an excellent job this night."

"I thank you, sire," Claudius bowed and took another sip of wine, raising his cup to Caracalla. "But it would not have been possible without your excellent performance. 'I have been wronged by Castor!' Truly, sire, even the divine Nero would have been jealous."

Caracalla's face darkened. "I am not, Nero. I prefer blood and battle to the stage, but your emperor will accept the compliment this time for the fruit his performance has borne." He motioned to the prisoners kneeling in the firelight. "But I can't see who is who with all the sacks over their heads."

"But that's all part of the game I have planned, sire!" Claudius said, his voice joyful, eager.

"What game?"

"Well, sire. I know you enjoy gladiatorial combat, almost as much as you enjoy the chariot races in the hippodrome. You've told me how often you have marvelled at the gladiators' skills in lopping off a head with one swing of a sword."

Caracalla's eyes lit up, and he became excited as he anticipated Claudius' next words.

"As you can see, sire, we have a variety of weapons upon the table here - gladii, battle axes, spathi, an Iberian falcata, a Gaulish longsword, and a Dacian falx."

"I've always wanted to try one of those," Caracalla said, standing from his chair and steadying himself on his feet.

More wine was poured and the two men drank again.

"We shall compete to see who can removed the most heads. My esteemed colleagues kneeling before us will help with the competition, and help you to hone your craft so that by the end of the game, you shall be expert at this precise technique."

"There are more than sixty men here, Claudius!"

"Sixty-eight to be precise, sire. Unfortunately, you had many enemies. But after tonight, Caesar shall be safe. I admit, it will be thirsty work, but we have plenty of wine left over."

"Wonderful." Caracalla began to stretch his wrists and arms as if he were preparing for his morning exercise at the gymnasium. Then he bent over and looked at the lists upon the table. "Who should we start with?" He ran his finger down the long list.

"Might I suggest starting with the names at the top, sire? The first dozen or so blows will be messy as you will be out of practice at first."

"Excellent idea!" Caracalla said, looking at the list. "Ah, the first name is 'Castor'." Caracalla looked up as if going a role call at camp. Castor! Where is Castor?"

Kneeling at the end of the first trench, a man in a black tunic whimpered with fear and Caracalla laughed.

"There he is!"

"Shall we begin, sire?" Claudius asked. "You should go first. Choose a weapon."

Caracalla looked at the assortment of deadly-sharp blades upon the table, his hand hovering over them, back and forth, before he picked up a gladius. "I'll go with what I am accustomed to, until I grow into the technique." He stepped forward and spun the gladius easily, the blade whistling as it twirled, the fire reflecting off of the blade.

Claudius picked up a gladius for himself and led Caracalla across the grass to the first trench. Once they arrived at the trembling man, the sack was ripped from his head and Castor's terrified face looked up.

The freedman was bruised and battered, and from the smell lingering about him, he had obviously urinated.

"You did very well this night, Castor," Caracalla said. "My father would have been proud of you."

"Sire...pl...please. Do not do this." He was weeping now. "I will serve you faithfully. I will, by the Gods I will."

"I think not, Castor. I cannot abide you. Your time has come." Caracalla leaned over to look straight in the man's eyes. "But you have the honour of helping Caesar one last time with his sword technique." Caracalla stood up and took aim with his gladius.

Castor began to scream, but for only a moment before Caracalla's blade swept down.

Blood squirted out as the blade became lodged in Castor's neck.

Caracalla pulled at it and took another swing, and then another, and another until the head fell over, hanging by tendon and skin and the weight of it pulled the body forward into the pit.

"I can't do this with all that screaming!" Caesar complained.

"It's all a part of the game, sire," Claudius said, stepping up with his own blade next. "Think of the screams as the roar of the crowd in the Colosseum that the gladiators must deal with. You did very well for the first go of it, sire."

"Thank you. It was much more difficult than I imagined." Caracalla looked at all the kneeling men around the cemetery. "Shall we just go down the rows? It may be faster that way."

"Whatever you wish, sire," Claudius said. "I think this first trench will hold the most interest for you." Claudius moved next to a row of three men in long grey tunicae, and unmasked the three of them at once.

"Ah!" Caracalla clapped. "My father's doctors!" He stood behind the men. "Gentlemen. You should have helped me to speed along my father's departure like I asked. Had you done, we might not find ourselves in this place. But, such as it is... Your turn Claudius."

Claudius Picus stepped behind the first doctor and took aim without speaking. Just as he was about to swing, the doctor began to shake his head and the blade crashed into the skull, cracking the side and sending him forward into the pit where he convulsed at the bottom.

"He ruined my swing, sire. Might I go again?"

Caracalla nodded. "Please do."

Claudius moved to the second doctor and without hesitation swung into the base of his neck. He hacked three times before the head came loose and the body toppled over. "That was better! Sire, your turn."

Caracalla stepped up to the third doctor, placed his feet carefully, checking the distance, and swung once, twice, three times. "Excellent! I've matched you, Claudius."

"A great improvement, sire." Claudius then moved to the next kneeling man. "I think you will have a better view of this one from the other side of the trench, sire. You can give the lesson, and he and I shall be the pupils."

Caracalla recognized the clothing of the man and smiled before running around the end of the trench to the other side and facing. He nodded and Claudius removed the hood. "Ah, Euodus! You are just in time for your lessons. Timely as ever!"

"Antoninus," Caracalla's teacher said. "Do not do this. Your father's shade will weep in Elysium."

Caracalla frowned, and the playful expression that had danced about his face turned to anger. "You are a poor student, Euodus. I'm very disappointed in you." He looked over the tutor at Claudius. "Now, Claudius, the key to this is the sweeping gesture of the blade. You must time it perfectly. Let us see if you can do it in three."

"Yes, sire!" Claudius said.

Euodus closed his eyes and Claudius swung.

"One! Two!"

"Claudius!" Caracalla said. "Two swings? You've done this before, haven't you?"

"I admit, sire, that I have had a bit of practice in the past."

"I'm impressed. Who's next?" Caracalla looked at the ornate armour of the next victim and nodded for Claudius to remove the sack before he came back around for his next turn.

Claudius removed the sack and there knelt Aemilius Papinianus, Prefect of the Praetorian Guard.

"There he is!" Caracalla said. The glade grew silent then as all strained to listen, even the kneeling men, for it had been Papinianus who had sought to oust Caracalla and Geta, who had promised the men loyal to him a long, rich retirement after their success. The mirth fled from Caracalla's face as he looked upon Papinianus. "You made such a mistake! Thought you would ignore my father's will? After he had such faith in you, my mother's cousin." Caracalla shook his head. "Such hubris, Papinianus. Such misguided arrogance and faith."

"Get on with it, coward!" Papinianus said. "Your reign will not last, for the Gods will despise you!"

"Ah, you see? That is where you are wrong. They despise you for being a traitor, for I am here with this," he held up the gladius, "and you are kneeling there, waiting to have that bald head of yours lopped off."

"Your mother would weep if she saw you now!"

"My mother is a weeper, and she is not here," Caracalla said. "You should have made your peace with me, Papinianus, rather than try to replace me, to sow rebellion."

"He would have been a better ruler than ever you will be."

"You discount the son of Severus too easily."

"Sons of Severus," Papinianus corrected. "You are not sole ruler."

Caracalla laughed. "Harmony only lasts so long as the players play together, Papinianus. And I am no musician." Caracalla stared across the pit at Papinianus. "I grow tired of you."

Papinianus spat across the pit at Caracalla's feet and shut his mouth, staring off into the sky above, as if trying to see far to the East, to home.

"I see you have nothing more to say," Caracalla held up the blade as he walked slowly back to the other side of the pit. "Claudius, I think I will try a different tool now. Bring me the Dacian falx."

"Right away, sire." Claudius took the bloody gladius from Caracalla and exchanged it with the long, curved blade of the Dacians. He handed it to Caracalla who was waiting behind Papinianus. "Here you go, sire."

Caracalla accepted the long, inwardly curved blade and hefted it from the double handle. He smiled. "This feels very strange, but I like it. I can see why the Dacians favoured it."

"It is a beautiful, terrible weapon, sire. But see how it works for you. Maybe we can institute it for the Praetorians."

"Let us see," Caracalla said, lining it up on the back of Papinianus' neck. "To Hades with you, Prefect!"

Papinianus closed his eyes and looked far away to the sun and sand of Syria, of home, and just as he imagined himself standing in the temple of Baal, darkness closed in and he was falling.

Caracalla swung with such fervour that the blade swept through Papinianus' neck with one stroke, but the blade was so long that the hook of the end caught the next man in the neck, sending blood spurting into his face.

"Excellent, sire!" Claudius cried. "Keep going!"

Caracalla swung again, and again with the falx, moving down the line of traitorous Praetorians until he reached the end of the first trench. He stopped, blood dripping from his face and armour, his hands sticky with gore.

"A towel and drink for Caesar!" Claudius ordered and one of the Praetorians by the table came over to offer such to Caracalla. "You're in the lead, sire! So many with one blow!"

Caracalla dried his hands and wiped his face. "The falx works well," he said. "But it is cumbersome. See what you think, Claudius. Take the next row while I have a drink."

"Thank you, sire." Claudius accepted a new falx from one of his men, and as Caracalla drank on the other side of the trench, Claudius went to work.

And so the night of blood wore on with Caracalla and Claudius taking turns. When the first trench was filled with bodies, they moved on to the second, and then the third and fourth, trying out different weapons and swings, joking about how heads fell away completely detached, or how bodies slumped over into darkness, pulled by the weight of each man's head.

The Praetorians who had sworn allegiance to Caracalla and not Papinianus, watched in stony silence as their comrades were executed like pigs at slaughter. Though many would have wished to run forward and stop the madness, they dared not move for fear of Claudius's retribution rather than Caracalla's. Instead, they watched and listened as their friends and colleagues' necks were severed, their faces drunkenly slashed and their eyes agape at the sad end of their Praetorian lives of glory.

Their leaders had expertly divided the men, and now the survivors would have to live with life in the service of the Caesar before them, having let die the brothers, husbands, and fathers whose bodies now lined the dark, twitching trenches of blood at their booted feet.

When the last body fell forward, Caracalla raised the battle axe he had come to favour and rested it upon his blood-soaked shoulder.

A trooper brought him a towel and a full cup of wine, and Caracalla reached for the wine first, downing it as Claudius did likewise. When Caracalla finished his drink, he stared at the fire of the nearest brazier for a moment, and in that light, he seemed to take on the appearance of some eastern demon of old, blood dripping in rivulets down his face and from the tight curls of his coarse hair. Finally, he reached for the towel the trooper still held out and wiped his face, hands, and the handle of the axe he held.

"Now you, Claudius. Kneel here." Caracalla said.

The troopers around the perimeter exchanged sudden glances and the dark, jovial mood of the necropolis turned stormy and serious.

Claudius laughed, the wine flowing freely in his veins at that point, as it had been in Caracalla's. "Sire? Your wit has no bounds!" he laughed again, the tip of the bloody falx he had enjoyed using coming off of the ground just slightly, ready. "Why would you say such a thing, sire? I have kept track of all your enemies for months now, carefully curated the proscription lists that filled these graves."

"You did well, Claudius. But you have not given me everyone, not least the most dangerous man who should have been at the top of the list. Papinianus would not have been so bold without him." Caracalla pointed the axe at Claudius and pointed for him to kneel. "You did not give me Lucius Metellus Anguis."

"I gave you every man who supported him. Even the legates who went to the Sarmatian camp lie in the second trench."

"It's all for nothing without the dragon, Claudius. And time and time again you've failed in that regard. Now kneel!!!"

"Sire. Before I do, I feel compelled to tell you that a special plan to ensnare the dragon is already underway. He will head straight for home in the South. In fact, I hear that he and his men have already fled."

Caracalla looked at him, the intensity in his eyes as volatile as an amphora of naphtha. "What are you talking about?"

"We will have him soon, sire!" Claudius spread his hands wide, palms up, as if offering something to the Gods themselves. "My men have been in the area of his home for a long while now, liaising with the ordo members of Lindinis whom I mentioned to you. There are only so many routes to his home, and for speed, he will stick to the road network. My men are waiting for him on every route. When they have him, they will hold him for me."

"I don't have time for your games, Claudius. I leave for Rome tomorrow!" He placed the axe on Claudius' neck, ready to swing, ignorant of the fact that the Praetorian still held the falx as he knelt.

"Sire. If you do this, Metellus will live to haunt you another day. He will regain support from the legions. My nets are already laid to catch a dragon, sire. Go to Rome tomorrow, and let me live so that I might follow with Metellus' head, and the heads of his wife and children."

The pressure of the axe blade where it rested on Claudius' skin, just above the collar of his cuirass, broke the skin, and it was then that Claudius wondered if he should strike, but he took the pain for a moment longer and then...

"Very well, Claudius. You may live for now," Caracalla said, withdrawing the axe. "But know this now. If you fail, your head will be the next one I remove. And believe me...I've had a lot of practice!"

Caracalla threw the axe onto the ground and walked away among the stinking, bloody trenches. A century of men who had been waiting outside the necropolis surrounded him as he walked back to the southern gate of Eburacum, a bloody Caesar striding through the streets at the start of his reign.

When Caracalla was gone, Claudius stood and turned to the men around the cemetery. "Fill in these trenches now!" he ordered. "Tomorrow, we ride south!"

XXIII

FURIAE

'Furies'

Armed centuries of Praetorians had surprised the Sarmatians upon the road not ten miles out of Eburacum, and it had been a bloody struggle for Lucius and his men to break free.

They had come from every direction with pilum and arrow, gladius and ballista bolt, and even though many Sarmatians fell in the charge, most of them managed to break through the chaos. As they rode for their lives, uncertain of who was friend or foe behind them, following their praefectus blindly into the deep night, they lost sight of each other and of the dragon banner.

"Where is the praefectus?" Dagon asked aloud as he led the charge, turning this way and that in his saddle, searching for any sign of Lucius by the light of the moon.

"I don't know, my lord!" said the decurion, Magar, his lungs heaving from the fighting. "He was with Barta last I saw him. After you shouted for him to ride on. They broke free and charged ahead."

Oh, Anguis...wait for us, I beg you! Dagon prayed to Epona, and his gods of sword and thunder as they set off once more, their horses' lungs heaving as they gobbled up the miles ahead. *Just wait!*

In the darkness, he did not see the milepost to Lindum on the road south, the way Lucius had gone, but charged headlong with the men to the southwest, to Rigodunum.

The night ride had been swift and full of terrors for Lucius and Barta. They had charged along the road south at a speed that even challenged the stride of their enormous mounts. When dawn came, casting a pink light over the variously rocky and rolling landscape of Britannia, they found themselves alone.

"Praefectus!" Barta said aloud as Lucius and Xanthus began to pull away. "We must stop to rest and water the horses! If we push them they will go on for you, but their hearts will burst in the process!"

Lucius turned in the saddle to look back at Barta who was waving at him. He felt Xanthus' coat, soaked with sweat, and reined in slowly, easing up on the speed. They stopped beside a stream, near a group of sycamore trees by the side of the road. The two men dismounted and led the horses to the water. The animals drank, and Lucius and Barta too bent down to cup their hands.

Lucius splashed his face and rubbed it roughly. *What has happened?* he wondered. *Everything happened so quickly.*

He went back onto the road and stared to the North where dark clouds were rolling swiftly over the fields and forests. It was a desolate spot, but the situation was even more so.

"They were waiting for us, Praefectus," Barta said as he came onto the road to stand beside Lucius.

"It's Claudius Picus' doing. It's been him all along, I'm certain." Lucius closed his eyes, trying desperately to calm himself, but he could not for all the fear he felt for his family. And for the guilt of having lost sight of Dagon and the men. He shook his head. "I should not have charged ahead."

"Yes. You should have, Praefectus," Barta said, his big bulk stepping in front of Lucius so that he had to look at him. "We have all sworn to protect you. You were the sole target of that attack. Claudius Picus has always sought to harm you. Success lies in your survival. With you alive, the legions will rally to your side."

"I'm not so sure, Barta." Lucius sighed. *How could I have been such an arrogant fool?* "With Papinianus gone - if he is indeed dead - I don't have the money to pay the legions. Yes, they honoured me, but will they follow me without pay until I'm sitting on the throne as Papinianus wanted?" Lucius reached up and touched Barta's shoulder. "By now, Caracalla and Claudius Picus have probably already threatened the officers, or killed them, and bribed the legions to stay loyal to them."

"I'll never understand Romans!" Barta growled. "No honour!"

"Most men follow power, Barta, not honour or the rightness of a cause. Especially if they are afraid."

"*We* do, Praefectus. The Sarmatians will never leave you."

Lucius hung his head. "I know." He gazed up the road again. "And I have let them down."

Now Barta took Lucius by the shoulders with his thick hands and shook him. "The Gods got you through the fighting back there for a reason, and my king told us to ride, so ride we did. You and I are here for a reason. You are the dragon, Praefectus, and we must ride for home to save your family, my queen, and my lord's unborn child." Barta whistled and the horses came trotting up the slope to their sides. "They have rested, and we must ride on."

"Thank you, Barta. You're right. We must get home. With hope, Vartan has reached them already, or soon will. But we must get to them."

"How great is the distance?" Barta asked as they climbed up into the saddles and straightened their cloaks in the chilly air.

"About two days at speed," Lucius said. "We should reach Lindum soon, but from there to Aquae Sulis there are several forts we'll have to avoid at Margidunum, Venonis, and Corinium. We don't know who we can trust."

"Lead the way, Praefectus, and with hope there are still men loyal to the Dragon!"

Together, they led their horses down the road to Lindum, and the South beyond.

Lucius and Barta's horses proved their pedigree on that ride, for they carried the two men without end, only stopping to rest and water when allowed, their pace never slackening.

Whether Epona rode with them, urging them on or not, Lucius could not tell, for his mind moved more swiftly than their mounts, charging in and out of panic, fear and anger. He knew he would not be able to rest until he saw his family safe. The world had turned upside down, and uncertainty had a stranglehold around his neck. At times, Lucius searched for the white stallion of his goddess, her hounds and birds charging in the fields and forests they passed in a blur, but he did not see her.

Merchants, farmers, and small detachments of men from nearby forts watched as the two men sped by, but none stopped them or challenged them. The troops they could not avoid had had no word from Eburacum, and so when Lucius told them that there was an emergency in the South, they wished him well.

The dragon still held sway in the hearts of some, it seemed.

After two days, coming over a wooded rise in the road, the city of Aquae Sulis appeared in a haze before them. They had by-passed Corinium Dobunnorum in the night, and now Lucius sought a way to avoid Aquae Sulis. They were close now to home.

"The road beyond Aquae Sulis will take us near to Ynis Wytrin," Lucius said, "but we should go straight home to the hillfort."

"I agree," Barta said as he chewed a piece of bread. "If they are in the Blessed Isle, they will be safe. But they are exposed at home."

"There's no time to waste!" Lucius kneed Xanthus' flanks and the great black stallion lunged down the hill. They left the road, seeking to go around the city. They would rejoin it afterward.

They did not see the man with a bow emerge from the woods then, a quickly-scrawled message tied to the shaft of an arrow which he loosed into the sky to reach another skulking man farther away. The lurkers had been waiting for days, weeks, for the man he had just seen. If the money had not been so good, they would not have hidden like thieves out of doors for so long. Now, the message had been passed along. The dragon praefectus was on his way.

The ride that day took some time, for the roads twisted and wound in an attempt to climb the line of hills where the lead mines were located. There was no way to avoid the roads, for all the cliffs and rocky outcrops flanking them on either side. It would have taken them an extra day to go around to the East.

By the time they came to the vast, watery, mist-covered levels surrounding Ynis Wytrin, night was falling.

"We can't stop now," Lucius said. "We're almost there." He looked around. The line of the Fosse Way was still just visible in the dim light as the mist began to thicken, a black line heading into white. "We won't have to go into Lindinis," Lucius said. "We're almost home!" He allowed himself to taste a little of the incredible relief he felt as they charged down the hill.

They passed through familiar ground now, a beacon to the East, a temple upon a hill to the West. The landscape rolled up and down, flanked by green trees and fields where young lambs bleated in the evening light. They were both tired, and the horses even more so.

As they rode, an inkling began in Lucius' gut, a warning in his mind like a mirage in the desert. Was it for real, or was he imagining it in his exhaustion?

The dark trees to either side of the steep stretch of road ahead seemed to crowd in on them, so thick that the darkness was deeper there than anywhere else.

651

It was then that a whistle flew from the trees and an arrow shaft planted itself in Barta's horse's flank.

"Attack!" Barta cried, his voice echoing over the road to be swallowed by the black trees.

"Ride! We'll outstrip them!" Lucius cried as they barrelled down the road, faster and faster as more arrows whistled through the misty air around them.

Barta cried out as a shaft pounded into his side and he was knocked from his saddle to the ground.

"NO!" Lucius cried, twisting in his saddle, trying to stop. "Barta!"

But the hill was steep and Xanthus still flew forward with momentum.

Lucius drew his sword, but he did not see the thick rope stretched across the road in the darkness. He turned to look forward too late, and the rope caught him in the chest throwing him from the saddle to land hard upon the road.

He cried out in pain, dazed, struggling to get up. He could hear Barta's raging voice far behind, but more than that the voices of several others, swarming like angry bees. Lucius rolled over and just as he was about to rise, something hard smashed into his head. A loud groaning sound that seemed utterly foreign burst from his own throat, another blow to his head hit home, and then...darkness.

The sounds were muffled, as if he were swimming in Neptune's dark deep realm, the surface above visible, but out of reach. Splashes of colour and of sound burst in his mind, and pain boiled in his head and body like water in a black cauldron.

It was the sound of a horse neighing violently in terror that roused him, and he knew the voice as well as any one of his men, better even.

Xanthus?

The sound was of pain, or torment. There was also laughter from several men, their loud voices making his head pound, grating on the senses as his mind swirled.

Then, the sound of a stallion in full anger, more like a primordial beast than something equine in nature. A cry of pain rang out, and curses from several men, and then the sound of galloping fading away into the night.

Was it night?

Run, Xanthus! Run!

Lucius tried to move, but something prevented him. Only his head lolled atop his shoulders as he tried to open his eyes. Slowly, the lids of his eyes cracked open and light burned through. He closed them again, reluctant to see what was about, but he forced himself to look slowly, to allow his vision to adapt to the grey light.

It's day.

His vision swirled for a moment, but as his sight adjusted, he could see better, feel more. He was tied to some sort of chair, his legs and arms bound by thick ropes. He strained at the bonds, but could not move them for the pain in his limbs. He gave up and looked around.

The floor was of dirt, and there was a musty smell of mould in the air, and of blood which, Lucius realized, was his own, crusted down the side of his head and face. Before him were double doors of wood, askew on their wooden hinges, the boards awkwardly spaced so that he could see the light outside, pouring into the place in streaks across the floor to his feet.

He looked up at the roof and noticed the blackened thatching rising to a peak in the middle, above the second level that went around the edges.

A roundhouse, he noted. *But where?*

Lucius tried to remember where they had been on the road last, before he had fallen from his saddle. *So close to home...* But he could not remember a roundhouse, did not know how long he had been out.

He looked around some more and noticed some baskets huddled together on either side of the house filled with grain, some with apples on the verge of rot. There were shelves to his right and left but from his vantage point they appeared to be empty. There was another smell though, a pungent odour that crept in from behind him. He strained to see what the source was, but all he could spot were a few amphora leaning against the back wall. He stopped suddenly, thinking of the moment he lost consciousness.

Barta!

Lucius strained at the ropes again, but could not find the strength to break them, the hemp only digging deeper into his skin.

"Barta!" he yelled, his voice hoarse before he tried again. "Barta!!!"

653

"Praefectus!" the Sarmatian's voice called back, some distance away.

"Shut up, you!" came another voice followed by the muffled sounds of clubbing.

"Leave him lone! We're Roman soldiers!" Lucius called. "You'll pay for this!"

The clubbing continued until Barta's defiant threats died down, and then there were footsteps coming, a shadow before the doors in front of Lucius.

The doors flew open and blinding light filled the house.

Lucius tried to look beyond the man coming toward him, but the light was so intense that he had to shut his eyes, until the door swung shut.

A man with a limp walked toward him. He was dressed all in black, and a pronounced scar ran down the side of his face.

"Why don't you shut up, Praefectus?" the man said, standing a little back from Lucius as if he were a cobra ready to strike.

"Do you know who I am?" Lucius said it as a threat, the timbre of his voice making it clear that retribution would be swift and painful.

But the man only laughed and spat at his feet.

"Of course I know who you are, Lucius Metellus Anguis. You're the 'Dragon Praefectus'."

"Do I know you?"

"No. But I know you. And I know your family."

Lucius lunged at the man, but was held in place by the ropes.

The man's arm swept in and the club he had been holding sent Lucius into darkness again.

Through the blood leaking down from his swollen brow, Barta watched the man come out of the roundhouse where Lucius was held. So many times he had tried to break the ropes that tied his arms and legs, splayed, between two trees, but he could not manage, no matter how hard he tried.

The beatings had been frequent, sometimes violent and brutal, sending him into unconsciousness, at other times more of a taunting entertainment for the large group of men who had attacked them.

Barta had noted early on that there were a few trained men among them, all dressed in plain uniforms of black or brown. Their weapons were professional. The rest of the mob were hired thugs.

The latter were the ones who enjoyed beating him, as if baiting a chained bear in the arena.

Barta assumed they were far from the road now, for he could not see the line of it anywhere. They were in the middle of a vast field, it seemed, and the wooded hills sloping upward behind the roundhouse seemed vaguely familiar.

Xanthus and Selene, Barta's own mount, had been tied to wooden posts farther down the field, but from where he was tied, he had been able to see them thrashing at the men whenever they approached them with clubs or spears.

He shut his eyes at the memory of those spears digging into Selene's flesh and muscled flanks, her cries of pain as she bled from a hundred wounds with no chance of fighting back.

Barta had roared threats at the men as they stabbed his horse, his friend, and as she fell to the ground in a pool of her own blood, weakened by the ordeal, her lifeblood pulsing its last, he wept tears of rage and anguish.

Xanthus had become enraged at that, as if some daemon had entered into him, lending him the strength of a chimera. He had broken the ropes, and when the men closed in, he kicked at them. They stabbed him next, sliced at him, but the stallion had reared, overpowered them, and charged.

But arrows had flown into him, and sent Xanthus into a rage so great that he had bolted as if furies hounded his back and clawed at his flanks.

It had been a relief to see the stallion run free, but Barta worried that he would only run to die alone in a far wood, full of worry for his rider.

Shortly after that, the praefectus' voice had called to him from the darkness of the roundhouse, and Barta had been clubbed again.

Never had he felt so helpless as he did tied between those two trees, Hercules hobbled, directly facing the roundhouse where Lucius was held captive.

As clouds moved in from the West, rain began to fall, light at first, but then increasingly heavy.

Barta looked up at the sky and allowed himself to drift off as the droplets fell upon his bloody face. He needed to rest, to regain strength for the moment when he would fight his way free and help the praefectus.

My King... Barta thought. *I will not let you down. I will protect him...*

It was night again when Lucius regained consciousness. He was unsure how long he had been out. It could have been a few hours, or a whole day. Time blurred as he fell in and out of consciousness with the rain and thunder outside. He thought only of home, of his family, of the Gods' warning that some roads, some ordeals, he was meant to endure alone.

Apollo...my lord...whatever happens to me, let my family be safe in Ynis Wytrin...

The thunder cracked loudly overhead, and lightning flashed several times, lighting the interior of the roundhouse momentarily.

In those fleeting flashes of light, Lucius thought he saw her, standing before him.

Morrigan.

She smiled at him, laughed, but no sound came from her black throat. Her deathly white skin was scarred beneath the oily strands of her black hair. She appeared to be in pain, but that pain was apparently doused as she gazed upon him. She reached out to his face with her pale hand.

Lucius tried to avoid her touch, but he could not.

She pressed her icy hand against the dried blood upon his face, and laughed.

Now, Dragon... You will die...

But then she disappeared as the lighting flashed again.

Lucius looked around, but could see nothing. He could, however, hear. Beneath the sound of the rain and thunder, voices came closer to the roundhouse, growing louder, accompanied by torches in the night.

No. It can't be...

The door opened, and a cloaked man walked in to stand before Lucius. When the door closed, he turned and pulled back his soaking hood.

"I can't tell you how happy I am to see you, Praefectus."

It was Marcus Claudius Picus.

XXIV

EX INVIDIA

'Of Hatred'

Claudius stood there, smiling, relishing the shock on Lucius' bloody and bruised features. For a few moments, he did not speak. He just smiled, looked Lucius over, looked at the chair, the ropes, and the ceiling of the roundhouse. Then his eyes fastened onto Lucius' own.

The eyes that Lucius looked into then were cold and blue, the sort of eyes that lit up when bad things happened, or when they were going to happen.

Claudius Picus' eyes were absolutely blazing with joy at that moment, and the sight of them struck fear deep inside Lucius' inner fortress.

"We never talk, you and I," Claudius said, walking over to the door where a wooden stool sat to the left, in front of the wall. He returned, set the stool down in front of Lucius, and sat. He removed his wet, mud-splattered cloak and let it fall to the ground in a pool of black. His ornate Praetorian armour was muddied as well, and he wiped the gorgon head in the middle as if to allow it to stare at Lucius with him. He looked up and smiled again, almost playfully. "You almost did it, didn't you?"

"What are you talking about?" Lucius answered, his voice deep and un-phased, despite the rising panic inside as his mind searched for some possible way out of the situation.

"Why…become emperor of Rome."

Lucius did not answer, not feeling the need to justify his reasons to such as Claudius. He knew the man was incapable of understanding the reasons he had decided to accept Papinianus' offer, for Claudius only ever did things for himself. "Does Caracalla suspect at all that you are using him?"

That smile again. "Bring a brazier!" he yelled back over his shoulder to the men standing guard outside. He turned back to Lucius. "It's getting a little dark and cold in here. We need some light."

Two Praetorians came in carrying a burning brazier which they set to Claudius' left, between him and Lucius. They then saluted and went out.

"You and I both know that Caracalla...the emperor...is a disappointment. And Geta!" he laughed. "He's still a child, really."

"Perhaps Caracalla's not as stupid as you hope?"

"He is not his father though, is he? If there's a truth I've noticed, it's that emperors and rulers are puppets. That others pull upon the strings. Those puppets believe they are ruling, true, but in point of fact, they are only carrying out the actions of others, those who stand in the shadows, dagger in hand."

Lucius shook his head. "Severus was no puppet."

"You disappoint me, Praefectus. His wife certainly controlled him to an extent, and do you forget the true man behind the power in the first years of his reign? You remember, Gaius Fulvius Plautianus, don't you?"

The anger spread on Lucius' face then as the memories of Plautianus flooded back, memories of being hunted, of Argus turning against the family, of...Alene killed, lying dead upon the desert sand.

"Oh...I've upset you. I see you remember well enough." Claudius stood and walked around the stool. "I've heard how Plautianus recruited your brother. I even met Argus once. Did you know that?" He looked at Lucius. "Good fighter, but not heartless enough for the job. Whatever did you do to him? He just disappeared?"

"Argus made his own way, and his actions determined his fate."

"I'm not much for philosophical discussion, but in this case, that rings true. Our actions do determine our fate. And so, here we find ourselves. Me, standing here. And you, tied to a chair, waiting and wondering what I'm going to do to you." He laughed. "But your actions have not only determined your fate, Praefectus. Your family's fate is tied to yours, is it not? The fate of your men too? So many people."

"And you are tied to no one. Must be lonely, Claudius. Have even the Gods abandoned you?"

"Some gods do not agree with me, it's true. But who says I have none? You may be blessed by the Gods as some say - though I don't see them helping you now - but I too have been blessed by some in this land. She has helped me, her anger has at least. Has she appeared to you yet?"

Lucius' eyes were wide then, and Claudius nodded.

"I see she has. I have to admit, she is no Venus, but when it comes to you, we are of the same mind. I wouldn't be surprised if she is standing in the shadows now, watching and waiting." Claudius made a show of looking at the back wall of the roundhouse, then shrugged. "But I don't care that you slew her son. The Wolf was a barbarian. A necessary evil. That was quite a feat, by the way. I thought for sure that when you and your men went into the highlands to find them, that you would not come back. Caracalla was so upset."

"He knew?" Lucius said.

"Of course, well…some of it. He knew what I wanted him to know. Her certainly knew that I was in touch with Argentocoxus."

"Traitors."

"Come now, Praefectus."

"Over fifty thousand men died in this war!" *I lost men and friends!*

"Casualties of the great game. You know, in a way, the fates of all those men who died were tied to your own actions."

"You're delusional. The emperor decided to campaign in Caledonia. Not me."

"Ah, you see? There you are mistaken. Yes, the emperor came to Caledonia, but he would not have if his own puppet master yet lived."

"What are you talking about?"

"Do you even know why I hate you so much, Praefectus?"

"Because I'm everything you have no hope of being."

Claudius rolled his eyes. "Ah, no. I'm quite certain I'm a better man than you are. No. The reason I came to hate you is that you took away the greatest opportunity of my career. One day, I was set to be at the very centre of power in the empire, and the next it all turned to ash in the wind." Claudius sat down again and removed the pugio from his cingulum to turn it over in his hands. He pointed it at Lucius, and for the first time, his smile faded. "The day you killed Plautianus was the day my own dreams burned before my eyes."

"Why does it not surprise me that you were one of Plautianus' men?" Lucius shook his head in contempt. "Of course you were."

"I wasn't just one of his men. He held the strings over the emperor, but I was just about to grip the strings holding him. I gave him so many names, helped him confiscate the estates and accounts of so many of my fellow patricians that he grew immensely rich. In exchange for helping him, he promised me wealth and power that you can only dream of. I would have been his advisor in all things...the real man holding the strings."

"Plautianus promised a lot of things to a lot of people. You were no exception. You're kidding yourself."

Claudius pointed the dagger at Lucius' face. "Am I?" His voice was angry, bitter. "I was the one who told him to promise all those things to all those people, including your brother." Claudius ran his finger along the sharp edge of the dagger, looking at the point as it pressed into his finger tip and broke the skin just a little so that a drop of blood appeared. "I started hating you the moment you killed Plautianus and tossed his body down from the Palatine palace. The only way I could survive the proscriptions after that was to ingratiate myself to our idiot emperor, Caracalla."

"Plautianus was a disgrace, Claudius. And you are a disgrace to that uniform, and to all good Romans."

"I did not survive this long by being good, Praefectus." Claudius calmed then, and his smile returned. "Ruthlessness is an often overlooked quality, don't you think? It should be used more often." He stood quickly then. "I think I know how to make the point." He turned to the doors behind him. "Open!"

The double doors of the roundhouse opened wide, and directly ahead, an avenue of torches held by Claudius' Praetorians led to the trees where Barta was tied by the arms and legs. Claudius turned to Lucius. "You didn't think they had already killed your man, did you?"

Lucius looked at Barta and felt his heart sink.

The big Sarmatian had been stripped bare, the tattoos covering his body - the bear, the lion, and the dragon - writhed as he strained at his bonds, trying to get to Lucius. His muscles bulged with the exhausted effort. "Anguis!" his deep voice called to Lucius, causing laughter among the Praetorians.

"Hercules bound, wouldn't you say?" Claudius said, smiling as he saw the desperation in Lucius' eyes as he looked upon his trusted bodyguard. "He is quite a specimen. A bit hairy, but strong and imposing. The lack of one eye adds to the effect too, wouldn't you say?"

"Let him go!" Lucius demanded.

Claudius only laughed. "I think not, Praefectus. He's already killed several men. He had to be beaten unconscious before they could tie him like that. I'm reluctant to untie him. The men spent so much time doing it." He laughed and disappeared outside the roundhouse for a moment. When he returned, he held Lucius' sword and pugio in his hands.

To see the golden-hilted blade Adara had given him in Claudius' hand made Lucius angry beyond reckoning, but when Claudius pointed the blade at Barta, he knew that worse was to come.

"I've often admired this sword, Praefectus," Claudius said, coming a little closer to Lucius. "Talk among the men is that the Gods themselves sent you this blade which was a gift from your lovely wife." He winked. "More on her later."

"If you hurt -"

"Please, Praefectus! Don't speak. You'll ruin the fun!" Claudius held up the sword and swung it around. "A blade made by the Gods. I wonder how it cuts? So many battles you've fought, and there isn't a chip or blemish upon the blade... You know, the night you fled Eburacum, I was playing a game with Caesar - Papinianus sends his greetings, by the way. Anyway, Caesar and I were testing a variety of weapons. Some of them cut very well - the Dacian falx was my favourite. But I wonder if any of them cut as well as this. So, I'd like to test it." He turned and stood still, stared at Lucius before walking slowly in Barta's direction, the flames of the Praetorian torches lighting his way.

Lucius strained at his bonds again. "You coward, Claudius! If you want a fight, untie me or Barta and we'll see how tough you really are!"

"Barta," Claudius muttered as he approached the naked Sarmatian. "What odd names you people have." Claudius walked slowly around Barta two times, gazing upon his body, picking a spot to start. He looked at Lucius one last time before disappearing behind Barta again. "Who wants a piece of rump for supper?" he asked his men and a moment later he swept the sword down and sliced through Barta's buttocks.

The Sarmatian howled in pain, and Lucius screamed with him.

"Claudius, stop it!"

"We're just getting started, Praefectus!" Claudius called back, holding up the blade in the firelight. "I've never seen such a clean cut. It's almost surgical!" He turned again to face Barta and the Sarmatian, through his painful grimace, managed to spit in Claudius' face.

661

Claudius raged and slashed again, this time cutting a long fine line down Barta's thigh, splitting it open like a roast.

The cries of pain emanating from deep in Barta's throat were a sort of torture for Lucius, but not so much as the anguish he felt for his friend. "Claudius!" Lucius yelled, calling him like a curse. "Take me instead!"

Claudius wheeled around after another slash across Barta's chest and smiled with blood lust in his eyes. "Do not fret, Praefectus. You're not going anywhere either. Your turn shall come!" He turned and slashed at Barta's groin this time.

Lucius wanted to turn away, to avoid the pained look upon the mighty warrior's face, his friend's face, but he could not. He forced himself to watch to take in what he was responsible for, to feel the anger and frustration and fear that were building up inside of him.

Barta howled like a wounded beast surrounded by huntsmen. His dark, wild eyes, set in his bleeding face, searched for a way out. His muscles strained with unimaginable power at his bonds, but the trees holding him were too large, too ancient and unswerving to care for his struggles as their ridged bark was filled with flying blood.

Claudius was breathing heavily now, and began to walk around Barta, assessing his work, the flow of blood from certain wounds, the convulsion of certain muscle groups set in the big man's body, especially the back. He did not care if his uniform were sprayed in blood and bits of skin. He was enjoying the feel of the sword in his hand too much, the cries of Lucius as he watched his man cut to ribbons and as the blood pooled in the grass about the feet of the barbarian's tattooed body.

"Praefectus! I wish I had borrowed your weapon a few nights ago, for I surely would have beat Caesar." He looked at the blade again, as he had before, and admired it, the bright glint of it in the darkness, the perfection of the blade. "Simply stunning," he muttered. Then, he sighed. "I've gotten carried away, haven't I?" He turned to Lucius. "Is it too much?" He pointed at Barta whose eyes rose to meet Lucius'.

The Sarmatian still strained to get to Lucius, as if he knew what was to come, that he had to protect Lucius even with the broken trunk of a body he yet possessed. His legs and arms strained and pulled, and he cried out loudly in the night as cracks began to form in the bodies of the trees.

Claudius spun around, his eyebrows up. "Impressive! I think we must help our barbarian friend along, don't you, Praefectus?" He walked around the back of Barta one more time and Lucius saw his blade poised in the dark behind.

Barta stared at Lucius. "Anguis!!!"

The blade swept round and an instant later Barta's bearded head was flying through the air to land in the mud before the round house.

"NOOOOO!!!" Lucius cried at the top of his lungs, his eyes wet with tears as he watched Barta's headless body slump and the head come to a stop, frozen in the mouthing of his name.

Claudius walked casually toward Lucius as rain began to fall more heavily, his face one of joy and wonder. "Can you imagine an emperor who weeps for his men?" he said. "Appalling! And from a man of your rank!"

Lucius looked up at him. "Coward."

"No, Praefectus. Just strategic. I've got much more work to do this night, and if I had fought your man there," he nodded toward Barta's body, "then I would have been injured, surely, and too much so to carry out my plans."

"Then fight me."

"Again, that is quite tempting. But I have nothing to prove to you, or my men out there. They know what I'm capable of, and they know I have the funds to donate to them for their service. Can you say the same?"

Lucius stared at the man before him and never before had he ever hated as much as he did at that moment.

Claudius suddenly cocked his ear as one of his men spoke out.

"Sir, riders approaching!"

"How many?" Claudius asked.

There was a pause, and then, "Two, sir!"

"Ah! My guests have arrived. Praefectus, you wait there while I greet them." Claudius went out and left Lucius to stare at the body of his friend.

Ride the wind, my brother, Lucius thought. *Forgive me, Barta...*

Outside, there were new voices added to the mix, Claudius' audible above them all. The new voices were of a man and a younger man. Lucius strained to hear, but could not tell until they came closer. As he listened he knew the voice then, just before a man appeared in the doorway beside a younger man.

"Crescens!" Lucius said. "What are you doing here?"

663

Serenus Crescens Nova of the Lindinis ordo now stood before Lucius with his son, the latter staring with hatred at Lucius.

Lucius had a sinking feeling as Claudius came in behind them and placed his blood-soaked arms over their shoulders.

Crescens flinched, but his son did not. The son only stared directly at Lucius.

"Praefectus..." Claudius said. "I believe you know Serenus Crescens Nova and his son? Of course you do." Claudius came around and stepped to the side between Lucius and the newcomers. "Crescens and I have been business partners for some time now, haven't we, Crescens?"

"We have," the ordo member said, his voice dark and resigned.

"Crescens, don't do this!" Lucius said.

"Oh, don't worry, Praefectus," Claudius said. "His role is done. He is only here to watch. After all, this is his land. He was kind enough to allow me to make use of it to host you."

"What?" Lucius stared at Crescens, but the man would not look at him. He ignored the son.

"Some time ago, my man made contact with Crescens and the ordo. I arranged with Caracalla to give Lindinis civitas status."

"He's lying, Crescens!" Lucius said loudly. "You cannot believe this man!"

"I believe him more than I do you, Praefectus Metellus," Crescens said. "You dismissed us out of hand, in favour of Ynis Wytrin, and now it has come time to pay for that decision."

"That's right." Claudius nodded. "For months now, Crescens has been reporting on the comings and goings of your family, Praefectus. He's been sending me reports, and quite detailed ones at that. I'm sure Caesar would be interested to know, for instance, that you have men who neglected the call to arms and stayed behind at your more or less fortified hillfort. Or that you have been catering to Britons over Romans. Or, my favourite, that your dear sweet wife is expecting a baby any day now!"

That got Lucius' attention, and when he whipped his head up to stare at Claudius, the man smiled.

"Yes, Praefectus. I know everything." He paused, his bloody fingers on his chin as if in deep thought. "Come to think of it, I remember hearing the name of Ynis Wytrin lately..." he rummaged around in his satchel, pulled out a letter, and held it up for Lucius to see. "I read about that place in an urgent missive most recently."

Lucius' heart sank and fear erupted throughout his body. It was the letter that he had sent with Vartan to give to Adara, asking her to go quickly to Ynis Wytrin where she and the children would be safe.

"I'm afraid that this never reached your wife, Praefectus," Claudius said, smiling, standing behind Crescens' son. He put his hands on the young man's shoulders.

Lucius could see Crescens felt a great discomfort in being there, in dealing with Claudius, but he could not pull out now. *He won't help me,* Lucius thought, knew. "Crescens... It wasn't Ynis Wytrin who sent men to your home to kill you that night. They were Claudius' men."

Crescens' face betrayed his knowledge.

"Oh Praefectus," Claudius laughed. "He already knows that. We have no secrets between us, Crescens and I. And I've been told about how you took it upon yourself to beat up on this young man and his friends." Claudius leaned over and whispered something in Crescens' son's ear.

The young man's face was full of determined anger as he stepped forward and stood in front of Lucius. He spat, and then his fist whipped out and took Lucius on the jaw. Then another hit, and another so that Lucius' head whipped side to side with each strike.

When Lucius looked up, the boy was smiling, rubbing his fist which he had hurt.

"Not bad, young man. You may have a future," Claudius said, stepping forward. "I'll bet that felt good. But you were hitting him all wrong. You need to use your whole body. Watch..." Claudius gazed down at Lucius and planted his feet, twisting his whole body and then swing his entire person from the waist, through the arm and down into the fist to take Lucius on the side of head.

Crescens' son hooted with glee as he saw Lucius' head snap sharply to one side and his eyes roll in his head.

"That's how you hit a man, boy," Claudius said.

"Can I kill him?" Crescens' son asked.

"No, no. I have something special in mind for him," Claudius answered. "But, if you like, you may come with us where we are going next. There will be plenty of killing, I suspect."

As the haze of his dizzying pain began to clear and he was able to focus on the men standing before him, Lucius heard part of what was said. *Where are they going?* But even as the words sprang to his mind, he began to understand. "Untie me," he muttered. "Fight me."

"I think not, Praefectus. Our time together is almost at an end. And we have a previous engagement that we must attend." Claudius turned to the door and called to his men. "It is time!"

Three Praetorians came into the roundhouse then, and Lucius braced for their attack. But they by-passed him and went to the back of the round house where the amphorae were lined up against the walls. Despite the heavy sound of the rain outside, Lucius could hear that they were pouring something around the perimeter of the house, along the base of the walls, and on the dirt floor surrounding him. It was the olive oil, but also that other, familiar scent which he now understood to be naphtha. The mingled scent of the two stung his nostrils as they poured it everywhere around him, the oil upon the ground and the naphtha upon the walls, its blackness staining them in horrible shapes.

"We must go now, Claudius Picus," Crescens said as he backed away toward the door, his hand firmly upon his son's arm.

Claudius did not turn. He continued to stare at Lucius. "You and your son will stay, Serenus Crescens. You may wait outside in the rain until we are done here. Then, you will accompany me."

Lucius tried to appear defiant as Claudius gazed down his aquiline nose at him, but as the latter's men poured oil and naphtha around him, the reality of fear and fire began to hack away at his courage. *Gods help me!* But he clung to a facade of calm strength as a man in a gale might cling to a single column out in the wind. "You won't get away with this, Claudius."

Claudius leaned down to speak so that only Lucius could hear him. "I already have. I have to admit that killing you has been high on my list of priorities. But come to think of it, killing your children and fucking your pregnant wife is my ultimate goal now. I will leave this cursed island quite sated." He smiled.

"AHHHHH!" Lucius screamed as he struggled to get at Claudius, to rip away his bonds, but it was futile. His facade crumbled with rage and fear.

Claudius laughed. "I'll bet Adara is sweet and plump right now, hmm? She's not expecting me, but I'm sure she'll be happy to see us."

Lucius was fuming, even as one of Claudius' men came back in to stand by the door holding a torch. "By the Gods, Claudius, I will die before I let you harm my family! I'll see you dead!"

"I think not, Praefectus." Claudius held up Lucius' sword and pointed it at him. "You'll be dead before I harm them! And I will! Oh, I will!"

Claudius' cool demeanour now broke and the wild, blood-loving man that he truly was came to the fore. He looked around the roundhouse one last time, happy with the dousing it had received, the spread of the oil and naphtha all the way to Lucius' feet and the legs of the chair to which he was tied. He sheathed Lucius' sword and then turned to take one of the amphorae by the door. He shook it and found it still had a little oil left in it.

"One final touch," he said as he walked up to Lucius and poured the remains on his lap over his pteruges, and upon the his armoured shoulders. "There. Perfect."

Lucius' head swept forward and nearly took Claudius on the jaw, but he was too quick and got out of the way.

"You're not a god. Just a man." Claudius pointed at the great symbol of the dragon with its outspread wings upon the chest of Lucius' cuirass. "Your time is at an end, Metellus." He reached back and his man at the door came forward to hand him the torch. "Dragons love fire, I hear. Well...it's time to see if a dragon can burn!"

With that, Claudius flung the torch to the far wall and flames erupted instantly, spreading as he and his man made their way to the door. "I'll let your family know how you're doing when I see them!" Claudius yelled as he closed and barred the doors of the roundhouse.

"I'll kill you!!!" Lucius screamed from inside the growing pyre of flame. "AHHHH!"

Outside, Claudius and his men, with Crescens and his son, sat atop their horses at a distance, watching the roundhouse go up in flames, great pillars of black smoke rising into the downpour of the night sky.

Claudius smiled and laughed wildly as Lucius' cries erupted from inside and then subsided. "I guess dragons do burn!" he said to his men, twenty or so of them. "It is done. The usurper Metellus is dead! Now, to his lair!"

The sound of hoofbeats faded into the night as Claudius led his deadly entourage away with Crescens and his son.

Behind them, the beacon of flame rose up into the night, a sacrificial fire visible for miles around.

XXV

UROBORUS

'Ouroboros'

Lucius felt utterly alone and defeated in that moment as the panic and fear became as oppressive as a tidal wave sent to destroy his psychic shore. He thought of Adara and the children, and the images of their faces flashed in his mind as the burning fires encircled him with greater intensity.

As smoke and flame swirled all around him, he knew his end was near.

Adara! Calliope! Phoebus! his soul cried out. *RUN!*

But his focus was pulled away by the raging flames all around him, for all he could feel was searing pain. He tried to peer into the light, to search for some sign of the Gods, but all he could see was a torrent of orange and yellow.

The circle of fire spread and joined, and as Lucius screamed and strained at the ropes, it appeared and enveloped him, a giant ouroboros of fire. The dragon before him roared in pain and anger, and when the great jaws turned from the doorway to open its maw, Lucius saw death before him.

"AHHHHHHH!" Lucius cried out, his lungs and eyes burning with smoke as the fiery beast threatened to swallow him, to burn him into oblivion. He began to pass into darkness…

Metellus! shouted a divine voice from somewhere beyond the fire.

Lucius roared back into consciousness and pain in the centre of that inferno which continued to burn, despite the pouring rain outside that came down like heavenly tears weeping for him.

Even the Gods could not douse the fire of his suffering.

His heart pounded in a panicked, erratic rhythm, and he coughed and spluttered.

He cried as he thought of how he had failed his family. All those years of wanting to keep them from harm, to protect them with all of his being, and now he would be there, trapped in that smouldering house, when death came for them.

His grief was beyond reckoning, but his anger was even more so, and he clung to that thread as the flames swept across the oiled, dirt floor of the roundhouse to light the feet of the chair and his own legs.

None were present to hear his deafening cries as the fire lapped at his body, burning his greaves, his leather skirt, and licking at the armoured cuirass that surrounded his torso. He was encased in an oven. The wet and sweaty wool of his tunic beneath began to singe and he felt the flames catch on his long hair before the fire went to work on his skin beneath his clothes.

"Gods, please!" he begged. "Why?"

You are a Dragon and fire is a part of the world! You are no mere mortal! Fight!

Lucius heard Apollo's crashing voice at the back of his mind, even as his skin blackened and he shut his eyes against the fire enveloping his face.

Fight Anguis!

Lucius strained under the weight of his fears, every limb stretching to its utmost, every tendon pulled to its extremity under the load of every vein that boiled and threatened to burst.

"AHHHHHHHH!" his voice called to the world around him, drowning out the roar of fire and rain. His burning bonds slackened little by little and then, his burning limbs snapped free of his promethean chains and he charged!

With his eyes shut, Lucius ran headlong into the dragon's mouth to crash through the blinding light and smouldering wood of the door to collapse in the mud and rain outside.

He strained to crawl away from the fires, pain everywhere in a body which he could no longer feel, even as cold mud spread over him. Then, he stumbled upon something hard and large and his eyes cracked open to see Barta's head cradled in his arms.

He wept then, holding the head of his friend, and screamed at the heavens for what had been done, and the fear of what he was now helpless to prevent.

Darkness closed in around the pain then, and he fell upon his back in the deep mud, his burned, convulsing body spread open to the falling sky.

It had been a mad ride out of Hades for Dagon and the Sarmatians. For days they had been riding like the wind, but it seemed that every god of darkness and death had tried to prevent them from going south.

When they realized they'd gone the wrong way, they rode hard to find Brencis and the others and to join up with them as they raced home to Briana and the Metelli.

Every step of the way, thunder and lightning had battered the landscape, terrifying the horses and blinding them as they charged over the land toward the South.

They were exhausted, but in his mind, Epona herself spoke to Dagon, urged him on to find Lucius.

The dragon needs you now! the goddess had cried.

No one challenged the hundreds of riders as they rode by, their faces affixed with fury and exhaustion as they sped down Rome's Britannic arteries, past black lakes and mountains, over rolling green landscapes dotted with forests, and across vast fields of green grass and tilled earth.

Not one of the men stopped or gave in to his exhaustion to be left behind or abandon his king or commander.

As they passed the outskirts of Aquae Sulis in the darkness of night, the riders cresting a hill and charging down, a beacon of fire seemed to rise up out of the land.

Dagon reined in hard and the riders behind him did likewise. In the pit of his stomach, he felt terror's raking claws slashing at his guts.

"Sire, over there!" one of the men yelled, pointing down the road.

Dagon drew his sword and the men around him levelled their kontoi at the great black and screaming shadow that charged toward them.

Dagon kicked his horse forward to meet it, and after a few strides, his mount reared in the face of the wild-eyed giant before him.

"It's Xanthus!" Brencis yelled above the pounding rain.

Lucius! Dagon felt the panic as the terrified animal screamed and reared before him, above him. "Whoa! Easy, boy!" he tried to grab the reins, but Xanthus would not let him near, thrashing and crying out as he was with black blood glistening on his flanks in the night's light.

The stallion reared another time, turned and charged away down the hill.

670

"Follow him!" Dagon ordered, kicking his horse forward with all the speed the animal could muster. *Hang on, Lucius! We're coming!*

The sky was black, veined with blinding flashes above the waves of orange heat that swept outward from the circle of fire in the middle of that distant field.

Barefoot, and from out of the shadows of the forest nearby, Epona stumbled toward the blackened and bloody form laying prostrate in the mud before the fire.

The goddess' eyes burned with tears, and as she walked, her three white hounds licked at her hands where she had wiped at her grief. She saw them standing there already - Apollo and Venus - and she felt anger toward them. Had she been fully healed from her own battle, she would have seen those who had done this bathed in blood and torn to pieces by her hounds.

How could you allow this to happen to him? she said to her divine peers as she knelt in the mud beside Lucius' body.

Venus wept as she looked down, silent in grief, in her feeling for Lucius and the rest of the Metelli. *It was a trial he had to endure,* Venus finally answered Epona.

You've killed him, Epona said, wanting to touch him but fearing to do so.

Apollo stood over Lucius, silent as he waded into the burned forest of the man's mind to find him, to lay hold of his consciousness in the dark. *Where are you, Anguis? It is not your time. Lucius Metellus Anguis!* The god's voice echoed in that vast and complicated realm. *Harken to me! Come back! Your family needs you!*

Lucius wandered weeping through a black forest in which he could barely see. He was weeping as he peered into the tangled labyrinth before him, like a child abandoned by his mother at birth, helpless. The fear in there was vast, with many levels of experience ranging from terror to utter and complete desolation and despair.

He tried to focus on a thought, but found it hard. Even his hands did not know what to do, for they opened and closed as he walked, grasped at any branch he could find to steady himself, or catch himself as he fell, tripping over root and rock in the darkness.

671

He had no sword in his hand, and without it, he felt powerless against the red eyes that peered at him out of the distant dark. His body was tired, so tired...and he would have lain down to eternal sleep in that place but for the faint breeze that found him, and the music upon that breeze...a voice.

Lucius pressed on, his hands steadying as he went in the direction of a minute, pin-point of light.

Your family needs you!

He heard the voice, and it roused him, somehow, from somewhere, he felt a familiarity. He fell though, onto his hands and knees, and never had the mossy ground looked so appealing. His eyes grew heavy, and all he wanted was to sleep...sleep...as the darkness closed in around him.

But that music! That light! It pulled at him still, and so he crawled now, his hands cut, his knees bruised and battered. He carried on, and the farther he went, the longer he held off sleep, the clearer the faces before him became, the more he remembered.

Calliope? Phoebus?...Adara? He tried reaching out to them, but the apparitions seemed to walk ahead in a middle distance he could not yet reach.

They need you, Anguis... the voice said again, the music.

Lucius grabbed hold of a solid oak branch and pulled, pushed up with his legs to lift himself, shaking as if the weight of an entire world pressed down upon him.

"Anguis?" he said the word aloud and it echoed in the forest.

A blue light began to shine around him when he said the word, and as he focussed his mind upon the word, the light intensified. He searched for its source, turned this way and that, until finally, he looked down to see it.

Upon his chest, the image of a dragon radiated with blue light. He touched it, and as he touched it with a trembling hand, he felt his limbs grow lighter and stronger, his determination sprouting inside him like an eager green shoot in spring.

"I'm coming!" he cried out, and he began to walk again, his eyes fixed on the point of light ahead, the music he heard his thread back to the world beyond the wood.

The edge of the wood came nearer and nearer, and he was running toward it now.

When he burst from the darkness of the forest onto the vast field beyond, he came to a stop and shielded his eyes.

Before him a great pyre burned with blinding light into a night sky of whirling stars.

Lucius shielded his eyes, took in the scene, and began to run like he had never run before, toward the light, toward the fire itself.

"I'm coming!" he yelled.

He could feel the rain falling, its cooling touch barely noticeable upon his skin.

The earth beneath him...it was shaking. He wondered if it would swallow him up then, but the music and light above him began to grow, and he strained to open his eyes, his cracked and aching lids resisting.

Rise...rise... the music said. *Go to them... Help is here.*

Lucius felt a warm soft touch upon his face and he looked up into the raindrops to see the black form above him.

"Anguis!" a panicked voice called out in the night. "Oh Gods!"

Dagon reined in when Xanthus stopped above the body in the mud, and he knew right away that it was Lucius.

Brencis and the other decurions dismounted and rushed to their praefectus' side where he lay, three of them leading Xanthus away.

"Form a perimeter!" Brencis ordered some of the men. "Whoever did this might still be near!"

The hoofbeats of the riders thundered off around the field.

"Anguis!" Dagon cried out as he knelt beside Lucius in the mud. "Stay with us!" He saw the head in the mud beside Lucius and closed his eyes in grief.

The men too saw this, and noted the trees nearby where Barta's body slumped against the thick ropes that had held him.

"Gods!" Dagon called to the sky in his anguish.

"What do we do?" Brencis asked Dagon as they looked over Lucius' body.

His armour and clothing was so charred and covered in mud, it appeared to have melded to his very skin like scales.

Dagon felt panic rising quickly, trying to arrest his own senses to render him dumb. But he fought it. "I'm here, Lucius. Who did this?"

Lucius stirred and his eyes opened again to look up at his friend.

"I'm here," Dagon repeated.

"Clau...Claudi-" His voice hurt, and his eyes would not stop watering.

673

"Claudius did this?" Dagon asked. "He's here?"

Lucius' head shook a little. "Ho...home..."

"They're going to the hillfort?"

Lucius blinked, his head nodding slightly in the mud.

"Our queen, Metella and the children went to Ynis Wytrin, did they not?" Brencis asked Dagon.

"Yes," Dagon said, relieved.

Lucius' eyes opened wider, their whites stained with blood, and shook his head again. "No. No...letter. Claudius. Ahh!" Lucius' breathing sped up and he struggled.

"No, Lucius! Stay down! You cannot move. We'll go to them now. You stay here."

"No!" The voice that came from Lucius' throat was not his own, but it was one of determination. *Gods,* he prayed. *Give me one last measure of strength to help my family before I die...*

The Sarmatian warriors gathered around then as the dragon struggled in the mud at their feet, and they wept to see him, to see the strength of his heart struggling to fill his broken body.

Dagon would have pressed him back down again to prevent him from moving, but he feared to touch him, to add to his pain. The life he saw kindled in Lucius' eyes then was something different, something he knew he should not interfere with.

Lucius' charred hands and arms reached out to grab Dagon and Brencis on either side of him. "Up!" his voice croaked.

They pulled him up out of the mud, slowly, and he stood for a moment, waving like a lone, surviving sapling in the desolation of a forest fire. *Gods, give me the strength I need...one last time...*

He took a few steps, his men around him, waiting to catch him, but he did not fall.

Dagon wiped his eyes as he watched Lucius move in the direction of Barta's body where he stopped before it and cried out in rage.

"AHHHH!!!" Lucius coughed and black bile burst from his mouth, from deep within his lungs. *Ride, Lucius!* he urged himself. *Ride home!* "Xanthus!"

The stallion pulled away from the men who had been holding him, tending to his wounds, and came to Lucius' side.

Lucius grabbed hold of the saddle horns, but could not pull himself up. He wanted to weep, but knew there was no time. He looked up however, and saw her.

674

On the other side of Xanthus stood Epona herself, her dazzling light soothing horse and rider. *One more ride, Lucius Metellus Anguis,* she said before whispering in Xanthus' ear.

The stallion knelt in the mud then and Lucius climbed onto his back, his aching legs locked between the saddle horns, his burned hands grasping the reins desperately.

The men all around them could see the goddess then, the true mother of their camp.

"Follow him!" Epona commanded, and every Sarmatian mounted up and charged after Lucius and Xanthus who were already speeding toward the road in the dim dawn light.

"On the Dragon!" Dagon cried as he and the men thundered after Lucius.

XXVI

FAMILIAE IRA

'A Family's Wrath'

Screams erupted in the darkness of the night.

Adara's heart leaped in her chest as her eyes shot open. Her baby kicked wildly in her swollen belly, but it was not the child in her womb who had woken her.

Calliope?

"Mama! Mama!" Phoebus called from the cubiculum next door. "Calliope's had another vision!"

Adara let her feet fall over the edge of the bed and got herself up, walking barefoot to the next room. She had not slept well, had had another chaotic dream that hounded her through the night. And throughout it all, she thought she could hear Lucius' voice.

She found Phoebus fully dressed, sitting on the edge of the bed, cradling Calliope. His eyes were wide, and scared as he held his sister, unsure of what to do.

"What is it, my love?" Adara asked, coming to the other side of the bed to sit awkwardly and hold her daughter.

Calliope wept hysterically and her face was a sad, sodden mess.

"She said something about Baba," Phoebus said.

Adara felt the first twinges of real panic, but they were nothing to what she saw in her daughter's eyes once she looked up at her in the lamp light. "Calliope, what did you see?"

"Fire, Mama," she wept. "I saw a roaring circle of fire, and Baba…he…he was in the middle of it. He was screaming for us!"

Adara's eyes began to burn and she pulled her daughter close to her chest. *No! Lucius, where are you?*

For a long while, Calliope had had visions, and for even longer, Adara had dreamed things she dreaded when it came to Lucius. But he had always come home. She had always put it down to a fear of losing the man she loved across time, her platonic other half. He was a man of war, and that fear was something the wives of soldiers were forced to deal with. Nightmares were a part of that reality.

But this time felt different.

Adara knew it...felt it. Her free hand cradled her belly where the baby kicked and churned, as if trying to reach out to its older sister who wept so near to it.

"Phoebus, why are you dressed?" Adara asked her son who was now standing at the far end of the room looking up at the early dawn sky of iron grey.

The rain was finally slowing down after what seemed days of it.

"I thought I should be ready in case something was wrong," he said. His head tilted quickly then to listen out the window, like a stag sniffing at the air in a wood. "I hear horses. Many of them."

Adara did not dare to hope that it was Lucius, though she longed to believe it with all her heart. "Calliope," she whispered, her hands holding her daughter's face as she kissed her forehead and eyes. "Can you get dressed?"

Calliope nodded silently, sniffling as she pulled back and sat up.

Adara stood and went to the window where Phoebus was standing. Together, they listened to the distant sound of horses. Fear did grasp at her then, and she took her son's hand.

"No dragons... It's not your father."

She looked at her two children, her hands cradling her third. She looked at Calliope, her fearful face and tired eyes. She had seen things before, and they had come to pass. Etain and Briana had both spoken of her gifts, and at the time, Adara had not fully believed it.

Calliope, however, was no Cassandra. Apollo loved their family and had not cursed her daughter like that ill-fated prophetess of Troy.

"Put your cloaks on and arm yourselves," Adara said, her mind racing as to what to do. "I'm going to get dressed." She made for the door and stopped at the railing overlooking the hall. "Briana!"

The Briton's cubiculum door swung open and she came out into the hall to look up at the railing. "I hear it too."

Their eyes met and they knew then that they felt the same fear.

"It's not Lucius and Dagon," Adara said seeing that Briana was almost fully dressed.

"What did Calliope see?"

Adara's lip began to tremble, so awash with emotion and fear was she, but she forced herself to focus, for her baby, for her children. "She saw fire."

There was a loud pounding at the barred door of the hall.

"My Queen! Lady Metella!" Lenya called from outside. "There are horsemen massing around the hillfort!"

677

"I'll go to him," Briana said. "You get dressed and armed."

Adara nodded and rushed into the room where she removed her sleeping shift and put on her long, blue wool tunica and wool socks. She did not fit into her leather breeches anymore and so she began to fasten her boots as best as she could.

Phoebus came running in, followed by his sister, and knelt on the floor to help his mother tie her boots. He made quick work of it and stood, his hand out to her. "We need to go down, Mama. Quickly!"

Adara belted her tunica as best she could and slung the sword Lucius had given her over her shoulder. "Come!" she said, taking Calliope's hand and following Phoebus out and down the stairs to the hall below.

Lenya was standing there with Briana, fully dressed in his scale armour and holding the long, iron club he favoured as a weapon over the sword hanging by his side. He bowed to Adara as she joined them. "My lady. Sigwyll is saddling yours and the children's horses for you."

"How can we leave if they're out there? We'll need to defend the fortress."

"There are many of them. Praetorians by the look of it."

Oh, Gods... Adara looked around the hall of their home. She could not abandon it. Not now. But her main goal was to keep her children safe.

Outside the open doors of the hall, horses rushed up and Badru came in quickly. He bowed and got to it. "They've set the bathhouse on fire!"

Lenya looked at Adara and Briana. "We need to get you away from here."

"But where? How?" Adara asked.

"They've scaled the wall at the southwest gate!" Vaclar yelled, and a few of the riders charged away.

Lenya ran outside to where Sigwyll Sloane was coming up with the horses. "Sigwyll, get them mounted!" he said as he climbed his own horse and hoisted his club.

Adara and Briana rushed outside with the children and saw the action being fought down the hill at the southwest gate.

The Sarmatians were slashing at the Praetorians who were pouring over the wall to form a front before the gate. The sound of steel on steel rang out in that early dawn greyness. Sigwyll helped

Adara and Briana into the saddles, and the children climbed onto the backs of their own ponies.

They turned to look around and then saw it. Down the slope of the central plateau where they stood, two Praetorians managed to push the bar up and the gates yawned open. Beyond, a rushing mass of horsemen with torches came charging in.

"Ride, children! Ride! Make for the northeast gate!" Adara kicked her horse's flanks and they followed.

"Try and make for the village, my lady!" Sigwyll yelled as he turned his horse to meet the charging Praetorians. "I'll hold them off!"

Adara glanced back at the man as they careened toward the northeast gate, past the stables and paddocks. Just as they reached the black outline of the supply depot, the sound of horses' hooves clattering on the pathway rushed up to meet their ears. Adara reined in, her panic acute now. "They're already coming!" she said to Briana.

The Briton looked around wildly, searching for a way out. "We can't ride out of here. "We'll have to scale down the fortifications. To the temple!" Briana kicked her horse and it leapt forward, followed by the others.

Praetorians burst out of the northeast gate passage and made directly for the hall upon the summit plateau. They waved burning brands and yipped as they rode, as if they were beating bushes to flush out quarry for the hunt.

It was then that the first torches alighted on the hall.

Down in the village far below, Alma woke early, as was normal, to begin the baking for the day. She stretched her tall frame, tied her long blonde hair back and fastened an apron around her waist.

When she opened the door onto the back to revive herself with fresh morning air, she stopped suddenly, her hands upon her gasping mouth. "Culhwch!"

Her husband came running out. "What is it, love?"

She pointed at the distant hillfort and the flames rising from the bathhouse on the east side. As they looked on, astonished, flames began to leap up from the hall on the summit plateau, then the stables and other buildings, each slowly lighting the early morning darkness with fire.

The faint sounds of battle reached their ears.

"We need to help them!" Alma said.

Culhwch was already rushing into the house. He knelt in the main room and removed a floor board to reach into the darkness below. His hands came out holding three linen bundles which he unwrapped quickly to reveal sheathed longswords. "Paulus, wake up!" he called to his son.

The boy came running down the stairs from the loft of their home. "What is it?"

"Our friends are in trouble! We need to help them!" Alma said to her son.

Culhwch tossed her one of the swords which she caught deftly. "I'll get the others!" he said, rushing out into the village street.

Adara wanted to scream as she saw the flames begin to lick up the walls of their home, to catch and fly up from the rooftops of the other buildings around the plateau.

From where they sat atop their horses behind the temple, they had gone unnoticed until then, but it was only a matter of time.

More Praetorians were riding up and around the hillfort, and then some others, men all in black, and then two that appeared to be civilians. The smaller of the civilians rode a short distance into the fort in their direction and then reined in hard.

"There they are!" the rider yelled, and several of the intruders' heads looked in the direction of the temple.

Adara gazed over the steep slope of the hillfort. It dropped away from her like a dark abyss.

"We need to go, Adara!" Briana said.

"Mama?" Calliope cried out.

"Phoebus! You and your sister need to climb down and run for the village as fast as you can. Don't stop! Just run!"

"I'm not leaving you, Mama!" the boy cried.

"My boy, I can't climb down this slope. I'll find another way."

"If we can break through, we may be able to ride out of here!" Briana said, watching as riders were speeding toward them.

"I love you!" Adara said to her children. "I'll see you at the village. Now go!"

Phoebus nodded and began to pull at his sister as she cried, still tortured by the visions she had had that night. "Come on, Calliope!" Phoebus said. "Let's go!" And together, they slid down the grassy slope of the first embankment.

Adara and Briana watched them go and then kicked their horses in the direction of the northeast gate. But as riders came at them from that direction, they changed course, and rode for the southwest. Their way was blocked there too.

"They're everywhere!" Briana said, and just as the two women drew their swords, the Sarmatians swept in to meet the attackers on both sides, joined by Sigwyll Sloane.

"Ride!" Sigwyll yelled as he slashed at two Praetorians with torches.

Adara watched as he was knocked from his horse's back by a pilum and swarmed by black-clad men whose blades plunged immediately into his body.

Hoof beats rushed up behind them and Adara and Briana turned quickly, their blades parrying the blades that came rushing toward them.

Then, all was chaos.

Their horses charged in separate directions, dodging, swerving, going anywhere to avoid the rush of the enemy.

Claudius Picus and Serenus Crescens watched from the summit plateau as the fires burned all around them.

"Was this completely necessary?" Crescens asked the Praetorian.

"Yes. It was," Claudius Picus said. "It's a pity you aren't enjoying yourself as much as your son, Crescens." Claudius pointed toward the temple where the ordo member's son was lighting the roof of the temple and whooping wildly into the dawn.

"I trust that you will begin the official process of making good on your promises soon," Crescens tried to look Claudius in those cold, pale eyes and the Patrician stared right back at him, blood still caked on Claudius' face from the night's activities. That was terrible enough, but the look he gave back, and the cold edge in his voice, made Crescens regret all that he had done to curry the man's favour.

"I think I'm done with you, Crescens. You and your little shit-hole-of-a-town can rot. After today, I'll be heading back to Rome." He smiled then, for he had seen her riding wildly about the fortress, flanked by two of the last Sarmatians. "Ah...there she is." Claudius kicked his horse and left Crescens in a pool of orange light cast by the burning hall.

681

"Claudius!" Crescens roared after the man. "You must honour our agreement!" But he only yelled to the wind and flame.

Phoebus and Calliope huddled in the shadows at the bottom of the first level of the ramparts. Calliope shook and wept as she stared up the slope at the orange glow above, the sounds of battle rattling her harshly - sword upon sword, the cries of men, the pained whinnying of horses.

"I want Mama," Calliope said.

Her brother ran to her side, his sword in one hand, and held her tightly. "We need to get to the village. Paulus and his parents will hide us. That's where Mama will look for us. We need to go."

Voices could be heard around the eastern curve of the rampart then, voices that seemed to be coming nearer.

"Go!" Phoebus said, and they began to run around the rampart's edge to a place where the trees were not dense and they could slide down to the next level easily.

Just ahead, Phoebus watched in horror as Calliope was knocked off of her feet, her cry sharp and full of pain. Immediately standing over her with a sword raised, was Serenus Crescens' son.

"NO!" Phoebus yelled, lunging in with his father's gladius to parry the blow.

The clang of steel was loud, and in the growing light of dawn, the young Crescens smiled at Phoebus. "Your father likes to harass those younger than himself. Let's see how that feels!"

The older boy attacked Phoebus whose blade parried wildly as he stumbled backward. He held his own, but the older boy had a longer reach and he followed up one attack with a left-handed blow across Phoebus' face, sending him reeling.

"Now, you can die like you father!" Crescens said.

Calliope cried out loud, and ran at him, her fingers scratching at his eyes.

Crescens turned and slapped her, then raised his blade again.

"Leave her alone!" Phoebus yelled through his blurring eyes.

The young Crescens turned to meet his attack, but Phoebus was full of fury in his thrusts and pushed back toward the oncoming voices of the Praetorian troops around the rampart's bend.

Crescens slashed across Phoebus chest, but the younger boy spun just in time and when he came around he plunged the point of his gladius into the older boy's ribs, screaming and pushing with all his might as he fell upon his adversary.

"Phoebus, look out!" Calliope cried as three oncoming Praetorians rushed in.

There was a loud war cry from above then, and Briana came sliding down the steep embankment with her sword arm reaching out. She landed hard, but took the Praetorians off guard from that side.

The first fell beneath her blade which sent his head tumbling down the steep hill, but the other two laughed and lunged at her.

They only got so far, for out of the darkness below, a chorus of warring voices rang out, followed by a small army of blades as Alma and Culhwch crashed into the other two Praetorians.

Two more of the enemy came running from the other direction, and Alma charged past Briana and the children to meet them, her sword quick as lightning as she danced around their death-dealing blades.

More villagers emerged at the top of the embankment, led by Paulus who went straight to Calliope and Phoebus.

"Paulus! You and Ula and Aina take them to safety. Fly, my boy, fly! We're going to help Metella!"

"Adara!" Briana cried into the grey light. "I lost her in the battle! She's still up there!"

"On me!" Culhwch cried, and he led the Durotrigans up the slope to help the surviving Sarmatians and find Adara Metella.

"Briana, go!" Alma called over her shoulder. "Keep the baby safe! Go!"

Briana limped after the children to follow them down the slope when she stopped.

"Listen!" she cried, her heart leaping.

They all stopped, their ears leaning to the sky above, and there they heard the sound of aid, of thunder and the wrath of the Gods themselves!

"The dragons!" Phoebus cried. "They're here!"

Dagon! Briana's heart cried out. "Come, children! Let's go. Help is here!"

Adara could see Claudius riding toward her from the top of the plateau beside their burning home. Praetorians closed in around her, toyed with her. To her right, pinned against the wall one of the

683

barracks, Lenya and Badru stood over the body of Vaclar, both wounded, both searching the darkness through blood-shaded eyes for Adara and Briana.

Adara spun Hyperion, and the stallion reared as she held on with all her strength to the saddle horn with her left hand, her right gripping the bloody sword she had been wielding.

She could see Lenya and Badru pointing in her direction and then, without a moment's hesitation, they ran toward her. The Praetorians surrounding Adara looked in their direction, and Lenya called out. "Ride Metella! Ride!"

Adara kicked Hyperion's flanks and the horse crashed into the enemies before her, trampling them as she sped toward the northeast gate.

As she exploded onto the ramp down the slope of the hillfort, she could hear the final battle cries of the Sarmatians who had fought to protect her and her family.

"I'm coming for you, Metella!" Claudius' voice echoed behind her, chased her as she careened down the rocky road, the steep, treed slopes on either side leaning in on her, the pathway choked by the smouldering remains of their bathhouse to her right.

Lucius! Adara thought.

In her desperation to escape, she did not hear the approach of the dragons, the thunder of familiar hooves, or the cries of the men sworn to protect her and her children. She only heard the man closing the distance between them, hunting her in that dark wood until she reached the open field below. She thought about riding to the village, but feared to lead him there, and so she charged across the valley toward the slope that curved up toward the rocky escarpment overlooking the hillfort. The farther she could lure that evil man away from her family, the better.

Hyperion raced across the field, and Claudius Picus' own horse raced after her.

Adara! Lucius screamed inwardly as his heart raced and panicked and threatened to explode with fear as he led the Sarmatians along the road directly for the burning hillfort.

They had seen the fires from a distance, and their pace had quickened to the point where even their horses surprised them by how much of a punishment they could take.

Lucius remembered very little of that ride as Xanthus charged for home, the cold wind and rain landing upon his burned and crusted skin. He did not care if the others could keep up with him, but charged on blindly to his family, his only concern for their safety which he knew could not be secured before Claudius was taken.

It was rage and a thirst for vengeance that kept Lucius in that saddle, his legs pounding Xanthus' flanks relentlessly, the stallion's flaring nostrils a sign of his own will to do so.

The flames rose higher and higher into the sky, and Lucius turned to see the blurry outline of Dagon riding beside him, leaning forward, low over the neck of his horse as he tried to keep up.

For Lucius then, the physical pain he felt, the clawing hands of death itself at his back, were nothing compared to the rage he felt upon seeing his distant, burning world, the panic that surged in every fibre of his being as he thought of his family and the ordeal of pain and death that only he and his men could prevent.

"Raise the dragons!" Dagon yelled, and the draco standards were lifted to howl into the sky as the earth shook beneath them.

Time had little meaning, only feeling and fear, and an anger to shake the walls of Olympus itself. The closer they got, the greater the fire burned and spread, the louder the sounds of battle in their ears, the screams, the clash of swords.

"Sarmatiana!" came the distant battle cry.

They heard it crash down from atop the fortress, and Dagon knew then that Lenya and the others were fighting their last.

"Sarmatiana!" they echoed back as the dragons roared.

"Brencis, take your men to the southwest gate!" Dagon ordered. "Lucius and I will hit them at the northeast!"

Brencis nodded and his men broke off toward the southwest corner, their speed increasing as they charged into darkness.

"Lucius, wait!" Dagon yelled as Xanthus pulled away.

I'm coming, Adara! Lucius pressed on, Xanthus' heart and lungs heaving so heavily that he felt the rumble beneath his broken body.

They raced along the northern ramparts, looking up where the fire burst into the sky from the destroyed buildings and the charring ruins of their home.

Finally they rounded the northeastern corner and burst onto the road up to the top.

But Lucius stopped suddenly, crying out in anger and pain as his skin cracked and bled.

685

The men sped past him and made for the top. Arrows shot from the wooded slopes as they rode, but their speed and armour protected them.

"Sarmatiana!" the first riders at the top yelled as they waded into the burning slaughter.

Lucius was about to follow when a loud cawing surrounded him and he looked up to see three white birds circling wildly, urging him on.

Epona?

They flew about him several times and then sped away to the East.

He watched them go and was about to ride on when he saw two dots racing up the distant hillside.

Go after her, Lucius! Ride! the voice of Epona burst in upon his chaotic thoughts.

He kicked Xanthus and sped after the distant riders, his heart ready to explode in his chest.

Adara kept glancing behind as she rode, faster than she had ever ridden before, but Claudius still followed, still hunted, still harangued her. She gripped one horn on Hyperion's saddle with her right hand, hanging on for her life, while her other hand cradled and held her belly as her sword in its sheath slapped against her side.

The baby churned violently, and she panicked, prayed to come out of the situation, though she had no idea what she would do.

Gods, help me! she pleaded as she kicked Hyperion around the curving, grassy slope that led upward. She could see the fires burning across the valley, and would have stopped to weep were she alone, but she could not. *Ride, Adara!* she chided herself. *Lucius, where are you?*

Sheep bleated in the darkness at the edge of the wood to her left, scattering at the hurried thumping of the horses' hooves.

The end of the path came up quickly, and Adara reined in at the top where a flat grassy area spilled away over a rocky precipice that looked down onto the hillfort. She looked out and saw a great battle raging around their home, upon it, and then she heard the Sarmatian war cry echo into the early morning as the sun fought to break into that cloudy sky. *Lucius!* She was so relieved, so grateful, that she almost forgot the sound of the hoofbeats rushing toward her. She turned in the saddle and looked toward the trees of the forest across

686

that high field, and thought of fleeing into them, but as she was about to kick Hyperion's flanks, Marcus Claudius Picus came into view and blocked the way.

Adara gasped when she saw him. He was covered in blood from head to foot, his ornate Praetorian armour caked with it. She prayed that none of that belonged to her children. Adara drew her sword and turned to face him.

"I've waited a long time for this, Metella," Claudius said, his voice eerily calm, a smug smile spread across his gory face. "You will want to put that down."

"Stay away from me!" she said, her voice and bearing defiant. She was an Antonina, a Metella...the wife of the Dragon. "My husband will be here soon. It's over. Leave while you can. Leave or I'll kill you."

He laughed, truly amused. And then he dismounted, dropped his horse's reins, and stood before her. "I don't think so." He looked over the cliff to see the hillfort on fire, the battle raging, and knew that the Sarmatians had indeed arrived. But he still laughed. "A dragon without its head, is no threat. The Sarmatians may have arrived, but without your husband, they will flee and be forgotten."

Claudius saw the flickering of momentary panic in Adara's eyes and then, to further emphasize the point, he reached beneath his cloak and drew Lucius' sword from his side. He held it up for her to see. "Recognize this?"

Adara could not help the cry of surprised anguish that burst from her throat as her sword lowered and her other hand covered her mouth. She wanted to weep, to comfort the baby that kicked even more in her as if it shared her despair. She shook her head. "You lie!"

"No, Metella. I don't. Your husband is dead. I burned him this night, not far from here, actually."

"No."

"He screamed quite loudly when the flames consumed his flesh." Claudius closed his eyes as if remembering a sweet memory. "I assure you, he is no god. Not even a dragon. 'Was', in fact. He was just a man. And now you and I are alone."

Adara felt her body begin to shudder, her world to turn in on itself. *Gods, keep my children safe...and help me to slay this man!*

687

With a speed that she had not expected, Claudius lunged first, darting forward, and with Lucius' sword, the blade slashed across Hyperion's neck like a butcher's knife through meat.

The stallion reared and Adara tumbled from the saddle, her sword clanging against a stone to stick in the grass, away from her hand where she landed, nearly pinned beneath the horse's body and flailing hooves.

"Ha, ha. This blade is truly amazing!" Claudius said, admiring it as Adara rolled on the ground, grabbing at her belly, groaning. He approached her slowly, taking in the sight of her bare legs and the swollen belly, the swollen breasts beneath her tunic.

Adara began to crawl away, but he followed, and soon she felt the cliff's edge behind her.

Claudius slammed the sword blade into the ground and removed his cloak. "Let us enjoy this moment, Metella."

And then he was on her, his hands grabbing at her kicking legs, scratching at her.

She pushed him back, but he came at her again, his strong arms trying to pry her legs apart.

"Don't you want to scream?" he said. "Call out for your husband! His shade can watch us!" he laughed as his hand grabbed her between the legs with bloody, probing fingers.

Adara let out a great, raging cry and her fist hammered the side of his nose, knocking it sideways with a crack. As he recoiled in pain, her legs pulled in and she pushed with all of her might into his chest, sending him flying backward.

She lunged toward her sword and felt her hand grip the handle swinging it immediately so that it cut across the chest of his cuirass. She found her feet, and tried to stand, one hand shielding her belly.

"You're quite a woman!" he nodded, his voice no longer laughing, but full of anger now. "Scream now, like your husband, Metella," he said as he circled around to pick up Lucius' sword from where it rose out of the ground.

"I will scream when I spit on your corpse."

"Why don't you drop your sword now? You can't win."

"Never."

"Then I guess I will have to fuck your dead body instead!" Claudius attacked, and the blade he wielded reached out with deadly precision, sweeping this way and that, pushing her backward, darting in and out, clanging upon her own blade as she parried wildly with every bit of skill she had learned.

Distant hoofbeats could be heard on the wind, but neither Adara nor Claudius noticed.

Adara crouched under a killing swipe and lunged in with her blade to cut across Claudius' thigh.

He grunted, but was quicker than her, and brought his elbow down on the back of her head, knocking her to the ground, following it up with a knee to her face.

Adara fell backward, groaning and stunned. Her sword arm rose up, but he parried it hard, and the blade fell away from her grasp, nearly falling off of the cliff's edge.

"This is now tiresome," he said, looking at her on the ground.

Claudius then walked in and kicked her belly, once, twice, three times, as hard as he could.

Adara screamed then, the pain too much to bear, the fear of what was happening, of dying, of leaving her children, strangling her.

Claudius dropped the sword and stood over her, ready to complete the conquest he had been thinking about for a long time, the final blow to the Metelli.

He did not see the speeding wraith rushing toward him in that dawn light as the sun began to rise over the valley, the great black shadow looming over him growling, and groaning. He spun as Lucius Metellus Anguis leapt from his horse's back to crash into him.

For a moment, fear and surprise paralyzed Claudius. *Impossible!* His mind reeled as the black form straddling him roared and charred hands fastened around his throat, squeezing with unimaginable strength and viciousness.

Adara pulled away, barely able to move for all the pain she felt. For a moment, she did not recognize the warrior who had Claudius pinned, but then the brilliant emblem of the dragon upon the man's chest told her it was her husband.

"Lucius!" she yelled.

"Run!" he yelled, but as he did so, black bile poured out of his mouth onto Claudius' face, the bloody whites of his eyes turning him to some enraged demon.

"I'm not leaving you!" Adara said, searching for her blade, even as she bled profusely beneath her tunic.

689

Claudius kicked and punched with what strength he had before he passed out. When his hand gripped Lucius' leg, a sheet of burned skin slid away.

Lucius' grip eased up as he screamed in pain, and Claudius rolled away.

Lucius glimpsed his sword and made for it, but Claudius charged and slammed into him, sending Lucius backward into Adara.

She cried out as she slipped and fell over the edge of the cliff.

Lucius reached out and caught her arm, his cry of pain echoing over the valley. But he had her, and he would not let go. *Gods!* "AHHH!"

"Don't let go, Lucius!" Adara said as she looked to the rocks and sloping grass far below. "Lucius!"

Lucius cried out again as Claudius coughed and laughed, with the blade poised above Lucius' back. He pressed his hobnail boot into Lucius' burned calf and Lucius' grip loosened, Adara's one arm beginning to slip away.

She screamed. Fearful for both of them, but then saw a glimmer of hope in the golden hilt of her sword jutting over the edge of the cliff.

"Goodbye again, Metellus!" Claudius said. "This time, you die!" The blade rose into the air and then stopped abruptly as Adara's sword swiped upward to slash beneath Claudius' cuirass into his guts, and then back to cut his hands off at the wrists sending Lucius' sword soaring over the cliff's edge, shining as it spun in the morning light.

Claudius screamed in pain as his body pitched forward, over Lucius and Adara to fall and crash onto the rocks far below.

"Ahhh!" Lucius yelled. "I can't hold on! Give me your other hand!" He looked into her teary eyes...those eyes he had always loved, that had given him strength in the darkest of times. "Please, my love..."

Adara threw her sword away onto the grass and gripped her husband's other forearm.

Lucius strained, pulled at her, but his strength was at its end. With one last, titanic effort, he heaved with both arms, his muscles and tissue tearing, his blackened skin falling away as his body slid forward more, the rocks digging into his stomach.

Adara clawed at the grass and pulled herself up, but as she did so, Lucius lost his desperate purchase on the cliff's edge and fell away from her, tumbling over in the air where she could not reach him.

The last thing Lucius saw was his wife at the top of the cliff as he fell away. *Safe...*

Adara's scream rang out over the entire valley. It erupted from her throat over...and over...and over. A keening cry to tear the hearts of the Gods out of themselves.

And they did weep, the Gods...for Adara, for the Metelli...for Lucius.

Even as the final Praetorians were slain by the Sarmatians and the Durotrigan villagers, all heads turned to that far cliff across the valley.

Adara stared at the body of her husband, her love, far below. Tears burned her eyes and her body shuddered with the oncoming waves of grief she knew would kill her. The willingness to live was leaving her...

"Lucius..." she wept when she could no longer scream. "Lucius..." before sunlight closed in on her, and her eyes slowly closed.

XXVII

FORTUNATI

'The Blessed'

The sound of weeping filled the world, it seemed.

And yet, it was quiet.

The barge carrying them glided through the mist-shrouded channels, the secret ways, from where the wagons the villagers had brought had left them off. Now, spirited away in the dusk light, watched by herons among the reedy banks, and fox or deer from the wild pathways that led to the water, the barge glided softly beneath the protective boughs of willow and beech trees.

Dagon sat on a bench with Briana. He gripped her hand, unable to speak, unwilling to, for all his speech poured into his thoughts and prayers. He was grateful that she was safe, that their child appeared unharmed by the battle. The feel of her beside him gave him hope.

And yet...

Laid out before him, seen through the blur of tears that tortured his eyes, Lucius lay near to death, falling in and out of unconsciousness, muttering incoherently through the pain that wracked his body.

The Gods had turned the world upside down and then set it ablaze,

Who will pick up the pieces? Dagon wondered. He had abandoned his men, and though it was out of necessity, forced upon him by the surviving men of the ala, it pained him to remember the words that he had spoken to them before boarding the barge.

Disband and disperse...disappear... Was he responsible for the erasure of his people then? Where would his brothers go? What king did such a thing? The image of his men standing along the misty shore, watching him float away would be one to haunt his days.

The men however, believed in Lucius and his family, in the Dragon. It was his own duty to try and save them, but how? The more Dagon looked upon Lucius' incinerated, battle-worn body, the more he realized that time was not on their side.

And what of Adara, and the children?

Calliope sat at the front of the barge, staring into the mist as if willing it to press on with her prayers, her weeping, while behind her, Phoebus sat with his father's sword across his lap, staring down at Lucius, and his mother who lay on her side, beside her husband.

Adara was a shadow of herself. Refusing to let sleep wash away the onslaught of grief that would soon overwhelm her, once the shock of events faded away. She lay beside her husband, speaking soft words to him, hoping that wherever he was, he could hear her. *How can I go on without you, Lucius... You are my life... Don't leave us...*

"We're almost there," said Olwyn Conn Coran, the young priestess whom Lucius had helped, so long ago, and whom Etain had sent with the barge when she had heard Calliope's fervent call for help as the fires burned.

"Please, Olwyn..." Briana said through her tears, her hand upon Adara's leg, trying to comfort her to let her know she was not alone. "We must help them."

The girl shook her head as she spread the cool marsh mud upon the burned man before her. "He is badly injured. I do not know that even Etain can help. But...if anyone can, it is she." The girl looked up. "It is in the hands of the Gods now."

"Please save them," Phoebus said to the priestess, the tears running down his cheeks as he stroked his mother's dark hair.

Lucius drifted in and out of consciousness, his awareness of time, of space, of anything but pain, fleeting. He felt as though he were floating in the sky at one point, but glimpses through his hurting eyes at the shoreline told him that he was upon the water. He could not hear, or speak, or turn his neck, but he felt his wife near, his children.

He heard a chorus of weeping, and wondered if he had stumbled into another realm, into Annwn. Then he saw them, the birds in the air, the pale hounds charging along the shoreline, and a woman with flaming red hair upon a white palfrey, racing along the water's edge, her eyes searching for his, willing him to see her, to stay with her.

Live, Dragon... You must live!

The barge sped up, the reeds flowing by faster, the mist thickening before it broke silently from the waterway into the broader expanse of the lake.

Epona reined in at the shoreline and, with tears in her eyes and upon her cheeks, she held up a hand to Lucius.

Goddess... his thoughts called to her as his eyes closed and his body began to shudder.

Epona then took up the golden hunting horn that hung at her side and blew.

The sound echoed across the water, swirling the mist around the barge as it sped toward Ynis Wytrin, toward the Isle of the Blessed.

They passed through a white world of water and mist, through the veil from one realm to another, and the weeping of the Dragon's children heralded their arrival at the gates of Annwn.

EPILOGUS

There was no more pain. Only joy and a feeling of wonder...of delight...of infinite possibility...

Lucius Metellus Anguis' lungs filled with fresh air, his chest rising and falling slowly, surely and without torment.

He was lying upon a soft expanse of emerald grass.

And there was sunlight. He could feel it on his skin, but it did not burn. He had missed sunlight.

He dared to open his eyes and there above him shuddered the delicate leaves of an olive tree, silver-green and full of beauty against the perfect blueness of the sky above.

There was also no longer a ringing in his ears, the roar of battle and flame. The soft lapping of the turquoise sea upon a pebbled shore far below filled his ears, and it reminded him of happy days long ago, but none so happy that they could halt the joy that now filled his heart.

He sat up easily, his muscles obeying the command. He was naked, but he did not care, for the feeling of youth and freedom that was woven through his being was something that all yearned for, but only few were blessed with. He felt like a...

"Welcome home."

Lucius turned away from the sea, and there before him, stood Apollo and Venus. He smiled and made to bow, but Venus stepped forward and raised him up.

"You need not bow, Lucius."

Her touch filled him with joy, unimaginable solace and love, and he wondered how ever he might have lived without it.

The gods smiled at him as he looked around, beyond them to the mountain rising up into the sky, its slopes and fertile terraces covered with white temples, arcades, and waterfalls. Music and birdsong was everywhere, and joyous laughter.

"Is this Elysium?" Lucius asked.

They shook their heads.

"It is the higher realm, beyond the Elysian Fields."

Lucius leaned on the shivering olive tree beside him as he gazed in wonder. There were no words available to him in that moment, for words were a mortal's tools.

Apollo stepped forward and placed his hand upon Lucius' head.

Venus smiled as he did so.

"This is where you belong now."

Lucius looked up at Apollo, his eyes wide and star-churned, as much as the god's before him. He shut his eyes suddenly as a memory exploded into his sight, of a dark forest glade ringed with fire and eyes. There was a feeling of unimaginable pain, a vision of blood. He opened his eyes and looked to the goddess beside him. "I heard you say it. I heard you ask him."

Venus nodded. "Yes, Lucius."

Lucius looked back to Apollo, and the silver-bowed god nodded and smiled, and gripped Lucius by both shoulders.

"This is where you belong now. With us."

Lucius pulled away.

Apollo and Venus watched him, their hearts filling with pity then, for even as they watched him, the joy, the life seemed to drain from him, even in that place of eternal beauty.

"My family..." Lucius said, his voice hoarse. He looked up. "Where is my family? My wife? My children?"

"They are safe," Apollo reassured him.

"But I am not with them," Lucius protested. He gripped the tree to steady himself, felt the Olympian ground turning beneath his feet. The stars in his eyes faded away, and all that was there now was sadness and longing, pleading. "Send me back to them, I beg you."

"You are the Dragon, Lucius. *Anguis*..." Apollo said, his voice kind, warm and full of care. "Here, you will no longer know pain or suffering. You can seek to create the world you dream of, to guide...to inspire..."

Lucius shook his head. "What is my life without them? They *are* my life."

Apollo looked at Venus, and the goddess reached out to take his hand. *Give him the choice...* she thought to him. He turned back to Lucius.

"Please," Lucius said. "I love them."

A tear ran down Venus' cheek then, for rarely did even she feel such a bond among those in the mortal realm.

"If you go back..." Apollo began, his voice a warning, a worry. "You will know greater pain than ever you have felt, and though you will be with them, your trials will push you to the brink, to the breaking point of your body, mind, and spirit." Apollo gripped Lucius again. "I do not want that for you, that pain, that suffering."

"None of us here do," Venus added.

Lucius nodded. He understood. "I understand," he said, though he shook as he said the words, for the image the Gods had just painted for him was one of terror.

"Very well," Apollo said, his hand still holding Lucius up. "Know that we will be with you, as ever...that we too are family..."

And Apollo let go. "Now...your trials begin."

Pain shot through the pathways of Lucius' body then as he watched the blue sky fall away, and the leaves upon the tree turn brown and blow away in the wind.

He fixed his gaze upon Apollo and Venus and the other gods who had come to see him. Their faces blurred as he fell to the crashing waves of the sea below.

He splashed into the water, upon his back, gazing up at them, his arms reaching, grasping for them to help free him of the pain that already harried his senses.

All around him the waters turned to red, contorting the Gods' faces.

Lucius gasped and sputtered beneath the surface, and then strong arms reached into the crimson depths to pull him out.

His voice and vision, his body came back into the world, and there he beheld many faces, young and old, including the faces he had longed for in paradise.

Through the pain he felt, never had the sound of weeping been more welcome.

Lucius Metellus Anguis was alive.

The End

Thank you for reading!

Did you enjoy *Isle of the Blessed*? Here is what you can do next.

If you enjoyed this adventure with Lucius Metellus Anguis, and if you have a minute to spare, please post a short review on the web page where you purchased the book.

Reviews are a wonderful way for new readers to find this series of books and your help in spreading the word is greatly appreciated.

If you would like to find out what happened to Lucius in Dumnonia, the story continues in *The Stolen Throne*, which is now available. More Eagles and Dragons novels will be coming soon, so be sure to sign-up for e-mail updates at:

https://eaglesanddragonspublishing.com/newsletter-join-the-legions/

Newsletter subscribers get a FREE BOOK, and first access to new releases, special offers, and much more.

To read more about the history, people and places featured in this book, check out *The World of Isle of the Blessed* blog series at https://eaglesanddragonspublishing.com/the-world-of-isle-of-the-blessed/

You can also check out the mini-documentary *In Insula Avalonia* here: https://eaglesanddragonspublishing.com/in-insula-avalonia-a-tour-of-glastonbury-with-author-and-historian-adam-alexander-haviaras/

Become a Patron of Eagles and Dragons Publishing!

If you enjoy the books that Eagles and Dragons Publishing puts out, our blogs about history, mythology, and archaeology, our video tours of historic sites and more, then you should consider becoming an official patron.

We love our regular visitors to the website, and of course our wonderful newsletter subscribers, but we want to offer more to our 'super fans', those readers and history-lovers who enjoy everything we do and create.

You can become a patron for as little as $1 per month. For your support, you will also get loads of fantastic rewards as tokens of our appreciation.

If you are interested, just visit the website below to go to the Eagles and Dragons Publishing Patreon page to watch the introductory video and check out the patronage levels and exciting rewards.

https://www.patreon.com/EaglesandDragonsPublishing

Join us for an exciting future as we bring the past to life!

AUTHOR'S NOTE

I wept when I finished this book. I am not ashamed to admit it. Not only is it because of the trials I have put beloved characters through - the Metelli, over the years have also become my family - but also because with this book, I have reached a critical point.

A long time ago, before I started writing the Eagles and Dragons series, I had a picture stuck in my head, a sort of dreamy image of pain and suffering, but also of unknown hope mixed with fear.

That image was of a man straining with all his might to hold onto the woman he loved as she dangled over the edge of a cliff.

The man and the woman, at the time, did not have names. The location of the cliff was unknown to me. But from this one haunting, recurring image, this entire series was born.

I don't know where it came from, but when such a thing happens, a sort of creative calling, I can't help but wonder if there is something greater out there, a Muse whispering inspiration into my ear in the dark of night.

I find that a truly awe-inspiring thing.

There was a lot of pressure to deliver on *Isle of the Blessed*, especially from myself. Years of plotting and research went into this, and when it came time to start writing, the words did not come easily. There were times when I thought I would never finish, when it felt like I was crawling on my hands and knees through a creative quagmire, with serpents striking at my flanks the whole of the way.

In a way, I turned to the goddess Disciplina, worshiped by the men of the legions, for aid. When I thought that I would never finish the book, I rallied myself and began getting up at 5 a.m. every morning, even on weekends, to press on, to achieve the momentum that I needed to power toward the finish.

And it worked.

But, as it is in life, so it is in fiction that the destination is not the goal, but rather it is the journey itself.

And what a journey this has been!

Once more, Cassius Dio has proved to be the most useful primary source in writing this novel, providing me with details that are both shocking and valuable to me as a writer. He writes of the second revolt of the Caledonians - after the first treaty in *Warriors of Epona* - and how they allied themselves with the Maeatae.

The Wolf of the Maeatae is, of course, a fictional character, but the tribe itself was very real, and their alliance with the Caledonians would have added new ferocity to the war with Rome. The orders that Severus gives in the book when he hears of the new rebellion and the breaking of the treaty are taken directly from Dio when he quotes the emperor as saying, "Let no one escape sheer destruction. No one our hands, not even the babe in the womb of the mother…" Chilling words that foreshadow the brutality of the campaign which saw over fifty-thousand Roman dead, and likely even more Maeatae and Caledonians.

If history teaches us anything, it is that in war, everyone loses something.

One of the main storylines in the novel is the ailing health of Septimius Severus, and both Cassius Dio and Herodian have been useful primary sources when it comes to his time in Eburacum (York). Severus' health was extremely bad at this time, and he was forced to remain in York with the empress and Geta, the latter helping to administer the empire. During this time, Caracalla was placed in charge of the campaign in Caledonia.

Septimius Severus is supposed to have died in York on February 4th, A.D. 211, and his passing was expected. According to Dio, Severus was ready for his death and even commissioned the urn of purple stone which was later interred in the tomb of the Antonines back in Rome. The funeral too was enormous and was supposed to have featured the largest funeral pyre ever.

During my research, I stumbled across a coin, later issued by Caracalla, with an image of the funeral pyre itself, and this provided a brilliant clue as to the appearance of the pyre. The location of the pyre at York was a bit trickier, but I did find one theory about a hill, in a flat area of the modern city, named Severus' Hill that is supposed to have been the site of the giant funeral pyre. There is some doubt about this explanation, but as the distance from the walls of the Roman settlement was not too big, I decided to set the scene there.

Despite his shortcomings, Dio and Herodian both portray Septimius Severus as an intelligent, strong, and good emperor. He did, perhaps, have too much faith in his sons, especially Caracalla, but the empire did reach its greatest extent under his rule. Herodian says that "No emperor before Severus won such outstanding victories

702

either in civil wars against political rivals or in foreign wars against barbarians."

There is no doubt he was a military emperor, and this is perhaps best exemplified not only in the quote from Herodian, but in the final advice Dio says Severus gave to his sons: "Be harmonious, enrich the soldiers, and scorn all other men."

I have to say that over the years, Septimius Severus has been a fascinating emperor to write about, and become acquainted with. I certainly will miss him.

Caracalla, however, provides a lot of fodder for story, and in *Isle of the Blessed*, we begin to really delve into his maniacal behaviour.

Herodian in particular highlights Caracalla's negative actions. He writes of how Caracalla tried to force his father's physicians to speed along the emperor's death so that he could take control, and how, after his father's death, he seized control and immediately began to murder many members of the court such as Euodus, his tutor, and Castor, Severus' loyal freedman. Cassius Dio backs this up. I included Papinianus in this slaughter as well, though he is supposed to have been done away with back in Rome.

The interesting thing here is that archaeology does appear to back up the idea that Caracalla ordered the execution by beheading of over sixty men after his father's death at York. In the early 2000s, archaeologists discovered a cemetery outside the walls of Roman York that contained the beheaded bodies of fifty men, plus eighteen more. All of these were supposed to be under the age of forty-five, and some bound by manacles. They were decapitated by sword or axe from behind. Another interesting discovery, besides the age of the victims, is that they were all large, strong specimens, and this has led to the supposition that they may have been Praetorian soldiers whose loyalty to Caracalla was in doubt.

This discovery was just too wonderful not to include in this novel, and thus was born the game that Marcus Claudius Picus 'played' with Caracalla.

Either way, it is the beginning of a troubled and bloody reign for the new emperor who did make a hurried treaty with the enemy and pull out of Caledonia so that he could rush back to Rome.

We move now from York to southern Britannia, where a large part of the novel takes place.

In *Warriors of Epona* and the author's note for that book, I spoke about Glastonbury (Ynis Wytrin) and the peaceful coexistence of the religious groups there. I have said it before, and I will say it again - Glastonbury was, and is, a very special place.

It was a joy to go back there for the research for this novel after so many years away, though every detail of the place was still burned into my memory, having lived just outside of the town for several years.

When it comes to Ynis Wytrin in the novel, we cannot know exactly how it appeared at that time. The Lady Chapel, of which Father Gilmore is the custodian, was likely there, but the rest of the abbey that most people are familiar with would have come much later in the Middle Ages. The Celts of the ancient world worshipped at sacred springs, and so the Well of the Chalice (today's Chalice Well and Gardens) was very likely one such sacred site. The water, due to the rich iron content, does indeed appear to be a rich, rusty red that stains the rock it runs over with time. I have spent many hours there in contemplation of various aspects of my own human experience, and it had indeed become one of my favourite places to visit. Whether there was an order of priestesses on site during the Roman period, I cannot say, but for the novel, I believed the character of Etain was the perfect custodian for such a sacred place.

At Glastonbury, there were, in ancient times, avenues of sacred trees that the druids supposedly used for processional ceremonies leading to the Tor, a sacred gateway to Annwn, the Celtic Otherworld. Most of the trees have been cut down, but you can still see two ancient yew trees in the Chalice Well gardens, as well as the majestic oaks named Gog and Magog a short walk away. As for Glastonbury Tor itself, there would not have been a tower upon it in the period in which this novel is set, for that tower of St. Michael is a medieval Christian construction. It is said that the processional way to the top of the Tor is a sort of labyrinthine path followed by the Druids, and when you stand at the top, or gaze at the Tor from the top of neighbouring Wearyall Hill, one can see the possibility of such a labyrinth.

In a way, we may never know the true Glastonbury of history, and to me, that is just as well. It is a place of mystery and legend, and like other such places, it is perhaps better to 'feel' the place than fully understand it. For those of you interested in seeing it, be sure to watch the mini-documentary I filmed there during my research: *In Insula Avalonia.*

The other site where much of the story takes place is, of course, the hillfort of South Cadbury Castle in Somerset. Most people know of this as one of the possible locations of the main fortress of the historical 'King' Arthur. Massive excavations were undertaken there during the sixties and seventies that revealed a large-scale refortification during the Arthurian period, part of the time commonly referred to as the Dark Ages. Some of the finds from this period included post holes of a large timber hall, storage pits, and a gatehouse at the southwest entrance to the fort. A bronze letter 'A' believed to be from a temple inscription to Mars was also found.

Obviously, I have taken some poetic license with this site in the story for *Isle of the Blessed*, but I felt compelled to include it. It is fiction to be sure, but there is some evidence that a Roman supply station was located on South Cadbury Castle at the time. In the story, the hillfort is land that Lucius and Adara receive from her father as a wedding gift in *Children of Apollo*. This, and most of the structures I have placed there in this story, such as the stables, barracks and baths, are fictional.

South Cadbury Castle was originally an Iron Age hillfort of the Durotriges, the Celtic tribe that inhabited the region. It was stormed by Vespasian during the assault on southern Britannia.

I love this site, and have spent much time there working as a volunteer archaeologist as part of the South Cadbury Environs Project team for a couple of seasons. Though we did not excavate or do geophysical survey of the hillfort itself, we did so on the surrounding fields, including the site of Sigwells, the village where the characters of Culhwch and Alma live in the novel.

I could go on about South Cadbury Castle, but will refrain from doing so here. If you would like to read more about it and the archaeology of the site, be sure to read the non-fiction work Historia IV, *Camelot: The Historical, Archaeological and Toponymic Considerations for South Cadbury Castle as King Arthur's Capital.* The latter also comes with a short video tour of this amazing site.

In writing *Isle of the Blessed*, I very much enjoyed delving into the world of Roman Somerset, a world which goes well beyond the confines of Aquae Sulis, modern Bath. Somerset has one of the highest concentrations of sacred Celtic and Roman sites in the UK, as well as a thriving villa economy that allowed towns such as Lindinis (not an official *civitas*) to thrive. Peter Leach's book, Roman Somerset, was an invaluable resource to understanding the setting and functioning of this beautiful part of England during this time period and before.

In the story, the villa of Serenus Crescens, where Lucius and Adara are invited to a banquet, is a sort of amalgamation of what is known from Pitney Roman villa, and Low Ham Roman villa, which is where the famous Aeneas and Dido mosaic was found. Both of these archaeological sites are located near the town of Ilchester, which is Roman Lindinis along the Fosse Way, the main Roman road that runs through Somerset.

For more about the history and archaeology of the places visited in this book, readers will want to check out the blog series, *The World of Isle of the Blessed* on the Eagles and Dragons Publishing website.

Many readers will find it odd, and perhaps be frustrated, that Lucius disappeared for a time to go to Dumnonia with Dagon and Einion to help the latter regain his family's kingdom. This episode in the broader story would have been too much of a deviation from the main storyline, making the book far too long. I also did not want to short-change that storyline, and so that is why I wrote *The Stolen Throne*, and why it was published at exactly the same time as *Isle of the Blessed*. I do hope that you enjoy both works, and that your questions about what happened to Lucius in that mysterious land are answered.

It goes without saying that the most difficult decision in writing *Isle of the Blessed* was to put Lucius and his family through hell, to hurt them.

Every hero on his journey must die in a way. Odysseus must go to the Underworld, and Jason is eaten and disgorged by the Colchian dragon. Though it was heartbreaking to do so, Lucius had to be burned, to die. It is so difficult doing this to beloved characters, and in a way, an author can feel like a traitor to his fictional family by doing such things. But a victory that is hard-won by the toils of life, that ancient concept of *ponos*, is the only real sort of victory. A character must sacrifice himself to be a hero.

There are many heroes in *Isle of the Blessed*.

Now, with the fires having burned their course, and rivers of blood having been spilt, the question of where to go next looms above me. Now that this book is finished, I find myself asking where my own creative hero's journey will take me. What will happen to Lucius Metellus Anguis and his family?

I have an inkling, and I hope you will continue to share this journey with me.

Adam Alexander Haviaras
Toronto, 2019

GLOSSARY

aedes – a temple; sometimes a room

aedituus – a keeper of a temple

aestivus – relating to summer; a summer camp or pasture

agora – Greek word for the central gathering place of a city or settlement

ala – an auxiliary cavalry unit

amita – an aunt

amphitheatre – an oval or round arena where people enjoyed gladiatorial combat and other spectacles

anguis – a dragon, serpent or hydra; also used to refer to the 'Draco' constellation

angusticlavius – 'narrow stripe' on a tunic; Lucius Metellus Anguis is a *tribunus angusticlavius*

anthemia – decorative roof finials made of terracotta

apodyterium – the changing room of a bathhouse

aquila – a legion's eagle standard which was made of gold during the Empire

aquilifer – senior standard bearer in a Roman legion who carried the legion's eagle

ara – an altar

armilla – an arm band that served as a military decoration

augur – a priest who observes natural occurrences to determine if omens are good or bad; a soothsayer

aureus – a Roman gold coin; worth twenty-five silver *denarii*

auriga – a charioteer

ava – grandmother

avus – grandfather

ballista – an ancient missile-firing weapon that fired either heavy 'bolts' or rocks

bireme – a galley with two banks of oars on either side

bracae – knee or full-length breeches originally worn by barbarians but adopted by the Romans

caldarium – the 'hot' room of a bathhouse; from the Latin *calidus*

caligae – military shoes or boots with or without hobnail soles

cardo – a hinge-point or central, north-south thoroughfare in a fort or settlement, the *cardo maximus* castrum – a Roman fort

cataphract – a heavy cavalryman; both horse and rider were armoured

cena- the principal, afternoon meal of the Romans

chiton – a long woollen tunic of Greek fashion

chryselephantine – ancient Greek sculptural medium using gold and ivory; used for cult statues

civica – relating to 'civic'; the civic crown was awarded to one who saved a Roman citizen in war

civitas – a settlement or commonwealth; an administrative centre in tribal areas of the empire

clepsydra – a water clock

cognomen – the surname of a Roman which distinguished the branch of a gens

collegia – an association or guild; e.g. *collegium pontificum* means 'college of priests'

colonia – a colony; also used for a farm or estate

consul – an honorary position in the Empire; during the Republic they presided over the Senate

contubernium – a military unit of ten men within a century who shared a tent

contus – a long cavalry spear

convivium – a banquet

cornicen – the horn blower in a legion

cornu – a curved military horn

cornucopia – the horn of plenty

corona – a crown; often used as a military decoration

cubiculum – a bedchamber

curule – refers to the chair upon which Roman magistrates would sit (e.g. *curule aedile*)

decumanus – refers to the tenth; the *decumanus maximus* ran east to west in a Roman fort or city

denarius – A Roman silver coin; worth one hundred brass *sestertii*

dignitas – a Roman's worth, honour and reputation

domus – a home or house

draco – a military standard in the shape of a dragon's head first used by Sarmatians and adopted by Rome

draconarius – a military standard bearer who held the draco

eques – a horseman or rider

equites – cavalry; of the order of knights in ancient Rome

fabrica – a workshop

fabula – an untrue or mythical story; a play or drama

familia – a Roman's household, including slaves

flammeum – a flame-coloured bridal veil

forum – an open square or marketplace; also a place of public business (e.g. the *Forum Romanum*)

fossa – a ditch or trench; a part of defensive earthworks

frigidarium – the 'cold room' of a bathhouse; a cold plunge pool

funeraticia – from *funereus* for funeral; the *collegia funeraticia* assured all received decent burial

garum – a fish sauce that was very popular in the Roman world

gladius – a Roman short sword

gorgon – a terrifying visage of a woman with snakes for hair; also known as Medusa

greaves – armoured shin and knee guards worn by high-ranking officers

groma – a surveying instrument; used for accurately marking out towns, marching camps and forts etc.

hasta – a spear or javelin

horreum – a granary

hydraulis – a water organ

hypocaust – area beneath a floor in a home or bathhouse that is heated by a furnace

imbrices – clay roof tile parts that fit together with *tegulae*

imperator – a commander or leader; commander-in-chief

insula – a block of flats leased to the poor

intervallum – the space between two palisades

itinere – a road or itinerary; the journey

lanista – a gladiator trainer

lectus imus – the 'low couch', or couch for the hosts in a Roman dining room, which allowed hosts to interact with honoured guests

lectus medius – the 'middle couch', or couch for honoured guests in a Roman dining room lectus summus – the 'high couch', or couch for lower-status guests and children, in a Roman dining room

lemure – a ghost

libellus – a little book or diary

lituus – the curved staff or wand of an augur; also a cavalry trumpet

lorica – body armour; can be made of mail, scales or metal strips; can also refer to a cuirass

lustratio – a ritual purification, usually involving a sacrifice

manica – handcuffs; also refers to the long sleeves of a tunic

marita - wife

maritus - husband

matertera – a maternal aunt

maximus – meaning great or 'of greatness'

missum – used as a call for mercy by the crowd for a gladiator who had fought bravely

murmillo – a heavily armed gladiator with a helmet, shield and sword

nomen – the gens of a family (as opposed to *cognomen* which was the specific branch of a wider gens)

nones – the fifth day of every month in the Roman calendar

novendialis – refers to the ninth day

nutrix – a wet-nurse or foster mother

nymphaeum – a pool, fountain or other monument dedicated to the nymphs

officium – an official employment; also a sense of duty or respect

onager – a powerful catapult used by the Romans; named after a wild ass because of its kick

oppidum – a large walled or fortified Iron Age settlement; these often became administrative centres under Roman rule

optio – the officer beneath a centurion; second-in-command within a century

ordo – a local council in charge of making decisions for a community

palaestra – the open space of a gymnasium where wrestling, boxing and other such events were practiced

palliatus – indicating someone clad in a pallium

711

pancration – a no-holds-barred sport that combined wrestling and boxing

parentalis – of parents or ancestors; (e.g. *Parentalia* was a festival in honour of the dead)

parma – a small, round shield often used by light-armed troops; also referred to as *parmula*

pater – a father

pax – peace; a state of peace as opposed to war

peregrinus – a strange or foreign person or thing

peristylum – a peristyle; a colonnade around a building; can be inside or outside of a building or home

phalerae – decorative medals or discs worn by centurions or other officers on the chest

philotimo – ancient Greek concept of 'love of honour'; philosophy that all one's actions should better the world around you and the lives of the people around you

pilum – a heavy javelin used by Roman legionaries

plebeius – of the plebeian class or the people

pontifex – a Roman high priest

popa – a junior priest or temple servant

primus pilus – the senior centurion of a legion who commanded the first cohort

pronaos – the porch or entrance to a building such as a temple

protome – an adornment on a work of art, usually a frontal view of an animal

pteruges – protective leather straps used on armour; often a leather skirt for officers

pugio – a dagger

quadriga – a four-horse chariot

quinqueremis – a ship with five banks of oars

retiarius – a gladiator who fights with a net and trident

rosemarinus – the herb rosemary

rusticus – of the country; e.g. a *villa rustica* was a country villa

sacrum – sacred or holy; e.g. the *via sacra* or 'sacred way'

schola – a place of learning and learned discussion

scutum – the large, rectangular, curved shield of a legionary secutor – a gladiator armed with a sword and shield; often pitted against a *retiarius*

sestertius – a Roman silver coin worth a quarter *denarius*

sica – a type of dagger

signum – a military standard or banner

signifer – a military standard bearer

spatha – an auxiliary trooper's long sword; normally used by cavalry because of its longer reach

spina – the ornamented, central median in stadiums such as the Circus Maximus in Rome

stadium – a measure of length approximately 607 feet; also refers to a race course

stibium – *antimony*, which was used for dyeing eyebrows by women in the ancient world

stoa – a columned, public walkway or portico for public use; often used by merchants to sell their wares

stola – a long outer garment worn by Roman women

strigilis – a curved scraper used at the baths to remove oil and grime from the skin

taberna – an inn or tavern

tabula – a Roman board game similar to backgammon; also a writing-tablet for keeping records

tegulae – clay roof tile parts that fit together with *imbrices*

tepidarium – the 'warm room' of a bathhouse

tessera – a piece of mosaic paving; a die for playing; also a small wooden plaque

testudo – a tortoise formation created by troops' interlocking shields

thraex – a gladiator in Thracian armour

titulus – a title of honour or honourable designation

torques – also 'torc'; a neck band worn by Celtic peoples and adopted by Rome as a military decoration

trepidatio – trepidation, anxiety or alarm

tribunus – a senior officer in an imperial legion; there were six per legion, each commanding a cohort

triclinium – a dining room

tunica – a sleeved garment worn by both men and women

ustrinum – the site of a funeral pyre

valitudinarium – a Roman military field hospital

vallum – an earthen wall or rampart with a palisade

veterinarius – a veterinary surgeon in the Roman army

vexillarius – a Roman standard bearer who carried the *vexillum* for each unit

vexillum – a standard carried in each unit of the Roman army

vicus – a settlement of civilians living outside a Roman fort

vigiles – Roman firemen; literally 'watchmen'

vitis – the twisted 'vinerod' of a Roman centurion; a centurion's emblem of office

vittae – a ribbon or band

ACKNOWLEDGEMENTS

In a way, I can't believe I've made it to this point in the journey of writing this novel. Writing *Isle of the Blessed* has been one of the most difficult periods in my career as a writer. I would not have made it through the fires of my own imagination and daily pressures without the help of many to whom I am extremely grateful.

First of all, I want to offer my heartfelt thanks to the fans and readers of the Eagles and Dragons series who have helped to make these books such a resounding success. I truly do feel blessed to be able to write these stories for you, stories that many of you have told me help you to escape the chaos of our modern world. A very special thank you to my staunchest followers and the patrons of Eagles and Dragons Publishing for their support, but also for their patience in waiting so long for this novel. I hope that the release of two at the same time is adequate recompense, and a sign of my gratitude. Special thanks to the following Eagles and Dragons Publishing patrons at the time of publication: A. Diassiti, Bonnie Miller, Dig it with Raven, J. Dagger, and Mayra Bone Voyage. I deeply appreciate your support and the faith you show in this series of books and what Eagles and Dragons Publishing is trying to achieve.

Thank you also to my fellow historians, archaeologists, and enthusiasts on-line and in various Facebook groups who always come through when a question is posed, or an historical conundrum surfaces. You're all brilliant!

What historical novel would be complete without loads of research up front, and that includes visits to various museums over the years. In particular, I would like to thank the staff and volunteers at the Trimontium Trust Museum in Melrose, Scotland, and the National Museum of Scotland in Edinburgh where I learned a great deal about the site of Trimontium, the Roman presence in Scotland, Roman cavalry, and the Votadini. In the South, I am once more indebted to the Museum of Somerset in Taunton for information about Roman Somerset, for showing me the finds from South Cadbury Castle, and for allowing me to see the faces of the Severans up close by viewing the Shapwick Coin Hoard. A special thank you must also go to Steve Minnitt, of the South West Heritage Trust and Taunton Museum, who sent me some important plans and reconstructions of the Roman villas at Pitney and Low Ham. While writing my dissertation on South Cadbury years ago, Steve was kind enough to show me the collections from South Cadbury Castle in the basement of the museum, so it was brilliant to connect once more.

When it comes to South Cadbury Castle and Celtic Britain, I cannot overstate the importance of the works of both Geoffrey Ashe and the late Professor Leslie Alcock. Not only did their books inspire me as a young, aspiring historian, they opened my eyes to a whole new world of research, a world that has inspired the Eagles and Dragons series itself and will continue to do so. Their research and excavations at South Cadbury Castle are invaluable in shedding light on the life of this magnificent site and the people who lived there. If you have not ready their books, then I highly recommend you do.

The good work at South Cadbury Castle was continued years later by Dr. Richard Tabor, from the University of Bristol, who headed the South Cadbury Environs Project team, and who gave me the chance of a lifetime to be a part of the excavations. I am grateful to Richard for taking a chance on me and for teaching me the ins and outs of test-pitting, excavation, analysis, and how to perform geophysical surveys of the areas around the hillfort itself. It was an experience I will not forget, and one that helped me to enrich the world of *Isle of the Blessed.*

When doing research for any historical novel, a good deal of travel away from home is required, a comfortable base from which to strike out. And so, I offer my thanks to our lovely host, Henrietta, at Castle Farmhouse Cottage, in the village of South Cadbury. It was amazing and inspiring to stay in such a beautiful place, directly beneath the ramparts of South Cadbury Castle, something I had been dreaming of for years since moving away from Somerset.

To Angus and Alison Gordon, the owners of Tiverton Castle in Devon, I want to say thank you for their friendship and the warm welcome they have given us over the years. It was a pleasure to return to stay at the castle with them while doing research for this book and finding sanctuary abroad. Tiverton has become a home away from home for me, a place full of wonderful memories, and I look forward to the next time we can meet.

Once more, I am indebted to my good friend, and fellow historian, Andrew Fenwick, who works at the Dundee Museum. He has always been a font of knowledge, and is the one who opened my eyes to the magnitude of the Roman presence in Scotland. He also introduced me to the crucial work and research of B. Hoffman and

D.J. Wooliscroft on the Gask Ridge frontier forts that were the front lines in the Roman invasion of Scotland. Thank you, Andy!

I would be remiss too, if I did not express my gratitude to my dear friends Jean-Francois and Heather Lamontagne for their support of these books, their valuable input as readers, and of course, their friendship. It is often surprising, as an author, how few of one's friends actually read one's books, and unbeknownst to me until recently, Jean-Francois and Heather had been following Lucius on his adventures for some time. Thank you both.

The Eagles and Dragons books would not be the same without the solid help of Kostis Diassitis of Athens, Greece. He is a scholar and historian in his own right, and I am always grateful to him for his revision of my Latin in the books, including *Isle of the Blessed*. As ever, any linguistic errors are entirely of my own making.

My sincere thanks to my cover designer, Laura, at LLPix Designs, for the beautiful cover designs she always manages to come up with. One of my favourite parts of the creative process is seeing that final book cover appear in my inbox and knowing 'That's the one!'. It is always a joy working with her.

To Catherine Comuzzi, my sincere thanks for becoming an ally toward the end of this journey. She helped me in the final stages of creation to gather the strength that helped me to face down my own ouroboros of fire and begin to understand my personal daemons.

I would also like to thank my brilliant editors, Angelina and Jeanette, at Eagles and Dragons Publishing, for their hard work and dedication, and for their belief in my books and the stories I'm trying to tell. I am eternally grateful to them, and I know that these stories would not be what they are without them. They had their work cut out for them with this novel!

Finally, and most importantly, I offer my love and gratitude to my wife and daughters for their love, support, patience, and understanding as I experienced the agony and ecstasy of creating this work. Truly, the journey is everything, and I am eternally grateful to have them with me upon the road.

Adam Alexander Haviaras
Toronto, 2019

ABOUT THE AUTHOR

Adam Alexander Haviaras is a writer and historian who has studied ancient and medieval history and archaeology in Canada and the United Kingdom. He currently resides in Toronto with his wife and children where he is continuing his research and writing other works of historical fantasy.

Other works by Adam Alexander Haviaras:

The Eagles and Dragons series

The Dragon: Genesis (Prequel)

A Dragon among the Eagles (Prequel)

Children of Apollo (Book I)

Killing the Hydra (Book II)

Warriors of Epona (Book III)

Isle of the Blessed (Book IV)

The Stolen Throne (Book V)

The Blood Road (Book VI)

The Carpathian Interlude Series

Immortui (Part I)

Lykoi (Part II)

Thanatos (Part III)

The Mythologia Series

Chariot of the Son

Heart of Fire: A Novel of the Ancient Olympics

Saturnalia: A Tale of Wickedness and Redemption in Ancient Rome

Titles in the Historia Non-fiction Series

Historia I: Celtic Literary Archetypes in *The Mabinogion*: A Study of the Ancient Tale of *Pwyll, Lord of Dyved*

Historia II: Arthurian Romance and the Knightly Ideal: A study of Medieval Romantic Literature and its Effect upon Warrior Culture in Europe

Historia III: *Y Gododdin*: The Last Stand of Three Hundred Britons - Understanding People and Events during Britain's Heroic Age

Historia IV: Camelot: The Historical, Archaeological and Toponymic Considerations for South Cadbury Castle as King Arthur's Capital

STAY CONNECTED

To connect with Adam and learn more about the ancient world visit www.eaglesanddragonspublishing.com

Sign up for the Eagles and Dragons Publishing Newsletter at www.eaglesanddragonspublishing.com/newsletter-join-the-legions/ to receive a FREE BOOK, first access to new releases and posts on ancient history, special offers, and much more!

Readers can also connect with Adam on Twitter @AdamHaviaras and Instagram @ adam_haviaras.

On Facebook you can 'Like' the Eagles and Dragons page to get regular updates on new historical fiction and fantasy from Eagles and Dragons Publishing.

Printed in Great Britain
by Amazon